# A House for Mr. Biswas

# A Bend in the River

# By V. S. NAIPAUL

## Nonfiction

Between Father and Son: Family Letters
Beyond Belief: Islamic Excursions Among the Converted Peoples
India: A Million Mutinies Now
A Turn in the South
Finding the Center
Among the Believers
The Return of Eva Perón (*with* The Killings in Trinidad)
India: A Wounded Civilization
The Overcrowded Barracoon
The Loss of El Dorado
An Area of Darkness
The Middle Passage

## Fiction

Half a Life
A Way in the World
The Enigma of Arrival
A Bend in the River
Guerrillas
In a Free State
A Flag on the Island
The Mimic Men
Mr. Stone and the Knights Companion
A House for Mr. Biswas
Miguel Street
The Suffrage of Elvira
The Mystic Masseur

# A House for Mr. Biswas

## A Bend in the River

# V. S. NAIPAUL

QUALITY PAPERBACK BOOK CLUB
NEW YORK

# A House for Mr. Biswas

# Contents

# Prologue

TEN WEEKS before he died, Mr Mohun Biswas, a journalist of
Sikkim Street, St James, Port of Spain, was sacked. He had been
ill for some time. In less than a year he had spent more than nine
weeks at the Colonial Hospital and convalesced at home for
even longer. When the doctor advised him to take a complete
rest the *Trinidad Sentinel* had no choice. It gave Mr Biswas three
months' notice and continued, up to the time of his death, to
supply him every morning with a free copy of the paper.

Mr Biswas was forty-six, and had four children. He had no
money. His wife Shama had no money. On the house in
Sikkim Street Mr Biswas owed, and had been owing for four
years, three thousand dollars. The interest on this, at eight per
cent, came to twenty dollars a month; the ground rent was
ten dollars. Two children were at school. The two older
children, on whom Mr Biswas might have depended, were
both abroad on scholarships.

It gave Mr Biswas some satisfaction that in the circumstances
Shama did not run straight off to her mother to beg for help.
Ten years before that would have been her first thought.
Now she tried to comfort Mr Biswas, and devised plans on
her own.

'Potatoes,' she said. 'We can start selling potatoes. The
price around here is eight cents a pound. If we buy at five and
sell at seven –'

'Trust the Tulsi bad blood,' Mr Biswas said. 'I know that
the pack of you Tulsis are financial geniuses. But have a good
look around and count the number of people selling potatoes.
Better to sell the old car.'

'No. Not the car. Don't worry. We'll manage.'

'Yes,' Mr Biswas said irritably. 'We'll manage.'

No more was heard of the potatoes, and Mr Biswas never
threatened again to sell the car. He didn't now care to do

anything against his wife's wishes. He had grown to accept her judgement and to respect her optimism. He trusted her. Since they had moved to the house Shama had learned a new loyalty, to him and to their children; away from her mother and sisters, she was able to express this without shame, and to Mr Biswas this was a triumph almost as big as the acquiring of his own house.

He thought of the house as his own, though for years it had been irretrievably mortgaged. And during these months of illness and despair he was struck again and again by the wonder of being in his own house, the audacity of it: to walk in through his own front gate, to bar entry to whoever he wished, to close his doors and windows every night, to hear no noises except those of his family, to wander freely from room to room and about his yard, instead of being condemned, as before, to retire the moment he got home to the crowded room in one or the other of Mrs Tulsi's houses, crowded with Shama's sisters, their husbands, their children. As a boy he had moved from one house of strangers to another; and since his marriage he felt he had lived nowhere but in the houses of the Tulsis, at Hanuman House in Arwacas, in the decaying wooden house at Shorthills, in the clumsy concrete house in Port of Spain. And now at the end he found himself in his own house, on his own half-lot of land, his own portion of the earth. That he should have been responsible for this seemed to him, in these last months, stupendous.

The house could be seen from two or three streets away and was known all over St James. It was like a huge and squat sentry-box: tall, square, two-storeyed, with a pyramidal roof of corrugated iron. It had been designed and built by a solicitor's clerk who built houses in his spare time. The solicitor's clerk had many contacts. He bought land which the City Council had announced was not for sale; he persuaded estate owners to split whole lots into half-lots; he bought lots of barely reclaimed swamp land near Mucurapo and got permission to build on them. On whole lots or three-quarter-lots he built one-storey houses, twenty feet by twenty-six, which could pass unnoticed; on half-lots he built two-storey houses, twenty feet by thirteen, which were distinctive. All his houses were assembled mainly from frames from the dismantled American Army camps at Docksite, Pompeii Savannah and Fort Read. The frames did not always match, but they enabled the solicitor's clerk to pursue his hobby with little professional help.

On the ground floor of Mr Biswas's two-storey house the solicitor's clerk had put a tiny kitchen in one corner; the remaining L-shaped space, unbroken, served as drawingroom and diningroom. Between the kitchen and the diningroom there was a doorway but no door. Upstairs, just above the kitchen, the clerk had constructed a concrete room which contained a toilet bowl, a wash-basin and a shower; because of the shower this room was perpetually wet. The remaining L-shaped space was broken up into a bedroom, a verandah, a bedroom. Because the house faced west and had no protection from the sun, in the afternoon only two rooms were comfortably habitable: the kitchen downstairs and the wet bathroom-and-lavatory upstairs.

In his original design the solicitor's clerk seemed to have forgotten the need for a staircase to link both floors, and what he had provided had the appearance of an afterthought. Doorways had been punched in the eastern wall and a rough wooden staircase – heavy planks on an uneven frame with one warped unpainted banister, the whole covered with a sloping roof of corrugated iron – hung precariously at the back of the house, in striking contrast with the white-pointed brickwork of the front, the white woodwork and the frosted glass of doors and windows.

For this house Mr Biswas had paid five thousand five hundred dollars.

Mr Biswas had built two houses of his own and spent much time looking at houses. Yet he was inexperienced. The houses he had built had been crude wooden things in the country, not much better than huts. And during his search for a house he had always assumed new and modern concrete houses, bright with paint, to be beyond him; and he had looked at few. So when he was faced with one which was accessible, with a solid, respectable, modern front, he was immediately dazzled. He had never visited the house when the afternoon sun was on it. He had first gone one afternoon when it was raining, and the next time, when he had taken the children, it was evening.

Of course there were houses to be bought for two thousand and three thousand dollars, on a whole lot, in rising parts of the city. But these houses were old and decaying, with no fences and no conveniences of any sort. Often on one lot there was a conglomeration of two or three miserable houses, with every room of every house let to a separate family who couldn't legally be got out. What a change from those backyards, overrun with chickens and children, to the drawingroom of the solicitor's clerk who, coatless, tieless and in slippers, looked relaxed and comfortable in his morris chair, while the heavy red curtains, reflecting on the polished floor, made the scene as cosy and rich as something in an advertisement! What a change from the Tulsi house!

The solicitor's clerk lived in every house he built. While he lived in the house in Sikkim Street he was building another a discreet distance away, at Morvant. He had never married, and lived with his widowed mother, a gracious woman who gave Mr Biswas tea and cakes which she had baked herself. Between mother and son there was much affection, and this touched Mr Biswas, whose own mother, neglected by himself, had died five years before in great poverty.

'I can't tell you how sad it make me to leave this house,' the solicitor's clerk said, and Mr Biswas noted that though the man spoke dialect he was obviously educated and used dialect and an exaggerated accent only to express frankness and cordiality. 'Really for my mother's sake, man. That is the onliest reason why I have to move. The old queen can't manage the steps.' He nodded towards the back of the house, where the staircase was masked by heavy red curtains. 'Heart, you see. Could pass away any day.'

Shama had disapproved from the first and never gone to see the house. When Mr Biswas asked her, 'Well, what you think?' Shama said, 'Think? Me? Since when you start thinking that I could think anything? If I am not good enough to go and see your house, I don't see how I could be good enough to say what I think.'

'Ah!' Mr Biswas said. 'Swelling up. Vexed. I bet you would be saying something different if it was your mother who was spending some of her dirty money to buy this house.'

Shama sighed.

'Eh? You could only be happy if we just keep on living with your mother and the rest of your big, happy family. Eh?'

'I don't think anything. *You* have the money, *you* want to buy house, and *I* don't have to think anything.'

The news that Mr Biswas was negotiating for a house of his own had gone around Shama's family. Suniti, a niece of twenty-seven, married, with two children, and abandoned for long periods by her husband, a handsome idler who looked after the railway buildings at Pokima Halt where trains stopped twice a day, Suniti said to Shama, 'I hear that you come like a big-shot, Aunt.' She didn't hide her amusement. 'Buying house and thing.'

'Yes, child,' Shama said, in her martyr's way.

The exchange took place on the back steps and reached the ears of Mr Biswas, lying in pants and vest on the Slumber-king bed in the room which contained most of the possessions he had gathered after forty-one years. He had carried on a war with Suniti ever since she was a child, but his contempt had never been able to quell her sarcasm. 'Shama,' he shouted, 'tell that girl to go back and help that worthless husband of hers to look after their goats at Pokima Halt.'

The goats were an invention of Mr Biswas which never failed to irritate Suniti. 'Goats!' she said to the yard, and sucked her teeth. 'Well, some people at least have goats. Which is more than I could say for some other people.'

'Tcha!' Mr Biswas said softly; and, refusing to be drawn into an argument with Suniti, he turned on his side and continued to read the *Meditations* of Marcus Aurelius.

The very day the house was bought they began to see flaws in it. The staircase was dangerous; the upper floor sagged; there was no back door; most of the windows didn't close;

one door could not open; the celotex panels under the eaves
had fallen out and left gaps between which bats could enter
the attic. They discussed these things as calmly as they could
and took care not to express their disappointment openly.
And it was astonishing how quickly this disappointment had
faded, how quickly they had accommodated themselves to
every peculiarity and awkwardness of the house. And once
that had happened their eyes ceased to be critical, and the
house became simply their house.

When Mr Biswas came back from the hospital for the first
time, he found that the house had been prepared for him.
The small garden had been made tidy, the downstairs walls
distempered. The Prefect motorcar was in the garage, driven
there weeks before from the *Sentinel* office by a friend. The
hospital had been a void. He had stepped from that into a
welcoming world, a new, ready-made world. He could not
quite believe that he had made that world. He could not see
why he should have a place in it. And everything by which
he was surrounded was examined and rediscovered, with
pleasure, surprise, disbelief. Every relationship, every possession.

The kitchen safe. That was more than twenty years old.
Shortly after his marriage he had bought it, white and new,
from the carpenter at Arwacas, the netting unpainted, the
wood still odorous; then, and for some time afterwards, sawdust stuck to your hand when you passed it along the shelves.
How often he had stained and varnished it! And painted it
too. Patches of the netting were clogged, and varnish and
paint had made a thick uneven skin on the woodwork. And
in what colours he had painted it! Blue and green and even
black. In 1938, the week the Pope died and the *Sentinel* came
out with a black border, he had come across a large tin of
yellow paint and painted everything yellow, even the typewriter. That had been acquired when, at the age of thirty-
three, he had decided to become rich by writing for
American and English magazines; a brief, happy, hopeful
period. The typewriter had remained idle and yellow, and its
colour had long since ceased to startle. And why, except that
it had moved everywhere with them and they regarded it as

one of their possessions, had they kept the hatrack, its glass now leprous, most of its hooks broken, its woodwork ugly with painting-over? The bookcase had been made at Short-hills by an out-of-work blacksmith who had been employed by the Tulsis as a cabinet-maker; he revealed his skill in his original craft in every bit of wood he had fashioned, every joint he had made, every ornament he had attempted. And the diningtable: bought cheaply from a Deserving Destitute who had got some money from the *Sentinel*'s Deserving Destitutes Fund and wished to show his gratitude to Mr Biswas. And the Slumberking bed, where he could no longer sleep because it was upstairs and he had been forbidden to climb steps. And the glass cabinet: bought to please Shama, still dainty, and still practically empty. And the morris suite: the last acquisition, it had belonged to the solicitor's clerk and had been left by him as a gift. And in the garage outside, the Prefect.

But bigger than them all was the house, his house.

How terrible it would have been, at this time, to be without it: to have died among the Tulsis, amid the squalor of that large, disintegrating and indifferent family; to have left Shama and the children among them, in one room; worse, to have lived without even attempting to lay claim to one's portion of the earth; to have lived and died as one had been born, unnecessary and unaccommodated.

# PART ONE

# 1. Pastoral

SHORTLY BEFORE he was born there had been another quarrel between Mr Biswas's mother Bipti and his father Raghu, and Bipti had taken her three children and walked all the way in the hot sun to the village where her mother Bissoondaye lived. There Bipti had cried and told the old story of Raghu's miserliness: how he kept a check on every cent he gave her, counted every biscuit in the tin, and how he would walk ten miles rather than pay a cart a penny.

Bipti's father, futile with asthma, propped himself up on his string bed and said, as he always did on unhappy occasions, 'Fate. There is nothing we can do about it.'

No one paid him any attention. Fate had brought him from India to the sugar-estate, aged him quickly and left him to die in a crumbling mud hut in the swamplands; yet he spoke of Fate often and affectionately, as though, merely by surviving, he had been particularly favoured.

While the old man talked on, Bissoondaye sent for the midwife, made a meal for Bipti's children and prepared beds for them. When the midwife came the children were asleep. Some time later they were awakened by the screams of Mr Biswas and the shrieks of the midwife.

'What is it?' the old man asked. 'Boy or girl?'

'Boy, boy,' the midwife cried. 'But what sort of boy? Six-fingered, and born in the wrong way.'

The old man groaned and Bissoondaye said, 'I knew it. There is no luck for me.'

At once, though it was night and the way was lonely, she left the hut and walked to the next village, where there was a hedge of cactus. She brought back leaves of cactus, cut them into strips and hung a strip over every door, every window, every aperture through which an evil spirit might enter the hut.

But the midwife said, 'Whatever you do, this boy will eat up his own mother and father.'                              .

The next morning, when in the bright light it seemed that all evil spirits had surely left the earth, the pundit came, a small, thin man with a sharp satirical face and a dismissing manner. Bissoondaye seated him on the string bed, from which the old man had been turned out, and told him what had happened.

'Hm. Born in the wrong way. At midnight, you said.'

Bissoondaye had no means of telling the time, but both she and the midwife had assumed that it was midnight, the inauspicious hour.

Abruptly, as Bissoondaye sat before him with bowed and covered head, the pundit brightened, 'Oh, well. It doesn't matter. There are always ways and means of getting over these unhappy things.' He undid his red bundle and took out his astrological almanac, a sheaf of loose thick leaves, long and narrow, between boards. The leaves were brown with age and their musty smell was mixed with that of the red and ochre sandalwood paste that had been spattered on them. The pundit lifted a leaf, read a little, wet his forefinger on his tongue and lifted another leaf.

At last he said, 'First of all, the features of this unfortunate boy. He will have good teeth but they will be rather wide, and there will be spaces between them. I suppose you know what that means. The boy will be a lecher and a spendthrift. Possibly a liar as well. It is hard to be sure about those gaps between the teeth. They might mean only one of those things or they might mean all three.'

'What about the six fingers, pundit?'

'That's a shocking sign, of course. The only thing I can advise is to keep him away from trees and water. Particularly water.'

'Never bath him?'

'I don't mean exactly that.' He raised his right hand, bunched the fingers and, with his head on one side, said slowly, 'One has to interpret what the book says.' He tapped the wobbly almanac with his left hand. 'And when the book says water, I think it means water in its natural form.'

'Natural form.'

'Natural form,' the pundit repeated, but uncertainly. 'I mean,' he said quickly, and with some annoyance, 'keep him away from rivers and ponds. And of course the sea. And another thing,' He added with satisfaction. 'He will have an unlucky sneeze.' He began to pack the long leaves of his almanac. 'Much of the evil this boy will undoubtedly bring will be mitigated if his father is forbidden to see him for twenty-one days.'

'That will be easy,' Bissoondaye said, speaking with emotion for the first time.

'On the twenty-first day the father *must* see the boy. But not in the flesh.'

'In a mirror, pundit?'

'I would consider that ill-advised. Use a brass plate. Scour it well.'

'Of course.'

'You must fill this brass plate with coconut oil – which, by the way, you must make yourself from coconuts you have collected with your own hands – and in the reflection on this oil the father must see his son's face.' He tied the almanac together and rolled it in the red cotton wrapper which was also spattered with sandalwood paste. 'I believe that is all.'

'We forgot one thing, punditji. The name.'

'I can't help you completely there. But it seems to me that a perfectly safe prefix would be *Mo*. It is up to you to think of something to add to that.'

'Oh, punditji, you must help me. I can only think of *hun*.'

The pundit was surprised and genuinely pleased. 'But that is excellent. Excellent. *Mohun*. I couldn't have chosen better myself. For Mohun, as you know, means the beloved, and was the name given by the milkmaids to Lord Krishna.' His eyes softened at the thought of the legend and for a moment he appeared to forget Bissoondaye and Mr Biswas.

From the knot at the end of her veil Bissoondaye took out a florin and offered it to the pundit, mumbling her regret that she could not give more. The pundit said that she had done her best and was not to worry. In fact he was pleased; he had expected less.

*

Mr Biswas lost his sixth finger before he was nine days old. It simply came off one night and Bipti had an unpleasant turn when, shaking out the sheets one morning, she saw this tiny finger tumble to the ground. Bissoondaye thought this an excellent sign and buried the finger behind the cowpen at the back of the house, not far from where she had buried Mr Biswas's navel-string.

In the days that followed Mr Biswas was treated with attention and respect. His brothers and sisters were slapped if they disturbed his sleep, and the flexibility of his limbs was regarded as a matter of importance. Morning and evening he was massaged with coconut oil. All his joints were exercised; his arms and legs were folded diagonally across his red shining body; the big toe of his right foot was made to touch his left shoulder, the big toe of his left foot was made to touch his right shoulder, and both toes were made to touch his nose; finally, all his limbs were bunched together over his belly and then, with a clap and a laugh, released.

Mr Biswas responded well to these exercises, and Bissoondaye became so confident that she decided to have a celebration on the ninth day. She invited people from the village and fed them. The pundit came and was unexpectedly gracious, though his manner suggested that but for his intervention there would have been no celebration at all. Jhagru, the barber, brought his drum, and Selochan did the Shiva dance in the cowpen, his body smeared all over with ash.

There was an unpleasant moment when Raghu, Mr Biswas's father, appeared. He had walked; his dhoti and jacket were sweated and dusty. 'Well, this is very nice,' he said. 'Celebrating. And where is the father?'

'Leave this house at once,' Bissoondaye said, coming out of the kitchen at the side. 'Father! What sort of father do you call yourself, when you drive your wife away every time she gets heavy-footed?'

'That is none of your business,' Raghu said. 'Where is my son?'

'Go ahead. God has paid you back for your boasting and your meanness. Go and see your son. He will eat you up. Six-fingered, born in the wrong way. Go in and see him. He has an unlucky sneeze as well.'

Raghu halted. 'Unlucky sneeze?'

'I have warned you. You can only see him on the twenty-first day. If you do anything stupid now the responsibility will be yours.'

From his string bed the old man muttered abuse at Raghu. 'Shameless, wicked. When I see the behaviour of this man I begin to feel that the Black Age has come.'

The subsequent quarrel and threats cleared the air. Raghu confessed he had been in the wrong and had already suffered much for it. Bipti said she was willing to go back to him. And he agreed to come again on the twenty-first day.

To prepare for that day Bissoondaye began collecting dry coconuts. She husked them, grated the kernels and set about extracting the oil the pundit had prescribed. It was a long job of boiling and skimming and boiling again, and it was surprising how many coconuts it took to make a little oil. But the oil was ready in time, and Raghu came, neatly dressed, his hair plastered flat and shining, his moustache trimmed, and he was very correct as he took off his hat and went into the dark inner room of the hut which smelled warmly of oil and old thatch. He held his hat on the right side of his face and looked down into the oil in the brass plate. Mr Biswas, hidden from his father by the hat, and well wrapped from head to foot, was held face downwards over the oil. He didn't like it; he furrowed his forehead, shut his eyes tight and bawled. The oil rippled, clear amber, broke up the reflection of Mr Biswas's face, already distorted with rage, and the viewing was over.

A few days later Bipti and her children returned home. And there Mr Biswas's importance steadily diminished. The time came when even the daily massage ceased.

But he still carried weight. They never forgot that he was an unlucky child and that his sneeze was particularly unlucky. Mr Biswas caught cold easily and in the rainy season threatened his family with destitution. If, before Raghu left for the sugar-estate, Mr Biswas sneezed, Raghu remained at home, worked on his vegetable garden in the morning and spent the afternoon making walking-sticks and sabots, or carving designs on the hafts of cutlasses and the heads of walking-sticks. His favourite design was a pair of wellingtons; he had never owned wellingtons but had seen them on the overseer. Whatever he did, Raghu never left the house. Even so, minor mishaps often followed Mr Biswas's sneeze: threepence lost in the shopping, the breaking of a bottle, the upsetting of a dish. Once Mr Biswas sneezed on three mornings in succession.

'This boy will eat up his family in truth,' Raghu said.

One morning, just after Raghu had crossed the gutter that ran between the road and his yard, he suddenly stopped. Mr Biswas had sneezed. Bipti ran out and said, 'It doesn't matter. He sneezed when you were already on the road.'

'But I heard him. Distinctly.'

Bipti persuaded him to go to work. About an hour or two later, while she was cleaning the rice for the midday meal, she heard shouts from the road and went out to find Raghu lying in an ox-cart, his right leg swathed in bloody bandages. He was groaning, not from pain, but from anger. The man who had brought him refused to help him into the yard: Mr Biswas's sneeze was too well known. Raghu had to limp in leaning on Bipti's shoulder.

'This boy will make us all paupers,' Raghu said.

He spoke from a deep fear. Though he saved and made himself and his family go without many things, he never ceased to feel that destitution was very nearly upon him. The more he hoarded, the more he felt he had to waste and to lose, and the more careful he became.

Every Saturday he lined up with the other labourers outside the estate office to collect his pay. The overseer sat at a little table, on which his khaki cork hat rested, wasteful of space, but a symbol of wealth. On his left sat the Indian clerk, important, stern, precise, with small neat hands that wrote small neat figures in black ink and red ink in the tall ledger. As the clerk entered figures and called out names and amounts in his high, precise voice, the overseer selected coins from the columns of silver and the heaps of copper in front of him, and with greater deliberation extracted notes from the blue one-dollar stacks, the smaller red two-dollar stack and the very shallow green five-dollar stack. Few labourers earned five dollars a week; the notes were there to pay those who were collecting their wives' or husbands' wages as well as their own. Around the overseer's cork hat, and seeming to guard it, there were stiff blue paper bags, neatly serrated at the top, printed with large figures, and standing upright from the weight of coin inside them. Clean round perforations gave glimpses of the coin and, Raghu had been told, allowed it to breathe.

These bags fascinated Raghu. He had managed to get a few and after many months and a little cheating – turning a shilling into twelve pennies, for example – he had filled them. Thereafter he had never been able to stop. No one, not even Bipti, knew where he hid these bags; but the word had got around that he buried his money and was possibly the richest man in the village. Such talk alarmed Raghu and, to counter it, he increased his austerities.

Mr Biswas grew. The limbs that had been massaged and oiled twice a day now remained dusty and muddy and un- washed for days. The malnutrition that had given him the sixth finger of misfortune pursued him now with eczema and sores that swelled and burst and scabbed and burst again, until they stank; his ankles and knees and wrists and elbows were in particular afflicted, and the sores left marks like vaccination scars. Malnutrition gave him the shallowest of chests, the thinnest of limbs; it stunted his growth and gave him a soft rising belly. And yet, perceptibly, he grew. He was never aware of being hungry. It never bothered him that he didn't go to school. Life was unpleasant only because the pundit had forbidden him to go near ponds and rivers. Raghu was an excellent swimmer and Bipti wished him to train Mr Biswas's brothers. So every Sunday morning Raghu took Pratap and Prasad to swim in a stream not far off, and Mr Biswas stayed at home, to be bathed by Bipti and have all his sores ripped open by her strong rubbing with the blue soap. But in an hour or two the redness and rawness of the sores had faded, scabs were beginning to form, and Mr Biswas was happy again. He played at house with his sister Dehuti. They mixed yellow earth with water and made mud fireplaces; they cooked a few grains of rice in empty condensed milk tins; and, using the tops of tins as baking-stones, they made rotis.

In these amusements Prasad and Pratap took no part. Nine and eleven respectively, they were past such frivolities, and had already begun to work, joyfully cooperating with the estates in breaking the law about the employment of children. They had developed adult mannerisms. They spoke with blades of grass between their teeth; they drank noisily and sighed, passing the back of their hands across their mouths; they ate enormous quantities of rice, patted their bellies and belched; and every Saturday they stood up in line to draw their pay. Their job was to look after the buffaloes that drew the cane-carts. The buffaloes' pleasance was a muddy, cloyingly sweet pool not far from the factory; here, with a dozen other thin-limbed boys, noisy, happy, over-energetic and with a full sense of their importance, Pratap and Prasad moved all day in the mud among the buffaloes. When they came home their legs were caked with the buffalo mud which, on drying, had turned white, so that they looked like the trees in fire-stations and police-stations which are washed with white lime up to the middle of their trunks.

Much as he wanted to, it was unlikely that Mr Biswas would have joined his brothers at the buffalo pond when he was of age. There was the pundit's ruling against water; and though it could be argued that mud was not water, and though an accident there might have removed the source of Raghu's anxiety, neither Raghu nor Bipti would have done anything against the pundit's advice. In another two or three years, when he could be trusted with a sickle, Mr Biswas would be made to join the boys and girls of the grass-gang. Between them and the buffalo boys there were constant disputes, and there was no doubt who were superior. The buffalo boys, with their leggings of white mud, tickling the buffaloes and beating them with sticks, shouting at them and controlling them, exercised power. Whereas the children of the grass-gang, walking briskly along the road single file, their heads practically hidden by tall, wide bundles of wet grass, hardly able to see, and, because of the weight on their heads and the grass over their faces, unable to make more than slurred, brief replies to taunts, were easy objects of ridicule.

And it was to be the grass-gang for Mr Biswas. Later he would move to the cane fields, to weed and clean and plant and reap; he would be paid by the task and his tasks would be measured out by a driver with a long bamboo rod. And there he would remain. He would never become a driver or a weigher because he wouldn't be able to read. Perhaps, after many years, he might save enough to rent or buy a few acres where he would plant his own canes, which he would sell to the estate at a price fixed by them. But he would achieve this only if he had the strength and optimism of his brother Pratap. For that was what Pratap did. And Pratap, illiterate all his days, was to become richer than Mr Biswas; he was to have a house of his own, a large, strong, well-built house, years before Mr Biswas.

But Mr Biswas never went to work on the estates. Events which were to occur presently led him away from that. They did not lead him to riches, but made it possible for him to console himself in later life with the *Meditations* of Marcus Aurelius, while he rested on the Slumberking bed in the one room which contained most of his possessions.

Dhari, the next-door neighbour, bought a cow in calf, and when the calf was born, Dhari, whose wife went out to work and who had no children of his own, offered Mr Biswas the job of taking water to the calf during the day, at a penny a week. Raghu and Bipti were pleased.

Mr Biswas loved the calf, for its big head that looked so insecurely attached to its slender body, for its knobbly shaky legs, its big sad eyes and pink stupid nose. He liked to watch the calf tugging fiercely and sloppily at its mother's udders, its thin legs splayed out, its head almost hidden under its mother's belly. And he did more than take water to the calf. He took it for walks across damp fields of razor grass and along the rutted lanes between the cane fields, anxious to feed it with grass of many sorts and unable to understand why the calf resented being led from one place to another.

It was on one of these walks that Mr Biswas discovered the stream. It could not be here that Raghu brought Pratap and Prasad to swim: it was too shallow. But it was certainly here that Bipti and Dehuti came on Sunday afternoons to do the washing and returned with their fingers white and pinched. Between clumps of bamboo the stream ran over smooth stones of many sizes and colours, the cool sound of water blending with the rustle of the sharp leaves, the creaks of the tall bamboos when they swayed and their groans when they rubbed against one another.

Mr Biswas stood in the stream and looked down. The swift movement of the water and the noise made him forget its shallowness, the stones felt slippery, and in a panic he scrambled up to the bank and looked at the water, now harmless again, while the calf stood idle and unhappy beside him, not caring for bamboo leaves.

He continued to go to the forbidden stream. Its delights seemed endless. In a small eddy, dark in the shadow of the bank, he came upon a school of small black fish matching their background so well that they might easily have been mistaken for weeds. He lay down on the bamboo leaves and stretched out a hand slowly, but as soon as his fingers touched the water, the fish, with a wriggle and flick, were away. After that, when he saw the fish, he did not try to catch them. He would watch them and then drop things on the water. A dry bamboo leaf might cause a slight tremor among the fish; a bamboo twig might frighten them more; but if he remained still after that and dropped nothing the fish would become calm again. Then he would spit. Though he couldn't spit as well as his brother Pratap who, with casual violence, could make his spit resound wherever it fell, it pleased Mr Biswas to see his spit circling slowly above the black fish before being carried away into the main stream. Fishing he sometimes tried, with a thin bamboo rod, a length of string, a bent pin and no bait. The fish didn't bite; but if he wiggled the string violently they became frightened. When he had gazed at the fish long enough he dropped a stick into the water; it was good then to see the whole school instantly streaking away.

Then one day Mr Biswas lost the calf. He had forgotten it, watching the fish. And when, after dropping the stick and scattering the fish, he remembered the calf, it had gone. He hunted for it along the banks and in the adjoining fields. He went back to the field where Dhari had left the calf that morning. The iron piquet, its head squashed and shiny from repeated poundings, was there, but no rope was attached to it, no calf. He spent a long time searching, in fields full of tall weeds with fluffy heads, in the gutters, like neat red gashes, between the fields, and among the sugarcane. He called for it, mooing softly so as not to attract the attention of people.

Abruptly, he decided that the calf was lost for good; that the calf was anyway able to look after itself and would somehow make its way back to its mother in Dhari's yard. In the meantime the best thing for him to do would be to hide until the calf was found, or perhaps forgotten. It was getting late and he decided that the best place for him to hide would be at home.

The afternoon was almost over. In the west the sky was gold and smoke. Most of the villagers were back from work, and Mr Biswas had to make his way home with caution, keeping close to hedges and sometimes hiding in gutters. Unseen, he came right up to the back boundary of their lot. On a stand between the hut and the cowpen he saw Bipti washing enamel, brass and tin dishes with ashes and water. He hid behind the hibiscus hedge. Pratap and Prasad came, blades of grass between their teeth, their close-fitting felt hats damp with sweat, their faces scorched by the sun and stained with sweat, their legs cased in white mud. Pratap threw a length of white cotton around his dirty trousers and undressed with expert adult modesty before using the calabash to throw water over himself from the big black oil barrel. Prasad stood on a board and began scraping the white mud off his legs.

Bipti said, 'You boys will have to go and get some wood before it gets dark.'

Prasad lost his temper; and, as though by scraping off the white mud he had lost the composure of adulthood, he flung his hat to the ground and cried like a child, 'Why do you ask me *now*? Why do you ask me *every* day? I am not going.'

Raghu came to the back, an unfinished walking-stick in one hand and in the other a smoking wire with which he had been burning patterns into the stick. 'Listen, boy,' Raghu said. 'Don't feel that because you are earning money you are a man. Do what your mother asks. And go quickly, before I use this stick on you, even though it is unfinished.' He smiled at his joke.

Mr Biswas became uneasy.

Prasad, still raging, picked up his hat, and he and Pratap went away to the front of the house.

Bipti took her dishes to the kitchen in the front verandah, where Dehuti would be helping with the evening meal. Raghu went back to his bonfire at the front. Mr Biswas slipped through the hibiscus fence, crossed the narrow, shallow gutter, grey-black and squelchy with the ashy water from the washing-up stand and the muddy water from Pratap's bath, and made his way to the small back verandah where there was a table, the only piece of carpenter-built furniture in the hut. From the verandah he went into his father's room, passed under the valance of the bed – planks resting on upright logs sunk into the earth floor – and prepared to wait.

It was a long wait but he endured it without discomfort. Below the bed the smell of old cloth, dust and old thatch combined into one overpoweringly musty smell. Idly, to pass the time, he tried to disentangle one smell from the other, while his ears picked up the sounds in and around the hut. They were remote and dramatic. He heard the boys return and throw down the dry wood they had brought. Prasad still raged, Raghu warned, Bipti coaxed. Then all at once Mr Biswas became alert.

'Ey, Raghu?' He recognized Dhari's voice. 'Where is that youngest son of yours?'

'Mohun? Bipti, where is Mohun?'

'With Dhari's calf, I suppose.'

'Well, he isn't,' Dhari said.

'Prasad!' Bipti called. 'Pratap! Dehuti! Have you seen Mohun?'

'No, mai.'

'No, mai.'

'No, mai.'

'No, mai. No, mai. No, mai,' Raghu said. 'What the hell do you think it is? Go and look for him.'

'Oh *God!*' Prasad cried.

'And you too, Dhari. It was your idea, getting Mohun to look after the calf. I hold you responsible.'

'The magistrate will have something else to say,' Dhari said. 'A calf is a calf, and for one who is not as rich as yourself –'

'I am sure nothing has happened,' Bipti said, 'Mohun knows he mustn't go near water.'

Mr Biswas was startled by a sound of wailing. It came from Dhari. 'Water, water. Oh, the unlucky boy. Not content with eating up his mother and father, he is eating me up as well. Water! Oh, Mohun's mother, what you have said?'

'Water?' Raghu sounded puzzled.

'The pond, the pond,' Dhari wailed, and Mr Biswas heard him shouting to the neighbours, 'Raghu's son has drowned my calf in the pond. A nice calf. My first calf. My only calf.'

Quickly a chattering crowd gathered. Many of them had been to the pond that afternoon; quite a number had seen a calf wandering about, and one or two had even seen a boy.

'Nonsense!' Raghu said. 'You are a pack of liars. The boy doesn't go near water.' He paused and added, 'The pundit especially forbade him to go near water in its natural form.'

Lakhan the carter said, 'But this is a fine man. He doesn't seem to care whether his son is drowned or not.'

'How do you know what he thinks?' Bipti said.

'Leave him, leave him,' Raghu said, in an injured, forgiving tone. 'Mohun is *my* son. And if I don't care whether he is drowned or not, that is *my* business.'

'What about my calf?' Dhari said.

'I don't care about your calf. Pratap! Prasad! Dehuti! Have you seen your brother?'

'No, father.'

'No, father.'

'No, father.'

'I will go and dive for him,' Lakhan said.

'You are *very* anxious to show off,' Raghu said.

'Oh!' Bipti cried. 'Stop this bickering-ickering and let us go to look for the boy.'

'Mohun is *my* son,' Raghu said. 'And if anybody is going to dive for him, it will be me. And I pray to God, Dhari, that when I get to the bottom of that pond I find your wretched calf.'

'Witnesses!' Dhari said. 'You are all my witnesses. Those words will have to be repeated in court.'

'To the pond! To the pond!' the villagers said, and the news was shouted to those just arriving: 'Raghu is going to dive for his son in the pond.'

Mr Biswas, under his father's bed, had listened at first with pleasure, then with apprehension. Raghu came into the room, breathing heavily and swearing at the village. Mr Biswas heard him undress and shout for Bipti to come and rub him down with coconut oil. She came and rubbed him down and they both left the room. From the road chatter and the sound of footsteps rose, and slowly faded.

Mr Biswas came out from under the bed and was dismayed to find that the hut was dark. In the next room someone began to cry. He went to the doorway and looked. It was Dehuti. From the nail on the wall she had taken down his shirt and two vests and was pressing them to her face.

'Sister,' he whispered.

She heard and saw, and her sobs turned to screams.

Mr Biswas didn't know what to do. 'It's all right, it's all right,' he said, but the words were useless, and he went back to his father's room. Just in time, for at that moment Sadhu, the very old man who lived two houses away, came and asked what was wrong, his words whistling through the gaps in his teeth.

Dehuti continued to scream. Mr Biswas put his hands into his trouser pockets and, through the holes in them, pressed his fingers on his thighs.

Sadhu led Dehuti away.

Outside, from an unknown direction, a frog honked, then made a sucking, bubbling noise. The crickets were already chirping. Mr Biswas was alone in the dark hut, and frightened.

*

The pond lay in swampland. Weeds grew all over its surface and from a distance it appeared to be no more than a shallow depression. In fact it was full of abrupt depths and the villagers liked to think that these were immeasurable. There were no trees or hills around, so that though the sun had gone, the sky remained high and light. The villagers stood silently around the safe edge of the pond. The frogs honked and the poor-me-one bird began to say the mournful words that gave it its name. The mosquitoes were already active; from time to time a villager slapped his arm or lifted a leg and slapped that.

Lakhan the carter said, 'He's been down there too long.'

Bipti frowned.

Before Lakhan could take off his shirt Raghu broke the surface, puffed out his cheeks, spat out a long thin arc of water and took deep resounding breaths. The water rolled off his oiled skin, but his moustache had collapsed over his upper lip and his hair fell in a fringe over his forehead. Lakhan gave him a hand up. 'I believe there is something down there,' Raghu said. 'But it is very dark.'

Far away the low trees were black against the fading sky; the orange streaks of sunset were smudged with grey, as if by dirty thumbs.

Bipti said, 'Let Lakhan dive.'

Someone else said, 'Leave it till tomorrow.'

'Till tomorrow?' Raghu said. 'And poison the water for everybody?'

Lakhan said, 'I will go.'

Raghu, panting, shook his head. '*My* son. *My* duty.'

'And my calf,' Dhari said.

Raghu ignored him. He ran his hands through his hair, puffed out his cheeks, put his hands to his sides and belched. In a moment he was in the water again. The pond didn't permit stylish diving; Raghu merely let himself down. The water broke and rippled. The gleam it got from the sky was fading. While they waited a cool wind came down from the hills to the north; between the shaking weeds the water shimmered like sequins.

Lakhan said, 'He's coming up now. I believe he's got something.'

They knew what it was from Dhari's cry. Then Bipti began to scream, and Pratap and Prasad and all the women, while the men helped to lift the calf to the bank. One of its sides was green with slime; its thin limbs were ringed with vinelike weeds, still fresh and thick and green. Raghu sat on the bank, looking down between his legs at the dark water.

Lakhan said, 'Let me go down now and look for the boy.'

'Yes, man,' Bipti pleaded. 'Let him go.'

Raghu remained where he was, breathing deeply, his dhoti clinging to his skin. Then he was in the water and the villagers were silent again. They waited, looking at the calf, looking at the pond.

Lakhan said, 'Something has happened.'

A woman said, 'No stupid talk now, Lakhan. Raghu is a great diver.'

'I know, I know,' Lakhan said. 'But he's been diving too long.'

Then they were all still. Someone had sneezed.

They turned to see Mr Biswas standing some distance away in the gloom, the toe of one foot scratching the ankle of the other.

Lakhan was in the pond. Pratap and Prasad rushed to hustle Mr Biswas away.

'That boy!' Dhari said. 'He has murdered my calf and now he has eaten up his own father.'

Lakhan brought up Raghu unconscious. They rolled him on the damp grass and pumped water out of his mouth and through his nostrils. But it was too late.

'Messages,' Bipti kept on saying. 'We must send messages.' And messages were taken everywhere by willing and excited villagers. The most important message went to Bipti's sister Tara at Pagotes. Tara was a person of standing. It was her fate to be childless, but it was also her fate to have married a man who had, at one bound, freed himself from the land and acquired wealth; already he owned a rumshop and a dry goods shop, and he had been one of the first in Trinidad to buy a motorcar.

Tara came and at once took control. Her arms were en-
cased from wrist to elbow with silver bangles which she had
often recommended to Bipti: 'They are not very pretty, but
one clout from this arm will settle any attacker.' She also wore
earrings and a *nakphul*, a 'nose-flower'. She had a solid gold
yoke around her neck and thick silver bracelets on her ankles.
In spite of all her jewellery she was energetic and capable, and
had adopted her husband's commanding manner. She left the
mourning to Bipti and arranged everything else. She had
brought her own pundit, whom she continually harangued;
she instructed Pratap how to behave during the ceremonies;
and she had even brought a photographer.

She urged Prasad, Dehuti and Mr Biswas to behave with
dignity and to keep out of the way, and she ordered Dehuti
to see that Mr Biswas was properly dressed. As the baby of the
family Mr Biswas was treated by the mourners with honour
and sympathy, though this was touched with a little dread.
Embarrassed by their attentions, he moved about the hut and
yard, thinking he could detect a new, raw smell in the air.
There was also a strange taste in his mouth; he had never
eaten meat, but now he felt he had eaten raw white flesh;
nauseating saliva rose continually at the back of his throat and
he had to keep on spitting, until Tara said, 'What's the matter
with you? Are you pregnant?'

Bipti was bathed. Her hair, still wet, was neatly parted
and the parting filled with red henna. Then the henna
was scooped out and the parting filled with charcoal dust.
She was now a widow forever. Tara gave a short scream and
at her signal the other women began to wail. On Bipti's
wet black hair there were still spots of henna, like drops of
blood.

Cremation was forbidden and Raghu was to be buried. He
lay in a coffin in the bedroom, dressed in his finest dhoti,
jacket and turban, his beads around his neck and down
his jacket. The coffin was strewed with marigolds which
matched his turban. Pratap, the eldest son, did the last rites,
walking round the coffin.

'Photo now,' Tara said. 'Quick. Get them all together. For
the last time.'

The photographer, who had been smoking under the mango tree, went into the hut and said, 'Too dark.'

The men became interested and gave advice while the women wailed.

'Take it outside. Lean it against the mango tree.'

'Light a lamp.'

'It *couldn't* be too dark.'

'What do you know? You've never had your photo taken. Now, what *I* suggest –'

The photographer, of mixed Chinese, Negro and European blood, did not understand what was being said. In the end he and some of the men took the coffin out to the verandah and stood it against the wall.

'Careful! Don't let him fall out.'

'Goodness. All the marigolds have dropped out.'

'Leave them,' the photographer said in English. 'Is a nice little touch. Flowers on the ground.' He set up his tripod in the yard, just under the ragged eaves of thatch, and put his head under the black cloth.

Tara roused Bipti from her grief, arranged Bipti's hair and veil, and dried Bipti's eyes.

'Five people all together,' the photographer said to Tara. 'Hard to know just how to arrange them. It look to me that it would have to be two one side and three the other side. You sure you want all five?'

Tara was firm.

The photographer sucked his teeth, but not at Tara. 'Look, look. Why nobody ain't put anything to chock up the coffin and prevent it from slipping?'

Tara had that attended to.

The photographer said, 'All right then. Mother and biggest son on either side. Next to mother, young boy and young girl. Next to big son, smaller son.'

There was more advice from the men.

'Make them look at the coffin.'

'At the mother.'

'At the youngest boy.'

The photographer settled the matter by telling Tara, 'Tell them to look at me.'

Tara translated, and the photographer went under his cloth. Almost immediately he came out again. 'How about making the mother and the biggest boy put their hands on the edge of the coffin?'

This was done and the photographer went back under his cloth.

'Wait!' Tara cried, running out from the hut with a fresh garland of marigolds. She hung it around Raghu's neck and said to the photographer in English, 'All right. Draw your photo now.'

Mr Biswas never owned a copy of the photograph and he did not see it until 1937, when it made its appearance, framed in passepartout, on the wall of the drawingroom of Tara's fine new house at Pagotes, a little lost among many other photographs of funeral groups, many oval portraits with blurred edges of more dead friends and relations, and coloured prints of the English countryside. The photograph had faded to the lightest brown and was partially defaced by the large heliotrope stamp of the photographer, still bright, and his smudged sprawling signature in soft black pencil. Mr Biswas was astonished at his own smallness. The scabs of sores and the marks of eczema showed clearly on his knobbly knees and along his very thin arms and legs. Everyone in the photograph had unnaturally large, staring eyes which seemed to have been outlined in black.

Tara was right when she said that the photograph was to be a record of the family all together for the last time. For in a few days Mr Biswas and Bipti, Pratap and Prasad and Dehuti had left Parrot Trace and the family split up for good.

It began on the evening of the funeral.

Tara said, 'Bipti, you must give me Dehuti.'

Bipti had been hoping that Tara would make the suggestion. In four or five years Dehuti would have to be married and it was better that she should be given to Tara. She would learn manners, acquire graces and, with a dowry from Tara, might even make a good match.

'If you are going to have someone,' Tara said, 'it is better to have one of your own family. That is what I always say. I don't want strangers poking their noses into my kitchen and bedroom.'

Bipti agreed that it was better to have servants from one's own family. And Pratap and Prasad and even Mr Biswas, who had not been asked, nodded, as though the problem of servants was one they had given much thought.

Dehuti looked down at the floor, shook her long hair and mumbled a few words which meant that she was far too small to be consulted, but was very pleased.

'Get her new clothes,' Tara said, fingering the georgette skirt and satin petticoat Dehuti had worn for the funeral. 'Get her some jewels.' She put a thumb and finger around Dehuti's wrist, lifted her face, and turned up the lobe of her ear. 'Earrings. Good thing you had them pierced, Bipti. She won't need these sticks now.' In the holes in her lobe Dehuti wore pieces of the thin hard spine of the blades of the coconut branch. Tara playfully pulled Dehuti's nose. 'Nakphul too. You would like a nose-flower?'

Dehuti smiled shyly, not looking up.

'Well,' Tara said, 'fashions are changing all the time these days. I am just oldfashioned, that is all.' She stroked her gold nose-flower. 'It is expensive to be oldfashioned.'

'She will satisfy you,' Bipti said. 'Raghu had no money. But he trained his children well. Training, piety –'

'Quite,' Tara said. 'The time for crying is over, Bipti. How much money did Raghu leave you?'

'Nothing. I don't know.'

'What do you mean? Are you trying to keep secrets from me? Everyone in the village knows that Raghu had a lot of money. I am sure he has left you enough to start a nice little business.'

Pratap sucked his teeth. 'He was a miser, that one. He used to hide his money.'

Tara said, 'Is this the training and piety your father gave you?'

They searched. They pulled out Raghu's box from under the bed and looked for false bottoms; at Bipti's suggestion they looked for any joint that might reveal a hiding-place in the timber itself. They poked the sooty thatch and ran their hands over the rafters; they tapped the earth floor and the bamboo-and-mud walls; they examined Raghu's walking-sticks, taking out the ferrules, Raghu's only extravagance; they dismantled the bed and uprooted the logs on which it stood. They found nothing.

Bipti said, 'I don't suppose he had any money really.'

'You are a fool,' Tara said, and it was in this mood of annoyance that she ordered Bipti to pack Dehuti's bundle and took Dehuti away.

Because no cooking could be done at their house, they ate at Sadhu's. The food was unsalted and as soon as he began to chew, Mr Biswas felt he was eating raw flesh and the nauseous saliva filled his mouth again. He hurried outside to empty his mouth and clean it, but the taste remained. And Mr Biswas screamed when, back at the hut, Bipti put him to bed and threw Raghu's blanket over him. The blanket was hairy and prickly; it seemed to be the source of the raw, fresh smell he had been smelling all day. Bipti let him scream until he was tired and fell asleep in the yellow, wavering light of the oil lamp which left the corners in darkness. She watched the wick burn lower and lower until she heard the snores of Pratap, who snored like a big man, and the heavy breathing of Mr Biswas and Prasad. She slept only fitfully herself. It was quiet inside the hut, but outside the noises were loud and continuous: mosquitoes, bats, frogs, crickets, the poor-me-one. If the cricket missed a chirp the effect was disturbing and she awoke.

She was awakened from a light sleep by a new noise. At first she couldn't be sure. But the nearness of the noise and its erratic sequence disturbed her. It was a noise she heard every day but now, isolated in the night, it was hard to place. It came again: a thud, a pause, a prolonged snapping, then a series of gentler thuds. And it came again. Then there was another noise, of bottles breaking, muffled, as though the bottles were full. And she knew the noises came from her garden. Someone was stumbling among the bottles Raghu had buried neck downwards around the flower-beds.

She roused Prasad and Pratap.

Mr Biswas, awaking to hushed talk and a room of dancing shadows, closed his eyes to keep out the danger; at once, as on the day before, everything became dramatic and remote.

Pratap gave walking-sticks to Prasad and Bipti. Carefully he unbolted the small window, then pushed it out with sudden vigour.

The garden was lit up by a hurricane lamp. A man was working a fork into the ground among the bottle-borders.

'Dhari!' Bipti called.

Dhari didn't look up or reply. He went on forking, rocking the implement in the earth, tearing the roots that kept the earth firm.

'Dhari!'

He began to sing a wedding song.

'The cutlass!' Pratap said. 'Give me the cutlass.'

'O God! No, no,' Bipti said.

'I'll go out and beat him like a snake,' Pratap said, his voice rising out of control. 'Prasad? Mai?'

'Close the window,' Bipti said.

The singing stopped and Dhari said, 'Yes, close the window and go to sleep. I am here to look after you.'

Violently Bipti pulled the small window to, bolted it and kept her hand on the bolt.

The digging and the breaking bottles continued. Dhari sang:

> In your daily tasks be resolute.
> Fear no one, and trust in God.

'Dhari isn't in this alone,' Bipti said. 'Don't provoke him.' Then, as though it not only belittled Dhari's behaviour but gave protection to them all, she added, 'He is only after your father's money. Let him look.'

Mr Biswas and Prasad were soon asleep again. Bipti and Pratap remained up until they had heard the last of Dhari's songs and his fork no longer dug into the earth and broke bottles. They did not speak. Only, once, Bipti said, 'Your father always warned me about the people of this village.'

Pratap and Prasad awoke when it was still dark, as they always did. They did not talk about what had happened and Bipti insisted that they should go to the buffalo pond as usual. As soon as it was light she went out to the garden. The flower-beds had been dug up; dew lay on the upturned earth which partially buried uprooted plants, already limp and quailing. The vegetable patch had not been forked, but tomato plants had been cut down, stakes broken and pumpkins slashed.

'Oh, wife of Raghu!' a man called from the road, and she saw Dhari jump across the gutter.

Absently, he picked a dew-wet leaf from the hibiscus shrub, crushed it in his palm, put it in his mouth and came towards her, chewing.

Her anger rose. 'Get out! At once! Do you call yourself a man? You are a shameless vagabond. Shameless and cowardly.'

He walked past her, past the hut, to the garden. Chewing, he considered the damage. He was in his working clothes, his cutlass in its black leather sheath at his waist, his enamel food-carrier in one hand, his calabash of water hanging from his shoulder.

'Oh, wife of Raghu, what have they done?'

'I hope you found something to make you happy, Dhari.'

He shrugged, looking down at the ruined flower-beds. 'They will keep on looking, *maharajin*.'

'Everybody knows you lost your calf. But that was an accident. What about –'

'Yes, yes. My calf. Accident.'

'I will remember you for this, Dhari. And Raghu's sons won't forget you either.'

'He was a great diver.'

'Savage! Get out!'

'Willingly.' He spat out the hibiscus leaf on to a flower-bed. 'I just wanted to tell you that these wicked men will come again. Why don't you help them, *maharajin*?'

There was no one Bipti could ask for help. She distrusted the police, and Raghu had no friends. Moreover, she didn't know who might be in league with Dhari.

That night they gathered all Raghu's sticks and cutlasses and waited. Mr Biswas closed his eyes and listened, but as the hours passed he found it hard to remain alert.

He was awakened by whispers and movement in the hut. Far away, it seemed, someone was singing a slow, sad wedding song. Bipti and Prasad were standing. Cutlass in hand, Pratap moved in a frenzy between the window and the door, so swiftly that the flame of the oil lamp blew this way and that, and once, with a plopping sound, disappeared. The room sank into darkness. A moment later the flame returned, rescuing them.

The singing drew nearer, and when it was almost upon them they heard, mingled with it, chatter and soft laughter.

Bipti unbolted the window, pushed it open a crack, and saw the garden ablaze with lanterns.

'Three of them,' she whispered. 'Lakhan, Dhari, Oumadh.'

Pratap pushed Bipti aside, flung the window wide open and screamed, 'Get out! Get out! I will kill you all.'

'Shh,' Bipti said, pulling Pratap away and trying to close the window.

'Raghu's son,' a man said from the garden.

'Don't sh me,' Pratap screamed, turning on Bipti. Tears came to his eyes and his voice broke into sobs. 'I will kill them all.'

'Noisy little fellow,' another man said.

'I will come back and kill you all,' Pratap shouted. 'I promise you.'

Bipti took him in her arms and comforted him, like a child, and in the same gentle, unalarmed voice said, 'Prasad, close the window. And go to sleep.'

'Yes, son.' They recognized Dhari's voice. 'Go to sleep. We will be here every night now to look after you.'

Prasad closed the window, but the noise stayed with them: song, talk, and unhurried sounds of fork and spade. Bipti sat and stared at the door, next to which, on the ground, Pratap sat, a cutlass beside him, its haft carved into a pair of wellingtons. He was motionless. His tears had gone, but his eyes were red, and the lids swollen.

*

In the end Bipti sold the hut and the land to Dhari, and she and Mr Biswas moved to Pagotes. There they lived on Tara's bounty, though not with Tara, but with some of Tara's husband's dependent relations in a back trace far from the Main Road. Pratap and Prasad were sent to a distant relation at Felicity, in the heart of the sugar-estates; they were already broken into estate work and were too old to learn anything else.

And so Mr Biswas came to leave the only house to which he had some right. For the next thirty-five years he was to be a wanderer with no place he could call his own, with no family except that which he was to attempt to create out of the engulfing world of the Tulsis. For with his mother's parents dead, his father dead, his brothers on the estate at Felicity, Dehuti as a servant in Tara's house, and himself rapidly growing away from Bipti who, broken, became increasingly useless and impenetrable, it seemed to him that he was really quite alone.

## 2. Before the Tulsis

MR BISWAS could never afterwards say exactly where his father's hut had stood or where Dhari and the others had dug. He never knew whether anyone found Raghu's money. It could not have been much, since Raghu earned so little. But the ground did yield treasure. For this was in South Trinidad and the land Bipti had sold so cheaply to Dhari was later found to be rich with oil. And when Mr Biswas was working on a feature article for the magazine section of the *Sunday Sentinel* – RALEIGH'S DREAM COMES TRUE, said the headline, 'But the Gold is Black. Only the Earth is Yellow. Only the Bush Green' – when Mr Biswas looked for the place where he had spent his early years he saw nothing but oil derricks and grimy pumps, see-sawing, see-sawing, endlessly, surrounded by red No Smoking notices. His grandparents' house had also disappeared, and when huts of mud and grass are pulled down they leave no trace. His navel-string, buried on that inauspicious night, and his sixth finger, buried not long after, had turned to dust. The pond had been drained and the whole swamp region was now a garden city of white wooden bungalows with red roofs, cisterns on tall stilts, and neat gardens. The stream where he had watched the black fish had been dammed, diverted into a reservoir, and its winding, irregular bed covered by straight lawns, streets and drives. The world carried no witness to Mr Biswas's birth and early years.

As he found at Pagotes.

'How old you is, boy?' Lal, the teacher at the Canadian Mission school, asked, his small hairy hands fussing with the cylindrical ruler on his roll-book.

Mr Biswas shrugged and shifted from one bare foot to the other.

'How you people want to get on, eh?' Lal had been converted to Presbyterianism from a low Hindu caste and held all unconverted Hindus in contempt. As part of this contempt he spoke to them in broken English. 'Tomorrow I want you to bring your buth certificate. You hear?'

'Buth suttificate?' Bipti echoed the English words. 'I don't have any.'

'Don't have any, eh?' Lal said the next day. 'You people don't even know how to born, it look like.'

But they agreed on a plausible date, Lal completed his roll-book record, and Bipti went to consult Tara.

Tara took Bipti to a solicitor whose office was a tiny wooden shed standing lopsided on eight unfashioned logs. The distemper on its walls had turned to dust. A sign, obviously painted by the man himself, said that F. Z. Ghany was a solicitor, conveyancer and a commissioner of oaths. He didn't look like all that, sitting on a broken kitchen chair at the door of his shed, bending forward, picking his teeth with a matchstick, his tie hanging perpendicular. Large dusty books were piled on the dusty floor, and on the kitchen table at his back there was a sheet of green blotting-paper, also dusty, on which there was a highly decorated metal contraption which looked like a toy version of the merry-go-round Mr Biswas had seen in the playground at St Joseph on the way to Pagotes. From this toy merry-go-round hung two rubber stamps, and directly below them there was a purple-stained tin. F. Z. Ghany carried the rest of his office equipment in his shirt pocket; it was stiff with pens, pencils, sheets of paper and envelopes. He needed to be able to carry his equipment about; he opened the Pagotes office only on market day, Wednesday; he had other offices, open on other market days, at Tunapuna, Arima, St Joseph and Tacarigua. 'Just give me three or four dog-case or cuss-case every day,' he used to say, 'and I all right, you hear.'

Seeing the group of three walking Indians file across the plank over the gutter, F. Z. Ghany got up, spat out the matchstick and greeted them with good-humoured scorn. '*Maharajin, maharajin,* and little boy.' He made most of his money from Hindus but, as a Muslim, distrusted them.

They climbed the two steps into his office. It became full. Ghany liked it that way; it attracted customers. He took the chair behind the table, sat on it, and left his clients standing.

Tara began to explain about Mr Biswas. She grew prolix, encouraged by the quizzical look on Ghany's heavy dissipated face.

During one of Tara's pauses Bipti said, 'Buth suttificate.'

'Oh!' Ghany said, his manner changing. 'Certificate of buth.' It was a familiar problem. He looked legal and said, 'Affidavit. When did the buth take place?'

Bipti told Tara in Hindi, 'I can't really say. But Pundit Sitaram should know. He cast Mohun's horoscope the day after he was born.'

'I don't know what you see in that man, Bipti. He doesn't *know* anything.'

Ghany could follow their conversation. He disliked the way Indian women had of using Hindi as a secret language in public places, and asked impatiently, 'Date of buth?'

'Eighth of June,' Bipti said to Tara. 'It *must* be that.'

'All right,' Ghany said. 'Eighth of June. Who to tell you no?' Smiling, he put a hand to the drawer of his table and pulled it this way and that before it came out. He took out a sheet of foolscap, tore it in half, put back one half into the drawer, pushed the drawer this way and that to close it, put the half-sheet on the dusty blotting-paper, stamped his name on it and prepared to write. 'Name of boy?'

'Mohun,' Tara said.

Mr Biswas became shy. He passed his tongue above his upper lip and tried to make it touch the knobby tip of his nose.

'Surname?' Ghany asked.

'Biswas,' Tara said.

'Nice Hindu name.' He asked more questions, and wrote. When he was finished, Bipti made her mark and Tara, with great deliberation and much dancing of the pen above the paper, signed her name. F. Z. Ghany struggled with the drawer once more, took out the other half-sheet, stamped his name on it, wrote, and then had everybody sign again.

Mr Biswas was now leaning forward against one of the dusty walls, his feet pushed far back. He was spitting carefully, trying to let his spittle hang down to the floor without breaking.

F. Z. Ghany hung up his name stamp and took down the date stamp. He turned some ratchets, banged hard on the almost dry purple pad and banged hard on the paper. Two lengths of rubber fell apart. 'Blasted thing bust,' he said, and examined it without annoyance. He explained, 'You could print the year all right, because you move that only once a year. But the dates and the months, man, you spinning them round all the time.' He took up the length of rubber and looked at them thoughtfully. 'Here, give them to the boy. Play with them.' He wrote the date with one of his pens and said, 'All right, leave everything to me now. Expensive business, affidavits. Stamps and thing, you know. Ten dollars in all.'

Bipti fumbled with the knot at the end of her veil and Tara paid.

'Any more children without certificate of buth?'

'Three,' Bipti said.

'Bring them,' Ghany said. 'Bring all of them. Any market day. Next week? Is better to straighten these things right away, you know.'

In this way official notice was taken of Mr Biswas's existence, and he entered the new world.

> *Ought oughts are ought,*
> *Ought twos are ought.*

The chanting of the children pleased Lal. He believed in thoroughness, discipline and what he delighted to call stick-to-it-iveness, virtues he felt unconverted Hindus particularly lacked.

> *One twos are two,*
> *Two twos are four.*

'Stop!' Lal cried, waving his tamarind rod. 'Biswas, ought twos are how much?'

'Two.'

'Come up here. You, Ramguli, ought twos are how much?'

'Ought.'

'Come up. That boy with a shirt that looks like one of his mother bodice. How much?'

'Four.'

'Come up.' He held the rod at both ends and bent it back and forth quickly. The sleeves of his jacket fell down past dirty cuffs and thin wrists black with hair. The jacket was brown but had turned saffron where it had been soaked by Lal's sweat. For all the time he went to school, Mr Biswas never saw Lal wearing any other jacket.

'Ramguli, go back to your desk. All right, the two of you. All-you decide now how much ought twos is?'

'Ought,' they whimpered together.

'Yes, ought twos are ought. You did tell me two.' He caught hold of Mr Biswas, pulled his trousers tight across his bottom, and began to apply the tamarind rod, saying as he beat, 'Ought twos are ought. Ought oughts are ought. *One* twos are two.'

Mr Biswas, released, went crying back to his desk.

'And now you. Before we talk about anything, tell me where you get that bodice from?'

With its flaming red colour and leg-of-mutton sleeves it was obviously a bodice and had, without comment, been recognized as such by the boys, most of whom wore garments not originally designed for them.

'Where you get it from?'

'My sister-in-law.'

'And you thank her?'

There was no reply.

'Anyway, when you see your sister-in-law, I want you to give her a message. I want you' – and here Lal seized the boy and started to use the tamarind rod – 'I want you to tell her that ought twos don't make four. I want you to tell her that ought oughts are ought, ought twos are ought, one twos are two, and *two* twos are four.'

Mr Biswas was taught other things. He learned to say the Lord's Prayer in Hindi from the *King George V Hindi Reader*, and he learned many English poems by heart from the *Royal Reader*. At Lal's dictation he made copious notes, which he never seriously believed, about geysers, rift valleys, watersheds, currents, the Gulf Stream, and a number of deserts. He learned about oases, which Lal taught him to pronounce 'osis', and ever afterwards an oasis meant for him nothing more than four or five date trees around a narrow pool of fresh water, surrounded for unending miles by white sand and hot sun. He learned about igloos. In arithmetic he got as far as simple interest and learned to turn dollars and cents into pounds, shilling and pence. The history Lal taught he regarded as simply a school subject, a discipline, as unreal as the geography; and it was from the boy in the red bodice that he first heard, with disbelief, about the Great War.

With this boy, whose name was Alec, Mr Biswas became friendly. The colours of Alec's clothes were a continual surprise, and one day he scandalized the school by peeing blue, a clear, light turquoise. To excited inquiry Alec replied, 'I don't know, boy. I suppose is because I is a Portuguese or something.' And for days he gave solemn demonstrations which filled most boys with disgust at their race.

It was to Mr Biswas that Alec first revealed his secret, and one morning recess, after Alec had given his demonstration, Mr Biswas dramatically unbuttoned and gave his. There was a clamour and Alec was forced to take out the bottle of Dodd's Kidney Pills. In no time the bottle was empty, except for some half a dozen pills which Alec said he had to keep. The pills, like the red bodice, belonged to his sister-in-law. 'I don't know what she going to do when she find out,' Alec said, and to those boys who still begged, he said, 'Buy your own. The drugstore full of them.' And many of them did buy their own, and for a week the school's urinals ran turquoise; and the druggist attributed the sudden rise in sales to the success of the Dodd's Kidney Pills Almanac which, in addition to jokes, carried story after story of the rapid cures the pills had effected on Trinidadians, all of whom had written the makers profusely grateful letters of the utmost articulateness, and been photographed.

With Alec Mr Biswas laid six-inch nails on the railway track at the back of the Main Road and had them flattened to make knives and bayonets. Together they went to Pagotes

River and smoked their first cigarettes. They tore off their shirt buttons, exchanged them for marbles and with these Alec won more, struggling continually to repair the depredations of Lal, who considered the game low and had forbidden it in the school grounds. They sat at the same desk, talked, were flogged and separated, but always came together again.

And it was through this association that Mr Biswas discovered his gift for lettering. When Alec tired of doing inaccurate erotic drawings he designed letters. Mr Biswas imitated these with pleasure and growing success. During an arithmetic test one day, finding himself with an astronomical number of hours in answer to a problem about cisterns, he wrote CANCELLED very neatly across the page and became absorbed in blocking the letters and shadowing them. When the period was over he had done nothing else.

Lal, who had noted Mr Biswas's industry with approval, flew into a rage. 'Ah! Sign-painter. Come up.'

He didn't flog Mr Biswas. He ordered him to write I AM AN ASS on the blackboard. Mr Biswas outlined stylish, contemptuous letters, and the class tittered approvingly. Lal, racing about the classroom, waving his tamarind rod for silence, brushed Mr Biswas's elbow and a stroke was spoilt. Mr Biswas turned this into an additional decoration which pleased him and impressed the class. It was too late for Lal to flog Mr Biswas or order him to clean the blackboard. Angrily he pushed him away, and Mr Biswas went back to his desk, smiling, a hero.

Mr Biswas went to Lal's school for nearly six years and for all that time he was friendly with Alec. Yet he knew little about Alec's home life. Alec never spoke about his mother or father and Mr Biswas knew only that he lived with his sister-in-law, the owner of the red bodice, an unphotographed user of Dodd's Kidney Pills, and, according to Alec, a great beater. Mr Biswas never saw this woman. He never went to Alec's home and Alec never came to his. There was a tacit agreement between them that they would keep their homes secret.

It would have pained Mr Biswas if anyone from the school saw where he lived, in one room of a mud hut in the back trace. He was not happy there and even after five years considered it a temporary arrangement. Most of the people in the hut remained strangers, and his relations with Bipti were unsatisfying because she was shy of showing him affection in a house of strangers. More and more, too, she bewailed her Fate; when she did this he felt useless and dispirited and, instead of comforting her, went out to look for Alec. Occasionally she had ineffectual fits of temper, quarrelled with Tara and muttered for days, threatening, whenever there was anyone to hear, that she would leave and get a job with the road-gang, where women were needed to carry stones in baskets on their heads. Continually, when he was with her, Mr Biswas had to struggle against anger and depression.

At Christmas Pratap and Prasad came from Felicity, grown men now, with moustaches; in their best clothes, their pressed khaki trousers, unpolished brown shoes, blue shirts buttoned at the collar, and brown hats, they too were like strangers. Their hands were as hard as their rough, sunburnt faces, and they had little to say. When Pratap, with many self-deprecating sighs, half-laughs and pauses which enabled him to deliver a short sentence in easy instalments without in any way damaging its structure, when Pratap told about the donkey he had bought and the current lengths of tasks, Mr Biswas was not really interested. The buying of a donkey seemed to him an act of pure comedy, and it was hard to believe that the dour Pratap was the frantic boy who had rushed about the room in the hut threatening to kill the men in the garden.

As for Dehuti, he hardly saw her, though she lived close, at Tara's. He seldom went there except when Tara's husband, prompted by Tara, held a religious ceremony and needed Brahmins to feed. Then Mr Biswas was treated with honour; stripped of his ragged trousers and shirt, and in a clean dhoti, he became a different person, and he never thought it unseemly that the person who served him so deferentially with food should be his own sister. In Tara's house he was respected as a Brahmin and pampered; yet as soon as the ceremony was over and he had taken his gift of money and cloth and left, he became once more only a labourer's child – *father's occupation: labourer* was the entry in the birth

certificate F. Z. Ghany had sent – living with a penniless
mother in one room of a mud hut. And throughout life his
position was like that. As one of the Tulsi sons-in-law and as
a journalist he found himself among people with money and
sometimes with graces; with them his manner was unforcedly
easy and he could summon up luxurious instincts; but always,
at the end, he returned to his crowded, shabby room.

Tara's husband, Ajodha, was a thin man with a thin, petulant face which could express benignity rather than warmth,
and Mr Biswas was not comfortable with him. Ajodha could
read but thought it more dignified to be read to, and Mr
Biswas was sometimes called to the house to read, for a
penny, a newspaper column of which Ajodha was particularly
fond. This was a syndicated American column called *That
Body of Yours* which dealt every day with a different
danger to the human body. Ajodha listened with gravity,
concern, alarm. It puzzled Mr Biswas that he should subject
himself to this torment, and it amazed him that the writer, Dr
Samuel S. Pitkin, could keep the column going with
such regularity. But the doctor never flagged; twenty years
later the column was still going, Ajodha had not lost his taste
for it, and occasionally Mr Biswas's son read it to him, for six
cents.

So, whenever Mr Biswas was in Tara's house, it was as a
Brahmin or a reader, with a status distinct from Dehuti's, and
he had little opportunity of speaking to her.

Bipti had a specific worry about her children: neither Pratap nor Prasad nor Dehuti was married. She had no plans for
Mr Biswas, since he was still young and she assumed that the
education he was receiving was provision and protection
enough. But Tara thought otherwise. And just when Mr
Biswas was beginning to do stocks and shares, transactions as
unreal to Lal as they were to him, and was learning 'Bingen
on the Rhine' from *Bell's Standard Elocutionist* for the visit of
the school inspector, he was taken out of school by Tara and
told that he was going to be made a pundit.

It was only when his possessions were being bundled that
he discovered he still had the school's copy of the *Standard
Elocutionist*. It was too late to return it, and he never did.

Wherever he went the book went with him, and ended in the blacksmith-built bookcase in the house at Sikkim Street.

For eight months, in a bare, spacious, unpainted wooden house smelling of blue soap and incense, its floors white and smooth from constant scrubbing, its cleanliness and sanctity maintained by regulations awkward to everyone except himself, Pundit Jairam taught Mr Biswas Hindi, introduced him to the more important scriptures and instructed him in various ceremonies. Morning and evening, under the pundit's eye, Mr Biswas did the *puja* for the pundit's household.

Jairam's children had all been married and he lived alone with his wife, a crushed, hard-working woman whose only duty now was to look after Jairam and his house. She didn't complain. Among Hindus Jairam was respected for his knowledge. He also held scandalous views which, while being dismissed as contentious, had nevertheless brought him much popularity. He believed in God, fervently, but claimed it was not necessary for a Hindu to do so. He attacked the custom some families had of putting up a flag after a religious ceremony; but his own front garden was a veritable grove of bamboo poles with red and white pennants in varying stages of decay. He ate no meat but spoke against vegetarianism: when Lord Rama went hunting, did they think it was just for the sport?

He was also working on a Hindi commentary on the *Ramayana*, and parts of this commentary were dictated to Mr Biswas to extend his own knowledge of the language. So that Mr Biswas could see and learn, Jairam took him on his rounds; and wherever he went with the pundit Mr Biswas, invested with the sacred thread and all the other badges of caste, found himself, as in Tara's house, the object of regard. It was his duty on these occasions to do the mechanical side of Jairam's offices. He took around the brass plate with the lighted camphor; the devout dropped a coin on the plate, brushed the flame with their fingers and took their fingers to their forehead. He took around the consecrated sweetened milk with strips of the tulsi leaf floating on its surface, and doled it out a teaspoonful at a time. When the ceremonies were over and the feeding of Brahmins began, he was seated next to Pundit Jairam; and when Jairam had eaten and belched and asked for more and eaten again it was Mr Biswas who mixed the bicarbonate of soda for him. Afterwards Mr Biswas went to the shrine, a platform of earth decorated with flour and planted with small banana trees, and pillaged it for the coins that had been offered, hunting carefully everywhere, showing no respect for the burnt offerings or anything else. The coins, dusted with flour or earth or ash, wet with holy water or warm from the sacred fire, he took to Pundit Jairam, who might then be engaged in some philosophical disputation. Jairam would wave Mr Biswas away without looking at him. As soon as they got home, however, Jairam asked for the money, counted it, and felt Mr Biswas all over to make sure he hadn't kept anything back. Mr Biswas also had to bring home all the gifts Jairam received, usually lengths of cotton, but sometimes cumbersome bundles of fruit and vegetables.

One particularly large gift was a bunch of Gros Michel bananas. They came to Jairam green and were hung in the large kitchen to ripen. In time the green became lighter, spotted, and soft yellow patches appeared. Rapidly the yellow spread and deepened, and the spots became brown and rich. The smell of ripening banana, overcoming the astringent smell of the glutinous sap from the banana stem, filled the house, leaving Jairam and his wife apparently indifferent, but rousing Mr Biswas. He reasoned that the bananas would become ripe all at once, that Jairam and his wife could not possibly eat them all, and that many would grow rotten. He also reasoned a banana or two would not be missed. And one day, when Jairam was out and his wife away from the kitchen, Mr Biswas picked two bananas and ate them. The gaps in the bunch startled him. They were more than noticeable; they offended the eye.

Jairam was no flogger. When he was in a rage he might box Mr Biswas on the ear; but usually he was less intemperate. For a badly conducted *puja*, for instance, he might make Mr Biswas learn a dozen couplets from the *Ramayana* by heart, confining him to the house until he had. All that day

Mr Biswas wondered what punishment the eating of the bananas would bring, while he copied out Sanskrit verses, which he couldn't understand, on strips of cardboard, having revealed to Jairam his skill in lettering.

Jairam came late that evening and his wife fed him. Then, as was his habit every evening after he had eaten and rested, he walked heavily about the bare verandah, talking to himself, going over the arguments he had had that day. First he quoted the opposing view. Then he tested various replies of his own; his voice rose shrill at the end of the final version of the repartee, which he said over and over, breaking off to sing a snatch of a hymn. Mr Biswas, lying on his sugarsack and floursack bed, listened. Jairam's wife was washing up the dishes in the kitchen; the waste water ran down a bamboo spout to a gutter, where it fell noisily among the bushes.

Waiting, Mr Biswas fell asleep. When he awoke it was morning and for a moment he had no fears. Then his error returned to him.

He had his bath in the yard, cut a hibiscus twig, crushed one end and cleaned his teeth with it, split the twig and scraped his tongue with the halves. Then he collected marigolds and zinnias and oleanders from the garden for the morning *puja*, and sat without religious fervour before the elaborate shrine. The smell of brass and stale sandalwood paste displeased him; it was a smell he was to recognize later in all temples, mosques and churches, and it was always disagreeable. Mechanically he cleaned the images, the lines and indentations of which were black or cream with old sandalwood paste; it was easier to clean the small smooth pebbles, whose significance had not yet been explained to him. At this stage Pundit Jairam usually came to see that he did not scamp the ritual, but this morning he did not come. Mr Biswas chanted from the prescribed scriptures, applied fresh sandalwood paste to the images and smooth pebbles, decked them with fresh flowers, rang the bell and consecrated the offering of sweetened milk. With the sandalwood marks still wet and tickling on his forehead, he sought out Jairam to offer him some of the milk.

Jairam, bathed and dressed and fresh, was sitting against some pillows in one corner of the verandah, spectacles low down on his nose, a brown Hindi book on his lap. When the verandah shook below Mr Biswas's bare feet Jairam looked up and then down through his spectacles, and turned a page of his dingy book. Spectacles made him look older, abstracted and benign.

Mr Biswas held the brass jar of milk toward him. 'Baba.'

Jairam sat up, rearranged a pillow, held a cupped palm, touching the elbow of the outstretched arm with the fingers of his free hand. Mr Biswas poured. Jairam brought the inside of his wrist against his forehead, blessed Mr Biswas, threw the milk into his mouth, passed his wet palm through his thin grey hair, readjusted his spectacles and looked down again at his book.

Mr Biswas went to his room, put on his workaday clothes and came out to breakfast. They ate in silence. Suddenly Jairam pushed his brass plate towards Mr Biswas.

'Eat this.'

Mr Biswas's fingers, ploughing through some cabbage, stood still.

'Of course you won't eat it. And I will tell you why. Because I have been eating from this plate.'

Mr Biswas's fingers, feeling dry and dirty, bent and straightened.

'Soanie!'

Jairam's wife thumped out from the kitchen and stood between them, with her back to Mr Biswas. He looked at the creases on the edge of her soles and saw that the soles were hard and dirty. This surprised him, because Soanie was always washing the floor and bathing herself.

'Go and bring the bananas.'

She pulled the veil over her forehead. 'Don't you think you had better forget it? It is such a small thing.'

'Small thing! A whole hand of bananas!'

She went to the kitchen and came back, cradling the bananas.

'Put them here, Soanie. Mohun, nobody else can touch these bananas now but yourself. When people, out of the

goodness of their hearts, give me gifts, they are for you. Eh?'
Then the edge went out of his voice and he became like the
benign, expounding pundit he was in company. 'We mustn't
waste, Mohun. I have told you that again and again. We
mustn't let these bananas get rotten. You must finish what
you have begun. Start now.'

Mr Biswas had been lulled by Jairam's calm, even manner,
and the abruptness of the command took him by surprise. He
looked down at his plate and flexed his fingers, the tips of
which were stuck with drying shreds of cabbage.

'Start now.'

Soanie stood in the doorway, blocking the light. Though
it was bright day, the room, with bedrooms on one side and
the low roof of the verandah on the other, was gloomy.

'Look. I have peeled one for you.'

The banana hovered in Jairam's clean hand before Mr
Biswas's face. He took it with his dirty fingers, bit and
chewed. Surprisingly, it tasted. But the taste was so localized
it gave no pleasure. He then discovered that chewing killed
the taste, and chewed deliberately, not tasting, only listening
to the loud squelchy sound that filled his head. He had never
heard bananas eaten with so much noise.

Presently the banana was finished, except for the hard little
cone buried at the heart of the banana skin, open like a huge
and ugly forest flower.

'Look, Mohun. I have peeled you another.'

And while he ate that, Jairam slowly peeled another. And
another, and another.

When he had eaten seven bananas, Mr Biswas was sick,
whereupon Soanie, silently crying, carried him to the back
verandah. He didn't cry, not from bravery: he was only bored
and uncomfortable. Jairam rose at once and walked heavily to
his room, suddenly in a great temper.

Mr Biswas never ate another banana. That morning also
marked the beginning of his stomach trouble; ever afterwards,
whenever he was excited or depressed or angry his stomach
swelled until it was taut with pain.

A more immediate result was that he became constipated.
He could no longer relieve himself in the mornings and he

was aware of the dishonour he did the gods by doing the *puja* unrelieved. The call came upon him at unpredictable times, and it was this which led to his departure from Jairam's, and took him back to that other world he had entered at Pagotes, the world signified by Lal's school and the effete rubber-stamps and dusty books of F. Z. Ghany.

One night he got up in a panic. The latrine was far from the house and to go there through the dark frightened him. He was frightened, too, to walk through the creaking wooden house, open locks, undo bolts and possibly waken Jairam who was fussy about his sleep and often flew into a rage even when awakened at a time he had fixed. Mr Biswas decided to relieve himself in his room on one of his handker-chiefs. He had scores of these, made from the cotton given him at the ceremonies he attended with Jairam. When the time came to dispose of the handkerchief, he left his room and tiptoed, the floor creaking, through the open doorway to the enclosed verandah at the back. He carefully unbolted the Demerara window, which hung on hinges at the top, and, keeping the window open with his left hand, flung the hand-kerchief as far as he could with his right. But his hands were short, the window was heavy, there was too little space for him to manoeuvre, and he heard the handkerchief fall not far off.

Not staying to bolt the window, he hurried back to his bed where for a long time he stayed awake, repeatedly imagining that a fresh call was upon him. He had just fallen asleep, it seemed, when someone was shaking him. It was Soanie.

Jairam stood scowling in the doorway. 'You are no Brahmin,' he said. 'I take you into my house and show you every consideration. I do not ask for gratitude. But you are trying to destroy me. Go and look at your work.'

The handkerchief had fallen on Jairam's cherished olean-der tree. Never again could its flowers be used at the *puja*.

'You will never make a pundit,' Jairam said. 'I was talking the other day to Sitaram, who read your horoscope. You killed your father. I am not going to let you destroy me. Si-taram particularly warned me to keep you away from trees. Go on, pack your bundle.'

The neighbours had heard and came out to watch Mr Biswas as, in his dhoti, with his bundle slung on his shoulder, he walked through the village.

Bipti was not in a welcoming mood when Mr Biswas, after walking and getting rides on carts, came back to Pagotes. He was tired, hungry and itching. He had expected her to welcome him with joy, to curse Jairam and promise that she would never allow him to be sent away again to strangers. But as soon as he entered the yard of the hut in the back trace he knew that he was wrong. She looked so depressed and indifferent, sitting in the sooty open kitchen with another of Ajodha's poor relations, grinding maize; and it did not then surprise him that, instead of being pleased to see him, she was alarmed.

They kissed perfunctorily, and she began to ask questions. He thought her manner was harsh and saw her questions as attacks. His replies were sullen, defensive, angry. Her fury rose and she shouted at him. She said that he was ungrateful, that all her children were ungrateful and didn't appreciate the trouble the rest of the world went to on their behalf. Then her rage spent itself and she became as understanding and protective as he hoped she would have been right at the beginning. But it was not sweet now. She poured water for him to wash his hands, sat him down on a low bench and gave him food – not hers to give, for this was the communal food of the house, to which she had contributed nothing but her labour in the cooking – and looked after him in the proper way. But she could not coax him out of his sullenness.

He did not see at the time how absurd and touching her behaviour was: welcoming him back to a hut that didn't belong to her, giving him food that wasn't hers. But the memory remained, and nearly thirty years later, when he was a member of a small literary group in Port of Spain, he wrote and read out a simple poem in blank verse about this meeting. The disappointment, his surliness, all the unpleasantness was ignored, and the circumstances improved to allegory: the journey, the welcome, the food, the shelter.

After the meal he learned that there was another reason for Bipti's annoyance. Dehuti had run away with Tara's yard boy, not only showing ingratitude to Tara and bringing disgrace to her, for the yard boy is the lowest of the low, but also depriving her at one blow of two trained servants.

'And it was Tara who wanted you to be a pundit,' Bipti said. 'I don't know what we are going to tell her.'

'Tell me about Dehuti,' he said.

Bipti had little to say. No one had been to see Dehuti; Tara had vowed never to mention her name again. Bipti spoke as if she herself deserved every reproach for Dehuti's behaviour; and though she declared she could have nothing more to do with Dehuti, her manner suggested that she had to defend Dehuti not only against Tara's anger, but also Mr Biswas's.

But he felt no anger or shame. When he asked about Dehuti he was only remembering the girl who pressed his dirty clothes to her face and wept when she thought her brother was dead.

Bipti sighed. 'I don't know what Tara is going to say now. You had better go and see her yourself.'

And Tara was not angry. True to her vow, she did not mention Dehuti. Ajodha, to whom Jairam had given only a hint of Mr Biswas's misdemeanour, laughed in his high-pitched, breathless way and tried to get Mr Biswas to tell exactly what had happened. Mr Biswas's embarrassment delighted Ajodha and Tara, until he was laughing too; and then, in the cosy back verandah of Tara's house – though it had mud walls it stood on proper pillars, had a neat thatched roof and wooden ledges on the half-walls, and was bright with pictures of Hindu gods – he told about the bananas, blusteringly at first, but when he noticed that Tara was giving him sympathy he saw his own injury very clearly, broke down and wept, and Tara held him to her bosom and dried his tears. So that the scene he had pictured as taking place with his mother took place with Tara.

Ajodha had bought a motorbus and opened a garage, and it was in the garage that Alec worked, no longer wearing red bodices or peeing blue, but doing mysterious greasy things. Grease blackened his hairy legs; grease had turned his white canvas shoes black; grease blackened his hands even beyond the wrist; grease made his short working trousers black and stiff. Yet he had the gift, which Mr Biswas admired, of being able to hold a cigarette between greasy fingers and greasy lips without staining it. His lips still twisted easily and his small humorous eyes still squinted; but the cheeks had already sunk on his small square face and he now had a perpetual air of abstraction and debauch.

Mr Biswas did not join Alec in the garage. Tara sent him to the rumshop. This had been Ajodha's first business venture and had provided the money for some of his subsequent exploits. But, with Ajodha's growing success, the importance of the rumshop had declined and it was now run by his brother Bhandat, about whom there were unpleasant rumours: Bhandat apparently drank, beat his wife and kept a mistress of another race.

Bipti, who had not been consulted, was very grateful to Tara. And Mr Biswas was thrilled at the thought of earning money. He was not going to earn much. He was to live at the shop and be fed by Bhandat's wife; he was to be given suits of clothes every now and then; and he was to get two dollars a month.

The rumshop was a long high building of simple design, flat to the ground, with a pitched roof of corrugated iron rising from concrete walls. Swing doors exposed only the wet floor of the shop and the feet of drinkers, and, in a land where all doors are wide open, gave a touch of vice to the building. The doors were needed, for many of the people who came past them meant to drink themselves into insensibility. At any time of the day there were people who had collapsed on the wet floor, men who looked older than they were, women too; useless people crying in corners, their anguish lost in the din and press of the standing drinkers who swallowed their rum at a gulp, made a face, hastily swallowed water, and bought more rum. There was swearing, boasting, threatening; fights, broken bottles, policemen; and steadily the coppers and the silver and the notes went into the greasy drawer below the shelves.

And every evening, when the shop was emptied, when the sleepers had been put outside and the broken bottles and glasses swept up, and the floor washed down – though no amount of water could get rid of the smell of raw rum – the drawer was pulled out and the Petromax gas lamp, taken down from the long wire hook that hung from the ceiling, was placed next to the drawer on the counter. The money was arranged in neat piles and Bhandat noted the day's takings on a sheet of stiff brown paper, smooth on one side, rough on the other. Bhandat wrote on the smooth side with a soft pencil that smudged easily. The shop had thick edges of darkness; the smell of dirty boards and stale rum was sharp; and Bhandat made his calculation in whispers against the noise of the Petromax whose hiss, lost in the din of the evening, had now in the silence swollen into a roar.

Bhandat's voice, even when low, was a whine with a querulous edge. He was a small man, with a nose as sharp as Ajodha's and a face as thin; but this face could never express benignity; always it looked harassed and irritable, and more so than ever at the end of the evening. He was going bald and the curve of his forehead repeated the curve of his nose. His thin upper lip was heavily outlined and had two neat and equal bumps in the middle which pressed in a swollen way over the lower lip and practically hid it. While Bhandat calculated Mr Biswas studied these bumps.

Bhandat made it clear that he regarded Mr Biswas as Tara's spy and distrusted him. And it was not long before Mr Biswas realized that Bhandat was stealing, and that these feverish nightly calculations were meant to frustrate Tara's weekly checks. He was not surprised or critical. Only, he was embarrassed by some of Bhandat's methods.

'When these people have three or four drinks and want another,' Bhandat said, 'don't give them full measure.'

Mr Biswas asked no questions.

Bhandat looked away and explained, 'It is for their own good really.'

Mr Biswas got to know when Bhandat felt he had given short measure often enough to risk pocketing the price of a drink. Bhandat stared straight at the man who had paid him, talked absurdly for a moment, then began to spin the coin. Whenever Mr Biswas saw a coin rising and falling through the air he knew that it would eventually land in Bhandat's pocket.

Directly afterwards Bhandat became as gay as he could with the customers, and suspicious and irritable with Mr Biswas. 'You,' he would say to Mr Biswas. 'What the hell are you looking at?' And sometimes he would say to people across the counter, 'Look at him. Always smiling, eh? As though he is smarter than everybody else. Look at him.'

'Yes,' the drinkers said. 'He is a real smart man. You better keep an eye on him, Bhandat.'

So to the drinkers Mr Biswas became 'smart man' or 'smart boy', someone who could be ridiculed.

He revenged himself by spitting in the rum when he bottled it, which he did early every morning. The rum was the same, but the prices and labels were different: 'Indian Maiden', 'The White Cock', 'Parakeet'. Each brand had its adherents, and to Mr Biswas this was a subsidiary revenge which gave a small but continuous pleasure.

The bottling-room was in the ancillary shop-buildings which formed a square about an unpaved yard. Bhandat lived with his family, and Mr Biswas, in two rooms. When it was dry Bhandat's wife cooked on the steps that led to one of these rooms; when it rained she cooked in a corrugated-iron shack, made by Bhandat during a period of sobriety and responsibility, in the yard. The other rooms were used as storerooms or were rented out to other families. The room in which Mr Biswas slept had no window and was perpetually dark. His clothes hung on a nail on one wall; his books occupied a small amount of floor space; he slept with Bhandat's two sons on a hard, smelly coconut fibre mattress on the floor. Every morning the mattress was rolled up, leaving a deposit of coarse fibre grit on the floor, and pushed under Bhandat's fourposter in the adjacent room. When this was done Mr Biswas felt he had no further claim to the room for the rest of the day.

On Sundays and on Thursday afternoons, when the shop was closed, he didn't know where to go. Sometimes he went to the back trace to see his mother. He was giving her a dollar a month, but she continued to make him feel helpless and unhappy, and he preferred to seek out Alec. But Alec was now seldom to be found and Mr Biswas often ended by going to Tara's. In the back verandah there the bookcase had been unexpectedly filled with twenty tall black volumes of the *Book of Comprehensive Knowledge*. Ajodha had agreed to buy the books from an American travelling salesman; even before he had paid a deposit the books had been delivered, and then apparently forgotten. The salesman never called again, no one asked to be paid, and Ajodha said happily that the company had gone bankrupt. He had no intention of reading the books, but they were a bargain; and when Mr Biswas proved the books' usefulness by coming week after week to read them, Ajodha was delighted.

Presently Mr Biswas fell into a Sunday routine. He went to Tara's in the middle of the morning, read for Ajodha all the *That Body of Yours* columns which had been cut out during the week, got his penny, was given lunch, and was then free to explore the *Book of Comprehensive Knowledge*. He read folk tales from various lands; he read, and quickly forgot, how chocolate, matches, ships, buttons and many other things were made; he read articles which answered, with drawings that looked pretty but didn't really help, questions like: Why does ice make water cold? Why does fire burn? Why does sugar sweeten?

'You must get Bhandat's boys to read these books too,' Ajodha said enthusiastically.

But Bhandat's boys refused to be enticed. They were learning to smoke; they were full of scandalous and incredible revelations about sex; and at night, in whispers, they wove lurid sexual fantasies. Mr Biswas had tried to contribute to these, but could never strike the correct note. He was either so tame or so ill-informed that they laughed, or so revolting that they threatened to tell. For weeks they tormented him with a particular indecency he had spoken until, in exasperation, he told them to go and tell and found, to his surprise, that he had put an end to their threats. And one night when he asked Bhandat's eldest boy how he had come by all his knowledge about sex, the boy said, 'Well, I have a mother, not so?'

Bhandat was spending more week-ends away from the shop. His sons talked openly of his mistress, at first with excitement and a little pride; later, when the rows between

Bhandat and his wife grew more frequent, with fear. There were moments of shock and humiliation when Bhandat shouted obscenities which his sons casually whispered at night. The silence of Bhandat's wife then was terrible. Occasionally things were thrown and the boys and Mr Biswas burst out screaming. Bhandat's wife would come, very calm, and try to quieten them. They wanted her to stay, but she always went back to Bhandat in the next room.

In the shop Bhandat was spinning more coins every day, and there were often scenes on Friday evening when Tara came to examine the accounts.

Then one week-end Mr Biswas had the two rooms to himself. One of Ajodha's relations died in another part of the island. The shop was not opened on Saturday and early that morning Bhandat and his family went to the funeral, with Ajodha and Tara. The empty rooms, usually oppressive, now held unlimited prospects of freedom and vice; but Mr Biswas could think of nothing vicious and satisfying. He smoked but that gave little pleasure. And gradually the rooms lost their thrill. Alec had given up his job in the garage, or had been sacked, and was not in Pagotes; Tara's house was closed; and Mr Biswas did not want to go to the back trace. But the feeling of freedom and urgency remained. He walked aimlessly, along the main road and down side streets he had never taken. He stopped buses and went for short rides. He had innumerable soft drinks and hard cakes at roadside shacks. The afternoon wore on. Groups of men, their week's work over, stood in week-end clothes at street corners, outside shops, around coconut-carts. As fatigue overcame him he began to long for the day to end, to relieve him of his freedom. He went back to the dark rooms tired, empty, miserable, yet still excited, still unwilling to sleep.

He awoke to find Bhandat standing over his mattress on the floor. Above red eyes Bhandat's lids were swollen, the way they became after he had been drinking. Mr Biswas had not expected anyone to return before evening; he had lost a whole day's freedom.

'Come on. Stop pretending. Where have you put it?' The bumps on Bhandat's top lip were quivering with anger.

'Put what?'

'Oh yes. Smart man. So you don't know?' And Bhandat pulled Mr Biswas off the mattress, grabbed him by the back of his trousers and lifted him to his toes. With this hold, widely known in Lal's school as the policeman's hold, Bhandat led Mr Biswas to the next room. No one else was there; Bhandat's wife and children had not come back from the funeral. A shirt hung on the back of a chair over a pair of neatly folded trousers. On the seat of the chair there were coins, keys and a number of crumpled dollar-notes.

'Last night I had twenty-six dollars in notes. This morning I have twenty-five. Eh?'

'I don't know. I didn't even know when you came in. I was sleeping all the time.'

'Sleeping. Yes, sleeping like the snake. With both eyes open. Big eyes and long tongue. Tongue wagging all the time to Tara and Ajodha. Do you think that has done you any good? You expect them to give you a pound and a crown for that?' He was shouting now, and pulling out his leather belt through the loops of his trousers. 'Eh? You will tell them you stole my dollar?' He raised his arm and brought the belt down on Mr Biswas's head. Whenever the buckle struck a bone it made a sharp sound.

Suddenly Mr Biswas howled. 'O God! O God! My eye! My eye!'

Bhandat stopped.

Mr Biswas had been cut on the cheek-bone and the blood had run below his eye.

'Get out, you nasty tale-carrying lout. Get out of here at once before I peel the skin off your back.' The bumps on Bhandat's lip were trembling again and his arm, when he raised it, was quivering.

The sun had not risen and the back trace was still and empty when Mr Biswas roused Bipti.

'Mohun! What has happened?'

'I fell down. Don't *ask* me.'

'Come, tell me. What's the matter?'

'Why do you keep on sending me to stay with other people?'

'Who beat you?' She pressed a finger under the cut on the cheek-bone and he winced. 'Bhandat beat you?' She undid his shirt and saw the weals on his back. 'He beat you? He beat you?'

She made him lie face down on the bed in her room, and, for the first time since he was a baby, rubbed his body down with oil. She gave him a cup of hot milk sweetened with brown sugar.

'I am never going back there,' Mr Biswas said.

Instead of giving the consolation he expected, Bipti said, as though arguing with him, 'Where will you go then?'

He became impatient. 'You have never done a thing for me. You are a pauper.'

He had meant to hurt her, but she was not hurt. 'It is my fate. I have had no luck with my children. And with you, Mohun, I have the least luck of all. Everything Sitaram said about you was true.'

'I have heard you and everybody else talking a lot about this Sitaram. What exactly did he say?'

'That you were going to be a spendthrift and a liar and that you were going to be lecherous.'

'Oh yes. Spendthrift with two dollars a month. Two whole dollars. Two hundred cents. Very heavy if you put that in a bag. And lecherous?'

'Leading a bad life. With women. But you are too small.'

'Bhandat's children are more lecherous than me. And with their mother too.'

'Mohun!' Then Bipti said, 'I don't know what Tara is going to say.'

'Again! Why do you keep on caring what Tara says? I don't want you to go and see Tara. I don't want anything from her. And Ajodha can keep that body of his. Let Bhandat's boys read to him. I am finished with that.'

But Bipti went to see Tara, and that afternoon Tara, still in her mourning clothes and her jewellery, fresh from her funeral duties and her struggles with the funeral photographer, came to the back trace.

'Poor Mohun,' Tara said. 'He's shameless, that Bhandat.'

'I am sure he stole the money himself,' Mr Biswas said. 'He's got a lot of practice. He steals all the time. And I can always tell when he is stealing. He spins the coin.'

'Mohun!' Bipti said.

'He's the lecher, spendthrift and liar. Not me.'

'Mohun!'

'And I know all about that other woman. His sons know about her too. They boast about it. He quarrels with his wife and beats her. I am not going back to that shop if he comes and asks me on bended knee.'

'I can't see Bhandat doing that,' Tara said. 'But he is sorry. The dollar wasn't missing. It was at the bottom of his trouser pocket and he didn't notice it.'

'He was too drunk, if you ask me.' Then the humiliation hurt afresh and he began to cry. 'You see, Ma. I have no father to look after me and people can treat me how they want.'

Tara became coaxing.

Mr Biswas, enjoying the coaxing and his misery, still spoke angrily. 'Dehuti was quite right to run away from you. I am sure you treated her badly.'

By mentioning Dehuti's name he had gone too far. Tara at once stiffened and, without saying more, left, her long skirt billowing about her, the silver bracelets on her arm clanking.

Bipti ran out after her to the yard. 'You mustn't mind the boy, Tara. He is young.'

'I don't mind, Bipti.'

'Oh Mohun,' Bipti said, when she came back to the room, 'you will reduce us all to pauperdom. You will see me spending the rest of my days in the Poor House.'

'I am going to get a job on my own. And I am going to get my own house too. I am finished with this.' He waved his aching arm about the mud walls and the low, sooty thatch.

On Monday morning he set about looking for a job. How did one look for a job? He supposed that one looked. He walked up and down the Main Road, looking.

He passed a tailor and tried to picture himself cutting khaki cloth, tacking, and operating a sewingmachine. He passed a barber and tried to picture himself stropping a razor; his mind wandered off to devise elaborate protections for his left thumb. But he didn't like the tailor he saw, a fat man sulkily sewing in a dingy shop; and as for barbers, he had never liked those who cut his own hair; he thought too how it would disgust Pundit Jairam to learn that his former pupil had taken up barbering, a profession immemorially low. He walked on.

He had no wish to enter any of the shops he saw and ask for a job. So he imposed difficult conditions on himself. He tried, for example, to walk a certain distance in twenty paces, and interpreted failure as a bad sign. For a moment he was perversely tempted by an undertaker's, a plain corrugated iron shed that made no concession to grief, smelling of new wood, fish-glue and french polish, with coffins lying on the floor among sawdust, shavings and unfashioned planks. Cheap coffins and raw wood stood in rows against one wall; expensive polished coffins rested on shelves; there were un-finished coffins around a work-bench and pieces of coffin everywhere else; in one corner there was a tottering stack of cheap toy coffins for babies. Mr Biswas had often seen babies' funerals; one in particular he remembered, where the coffin was carried under the arm of a man who rode slowly on a bicycle. 'Get a job there,' he thought, 'and help to bury Bhandat.' He passed dry goods shops – strange name: dry goods – and the rickety little rooms bulged with dry goods, things like pans and plates and bolts of cloth and cards of bright pins and boxes of thread and shirts on hangers and brand-new oil lamps and hammers and saws and clothes-pegs and everything else, the wreckage of a turbulent flood which appeared to have forced the doors of the shops open and left deposits of dry goods on tables and on the ground outside. The owners remained in their shops, lost in the gloom and wedged between dry goods. The assistants stood outside with pencils behind their ears or pencils tapping bill-pads with the funereally-coloured carbon paper peeping out from under the first sheet. Grocers' shops, smelling damply of oil, sugar and salted fish. Vegetable stalls, damp but fresh, and smelling of earth. Grocers' wives and children stood oily and confident behind counters. The women behind the vegetable stalls were old and correct with thin mournful faces; or they were young and plump with challenging and quarrelsome stares; with a big-eyed child or two hanging about behind the purple sweet potatoes to which dirt still clung; and babies in the background lying in condensed milk boxes. And all the time donkey-carts, horse-carts and ox-carts rumbled and jangled in the roadway, the heavy iron-rimmed wheels grating over gravel and sand and wobbling over the bumpy road. Continually long whips with knotted ends whistled and cracked, arousing brief enthusiasm in the animals. The men drivers sat on their carts; the boy drivers stood, shouting and whistling at their animals and their rivals; half a dozen races were always in progress.

Mr Biswas returned to the back trace, his resolution shaken. 'I am not going to take any job at all,' he told Bipti.

'Why don't you go and make it up with Tara?'

'I don't want to see Tara. I am going to kill myself.'

'That would be the best thing for you. And for me.'

'Good. *Good*. I don't want any food.' And in a great rage he left the hut.

Anger gave him energy, and he determined to walk until he was tired. On the Main Road he took the other direction now and went past the office of F. Z. Ghany, dingier but still intact, closed because it wasn't market day; past the same array of shops, it seemed, the same owners, the same goods, the same assistants; and it all filled him with the same depression.

Late in the afternoon, when he was some miles out of Pagotes, a slender young man with shining eyes and a thick shining moustache came up to Mr Biswas and tapped him on the shoulder. He was embarrassed to recognize Ramchand, Tara's delinquent yard boy, now Dehuti's husband. He had sometimes seen him at Tara's, but they had not spoken.

Ramchand, so far from showing embarrassment, behaved as though he had known Mr Biswas well for years. He asked so many questions so quickly that Mr Biswas had time only to nod. 'How is everything? It is good to see you. And your mother? Well? Nice to hear. And the shop? A funny thing. You know Parakeet and Indian Maiden and The White Cock? I make that rum now. They are the same, you know.'

'I know.'

'No future working for Tara, I can tell you. As you know, I am working at this rum place now, and do you know how much I am getting? Come on. Guess.'

'Ten dollars.'

'Twelve. With a bonus every Christmas. And rum at the wholesale price into the bargain. Not bad, eh?'

Mr Biswas was impressed.

'Dehuti talks about you all the time. At one time everybody thought you were drowned, remember?' Then, as though this knowledge had removed whatever unfamiliarity remained between them, Ramchand added, 'Why don't you come and see Dehuti? She was talking about you only last night.' He paused. 'And perhaps you could eat something as well.'

Mr Biswas noticed the pause. It reminded him that Ramchand was of a low caste; and though it was absurd in the Main Road to think that of a man earning twelve dollars a month in addition to bonuses and other advantages, Mr Biswas was flattered that Ramchand looked upon him as someone to be flattered and conciliated. He agreed to go to see Dehuti. Ramchand, delighted, talked on, revealing much knowledge of other members of the family. He told Mr Biswas that Ajodha's finances were not as sound as they appeared, and that Tara was offending too many people. Tara may have vowed never to mention Ramchand's name again; he appeared anxious to mention hers as often as possible.

Mr Biswas had never questioned the deference shown him when he had gone to Tara's to be fed as a Brahmin and on his rounds with Pundit Jairam. But he had never taken it seriously; he had thought of it as one of the rules of a game that was only occasionally played. When he got to Ramchand's he thought it even more of a game. The hut indicated lowness in no way. The mud walls had been freshly whitewashed and decorated with blue and green and red palm-prints (Mr Biswas recognized Ramchand's broad palm and stubby fingers); the thatch was new and neat; the earth floor was high and had been packed hard; pictures from calendars were stuck on the walls, and in the verandah there was a hatrack. It was altogether less depressing than the crumbling, neglected hut in the back trace.

But it seemed that to Dehuti marriage had brought no joy. She was uneasy at being caught among her household possessions, and tried to hint that they had nothing to do with her. When Ramchand started to point out some attractive feature of the hut, she sucked her teeth and he desisted. Mr Biswas couldn't believe that Dehuti had ever spoken about him, as Ramchand had said. She hardly spoke, hardly looked at him. Without expression she brought out an ugly baby from an inner room, asleep, and showed it, suggesting at the same time that she had not brought it out to show it. She looked careworn and sulky, untouched by her husband's bubbling desire to please. Yet in her unhurried way she did what she could to make Mr Biswas welcome. He understood that she feared rebuff and the reports he might take back, and this made him uncomfortable.

Dehuti, never pretty, was now frankly ugly. Her Chinese eyes looked sleepy, the pupils without a light, the whites smudged. Her cheeks, red with pimples, bulged low and drooped around her mouth. Her lower lip projected, as though squashed out by the weight of her cheeks. She sat on a low bench, the back of her long skirt caught tightly between her calves and the backs of her thighs, the front draped over the knees. Mr Biswas was surprised by her adulthood. It was the way she sat, knees apart, yet so decorously covered; he had associated that only with mature women. He tried to find in the woman the girl he had known. But seeing her growing needlessly impatient while Ramchand, at her instructions, lit the fire and prepared to boil the rice, Mr Biswas felt that this sight of Dehuti had wiped out the old picture. This was a loss; it added to the unhappiness he had begun to feel as soon as he entered the hut.

Ramchand came from the kitchen and sank in the most relaxed way on to the earth floor. He stretched out one short-trousered leg and held his hands around his upright knee. The corrugations of his thick hair glinted with oil. He smiled at Mr Biswas, smiled at the baby, smiled at Dehuti. He asked Mr Biswas to read the writing on the calendar pictures and the Sunday school cards on the walls, and listened in pure pleasure while Mr Biswas did so.

'You are going to be a great man,' Ramchand said. 'A great man. Reading like that at your age. Used to hear you reading those things to Ajodha. Never known a healthier man in all my life. But one day he is going to fall really sick, let him watch out. He's just asking for it. I feel sorry for him, to tell you the truth. I feel sorry for all these rich fellows.' It turned out that Ramchand felt sorry for many other people as well. 'Pratap now. He's got himself into a mess because of these donkeys he keeps on buying, heaven knows why. The last two died. Did you hear about it?' Mr Biswas hadn't, and Ramchand told of the bloody end of the donkeys; one had speared itself on a bamboo stake. He also spoke of Prasad and his search for a wife; with tolerant amusement he mentioned Bhandat and his mistress. He became increasingly avuncular; it was clear he thought his own condition perfect, and this perfection delighted him. 'Not finished with these decorations,' he said, pointing to the walls. 'Getting some more of those Sunday school pictures. Jesus and Mary. Eh, Dehuti?' Laughingly he flung the matchstick he had been chewing at the baby.

Dehuti closed her eyes in annoyance, puffed out her pimply cheeks a little more and turned her face away. The matchstick fell harmlessly on the baby.

'Making some improvements too,' Ramchand said. 'Come.'

This time Dehuti did not suck her teeth. They went to the back and Mr Biswas saw another room being added to the hut. Trimmed tree-branches had been buried in the earth; the rafters, of lesser boughs, were in place; between the uprights the bamboo had been plaited; the earth floor was raised but not yet packed. 'Extra room,' Ramchand said. 'When it is finished you can come and stay with us.'

Mr Biswas's depression deepened.

They went on a tour of the small hut, Ramchand pointing out the refinements he had added: shelves set in the mud walls, tables, chairs. Back in the verandah Ramchand pointed to the hatrack. There were eight hooks on it symmetrically arranged about a diamond-shaped glass. 'That is the only thing here I didn't make myself. Dehuti set her heart on it.' He slumped down on the floor again and flung the little ball of earth he had been rolling between his fingers at the baby.

Dehuti closed her eyes and pouted. 'Me? I didn't want it. I wish you would stop running round giving people the idea that I have modern ambitions.'

He laughed uneasily and scratched his bare leg; the nails left white marks.

'I have no hat to hang on a hatrack,' Dehuti said. 'I don't want a mirror to show me my ugly face.'

Ramchand scratched and winked at Mr Biswas. 'Ugly face? Ugly face?'

Dehuti said, 'I don't stand up in front of the hatrack combing my hair for hours. My hair is not pretty and curly enough.'

Ramchand accepted the compliment with a smile.

In the verandah, black and yellow in the light of the oil lamp, they sat down on low benches to eat. But although he was hungry, and although he knew that both Dehuti and Ramchand had much affection for him, Mr Biswas found that his belly was beginning to rise and hurt, and he couldn't eat. Their happiness, which he couldn't share, had upset him. And it pained him more then to see Ramchand's jumpy enthusiasm replaced by uncertainty. Dehuti's sullen expression never changed; it was for just such a rebuff that she had been prepared.

He left soon after, promising to come back and see them one day, knowing that he wouldn't, that the links between Dehuti and himself, never strong, had been broken, that from her too he had become separate. The desire to keep on looking for a job had left him. He supposed he had always known he would fall back on Tara for help. She liked him; Ajodha liked him. Perhaps he would apologize, and they would put him in the garage.

Then Alec reappeared in Pagotes, and there was no sign of engine grease on him. His hands and arms and face were spotted and streaked with paint of various colours, as were his long khaki trousers and white shirt, where each stain was rimmed with oil. When, at the end of a long, idle and uncertain week, Mr Biswas saw him, Alec had a small tin of paint in one hand and a small brush in the other; he was standing on a ladder against a café in the Main Road and painting a sign, of which he had already achieved THE HUMMING BIRD CA.

Mr Biswas was full of admiration.

'You like it, eh?' Alec came down the ladder, pulled out a large paint-spotted cloth from his back pocket and wiped his hands. 'Got to shadow them. In two colours. Blue across, green down.'

'But that will spoil it, man.'

Alec spat out a cigarette that had burned down to his lips and gone dead. 'It will look like a little carnival when I finish. But that is the way they want it.' He jerked his head contemptuously towards the proprietor of the Humming Bird Café who was leaning on his counter and looking at them suspiciously. The shelves at his back were half filled with bottles of aerated water. Flies buzzed about him, attracted by the sweat on his neck and those parts of his body exposed by his vest; flies with different tastes had settled on the coarse sugar on the rock cakes in his showcase.

To Alec Mr Biswas explained his problem, and they talked for a while. Then they went into the tiny café and Alec bought two bottles of aerated water.

Alec said to the proprietor, 'This is my assistant.'

The proprietor looked at Mr Biswas. 'How he so small?'

'Young firm,' Alec said. 'Give youth a chance.'

'He could paint humming birds?'

'He want a lot of humming birds in the sign,' Alec explained to Mr Biswas. 'Hanging about and behind the lettering.'

'Like the Keskidee Café,' the proprietor said. 'You see the sign he got?' He pointed obliquely across the road to another refreshment shack, and Mr Biswas saw the sign. The letters were blocked in three colours and shadowed in three other colours. Keskidee birds stood on the K, perched on the D, hung from the C; on EE two keskidees billed.

Mr Biswas couldn't draw.

Alec said, ' 'Course he could paint humming birds, if you really want them. The only thing is, it would look a little follow-fashion.'

'And too besides, it oldfashion,' Mr Biswas said.

'I glad you say that,' Alec said. 'Was what I been trying to tell him. The modern thing is to have lots of words. All the shops in Port of Spain have signs with nothing but words. Tell him.'

'What sort of words?' the proprietor said.

'Sweet drinks, cakes and ice,' Mr Biswas said.

The proprietor shook his head.

'Beware of the dog,' Alec said.

'I ain't got a dog.'

'Fresh fruits daily,' Alec went on. 'Stick no bills by order.'

The proprietor shook his head.

'Trespassers will be prosecuted. Overseas visitors welcomed. If you don't see what you require please ask. Our assistants will be pleased to help you with your inquiries.'

The proprietor was thinking.

'No hands wanted,' Alec said. 'Come in and look around.'

The proprietor became alert. 'Is exactly what I have to fight in this place.'

'Idlers keep out,' Mr Biswas said.

'By order,' the proprietor said.

'Idlers keep out by order. A good sign,' Alec said. 'This boy will do it for you in two twos.'

So Mr Biswas became a sign-writer and wondered why he had never thought of using this gift before. With Alec's help he worked on the café sign and to his delight and amazement it came out well enough to satisfy the proprietor. He had been used to designing letters with pen and pencil and was afraid that he would not be able to control a brush with paint. But he found that the brush, though flattening out disconcertingly at first, could be made to respond to the gentlest pressure; strokes were cleaner, curves truer. 'Just turn the brush slowly in your fingers when you come to the curve,' Alec said; and curves held fewer problems after that. After IDLERS KEEP OUT BY ORDER he did more signs with Alec; his hand became surer, his strokes bolder, his feeling for letters finer. He thought R and S the most beautiful of Roman letters; no letter could express so many moods as R, without losing its beauty; and what could compare with the swing and rhythm of S? With a brush, large letters were easier than small, and he felt much satisfaction after he and Alec had covered long stretches of palings with signs for Pluko, which was good for the hair in various ways, and Anchor Cigarettes. There was some worry about the cigarette packet; they would have preferred to draw it closed, but the contractors wanted it open, condemning Mr Biswas and Alec to draw not only the packet, but the silver foil, crumpled, and eight cigarettes, all marked ANCHOR, pulled out to varying lengths.

After a time he started to go again to Tara's. She bore him no ill-will but he was disappointed to find that Ajodha no longer required him to read *That Body of Yours*. One of Bhandat's sons now did that. Two things had happened in the rum-shop. Bhandat's wife had died in childbirth, and Bhandat had left his sons and gone to live with his mistress in Port of Spain. The boys were taken in by Tara, who added Bhandat's name to those never mentioned by her again. For years afterwards no one knew where or how Bhandat lived, though there were rumours that he lived in a slum in the city centre, surrounded by all sorts of quarrelling and disreputable people.

So Bhandat's sons moved from the squalor of the rum-shop to the comfort of Tara's house. It was a passage that Mr Biswas had made often himself, and it was no surprise to him that the boys had soon settled in so well that Bhandat was forgotten and it was hard to think of his sons living anywhere else.

Mr Biswas continued to paint signs. It was satisfying work, but it came irregularly. Alec wandered from district to district, sometimes working, sometimes not, and the partnership was spasmodic. There were many weeks when Mr Biswas was out of work and could only read and design letters and practise his drawing. He learned to draw bottles, and in preparation for Christmas drew one Santa Claus after another until he had reduced it to a simple design in red, pink, white and black. Work, when it came, came in a rush. In September most shopkeepers said that they wanted no Christmas-signs nonsense that year. By December they had changed their minds, and Mr Biswas worked late into the night doing Santa Clauses and holly and berries and snow-capped letters; the finished signs quickly blistered in the blazing sun. Occasionally there were inexplicable rashes of new signs, and a district was thronged for a fortnight or so with sign-writers, for no shopkeeper wished to employ a man who had been used by his rival. Every sign then was required to be more elaborate than the last, and for stretches the Main Road was dazzling with signs that were hard to read. Plainness was required only for the posters for Local Road Board Elections. Mr Biswas did scores of these, many on cotton, which he had to stretch and pin to the mud wall of the verandah in the back trace. The paint leaked through and the wall became a blur of conflicting messages in different colours.

To satisfy the extravagant lettering tastes of his shopkeepers he scanned foreign magazines. From looking at magazines for their letters he began to read them for their stories, and during his long weeks of leisure he read such novels as he could find in the stalls of Pagotes. He read the novels of Hall Caine and Marie Corelli. They introduced him to intoxicating worlds. Descriptions of landscape and weather in particular excited him; they made him despair of finding romance in his own dull green land which the sun scorched every day; he never had much taste for westerns.

He became increasingly impatient at living in the back trace; and although his income, despite Christmas, elections and shopkeepers' jealousies, was small and uncertain, he would have liked to risk moving. But Bipti, who had always talked of moving, now said she had lived there too long and did not want to be among strangers in her old age. 'I leave here. One day you will get married, and where shall I be then?'

'I am never going to get married.' It was his usual threat, for Bipti had begun to say that she had only to see Mr Biswas married and her life's work would be complete. Pratap and Prasad were already married, Pratap to a tall, handsome woman who was bearing a child every eighteen months, Prasad to a woman of appalling ugliness who was mercifully barren.

'You mustn't say things like that,' Bipti said. She could still irritate him by taking everything he said seriously.

'So what? You expect me to bring a wife here?' He walked about the cluttered room, always smelling now of paint and oil and turpentine, and kicked at the dusty brown piles of his magazines and books on the floor.

He stayed in the back trace and read Samuel Smiles. He had bought one of his books in the belief that it was a novel, and had become an addict. Samuel Smiles was as romantic and satisfying as any novelist, and Mr Biswas saw himself in many Samuel Smiles heroes: he was young, he was poor, and he fancied he was struggling. But there always came a point when resemblance ceased. The heroes had rigid ambitions and lived in countries where ambitions could be pursued and had a meaning. He had no ambition, and in this hot land, apart from opening a shop or buying a motorbus, what could he do? What could he invent? Dutifully, however, he tried. He bought elementary manuals of science and read them; nothing happened; he only became addicted to elementary manuals of science. He bought the seven expensive volumes of *Hawkins' Electrical Guide*, made rudimentary compasses, buzzers and doorbells, and learned to wind an armature. Beyond that he could not go. Experiments became more complex, and he didn't know where in Trinidad he could find the equipment mentioned so casually by Hawkins. His interest in electrical matters died, and he contented himself with reading about the Samuel Smiles heroes in their magic land.

And yet there were moments when he could persuade himself that he lived in a land where romance was possible. When, for instance, he had to do a rush job and worked late into the night by the light of a gas lamp, excitement and the light transforming the hut; able then to forget that ordinary morning would come and the sign would hang over a cluttered little shop with its doors open on to a hot dusty road.

There were the days when he became a conductor on one of Ajodha's buses which ran in competition with other buses on a route without fixed stops. He enjoyed the urgent motion and noisy rivalry, and endangered himself needlessly by hanging far out from the running-board to sing to people on the road, 'Tunapuna, Naparima, Sangre Grande, Guayaguayare, Chacachacare, Mahatma Gandhi and back,' the glorious Amerindian names forming an imaginary route that took in the four corners of the island and one place, Chacachacare, across the sea.

And there were times when elusive Alec, with a face that hinted of debauch, came to Pagotes, spoke of pleasures and took Mr Biswas to certain houses which terrified, then attracted, and finally only amused him. With Bhandat's boys he also went; but they seemed to get most of their pleasure from the thought that they were being vicious.

And now too there were other occasions of excitement, unrelated to the excitements of books and magazines, unrelated to the visits to those houses: the glimpse of a face, a smile, a laugh. But his experiences had taken him beyond the stage when a girl was something of painful loveliness, and it was a marvel that any creature so soft and lovely could welcome the attentions of hard, ugly men; and few persons now held him. Some features always finally repelled, a tone of voice, a quality of skin, an over-sensuous hang of lip; one such lip had grown gross and obscene in a dream which left him feeling unclean. Love was something he was embarrassed to think about; the very word he mentioned seldom, and then as mockingly as Alec and Bhandat's boys. But secretly he believed.

Alec, misunderstanding, said, 'You worry too much. These things come when you least expect them.'

But he never ceased to worry. He no longer simply lived. He had begun to wait, not only for love, but for the world to yield its sweetness and romance. He deferred all his pleasure in life until that day. And it was in this mood of expectation that he went to Hanuman House at Arwacas, and saw Shama.

# 3. The Tulsis

AMONG THE tumbledown timber-and-corrugated-iron buildings in the High Street at Arwacas, Hanuman House stood like an alien white fortress. The concrete walls looked as thick as they were, and when the narrow doors of the Tulsi Store on the ground floor were closed the House became bulky, impregnable and blank. The side walls were window-less, and on the upper two floors the windows were mere slits in the façade. The balustrade which hedged the flat roof was crowned with a concrete statue of the benevolent monkey-god Hanuman. From the ground his whitewashed features could scarcely be distinguished and were, if anything, slightly sinister, for dust had settled on projections and the effect was that of a face lit up from below.

The Tulsis had some reputation among Hindus as a pious, conservative, landowning family. Other communities, who knew nothing of the Tulsis, had heard about Pundit Tulsi, the founder of the family. He had been one of the first to be killed in a motorcar accident and was the subject of an ir-reverent and extremely popular song. To many outsiders he was therefore only a creature of fiction. Among Hindus there were other rumours about Pundit Tulsi, some romantic, some scurrilous. The fortune he had made in Trinidad had not come from labouring and it remained a mystery why he had emigrated as a labourer. One or two emigrants, from criminal clans, had come to escape the law. One or two had come to escape the consequences of their families' participa-tion in the Mutiny. Pundit Tulsi belonged to neither class. His family still flourished in India – letters arrived regularly – and it was known that he had been of higher standing than most of the Indians who had come to Trinidad, nearly all of whom, like Raghu, like Ajodha, had lost touch with their families and wouldn't have known in what province to find them. The deference paid Pundit Tulsi in his native district had followed him to Trinidad and now that he was dead attached to his family. Little was really known about this family; outsiders were admitted to Hanuman House only for certain religious celebrations.

Mr Biswas went to Hanuman House to paint signs for the Tulsi Store, after a protracted interview with a large, moustached, overpowering man called Seth, Mrs Tulsi's brother-in-law. Seth had beaten down Mr Biswas's price and said that Mr Biswas was getting the job only because he was an Indian; he had beaten it down a little further and said that Mr Biswas could count himself lucky to be a Hindu; he had beaten it down yet further and said that signs were not really needed but were being commissioned from Mr Biswas only because he was a Brahmin.

The Tulsi Store was disappointing. The façade that promised such an amplitude of space concealed a building which was trapezoid in plan and not deep. There were no windows and light came only from the two narrow doors at the front and the single door at the back, which opened on to a covered courtyard. The walls, of uneven thickness, curved here and jutted there, and the shop abounded in awkward, empty, cobwebbed corners. Awkward, too, were the thick ugly columns, whose number dismayed Mr Biswas because he had undertaken, among other things, to paint signs on all of them.

He began by decorating the top of the back wall with an enormous sign. This he illustrated meaninglessly with a drawing of Punch, who appeared incongruously gay and roguish in the austere shop where goods were stored rather than displayed and the assistants were grave and unenthusiastic.

These assistants, he had learned with surprise, were all members of the House. He could not therefore let his eyes rove as freely as usual among the unmarried girls. So, as circumspectly as he could, he studied them while he worked, and decided that the most attractive was a girl of about sixteen, whom the others called Shama. She was of medium height, slender but firm, with fine features, and though he disliked her voice, he was enchanted by her smile. So en-

chanted, that after a few days he would very much have liked
to do the low and possibly dangerous thing of talking to her.
The presence of her sisters and brothers-in-law deterred him,
as well as the unpredictable and forbidding appearances of
Seth, dressed more like a plantation overseer than a store
manager. Still, he stared at her with growing frankness. When
she found him out he looked away, became very busy with
his brushes and shaped his lips as though he were whistling
softly. In fact he couldn't whistle; all he did was to expel air
almost soundlessly through the lecherous gap in his top teeth.

When she had responded to his stares a few times he felt
that a certain communion had been established between
them; and, meeting Alec in Pagotes, where Alec was working
in Ajodha's garage once again, as a mechanic and a painter of
buses and signs, Mr Biswas said, 'I got a girl in Arwacas.'

Alec was congratulatory. 'Like I did say, these things come
when you least expect them. What you was fussing so for?'

And a few days later Bhandat's eldest boy said, 'Mohun, I
hear you got a girl at long last, man.' He was patronizing; it
was well known that he was having an affair with a woman of
another race by whom he had already had a child; he was
proud both of the child and its illegitimacy.

The news of the girl at Arwacas spread and Mr Biswas enjoyed some glory at Pagotes until Bhandat's younger son, a
prognathous, contemptuous boy, said, 'I feel you lying like
hell, you know.'

When Mr Biswas went to Hanuman House the next day
he had a note in his pocket, which he intended to give to
Shama. She was busy all morning, but just before noon, when
the store closed for lunch, there was a lull and her counter was
free. He came down the ladder, whistling in his way. Unnecessarily, he began stacking and restacking his paint tins.
Then, preoccupied and frowning, he walked about the store,
looking for tins that were not there. He passed Shama's
counter and, without looking at her, placed the note under a
bolt of cloth. The note was crumpled and slightly dirty and
looked ineffectual. But she saw it. She looked away and
smiled. It was not a smile of complicity or pleasure; it was a
smile that told Mr Biswas he had made a fool of himself. He

felt exceedingly foolish, and wondered whether he shouldn't take back his note and abandon Shama at once.

While he hesitated a fat Negro woman went to Shama's counter and asked for flesh-coloured stockings, which were then enjoying some vogue in rural Trinidad.

Shama, still smiling, took down a box and held up a pair of black cotton stockings.

'Eh!' The woman's gasp could be heard throughout the shop. 'You playing with me? How the hell all-you get so fresh and conceited?' She began to curse. 'Playing with me!' She pulled boxes and bolts of cloth off the counter and hurled them to the floor and every time something crashed she shouted, 'Playing with me!' One of the Tulsi sons-in-law ran up to pacify her. She cuffed him back. 'Where the old lady?' she called, and screamed, 'Mai! Mai!' as though in great pain.

Shama had ceased to smile. Fright was plain on her face. Mr Biswas had no desire to comfort her. She looked so much like a child now that he only became more ashamed of the note. The bolt of cloth which concealed it had been thrown to the ground, and the note was exposed, caught at the end of the brass yardstick that was screwed to the counter.

He moved towards the counter, but was driven back by the woman's fat flailing arms.

Then silence fell on the shop. The woman's arms became still. Through the back doorway, to the right of the counter, Mrs Tulsi appeared. She was as laden as Tara with jewellery; she lacked Tara's sprightliness but was statelier; her face, though not plump, was slack, as if unexercised.

Mr Biswas moved back to his tins and brushes.

'Yes, ma'am, I want to see you.' The woman was breathless with anger. 'I want to see you. I want you to beat that child, ma'am. I want you to beat that conceited, rude child of yours.'

'All right, miss. All right.' Mrs Tulsi pressed her thin lips together repeatedly. 'Tell me what happened.' She spoke English in a slow, precise way which surprised Mr Biswas and filled him with apprehension. She was now behind the counter and her fingers which, like her face, were creased rather than wrinkled, rubbed along the brass yardstick. From time to time, while she listened, she pressed the corner of her veil over her moving lips.

Mr Biswas, now busily cleaning brushes, wiping them dry, and putting soap in the bristle to keep it supple, was sure that Mrs Tulsi was listening with only half a mind, that her eyes had been caught by the note: *I love you and I want to talk to you.*

Mrs Tulsi spoke some abuse to Shama in Hindi, the obscenity of which startled Mr Biswas. The woman looked pacified. Mrs Tulsi promised to look further into the matter and gave the woman a pair of flesh-coloured stockings free. The woman began to retell her story. Mrs Tulsi, treating the matter as closed, repeated that she was giving the stockings free. The woman went on unhurriedly to the end of the story. Then she walked slowly out of the shop, muttering, exaggeratedly swinging her large hips.

The note was in Mrs Tulsi's hand. She held it just above the counter, far from her eyes, and read it, patting her lips with her veil.

'Shama, that was a shameless thing to do.'

'I wasn't thinking, Mai,' Shama said, and burst into tears, like a girl about to be flogged.

Mr Biswas's disenchantment was complete.

Mrs Tulsi, holding her veil to her chin, nodded absently, still looking at the note.

Mr Biswas slunk out of the store. He went to Mrs Seeung's, a large café in the High Street, and ordered a sardine roll and a bottle of aerated water. The sardines were dry, the onion offended him, and the bread had a crust that cut the inside of his lips. He drew comfort only from the thought that he had not signed the note and could deny writing it.

When he went back to the store he was determined to pretend that nothing had happened, determined never to look at Shama again. Carefully he prepared his brushes and set to work. He was relieved that no one showed an interest in him; and more relieved to find that Shama was not in the store that afternoon. With a light heart he outlined Punch's dog on the irregular surface of the whitewashed column. Below the dog he ruled lines and sketched BARGAINS!

BARGAINS! He painted the dog red, the first BARGAINS! black, the second blue. Moving a rung or two down the ladder he ruled more lines, and between these lines he detailed some of the bargains the Tulsi Store offered, in letters which he 'cut out', painting a section of the column red, leaving the letters cut out in the whitewash. Along the top and bottom of the red strip he left small circles of whitewash; these he gashed with one red stroke, to give the impression that a huge red plaque had been screwed on to the pillar; it was one of Alec's devices. The work absorbed him all afternoon. Shama never appeared in the store, and for minutes he forgot about the morning's happenings.

Just before four, when the store closed and Mr Biswas stopped work, Seth came, looking as though he had spent the day in the fields. He wore muddy bluchers and a stained khaki topee; in the pocket of his sweated khaki shirt he carried a black notebook and an ivory cigarette holder. He went to Mr Biswas and said, in a tone of gruff authority, 'The old lady want to see you before you go.'

Mr Biswas resented the tone, and was disturbed that Seth had spoken to him in English. Saying nothing, he came down the ladder and washed out his brushes, doing his soundless whistling while Seth stood over him. The front doors were bolted and barred and the Tulsi Store became dark and warm and protected.

He followed Seth through the back door to the damp, gloomy courtyard, where he had never been. Here the Tulsi Store felt even smaller: looking back he saw lifesize carvings of Hanuman, grotesquely coloured, on either side of the shop doorway. Across the courtyard there was a large, old, grey wooden house which he thought must be the original Tulsi house. He had never suspected its size from the store; and from the road it was almost hidden by the tall concrete building, to which it was connected by an unpainted, new-looking wooden bridge, which roofed the courtyard.

They climbed a short flight of cracked concrete steps into the hall of the wooden house. It was deserted. Seth left Mr Biswas, saying he had to go and wash. It was a spacious hall, smelling of smoke and old wood. The pale green paint had grown dim and dingy and the timbers revealed the ravages of woodlice which left wood looking so new where it was rotten. Then Mr Biswas had another surprise. Through the doorway at the far end he saw the kitchen. And the kitchen had mud walls. It was lower than the hall and appeared to be completely without light. The doorway gaped black; soot stained the wall about it and the ceiling just above; so that blackness seemed to fill the kitchen like a solid substance.

The most important piece of furniture in the hall was a long unvarnished pitchpine table, hard-grained and chipped. A hammock made from sugarsacks hung across one corner of the room. An old sewingmachine, a baby-chair and a black biscuit-drum occupied another corner. Scattered about were a number of unrelated chairs, stools and benches, one of which, low and carved with rough ornamentation from a solid block of cyp wood, still had the saffron colour which told that it had been used at a wedding ceremony. More elegant pieces – a dresser, a desk, a piano so buried among papers and baskets and other things that it was unlikely it was ever used – choked the staircase landing. On the other side of the hall there was a loft of curious construction. It was as if an enormous drawer had been pulled out of the top of the wall; the vacated space, dark and dusty, was crammed with all sorts of articles Mr Biswas couldn't distinguish.

He heard a creak on the staircase and saw a long white skirt and a long white petticoat dancing above silver-braceleted ankles. It was Mrs Tulsi. She moved slowly; he knew from her face that she had spent the afternoon in bed. Without acknowledging his presence she sat on a bench and, as if already tired, rested her jewelled arms on the table. He saw that in one smooth ringed hand she was holding the note.

'You wrote this?'

He did his best to look puzzled. He stared hard at the note and stretched a hand to take it. Mrs Tulsi pulled the note away and held it up.

'That? I didn't write that. Why should I want to write that?'

'I only thought so because somebody saw you put it down.'

The silence outside was broken. The tall gate in the corrugated iron fence at the side of the courtyard banged repeatedly, and the courtyard was filled with the shuffle and chatter of the children back from school. They passed to the side of the house, under the gallery formed by the projecting loft. A child was crying; another explained why; a woman shouted for silence. From the kitchen came sounds of activity. At once the house felt peopled and full.

Seth came back to the hall, his bluchers resounding on the floor. He had washed and was without his topee; his damp hair, streaked with grey, was combed flat. He sat down across the table from Mrs Tulsi and fitted a cigarette into his cigarette holder.

'What?' Mr Biswas said. 'Somebody saw me put *that* down?'

Seth laughed. 'Nothing to be ashamed about.' He clenched his lips over the cigarette holder and opened the corners of his mouth to laugh.

Mr Biswas was puzzled. It would have been more understandable if they had taken his word and asked him never to come to their house again.

'I believe I know your family,' Seth said.

In the gallery outside and in the kitchen there was now a continual commotion. A woman came out of the black doorway with a brass plate and a blue-rimmed enamel cup. She set them before Mrs Tulsi and, without a word, without looking right or left, hurried back to the blackness of the kitchen. The cup contained milky tea, the plate *roti* and curried beans. Another woman brought similar food in an equally reverential way to Seth. Mr Biswas recognized both women as Shama's sisters; their dress and manner showed that they were married.

Mrs Tulsi, scooping up some beans with a shovel of *roti*, said to Seth, 'Better feed him?'

'Do you want to eat?' Seth spoke as though it would have been amusing if Mr Biswas did want to eat.

Mr Biswas disliked what he saw and shook his head.

'Pull up that chair and sit here,' Mrs Tulsi said and, barely raising her voice, called, 'C, bring a cup of tea for this person.'

'I know your family,' Seth repeated. 'Who's your father again?'

Mr Biswas evaded the question. 'I am the nephew of Ajodha. Pagotes.'

'Of course.' Expertly Seth ejected the cigarette from the holder to the floor and ground it with his bluchers, hissing smoke down from his nostrils and up from his mouth. 'I know Ajodha. Sold him some land. Dhanku's land,' he said, turning to Mrs Tulsi.

'O yes.' Mrs Tulsi continued to eat, lifting her armoured hand high above her plate.

C turned out to be the woman who had served Mrs Tulsi. She resembled Shama but was shorter and sturdier and her features were less fine. Her veil was pulled decorously over her forehead, but when she brought Mr Biswas his cup of tea she gave him a frank, unimpressed stare. He attempted to glare back but was too slow; she had already turned and was walking away briskly on light bare feet. He put the tall cup to his lips and took a slow, noisy draught, studying his reflection in the tea and wondering about Seth's position in the family.

He put the cup down when he heard someone else come into the hall. This was a tall, slender, smiling man dressed in white. His face was sunburnt and his hands were rough. Breathlessly, with many sighs, laughs and swallows, he reported to Seth on various animals. He seemed anxious to appear tired and anxious to please. Seth looked pleased. C came from the kitchen again and followed the man upstairs; he was obviously her husband.

Mr Biswas took another draught of tea, studied his reflection and wondered whether every couple had a room to themselves; he also wondered what sleeping arrangements were made for the children he heard shouting and squealing and being slapped (by mothers alone?) in the gallery outside, the children he saw peeping at him from the kitchen doorway before being dragged away by ringed hands.

'So you really do like the child?'

It was a moment or so before Mr Biswas, behind his cup, realized that Mrs Tulsi had addressed the question to him, and another moment before he knew who the child was.

He felt it would be graceless to say no. 'Yes,' he said, 'I like the child.'

Mrs Tulsi chewed and said nothing.

Seth said: 'I know Ajodha. You want me to go and see him?'

Incomprehension, surprise, then panic, overwhelmed Mr Biswas. 'The child,' he said desperately. 'What about the child?'

'What about her?' Seth said. 'She is a good child. A little bit of reading and writing even.'

'A little bit of reading and writing –' Mr Biswas echoed, trying to gain time.

Seth, chewing, his right hand working dexterously with *roti* and beans, made a dismissing gesture with his left hand. 'Just a little bit. So much. Nothing to worry about. In two or three years she might even forget.' And he gave a little laugh. He wore false teeth which clacked every time he chewed.

'The child – ' Mr Biswas said.

Mrs Tulsi stared at him.

'I mean,' said Mr Biswas, 'the child knows?'

'Nothing at all,' Seth said appeasingly.

'I mean,' said Mr Biswas, 'does the child like me?'

Mrs Tulsi looked as though she couldn't understand. Chewing, with lingering squelchy sounds, she raised Mr Biswas's note with her free hand and said, 'What's the matter? *You* don't like the child?'

'Yes,' Mr Biswas said helplessly. 'I like the child.'

'That is the main thing,' Seth said. 'We don't want to force you to do anything. Are we forcing you?'

Mr Biswas remained silent.

Seth gave another disparaging little laugh and poured tea into his mouth, holding the cup away from his lips, chewing and clacking between pours. 'Eh, boy, are we forcing you?'

'No,' Mr Biswas said. 'You are not forcing me.'

'All right, then. What's upsetting you?'

Mrs Tulsi smiled at Mr Biswas. 'The poor boy is shy. *I* know.'

'I am *not* shy and I am *not* upset,' Mr Biswas said, and the aggression in his voice so startled him that he continued softly, 'It's only that – well, it's only that I have no money to start thinking about getting married.'

Mrs Tulsi became as stern as he had seen her in the store that morning. 'Why did you write this then?' She waved the note.

'Ach! Don't worry with him,' Seth said. 'No money! Ajodha's family, and no money!'

Mr Biswas thought it would be useless to explain.

Mrs Tulsi became calmer. 'If your father was worried about money, he wouldn't have married at all.'

Seth nodded solemnly.

Mr Biswas was puzzled by her use of the words 'your father'. At first he had thought she was speaking to Seth alone, but then he saw that the statement had wider, alarming implications.

Faces of children and women peeped out from the kitchen doorway.

The world was too small, the Tulsi family too large. He felt trapped.

How often, in the years to come, at Hanuman House or in the house at Shorthills or in the house in Port of Spain, living in one room, with some of his children sleeping on the next bed, and Shama, the prankster, the server of black cotton stockings, sleeping downstairs with the other children, how often did Mr Biswas regret his weakness, his inarticulateness, that evening! How often did he try to make events appear grander, more planned and less absurd than they were!

And the most absurd feature of that evening was to come. When he had left Hanuman House and was cycling back to Pagotes, he actually felt elated! In the large, musty hall with the sooty kitchen at one end, the furniture-choked landing on one side, and the dark, cobwebbed loft on the other, he had been overpowered and frightened by Seth and Mrs Tulsi and all the Tulsi women and children; they were strange and had appeared too strong; he wanted nothing so much then as to be free of that house. But now the elation he felt was not that of relief. He felt he had been involved in large events. He felt he had achieved status.

His way lay along the County Road and the Eastern Main Road. Both were lined for stretches with houses that were ambitious, incomplete, unpainted, often skeletal, with wooden frames that had grown grey and mildewed while their owners lived in one or two imperfectly enclosed rooms. Through unfinished partitions, patched up with box-boards, tin and canvas, the family clothing could be seen hanging on lengths of string stretched across the inhabited rooms like bunting; no beds were to be seen, only a table and chair perhaps, and many boxes. Twice a day he cycled past these houses, but that evening he saw them as for the first time. From such failure, which until only that morning awaited him, he had by one stroke made himself exempt.

And when that evening Alec asked in his friendly mocking way, 'How the girl, man?' Mr Biswas said happily, 'Well, I see the mother.'

Alec was stupefied. 'The mother? But what the hell you gone and put yourself in?'

All Mr Biswas's dread returned, but he said, 'Is all right. I got my eyes open. Good family, you know. Money. Acres and acres of land. No more sign-painting for me.'

Alec didn't look reassured. "How you manage this so quick?'

'Well, I see this girl, you know. I see this girl and she was looking at me, and I was looking at she. So I give she a little of the old sweet talk and I see that she was liking me too. And, well, to cut a long story short, I ask to see the mother. Rich people, you know. Big house.'

But he was worried, and spent much time that evening wondering whether he should go back to Hanuman House. He began feeling that it was he who had acted, and was unwilling to believe that he had acted foolishly. And, after all, the girl was good-looking. And there would be a handsome dowry. Against this he could set only his fear, and a regret he could explain to no one: he would be losing romance forever, since there could be no romance at Hanuman House.

In the morning everything seemed so ordinary that both his fear and regret became unreal, and he saw no reason why he should behave unusually.

He went back to the Tulsi Store and painted a column.

He was invited to lunch in the hall, off lentils, spinach and a mound of rice on a brass plate. Flies buzzed on fresh food-stains all along the pitchpine table. He disliked the food and disliked eating off brass plates. Mrs Tulsi, who was not eating herself, sat next to him, stared at his plate, brushed the flies away from it with one hand, and talked.

At one stage she directed his attention to a framed photo-graph on the wall below the loft. The photograph, blurred at the edges and in many other places, was of a moustached man in turban, jacket and dhoti, with beads around his neck, caste-marks on his forehead and an unfurled umbrella on the crook of his left arm. It was Pundit Tulsi.

'We never had a quarrel,' Mrs Tulsi said. 'Suppose I wanted to go to Port of Spain, and he didn't. You think we'd quarrel about a thing like that? No. We would sit down and talk it over, and he would say, "All right, let us go." Or I would say, "All right, we *won't* go." That's the way we were, you know.'

She had grown almost maudlin, and Mr Biswas was trying to appear solemn while chewing. He chewed slowly and wondered whether he shouldn't stop altogether; but when-ever he stopped eating Mrs Tulsi stopped talking.

'This house,' Mrs Tulsi said, blowing her nose, wiping her eyes with her veil and waving a hand in a fatigued way, 'this house – he built it with his own hands. Those walls aren't concrete, you know. Did you know that?'

Mr Biswas went on eating.

'They looked like concrete to you, didn't they?'

'Yes, they looked like concrete.'

'It looks like concrete to *everybody*. But everybody is wrong. Those walls are really made of clay bricks. Clay bricks,' she repeated, staring at Mr Biswas's plate and waiting for him to say something.

'Clay bricks!' he said. 'I would never have thought that.'

'Clay bricks. And he made every brick himself. Right here. In Ceylon.'

'Ceylon?'

'That is how we call the yard at the back. You haven't seen it? Nice piece of ground. Lots of flower trees. He was a great

one for flowers, you know. We still have the brick-factory and
everything there as well. There's a lot of people don't know
about this house. Ceylon. You'd better start getting to know
these names.' She laughed and Mr Biswas felt a little stab of
fear. 'And then,' she went on, 'he was going to Port of Spain
one day, to make arrangements to take us all back to India. Just
for a trip, you know. And this car came and knocked him
down, and he died, Died,' she repeated, and waited.

Mr Biswas swallowed hurriedly and said, 'That must have
been a blow.'

'It was a blow. Only one daughter married. Two sons to
educate. It was a blow. And we had no money, you know.'

This was news to Mr Biswas. He hid his perturbation by
looking down at his brass plate and chewing hard.

'And Seth says, and I agree with him, that with the father
dead, one shouldn't make too much fuss about marrying
people off. You know' – she lifted her heavy braceleted arms
and made a clumsy dancer's gesture which amused her a good
deal – 'drums and dancing and big dowry. We don't believe
in that. We leave that to people who want to show off. You
know the sort of people. Dressed up to kill all the time. Yet
go and see where they come out from. You know those
houses in the County Road. Half built. No furniture. No, we
are not like that. Then, all this fuss about getting married was
more suitable for oldfashioned people like myself. Not for
you. Do you think it matters how people get married?'

'Not really.'

'You remind me a little of *him*.'

He followed her gaze to other photographs of Pundit Tulsi
on the wall. There was one of him flanked by potted palms
against the sunset of a photographer's studio. In another
photograph he stood, a small indistinct figure, under the arcade of Hanuman House, beyond the High Street that was
empty except for a broken barrel which, because it was nearer
the camera, stood out in clear detail. (How did they empty
the street, Mr Biswas wondered. Perhaps it was a Sunday
morning, or perhaps they had roped the populace off.) There
was another photograph of him behind the balustrade. In
every photograph he carried the unfurled umbrella.

'He would have liked you,' Mrs Tulsi said. 'He would have been proud to know that you were going to marry one of his daughters. He wouldn't have let things like your job or your money worry him. He always said that the only thing that mattered was the blood. I can just look at you and see that you come from good blood. A simple little ceremony at the registrar's office is all that you need.'

And Mr Biswas found that he had agreed.

At Hanuman House everything had appeared simple and reasonable. Outside, he was stunned. He had not had time to think about the problems marriage would bring. Now they seemed enormous. What would happen to his mother? Where would he live? He had no money and no job, for sign-writing, while good enough for a boy living with his mother, was hardly a secure profession for a married man. To get a house he would first have to get a job. He needed much time, but the Tulsis were giving him none at all, though they knew his circumstances. He assumed that they had decided to give more than a dowry, that they would help with a job or a house, or both. He would have liked to talk things over with Seth and Mrs Tulsi; but they had become unapproachable as soon as notice had been given at the registrar's.

There was no one in Pagotes he could talk to, for pure shame had kept him from telling Tara or Bipti or Alec that he was going to be married. At Hanuman House, in the press of daughters, sons-in-law and children, he began to feel lost, unimportant and even frightened. No one particularly noticed him. Sometimes, during the general feeding, he might be included; but as yet he had no wife to single him out for attention, to do the little services he saw Shama's sisters doing for their husbands: the ready ladle, the queries, the formal concern. Shama he seldom saw, and when he did, she ostentatiously ignored him.

It never occurred to him that he might withdraw. He felt he had committed himself in every legal and moral way. And, telling Bipti one morning that he would be away for a short time on a job, he took some of his clothes and moved to Hanuman House. It was only half a lie: he could not believe that the events he was taking part in had any solidity, and could change him in any way. The days were too ordinary for that; nothing unusual could befall him. And shortly, he knew, he would return, unchanged, to the back trace. As a guarantee of that return, he left most of his clothes and all of his books in the hut; it was partly, too, to guarantee this return that he lied to Bipti.

After a brief ceremony at the registrar's, as make-believe as a child's game, with paper flowers in dissimilar vases on a straw-coloured, official-looking desk, Mr Biswas and Shama were given part of a long room on the top floor of the wooden house.

And now he became cautious. Now he thought of escape. To leave the way clear for that he thought it important to avoid the final commitment. He didn't embrace or touch her. He wouldn't have known, besides, how to begin, with someone who had not spoken a word to him, and whom he still saw with the mocking smile she had given that morning in the store. Not wishing to be tempted, he didn't look at her, and was relieved when she left the room. He spent the rest of that day imprisoned where he was, listening to the noises of the house.

Neither on that day nor on the following days did anyone speak to him of dowry, house or job; and he realized that there had been no discussions because Mrs Tulsi and Seth didn't see that there were any problems to discuss. The organization of the Tulsi house was simple. Mrs Tulsi had only one servant, a Negro woman who was called Blackie by Seth and Mrs Tulsi, and Miss Blackie by everyone else. Miss Blackie's duties were vague. The daughters and their children swept and washed and cooked and served in the store. The husbands, under Seth's supervision, worked on the Tulsi land, looked after the Tulsi animals, and served in the store. In return they were given food, shelter and a little money; their children were looked after; and they were treated with respect by people outside because they were connected with the Tulsi family. Their names were forgotten; they became Tulsis. There were daughters who had, in the Tulsi marriage lottery, drawn husbands with money and position; these daughters followed the Hindu custom of living with their husband's families, and formed no part of the Tulsi organization.

Up to this time Mr Biswas thought he had been especially favoured by the Tulsis. But when he came to see how the family disposed of its daughters, he wondered that Seth and Mrs Tulsi had gone to such trouble on two consecutive days to make marriage attractive to him. They had married Shama to him simply because he was of the proper caste, just as they had married the daughter called C to an illiterate coconut-seller.

Mr Biswas had no money or position. He was expected to become a Tulsi.

At once he rebelled.

Pretending not to know what was expected of him, he finished the signs for the Tulsi Store and decided that the time had come to escape, with Shama or without her. It looked as though it would have to be without her. They still had not spoken; and, following his policy of caution, he had not attempted to establish any relations with her in the long room. He was convinced that she was a thorough Tulsi. And he was glad of his caution when she took to crying openly in the hall, surrounded by sisters, brothers-in-law, nephews and nieces, saying that Mr Biswas had been married less than a fortnight but was already doing his best to break her heart and create trouble in the family.

In a tremendous temper Mr Biswas began packing his brushes and clothes.

'Yes, take up your clothes and go,' Shama said. 'You came to this house with nothing but a pair of cheap khaki trousers and a dirty old shirt.'

He left Hanuman House and went back to Pagotes.

He felt unchanged, unmarried. He had simply had a good fright, but had managed things well and escaped.

In Pagotes, however, he found that his marriage was not a secret. Bipti welcomed him with tears of joy. She said she had always known that he wouldn't let her down. She had never said it, but she had always felt he would marry into a good family. She could now die happily. If she lived she had something to brighten her old age. Mr Biswas must not reproach himself for his secrecy; he was not to worry about her at all; he had his own life to live.

And despite his protests she put on her best clothes and went to Arwacas the next day. She came back overwhelmed by the graciousness of Mrs Tulsi, the diffidence of Shama and the splendour of Hanuman House.

She described a house he hardly knew. She spoke of a drawingroom with two tall thronelike mahogany chairs, potted palms and ferns in huge brass vases on marble topped tables, religious paintings, and many pieces of Hindu sculpture. She spoke of a prayer-room above that, which, with its slender columns, was like a temple: a low, cool, white room, empty except for the shrine in the centre.

She had seen only the upper floors of the concrete or rather, clay-brick, building. He didn't tell her that that part of the house was reserved for visitors, Mrs Tulsi, Seth and Mrs Tulsi's two younger sons. And he thought it better to keep silent about the old wooden house which the family called 'the old barracks'.

He spent two days in hiding at the back trace, not caring to face Alec or Bhandat's boys. On the third day he felt the need of greater comfort than Bipti could give, and that evening he went to Tara's. He entered by the side gate. From the cowpen came a familiar early evening sound: the unhurried stir and rustle of cows in stalls laid with fresh straw. The back verandah outside Tara's kitchen was warm with light. He heard the steady drone of someone reading aloud.

He found Ajodha rocking slowly, his head thrown back, frowning, his eyes closed, his eyelids palpitating with anguish while Bhandat's younger boy read *That Body of Yours*.

Bhandat's boy stopped reading when he saw Mr Biswas. His eyes became bright with amusement and his prognathous smile was a sneer.

Ajodha opened his eyes and gave a shriek of malicious delight. 'Married man!' he cried in English. 'Married man!'

Mr Biswas smiled and looked sheepish.

'Tara, Tara,' Ajodha called. 'Come and look at your married nephew.'

She came out gravely from the kitchen, embraced Mr Biswas and wept for so long that he began to feel, with sadness and a deep sense of loss, that he really was married, that in some irrevocable way he had changed. She undid the knot at the end of her veil and took out a twenty-dollar note. He objected for a little, then took it.

'Married man!' Ajodha cried again.

Tara took Mr Biswas to the kitchen and gave him a meal. And while, in the verandah, Bhandat's boy continued to read *That Body of Yours*, with the moths striking continually against the glass chimney of the oil lamp, she and Mr Biswas talked. She could not keep the unhappiness and disappointment out of her face and voice, and this encouraged him to be bitter about the Tulsis.

'And what sort of dowry did they give you?' she asked.

'Dowry? They are not so oldfashioned. They didn't give me a penny.'

'Registry?'

He bit at a slice of pickled mango and nodded.

'It is a modern custom,' Tara said. 'And like most modern customs, very economical.'

'They didn't even pay me for the signs.'

'You didn't ask?'

'Yes,' he lied. 'But you don't know those people.' He would have been ashamed to explain the organization of the Tulsi house, and to say that his signs were probably considered contributions to the family endeavour.

'You just leave this to me,' Tara said.

His heart sank. He had wanted her to declare that he was free, that he needn't go back, that he could forget the Tulsis and Shama.

And he was no happier when she went to Hanuman House and came back with what she said was good news. He was not to live at Hanuman House forever; the Tulsis had decided to set him up as soon as possible in a shop in a village called The Chase.

He was married. Nothing now, except death, could change that.

'They told me that they only wanted to help you out,'
Tara said. 'They said you didn't want any dowry or big wed-
ding and they didn't offer because it was a love match.'
Reproach was in her voice.

'Love match!' Ajodha cried. 'Rabidat, listen to that.' He
punched Bhandat's younger boy in the belly. 'Love match!'

Rabidat gave his contemptuous smile.

Mr Biswas looked angrily and accusingly at Rabidat. He
held Rabidat, more than anyone else, responsible for his marriage and wanted to say it was Rabidat's taunt which had
made him write that note to Shama. Instead, ignoring
Ajodha's chuckles and shrieks, he said, 'Love match? What
love match? They are lying.'

In a disappointed, tired way Tara said, 'They showed me a
love letter.' She used the English word; it sounded vicious.

Ajodha shrieked again. 'Love letter! Mohun!'

Bhandat's boy continued to smile.

Their mood seemed to infect Tara. 'Mrs Tulsi told me that
she believed you wanted to go on with your sign-writing and
that Hanuman House was the best place to work from.' She
had begun to smile. 'Everything's all right now, boy. You can
go back to your wife.'

The stress she gave to the word 'wife' wounded Mr
Biswas.

'You have got yourself into a real gum-pot,' she added,
more sympathetically. 'And I had such nice plans for you.'

'I wish you had told me,' he said, without irony.

'Go back and get your wife!' Ajodha said.

He paid no attention to Ajodha and asked Tara in English,
'You like she?' Hindi was too intimate and tender.

Tara shrugged, to say that it was none of her business; and
this hurt Mr Biswas, for it emphasized his loneliness: Tara's
interest in Shama might have made everything more bearable.
He thought he would show an equal unconcern. Lightly,
smiling back at Ajodha, he asked Tara, 'I suppose they vex
with me now over there, eh?'

His tone angered her. 'What's the matter? Are you afraid
of them already, like every other man in that place?'

'Afraid? No. You don't know me.'

But it was some days before he could make up his mind to go back. He didn't know what his rights were, didn't believe in the shop at The Chase, and his plans were vague. Only, he doubted that he would return to the back trace, and when he packed, he packed everything, Bipti crying happily all the while. As he cycled past the unfinished, open houses on the County Road, he wondered how many nights he would spend behind the closed façade of Hanuman House.

'What?' Shama said in English. 'You come back already? You tired catching crab in Pagotes?'

Despite the adventurousness and danger of his calling, the crab-catcher was considered the lowest of the low.

'I thought I would come and help all-you catch some here,' Mr Biswas replied, and killed the giggles in the hall.

No other comment was made. He had expected to be met by silence, stares, hostility and perhaps a little fear. He got the stares; the noise continued; the fear was, of course, only a wild hope; and he couldn't be sure of the hostility. The interest in his return was momentary and superficial. No one referred to his absence or return, not Seth, not Mrs Tulsi, both of whom continued, as they had done even before he left, hardly to notice him. He heard nothing about the visits of Bipti and Tara. The house was too full, too busy; such events were insignificant because he mattered little to the house. His status there was now fixed. He was troublesome and disloyal, and could not be trusted. He was weak and therefore contemptible.

He had not expected to hear any more about the shop in The Chase. And he didn't. He began to doubt that it existed. He went on with his sign-writing and spent as much time as he could out of the house. But he was unknown in Arwacas and jobs were scarce. Time hung heavily on his hands until he met an equally underemployed man called Misir, the Arwacas correspondent of the *Trinidad Sentinel*. They discussed jobs, Hinduism, India and their respective families.

Every afternoon Mr Biswas had to prepare afresh for his return to Hanuman House, though once he had pushed open the tall gate at the side it was a short journey, across the courtyard, through the hall, up the steps, along the verandah, through the Book Room, to his share of the long room. There he stripped to pants and vest, lay down on his bedding and read, leaning on one elbow. His pants, made by Bipti from floursacks, were unfortunate. Despite many washings they were still bright with letters and even whole words; they went down to his knees and made him look smaller than he was. It was not long before the children got to know about these pants, but Mr Biswas, refusing to yield to laughter, comments from the hall and Shama's pleas, continued to parade them.

It was impossible to keep anything secret from the children. As soon as darkness fell beds were made for them in the Book Room and all along the verandah upstairs. As the evening wore on, more and more beds were unrolled and the old upstairs became choked with sleepers; sleepers filled the wooden bridge that connected the old upstairs with the concrete house. Beyond the bridge, called 'the new room', lay the seclusion and space of the drawingroom that had impressed Bipti. But even if that part of the house was not reserved for Seth, Mrs Tulsi and her two sons, Mr Biswas would not have cared to go there. It was a forbidding room, with its large brass pots and marble topped tables. There was nothing to sit on apart from the two chairs which Bipti had described as thronelike. And the room was made oppressive by the many statues of Hindu gods, heavy and ugly, which Pundit Tulsi had brought back from his Indian visits. 'He must have bought them wholesale from some godshop,' Mr Biswas told Shama later. Above that was the greater seclusion of the prayer-room, reached from the drawingroom by a staircase as steep as a ship's companionway (a means of testing the faithful, or it might simply have been that Pundit Tulsi, like most builders in the island, got ideas as he went along). But in the prayer-room there was no furniture at all, the ground was of course sacred, and he found the smell of incense and sandalwood insupportable.

So, besieged by sleepers, he remained in the long room. His share of it was short and narrow: the long room, originally a verandah, had been enclosed and split up into bedrooms. He had Shama bring up his food there and he ate, squatting on his pants-clad haunches, his left hand squashed between his calf and the back of his thigh. At these times Shama was not the Shama he saw downstairs, the thorough Tulsi, the antagonist the family had assigned him. In many subtle ways, but mainly by her silence, she showed that Mr Biswas, however grotesque, was hers and that she had to make do with what Fate had granted her. But there was as yet little friendliness between them. They spoke in English. She seldom asked about his work and he was cautious about revealing information which might later be used against him, although shame alone might have kept him from telling her what he earned.

And it was at these eating sessions that Mr Biswas took his revenge on the Tulsis.

'How the little gods getting on today, eh?' he would ask.

He meant her brothers. The elder attended the Roman Catholic college in Port of Spain and came home every week-end; the younger was being coached to enter the college. At Hanuman House they were kept separate from the turbulence of the old upstairs. They worked in the drawing-room and slept in one of the bedrooms off it; these bedrooms were small and badly lighted, but their walls felt thick and their very gloom suggested richness and security. The brothers often did the *puja* in the prayer-room. Despite their age they were admitted into the councils of Seth and Mrs Tulsi and their views were quoted with respect by sisters and brothers-in-law. To assist their scholarship, the best of the food was automatically set aside for them and they were given special brain-feeding meals, of fish in particular. When the brothers made public appearances they were always grave, and sometimes stern. Occasionally they served in the store, sitting near the cashbox, with open textbooks before them.

'How the gods, eh?'

Shama wouldn't reply.

'And how the Big Boss getting on today?' That was Seth.

Shama wouldn't reply.

'And how the old queen?' That was Mrs Tulsi. 'The old hen? The old cow?'

'Well, nobody didn't *ask* you to get married into the family, you know.'

'Family? Family? This blasted fowlrun you calling family?'

And with that Mr Biswas took his brass jar and went to the Demerara window, where he gargled loudly, indulging at the same time in vile abuse of the family, knowing that the gargling distorted his words. Then he spat the water down venomously to the yard below.

'Careful, man. The kitchen just down there.'

'I know that. I just hoping I spit on some of your family.'

'Well, you should be glad that nobody would bother to spit on yours.'

It was a strain, living in a house full of people and talking to one person alone, and after some weeks Mr Biswas decided to look around for alliances. Relationships at Hanuman House were complex and as yet he understood only a few, but he had noted that two friendly sisters made two friendly husbands, and two friendly husbands made two friendly sisters. Friendly sisters exchanged stories of their husbands' disabilities, the names of illnesses and remedies forcing such discussions to be in English.

'He got one backache these days.'

'You must use hartshorn. He did have backache too. He try Dodd's Kidney Pills and Beecham's and Carter's Little Liver Pills and a hundred and one other little pills. But hartshorn did cure him.'

'He don't like hartshorn. He prefer Sloan's Liniment and Canadian Healing Oil.'

'And *he* don't like Sloan's Liniment.'

Friendly sisters sealed their friendship by being frank about the other's children and even by flogging them on occasion. When the flogged child, unaware of the relationship between the mothers, complained, his mother would say, 'Serve you right. I am glad your aunt is laying her hand on you. *She* will keep you straight.' And the mother of the beaten child would wait her turn to do some beating among the other's children.

Between Shama and C there was a noticeable friendship and Mr Biswas decided to make overtures to C's husband, the former coconut-seller, whose name was Govind. He was tall and well-built and handsome, though in a conventional, unremarkable way. Mr Biswas thought it unseemly that someone so well-made should have been a coconut-seller, and should now do manual work in the fields. And Mr Biswas was pained to see Govind in the presence of Seth. His handsome face became weak in every way. His eyes became small and bright and restless; he stammered and swallowed and gave nervous little laughs. And afterwards, when, released, he sat down at the long pitchpine table to eat, he changed again. Talking loudly and breathlessly, snorting and sighing, he assaulted his food, as though anxious to show enthusiasm even in that activity, anxious to prove that hard work had given him an indiscriminate appetite, and anxious at the same time to proclaim that food didn't matter to him.

Mr Biswas thought of Govind as a fellow sufferer, but one who had surrendered to the Tulsis and been degraded. He had forgotten his own reputation as a buffoon and troublemaker, however, and found Govind wary of his approaches. On a few evenings Govind suffered himself to be led outside by Mr Biswas. Sitting under the arcade, nervously swinging his long legs and smiling, sucking his teeth and exploring them with his jagged, dirt-stained fingernails, Govind didn't appear at ease. There was little to talk about. Women, of course, could not be discussed, and Govind didn't wish to discuss India or Hinduism. So Mr Biswas could talk only of the Tulsis. He asked what it was like to work under Seth. Govind said it was all right. He asked what Govind thought of Mrs Tulsi. She was all right. Her two sons were all right. Everybody was all right. So Mr Biswas talked of jobs. Govind showed a little more interest.

'You should give up that sign-painting,' he said one evening, and Mr Biswas was surprised and even slightly annoyed that Govind, of all people, should offer him advice, and so positively.

'They looking for good drivers on the estate,' Govind said.

'Give up sign-painting? And my independence? No, boy. My motto is: paddle your own canoe.' Mr Biswas began to quote from the poem in *Bell's Standard Elocutionist*.

'What about you? How much they paying you?'

'They paying me enough.'

'So you say. But those people are bloodsuckers, man. Rather than work for them, I would catch crab or sell coconut.'

At the mention of his former profession Govind gave a nervous laugh and swung his legs agitatedly.

'You wouldn't see the little gods in the field, I bet.'

'Lil gods?'

Mr Biswas explained. He explained a lot more. Govind, smiling, sucking his teeth and laughing from time to time, didn't say anything.

Late one afternoon Shama came up with food for Mr Biswas and said, 'Uncle want to see you.' Uncle was Seth.

'Uncle want to see me? Man, go back and tell Uncle that if he want to see me, he must come up here.'

Shama grew serious. 'What you been doing and saying? You getting everybody against you. You don't mind. But what about me? You can't give me anything and you want to prevent everybody else from doing anything for me. Is all right for you to say that you going to pack up and leave. But you know that is only talk. What you got?'

'I ain't got a damned thing. But I not going down to see Uncle. I not at his beck and call, like everybody else in this house.'

'Go down and tell him so yourself. You talking like a man, go down and behave like one.'

'I not going down.'

Shama cried, and in the end Mr Biswas put on his trousers. As he went down the stairs his courage began to leave him, and he had to tell himself that he was a free man and could leave the house whenever he wished. In the hall, to his shame, he heard himself saying, 'Yes, Uncle?'

Seth was fixing a cigarette in his long ivory holder, an exquisiteness which no longer seemed an affectation to Mr Biswas. It no longer contrasted with his rough estate clothes and rough, unshaved, moustached face; it had become part of his appearance. Mr Biswas, concentrating on the delicate activity of Seth's thick, bruised fingers, could feel that the hall was full. But no one was raising his voice; the whispers, the sounds of eating, the muted and seemingly distant scuffles, amounted to silence.

'Mohun,' Seth said at last, 'how long you been living here?'

'Two months, Uncle.' And he couldn't help noticing how much he sounded like Govind.

Mrs Tulsi was there, sitting on a bench at the long table. Unusually, the two gods, unsmiling boys, were there, sitting together in the sugarsack hammock, their feet on the floor. Sisters were feeding husbands at the other end of the table. Sisters and their children were thick about the black entrance to the kitchen.

'You been eating well?'

In Seth's presence Mr Biswas felt diminished. Everything about Seth was overpowering: his calm manner, his smooth grey hair, his ivory holder, his hard swollen forearms: after he spoke he stroked them, and looked at the hairs springing back into their original posture.

'Eating well?' Mr Biswas thought about the miserable meals, the risings of his belly, the cravings which were seldom satisfied. 'Yes. I been eating well.'

'You know who provide all the food you been eating?'

Mr Biswas didn't answer.

Seth laughed, took the cigarette holder out of his mouth and coughed, from a deep chest. 'This is a helluva man. When a man is married he shouldn't expect other people to feed him. In fact, he should be feeding his wife. When I got married you think I did want Mai mother to feed me?'

Mrs Tulsi rubbed her braceleted arms on the pitchpine table and shook her head.

The gods were grave.

'And yet I hear that you not happy here.'

'I didn't tell anybody anything about not being happy here.'

'I is the Big Boss, eh? And Mai is the old queen and the old hen. And these boys is the two gods, eh?'

The gods became stern.

Looking away from Seth, and causing a dozen or more faces instantly to turn away, Mr Biswas saw Govind among eaters at the far end of the table, going at his food in his smiling savage way, apparently indifferent to the inquisition, while C, bowed and veiled, stood dutifully over him.

'Eh?' For the first time there was impatience in Seth's voice, and, to show his displeasure, he began talking Hindi. 'This is gratitude. You come here, penniless, a stranger. We take you in, we give you one of our daughters, we feed you, we give you a place to sleep in. You refuse to help in the store, you refuse to help on the estate. All right. But then to turn around and insult us!'

Mr Biswas had never thought of it like that. He said, 'I sorry.'

Mrs Tulsi said, 'How can anyone be sorry for something he *thinks*?'

Seth pointed to the eaters at the end of the table. 'What names have you given to those, eh?' The eaters, not looking up, ate with greater concentration.

Mr Biswas said nothing.

'Oh, you haven't given them names. It's only to me and Mai and the two boys that you have given names?'

'I sorry.'

Mrs Tulsi said, 'How can anyone be sorry –'

Seth interrupted her. 'So we want someone to work on the estate. Is nice to keep these things in the family. And what you say? You want to paddle your own canoe. Look at him!' Seth said to the hall. 'Biswas the paddler.'

The children smiled; the sisters pulled their veils over their foreheads; their husbands ate and frowned; the gods in the hammock, rocking very slowly with their feet on the floor, glowered at the staircase landing.

'It runs in the family,' Seth said. 'They tell me your father was a great diver. But where has all your paddling got you so far?'

Mr Biswas said, 'Is just that I don't know anything about estate work.'

'Oho! Is because you can read and write that you don't want to get dirt on your hands, eh? Look at my hands.' He showed nails that were corrugated, warped and surprisingly short. The hairy backs of his hands were scratched and discoloured; the palms were hardened, worn smooth in some places, torn in others. 'You think I can't read and write? I can read and write better than the whole lot of them.' He waved one hand to indicate the sisters, their husbands, their children; he held the other palm open towards the gods in the hammock, to indicate that they were excepted. There was amusement in his eyes now, and he opened his mouth on either side of the cigarette holder to laugh. 'What about these boys here, Mohun? The gods.'

The younger god furrowed his brow, opened his eyes wider and wider until they were expressionless, and attempted to set his small, plump-lipped mouth.

'You think *they* can't read and write too?'

'See them in the store,' Mrs Tulsi said. 'Reading and selling. Reading and eating and selling. Reading and eating and counting money. They are not afraid of getting their hands dirty.'

Not with money, Mr Biswas told her mentally.

The younger god got up from the hammock and said, 'If he don't want to take the job on the estate, that is his business. It serve you right, Ma. You choose your son-in-laws and they treat you exactly how you deserve.'

'Sit down, Owad,' Mrs Tulsi said. She turned to Seth. 'This boy has a terrible temper.'

'I don't blame him,' Seth said. 'These paddlers go away, paddling their own canoe – that is how it is, eh, Biswas? – and as soon as trouble start they will be running back here. Seth is just here for people to insult, the same people, mark you, who he trying to help. *I* don't mind. But that don't mean I can't see why the boy shouldn't mind.'

The younger god frowned even more. 'Is not because my father dead that people who eating my mother food should feel that they could call she a hen. I want Biswas to apologize to Ma.'

'Apologize-ologize,' Mrs Tulsi said. 'It wouldn't make any difference. I don't see how anyone can be sorry for something he *feels*.'

There is, in some weak people who feel their own weakness and resent it, a certain mechanism which, operating suddenly and without conscious direction, releases them from final humiliation. Mr Biswas, who had up till then been viewing his blasphemies as acts of the blackest ingratitude, now abruptly lost his temper.

'The whole pack of you could go to hell!' he shouted. 'I not going to apologize to one of the damn lot of you.'

Astonishment and even apprehension appeared on their faces. He noted this for a lucid moment, turned and ran up the stairs to the long room, where he began to pack with unnecessary energy.

'You don't care what mess you get other people in, eh?'

It was Shama, standing in the doorway, barefooted, veil low over her forehead, looking as frightened as on that morning in the store.

'Family! Family!' Mr Biswas said, stuffing clothes and books – *Self Help, Bell's Standard Elocutionist*, the seven volumes of *Hawkins' Electrical Guide* – into a cardboard box whose top flaps bore the circular impressions of tins of condensed milk. 'I not staying here a minute longer. Having that damn little boy talk to me like that! He does talk to all your brother-in-laws like that?'

He packed with such energy that he was soon finished. But his anger had begun to cool and he reflected that by leaving the house again so soon he would be behaving absurdly, like a newly-married girl. He waited for Shama to say something that would rekindle his anger. She remained silent.

'Before I go,' he said, unpacking and re-packing the condensed milk case, 'I want you to tell the Big Boss – because it is clear that he is the big bull in the family – I want you to go and tell him that he ain't pay me for the signs I do in the store.'

'Why you don't go and tell him yourself?' Shama was now angry and near to tears.

He tried to see himself asking Seth for money. He couldn't. 'You and all,' he said, 'don't start provoking me. You think I want to talk to that man? *You* know him for a long time. He is like a second father to you. You must ask him.'

'And suppose he ask for what you owe him?'

'I would give you straight back to him.'

'You owe him more than he owe you.'

'He owe me more than I owe him.'

They reduced it to a plain argument, which not only killed what remained of his anger, but even left him exhilarated, though a little puzzled as to what he should do next.

Before he could decide, C and Padma, Seth's wife, came without knocking into the room. C was crying. Padma begged Mr Biswas, for the sake of family unity and the family name, not to do anything in a temper.

He became very offended, turned his back to Padma and C and walked heavily up and down the small room.

With the arrival of the women Shama's attitude changed. She ceased to be irritated and suppliant and instead looked martyred. She sat stiffly on a low bench, thumb under her chin, elbow on her knee, and opened her eyes until they were as wide and empty as the younger god's had been a few minutes before in the hall.

'Don't go, brother,' C sobbed. 'Your sister is begging you.' She tried to grab his ankles.

He skipped away and looked puzzled.

C, sobbing, noticed his puzzlement and elucidated: 'Chinta is begging you.' She mentioned her own name to indicate the depth of her unhappiness and the sincerity of her plea; and she began to wail.

By coming up to plead with him Chinta had as good as confessed that it was her husband Govind who had reported Mr Biswas's blasphemies to Seth; she was also claiming that Govind had triumphed. Mr Biswas knew that when husbands quarrelled it was the duty of the wife of the victorious husband to placate the defeated husband, and the duty of the wife of the defeated husband not to display anger, but skilfully to suggest that her unhappiness was due, in equal measure, to both husbands. Shama, following Chinta's arrival, had cast herself as the defeated wife and was making a commendable first attempt at this difficult role.

There was no means of protesting at this subtle humiliation. Up to that moment Mr Biswas had never felt that he had
enemies. People were simply indifferent to him. But now an
enemy, the enemy, had declared itself. And he resolved not
to run away.

And having made his resolve, he felt he had already won.
And, already a winner, he looked upon Chinta and Padma
with charity. Chinta was sobbing to herself, dabbing at her
eyes with her veil. He said to her, kindly, 'Why your husband
don't take a job with the *Gazette*, eh? He is a born reporter.'
This had no effect on the flow of tears from Chinta's bright
eyes. Shama still sat martyred and unmoving, eyes wide,
knees apart, skirt draped over knees. 'What the hell you
playing you thinking, eh?' She didn't hear. Padma continued
to behave with fatigued dignity. He said nothing to her. She
resembled Mrs Tulsi but was fatter and looked older. Her
sallow, unhealthy skin was oily, and she continually fanned
herself, as though tormented by some inner heat. After her
first plea she hadn't looked at Mr Biswas or spoken to him.
She didn't cry or look sadder than usual. She had come on too
many of these missions for them to thrill her the way they still
thrilled Chinta: there was not a man in the house with whom
Seth had not quarrelled at some time or other. Padma simply
came, made her plea, sat and looked unwell. She never, in the
hall or elsewhere, expressed approval of Seth's actions or disapproval of those of her nieces' husbands; this won her much
respect and made her a good peacemaker.

Sternly and impatiently Mr Biswas said, 'All right. All
right. Dry your tears. I not going.'

Chinta gave a short loud sob; it marked the end of her
tears.

'But just tell them not to provoke me, that's all.'

Sighing, Padma rose, heavily and unhealthily; and without
another word she and Chinta left the room.

Shama unstiffened. Her eyes narrowed a little, her fingers
left her chin. She began to cry, silently, and her body under-
went a relaxing, melting process which fascinated Mr Biswas
and infuriated him. Her arms seemed to grow rounder; her
shoulders rounded and drooped; her back curved; her eyes

softened until they were quite liquid with tears; her wrists rested on her knees as if broken; her hands flapped loose; her long fingers swung lifelessly, as if broken at every joint.

'Talk about bad blood,' Mr Biswas said. '*Talk* about bad blood!'

Disappointed in Govind, Mr Biswas began to find virtues in brothers-in-law he had disregarded. There was Hari, a tall, pale, quiet man who spent much time at the long table, working through mounds of rice in a slow, unenthusiastic but efficient way, watched over by his pregnant wife. He spent even more time in the latrine, and this made him feared. 'They should ring a bell when Hari decide to go to the latrine,' Mr Biswas told Shama, 'just as how they ring a bell to tell people they cutting off the water.' It was generally accepted at Hanuman House that Hari was a sick man; his wife told with sorrow and pride of the terrifying diagnoses of various doctors. No man looked less suitable for work on the estate; it was hard to imagine that thin, gentle voice ordering labourers about, reproving the idle and shouting down the argumentative. He was in fact a pundit, by training and inclination, and never looked so happy as when he changed from estate clothes into a dhoti and sat in the verandah upstairs reading from some huge, ungainly Hindi book that rested on a stylishly carved Kashmiri bookrest. He did the *puja* when the gods were away and he still conducted occasional ceremonies for close friends. He offended no one and amused no one. He was obsessed with his illnesses, his food and his religious books.

Between his estate duties, his reading in the verandah and his visits to the latrine, Hari had little free time, and was open to approach only at the long table. But then conversation was not easy. Hari believed in chewing every mouthful forty times, and was a noisy and preoccupied eater.

Sitting next to Hari one evening, receiving a brief ruminant glance from him and a concerned stare from his wife, Mr Biswas waited until Hari had champed and ground and squelched through a mouthful. Then he hurriedly asked, 'What do you feel about the Aryans?'

He was speaking of the protestant Hindu missionaries who had come from India and were preaching that caste was unimportant, that Hinduism should accept converts, that idols should be abolished, that women should be educated, preaching against all the doctrines the orthodox Tulsis held dear.

'What do you feel about the Aryans?' Mr Biswas asked.

'The Aryans?' Hari said, and started on another mouthful. His tone declared that it was a frivolous question raised by a mischievous person.

A look of anguish came over the face of Hari's wife.

'Yes,' Mr Biswas said, despairingly filling in the pause. 'The Aryans.'

'I don't think much about them.' Hari bit at a pepper, baring sharp little white teeth, like a rat's, and surprising in such a tall and sluggish man. 'I hear,' he went on, the merest hint of amusement and reproof in his voice, 'that you have been doing a lot of thinking about them.'

Mr Biswas was almost an Aryan convert.

It was Misir, the idle journalist, who had encouraged him to go to hear Pankaj Rai. 'He is not one of those illiterate Trinidad pundits, you know,' Misir said. 'Pankaj is a BA and a LLB into the bargain. The man is a real orator. A purist, man.' Mr Biswas had not asked what a purist was, but the word, pronounced with reverence by Misir, appealed strongly to him, suggesting not only purity and fastidiousness, but also elegance and breeding.

He had an additional inducement: the meeting was to be held at the home of the Naths. The Naths owned land and a soap factory, and were the Tulsis' most important rivals in Arwacas. Between Naths and Tulsis of all ages there was an enmity as established and unexamined as the enmity between Hindu and Muslim. The enmity had grown more acrimonious since the Naths had built a new house in the modern Port of Spain style.

Purist, Mr Biswas thought, when he saw Pankaj Rai. The man *is* a purist. He was elegant in a long, black, close-fitting Indian coat; and when he shook Mr Biswas by the hand Mr Biswas surrendered to his graciousness, at the same time not-

ing with satisfaction that Pankaj Rai was as short as himself
and had an equally ugly nose. He also had unusually heavy,
drooping eyelids which could make him look comic or sinister, benevolent or supercilious. They dropped a fraction of an
inch and converted a smile into a faint but devastating sneer.
This was particularly effective when he began to ridicule the
practices of orthodox Hinduism. He spoke without flourish,
and slowly, as if tasting the phrases beforehand, like a good
purist; and it was a revelation to Mr Biswas that words and
phrases which by themselves were commonplace could be
welded into sentences of such balance and beauty. He found
he agreed with everything Pankaj Rai said: after thousands of
years of religion idols were an insult to the human intelligence and to God; birth was unimportant; a man's caste
should be determined only by his actions.

After he had spoken Pankaj Rai distributed copies of his
book, *Reform the Only Way*, and Mr Biswas asked for his to be
autographed. Pankaj Rai did more. He wrote Mr Biswas's
name as well, describing him as a 'dear friend'. Below this
inscription Mr Biswas wrote: 'Presented to Mohun Biswas by
his dear friend Pankaj Rai, BA LLB.'

He showed book and inscriptions to Shama when he got
back to Hanuman House.

'Go ahead,' Shama said.

'Let me hear what you have against him. You people say
you are high-caste. But you think Pankaj would call you that?
Let me see. I wonder where Pankaj would place the Big Bull.
Ha! With the cows. Make him a cowherd. No. That is a good
job.' He remembered his own cowherd days. 'Better make
him a leather-worker, skinning dead animals. Yes, that's it.
The Big Bull is a member of the leather-worker caste. And
what about the two gods? Where you think Pankaj would
place them?'

'Just where you would place your brothers.'

'Road-sweeper? Little washerboys? Barber? Yes, little barbers. Pankaj would just look at them and feel that he want a
trim. And what about your mother?' He paused. 'Sha-ma! It
just hit me. Pankaj would say that your mother ain't a Hindu
at all! I mean, look at the facts. Marrying off her favourite

daughter in a registry office. Sending the two little barbers to a Roman Catholic college. As soon as Pankaj see your mother he would start making the sign of the cross. Roman Catholic, that's what she is!'

'Why don't you shut your mouth?' Shama tried to sound amused, but he could tell that she was getting angry.

'Ro-man Cat-o-lic! Roman cat, the bitch. You think she could fool Pankaj? And here you have Pankaj bringing the woman a message of hope, saying that Hindus should take in converts and treat them like their own, saying that it is not necessary to be born a high-caste to be a high-caste. A message of hope, man. And what? Your mother running the man down, when she should be grateful like hell, kissing the man foot. Gratitude, eh?'

'I just hope this Pankaj Rai come to lift you out of this gum-pot you surely going to land yourself in. Go ahead.'

'Shama.'

'Why you don't wrap your little tail up and go to sleep?'

'Shama, we have another problem, girl. You think any good Hindu would get married to a Roman Catholic girl, if he was really a good Hindu? Shama, you know what? It look to me that your whole family is just one big low-caste bunch.'

'You should know. You married into it.'

'Married into it. Ha! You think that make me happy. I *look* as if I happy?'

'Why you should look as if you happy? It should make you miserable. Is the first time in your life you eating three square meals a day. It giving your stomach too much exercise, I should say.'

'Licking up my stomach, you mean. My biggest item of food and drink in this house is soda powder and water.'

He pressed his foot against the wall and with his big toe drew circles around one of the faded lotus decorations.

He intended to discuss the Aryans less flippantly with Hari. He imagined that Hari, like Pundit Jairam and many other pundits, would welcome disputation. But at the long table Hari remained cold, his wife looked aghast, and Mr Biswas left him to his food.

When Hari had changed and was sitting in the verandah upstairs, humming from some holy book in his cheerless way, Mr Biswas, piqued and anxious to provoke some reaction, brought out his copy of *Reform the Only Way* and showed it, drawing Hari's attention to the inscriptions. Hari looked briefly at the book and said, 'Mm.'

Having failed with Hari, Mr Biswas decided that it would be prudent to withhold the message of hope from the other brothers-in-law, who were less intelligent and more temperamental.

About a week later Seth met Mr Biswas in the hall and said, laughing, 'How is your *dear* friend Pankaj Rai?'

'What you asking me for?' Mr Biswas nearly always spoke English at Hanuman House, even when the other person spoke Hindi; it had become one of his principles. 'Why you don't ask Hari, the stargazer?'

'You know Rai nearly went to jail?'

'Some people would say anything.' But Mr Biswas was disturbed by this news about the purist.

'These Aryans say all sorts of things about women,' Seth said. 'And you know why? They want to lift them up to get on top of them. You know Rai was interfering with Nath's daughter-in-law? So they asked him to leave. But a lot of other things left the house when he left.'

'But the man is a BA.'

'And LLB. I know. I wouldn't trust an Aryan with my great-grandmother.'

'Is a trick. The man is a dear friend. A purist. Pankaj wouldn't do a thing like that. You never hear him talk, that's why.'

'Nath's daughter-in-law heard, though. She didn't like what she heard.'

'Scandal, scandal. Is just a piece of scandal you stick-in-the-mud Sanatanists dig up.'

'If I had my way,' Seth said, 'I would cut the balls off all these Aryans. Have they converted you yet?'

'That is my own business.'

'I hear they have made some creole converts. Brothers for you, Mohun!'

In the verandah Mr Biswas saw Hari in dhoti, vest and beads, reading.

'He*llo*, pun*dit!*' Mr Biswas said.

Hari stared blankly at Mr Biswas and returned to his book.

Mr Biswas went past a door with glass panes of many colours into the Book Room. Here, along the length of one wall, was a bookcase choked with the religious literature Hari was working through. Few of the books were bound. Many were simply stacks of large loose brown-edged sheets which looked stained rather than printed. Each sheet carried partial impressions of the sheet above and the sheet below; the ink had turned russet; and each letter lay in a patch of oil.

Mr Biswas turned and walked back to the verandah. He put his head around a brilliant blue pane and whispered loudly down the verandah to Hari, 'Hello, Mr God.'

Hari, humming, didn't hear.

'I got a name for another one of your brother-in-laws,' he told Shama that evening, lying on his blanket, his right foot on his left knee, peeling off a broken nail from his big toe. 'The constipated holy man.'

'Hari?' she said, and pulled herself up, realizing that she had begun to take part in the game.

He slapped his yellow, flabby calf and pushed his finger into the flesh. The calf yielded like sponge.

She pulled his hand away. 'Don't do that. I can't bear to see you do that. You should be ashamed, a young man like you, being so soft.'

'That is all the bad food I eating in this place.' He was still holding her hand. 'Well, as a matter of fact, I have quite a few names for him. The holy ghost. You like that?'

'Man!'

'And what about the two gods? It ever strike you that they look like two monkeys? So, you have one concrete monkey-god outside the house and two living ones inside. They could just call this place the monkey house and finish. Eh, monkey, bull, cow, hen. The place is like a blasted zoo, man.'

'And what about you? The barking puppy dog?'

'Man's best friend.' He flung up his legs and his thin slack calves shook. With a push of his finger he kept the calves swinging.

'Stop doing that!'

By now Shama's head was on his soft arm, and they were lying side by side.

Abandoning the brothers-in-law altogether, Mr Biswas contented himself with the company of the Aryans at the Naths'. Pankaj Rai was no longer with them and no one was willing to talk about him. His place had been taken by a man who introduced himself as Shivlochan, BA (Professor). He was no purist. He spoke pompous Hindi and little English, and continually allowed himself to be bullied by Misir. Misir was keen on discussions and resolutions, and under his guidance they passed resolutions that education was important, that child marriage should be abolished, that young people should choose their own spouses.

Misir, who had suffered from his parents' choice, said, 'The present system is nothing more than cat-in-bag.'

(Mr Biswas loved Misir's phrases. 'That is all your family do for you,' he said to Shama that evening. 'Marry off the whole pack of you cat-in-bag.'

'Don't think I don't know where you picking up all that,' Shama said. 'Go ahead.')

'Look what I got,' Misir said, 'from marrying cat-in-bag. What about you, Mohun? You happy about this cat-in-bag business?'

'As a matter of fact,' Mr Biswas said, 'I didn't get married cat-in-bag. I did see the girl first.'

'You mean they let you see the child first?' Whatever remained of Misir's orthodox instincts was clearly outraged.

'Well, she was just there, you know, in the shop, selling cloth and socks and ribbon. And I see her and then –'

'All the old confusion, eh?'

'Well, not exactly. Things just happen after that.'

'I didn't know,' Misir said. 'Well, you ask for what you get. Anyway, I think we could say we are against this early cat-in-bag marriage business.'

'We could say that,' Mr Biswas said.

'Now, how are we going to put our ideas across to the masses?' Misir said, and Mr Biswas noted that Misir's manner was growing more and more like Pankaj Rai's. 'I suggest persuasion.'

'Peaceful persuasion,' Shivlochan said.

'Peaceful persuasion. Start like Mohammed. Start small. Start with your own family. Start with your own wife. Then move on. I want everybody here to go home this evening determined to pass the word on to his neighbours. And I promise you, my friends, that in no time Arwacas will become a stronghold of Aryanism.'

'Just a moment,' Mr Biswas said. 'Not so fast. Start with your own family? You don't know my family. I think we better leave them out.'

'This is a helluva man,' Misir said. 'You want to convert three hundred million Hindus and you let one backward little family of country bookies frighten you?'

'I telling you, man. You don't know my family.'

'All right,' Misir said, a little of his bounce gone. 'Now, supposing peaceful persuasion doesn't work. Just supposing. What do you suggest, my friends? By what means can we bring about the conversion we so earnestly desire?' The last two sentences had occurred in one of Pankaj Rai's speeches.

'By the sword,' Mr Biswas said. 'The only thing. Conversion by the sword.'

'That's how I feel too,' Misir said.

'Just a minute, gentlemen,' Shivlochan, BA (Professor), said, rising. 'You are rejecting the doctrine of non-violence. Do you realize that?'

'Rejecting it just for a short time,' Misir said impatiently. 'Short short time.'

Shivlochan sat down.

'I think, then, that we could pass a resolution to the effect that peaceful persuasion should be followed by militant conversion. All right?'

'I think so,' Mr Biswas said.

'I think this would make a good little story,' Misir said. 'Going to telephone it in to the *Sentinel* straight away.'

On the country page of the *Sentinel* the next day there was
an item, two inches high, about the proceedings of the
Arwacas Aryan Association, the AAA. Mr Biswas's name was
mentioned, as was his address.

He left an open and marked copy of the paper on the long
table in the hall. And when that evening Shama came up as
he was reading *Reform the Only Way* and said that Seth wanted
to see him, Mr Biswas didn't argue. Whistling in his soundless
way, he put on his trousers and ran down to face the family
tribunal.

'I see you have got your name in the papers,' Seth said.

Mr Biswas shrugged.

The gods swung slowly in the hammock, frowning.

'What are you trying to do? Disgrace the family? Here you
have these boys trying to get on in the Catholic college. Do
you believe this sort of thing is going to help them in any
way?'

The gods looked injured.

'Jealous,' Mr Biswas said. 'Everybody just jealous.'

'What have you got for them to be jealous of?' Mrs Tulsi
asked.

The elder god got up, in tears. 'I not going to remain sitting down in this hammock and have any-and-everybody in
this house insulting me. Is your fault, Ma. Is your son-in-law.
You just bring them in here to eat all the food my father
money buy and then to insult your sons.'

It was a grave charge, and Mrs Tulsi held the boy
to her and embraced him and wiped away his tears with her
veil.

'It's all right, son,' Seth said. 'I am still here to look after
you.' He turned to Mr Biswas. 'All right,' he said in English.
'You see what you cause. You want to get the family in
trouble. You want to see them go to jail. They feeding you,
but you want to see me and Mai go to jail. You want to see
the two boys, who ain't got no father, go through life without
a education. All that is all right. This house is like a republic
already.'

Sisters and brothers-in-law froze into attitudes of sullen
penitence. Seth's gratuitous remark about the republic was a

rebuke to them all; it meant that Mr Biswas's behaviour was bringing discredit upon the other brothers-in-law.

'So,' Seth went on. 'You want to see girl children educated and choosing their own husband, eh? The same sort of thing that your sister do.'

The sisters and their husbands relaxed.

Mr Biswas said, 'My sister better than anybody here, and better off too. And too besides, she living in a house a lot cleaner.'

Seth rested his elbow on the table and smoked sadly, looking down at his bluchers. 'The Black Age,' he said softly in Hindi. 'The Black Age has come at last. Sister, we have taken in a serpent. It is my fault. You must blame me.'

'I not asking to stay here, you know,' Mr Biswas said. 'I believe in the old ways too. You make me marry your daughter, you promise to do this and do that. So far I ain't got nothing. The day you give me what you promise me, I gone.'

'So you want girl children learning to read and write and picking up boy-friends? You want to see them wearing short frocks?'

'I ain't say a thing about short frocks. I talking about what you promise me.'

'Short frocks. And love letters. Love letters! Remember the love letter you write Shama?'

Shama giggled. The sisters and their husbands, more at ease now, giggled. Mrs Tulsi gave a short explosive laugh. Only the gods remained stern; but Mrs Tulsi, still embracing the elder god, coaxed a smile from him.

So the encounter was a defeat. But Mr Biswas, so far from being cast down, was exhilarated. He had no doubt now that in his campaign against the Tulsis – for that was how he thought of it – he was winning.

Unexpected support came through the Aryan Association.

The Association attracted the attention of Mrs Weir, the wife of the owner of a small sugar-estate. She didn't pay her labourers well but was respected by them for her interest in religion and the concern she showed for their spiritual welfare. Most of her labourers were Hindus and Mrs Weir was particularly interested in Hinduism. It was rumoured that her purpose was an eventual wholesale conversion of Hindus, but Misir denied this. He said he had practically converted *her*. She did indeed come to an Aryan meeting. And she invited some of the Aryans to tea. Mr Biswas, Misir, Shivlochan and two others went. Misir talked. Mrs Weir listened and never disagreed. Misir gave books and pamphlets. Mrs Weir said she looked forward to reading them. Just before they left, Mrs Weir presented everyone with copies of the *Meditations* of Marcus Aurelius, the *Discourses* of Epictetus, and a number of other booklets.

For days afterwards Hanuman House was subjected to the propaganda of a little-known Christian sect. Mrs Weir's booklets turned up on the long table, in the Tulsi Store, in the kitchen, in bedrooms. A religious picture was nailed on the inside of the latrine-door. When a booklet was found on the prayer-room shrine, Seth summoned Mr Biswas and said, 'The next thing will be for you to start teaching the children hymns. I can't understand how anyone could have even tried to turn you into a pundit.'

Mr Biswas said, 'Well, since I been in this house I begin to get the feeling that to be a good Hindu you must be a good Roman Catholic first.'

The elder god, seeing himself attacked, got up from the hammock, already prepared to cry.

'Look at him,' Mr Biswas said. 'Little Jack Horner. If he just put his hand in his shirt he pull up a crucifix.'

The elder god did wear a crucifix. It was regarded in the house as an exotic and desirable charm. The elder god wore many charms and it was thought fitting that someone so valuable should be well protected. On the Sunday before examination week he was bathed by Mrs Tulsi in water consecrated by Hari; the soles of his feet were soaked in lavender water; he was made to drink a glass of Guinness stout; and he left Hanuman House, a figure of awe, laden with crucifix, sacred thread and beads, a mysterious sachet, a number of curious armlets, consecrated coins, and a lime in each trouser pocket.

'You call yourself Hindus?' Mr Biswas said.

Shama tried to silence Mr Biswas.

The younger god got out of the hammock and stamped. 'I not going to remain in this hammock and hear my brother insulted, Ma. *You* don't care.'

'What?' said Mr Biswas. 'I insult somebody? At the Catholic college they make him close his eyes and open his mouth and say Hail Mary. What about that?'

'Man!' Shama said.

The elder god was crying.

The younger god said, '*You* don't care, Ma.'

'Biswas!' Seth said. 'You want to feel my hand?'

Shama pulled at Mr Biswas's shirt and he struggled as though he were being pulled away from a physical fight which he was winning and wanted to continue. But he had noted Seth's threat and allowed himself to be pushed slowly up the stairs.

Halfway up they heard Seth calling for his wife. 'Padma! Come quickly and look after your sister. She is going to faint.'

Someone raced up the steps. It was Chinta. She ignored Mr Biswas and said accusingly to Shama, 'Mai faint.'

Shama looked hard at Mr Biswas.

'Faint, eh?' Mr Biswas said.

Chinta didn't say any more. She hurried on to the concrete house to prepare Mrs Tulsi's bedroom, the Rose Room.

As soon as Shama had seen Mr Biswas safely to their room she left him, and he heard her running across the Book Room and down the stairs.

Mrs Tulsi often fainted. Whenever this happened a complex ritual was at once set in motion. One daughter was despatched to get the Rose Room ready, and Mrs Tulsi was taken there by other daughters working under the direction of Padma, Seth's wife. If, as often happened, Padma was ill herself, Sushila took her place. Sushila's position in the family was unique. She was a widowed daughter whose only child had died. Because of her suffering she was respected, but though she gave herself the airs of authority her status was undefined, at times appearing as high as Mrs Tulsi's, at times lower than Miss Blackie's. It was only during Mrs Tulsi's illnesses that anyone could be sure of Sushila's power.

In the Rose Room, then, after a faint, one daughter fanned Mrs Tulsi; two massaged her smooth, shining and surprisingly firm legs; one soaked bay rum into her loosened hair and massaged her forehead. The other daughters stood by, ready to carry out the instructions of Padma or Sushila. The gods were often there as well, looking grimly on. When the massage and the bay rum-soaking was over Mrs Tulsi turned on her stomach and asked the younger god to walk on her, from the soles of her feet to her shoulders. The elder god had done this duty in the past but had grown too heavy.

The sons-in-law found themselves alone in the wooden house with the children, who knew without being told that they had to be silent. All activity was suspended; the house became dead. One of the sons-in-law was invariably responsible for precipitating Mrs Tulsi's faint. He was now hounded by silence and hostility. If he attempted to make friendly talk many glances instantly reproved him for his frivolity. If he moped in a corner or went up to his room he was condemned for his callousness and ingratitude. He was expected to stay in the hall and show all the signs of contrition and unease. He waited for the sounds of footsteps coming from the Rose Room; he accosted a busy, offended sister and, ignoring snubs, made whispered inquiries about Mrs Tulsi's condition. Next morning he came down, shy and sheepish. Mrs Tulsi would be better. She would ignore him. But that evening forgiveness would be in the air. The offender would be spoken to as if nothing had happened, and he would respond with eagerness.

Mr Biswas didn't go to the hall. He remained on his blanket in the long room, doodling and thinking out subjects for the articles he had promised to write for the New Aryan, a magazine Misir was planning. He couldn't concentrate, and soon the paper was covered with repetitions, in various styles, of the letters RES, a combination he had found challenging and beautiful ever since he had done a sign for a restaurant.

The room smelled of hartshorn.

'You happy, eh, now that you make Mai faint?'

It was Shama. Her hands were still oily.

'Which foot you rub?' Mr Biswas asked. 'You should be glad they allow you to touch a foot. You know, it does beat me why all you sisters so anxious to look after the old hen. She did look after you? She just pick you up and marry you off to any old coconut-seller and crab-catcher. And still everybody rushing up to rub foot and squeeze head and hand smelling-salts.'

'You know, nobody hearing you talk would believe that you come to this house with no more things than you could hang up on a one-inch nail.'

It was a familiar attack. He ignored it.

Next morning he went down to the hall and called briskly, 'Morning, morning. Morning, everybody.' He got no reply. He said, 'Shama, Shama. Food, girl. Food.' She brought him a tall cup of tea. Breakfast was tea and biscuits. The biscuits came in a vast drum, returnable to the biscuit makers: the largest economy size, the method of bulk-purchase used by café-owners. While he was diving into the drum, turning away straw, feeling for biscuits – a pleasant task, for the straw and biscuits together had a smell that was good and even better than the meal – while he was doing this, Mrs Tulsi came into the hall, fatigued and heavy, looking almost as old as Padma. Her veil was low over her forehead and every now and then she pressed a handkerchief soaked in eau-de-Cologne to her nose. Without her teeth she looked decrepit, but there was about her decrepitude a quality of everlastingness.

'You feeling better, Mai?' Mr Biswas asked, stacking some biscuits on a chipped enamel plate. He spoke very cheerfully.

The hall was hushed.

'Yes, son,' Mrs Tulsi said. 'I am feeling better.'

And it was Mr Biswas's turn to be astonished.

('I was wrong about your mother,' he told Shama before he left that morning. 'She is not a old hen at all. Nor a old cow.'

'I glad you learning gratitude,' Shama said.

'She is a she-fox. A old she-fox. What they call that? You know what I mean, man. You remember your *Macdougall's Grammar*. Abbot, abbess. Stag, roe, Hart, hind. Fox, what?'

'I not going to tell you.'

'I going to find out. In the meantime, remember the name change. She is the old she-fox.')

He remained on the staircase landing, sinking lower and lower through the torn seat of a cane-bottomed chair in front of the stained, battered, disused and useless piano, sipping his tea, cracking biscuits and dropping the pieces into the tea. He watched the pieces swell out and rescued them with his spoon just when they started to sink. Then swiftly, before the soggy biscuit that drooped over the spoon could fall off, he thrust the spoon into his mouth. All around him children were doing the same.

The younger god came down the stairs. He had been doing the morning *puja*. With his small dhoti, small vest, beads and miniature caste-marks he looked like a toy holy man. He carried a brass plate on which there was a cube of burning camphor. The camphor had been used to give incense to the images in the prayer-room; now it was to be offered to every member of the family.

The god went first to Mrs Tulsi. She put her handkerchief in her bosom, touched the camphor flame with her fingertips and carried her fingertips to her forehead. 'Rama, Rama,' she said. Then she added, 'Take it to your brother Mohun.'

The hall was hushed again. And again Mr Biswas was astonished.

Sushila, clinging to her sickroom authority of the previous evening, said, 'Yes, Owad. Take it to your brother Mohun.'

The god hesitated, frowning. Then he sucked his teeth, stamped up to the landing and offered the aromatic camphor flame to Mr Biswas. Mr Biswas rescued more sodden biscuit from the enamel cup. He put his mouth under the spoon, caught the biscuit that broke off, chewed noisily and said, 'You could take that away. You know I don't hold with this idol worship.'

The god, annoyed just the moment before, was stupefied almost into argument and coaxing before the full horror of Mr Biswas's rejection came to him. He stood still, the camphor burning, melting on the plate.

The hall was still.

Mrs Tulsi was silent. Forgetting her frailty and fatigue, she got up and walked slowly up the stairs.

'Man!' Shama cried.

Shama's shout aroused the god. He walked down to the hall, tears of anger in his eyes, saying, '*I* didn't want to go and offer him anything. I didn't. I know the amount of respect he have for people.'

Sushila said, 'Shh. Not while you are carrying the plate.'

'Man!' Shama said. 'What you go and do now?'

Mr Biswas drained his cup, used his spoon to scrape up the mess of biscuit at the bottom, ate that and, getting up, said, 'What I do? I ain't do nothing. I just don't believe in this idol worship, that is all.'

'M-m-m-m. *Mm!*' Miss Blackie made a loud purring noise. She was offended. She was a Roman Catholic and went to mass every morning, but she had seen the Hindu rites performed every day for many years and regarded them as inviolate as her own.

'Idols are stepping-stones to the worship of the real thing,' Mr Biswas said, quoting Pankaj Rai to the hall. 'They are necessary only in a spiritually backward society. Look at that little boy down there. You think he know what he was doing this morning?'

The god stamped and said shrilly, 'I know a lot more about it than you, you – you *Christian!*'

Miss Blackie purred again, now deeply offended.

Sushila said to the god, 'You must never lose your temper when you are doing *puja*, Owad. It isn't nice.'

'It nice for him to insult me and Ma and everybody else the way he doing?'

'Just give him enough rope. He will hang himself.'

In the long room Mr Biswas gathered his painting equipment and sang over and over:

> *In the snowy and the blowy,*
> *In the blowy and the snowy.*

Words and tune were based, remotely, on *Roaming in the Gloaming*, which the choir at Lal's school had once sung to entertain important visitors from the Canadian Mission.

Yet almost as soon as he had left Hanuman House through the side gate, Mr Biswas's high spirits vanished, and a depression fell upon him and lasted all day. He worked badly. He had to paint a large sign on a corrugated iron paling. Doing letters on a corrugated surface was bad enough; to paint a cow and a gate, as he had to, was maddening. His cow looked stiff, deformed and sorrowful, and undid the gaiety of the rest of the advertisement.

He was strained and irritable when he went back to Hanuman House. The aggrieved and aggressive stares he received in the hall reminded him of his morning triumph. All his joy at that had turned into disgust at his condition. The campaign against the Tulsis, which he had been conducting with such pleasure, now seemed pointless and degrading. Suppose, Mr Biswas thought in the long room, suppose that at one word I could just disappear from this room, what would remain to speak of me? A few clothes, a few books. The shouts and thumps in the hall would continue; the *puja* would be done; in the morning the Tulsi Store would open its doors.

He had lived in many houses. And how easy it was to think of those houses without him! At this moment Pundit Jairam would be at a meeting or he would be eating at home, looking forward to an evening with his books. Soanie stood in the doorway, darkening the room, waiting for the least gesture of command. In Tara's back verandah Ajodha sat relaxed in his rockingchair, his eyes closed, listening perhaps to *That Body of Yours* being read by Rabidat, who sat at an awkward angle, trying to hide the smell of drink and tobacco on his breath. Tara was about, harrying the cowman (it was milking-time) or harrying the yard boy or the servant girl, harrying somebody. In none of these places he was being missed because in none of these places had he ever been more than a visitor, an upsetter of routine. Was Bipti thinking of him in the back trace? But she herself was a derelict. And, even more remote, that house of mud and grass in the swamplands: probably pulled down now and ploughed up. Beyond that, a void. There was nothing to speak of him.

He heard footsteps and Shama came into the room with a brass plate loaded with rice, curried potatoes, lentils and coconut chutney.

'How often you want me to tell you that I hate those blasted brass plates?'

She put the plate on the floor.

He walked round it. 'Nobody ever teach you hygiene at school? Rice, potatoes. All that damn starch.' He tapped his belly. 'You want to blow me up?' At the sight of Shama his depression had turned to anger, but he spoke jocularly.

'I always say,' Shama said, 'that you must complain only when you start providing your own food.'

He went to the window, washed his hands, gargled and spat.

Someone shouted from below, 'Up there! Look what you doing!'

'I know, I know,' Shama said, running to the window. 'I know this was bound to happen one day. You spit on somebody.'

He looked out with interest. 'Who it is? The old she-fox, or one of the gods?'

'You spit on Owad.'

They heard him complaining.

Mr Biswas took another mouthful of water and gargled. Then, with cheeks puffed out, he leaned as far out of the window as he could.

'Don't think I not seeing you,' the god shouted. 'I marking what you doing, Mr Biswas. But I standing up right here and if you spit on me again I going to tell Ma.'

'Tell, you little son of a bitch,' Mr Biswas muttered, spitting.

'Man!'

'O God!' the god exclaimed.

'You lucky little monkey,' Mr Biswas said. He had missed.

'Man!' Shama cried, and dragged him from the window.

He walked slowly around the brass plate.

'Walk,' Shama said. 'You walk until you tired. But wait until you provide your own food before you start criticizing the food other people give you.'

'Who give you that message to give me? Your mother?'
He pulled his top teeth behind his lower teeth, but his long
floursack pants prevented him from looking menacing.

'Nobody didn't give me any message to give you. It is just
something I think of myself.'

'You think of it yourself, eh?'

He had seized the brass plate, spilling rice on the floor, and
was rushing to the Demerara window. Going to throw the
whole damned thing out, he had decided. But his violence
calmed him, and at the window he had another thought:
throw the plate out and you could kill somebody. He arrested
his hurling gesture, and merely tilted the plate. The food
slipped off easily, leaving a few grains of rice sticking to
streaks of lentils and oily, bubble-ridden trails of curry.

'O God! Oo – Go-o-od!'

It began as a gentle cry and rose rapidly to a sustained
bawling which aroused sympathetic shrieks from babies all
over the house. All at once the bawling was cut off, and seconds later – it seemed much later – Mr Biswas heard a deep,
grating, withdrawing snuffle. 'I going to tell Ma,' the god
cried. 'Ma, come and see what your son-in-law do to me. He
cover me down with his dirty food.' After a sirenlike intake
of breath the bawling continued.

Shama looked martyred.

There was considerable commotion below. Several people
were shouting at once, babies screamed, there was much
subsidiary bawling and chatter, and the hall resounded with
agitated movements.

Heavy footsteps made the stairs shake, rattled the glass
panes on doors, drummed across the Book Room, and
Govind was in Mr Biswas's chamber.

'Is you!' Govind shouted, breathing hard, his handsome
face contorted. 'Is you who spit on Owad.'

Mr Biswas was frightened.

He heard more footsteps on the stairs. The bawling drew
nearer.

'Spit?' Mr Biswas said. 'I ain't spit on anybody. I just gargle
out of the window and throw away some bad food.'

Shama screamed.

Govind threw himself on Mr Biswas.

Caught by surprise, stupefied by fear, Mr Biswas neither shouted nor hit back at Govind, and allowed himself to be pummelled. He was struck hard and often on the jaw, and with every blow Govind said, 'Is you.' Vaguely Mr Biswas was aware of women massing in the room, screaming, sobbing, falling upon Govind and himself. He was acutely aware of the god bawling, right in his ear, it seemed: a dry, deliberate, scraping noise. Abruptly the bawling ceased. 'Yes, is he!' the god said. 'Is he. He asking for this a long time now.' And at every cuff and kick Govind gave, the god grunted, as though he himself had given the blow. The women were above Mr Biswas and Govind, their hair and veils falling loose. One veil tickled Mr Biswas's nose.

'Stop him!' Chinta cried. 'Govind will kill Biswas if you don't stop him. He is a terrible man, I tell you, when his temper is up.' She burst into a short, sharp wail. 'Stop it, stop it. They will send Govind to the gallows if you don't stop it. Stop it before they make me a widow.'

Punched on his hollow chest, short-jabbed on his soft, rising belly, Mr Biswas found, to his surprise, that his mind remained quite clear. What the hell is that woman crying for? he thought. She is going to be a widow all right, but what about me? He was trying to encircle Govind with his arms, but was unable to do more than tap him on the back. Govind didn't appear to notice the taps. Mr Biswas would have been surprised if he had. He wanted to scratch and pinch Govind, but reflected that it would be unmanly to do so.

'Kill him!' the god shouted. 'Kill him, Uncle Govind.'

'Owad, Owad,' Chinta said. 'How can you say a thing like that?' She pulled the god to her and pressed his head against her bosom. 'You too? Do you *want* to make me a widow?'

The god allowed himself to be embraced, but twisted his head to see the struggle and kept on shouting, 'Kill him, Uncle Govind. Kill him.'

The women were having little effect on Govind. They had succeeded only in lessening the swing of his arms, but his short jabs were powerful. Mr Biswas felt them all. They no longer caused pain.

'Kill him, Uncle Govind!'

He doesn't want any encouragement, Mr Biswas thought. Neighbours were shouting.

'What happening, Mai? Mai! Mrs Tulsi! Mr Seth! What happening?'

Their urgent, frightened voices frightened Mr Biswas. Suddenly he heard himself bawling, 'O God! I dead. I dead. He will kill me.'

His terror silenced the house.

It stilled Govind's arms. It stilled the god, and gave him a fleeting vision of black policemen, courthouses, gallows, graves, coffins.

The women lifted themselves off Govind and Mr Biswas. Govind, breathing heavily, lifted himself off Mr Biswas.

How I hate people who breathe like that, Mr Biswas thought. And how that Govind smells! It wasn't a smell of sweat, but of oil, body oil, associated in Mr Biswas's mind with the pimples on Govind's face. How unpleasant it must be, to be married to a man like that!

'Has he killed him?' Chinta asked. She was calmer; her voice held pride and genuine concern. 'Talk, brother. Talk. Talk to your sister. Get him to say something, somebody.'

Now that Govind was off his chest Mr Biswas's only concern was to make sure that he was properly dressed. He hoped nothing had happened to his pants. He moved a hand down to investigate.

'He is all right,' Sushila said.

Someone bent over him. That smell of oil, Vick's Vaporub, garlic and raw vegetables told him it was Padma. 'Are you all right?' she asked, and shook him.

He turned over on his side, his face to the wall.

'He is all right,' Govind said, and added in English, 'Is a good thing all you people did come, otherwise I woulda be swinging on the gallows for this man.'

Chinta gave a sob.

Shama had maintained her martyr's attitude throughout, sitting on the low bench, her skirt draped over her knees, one hand supporting her chin, her staring eyes misting over with tears.

'Spitting on me, eh?' the god said. 'Go ahead. Why you don't spit now? Coming and laughing at our religion. Laughing at me when I do *puja*. *I* know the good I doing myself when I do *puja*, you hear.'

'It's all right, son,' Govind said. 'Nobody can insult you and Mai when I am around.'

'Leave him alone, Govind,' Padma said. 'Leave him, Owad.'

The incident was over. The room emptied.

Left alone, Shama and Mr Biswas remained as they were, Shama staring through the doorway, Mr Biswas considering the lotuses on the pale green wall.

They heard the hall return to life. The evening meal, delayed, was being laid out with unusual zest. Babies were consoled with songs, clapping, chuckles and baby-talk. Children were scolded with exceptional good humour. Between everyone downstairs there was for the moment a new bond, and Mr Biswas recognized this bond as himself.

'Go and get me a tin of red salmon,' he said to Shama, without turning from the wall. 'And some hops bread.'

Her throat was tickling. She coughed and tried to hide the swallow by sighing.

This wearied him further. He got up, his pants hanging loose, and looked at her. She was still staring through the doorway into the Book Room. His face felt heavy. He put a hand to one cheek and worked his jaw. It moved stiffly.

Tears spilled over from Shama's big eyes and ran down her cheeks.

'What happen? Somebody beat you too?'

She shook her tears away, without removing her hand from her chin.

'Go and get me a tin of salmon. Canadian. And get some bread and peppersauce.'

'What happen? You have a craving? You making baby?'

He would have liked to hit her. But that would have been ridiculous after what had just happened.

'You making baby?' Shama repeated. She rose, shook down her skirt and straightened it. Loudly, as though trying to catch the attention of the people downstairs, she said, 'Go and get it yourself. You not going to start ordering *me* around, you hear.' She blew her nose, wiped it, and left.

He was alone. He gave a kick at a lotus on the wall. The noise startled him, his toe hurt, and he aimed another kick at his pile of books. He sent them toppling and marvelled at the endurance and uncomplainingness of inanimate objects. The bent corner of the cover of *Bell's Standard Elocutionist* was like a wound silently, accusingly borne. He stooped to pick the books up, then decided it would be a sign of self contempt to do so. Better for them to lie like that for Shama to see and even rearrange. He passed a hand over his face. It felt heavy and dead. Squinting downwards, he could see the rise of cheek. His jaw ached. He was beginning to ache all over. It was odd that the blows had made so little impression at the time. Surprise was a good neutralizer. Perhaps it was the same with animals. Jungle life could be bearable, then; it was part of God's plan. He went over to the cheap mirror hanging at the side of the window. He had never been able to see properly in it. It was an idiotic place to put a mirror, and he was mad enough to pull it down. He didn't. He stepped to one side and looked over his shoulder at his reflection. He knew his face felt heavy; he had no idea it looked so absurd. But he had to go out, leave the house for the time being, get his salmon, bread and peppersauce – bad for him, but the suffering would come later. He put on his trousers, and the rattle of the belt buckle was such a precise, masculine sound that he silenced it at once. He put on his shirt and opened the second button to reveal his hollow chest. But his shoulders were fairly broad. He wished he could devote himself to developing his body. How could he, though, with all that bad food from that murky kitchen? They had salmon only on Good Friday: the influence, doubtless, of the orthodox Roman Catholic Hindu Mrs Tulsi. He pulled his hat low over his forehead and thought that in the dark he might just get away with his face.

As he went down the stairs the chatter became a babel. Past the landing, he waited for the silence, the reanimation.

It happened as he feared.

Shama didn't look at him. Among gay sisters she was the gayest.

Padma said. 'You better feed Mohun, Shama.'

Govind didn't look up. He was smiling, at nothing, it seemed, and was eating in his savage, noisy way, rice and curry spilled all over his hairy hand and trickling down to his wrist. Soon, Mr Biswas knew, he would clean his hand with a swift, rasping lick.

Mr Biswas, his back to everyone in the hall, said, 'I not eating any of the bad food from this house.'

'Well, nobody not going to beg you, you hear,' Shama said.

He curled the brim of his hat over his eye and went down into the courtyard, lit only by the light from the hall.

The god said, 'Anyone see a spy pass through here?'

Mr Biswas heard the laughter.

Under the eaves of a bicycle shop across the High Street an oyster stall was yellowly, smokily lit by a flambeau with a thick spongy wick. Oysters lay in a shining heap, many-faceted, grey and black and yellow. Two bottles, stopped with twists of brown paper, contained red peppersauce.

Postponing the salmon, Mr Biswas crossed the road and asked the man, 'How the oysters going?'

'Two for a cent.'

'Start opening.'

The man shouted, released into happy activity. From somewhere in the darkness a woman came running up. 'Come on,' the man said. 'Help open them.' They put a bucket of water on the stall, washed the oysters, opened them with short blunt knives, and washed them again. Mr Biswas poured peppersauce into the shell, swallowed, held out his hand for another. The peppersauce scalded his lips.

The oyster man was talking drunkenly, in a mixture of Hindi and English. 'My son is a helluva man. I feel that something is seriously wrong with him. One day he put a tin can on the fence and come running inside the house. "The gun, Pa," he said. "Quick, give me the gun." I give him the gun. He run to the window and shoot. The tin can fall. "Pa," he say. "Look. I shoot work. I shoot ambition. They dead." '

The flambeau dramatized the oyster man's features, filling hollows with shadow, putting a shine on his temples, above his eyebrows, along his nose, along his cheek-bones. Suddenly he flung down his knife and pulled out a stick from below his stall. He waved the stick in front of Mr Biswas. 'Anybody!' he said. 'Tell anybody to come!'

The woman didn't notice. She went on opening oysters, laying them in her scratched, red palms, prising the ugly shells open, cutting the living oysters from their moorings to the pure, just-exposed inside shell.

'Tell anybody,' the man said. 'Anybody at all.'

'Stop!' Mr Biswas said.

The woman took her hand out of the bucket and replaced a dripping oyster on the heap.

The man put away his stick. 'Stop?' He looked saddened, and ceased to be frightening. He began to count the empty shells.

The woman disappeared into the darkness.

'Twenty-six,' the man said. 'Thirteen cents.'

Mr Biswas paid. The raw, fresh smell of oysters was now upsetting him. His stomach was full and heavy, but unsatisfied. The peppersauce had blistered his lips. Then the pains began. Nevertheless he went on to Mrs Seeung's. The high, cavernous café was feebly lit. Flies were asleep everywhere, and Mr Seeung was half-asleep behind the counter, his porcupinish head bent over a Chinese newspaper.

Mr Biswas bought a tin of salmon and two loaves of bread. The bread looked and smelled stale. He knew that in his present state bread would only bring on nausea, but it gave him some satisfaction that he was breaking one of the Tulsi taboos by eating shop bread, a habit they considered feckless, negroid and unclean. The salmon repelled him; he thought it tasted of tin; but he felt compelled to eat to the end. And as he ate, his distress increased. Secret eating never did him any good.

Yet what he considered his disgrace was in fact his triumph.

The next morning Seth summoned him and said in English, 'I come back late last night from Carapichaima, just looking for my food and my bed and the first thing I hear is

that you try to beat up Owad. I don't think we could stand
you here any longer. You want to paddle your own canoe.
All right, go ahead and paddle. When you start getting your
tail wet, don't bother to come back to me or Mai, you hear.
This was a nice united family before you come. You better
go away before you do any more mischief and *I* have to lay
my hand on you.'

So Mr Biswas moved to The Chase, to the shop. Shama
was pregnant when they moved.

# 4. The Chase

THE CHASE was a long, straggling settlement of mud huts in the heart of the sugarcane area. Few outsiders went to The Chase. The people who lived there worked on the estates and the roads. The world beyond the sugarcane fields was remote and the village was linked to it only by villagers' carts and bicycles, wholesalers' vans and lorries, and an occasional private motorbus that ran to no timetable and along no fixed route.

For Mr Biswas it was like returning to the village where he had spent his early years. Only, now the surrounding darkness and mystery had gone. He knew what lay beyond the sugarcane fields and where the roads went. They went to villages which were just like The Chase; they went to ramshackle towns where, perhaps, some store or café was decorated by his signs.

To such towns the villagers made arduous and infrequent excursions to obtain dry goods, to make complaints to the police, to appear in court; for The Chase could support neither a dry goods store nor a police station nor even a school. Its two most important public buildings were the two rumshops. And it abounded in small food-shops, one of which was Mr Biswas's.

Mr Biswas's shop was a short, narrow room with a rusty galvanized iron roof. The concrete floor, barely higher than the earth, was abraded to a pebbly roughness and encrusted with dirt. The walls leaned and sagged; the concrete plaster had cracked and flaked off in many places, revealing mud, tapia grass and bamboo strips. The walls shook easily, but the tapia grass and bamboo strips had given them an astonishing resilience; so that although for the next six years Mr Biswas never ceased to feel an anxiety when someone leaned on the walls or flung sacks of sugar or flour against them, the walls never fell down, never deteriorated beyond the limberness in which he had found them.

At the back of the shop there were two rooms with un-plastered mud walls and a roof of old, rough thatch that extended over an open gallery at one side. The floor of beaten earth had disintegrated and the chickens of the neighbour-hood came there to take dust-baths during the heat of the day.

The kitchen was a derelict makeshift structure in the yard. It had crooked tree branches for uprights, assorted bits of corrugated iron for roof, and almost anything for walls: sections of tin, strips of canvas and bamboo, boards from shop boxes. One wall had a space for a window, but the rectangular shape that had been intended had become a rhomboid. The window itself, ill-fitting lengths of unmatched wood held together by two crossbars split by massive nails that had been hammered back flat and grown rusty, the window itself was rectangular and was unable to fill the rhomboid vacancy. Though it was small and stood in the open, the kitchen was always dark. The window by day and the flambeau or fire by night showed that the walls were black and fluffy with soot, as though a new species of spider had been bred there, with the ability to spin webs as black and furry as its legs. Everything smelled of woodsmoke.

But there was space. Space to the back, right up to a boundary that was lost amid a tangle of tall bush, abandoned land called by the villagers and later by Mr Biswas 'the 'bandon'. There was more abandoned land to one side; once a well-tilled field, it was now a pasture for those cows of the village that could feed on its weeds and nettles and razor-sharp grass, wild, scrambling growths.

The Tulsis had bought this unprofitable property on the advice of Seth. He was a member of a Local Road Board and had received information, later proved to be worthless, that a trunk road was to be driven through the very spot on which Mr Biswas's shop stood.

Mr Biswas moved from Hanuman House with little trouble. He had little to move: his clothes, a few books and magazines, his painting equipment. Shama had much more. She had many clothes; and just before she left, she was given bolts of cloth by Mrs Tulsi straight from the shelves of the Tulsi Store. It was Shama, too, who thought of buying pots and pans and cups and plates; and though she got them at cost price from the Tulsi Store, Mr Biswas was disturbed to see that his savings, sign-writing money accumulated during his stay at Hanuman House, had begun to melt even before he had moved.

Their goods barely filled a donkey-cart, and their arrival at The Chase was noted by a waiting crowd with pity and some hostility. The hostility came from rival shopkeepers. And Mr Biswas, shakily perched on one of Shama's bundles, with the clang of those cost-price but expensive pans in his ears, was unable to ignore the hostility of Shama herself. She had kept up her martyr's attitude throughout the journey, silently staring at the road through the piquets of the cart, holding on her lap a box containing a Japanese coffee-set of intricate and fantastic design, part of a consignment the Tulsi Store had not been able to sell after three years, and given by Seth as a belated wedding present. Nor did Mr Biswas fail to notice that The Chase appeared to be managing quite well without his shop, which had been closed, as he knew, for many months.

'Is the sort of place you could build up,' he said to the carter.

The carter nodded non-committally, looking neither at Mr Biswas nor at the crowd but straight at his donkey, and aiming a gentle lash at the animal's eye.

And Shama sighed: the sigh which now told Mr Biswas that she thought him stupid, boring and shaming.

The cart stopped.

'Whoa!' some boys shouted.

Looking stern, preoccupied and, as he hoped, dangerous, Mr Biswas became very busy, helping the carter to unload. They carried bundles and boxes through the back rooms smelling of dust to the dark shop, warm in the late afternoon with the smell of coarse brown sugar and stale coconut oil. The white lines of light between the boards of the front door came from a bright, open world; movements inside the shop sounded furtive.

Their possessions, spread out on the counter, didn't take up much space.

'Only the first load,' Mr Biswas said to the carter. 'Have a pile of other stuff to come.'

The carter said nothing.

'Oh.' Mr Biswas remembered the carter had to be paid. More money.

The man took the dirty blue dollar-note and left.

'Is the last time *he* carry anything for me,' Mr Biswas said. 'I could tell him that.'

There was silence in the closed, stuffy shop.

'Is the sort of place you could build up,' Mr Biswas said.

His eyes became accustomed to the darkness and he looked about him. On a top shelf he saw some tins, apparently abandoned by the previous shopkeeper. About this person Mr Biswas now began to speculate. There was ambition and despair in these tins: their faded labels had been nibbled by rats and stained by flies; some tins had no labels at all.

He heard the carter shouting at his donkey as the cart turned in the narrow road; villagers gave advice, boys shouted encouragement, a whip repeatedly cracked, hoofbeats sounded awkward and irregular; then, with a jangle of harness, a cracking of the whip and a shout, the cart was off, cheered by the village boys.

Shama started to cry. But this time she didn't cry silently, with the tears running down from the expressionless eyes. She sobbed like a child, leaning over the box with the Japanese coffee-set on the counter. 'You wanted this. You wanted to paddle your own canoe. In all my life I never was so shamed as today. People standing up and laughing. *This* is what you want to paddle your own canoe with.' She covered her eyes with one hand and waved at the bundles on the counter with the other.

He wanted to comfort her. But he needed comfort himself. How lonely the shop was! And how frightening! He had never thought it would be like this when he found himself in an establishment of his own. It was late afternoon; Hanuman

House would be warm and noisy with activity. Here he was afraid to disturb the silence, afraid to open the door of the shop, to step into the light.

And in the end it was Shama who gave him comfort. For presently she stopped crying, gave a long, decisive blow to her nose and began sweeping, setting up, putting away. He followed her about, watching, offering help, glad to be told to do something and enjoying it when she reproved him for doing it badly.

In his careless retreat the previous tenant had abandoned two articles of furniture to the Tulsis; these had now passed to Mr Biswas. In one of the back rooms there was a large, canopy-less cast iron fourposter whose black enamel paint was chipped and lacklustre.

'Smell,' Shama said, holding a bedboard to Mr Biswas's nose. It had the piercing acrid smell of bedbugs. She doused the boards with kerosene. It wouldn't kill the bugs, she said. But it would keep them quiet for the time being.

And for years Mr Biswas was to know, particularly on a Saturday morning, the smell of kerosene and bedbugs. The boards changed; the mattress changed; but the bugs remained, following the fourposter wherever it went, from The Chase to Green Vale to Port of Spain to the house at Shorthills and, finally, to the house in Sikkim Street, where it nearly filled one of the two bedrooms on the upper floor.

The other piece of furniture that came with the shop was a kitchen table, small, low, and so neatly made that it stood, not in the kitchen in the yard, but in a bedroom. It was on this table, after much dusting and washing and wiping, that Shama placed her clothes and bolts of cloth; the parcel with the Japanese coffee-set she put below it, on the earth floor. Mr Biswas no longer thought the coffee-set, and Shama's attitude to it, absurd. Feeling grateful to Shama, he felt tender towards her coffee-set. He was not prepared for such a change in himself; but then he was astonished at the change in Shama. Till the last she had protested at leaving Hanuman House, but now she behaved as though she moved into a derelict house every day. Her actions were assertive, wasteful and unnecessarily noisy. They filled shop and house; they banished silence and loneliness.

And, further miracle, she produced a meal from that kitchen in the yard. He could not look on it as simply food. For the first time a meal had been prepared in a house which was his own. He felt abashed; and was glad that Shama did not treat it as an occasion. Only, feeding him at the table in the bedroom, by the light of a brand-new cost-price oil lamp from the Tulsi Store, she didn't sigh or stare or look weary and impatient as she had done in the lotus-decorated long room at Hanuman House.

In a few weeks the house became cleaner and habitable. The atmosphere of decay and disuse, while not disappearing, was made to retreat and held in check. Nothing could be done about the walls of the shop; no amount of washing could remove the smell of oil and sugar; the lower shelves and the two planks on the concrete floor behind the counter remained black with grease that had dried, and rough with dust that had stuck. They poured disinfectant everywhere, until they were almost choked by its fumes. But as the days passed, their zeal abated. They remembered the previous tenants less and less; and the grime, increasingly familiar, eventually became their own, and therefore supportable. Only slight improvements were made to the kitchen. 'It standing up just by the grace of God,' Mr Biswas said. 'Pull out one board, and the whole thing tumble down.' The earth floor of the bedrooms and gallery was mended, packed a little higher and plastered to a smooth, grey dustlessness. The Japanese coffee-set was taken out of its box and displayed on the table, where it appeared to be in peril; but Shama said it would remain there only until a better place was found.

And that was what Mr Biswas continued to feel about their venture: that it was temporary and not quite real, and it didn't matter how it was arranged. He had felt that on the first afternoon; and the feeling lasted until he left The Chase. Real life was to begin for them soon, and elsewhere. The Chase was a pause, a preparation.

In the meantime he became a shopkeeper. Selling had seemed to him such an easy way of making a living he had often wondered why people bothered to do anything else. On market days in Pagotes, for instance, you could buy a bag of flour, open it, sit down before it with a scoop and a set of scales on one side; and, ridiculously, people came and bought your flour and put money in your pocket. It looked such a simple process that Mr Biswas felt it wouldn't work if he tried it. But when he had stocked the shop, using the rest of his savings, and opened his doors, he found that people did come to him and buy and hand over real money. After every sale in those early days he felt he had pulled off a deep confidence trick, and had difficulty in hiding his exultation.

He thought of the tins on the top shelf – he had not got around to taking them down – and was as puzzled by his success as he was delighted by it. At the end of the first month he found he had made the vast profit of thirty-seven dollars. He knew nothing about keeping books and it was Shama who had suggested that he should make notes of goods given on credit on squares of brown shop-paper. It was Shama who suggested that these squares should be spiked. It was Shama who made the spike. And it was Shama who kept the accounts, writing in her round, stylish, slow Mission-school hand in a Shorthand Reporter's Notebook (the words were printed on the cover).

During these weeks the strangeness of their solitude lessened. But they were as yet unused to their new relationship and though they never quarrelled their talk remained impersonal and constrained. The solitude embarrassed Mr Biswas by the intimacy it imposed, especially during the serving of food. The atmosphere of service and devotion was flattering, but at the same time unsettling. It strained Mr Biswas and he was even glad when abruptly, it broke.

One evening Shama said, 'We must have a house-blessing ceremony, and get Hari to bless the shop and house, and have Mai and Uncle and everybody else here.'

He was taken completely by surprise, and lost his temper. 'What the hell you think I look like?' he asked in English. 'The Maharajah of Barrackpore? And what the hell for I should get Hari to come and bless this place? *This* place? Look for yourself.' He pointed to the kitchen and slapped the wall of the shop. 'Is bad enough as it is. To feed your family on top of all this is really going too damn far.'

And Shama did something he hadn't heard for weeks: she sighed, the old weary Shama sigh. And she said nothing.

In the days that followed he learned something new: how a woman nagged. The very word, nag, was known to him only from foreign books and magazines. It had puzzled him. Living in a wife-beating society, he couldn't understand why women were even allowed to nag or how nagging could have any effect. He saw that there were exceptional women, Mrs Tulsi and Tara, for example, who could never be beaten. But most of the women he knew were like Sushila, the widowed Tulsi daughter. She talked with pride of the beatings she had received from her short-lived husband. She regarded them as a necessary part of her training and often attributed the decay of Hindu society in Trinidad to the rise of the timorous, weak, non-beating class of husband.

To this class Mr Biswas belonged. So Shama nagged; and nagged so well that from the first he knew she was nagging. It amazed him that someone so young should show herself so competent in such an alien skill. But there were things which should have warned him. She had never run a house, but at The Chase she had always behaved like an experienced housewife. Then there was her pregnancy. She took that as easily as if she had borne many children; she never spoke about it, ate no special foods, made no special preparations, and generally behaved so normally that at times he forgot she was pregnant.

So Shama nagged. With her gloom and a refusal to speak, first of all; then with a precise, economical and noisy efficiency. She didn't ignore Mr Biswas. She made it clear that she noted his presence, and that it filled her with despair. At nights, next to him, but without touching him, she sighed loudly and blew her nose just at those moments when he was dropping off to sleep. She turned heavily and impatiently from side to side.

For the first two days he pretended not to notice.

On the third day he asked, 'What happen to you?'

She didn't reply, sitting next to him at the table, sighing, watching him while he ate.

He asked again.

She said, 'Talk about ungrateful!' and was up and out of the room.

He ate with diminished appetite.

That night Shama blew her nose repeatedly, and turned over in bed.

Mr Biswas prepared to stick it out.

Then Shama was silent.

Mr Biswas thought he had won.

Then Shama snuffled, very low, as though ashamed that the sound had escaped her.

Mr Biswas grew very still, and listened to his own breathing. It sounded regular and unnatural. He opened his eyes and looked up at the thatched roof. He could make out the rafters and the loose straws that hung straight down, threatening to fall into his eyes.

Shama groaned and blew her nose loudly, once, twice, three times. Then she got out of the cast iron fourposter and it rattled. Suddenly silent and energetic, she went out of the room. The latrine was right at the back of her yard.

When she came back, minutes later, he acknowledged defeat. 'What happen, man?' he asked. 'You can't sleep?'

'I been sleeping sound sound,' she said.

The next morning he said, 'All right, send for the old queen and the big boss and Hari and the gods and everybody else and get the shop bless.'

Shama was determined to do things well. Three labourers worked for three days to put up a large tent in the yard. It was a simple affair, with bamboo uprights and a roof of coconut branches; but the bamboos had to be transported from a neighbouring village, and the labourers, after many aggrieved and unintelligible mutterings about the Workmen's Compensation Act, had to be paid extra for climbing the coconut trees to get branches. Enormous quantities of food were bought; and, to assist in its preparation, sisters began arriving at The Chase three days before the house-blessing ceremony.

With their arrival Mr Biswas's protests ceased. He consoled himself with the thought that not all of the Tulsis would come.

They all came, except Seth, Miss Blackie and the two gods.

'Owad and Shekhar learning,' Mrs Tulsi said in English, meaning only that the gods were at school.

She wandered about the yard, opening doors, inspecting, no expression on her face.

Hari, the holy man, who was to be the pundit that day, was just as Mr Biswas remembered him, just as soft-spoken and lymphatic. His felt hat sat softly on his head. He greeted Mr Biswas without rancour, without pleasure, without interest. Then he went into the bedroom that was reserved for him and changed into his pundit's garb, which he had brought in a small cardboard suitcase. When he emerged as a pundit everyone treated him with a new respect.

Children, most of whom Mr Biswas could associate with no particular parent, swarmed everywhere, the girls in stiff satin dresses and with large rayon bows in long, dank hair, the boys in pantaloons and bright shirts. And there were babies: asleep in mothers' arms, asleep on blankets and sacks under the tent, asleep in various corners of the shop; babies crying and being energetically walked in the yard; babies crawling, babies bawling, babies simply silent; babies performing every babylike function.

Govind nodded to Mr Biswas, but didn't speak, and went and sat in the tent, where he talked and laughed loudly with the brothers-in-law.

Chinta and Padma asked without warmth after Mr Biswas's health. Padma asked because it was her duty, as Seth's representative; Chinta asked because Padma had done so. The two women were together for much of the time, and Mr Biswas suspected that an equally close relationship existed between Govind and Seth.

It seemed, too, that Sushila, the childless widow, was enjoying one of her periods of authority. She had now joined Mrs Tulsi and they both wandered about, peering and prodding and holding muted discussions in Hindi.

Mr Biswas found himself a stranger in his own yard. But
was it his own? Mrs Tulsi and Sushila didn't appear to think
so. The villagers didn't think so. They had always called the
shop the Tulsi Shop, even after he had painted a sign and
hung it above the door:

THE BONNE ESPERANCE GROCERY
M. Biswas Prop
Goods at City Prices

With one bedroom reserved for Hari, the other for Mrs
Tulsi, and with the shop full of babies, Mr Biswas could retreat nowhere. He stood before the shop, fondling his belly
under his shirt and working out the quarrel he would have
with Shama afterwards.

A scampering and a series of cries came from the shop.

Then Sushila's voice was heard, raised in undoubted authority. 'Get away from here. Go and play in the open. Can't
you see you are waking up the babies? Why do you big children like the dark so much?'

Every sister was perpetually on the alert for any sign, however slight or veiled, of sexual inclination among the children.

Mr Biswas knew the disagreeable rumpus that would follow. He had no taste for it, and walked away from the shop
to the boundary of the lot. Here, under a hedge, he came
upon a group of children playing house.

'You are Mai,' a girl said to another girl. And to a boy,
'You are Seth.'

Mr Biswas withdrew. But the girl – whose litter did she
belong to? – saw him and, raising her voice from the whisper
with which games of house should be played, said with un-
mistakable malice, 'And who will be Mohun? You, Bhoj.
You have three-quarter white pants. And you are a great
fighter.'

There was a round of childish laughter which filled Mr
Biswas's mind with thoughts of murder, though even as
he hurried away he felt some desire to see what Bhoj looked
like.

For the last three days, since the arrival of her sisters,
Shama had become a Tulsi and a stranger again. Now she was

unapproachable. The ceremony in the tent was about to begin and she sat in front of Hari, listening to his instructions with bowed head. Her hair was still wet from her ritual bath and she was dressed in white from top to toe. She looked like someone waiting to be sacrificed and Mr Biswas thought he could detect pleasure in the curve of her back. Her status, like Hari's, was only temporary; but while the ceremony lasted, it was paramount.

Mr Biswas didn't want to witness the ceremony. It meant sitting with the brothers-in-law in the tent; and he was sure that the sight of Shama's submissive and exultant back would eventually infuriate him. Also, it occurred to him that if he kept moving about he might prevent some of the Tulsi army from looting.

It was then that he thought of the shop.

He nearly ran there. It was dark, with the front doors closed, and he had to be careful. The shop smelled of babies, who were asleep everywhere: on the counter, flanked by pillows and boxes to keep them from rolling off; under the counter; on the floor planks behind the counter. Then, slowly in the darkness, a group of squatting children defined itself in one corner. They were silent and intent. With equal silence and intentness Mr Biswas picked his way past the babies to the counter.

The little group was methodically breaking soda water bottles and extracting the crystal marbles from the necks. The bottles were wrapped in sacking to muffle the noise. There was a deposit of eight cents on every bottle. The sweet jars on the bottom shelf were disarrayed. The Paradise Plums had dwindled substantially. So had the Mintips, a mint sweet with the elasticity and lastingness of rubber. So had the salted prunes. Many tin-lids had not been screwed on properly. Mr Biswas put out a hand to straighten a lid. It felt sticky. He dropped it. A baby bawled, the children in the corner became alert, and Mr Biswas shouted, 'Get out of here before I lay my hand on some of you.' And at the same time, with the dexterity of the practised shopkeeper, he lifted the flap of the counter and opened the little door, almost in one action, and was on the group in the corner.

He lifted a boy by the collar. The boy bawled, the girls with him bawled, the babies in the shop bawled.

From outside a woman asked, 'What's happening? What's happening?'

Mr Biswas dropped the boy he had seized, and the boy ran outside, screaming louder than the babies.

'Uncle Mohun beat me. Ma, Uncle Mohun beat me.'

Another woman, doubtless the mother, said, 'But he wouldn't touch you for nothing.' Her tone indicated that Mr Biswas wouldn't dare. 'You must have been doing something.'

'I wasn't doing nothing, Ma,' the boy wailed in English.

'He wasn't doing nothing, Ma.' This was from one of the girls. Mr Biswas knew her: a dumpy little thing, with big contemptuous eyes and full, pendulous lips; she was capable of fantastic physical contortions and often performed for visitors at Hanuman House.

'Blasted liar!' Mr Biswas said. He ran out of the shop, past a woman who was coming, cooing, to a bawling baby. 'Wasn't doing nothing? And who break up all those soda water bottles?'

In the tent Hari droned imperturbably on. Shama remained bowed in her white cocoon. The brothers-in-law sat on their blankets, reverentially still.

Mr Biswas was lucid enough to hope that he wasn't antagonizing a father.

Padma went into the shop in her slow way and came out and said judicially. '*Some* bottles have been broken.'

'And is eight cents a bottle,' Mr Biswas said. 'Wasn't doing nothing!'

The mother of the boy, suddenly enraged, flew to a hibiscus bush and began breaking off a switch. It was a tough bush and she had to bend the switch back and forth several times. Torn leaves fell on the ground.

The boy's bawls were now touched with genuine anguish.

The mother broke two switches on the boy, speaking as she beat. '*This* will teach you not to meddle with things that don't belong to you. *This* will teach you not to provoke people who don't make any allowances for children.' She caught sight of the marks left on the boy's collar by Mr Biswas's fingers, sticky from the tin-lid. 'And *this* will teach you not to let big people make your clothes dirty. *This* will teach you that they don't have to wash them. *You* are a big man. You know *right*. You know *wrong*. *You* are not a child. *That* is why *I* am beating *you* as though you are a *big* man and can take a *big* man's blows.'

The beating had ceased to be a simple punishment and had become a ritual. Sisters came out to witness, rocking crying babies in their arms, and said without urgency, 'You will damage the boy, Sumati.' And: 'Stop it now, Sumati. You have beaten him enough.'

Sumati continued to beat, and didn't stop talking.

In the tent Hari intoned. From the set of Shama's back Mr Biswas could divine her displeasure.

'House-blessing party!' Mr Biswas said.

The beating went on.

'Is just a form of showing-off,' Mr Biswas said. He had seen enough of these beatings to know that later it would be said admiringly, 'Sumati beats her children really well'; and that the sisters would say to their children, 'Do you want to be beaten the way Sumati beat her son that day at The Chase?'

The boy, no longer crying, was at last released. He sought comfort from an aunt, who calmed her baby, calmed the boy, said to the baby, 'Come, kiss him. His mother has beaten him really badly today'; then to the boy, 'Come, look how you are making him cry.' The whimpering boy kissed the crying baby and slowly the noise subsided.

'Good!' Sumati said, tears in her eyes. 'Good! Everyone is satisfied now. And I suppose the soda water bottles have been made whole again. Nobody is losing eight cents a bottle now.'

'I didn't ask anybody to beat their child, you hear,' Mr Biswas said.

'Nobody asked,' Sumati said, to no one in particular. 'I am just saying that everybody is now satisfied.'

She went to the tent and sat down in the section set aside for women and girls. The boy sat among the men.

The road was now lined with villagers and a few outsiders as well. They had not been attracted by the flogging, though that had encouraged the children of the village to gather a little earlier than might have been expected. They came for the food that would be distributed after the ceremony. Among these expectant uninvited guests Mr Biswas noticed two of the village shopkeepers.

The cooking was being done, under the superintendence of Sushila, over an open fire-hole in the yard. Sisters stirred enormous black cauldrons brought for the occasion from Hanuman House. They sweated and complained but they were happy. Though there was no need for it, some had stayed awake all the previous night, peeling potatoes, cleaning rice, cutting vegetables, singing, drinking coffee. They had prepared bin after bin of rice, bucket upon bucket of lentils and vegetables, vats of tea and coffee, volumes of chapattis.

Mr Biswas had given up trying to work out the cost. 'Just going to leave me a damn pauper,' he said. He walked along the hibiscus hedge, plucked leaves, chewed them and spat them out.

'You have a nice little property here, Mohun.'

It was Mrs Tulsi, looking tired after her rest on the cast iron fourposter. She had used the English word 'property'; it had an acquisitive, self-satisfied flavour; he would have preferred it if she had said 'shop' or 'place'.

'Nice?' he said, not sure whether she was being satirical or not.

'Very nice little property.'

'Walls falling down in the shop.'

'They wouldn't fall.'

'Roof leaking in the bedroom.'

'It doesn't rain all the time.'

'And I don't sleep all the time either. Want a new kitchen.'

'The kitchen looks all right to me.'

'And who does eat all the time, eh? We could do with a extra room.'

'What's the matter? You want a Hanuman House right away?'

'I don't want a Hanuman House at all.'

'Look,' Mrs Tulsi said. They were in the gallery now. 'You don't want an extra room at all. You could just hang some sugarsacks on these posts during the night, and you have your extra room.'

He looked at her. She was in earnest.

'Take them away in the morning,' she said, 'and you have your gallery again.'

'Sugarsack, eh?'

'Just six or seven. You wouldn't need any more.'

I would like to bury you in one, Mr Biswas thought. He said, 'You going to send me some of these sugarsacks?'

'You're a shopkeeper,' she said. 'You have more than me.'

'Don't worry. I was just joking. Just send me a coal barrel. You could get a whole family in a coal barrel. You didn't know that?'

She was too surprised to speak.

'I don't know why they still building houses,' Mr Biswas said. 'Nobody don't want a house these days. They just want a coal barrel. One coal barrel for one person. Whenever a baby born just get another coal barrel. You wouldn't see any houses anywhere then. Just a yard with five or six coal barrels standing up in two or three rows.'

Mrs Tulsi patted her lips with her veil, turned away and stepped into the yard. Faintly she called, 'Sushila.'

'And you could get Hari to bless the barrels right in Hanuman House,' Mr Biswas said. 'No need to bring him all the way to The Chase.'

Sushila came and, giving Mr Biswas a hard stare, offered her arm to Mrs Tulsi. 'What has happened, Mai?'

In the shop a baby woke and screamed and drowned Mrs Tulsi's words.

Sushila led Mrs Tulsi to the tent.

Mr Biswas went to the bedroom. The window was closed and the room was dark, but enough light came in to make everything distinct: his clothes on the wall, the bed rumpled from Mrs Tulsi's rest. Violating his fastidiousness, he lay down on the bed. The musty smell of old thatch was mingled with the smell of Mrs Tulsi's medicaments: bay rum, soft candles, Canadian Healing Oil, ammonia. He didn't feel a small man, but the clothes which hung so despairingly from the nail on the mud wall were definitely the clothes of a small man, comic, make-believe clothes.

He wondered what Samuel Smiles would have thought of him.

But perhaps he could change. Leave. Leave Shama, forget the Tulsis, forget everybody. But go where? And do what? What could he do? Apart from becoming a bus-conductor, working as a labourer on the sugar-estates or on the roads, owning a shop. Would Samuel Smiles have seen more than that?

He was in a state between waking and sleeping when there was a rattling on the door: no ordinary rattling: this was rattling with a purpose: he recognized Shama's hand. He shut his eyes and pretended to be asleep. He heard the hook lift and fall. She came into the room and even on the earth floor her footsteps were heavy, meant to be noticed. He felt her standing at the side of the fourposter, looking down at him. He stiffened; his breathing changed.

'Well, you make me really proud of you today,' Shama said.

And, really, it wasn't what he was expecting at all. He had grown so used to her devotion at The Chase that he expected her to take his side, if only in private. All the softness went out of him.

Shama sighed.

He got up. 'The house done bless?'

She flung back her long hair, still damp and straight, and he could see the sandalwood marks on her forehead: so strange on a woman. They made her look terrifyingly holy and unfamiliar.

'What you waiting for? Get out and make sure it properly bless.'

She was surprised by his vehemence and, without sighing or speaking, left the room.

He heard her making excuses for him.

'He has a headache.'

He recognized the tone as the one used by friendly sisters to discuss the infirmities of their husbands. It was Shama's plea to a sister to exchange intimacies, to show support.

He hated Shama for it, yet found himself anxiously waiting for someone to reply, to discuss his illness sympathetically, headache though it was.

But no one even said, 'Give him an aspirin.'

Still, he was pleased that Shama had tried.


The house-blessing seriously depleted Mr Biswas's resources; and after the ceremony, affairs in the shop began to go less well. One of the shopkeepers Mr Biswas had fed sold his establishment. Another man moved in; his business prospered. It was the pattern of trade in The Chase.

'Well, one thing sure,' Mr Biswas said. 'The house bless. You think everybody was just waiting for all that free food to stop coming here?'

'You give too much credit,' Shama said. 'You must get those people to pay you.'

'You want me to go and beat them?'

And when she took out the Shorthand Reporter's Notebook, he said, 'What you want to bust your brains adding up accounts for? I could tell you straight off. Ought oughts are ought.'

She worked out the expenses of the house-blessing and added up the outstanding credit.

'I don't want to know,' Mr Biswas said. 'I just don't want to know. How about getting the house un-bless? You think Hari could manage that?'

She had a theory. 'The people feeling shame. They owe too much. It used to happen in the store at home.'

'You know what *I* think it is? Is my face. I don't think I have the face of a shopkeeper. I have the sort of face of a man who does give credit but can't get it.' He got a mirror and studied his face. 'That nose, with that ugly lump on top of it. Those Chinese eyes. Look, girl, suppose – I mean, just supposing you see me for the first time. Look at me and try to imagine that.'

She looked.

'All right. Close your eyes. Now open them. First time you see me. You just see me. What you would say I was?'

She couldn't say.

'That is the whole blasted trouble,' he said. 'I don't look like anything at all. Shopkeeper, lawyer, doctor, labourer, overseer – I don't look like any of them.'

The Samuel Smiles depression fell on him.

Shama was a puzzle. Within the girl who had served in the Tulsi Store and romped up and down the staircase of Hanuman House, the wit, the prankster, there were other Shamas, fully grown, it seemed, just waiting to be released: the wife, the housekeeper, and now the mother. With Mr Biswas she continued to be brisk, uncomplaining and almost unaware of her pregnancy. But when she was visited by her sisters, who made it plain that the pregnancy was their business, Tulsi business, and had little to do with Mr Biswas, a change came over her. She did not cease to be uncomplaining; but she also became someone who not so much suffered as endured. She fanned herself and spat often, which she never did when she was alone; but pregnant women were supposed to behave in this way. It was not that she was trying to impress the sisters and get their sympathy; she was anxious not to disappoint them or let herself down. And when her feet began to swell, Mr Biswas wanted to say, 'Well, you are complete and normal now. Everything is going as it should. You are just like your sisters.' For there was no doubt that this was what Shama expected from life: to be taken through every stage, to fulfil every function, to have her share of the established emotions: joy at a birth or marriage, distress during illness and hardship, grief at a death. Life, to be full, had to be this established pattern of sensation. Grief and joy, both equally awaited, were one. For Shama and her sisters and women like them, ambition, if the word could be used, was a series of negatives: not to be unmarried, not to be childless, not to be an undutiful daughter, sister, wife, mother, widow.

Secretly, with the help of her sisters, the baby clothes were made. A number of Mr Biswas's floursacks disappeared; later they turned up as diapers. And the time came for Shama to go to Hanuman House. Sushila and Chinta came to fetch her;

the pretence was still maintained that Mr Biswas didn't know why.

Then he discovered that Shama had made preparations for him as well. His clothes had been washed and darned; and he was moved, though not surprised, to find on the kitchen shelf little squares of shop-paper on which, in her Mission-school script that always deteriorated after the first two or three lines, Shama had pencilled recipes for the simplest meals, writing with a disregard for grammar and punctuation which he thought touching. How quaint, too, to find phrases he had only heard her speak committed to paper in this handwriting! In her instructions for the boiling of rice, for example, she told him to 'throw in just a little pinch of salt' – he could see her bunching her long fingers – and to use 'the blue enamel pot without the handle'. How often, crouched before the *chulha* fire, she had said to him, 'Just hand me the blue pot without the handle.'

During the idle hours in the shop he had begun to choose names, mostly male ones: he never thought anything else likely. He wrote them on shop-paper, rolled them on his tongue, and tried them out on customers.

'Krishnadhar Haripratap Gokulnath Damodar Biswas. What do you think of that for a name? K. H. G. D. Biswas. Or what about Krishnadhar *Gokul*nath Haripratap Damodar Biswas. K. G. H. D.'

'You are not leaving much room for the pundit to give the child a name.'

'No pundit is giving any name to any child of mine.'

And on the back endpaper of the *Collins Clear-Type Shakespeare*, a work of fatiguing illegibility, he wrote the names in large letters, as though his succession had already been settled. He would have used *Bell's Standard Elocutionist*, still his favourite reading, if it had not suffered so much from the kick he had given it in the long room at Hanuman House; the covers hung loose and the endpapers had been torn, exposing the khaki-coloured boards. He had bought the *Collins Clear-Type Shakespeare* for the sake of *Julius Caesar*, parts of which he had declaimed at Lal's school. Every other play defeated him; the volume remained virtually unread and now, as a repository of the family records, proved to be a mistake. The endpaper blotted atrociously.

And the baby was a girl. But it was born at the correct time; it was born without difficulty; it was healthy; and Shama was absolutely well. He expected no less from her. He closed the shop and cycled to Hanuman House, and found that his daughter had already been named.

'Look at Savi,' Shama said.

'Savi?'

They were in Mrs Tulsi's room, the Rose Room, where all the sisters spent their confinements.

'It is a nice name,' Shama said.

Nice name; when all the way from The Chase he had been working on names, and had decided on Sarojini Lakshmi Kamala Devi.

'Seth and Hari chose it.'

'You don't have to tell me.' Jerking his chin towards the baby, he asked in English, 'They had it register?'

On the marble topped table next to the bed there was a sheet of paper under a brass plate. She handed that to him.

'Well! I glad she register. You know the government and nobody else did want to believe that I was even born. People had to swear and sign all sort of paper.'

'All of we was register,' Shama said.

'All of all-you *would* be register.' He looked at the certificate. 'Savi? But I don't see the name here at all. I only see Basso.'

She widened her eyes. 'Shh!'

'I not going to let anybody call my child Basso.'

'Shh!'

He understood. Basso was the real name of the baby, Savi the calling name. The real name of a person could be used to damage that person, whereas the calling name had no validity and was only a convenience. He was relieved he wouldn't have to call his daughter Basso. Still, what a name!

'Hari make that one up, eh? The holy ghost.'

'And Seth.'

'Trust the pundit and the big thug.'

'Man, what you doing?'

He was scribbling hard on the birth certificate.

'Look.' At the top of the certificate he had written: *Real calling name: Lakshmi. Signed by Mohun Biswas, father.* Below that was the date.

They both felt that a government document, which should have remained inviolate, had been challenged.

He enjoyed her alarm, and looked at her closely for the first time since he had come. Her long hair was loose and spread about her pillow. To look at him she had to press her chin into her neck.

'You got a double chin,' he said. She didn't reply.

Suddenly he jumped up. 'What the hell is this?'

'Show me.'

He showed her the certificate. 'Look. Occupation of father. Labourer. Labourer! Me! Where your family get all this bad blood, girl?'

'I didn't see that.'

'Trust Seth. Look. Name of informant: R. N. Seth. Occupation: Estate Manager.'

'I wonder why he do that.'

'Look, the next time you want a informant, eh, just let me know. Calling Lakshmi Basso and Savi. Hello, Lakshmi. Lakshmi, is me, your father, occupation — occupation what, girl? Painter?'

'It make you sound like a house painter.'

'Sign-painter? Shopkeeper? God, not that!' He took the certificate and began scribbling. 'Proprietor,' he said, passing the certificate to her.

'But you can't call yourself a proprietor. The shop belong to Mai.'

'You can't call me a labourer either.'

'They could bring you up for this.'

'Let them try.'

'You better go now, man.'

The baby was stirring.

'Hello, Lakshmi.'

'Savi.'

'Basso.'

'Shh!'

'Talk about the old thug. The old scorpion, if you ask me. The old Scorpio.'

He left the dark room with its close medicinal smells, its basins and its pile of diapers and came out into the drawing-room where at one end the two tall chairs stood like thrones. He went through the wooden bridge to the verandah of the old upstairs where Hari usually sat reading his unwieldy scriptures. Shyly, he came down the stairs into the hall, anticipating much attention as the father of the newest baby in Hanuman House. No one particularly looked at him. The hall was full of children eating gloomily. Among them he recognized the contortionist and the girl who had been running the house-game at The Chase. He smelled sulphur and saw that the children were not eating food but a yellow powder mixed with what looked like condensed milk.

He asked, 'What is that, eh?'

The contortionist grimaced and said, 'Sulphur and condensed milk.'

'Food getting expensive, eh?'

'Is for the eggzema,' the house-player said.

She dipped her finger in condensed milk, in sulphur, then put her finger in her mouth. Hurriedly she repeated the action.

Mrs Tulsi had come out of the black kitchen doorway.

'Sulphur and condensed milk,' Mr Biswas said.

'To sweeten it,' Mrs Tulsi said. Again she had forgiven him.

'Sweeten!' the contortionist whispered loudly. 'My foot.' Her achievements gave her unusual licence.

'Very good for the eczema.' Mrs Tulsi sat down next to the contortionist, took up her plate and shook back the sulphur from the rim, over which the contortionist had been steadily spilling sulphur on to the table. 'Have you seen your daughter, Mohun?'

'Lakshmi?'

'Lakshmi?'

'Lakshmi. My daughter. That is the name *I* choose.'

'Shama looks well.' Mrs Tulsi brushed the spilled sulphur off the table on to her palm and shook the palm over the condensed milk, which the contortionist had so far kept virgin. 'I have put her in the Rose Room. My room.'

Mr Biswas said nothing.

Mrs Tulsi patted the bench. 'Come and sit here, Mohun.'

He sat beside her.

'The Lord gives,' Mrs Tulsi said abruptly in English.

Concealing his surprise, Mr Biswas nodded. He knew Mrs Tulsi's philosophizing manner. Slowly, and with the utmost solemnity, she made a number of simple, unconnected statements; the effect was one of puzzling profundity.

'Everything comes, bit by bit,' she said. 'We must forgive. As your father used to say' – she pointed to the photographs on the wall – 'what is for you is for you. What is not for you is not for you.'

Against his will Mr Biswas found himself listening gravely and nodding in agreement.

Mrs Tulsi sniffed and pressed her veil to her nose. 'A year ago, who would have thought that you would be sitting here, in this hall, with these children, as my son-in-law and a father? Life is full of these surprises. But they are not really surprising. You are responsible for a life now, Mohun.' She began to cry. She put her hand on Mr Biswas's shoulder, not to comfort him, but urging him to comfort her. 'I let Shama have my room. The Rose Room. I know that you are worried about the future. Don't tell me. I know.' She patted his shoulder.

He was trapped by her mood. He forgot the children eating sulphur and condensed milk, and shook his head as if to admit that he had thought profoundly and with despair of the future.

Having trapped him in the mood, she removed her hand, blew her nose and dried her eyes. 'Whatever happens, you keep on living. Whatever happens. Until the Lord sees fit to take you away.' The last sentence was in English; it took him aback, and broke the spell. 'As He did with your dear father. But until that time comes, no matter how they starve you or how they treat you, they can never kill you.'

They, Mr Biswas thought, who are they?

Then Seth stamped into the hall with his muddy bluchers and the children applied themselves with zeal to the sulphur powder.

'Mohun,' Seth said. 'See your daughter? You surprise me, man.'

The contortionist giggled. Mrs Tulsi smiled.

You traitor, Mr Biswas thought, you old she-fox traitor.

'Well, you are a big man now, Mohun,' Seth said. 'Husband and father. Don't start behaving like a little boy again. The shop gone bust yet?'

'Give it a little time,' Mr Biswas said, standing up. 'After all, is only about four months since Hari bless it.'

The contortionist laughed; for the first time Mr Biswas felt charitably towards this girl. Encouraged, he added, 'You think we could get him to un-bless it?'

There was more laughter.

Seth shouted for his wife and food.

At the mention of food the children looked up longingly.

'No food for none of all-you today,' Seth said. 'This will teach you to play in dirt and give yourself eggzema.'

Mrs Tulsi was at Mr Biswas's side. She was solemn again. 'It comes bit by bit.' She was whispering now, for sisters were coming out of the kitchen with brass plates and dishes. 'You never thought, I expect, that your own first child would be born in a place like this.'

He shook his head.

'Remember, they can't kill you.'

That 'they' again.

'Oh,' Mr Biswas said. 'So it have three in the family now.'

She was warned by his tone.

'Send me a barrel,' he said loudly. 'A small coal barrel.'

He came out through the side gate and wheeled his cycle past the arcade, which was already filling up with the evening crowd of old India-born men who came there to smoke and talk. He cycled to Misir's rickety little wooden house and called at the lighted window.

Misir pushed his head past the lace curtain and said, 'Just the man I want to see. Come in.'

Misir said he had packed his wife and children off to his mother-in-law. Mr Biswas guessed the reason to be a quarrel or a pregnancy.

'Been working like hell without them, too,' Misir said. 'Writing stories.'

'For the *Sentinel*?'

'*Short* stories,' Misir said with his old impatience. 'Just sit down and listen.'

Misir's first story was about a man who had been out of work for months and was starving. His five children were starving; his wife was having another baby. It was December and the shops were full of food and toys. On Christmas eve the man got a job. Going home that evening, he was knocked down and killed by a motorcar that didn't stop.

'Helluva thing,' Mr Biswas said. 'I like the part about the car not stopping.'

Misir smiled, and said fiercely, 'But life is like that. Is not a fairy-story. No once-upon-a-time-there-was-a-rajah nonsense. Listen to this one.'

Misir's second story was about a man who had been out of work for months and was starving. To keep his large family he began selling his possessions, and finally he had nothing left but a two-shilling sweepstake ticket. He didn't want to sell it, but one of his children fell dangerously ill and needed medicine. He sold the ticket for a shilling and bought medicine. The child died; the ticket he had sold won the sweepstake.

'Helluva thing,' Mr Biswas said. 'What happen?'

'To the man? Why you asking *me*? Use your imagination.'

'Hell, hell, helluva thing.'

'People should know about these things,' Misir said. 'Know about life. You should start writing some stories yourself.'

'I just don't have the time, boy. Have a little property in The Chase now.' Mr Biswas paused, but Misir didn't react. 'Married man, too, you know. Responsibilities.' He paused again. 'Daughter.'

'God!' Misir exclaimed in disgust. *'God!'*

'Just born.'

Misir shook his head, sympathizing. 'Cat in bag, cat in bag. That is all we get from this cat-in-bag business.'

Mr Biswas changed the subject. 'What about the Aryans?'

'Why you asking? You don't really care. Nobody don't care. Just tell them a few fairy-stories and they happy. They don't want to face facts. And this Shivlochan is a damn fool. You know they send Pankaj Rai back to India? Sometimes I stop and wonder what happening to him over there. I suppose the poor man in rags, starving in some gutter, can't get a job or anything. You know, you could make a good story out of Pankaj.'

'Just what I was going to say. The man was a purist.'

'A born purist.'

'Misir, you still working for the *Sentinel*?'

'Blasted cent a line still. Why?'

'A damn funny thing happen today. You know what I see? A pig with two heads.'

'Where?'

'Right here, Hanuman House. From their estate.'

'But Hindus like the Tulsis wouldn't keep pigs.'

'You would be surprised. Of course it was dead.'

For all his reforming instincts, Misir was clearly disappointed and upset. 'Anything for the money these days. Still, is a story. Going to telephone it in straight away.'

And when he left Misir, Mr Biswas said, 'Occupation labourer. This will show them.'

It would be three weeks before Shama returned to The Chase. He put up a hammock for the baby in the gallery and waited. The shop and the back rooms became increasingly disordered, and felt cold, like an abandoned camp. Yet as soon as Shama came with Lakshmi – 'Her name is Savi,' Shama insisted, and Savi it remained – those rooms again became the place where he not only lived, but had status without having to assert his rights or explain his worth.

He immediately began complaining of the very things that pleased him most. Savi cried, and he spoke as though she were one of Shama's indulgences. Meals were late, and he exhibited an annoyance which concealed the joy he felt that there was someone to cook meals with him in mind. To these outbursts Shama didn't reply, as she would have done before.

She was morose herself, as though she preferred this bond to
the bond of sentimentality.

He liked to watch when the baby was bathed. Shama did
this expertly; she might have been bathing babies for years.
Her left arm and hand supported the baby's back and wobbly
head; her right hand soaped and washed; finally there was the
swift, gentle gesture which transferred the baby from basin
to towel. He marvelled that someone who had come out
of Hanuman House with hands torn by housework could
express so much gentleness through those same hands. Afterwards Savi was rubbed with coconut oil and her limbs exercised, to certain cheerful rhymes. The same things had been
done to Mr Biswas and Shama when they were babies; the
same rhymes had been said; and possibly the ritual had been
evolved a thousand years before.

The anointing was repeated in the evening, when the sun
had dropped and the surrounding bush had begun to sing.
And it was at this time, some six months later, that Moti came
to the shop and rapped hard on the counter.

Moti did not belong to the village. He was a small
worried-looking man with grey hair and bad teeth. He was
dressed in a dingy clerkish way. His dirty shirt sat neatly on
him and the creases on his trousers could just be seen. In his
shirt pocket he carried a fountain pen, a stunted pencil and
pieces of soiled paper, the equipment and badge of the rural
literate.

He asked nervously for a pennyworth of lard.

Mr Biswas's Hindu instincts didn't permit him to stock
lard. 'But we have butter,' he said, thinking of the tall smelly
tin full of red, runny, rancid butter.

Moti shook his head and took off his bicycle clips. 'Just
give me a cent Paradise Plums.'

Mr Biswas gave him three in a square of white paper.

Moti didn't go away. He put a Paradise Plum in his mouth
and said, 'I am glad you don't stock lard. I respect you for it.'
He paused and, closing his eyes, crushed the Paradise Plum
between his jaws. 'I am glad to see a man in your position not
giving up his religion for the sake of a few cents. Do you

know that these days some Hindu shopkeepers are actually selling salt beef with their own hands? Just for the few extra cents.'

Mr Biswas knew, and regretted the squeamishness which
prevented him from doing the same.

'And look at that other thing,' Moti said, talking through
the crushed Paradise Plum. 'Did you hear about the pig?'

'The Tulsi pig? Doesn't surprise me at all.'

'Still, the blessing is that not everyone is like that. You, for
instance. And Seebaran. Do you know Seebaran?'

'Seebaran?'

'Don't know Seebaran! L. S. Seebaran? The man who has
been handling practically all the work in the Petty Civil.'

'Oh, him,' Mr Biswas said, still in the dark.

'Very strict Hindu. And one of the best lawyers here too,
I can tell you. We should be proud of him. The man who was
here before you – what's his name? – anyway, the man before
you had a lot to thank Seebaran for. He would be a pauper
today if it hadn't been for Seebaran.'

Moti put another Paradise Plum in his mouth and absently
considered the meagrely filled shelves. Mr Biswas followed
Moti's gaze, which came to rest on the tins with half-eaten
labels, left there by the man Seebaran had assisted.

'So everybody going to Dookhie, eh?' Moti said,
more familiar now, and speaking in English. Dookhie was
the newest shopkeeper in The Chase. 'Is a shame. Is a shame
the way some people spend their whole life living on
credit. Is a form of robbery. Take Mungroo. You know
Mungroo?'

Mr Biswas knew him well.

'A man like Mungroo should be in jail,' Moti said.

'I think so too.'

'Is not,' Moti said judiciously, closing his eyes and cracking
the Paradise Plum, 'as if he was a pauper and can't afford to
pay. Mungroo richer than you and me could ever hope to be,
you hear.' This was news to Mr Biswas.

'Man should be in jail,' Moti repeated.

Mr Biswas was about to say that he hadn't been fooled by
Mungroo when Moti said, 'He don't rob the rude and crude
shopkeepers, people like himself. He frighten they give him a

good dose of licks. No, he does look for nice people with nice soft heart, and is them he does rob. Mungroo see you, he think you look nice, and *next* day his wife come round for two cents this and three cents that, and she forget that she ain't got no money, and if you could wait till next pay day. Well, you wrap up the goods in good strong paper-bag, you send she home happy, and you sit down and wait till next day. Next pay day Mungroo forget. His wife forget. They too busy killing chicken and buying rum to remember you. Two-three days later, eh-eh, wife suddenly remember you. She bawling again. She want more trust. Don't tell me about Mungroo. I know him too good. Man should be in jail, if anybody had the guts to throw him there.'

The account was telescoped and dramatized, but Mr Biswas recognized its truth. He felt exposed, and said nothing.

'Just show me your accounts,' Moti said. 'Just to see how much Mungroo owe you.'

Mr Biswas took down the spike from the nail between the shelves where it hung above a faded advertisement for Cydrax, a beverage which had not caught the village's fancy. The spike was now a tall, feathery, multi-coloured brush, with the papers at the bottom as brittle and curling as dead leaves.

'Pappa!' Moti said, and became graver and graver as he looked through the papers. He could not look very far because to get at the lower papers he would have had to remove those at the top altogether. He turned away from Mr Biswas and contemplated the blackness outside, staring past the doorway against which the rear wheel of his decrepit bicycle could be seen. Sadly he sucked his Paradise Plum. 'Pity you don't know Seebaran. Seebaran woulda fix you up in two twos. He help out the man before you. Otherwise the man would be a pauper now, man. A pauper. Is a funny thing, but you don't expect to find people getting fat and rich on credit while the poor shopkeeper, who give the credit, not getting enough to eat, wearing rags, watching his children starve, watching them sick.'

Mr Biswas, seeing himself as the hero of one of Misir's stories, could scarcely hide his alarm.

'All right, then, man.' Moti fixed his bicycle clips around his ankles. 'I got to go. Thanks for the chat. I hope everything go all right with you.'

'But you know Seebaran,' Mr Biswas said.

'Know him, yes. But I don't know whether I could just go and ask him to help out a friend of mine. Busy man, you know. Handling nearly all the work in the Petty Civil.'

'Still, you could tell him?'

'Yes,' Moti said, without conviction. 'I could tell him. But Seebaran is a big man. You can't go troubling him with just one or two little things.'

Mr Biswas brushed his hand up and down the papers on the spike. 'It have a *lot* of work here for him,' he said aggressively. 'You tell him.'

'All right. I go tell him.' Moti got on his cycle. 'But I ain't promising nothing.'

Savi was asleep when Mr Biswas went to the back room.

'Going to settle Mungroo and the rest of them,' Mr Biswas said to Shama. 'Putting Seebaran on their tail.'

'Who is Seebaran?'

'Who is Seebaran! You mean you don't know Seebaran? The man who handling practically all the work in the Petty Civil.'

'I know all that. I hear what the man was saying too.'

'Why the hell you ask me then for?'

'You don't think you better get advice before you start bringing up people?'

'Advice? Who from? The old thug and the old she-fox? I know they know everything. You don't have to tell me that. But they know law?'

'Seth bring up a lot of people.'

'And every time he bring somebody up, he lose. You don't have to tell me that either. Everybody in Arwacas know about Seth and the people he bring up. He don't know everything.'

'He used to study doctor. Doctor or druggist.'

'Used to study doctor! Horse-doctor, if you ask me. He look like a doctor to you? You ever look at his hands? Fat, thick. Can't even hold a pencil properly.'

'He cut open that boil Chanrouti had the other day.'

'And yes. That is another thing I want to tell you, eh. In advance. In ad*vance*. I don't want Seth cutting open any boil on any of my children. And I don't want him prescribing any blasted sulphur and condensed milk for any of them either.'

Mungroo was the leader of the village stick-fighters. He was a tall, wiry, surly man, made ferocious in appearance by a large handlebar moustache, for which the villagers called him Moush, then Moach. As a stickman he was a champion. He had reach and skill, and his responses were miraculous. He converted a parry into a lunge so fluently it seemed to be a single action. He fought every duel as though he had rehearsed its every development. It was Mungroo who had organized the young men of The Chase into a fighting band, ready to defend the honour of the village on the days of the Christian Carnival and the Muslim Hosein. Under his direction and in his yard they practised assiduously in the evenings by the light of flambeaux. The village boys went to watch this evening practice. So, despite Shama's disapproval, did Mr Biswas.

As much as the game he liked the making of the sticks. Designs were cut into the bark of the *poui*, which was then roasted in a bonfire; the burnt bark was peeled off, leaving the design burnt into the white wood. There was no scent as pleasant as that of barely roasted *poui*: faint, yet so lasting it seemed to come from afar, from some immeasurable depth captive within the wood: as faint as the scent of the *pouis* Raghu roasted in the village like this, in a yard like this, in a bonfire like this: bringing sensations, not pictures, of an evening meal being cooked over a fire that shone on a mud wall and kept out the night, of cool, new, unused mornings, of rain muffled on a thatched roof and warmth below it: sensations as faint as the scent of the *poui* itself, but sadly evanescent, refusing to be seized or to be translated into a concrete memory.

Afterwards, the sticks, their heads carved, were soaked in coconut oil in bamboo cylinders, to give them greater strength and resilience. Then Mungroo took the sticks to an old stickman he knew, to have them 'mounted' with the spirit of a dead Spaniard. So that the ritual ended in romance, awe and mystery. For the Spaniards, Mr Biswas knew, had surrendered the island one hundred years before, and their descendants had disappeared; yet they had left a memory of reckless valour, and this memory had passed to people who came from another continent and didn't know what a Spaniard was, people who, in their huts of mud and grass where time and distance were obliterated, still frightened their children with the name of Alexander, of whose greatness they knew nothing.

By profession Mungroo was a roadmender. He preferred to say that he worked for the government, and he preferred not to work at all. He made it plain that because he defended the honour of the village, the village owed him a living. He exacted contributions for pitch-oil for the flambeaux, for the 'mounting' fees, and for the expensive costumes the stick-fighters wore on days of battle. At first Mr Biswas contributed willingly. Then Mungroo, the better to devote himself to his art, abandoned the road-gang for weeks at a time and lived on credit from Mr Biswas and other shopkeepers. Mr Biswas admired Mungroo. He felt it would be disloyal to refuse Mungroo credit, unbecoming to remind him of his debts, and dangerous to do either. Mungroo became steadily more demanding. Mr Biswas complained to other customers; they told Mungroo. Mungroo didn't reply, as Mr Biswas had feared, with violence, but with a dignity which, though it struck Mr Biswas as hollow, hurt him as deeply as the silences and sighs of Shama. Mungroo refused to speak to Mr Biswas and spat, casually, whenever he passed the shop. Mungroo's bills remained unpaid; and Mr Biswas lost a few more customers.

Earlier than Mr Biswas had expected, Moti returned and said, 'You are a lucky man. Seebaran has decided to help you. I told him you were a friend of mine and a good Hindu, and he's a very strict Hindu himself, as you know. He is going to help you. Even though he's busy.' He took out the papers from his shirt pocket, found the one he wanted and slapped it down on the counter. At the top a mauve stamp, slightly askew, said that L. S. Seebaran was a solicitor and convey-ancer. Below that there were many dotted lines between printed sentences. 'Seebaran going to full up those for you as soon as he get your papers,' Moti said, using English, the lan-guage of the law.

*Unless this sum*, Mr Biswas read with a thrill, *together with One Dollar and Twenty Cents ($1.02c), the cost of this letter, is paid within ten days, legal proceedings shall be instituted against you.* And there was another dotted line below that, where L. S. Seebaran was to sign himself yours faithfully.

'Powerful, powerful, man,' Mr Biswas said. 'Legal proceedings, eh. I didn't know it was so easy to bring people up.'

Moti gave a knowing little grunt.

'One dollar and twenty cents, the cost of this letter,' Mr Biswas said. 'You mean I don't even have to pay that?'

'Not with Seebaran fighting your case for you.'

'One dollar and twenty cents. You mean Seebaran getting that just for fulling up those dotted lines? Education, boy. It have nothing like a profession.'

'You is your own boss, if you is a professional man,' Moti said, his voice touched with a remote sadness.

'But one twenty, man. Five minutes' writing for one twenty.'

'You forgetting that Seebaran had to spend years and years studying all sort of big and heavy books before they allow him to send out papers like this.'

'You know, the thing to do is to have three sons. Make one a doctor, one a dentist, and one a lawyer.'

'Nice little family. If you have the sons. And if you have the money. They don't give trust in *those* places.'

Mr Biswas brought out Shama's accounts. Moti asked to see the credit slips again, and his face fell as he looked through them. 'A lot of these ain't signed,' he said.

Mr Biswas had for long thought it discourteous to ask his creditors to do so. He said, 'But they wasn't signed the last time either.'

Moti gave a nervous laugh. 'Don't worry. I know cases where Seebaran recover people money even without paper or anything. But is a lot of work here, you know. You got to show Seebaran that you serious.'

Mr Biswas went to the drawer below the shelves. The drawer was large but not heavy, and pulled out in an easy, awkward way; the wood inside was oily but surprisingly white. 'A dollar and twenty cents?' he said.

A throat was cleared. Shama's.

'*Maharajin,*' Moti said.

There was no reply.

Mr Biswas didn't turn. 'One twenty?' he repeated, rattling the coins in the drawer.

Moti said unhappily, 'You can't give a man like Seebaran one twenty to fight a case for you.'

'Five,' Mr Biswas said.

'That would be good,' Moti said, as though he had hoped to get ten.

'Two,' Mr Biswas said, walking briskly to the counter and laying down a red note.

'Is all right,' Moti said. 'Don't bother to count it.'

'And one is three.' Mr Biswas put down a blue note. 'And one is four. And one is five.'

'Five,' Moti said.

'Tell Seebaran I send that.'

Moti put the notes in his side pocket and Shama's Shorthand Reporter's Notebook in his hip pocket. He fixed on his bicycle clips and, looking up, said, '*Maharajin,*' directing a brief smile over Mr Biswas's shoulder. Then, briskly, not looking back, he wheeled his shaky bicycle across the yellow dirt yard, dusty and cracked, with here and there a bleached and flattened Anchor cigarette packet. 'Right,' he called from the road, hopping on the saddle and pedalling rapidly away.

'Right, man, Moti!' Mr Biswas called back.

He remained where he was, palms pressed against the edge of the counter, staring at the road, at the mango tree and the side wall of the hut in the lot obliquely opposite, and the sugarcane fields stretching away with an occasional blob of trees, to the low hills of the Central Range.

'All right!' he said. 'Somebody turn you into a statue?'

Shama sighed.

'I suppose I is my own boss.'

'And a professional man,' she said.

'Shoulda give him ten dollars.'

'Is not too late. Why you don't empty the drawer and run after him?'

And having stimulated his rage and his appetite for argument, she left the doorway and went to the back room, where after much thumping and sighing she began to sing a popular Hindi song:

> Slowly, slowly,
> Brothers and sisters,
> Bear his corpse to the water's edge.

He didn't have the Hindu delight in tragedy and the details of death, and he had often asked Shama not to sing this cremation song. Now he had to listen while she sang with sweet lugubriousness to the end. And when, fretted to defeat, he went to the back room, he found Shama, in her best satin bodice and most elaborately worked veil, putting bootees on a fully dressed Savi.

'Hello!' he said.

Shama tied one bootee and slipped on the other.

'Going somewhere?'

She tied the other bootee.

At last she said in Hindi, 'You may have lost all shame. But everyone hasn't. Just remember that.'

He knew that the Tulsi daughters who lived with their husbands often went back after a quarrel to Hanuman House, where they complained and got sympathy and, if they didn't stay too long, respect. 'All right,' he said. 'Pack up and go. I suppose they are going to give you some medal at the monkey house.'

After she left, he stood in the shop doorway, fondling his belly and watching his creditors coming back from the fields. The only thing that gave him pleasure was the thought of the surprise these people were going to get in a few days: a flutter of disturbances throughout The Chase for which he, inactive in his shop, would be responsible.

*

'Biswas!' Mungroo shouted from the road. 'Come out, before I come in.'

The day had arrived. Mungroo was holding a sheet of paper in one hand and slapping at it with the other.

'Biswas!'

A crowd was beginning to gather. Many held papers.

'Paper,' Mungroo said. 'He has sent me a paper. I am going to make him eat this piece of paper. Biswas!'

Unhurriedly Mr Biswas lifted the counter-flap, pulled the little door open and passed to the front of the shop. The law was on his side – he had, indeed, brought it into play – and he felt this gave him complete protection. He leaned against the doorpost, felt the wall quiver, stifled his fear about the wall tumbling down, and crossed his legs.

'Biswas! I am going to make you eat this paper.'

Women screamed from the road.

'Touch me,' Mr Biswas said.

'Paper,' Mungroo said, stepping into the yard.

'Touch me and I bring you up.'

Still Mungroo advanced.

'I bring you up and you spend Carnival in jail.'

The effect was startling. Carnival was less than a month away. Mungroo halted. His followers, seeing themselves leaderless during the two most important days of the stick-fighting year, at once ran to Mungroo and held him back.

'I call all of all-you as witnesses,' Mr Biswas said, unaware of the reasons for his deliverance. 'Let him touch me. And all of all-you have to come to court to be *my* witnesses.' He believed that by being the first to ask them he had bound them legally. 'Can't ask my wife,' he went on. 'They don't take wife as witness. But I asking all of all-you here.'

'Paper. The man has sent me a paper,' Mungroo muttered, while he allowed himself, without loss of prestige, to be pushed slowly back to the road by his followers.

'Well,' Mr Biswas said. 'One man get his paper. He had it coming to him a long time. Let me tell you, eh. Don't let Tom, Dick or Harry think he can play with me, you hear. One man get his paper. A lot more going to get *their* paper before I finish. And don't come to talk to me. Go and talk to Seebaran.'

When he came to the shop, a week later, Moti was businesslike. As soon as he greeted Mr Biswas he took out a sheet of paper from his shirt pocket, spread it on the counter and began ticking off names with his fountain pen. 'Well, Ratni pay up,' he said. 'Dookhni pay. Sohun pay. Godberdhan pay. Rattan pay.'

'We frighten them, eh? So, no legal proceedings against them, then?'

'Jankie ask for time. Pritam too. But they going to pay, especially as they see the others paying up.'

'Good, good,' Mr Biswas said. 'I could do with their money right now.'

Moti folded the sheet of paper.

'So?' Mr Biswas said.

Moti put the paper in his pocket.

Mr Biswas pretended he hadn't been waiting for anything. 'And Mungroo?'

'I glad you ask about him. As a matter of fact, he giving us a little trouble.' Moti took out a long envelope from his trouser pocket and handed it to Mr Biswas. 'This is for you.'

It was a communication, on stiff paper, from the Attorney-General.

Mr Biswas read with disbelief, annoyance and distress.

'Who is this damn Muslim Mahmoud who stamp his dirty name down here? He is a solicitor and conveyancer too, eh? I thought Seebaran was handling all the work in the Petty Civil.'

'No, no,' Moti said soothingly. 'This is Assize Court business.'

'Assize. *Assize!* So this is what Seebaran land me up in!'

'Seebaran ain't land you up in nothing. You land yourself. Read the schedule.'

'O God! Look, look. Mungroo bringing *me* up for damaging *his* credit!'

'And he have a good case too. You shouldn't go around telling people he owe you money. Over and over I hear Seebaran telling clients, "Leave everything to me and keep your mouth shut. Keep your mouth shut. Keep your mouth shut and leave everything to me." Over and over. But clients don't listen. I know clients who talk their way straight to the gallows.'

'Seebaran didn't tell me a damn thing. I ain't even see the blasted man yet.'

'He want to see you now.'

'Just let me get this straight. Mungroo owe me money. I say so and I damage his credit. So now he can't go around taking goods on trust and not paying. So he bring me up. Exactly what the hell this is? And what about those slips?'

'They wasn't signed. I did warn you about that, remember. But you didn't listen. Clients don't listen. Is a serious business, man. It got Seebaran worried like anything. I could tell you.'

'Hear you. It got Seebaran worried. What about me?'

'Seebaran don't think you would have a chance in court. He say it would be better to settle outside.'

'You mean shell out. All right. Pounds, shillings and pence, dollars and cents. Let me hear who have to get how much. This is the way Seebaran handling all the work in the Petty Civil, eh?'

'Seebaran only want to help you out, you know. You could take your case to some K C or the other and pay him a hundred guineas before he ask you to sit down. Nobody stopping you.'

Mr Biswas listened. He learned with surprise that there had already been friendly discussions between Mungroo's lawyer, Mahmoud, and Seebaran; so that the case had been raised and virtually settled without his knowing anything about it at all. It appeared that Mungroo was willing, for one hundred dollars, to call off the action. The fees of both lawyers came to a hundred dollars as well, though Seebaran, appreciating Mr Biswas's position, had said he would accept only such money as he could recover from Mr Biswas's creditors.

'Suppose,' Mr Biswas said, 'that all the others decide to behave like Mungroo. Suppose that every manjack bring me up.'

'Don't think about it,' Moti said. 'You would make your-self sick.'

As soon as he could, Mr Biswas cycled to Arwacas to ask Shama to come back. He did not tell her what had happened. And it was not from Mrs Tulsi or Seth that he borrowed the money, but from Misir, who, in addition to his journalistic, literary and religious activities, had set up as a usurer, with a capital of two hundred dollars.

More than half the time that remained to Mr Biswas in The Chase was spent in paying off this debt.

In all Mr Biswas lived for six years at The Chase, years so squashed by their own boredom and futility that at the end they could be comprehended in one glance. But he had aged. The lines which he had encouraged at first, to give him an older look, had come; they were not the decisive lines he had hoped for that would give a commanding air to a frown; they were faint, fussy, disappointing. His cheeks began to fall; his cheek bones, in a proper light, jutted slightly; and he de-veloped a double chin of pure skin which he could pull down so that it hung like the stiff beard on an Egyptian statue. The skin loosened over his arms and legs. His stomach was now perpetually distended; not fat: it was his indigestion, for that affliction had come to stay, and bottles of Maclean's Brand Stomach Powder became as much part of Shama's purchases as bags of rice or flour.

Though he never ceased to feel that some nobler purpose awaited him, even in this limiting society, he gave up reading Samuel Smiles. That author depressed him acutely. He turned to religion and philosophy. He read the Hindus; he read the Marcus Aurelius and Epictetus which Mrs Weir had given him; he earned the gratitude and respect of a stall-keeper at Arwacas by buying an old and stained copy of *The Supersensual Life*; and he began to dabble in Christianity, acquiring a volume, written mostly in capital letters, called *Arise and Walk*. As a boy he had liked to read descriptions of bad weather in foreign countries; they made him forget the heat and sudden rain which was all he knew. But now, though his philosophical books gave him solace, he could never lose the feeling that they were irrelevant to his situation. The books had to be put down. The shop awaited; money problems awaited; the road outside was short, and went through flat fields of dull green to small, hot settlements.

And at least once a week he thought of leaving the shop, leaving Shama, leaving the children, and taking that road.

Religion was one thing. Painting was the other. He brought out his brushes and covered the inside of the shop doors and the front of the counter with landscapes. Not of the abandoned field next to the shop, the intricate bush at the back, the huts and trees across the road, or the low blue mountains of the Central Range in the distance. He painted cool, ordered forest scenes, with gracefully curving grass, cultivated trees ringed with friendly serpents, and floors bright with perfect flowers; not the rotting, mosquito-infested jungle he could find within an hour's walk. He attempted a portrait of Shama. He made her sit on a fat sack of flour – the symbolism pleased him: 'Suit your family to a T,' he said – and spent so much time on her clothes and the sack of flour that before he could begin on her face Shama abandoned him and refused to sit any more.

He read innumerable novels, particularly those in the Reader's Library; and he even tried to write, encouraged by the appearance in a Port of Spain magazine of a puzzling story by Misir. (This was a story of a starving man who was rescued by a benefactor and after some years rose to wealth. One day, driving along the beach, the man heard someone in the sea shouting for help, and recognized his former benefactor in difficulties. He instantly dived into the water, struck his head on a submerged rock and was drowned. The benefactor survived.) But Mr Biswas could never devise a story, and he lacked Misir's tragic vision; whatever his mood and however painful his subject, he became irreverent and facetious as soon as he began to write, and all he could manage were distorted and scurrilous descriptions of Moti, Mungroo, Seebaran, Seth and Mrs Tulsi.

And there were whole weeks when he devoted himself to some absurdity. He grew his nails to an extreme length and held them up to startle customers. He picked and squeezed at his face until his cheeks and forehead were inflamed and the rims of his lips were like welts. When his skin became pitted with little holes, he studied these with interest and found the perfection of their shape pleasing. And once he dabbed healing ointments of various colours on his face and went and stood in the shop doorway, greeting people he knew.

He did these things when Shama was away. And more and more frequently she went to Hanuman House, even when there was no quarrel, and stayed longer.

Three years after Savi was born, Shama gave birth to a son. He was not given the names that had been written on the endpaper of the *Collins Clear-Type Shakespeare*. Seth suggested that the boy should be called Anand, and Mr Biswas, who had prepared no new names, agreed. Then it was Anand who travelled with Shama. Savi stayed at Hanuman House. Mrs Tulsi wanted this; so did Shama; so did Savi herself. She liked Hanuman House for its activity and its multitude of children; at The Chase she was restless and badly behaved.

'Ma,' Savi said to Shama one day, 'couldn't you give me to Aunt Chinta and take Vidiadhar in exchange?'

Vidiadhar was Chinta's newest baby, born a few months before Anand. And the reason for Savi's request was this: by virtue of a tradition whose beginnings no one could trace, Chinta was the aunt who distributed all the delicacies that were given to the House by visitors.

Shama told the story as a joke, and couldn't understand it when Mr Biswas became annoyed.

Once a week he rode his Royal Enfield bicycle to Hanuman House to see Savi. Often he didn't have to go inside; Savi was waiting for him in the arcade. At every visit he gave her a silver six-cents piece and asked anxious questions.

'Who beat you?'

Savi shook her head.

'Who shouted at you?'

'They shout at everybody.'

She didn't seem to need a protector.

One Saturday he found her wearing heavy boots with long iron bands down the side of her legs and straps over her knees.

'Who put these on you?'

'Granny.' She was not aggrieved. She was proud of the boots, the iron, the straps. 'They are heavy, heavy.'

'Why did she put them on? To punish you?'

'Only to straighten my legs.'

She had bow-legs. He didn't believe anything could be done about them and had never tried to find out.

'They are ugly.' That was all he could say. 'They make you look like a cripple.'

She frowned at the word. 'Well, I like it.' Then, taking the six cents, 'At least, I don't mind.' She threw out her hands, then put them on her hips and looked away, just like one of the aunts.

The numbers of the Tulsis swelled continually. Fresh children were born to the resident daughters. A son-in-law who lived away died, and his brood came to Hanuman House, where they were distinguished and made glamorous by their mourning clothes of black, white and mauve. This Christian custom did not please everyone. And almost at once Shama had tales to take back to The Chase about the low manners and language of the new arrivals. There were even whispers of theft and obscene practises, and Shama reported the general approval when the widow, anxious to appease, took to inflicting spectacular punishments on her bereaved children.

All this made Mr Biswas uneasy, and he was mortified to find that Savi now talked of nothing but the mourners, their misdeeds and their punishments.

'Sometimes,' Savi said, 'their mother simply hands over to Granny.'

'Look, Savi. If Granny or anybody else touches you, you just let me know. Don't let them frighten you. I will take you home right away. You just let me know.'

'And Granny tied Vimla to the bed in the Rose Room and blindfolded her and pinched her all over.'

'God!'

'It serves Vimla right. The language that girl has picked up.'

Mr Biswas wanted to know whether Savi had been blindfolded and pinched herself; but he was afraid to ask.

'Oh, I like Granny,' Savi said. 'I think she is very funny. And she likes me.'

'Yes?'

'She calls me the little paddler.'

He made no comment.

Another day Savi said, 'Granny is making me eat fish. I hate it.'

'Well, you just don't eat it. Throw it away. Don't let them feed you any of their bad food.'

'But I can't refuse. Granny takes out all the bones and feeds me herself.'

When he got back to The Chase he told Shama, 'Look, I want you to get your mother to stop trying to feed my daughter all sort of bad food, you hear.'

She knew about it. 'Fish? But the brains good for the brain, you know.'

'It look to me that your family just eat too much damn fish brains, you hear. And I want them to stop calling the girl the little paddler. I don't want anybody to give names to my child.'

'And what about the names you give?'

'I just want them to stop it, that is all.'

Never ceasing to believe that their stay at The Chase was only temporary, he had made no improvements. The kitchen remained askew and rickety; he did not wall off part of the gallery to make a new room; and he had not thought it worth while to plant trees that would bear flowers or fruit in two or three years.

It was strange, then, for him to find one day that house and shop bore so many marks of his habitation. No one might have lived there before him, and it was hard to imagine anyone after him moving about these rooms and getting to know them as he had done. The hammock rope had worn polished indentations in the rafters from which it hung. The rope itself had grown darker; where his hands and Shama's had held it there were glints like those on the bumps on the lower half of the mud walls. The thatch was sootier and more bearded; the back rooms smelled of his cigarettes and his paint; window-sills and the gallery uprights had been made clean by constant leaning. The shop was gloomier, dingier, smellier, but entirely supportable. The table that had come with the shop had been so transformed that he felt it had always been his. He had tried to varnish it, but the wood, a local cedar, was absorbent and never sated, drinking in coat after coat of stain and varnish until, in exasperation, he painted it one of his forest greens, and had to be dissuaded by Shama from doing a landscape on it.

And it was strange, too, to find that these disregarded years had been years of acquisition. They could not move from The Chase on a donkey-cart. They had acquired a kitchen safe of white wood and netting. This too had been awkward to varnish and had been painted. One leg was shorter than the others and had to be propped up; now they knew without thinking that they must never lean on the safe or handle it with violence. They had acquired a hatrack, not because they possessed hats, but because it was a piece of furniture all but the very poor had. As a result, Mr Biswas acquired a hat. And they had acquired, at Shama's insistence, a dressingtable, the work of a craftsman, french-polished, with a large, clear mirror. To protect it, they had placed it on lengths of wood in a dark corner of their bedroom, so that the mirror was almost useless. The first scratches had been treated as disasters. It had since suffered many more scratches and one major excision, and Shama polished it less often; but it still looked new and surprisingly rich in that low thatched room. Shama, never afraid of debt, had wanted a wardrobe as well, but Mr Biswas said that wardrobes reminded him of coffins, and their clothes remained in the drawers of the dressingtable, on nails on the wall and in suitcases under the fourposter.

Though Hanuman House had at first seemed chaotic, it was not long before Mr Biswas had seen that in reality it was ordered, with degrees of precedence all the way down, with Chinta below Padma, Shama below Chinta, Savi below Shama, and himself far below Savi. With no child of his own, he had wondered how the children survived. Now he saw that in this communal organization children were regarded as assets, a source of future wealth and influence. His fears that Savi would be badly treated were absurd, as was his surprise that Mrs Tulsi should go to such trouble to get Savi to overcome her dislike of fish.

It was not for this reason alone that his attitude to Hanuman House changed. The House was a world, more real than The Chase, and less exposed; everything beyond its gates was foreign and unimportant and could be ignored. He needed such a sanctuary. And in time the House became to him what Tara's had been when he was a boy. He could go to Hanuman House whenever he wished and become lost in the crowd, since he was treated with indifference rather than hostility. And he went there more often, held his tongue and tried to win favour. It was an effort, and even at times of great festivity, when everyone worked with energy and joy, enthusiasm reacting upon enthusiasm, in himself he remained aloof.

Indifference turned to acceptance, and he was pleased and surprised to find that because of his past behaviour he, like the girl contortionist, now being groomed for marriage, had a certain licence. On occasion pungent remarks were invited from him, and then almost anything he said raised a laugh. The gods were away most of the time and he seldom saw them. But he was glad when he did; for his relationship with them had changed also, and he considered them the only people he could talk to seriously. Now that he had dropped his Aryan iconoclasm, they discussed religion, and these discussions in the hall became family entertainments. He invariably lost, since his telling points could be dismissed as waggishness; which satisfied everybody. His standing rose even higher when there were guests for important religious ceremonies. It was soon established that Mr Biswas, like Hari, was too incompetent, and too intelligent, to be given the menial tasks of the other brothers-in-law. He was deputed to have disputations with the pundits in the drawingroom.

He took to going to Hanuman House the afternoon before these ceremonies, so that he spent the night there. And it was then that he was reminded of an old, secret ambition. As a boy he had envied Ajodha and Pundit Jairam. How often, of an evening, he had seen Jairam bath and put on a clean dhoti and settle down among the pillows in his verandah with his book and spectacles, while his wife cooked in the kitchen! He had thought then that to be grown up was to be as contented and comfortable as Jairam. And when Ajodha sat on a chair and threw his head back, that chair at once looked more comfortable than any. Despite his hypochondria and fastidiousness Ajodha ate with so much relish that Mr Biswas used to feel, even when eating with him, that the food on Ajodha's plate had become more delicious. Late in the evenings, before he went to bed, Ajodha let his slippers fall to the floor, drew up his legs on to the rockingchair and, rocking slowly, sipped a glass of hot milk, closing his eyes, sighing after every sip; and to Mr Biswas it had seemed that Ajodha was relishing the most exquisite luxury. He believed that when he became a man it would be possible for him to enjoy everything the way Ajodha did, and he promised himself to buy a rockingchair and to drink a glass of hot milk in the evenings. But on these evenings when Hanuman House was bright with lights and hummed with happy activity, when he was able to sit among the cushions on the polished floor of the drawingroom and call for a glass of hot milk, he experienced no sharp pleasure, and was instead nagged by the uneasiness he had felt when he visited Tara's and read *That Body of Yours* to Ajodha. Then he knew that as soon as he stepped out of the yard he returned to nonentity, the rumshop on the Main Road and the hut in the back trace. Now it was the thought of the shop in darkness at The Chase, the shelves of tinned foods that wouldn't sell, the display boards that had lost their pleasant smell of new cardboard and printer's ink and had grown flyblown and dim, the oily drawer that rocked in its socket and held so little money. And always the thought, the fear about the future. The future wasn't the next day or the next week or even the next year, times within his comprehension and therefore without dread. The future he feared could not be thought of in terms of time. It was a blankness, a void like those in dreams, into which, past tomorrow and next week and next year, he was falling.

Once, years before, he was conducting one of Ajodha's motorbuses that ran its erratic course to remote and unsuspected villages. It was late afternoon and they were racing back along the ill-made country road. Their lights were weak and they were racing the sun. The sun fell; and in the short dusk they passed a lonely hut set in a clearing far back from the road. Smoke came from under the ragged thatched eaves: the evening meal was being prepared. And, in the gloom, a boy was leaning against the hut, his hands behind him, staring at the road. He wore a vest and nothing more. The vest glowed white. In an instant the bus went by, noisy in the dark, through bush and level sugarcane fields. Mr Biswas could not remember where the hut stood, but the picture remained: a boy leaning against an earth house that had no reason for being there, under the dark falling sky, a boy who didn't know where the road, and that bus, went.

And often, among the pundits and the cushions and the statuary in the drawingroom, eating the enormous meals the Tulsis provided on these occasions, he was assailed by this sense of utter desolation. Then, without conviction, he counted his blessings and ordered himself to enjoy the moment, like the others.

And while he made greater efforts to please at Hanuman House, with Shama, at The Chase, he became increasingly irritable. After every visit he abused the Tulsis to her, and his invective was without fantasy or humour.

'Talk about hypocrisy,' Shama said. 'Why you don't tell them so to their face?'

He began to think that she was plotting to get him back to Hanuman House, and he wondered whether she hadn't encouraged him to believe that The Chase was temporary. She had never urged him to make improvements, and was always interested when something was done at Hanuman House, when the famous clay-brick factory was pulled down or when awnings were put up over the windows. More and more The Chase was a place where Shama only spent time; she had always called Hanuman House home. And it was her home, and Savi's, and Anand's, as it could never be his. As he realized every Christmas.

The Tulsis celebrated Christmas in their store and, with equal irreligiosity, in their home. It was a purely Tulsi festival.

All the sons-in-law, and even Seth, were expelled from Hanuman House and returned to their own families. Even Miss Blackie went to her own people.

For Mr Biswas Christmas was a day of tedious depression. He went to Pagotes to see his mother and Tara and Ajodha, none of whom recognized Christmas. His mother cried so much and with so much feeling he was never sure whether she was glad to see him. Every Christmas she said the same things. He sounded like his father; if she closed her eyes while he spoke she could imagine that his father was alive again. She had little to say about herself. She was happy where she was and did not want to be a burden to any of her sons; her life was over, she had nothing more to do, and was waiting for death. To feel sympathy for her he had to look, not at her face, but at the thinness of her hair. It was still black, however: which was a pity, for grey hair would have helped to put him in a more tender mood. Suddenly she got up and said she was going to make him tea; she was poor, that was all she could offer. She went out to the gallery and he heard her talking to someone. Her voice was quite different; it was firm, without a whine, the voice of a woman still energetic and capable. She brought tea that was lukewarm, with too little tea, too much milk and a taste of woodsmoke. She told him he needn't drink it. Dutifully he put his arm around her. The gesture caused him pain, making him feel his own worthlessness. She didn't respond, and wept and talked as before. She said she was going to give him tomatoes and cabbages and lettuces to take home. When she went out her voice and manner changed again. He gave her a dollar, which he could scarcely afford. She took it without showing surprise and without a word of thanks. He was always glad when he could leave the back trace to go to Tara's.

At last Shama said she could stand The Chase no more. She wanted them to give up the shop and return to Hanuman House. This re-opened all their old quarrels. Only, now everything Shama said was true and cutting.

'We are not doing anything here,' she said.

'All right, Mrs Samuel Smiles. Look, I standing up in this shop, behind this dirty old counter. Tell me exactly what it have for me to do. You tell me.'

'You know it isn't that I mean.'

'You want me to make the spinning-jenny and the flying shuttle? Invent the steam-engine?'

And these arguments ended in insults and were followed by days of silence.

They spent their last two years at The Chase in this state of mutual hostility; at peace only in Hanuman House.

She became pregnant for the third time.

'Another one for the monkey house,' he said, passing his hands over her belly.

'You had nothing to do with it.'

And though he had spoken humorously, this led to another serious quarrel, which went over the same limited ground until, unable to control his rage, he hit her.

They were both astonished. She was silenced in the middle of a sentence; for some time afterwards the unfinished sentence remained in his mind, as though it had just been spoken. She was stronger than he. Her silence and her refusal to retaliate made his humiliation complete. She dressed Anand and went to Arwacas.

It was the kite-flying season and in the afternoons, when the wind came from the hills to the north, for miles around multi-coloured kites with long tails plunged and wriggled like tadpoles in the clear sky above the plain. He had been thinking that in two or three years he and Anand would fly kites together.

He decided that this time Shama would have to make the first move. So for many months he didn't go to Hanuman House, not even to see Savi. When, however, he judged that the baby was born, he broke his resolution and closed the shop – what was it that made him know, as he put the bar into place, that he was closing the doors for the last time? – and wheeled out the Royal Enfield from the bedroom and cycled to Arwacas, a small man made conspicuous by the exaggeratedly upright way he sat on the low saddle (to tauten his stomach and relieve his indigestion pains), with his palms pressing hard on the handgrips and the inside of his wrists turned outwards. He cycled slowly and steadily, his feet flat on the pedals. From time to time he inclined his head, arched his back and gave a series of small belches. This gave him some relief.

He reached Arwacas when it was dark, suffering an additional anxiety because he rode without bicycle lights, an offence zealously pursued by idle policemen. There were no street lamps, only the yellow smoky flames of flambeaux on night stalls and the dim lights of houses coming through curtained doorways and windows. In the arcade of Hanuman House, grey and substantial in the dark, there was already the evening assembly of old men, squatting on sacks on the ground and on tables now empty of Tulsi Store goods, pulling at clay *cheelums* that glowed red and smelled of ganja and burnt sacking. Though it wasn't cold, many had scarves over their heads and around their necks; this detail made them look foreign and, to Mr Biswas, romantic. It was the time of day for which they lived. They could not speak English and were not interested in the land where they lived; it was a place where they had come for a short time and stayed longer than they expected. They continually talked of going back to India, but when the opportunity came, many refused, afraid of the unknown, afraid to leave the familiar temporariness. And every evening they came to the arcade of the solid, friendly house, smoked, told stories, and continued to talk of India.

Mr Biswas went in by the tall side gate. The hall was lit by one oil lamp. Despite the late hour children were still eating. Some were at the long table, some on benches and chairs about the hall, two in the hammock, some on the steps, some on the landing, and two on the disused piano. Two of the lesser Tulsi sisters and Miss Blackie were supervising.

No one seemed surprised to see him. He was grateful for that. He looked for Savi and had trouble in locating her. She saw him first, smiled, but didn't leave the table. He went up to her.

'I haven't seen you for a long time,' she said, and he couldn't tell whether she was disappointed or not.

'Missing your six cents, eh?' He studied the food on Savi's enamel plate: curried beans, fried tomatoes and a dry pancake. 'Where's your mother?'

'She had another baby. Did you know?'

He noticed the fatherless children. They had given up their offending mourning suits; even so, their clothes were different. He didn't know these children very well and they regarded him, a visiting father, with curiosity.

'Ma said you beat her,' Savi said.

The fatherless children looked at Mr Biswas with dread and disapproval. They all had large eyes: another distinguishing feature.

Mr Biswas laughed. 'She was only joking,' he said in English.

'She upstairs, rubbing down Myna,' Savi said, in English as well.

'Myna, eh? Another girl.' He spoke light-heartedly, trying to get the attention of the two Tulsi sisters. 'This family just full of girl children.'

The sisters tittered. He turned to them and smiled.

Shama was not in the Rose Room, but in the wooden bridge between the two houses. A basin with soapy, baby-smelling water was on the floor and, as Savi had said, Shama was rubbing down Myna, the way she had rubbed down Savi herself and Anand (asleep on the bed: no more rubbing for him, for the rest of his life).

Shama saw him, but concentrated on the baby, folding limbs this way and that, saying the rhyme that was to end in a laugh, a bunching of the limbs over the belly, a clap, and a release of the limbs.

Mr Biswas watched.

While she was dressing Myna, Shama said, 'Have you eaten?'

He shook his head. They might have parted only the hour before. And not only that. She had spoken about eating, and there was nothing in her voice to hint at the innumerable quarrels they had had about food. He had often opened tins of salmon and sardines from the shop after refusing to eat her food and sometimes throwing it away, food as unimaginative as that he had just seen on Savi's plate. It wasn't that the Tulsis couldn't cook. They thought appetizing food should be reserved for religious festivals; at other times it was a carnal indulgence. Mr Biswas's digestion had been repeatedly shocked to move from plain food before a ceremony to excessively rich food on the day of the ceremony and promptly back to plain food the day after.

Myna fell asleep at Shama's breast and was laid on the bed next to Anand. A pillow was placed at her side to keep her from rolling off, and the oil lamp in the bracket on the unpainted wall was turned down.

When Mr Biswas and Shama passed through the verandah it was thronged with children sitting on mats, reading or playing cards or draughts. These games had been recently introduced and were taken with the utmost seriousness; they were regarded as intellectual disciplines particularly suitable for children. Savi, too small for books, was playing Go-to-Pack with one of the large-eyed children. Everyone talked in whispers. Shama walked on tiptoe.

'Mai sick,' she said.

Which accounted for the children's late dinner and the absence of so many of the sisters.

Shama laid out food for Mr Biswas in the hall. The food might be bad at Hanuman House, but there was always some for unexpected visitors. Everything was cold. The pancakes were sweating, hard on the outside and little better than dough inside. He did not complain.

'You going back tonight?' she asked in English.

He knew then that he hadn't intended to go back, ever. He said nothing.

'You better sleep here then.'

As long as there was floor space, there was bed space.

Some sisters came into the hall. Packs of cards were brought out; the sisters split into groups and gravely settled down to play. Chinta played with style. She fussed with her cards, rearranged them often, stared blankly and disconcertingly at the other players, hummed and never spoke; before she played a telling card she frowned at it, pulled it up a little, tapped it down and kept on tapping it; then, suddenly, she threw it on the table with a crack and, still frowning, collected her trick. She was a magnanimous winner and a bad loser.

Mr Biswas watched.

Shama made a bed for him in the verandah upstairs, among the children.

He woke to a babel the next morning and when he went down to the hall found the sisters getting their children ready for school. It was the only time of day when it was reasonably easy to tell which child belonged to which mother. He was surprised to see Shama filling a satchel with a slate, a slate pencil, a lead pencil, an eraser, an exercise book with the Union Jack on the cover, and *Nelson's West Indian Reader*, First Stage, by Captain J. O. Cutteridge, Director of Education, Trinidad and Tobago. Lastly Shama wrapped an orange in tissue paper and put it in the satchel. 'For teacher,' she said to Savi.

Mr Biswas didn't know that Savi had begun to go to school.

Shama sat on a bench, held Savi between her legs, combed her hair, plaited it, straightened the pleats on her navy-blue uniform, and adjusted her Panama hat.

Mother and daughter had been doing this for many weeks. And he had known nothing.

Shama said, 'If your shoelaces come loose again today, you think you would be able to tie them back?' She bent down and undid Savi's shoelaces. 'Let me see you tie them.'

'You know I can't tie them.'

'Do it quick sharp, or I give you a dose of licks.'

'I can't tie them.'

'Come,' Mr Biswas said, shamelessly paternal in the bustling hall. 'I will tie them for you.'

'No,' Shama said. 'She must learn to tie her laces. Otherwise I will keep her at home and beat her until she can tie them.'

It was standard talk at Hanuman House. At The Chase Shama had never spoken like that.

As yet no one was paying attention. But when Shama started to hunt for one of the many hibiscus switches which always lay about the hall, sisters and children became less noisy and good-humouredly waited to see what would happen. It was not going to be a serious flogging since ineptitude rather than criminality was being punished; and Shama moved about with a comic jerkiness, as though she knew she was only an actor in a farce and not, like Sumati at the house-blessing in The Chase, a figure of high tragedy.

Mr Biswas, his eyes fixed on Savi, found himself tittering nervously. Still wearing her Panama hat, Savi squatted on the floor, tangling laces and watching them fall apart, or knotting them double, tight and high, and having to undo them with her nails and teeth. She, too, was partly acting for the audience. Her failures were greeted with approving laughter. Even Shama, standing by with whip in hand, allowed amusement to invade her playacting annoyance.

'All right,' Shama said. 'Let me show you for the last time. Watch me. Now try.'

Savi fumbled ineffectually again. This time there was less laughter.

'You just want to shame me,' Shama said. 'A big girl like you, five going on six, can't tie her own laces. Jai, come here.'

Jai was the son of an unimportant sister. He was pushed to the front by his mother, who was dandling another baby on her hip.

'Look at Jai,' Shama said. 'His mother don't have to tie his shoelaces. And he is a whole year younger than you.'

'Fourteen months younger,' Jai's mother said.

'Well, fourteen months younger,' Shama said, directing her annoyance to Savi. 'You want to defy me?'

Savi was still squatting.

'Hurry up now!' Shama said, so loudly and suddenly that Savi jumped and began playing stupidly with the laces.

No one laughed.

Stooping, Shama brought the hibiscus switch down on Savi's bare legs.

Mr Biswas looked on, a fixed smile on his face. He made phlegmy little noises, urging Shama to stop.

Savi was crying.

Sushila, the widow, came to the top of the stairs and said authoritatively, 'Remember Mai.'

They all remembered. Silence for the sick. The scene was over.

Shama, trying too late to turn comedy into tragedy, developed a sudden temper and stamped off, almost unnoticed, to the kitchen.

Sumati, the flogger at The Chase, pulled Savi to her long skirt. Savi cried into it and used it to wipe her nose and dry her eyes. Then Sumati tied Savi's laces and sent her off to school.

At The Chase Shama had seldom beat Savi, and then it had been only a matter of a few slaps. But at Hanuman House the sisters still talked with pride of the floggings they had received from Mrs Tulsi. Certain memorable floggings were continually recalled, with commonplace detail made awful and legendary by its association with a stupendous event, like the detail in a murder case. And there was even some rivalry among the sisters as to who had been flogged worst of all.

Mr Biswas had breakfast: biscuits from the big black drum, red butter, and tea, lukewarm, sugary and strong. Shama, though indignant, was dutiful and correct. As she watched him eat, her indignation became more and more defensive. Finally she was only grave.

'You see Mai yet?'

He understood.

They went to the Rose Room. Sushila admitted them and at once went outside. A shaded oil lamp burned low. The jalousied window in the thick clay-brick wall was closed, keeping out daylight; cloth was wedged around the frame, to keep out draughts. There was a smell of ammonia, bay rum, rum, brandy, disinfectant, and a variety of febrifuges. Below a white canopy with red appliqué apples Mrs Tulsi lay, barely recognizable, a bandage around her forehead, her temples dotted with lumps of soft candle, her nostrils stuffed with some white medicament.

Shama sat on a chair in a shadowed corner, effacing herself.

The marble topped bedside table was a confusion of bottles, jars and glasses. There were little blue jars of medicated rubs, little white jars of medicated rubs; tall green bottles of bay rum and short square bottles of eyedrops and nosedrops; a round bottle of rum, a flat bottle of brandy and an oval royal blue bottle of smelling-salts; a bottle of Sloan's Liniment and a tiny tin of Tiger Balm; a mixture with a pink sediment and one with a yellow-brown sediment, like muddy water left to stand from the previous night.

Mr Biswas didn't want to talk to Mrs Tulsi in Hindi, but the Hindi words came out. 'How are you, Mai? I couldn't come to see you last night because it was too late and I didn't want to disturb you.' He hadn't intended to give any explanations.

'How are *you*?' Mrs Tulsi said nasally, with unexpected tenderness. 'I am an old woman and it doesn't matter how I am.'

She reached out for the bottle of smelling salts and sniffed at it. The bandage around her forehead slipped down to her eyes. Adapting her tone of tenderness to one of distress and authority, she said, 'Come and squeeze my head, Shama.'

Shama obeyed with alacrity. She sat on the edge of the bed and undid the bandage, undid Mrs Tulsi's hair, parted it in several places, poured bay rum into her palms and from there into the partings. She worked the bay rum into Mrs Tulsi's scalp and the soaked hair squelched. Mrs Tulsi looked comforted. She closed her eyes, screwed the white medicament a little further up her nostrils, and patted her lips with a thin shawl.

'You have seen your daughter?'

Mr Biswas laughed.

'Two girls,' Mrs Tulsi said. 'Our family is unlucky that way. Think of the worry I had when your father died. Fourteen daughters to marry. And when you marry your girl children you can't say what sort of life you are letting them in for. They have to live with their Fate. Mothers-in-law, sisters-in-law. Idle husbands. Wife-beaters.'

Mr Biswas looked at Shama. She was concentrating on Mrs Tulsi's head. At every press of Shama's long fingers Mrs Tulsi closed her eyes, interrupted what she was saying and groaned, 'Aah.'

'That is what a mother has to put up with,' Mrs Tulsi said. 'I don't mind. I have lived long enough to know that you can't expect anything from anybody. I give you five hundred dollars. Do you think I want you to bow and scrape and touch my feet whenever you see me? No. I expect you to spit on me. I *expect* that. When you want five hundred dollars again you come back to me. Do you want me to say, "The last time I gave you five hundred dollars you spat on me. Therefore I can't give you five hundred dollars this time"? Do you want me to say that? No. I *expect* the people who spit on me to come to me again. I have a soft heart. And when you have a soft heart, you have a soft heart. Your father used to say to me, "My bride" – that was the way he called me until the day he died – "my bride," he used to say, "you have the softest heart of any person I know. Be careful of that soft heart. People will take advantage of that soft heart and trample on it." And I used to say, "When you have a soft heart, you have a soft heart." '

She pressed her eyes till tears ran down her cheeks. Her damp grey hair was spread out on the pillow. Now here was a woman with grey hair, and he felt little tenderness towards her.

Then he noted, what he had missed in the darkness, that Shama's cheeks were also wet. She must have been crying silently all along.

'I don't mind,' Mrs Tulsi said. She blew her nose and called for bay rum. Shama filled her palm with bay rum, drenched Mrs Tulsi's face and pressed her palm over Mrs Tulsi's nose. Mrs Tulsi's face shone; she screwed up her eyes to prevent the bay rum going into them and breathed loudly through her mouth. Shama removed her hand and Mrs Tulsi said, 'But I don't know what Seth will say.'

As at a cue Seth came in. He ignored Mr Biswas and Shama and asked Mrs Tulsi how she was, expressing in those words his concern for Mrs Tulsi and his impatience with the people who were disturbing her. He sat on the other side of the bed. The bed creaked; he sighed; he shifted his feet and his bluchers drummed on the floor in annoyance.

'We've been talking,' Mrs Tulsi said gently.

Shama gave a little sob.

Seth sucked his teeth. He sounded extremely irritable; it was as if he too were unwell, with a cold or a headache. 'Paddling-addling,' he said. His voice was gruff and indistinct.

'You mustn't mind,' Mrs Tulsi said.

Seth held his thigh and looked at the floor.

And Mr Biswas was convinced of what he had already guessed from Mrs Tulsi's speech and Shama's tears: that the scene had been arranged, that there had been not only discussions, but decisions. And Shama, who had arranged the scene, was crying to lessen his humiliation, to shift some of it to herself. Her tears were ritual in another way: they were tears for the hardships that had come to her with a husband she had been given by Fate.

'So what we going to do about the shop?' Seth asked in English. He was still irritable and his voice, though business-like, was weary.

Mr Biswas couldn't think. 'Is a bad site for a shop,' he said.

'A bad site today could be a good site tomorrow,' Seth said. 'Suppose I drop a few cents here and there and get the Public Works to run the trunk road through there after all? Eh?'

Shama's sobs mingled with the squelch of bay rum in Mrs Tulsi's hair.

'You got any debts?'

'Well, a lot of people owing me but they won't pay.'

'Not after what happen with Mungroo. I suppose you was the only man in Trinidad who didn't know about Seebaran and Mahmoud.'

Shama was crying openly.

Abruptly Seth lost interest in Mr Biswas. He said, 'Tcha!' and looked at his bluchers.

'You mustn't mind,' Mrs Tulsi said. 'I know you haven't got a soft heart. But you mustn't mind.'

Seth sighed. 'So what we going to do with the shop?'

Mr Biswas shrugged.

'Insure-and-burn?' Seth said, making it one word: *insuranburn*.

Mr Biswas felt that talk like this belonged to the realms of high finance.

Seth crossed his big arms high over his chest. 'Is the only thing for you to do now.'

'Insuranburn,' Mr Biswas said. 'How much I going to make out of that?'

'More than you would make if you *don't* insuranburn. The shop is Mai own. The goods is yours. For the goods you ought to get about seventy-five, a hundred dollars.'

It was a large sum. Mr Biswas smiled.

But Seth only said, 'And after that, what?'

Mr Biswas tried to look thoughtful.

'You still too proud to get your hands dirty in the fields?' And Seth displayed his own hands.

'Soft heart,' Mrs Tulsi muttered.

'I want a driver at Green Vale,' Seth said.

Shama gave a loud sob and, suddenly leaving Mrs Tulsi's head, rushed to Mr Biswas and said, 'Take it, man. Take it, I beg you.' She was making it easy for him to accept. 'He will take it,' she cried to Seth. 'He will take it.'

Seth looked irritable and turned away.

Mrs Tulsi groaned.

Shama, still crying, went back to the bed and pressed her fingers into Mrs Tulsi's hair.

Mrs Tulsi said, 'Aah.'

'I don't know anything about estate work,' Mr Biswas said, trying to salvage some of his dignity.

'Nobody begging you,' Seth said.

'You mustn't mind,' Mrs Tulsi said. 'You know what Owad always tells me. He always blames me for the way I married off my daughters. And I suppose he is right. But then Owad is going to college, reading and learning all the time. And I am very oldfashioned.' She spoke with pride in Owad and pride in her oldfashionedness.

Seth stood up. His bluchers scraped on the floor, the bed made noises, and Mrs Tulsi was slightly disturbed. But Seth's irritability had disappeared. He took out the ivory cigarette holder which had been pushing up through the buttoned flap of the pocket on his khaki shirt, put it in his mouth and blew whistlingly through it. 'Owad. You remember him, Mohun?' He laughed, opening his mouth on either side of the holder. 'The old hen son.'

'What is past is past,' Mrs Tulsi said. 'When people are boys they behave like boys. When they are men they behave like men.'

Shama squeezed vigorously at Mrs Tulsi's head and succeeded in reducing Mrs Tulsi's speech to a series of 'Aah. Aah.' She washed bay rum into Mrs Tulsi's hair and face and held her palm over Mrs Tulsi's nose and mouth.

'This insuranburning,' Mr Biswas said, and his tone was light, 'who going to see about it? Me?' He was putting himself back into the role of the licensed buffoon.

Shama was the first to laugh. Seth followed. A croak came from Mrs Tulsi and Shama took away her hand from Mrs Tulsi's mouth to allow her to laugh.

Mrs Tulsi began to splutter. 'He want,' she said in English, choking with laughter, 'to jump – from – the fryingpan – into – into –'

They all roared.

'– into – the fire!'

The witty mood spread.

'No more paddling,' Seth said.

'We insuranburning right away?' Mr Biswas asked, pitching his voice high and speaking quickly.

'You got to get your furniture out first,' Seth said.

'My bureau!' Shama exclaimed, and put her hand to her own mouth, as though astonished that, when she had left Mr Biswas, she had forgotten to take that piece of furniture with her.

'You know,' Seth said, 'the best thing would be for you to do the insuranburning.'

'No, Uncle,' Shama said. 'Don't start putting ideas in his head.'

'Don't worry with the child,' Mr Biswas said. 'You just tell me.'

Seth sat on the bed again. 'Well, look,' he said, and his voice was amused and avuncular. 'You had this trouble with Mungroo. You go to the police station and lay your life on Mungroo head.'

'Lay my what on Mungroo head?'

'Tell them about the row. Tell them that Mungroo threatening to kill you. And the moment anything happen to you, the first person they would pick up would be Mungroo.'

'You mean the first person they would pick up would be me. But let me get this straight. When I dead, like a cockroach, lying on my back with my four foot throw up straight and stiff and high in the air, you want me to walk to the police station and say, "I did tell all-you so." '

Mrs Tulsi, still chuckling over her own joke, the first she had managed in English, made Mr Biswas's an excuse to burst out laughing again.

'Well, you lay your life on Mungroo head,' Seth said. 'You go back to The Chase and stay quiet. You let one week pass, two weeks, even three. Then you make your little preparations. You let Shama collect her bureau. On Thursday, half-day, you drop pitch-oil all over the shop – not where you sleeping – and in the night-time you set a match to it. You give it a little time – not too much – and then you run outside and start bawling for Mungroo.'

'You mean,' Mr Biswas said, 'that this is why all those motorcars burning up every day in this place? And all those houses?'

# 5. Green Vale

WHENEVER AFTERWARDS Mr Biswas thought of Green Vale he thought of the trees. They were tall and straight, and so hung with long, drooping leaves that their trunks were hidden and appeared to be branchless. Half the leaves were dead; the others, at the top, were a dead green. It was as if all the trees had, at the same moment, been blighted in luxuriance, and death was spreading at the same pace from all the roots. But death was forever held in check. The tonguelike leaves of dead green turned slowly to the brightest yellow, became brown and thin as if scorched, curled downwards over the other dead leaves and did not fall. And new leaves came, as sharp as daggers; but there was no freshness to them; they came into the world old, without a shine, and only grew longer before they too died.

It was hard to imagine that beyond the trees on every side lay the clear plain. Green Vale was damp and shadowed and close. The trees darkened the road and their rotting leaves choked the grass gutters. The trees surrounded the barracks.

As soon as he saw the barracks Mr Biswas decided that the time had come for him to build his own house, by whatever means. The barracks gave one room to one family, and sheltered twelve families in one long room divided into twelve. This long room was built of wood and stood on low concrete pillars. The whitewash on the walls had turned to dust, leaving stains like those left on stones by bleaching clothes; and these stains were mildewed and sweated and freckled with grey and green and black. The corrugated iron roof projected on one side to make a long gallery, divided by rough partitions into twelve kitchen spaces, so open that when it rained hard twelve cooks had to take twelve coal-pots to twelve rooms. The ten middle rooms each had a front door and a back window. The rooms at the end had a front door, a back window, and a side window. Mr Biswas, as a driver, was given an end room. The back window had been nailed shut by the previous tenant and plastered over with newspaper. Its position could only be guessed at, since newspaper covered the walls from top to bottom. This had obviously been the work of a literate. No sheet was placed upside down, and Mr Biswas found himself continuously exposed to the journalism of his time, its bounce and excitement bottled and made quaint in these old newspapers.

Into this room they moved all their furniture: the kitchen safe, the green kitchen table, the hatrack, the iron fourposter, a rockingchair Mr Biswas had bought in the last days at The Chase, and the dressingtable which, during Shama's long absences at Hanuman House, had come to stand for Shama.

Only one small drawer of the dressingtable was Mr Biswas's. The others were alien and if by some chance he opened one he felt he was intruding. It was during the move to Green Vale that he discovered that, in addition to the finer clothes of Shama and the children, those drawers contained Shama's marriage certificate and the birth certificates of her children; a Bible and Bible pictures she had got from her mission school and kept, not for their religious content, but as reminders of past excellence; and a packet of letters from a pen-pal in Northumberland, the result of one of the headmaster's schemes. Mr Biswas yearned after the outside world; he read novels that took him there; he never suspected that Shama, of all persons, had been in contact with this world.

'You didn't by any chance keep the letters you did write back?'

'Headteacher used to read them and post them.'

'I woulda *like* to read your letters.'

So Mr Biswas became a driver, or sub-overseer, at a salary of twenty-five dollars a month, which was twice as much as the labourers got. As he had told Seth, he knew nothing about estate work. He had been surrounded by sugarcane all his life; he knew that the tall fields shot up grey-blue, arrow-like flowers just when shop signs were bursting into green and red gaiety, with holly and berries and Santa Claus and snow-capped letters; he knew the 'crop-over' harvest festival; but he didn't know about burning or weeding or hoeing or trenching; he didn't know when new cuttings had to be put in or mounds of trash built around new plants. He got instructions from Seth, who came to Green Vale every Saturday to inspect, and pay the labourers, which he did from the kitchen space outside Mr Biswas's room, using the green kitchen table, and having Mr Biswas sit beside him to read out the number of tasks each labourer had worked.

Mr Biswas didn't know the admiration and respect his father Raghu had had for drivers. But he could feel the awe the labourers had for the blue and green moneybags with serrated edges and small circular holes for the money to breathe, and he took some pleasure in handling these bags casually, as though they were a bother. It sometimes occurred to him that, perhaps at that very moment, his brothers were standing in similar slow submissive queues on other estates.

On Saturdays, then, he enjoyed power. But on the other days it was different. True, he went out early every morning with his long bamboo rod and measured out the labourers' tasks. But the labourers knew he was unused to the job and was there simply as a watchman and Seth's representative. They could fool him and they did, fearing more a single rebuke of Seth's on Saturday than a week of shy remonstrance from Mr Biswas. Mr Biswas was ashamed to complain to Seth. He bought a topee; it was too big for his head, which was rather small, and he adjusted the topee so badly that it fell down to his ears. For some time after that, whenever the labourers saw Mr Biswas they pulled their hats over their eyes, tilted their heads backwards and looked in his direction. Two or three of the young and impudent even talked to him in this way. He thought he ought to ride a horse, as Seth did; and he was beginning to feel sympathy for those overseers of legend who rode on horseback and lashed labourers on either side. Then, being the buffoon with Seth one Saturday, he mounted Seth's horse, was thrown after a few yards, and said, 'I didn't want to go where he was going.'

'Gee up!' one labourer shouted to another on Monday.

'Oops!' the second labourer replied.

Mr Biswas told Seth, 'I got to stop living next door to these people.'

Seth said, 'We are going to build a house for you.'

But Seth was only talking. He never mentioned the house again, and Mr Biswas remained in the barracks. He began to speak about the brutishness of labourers; and instead of wondering, as he had done at the beginning, how they lived on three dollars a week, he wondered why they got so much. He took it out on Shama.

'Is you who get me in this. You and your family. Look at me. I look like Seth? You could look at me and say that this is my sort of work?'

He came back from the fields sweated, itching and dusty, bitten by flies and other insects, his skin torn and tender. He welcomed the sweating and the fatigue and the sensation of burning on his face. But he hated the itching, and dried dirt on his fingernails tortured him as acutely as the sound of slate pencils on slates or shovels on concrete.

The barrackyard, with its mud, animal droppings and the quick slime on stale puddles, gave him nausea, especially when he was eating fish or Shama's pancakes. He took to eating at the green table in the room, hidden from the front door, his back to the side window, and determined not to look up at the black, furry underside of the galvanized iron roof. As he ate he read the newspapers on the wall. The smell of damp and soot, old paper and stale tobacco reminded him of the smell of his father's box, under the bed which rested on tree-branches buried in the earth floor.

He bathed incessantly. The barracks had no bathroom but at the back there were waterbarrels under the spouts which drained off the water from the roof. However quickly the water was used, there were always larvae of some sort on its surface, jumpy jellylike whiskery things, perfection in their way. Mr Biswas stood in pants and sabots on a length of board next to a barrel and threw water over himself with a calabash dipper. He sang Hindi songs and *In the snowy and the blowy* while he did so. Afterwards he wrapped a towel around his waist, took off his pants and then, in towel and sabots, made a dash for his room.

Since there was no side door to his room, he had to run around to the front, come into full view of all twelve kitchens and all twelve rooms, then bound into his own.

One day the towel dropped off.

'Is you,' he told Shama, after a terrible day in the fields. 'Is you and your family who get me in this.'

Shama, who had herself spent a day of humiliation at the barracks, cooked one of her especially bad meals, dressed Anand, a boy now big enough to talk, and took him to Hanuman House.

On Saturday, after he had paid the labourers, Seth smiled and said, 'Your wife say to look in the top righthand drawer of her bureau and get her pink bodice, and look in the bottom of the lefthand corner of the middle drawer for the pantaloons for the boy.'

'Ask my wife, which boy?'

But Mr Biswas explored the alien drawers.

'I nearly forget,' Seth said, just before he left. 'That shop at The Chase. Well, it insuranburn now.'

Seth took out a roll of dollar notes from his trouser pocket and displayed it like a magician. Note by note, he counted the roll into Mr Biswas's hand. It came to seventy-five dollars, the sum he had mentioned in the Rose Room at Hanuman House.

Mr Biswas was impressed and grateful. He determined to put his money aside, and add to it, until he had enough to build his house.

He had thought deeply about this house, and knew exactly what he wanted. He wanted, in the first place, a real house, made with real materials. He didn't want mud for walls, earth for floor, tree branches for rafters and grass for roof. He wanted wooden walls, all tongue-and-groove. He wanted a galvanized iron roof and a wooden ceiling. He would walk up concrete steps into a small verandah; through doors with coloured panes into a small drawingroom; from there into a small bedroom, then another small bedroom, then back into the small verandah. The house would stand on tall concrete pillars so that he would get two floors instead of one, and the way would be left open for future development. The kitchen

would be a shed in the yard; a neat shed, connected to the
house by a covered way. And his house would be painted.
The roof would be red, the outside walls ochre with chocolate facings, and the windows white.

His talk about houses made Shama fearful and impatient
and had even caused quarrels. So he did not tell her of this
picture or of his plan, and she continued to live for long
periods at Hanuman House. She needed to give no explanations to her sisters now. Green Vale, part of the Tulsi lands and
just outside Arwacas, was considered almost an extension of
Hanuman House.

Rejecting the stone-cold food Shama occasionally sent
from Hanuman House, and tired of tins, Mr Biswas learned
to cook for himself; and he bought a primus, since he
couldn't manage the coal-pot. Sometimes he went for a walk
in the early evening; sometimes he stayed in his room and
read. But there were times when, without being fatigued, he
could do nothing, when neither food nor tobacco tasted, and
he could only lie on the fourposter and read the newspapers
on the wall. He soon had many of the stories by heart. And
the first line of one story, in breathless capitals, came to
possess his mind: AMAZING SCENES WERE WITNESSED
YESTERDAY WHEN. Absently he spoke the words aloud, by
himself, with the labourers, with Seth. On some evenings, in
his room, the words came into his head and repeated themselves until they were meaningless and irritating and he
longed to drive them away. He wrote the words on packets
of Anchor cigarettes and boxes of Comet matches. And, to
fight this exhausting vacancy that left him with the feeling
that he had drunk gallons of stale, lukewarm water, he took
to lettering religious tags on strips of cardboard, which he
hung on the walls against the newspapers. From a Hindi magazine he copied a sentence which, on cardboard, stretched
right across one wall, above the papered window: HE WHO
BELIEVETH IN ME OF HIM I WILL NEVER LOSE HOLD
AND HE SHALL NEVER LOSE HOLD OF ME.

The sugarcane was in arrow. The lanes and roads between
the fields were clean green canyons. And at Arwacas the
shop-signs celebrated snow and Santa Claus. The Tulsi Store

was hung with paper holly and berries, but carried no Christmas signs. Mr Biswas's old signs still served. They had faded; the distemper on the wall and columns had flaked off in places and Punch had lost a piece of his nose; near the ceiling the letters were dim with dust and soot. Savi knew, and was proud, that the signs had been done by her father. But their gaiety puzzled her; she couldn't associate them with the morose man she went to see in the dingy barrackroom and who sometimes came to see her. She felt, with a sense of loss that became sharper as Christmas drew nearer, that the signs had been done at some time beyond her memory when her father lived happily at Hanuman House with her mother and everyone else.

Christmas was the only time of the year when the gaiety of the signs had some meaning. Then the Tulsi Store became a place of deep romance and endless delights, transformed from the austere emporium it was on other days, dark and silent, its shelves crammed with bolts of cloth that gave off acrid and sometimes unpleasant smells, its tables jumbled with cheap scissors and knives and spoons, towers of dusty blue-rimmed enamel plates interleaved with ragged grey paper, and boxes of hairpins, needles, pins and thread. Now all day there was noise and bustle. Gramophones played in the Tulsi Store and all the other stores and even from the stalls in the market. Mechanical birds whistled; dolls squeaked; toy trumpets were tried out; tops hummed; cars shot across counters, were seized by hands, and held whining in mid-air. The enamel plates and the hairpins were pushed to the back, and their place was taken by black grapes in white boxes filled with aromatic sawdust; red Canadian apples whose scent overrode every other; by a multitude of toys and dolls and games in boxes, new and sparkling glassware, new china, all smelling of their newness; by Japanese lacquered trays, stacked one on top the other like a pack of cards, so elegant as they stood that it was sad to think of them being sold one by one, leaving the store in brown paper and string, and ending drab, broken and disregarded in ugly kitchens and tumbledown houses. There were stacks, too, of the Bookers Drug Stores Almanac, with art paper tickling smooth to the touch and a smell of corresponding richness, with jokes, stories, photographs, quizzes, puzzles, and prizes for competitions which the Tulsi children were all going to enter but never would, though they had already inked in their names and addresses on dotted lines. And the decorations: the paper holly and berries, the spiralling streamers of crêpe paper, the cotton wool and the Jack Frost that stuck to fingers and clothes, the balloons, the lanterns.

The sisters masked their excitement by frowns and complaints of fatigue that fooled no one. Mrs Tulsi herself came to the store from time to time, spoke to people she knew, and on occasion even sold something. The two gods strode sternly about, superintending, signing bills, checking money. The elder god was especially stern this Christmas and the children were afraid of him. His behaviour had grown a little strange. He had not yet left the Roman Catholic college, but efforts were being made to find him a wife from among the handful of eligible families. He expressed his disapproval by random angry outbursts, tears and threats of suicide. This was construed as a conventional shyness and, as such, was a source of amusement to sisters and brothers-in-law. But the children were frightened when he talked of leaving the house and buying rope and soft candle; they were not sure what he wanted the soft candle for; and they stayed out of his way.

On the morning of Christmas Eve excitement was at its height, but before the afternoon was out had subsided so far that the displays had ceased to be magical, their gaiety became disorder, and the disorder could be seen to be superficial. So that before Christmas came, in the shop it was felt to be over. And throughout the afternoon attention turned more and more to the hall and kitchen where Sumati, the flogger, was in charge of the baking, and Shama, who had no recognized talents, was one of her many helpers. The smells from the kitchen had an added savour because, as always at Hanuman House, the food continued to be ordinary and bad up to the very day of a festival.

The Tulsi Store was closed, the toys left in darkness which would transform them into stock and the brothers-in-law prepared to leave Hanuman House for their families. As Mr

Biswas cycled through the night to Green Vale, he remembered he had not got presents for Savi and Anand. But they expected none from him; they knew they would find their presents in their stockings on Christmas morning.

Because the sisters were busy the children were given a skimpier dinner than usual. Then hunts were started for stockings. There were none to be had. The providential, mostly the girls, had acquired theirs days before, and the boys had to be content with pillowcases. There was talk of staying awake, but one by one the children dropped out of card games and fell asleep to the songs that came from their mothers in the kitchen.

Anand had a moment of alarm when he got up. His pillowcase, lying at the foot of his bedding on the floor, looked empty. But when he shook the pillowcase out he found he had got what the other boys had: a balloon, one of those he had seen for weeks past in the store, a red apple in a dark blue wrapper, one of those he had seen in the boxes in the store, and a tin whistle. In her stocking Savi found a balloon, an apple and a tiny rubber doll. Presents were compared, and when it was established that there was no cause for jealousy, the children ate their apples, blew up balloons, and raised a feeble chirruping with tin whistles. Many whistles were soon silenced by spittle or some fundamental mechanical defect, and most of the boys burst their balloons before going downstairs to kiss Mrs Tulsi. Those boys who were to grow up into detestable men gave a single toot on their whistles, nibbled at their apples and blew up their balloons hardly at all, in this resembling the girls, who already showed their pleasure in possession and anticipation rather than fulfilment. Then the children, in varying degrees of contentment, went downstairs and found Mrs Tulsi waiting at the long pitchpine table. Their mothers were waiting as well, happy Santa Clauses. When a discontented child forgot to kiss Mrs Tulsi and impatiently hurried off to see about food, his mother called him back.

After breakfast – tea and biscuits from the drum – the children waited for lunch. More whistles were silenced; more balloons burst. The girls seized the scraps of the boys' burst balloons and blew them up into many-coloured bunches of grapes which they rubbed against their cheeks to make a noise like heavy furniture dragging on an unpolished floor. Lunch was good. And after lunch they waited for tea: Sumati's cakes, a local and fraudulent cherry brandy doled out by Chinta, and icecream, made by Chinta again, who, against annual evidence, was supposed to have an especial gift for making icecream. And that was that. Dinner was as bad as usual. Christmas was over. And, like all other Christmases at Hanuman House, it had turned out to be only a series of anticipations.

At the barracks there were no apples, no stockings, no baking of cakes, no churning of icecream, no refinements to be waited for. It was from the start a day of abandoned eating and drinking and was to end, not with the beating of children, but with the beating of wives. Mr Biswas went to see his mother and had dinner at Tara's. On Boxing-day he visited his brothers; they had married nondescript women from nondescript families and spent Christmas with their wives.

The following day Mr Biswas cycled from Green Vale to Arwacas. When he turned into the High Street the sight of the stores, open again and carelessly displaying Christmas goods at bargain prices, reminded him of the presents he had forgotten. He got off his bicycle and leaned it against the kerb. Before he had taken off his bicycle clips he was accosted by a heavy-lidded shopman who repeatedly sucked his teeth. The shopman offered Mr Biswas a cigarette and lit it for him. Words were exchanged. Then, with the shopman's arm around his shoulders, Mr Biswas disappeared into the shop. Not many minutes later Mr Biswas and the shopman reappeared. They were both smoking and excited. A boy came out of the shop partly hidden by the large doll's house he was carrying. The doll's house was placed on the handlebar of Mr Biswas's cycle and, with Mr Biswas on one side and the boy on the other, wheeled down the High Street.

Every room of the doll's house was daintily furnished. The kitchen had a stove such as Mr Biswas had never seen in real life, a safe and a sink. As they progressed towards Hanuman

House Mr Biswas's excitement cooled; his extravagance astonished, then frightened him. He had spent more than a month's wages. He couldn't take back the doll's house now; he was attracting continuous attention. And he had bought nothing for Anand. It was always like this. When he thought of his children he thought mainly of Savi. She was part of those early months at The Chase and he knew her. Anand belonged completely to the Tulsis.

At Hanuman House they knew about the doll's house before it arrived. The hall was packed with sisters and their children. Mrs Tulsi sat at the pitchpine table patting her lips with her veil.

The children exclaimed when the doll's house was set down, and in the hush that followed Savi came forward and stood near it proprietorially.

'Well, what you think?' Mr Biswas asked the hall, using his quick, high-pitched voice.

The sisters were silent.

Then Padma, Seth's wife, usually taciturn and oppressed and unwell, began on a long and involved story, which Mr Biswas refused to believe, about an incredible doll's house one of Seth's brothers had made for somebody's daughter, a girl of exceptional beauty who had died shortly afterwards.

As Padma spoke, the children, boys and girls, gathered round the house. Mr Biswas was not altogether happy about this, but was pleased when the children acknowledged Savi's ownership by asking her permission to open doors and touch beds. Even as she explored, Savi tried to give the impression that she was familiar with everything.

'What have you brought for the others?'

It was Mrs Tulsi.

'Didn't have room,' Mr Biswas said gaily.

'When I give, I give to all,' Mrs Tulsi said. 'I am poor, but I give to all. It is clear, however, that I cannot compete with Santa Claus.'

Her voice was even and he would have smiled, as at a witticism, but when he looked at her he saw that her face was tight with anger.

'Vidiadhar and Shivadhar!' Chinta shouted. 'Come here at once. Stop interfering with what doesn't belong to you.'

As at a signal the sisters pounced on their children, threatening horrible punishments on those who interfered with what didn't belong to them.

'I will peel your backside.'

'I will break every bone in your body.'

And Sumati the flogger said, 'I will make you heavy with welts.'

'Savi, go and put it away,' Shama whispered. 'Take it up-stairs.'

Mrs Tulsi, rising, patting her lips, said, 'Shama, I hope you will have the grace to give me notice before you move to your mansion.' She laboured up the stairs, and Sushila, the widow who ruled the sickroom, followed solic-itously.

The affronted sisters drew closer together, and Shama stood alone. Her eyes were wide with dread. She stared ac-cusingly at Mr Biswas.

'Well,' he said briskly. 'I better go back home – to the barracks.'

He urged Savi and Anand to come with him out to the arcade. Savi came willingly. Anand was, as usual, embar-rassed. Mr Biswas couldn't help feeling that, compared with Savi, the boy was a disappointment. He was small for his age, thin and sickly, with a big head; he looked as though he needed protection, but was shy and tongue-tied with Mr Biswas and always seemed anxious to be free of him. Now, when Mr Biswas put his arms around him, Anand sniffed, rubbed a dirty face against Mr Biswas's trousers, and tried to pull away.

'You must let Anand play with it,' Mr Biswas said to Savi.

'He is a boy.'

'Don't worry.' Mr Biswas rubbed Anand's bony back. 'You are going to get something next time.'

'I want a car,' Anand said to Mr Biswas's trousers. 'A big one.'

Mr Biswas knew the sort he meant. 'All right,' he said. 'Going to get you a car.'

Immediately Anand broke away and ran back through the gate to the yard, riding an imaginary horse, wielding an imaginary whip and shouting, 'And I going to get a car! I going to get a car!'

He bought the car; not, despite his promise, the big one Anand wanted, but a clockwork miniature; and on Saturday, after the labourers had been paid, he took it to Arwacas. His arrival was noted from the arcade and, as he pushed the side gate open, he heard the message being relayed by the children in awed and expectant tones: 'Savi, your pappa come to see you.'

She came crying to the doorway of the hall. When he embraced her she burst into loud sobs.

The children were silent. He heard the stairs creaking continually, and he became aware of a thick shuffling and whispering in the black kitchen at the far end.

'Tell me,' he said.

She stifled her sobs. 'They break it up.'

'Show me!' he cried. 'Show me!'

His rage shocked her out of her tears. She came down the steps and he followed her through the gallery at the end of the hall into the yard, past a half-full copper reflecting a deep blue sky, and a black riveted tank where fish, bought alive from the market, swam until the time came for them to be eaten.

And there, below the almost bare branches of the almond tree that grew in the next yard, he saw it, thrown against a dusty leaning fence made of wood and tin and corrugated iron. A broken door, a ruined window, a staved-in wall or even roof – he had expected that. But not this. The doll's house did not exist. He saw only a bundle of firewood. None of its parts was whole. Its delicate joints were exposed and useless. Below the torn skin of paint, still bright and still in parts imitating brickwork, the hacked and splintered wood was white and raw.

'O God!'

The sight of the wrecked house and the silence of her father made Savi cry afresh.

'Ma mash it up.'

He ran back to the house. The edge of a wall scraped against his shoulder, tearing his shirt and tearing the skin below.

Sisters had now left the stairs and kitchen and were sitting about the hall.

'Shama!' he bawled. 'Shama!'

Savi came slowly up the steps from the courtyard. Sisters shifted their gaze from Mr Biswas to her and she remained in the doorway, looking down at her feet.

'Shama!'

He heard a sister whisper, 'Go and call your aunt Shama. Quick.'

He noticed Anand among the children and sisters.

'Come here, boy!'

Anand looked at the sisters. They gave him no help. He didn't move.

'Anand, I call you! Come here quick sharp.'

'Go, boy,' Sumati said. 'Before you get blows.'

While Anand hesitated, Shama came. She came through the kitchen doorway. Her veil was pulled over her forehead. This unusual touch of dutifulness he noted. She looked frightened yet determined.

'You bitch!'

The silence was absolute.

Sisters shooed away their children up the stairs and into the kitchen.

Savi remained in the doorway behind Mr Biswas.

'I don't mind what you call me,' Shama said.

'You break up the dolly house?'

Her eyes widened with fear and guilt and shame. 'Yes,' she said, exaggeratedly calm. Then casually, 'I break it up.'

'To please who?' He was losing control of his voice.

She didn't answer.

He noticed that she looked lonely. 'Tell me,' he screamed. 'To please *these* people?'

Chinta got up, straightened out her long skirt and started to walk up the stairs. 'Let me go away, eh, before I hear something I don't like and have to answer back.'

'I wasn't pleasing anybody but myself.' Shama was speaking more surely now and he could see that she was gaining strength from the approval of her sisters.

'You know what I think of you and your family?'

Two more sisters went up the stairs.

'I don't care what you think.'

And suddenly his rage had gone. His shouts rang in his head, leaving him startled, ashamed and tired. He could think of nothing to say.

She recognized the change in his mood and waited, at ease now.

'Go and dress Savi.' He spoke quietly.

She made no move.

*'Go and dress Savi!'*

His shout frightened Savi and she began to scream. She was trembling and when he touched her she felt brittle.

Shama at last moved to obey.

Savi pulled away. 'I don't want anybody to dress me.'

'Go and pack her clothes.'

'You are taking her with you?'

It was his turn to be silent.

The children who had been shooed away into the kitchen pushed their faces out of the doorway.

Shama walked the length of the hall to the stairs, where sisters, sitting on the lower steps, pulled their knees in to let her pass.

At once everybody relaxed.

Sumati said in an amused voice, 'Anand, are you going with your father too?'

Anand pulled his head back into the kitchen.

The hall became active again. Children drifted back, and sisters hurried between kitchen and hall, laying out the evening meal. Chinta returned and started on a light-hearted song, which was taken up by other sisters.

The drama was over, and Shama's re-entry, with ribbons, comb and a small cardboard suitcase, did not have the same attention as her exit.

Offering the suitcase with outstretched hand, Shama said, 'She is your daughter. You know what is good for her. You have been feeding her. You know –'

He set his mouth, pulling his upper teeth behind his lower.

Chinta broke off her singing to say to Savi, 'Going home, girl?'

'Put some shoes on her feet,' Shama said.

But that meant washing Savi's feet, and that meant delay; and, pushing away Shama when she tried to comb Savi's hair, he led Savi outside. It was only when they were in the High Street that he remembered Anand.

Market day was over and the street was littered with broken boxes, torn paper, straw, rotting vegetables, animal droppings and, though it hadn't rained, a number of puddles. By the light of flambeaux stalls were being stripped and carts loaded by vendors, their wives and tired children.

Mr Biswas tied the suitcase to the carrier of his bicycle, and he and Savi walked in silence to the end of the High Street.

When the red and ochre police station was out of sight, he put Savi on the crossbar of the cycle, took a short run and, with difficulty and some nervousness, hopped on to the saddle. The cycle wobbled; Savi held on to his left arm and made balance more uncertain. Presently, however, they had left Arwacas and there was nothing but silent sugarcane on either side of the road. It was pitch black. The bicycle had no lights and they couldn't see for more than a few yards ahead. Savi was trembling.

'Don't frighten.'

A light flashed in front of them. A gritty male voice said harshly, 'Where you think you going?'

It was a Negro policeman. Mr Biswas pulled at his hand-brakes. The bicycle leaned to the left and Savi slipped to the ground.

The policeman examined the bicycle. 'No licence, eh? No licence. No lights. And you was towing. You have a nice little case coming up.' He paused, waiting to be bribed. 'All right, then. Name and address.' He wrote in his book. 'Good. You go be getting a summons.'

So they walked the rest of the way to Green Vale, through the darkness, and then below the dead trees to the barracks.

They spent a miserable week. Mr Biswas left the barracks early in the morning and returned in the middle of the afternoon. All that time Savi was alone. An old woman, who was spending time with her son, his wife and five children in a barrackroom, took pity on Savi and gave her food at midday. This food Savi never ate; hunger could not overcome her distrust of food cooked by strangers. She took the plate to the room, emptied it on to a sheet of newspaper, washed the plate, took it back to the old woman, thanked her, and waited for Mr Biswas. When he came she waited for the night; when the night came she waited for the morning.

To amuse her, he read from his novels, expounded Marcus Aurelius and Epictetus, made her learn the quotations hanging on the walls, and made her sit still while he unsuccessfully tried to sketch her. She was dispirited and submissive. She was also afraid. Sometimes, especially during walks under the trees, he suddenly seemed to forget her, and she heard him muttering to himself, holding bitter, repetitive arguments with unseen persons. He was 'trapped' in a 'hole'. 'Trap,' she heard him say over and over. 'That's what you and your family do to me. Trap me in this hole.' She saw his mouth twist with anger; she heard him curse and threaten. When they got back to the barracks he asked her to mix him doses of Macleans' Brand Stomach Powder.

They were both looking forward to Saturday afternoon, when Seth would come and take her back to Hanuman House. There was a good reason why she couldn't stay any longer: her school was opening on Monday.

On Saturday Seth came. He was not alone. Shama, Anand and Myna came with him. Savi ran to the road to meet them. Mr Biswas pretended he didn't see, and Seth smiled, as at the antics of children. Quarrels between Seth and his wife were unknown, and it was his policy never to interfere in quarrels between sisters and their husbands. But Mr Biswas knew that despite the smile Seth had come as Shama's protector.

He immediately took out the green table to the yard, setting it some distance away from the room, and the labourers queued up, screening him from Shama. While he sat beside Seth, calling out tasks and wages and making entries in the ledger, he listened to Savi talking excitedly to Shama and Anand. He heard Shama's cooing replies. Soon she was so sure of the children's affection that she was even scolding them. What a difference there was, though, in the voice she used now and the voice she used at Hanuman House!

And even while he noted Shama's duplicity, he felt that Savi had betrayed him.

The labourers were paid. Seth said he wanted to have a look at the fields; it was not necessary for Mr Biswas to come with him.

Shama was sitting in the kitchen area. She held Myna in her arms and was playing with her, talking baby-talk. Savi and Anand looked on. When Mr Biswas passed, Shama glanced at him but did not stop talking to Myna.

Savi and Anand looked up apprehensively.

Mr Biswas went into the room and sat in the rocking-chair.

Shama said loudly, 'Anand, go and ask your father if he would like a cup of tea.'

Anand came, shy and worried, and mumbled the message.

Mr Biswas did not reply. He studied Anand's big head and thin arms. The skin at the elbow was baggy, and scarred purple with eczema. Had he too been fed on sulphur and condensed milk?

Anand waited, then went outside.

Mr Biswas rocked. The floor-planks were wide and rough. One had cambered and cracked; whenever the rockers came down on it, it squeaked and snapped.

Savi, not looking at Mr Biswas, brought Myna into the room and laid her carefully on the bed.

Shama was fanning the coal-pot.

Savi, her pyromaniacal instincts aroused, hurried out of the room, saying, 'Ma, you getting coal all over your clothes. Let me.'

So. They had all forgotten the doll's house. He drew up his feet on to the chair, leaned his head back, closed his eyes and rocked. The board replied.

'Anand, take this to your father.'

He heard Anand approaching but didn't open his eyes. He wondered whether he shouldn't take the tea and fling it over Shama's fussy embroidered dress and smiling, uncertain face.

He opened his eyes, took the cup from Anand, and sipped.

When Seth came back he smiled at everyone benevolently and sat down on the steps. Shama gave him a large cup of tea and he drank it in three gurgling draughts, snorting and sighing in between. He took off his hat and smoothed his damp hair. Suddenly he began to laugh. 'Mohun, I hear you have a case.'

'Case? Oh, *case!* Small one. Tiny tiny. Baby case, really.'

'You are a funny sort of paddler. Get your summons yet?'

'Waiting for it.'

'And Savi. You get your summons yet?'

Savi smiled, as though there had been no terror in the dark road and the flash of the policeman's torch.

'Well, don't worry.' Seth got up. 'These people just want to see whether your dollar-notes look any different from theirs. I settle it up. Wouldn't do anybody any good for your case to come up.'

And he was gone.

Mr Biswas closed his eyes, rocked on the noisy board, and the children became anxious again.

He remained in the chair until it was dark and time to eat. Oil lamps were lighted in many barrackrooms. Far down a drunk man was swearing.

Savi and Anand ate sitting on the steps. As he ate at the green table Mr Biswas became less torpid, and Shama correspondingly gloomier. Towards the end of the meal he even began to clown. He squatted on the chair, with his left hand squashed between calf and thigh, and asked banteringly, 'Why you didn't stay at the monkey house, eh?'

She didn't reply.

After he had washed his hands and gargled out of the side window, Shama sat down on the steps to eat. He watched her.

'Crying, eh?'

Slowly the tears flowed out of her wide eyes.

'So you vex up then?'

One tear raced down her cheek and hung trembling over her top lip.

'It tickling?'

Her mouth was half full but she stopped chewing.

'Don't tell me the food so bad.'

She said, as though to herself, 'If it wasn't for the children –'

'If it wasn't for the children, what?'

She continued to chew with a loud and morose deliberation.

In one corner Savi and Anand were rolling out sacks and sheets on which to sleep.

'You come,' Shama said. 'You come, you didn't look right, you didn't look left, you start getting on, you curse me upside down –'

It was the beginning of her apology. He didn't interrupt.

'You didn't know what I had to put up with. Talking night and day. Puss-puss here. Puss-puss there. Chinta dropping remarks all the time. Everybody beating their children the moment they start talking to Savi. Nobody wanting to talk to me. Everybody behaving as though I kill their father.' She stopped, and cried. 'So I had to satisfy them. I break up the dolly-house and everybody was satisfied. And then you come. You didn't look right, you didn't look left –'

'Charge of the Light Brigade. You think Chinta would break up a dolly-house Govind buy? If you could imagine Govind doing anything like that. Tell me, what does that brother-in-law of yours use for food, eh? Dirt? You think Chinta would break up a dolly-house Govind buy?'

She wept over her plate.

Later she wept over the washingup, repeatedly interrupting her tears, first to blow her nose, then to sing sad songs softly, and finally to ask about Savi's behaviour during the week.

He told how Savi had thrown away the old woman's food. Shama was gratified, and told other stories of the girl's sensibility. Savi, still anxiously awake and only pretending to be asleep, listened with pleasure. Again Shama told of Savi's dislike for fish and how Mrs Tulsi had overcome that dislike. She also spoke of Anand, who was so sensitive that biscuits made his mouth bleed.

Mr Biswas, his mood now soft as hers, did not say that he thought this to be a sign of undernourishment. Instead he began to talk about his house and Shama listened without enthusiasm but without objection.

'And as soon as the house finish, going to buy that gold brooch for you, girl!'

'I would like to see the day.'

They had come on Saturday. On Monday Savi had to go back to school.

'Stay here,' Mr Biswas said. 'They don't teach much on the first day.'

'How you know?' Savi said. 'You ever went to school?'

'Yes, miss. I went to school. You are not the only one to go to school, you know.'

'If I stay I will have to have an excuse to give Teacher.'

'I will write one for you in two twos. Dear Teacher, My daughter Savi is unable to attend school for the first week because she has been staying with her grandmother and is suffering from serious undernourishment.'

On Sunday evening Shama took Savi and Anand back to Arwacas. She went to Hanuman House again. And so for the rest of the term she came and left; and he never ceased to feel that he was alone, with the trees, the newspapers on the wall, the religious quotations, his books.

One thing gave him comfort. He had claimed Savi.

At Easter he learned that Shama was pregnant for the fourth time.

One child claimed; one still hostile; one unknown. And now another.

Trap!

The future he feared was upon him. He was falling into the void, and that terror, known only in dreams, was with him as he lay awake at nights, hearing the snores and creaks and the occasional cries of babies from the other rooms. The relief that morning brought steadily diminished. Food and tobacco were tasteless. He was always tired, and always restless. He went often to Hanuman House; as soon as he was there he wanted to leave. Sometimes he cycled to Arwacas without going to the house, changing his mind in the High Street, turning round and cycling back to Green Vale. When he closed the door of his room for the night it was like an imprisonment.

He talked to himself, shouted, did everything as noisily as he could.

Nothing replied. Nothing changed. *Amazing scenes were witnessed yesterday when.* The newspapers remained as jaunty as they had been, the quotations as sedate. *Of him I will never lose hold and he shall never lose hold of me.* But now in the shape and position of everything around him, the trees, the furniture, even those letters he had made with brush and ink, there was an alertness, an expectancy.

Seth announced one Saturday that there were to be changes on the estate at the end of the crop season. Some twenty acres which had for many years been rented to labourers were to be taken over. Seth and Mr Biswas went from hut to hut, breaking the news. As soon as he entered a labourer's hut Seth lost his briskness. He looked tired and sounded tired; he accepted a cup of tea and drank it wearily; then he spoke, as though the matter was trivial, burdensome only to him, and the land was being taken from the labourers purely for their benefit. The labourers listened politely and asked Seth and Mr Biswas whether they wanted more tea. Seth accepted at once, saying it was very good tea. He played with the thin-limbed, big-eyed children, made them laugh and gave them coppers to buy sweeties. Their parents protested he was spoiling them.

Afterwards Seth said to Mr Biswas, 'You can't trust those buggers. They are going to give a lot of trouble. You better watch out.'

The labourers never spoke about the land to Mr Biswas, and while the crop was being reaped there was no trouble.

When the land was bare Seth said, 'They will want to dig up the roots. Don't let them.'

It was not long before Mr Biswas had to report that some roots had been dug up.

Seth said, 'It looks as though I will have to horsewhip one or two of them.'

'No, not that. You go back every night to sleep safe and sound in Arwacas. I have to stay here.'

In the end they decided to employ a watchman, and the land was prepared, without further trouble, for the new crop.

'You think the whole thing worth it?' Mr Biswas asked. 'Paying watchman and everything?'

'In a year or so we wouldn't have any trouble,' Seth said. 'People get used to everything.'

And it seemed that Seth was right. The dispossessed labourers, though they saw Mr Biswas every day, contented themselves with sending him messages by other labourers.

'Dookinan says that he know you have a kind heart and wouldn't want to do anything to harm him. Five children, you know.'

'Is not me,' Mr Biswas said. 'Is not my land. I just doing a job and drawing a salary.'

The labourers' acceptance, at first touched with hope, turned to resignation. And resignation turned to hostility, directed not against Seth, who was feared, but against Mr Biswas. He was no longer mocked; but no one smiled at him, and outside the fields he was ignored.

Every night he bolted himself in his room. As soon as he was still he felt the stillness around him and he had to make movements to destroy the stillness, to challenge the alertness of the room and the objects in it.

He was rocking hard on the creaking board one night when he thought of the power of the rockers to grind and crush and inflict pain, on his hands and toes and the tenderer parts of his body. He rose at once in agony, covering his groin with his hands, sucking hard on his teeth, listening to the chair as, rocking, it moved sideways along the cambered plank. The chair fell silent. He looked away from it. On the wall he saw a nail that could puncture his eye. The window could trap and mangle. So could the door. Every leg of the green table could press and crush. The castors of the dressing-table. The drawers. He lay face down on the bed, not wanting to see and, to drive out the shapes of objects from his head, he concentrated on the shapes of letters, working out design after design for the letter R. At last he fell asleep, with his hands covering the vulnerable parts of his body, and wishing he had hands to cover himself all over. In the morning he was better; he had forgotten his fears.

There had been many changes at Hanuman House, but though he went there two or three times a week he noticed the changes as from a distance and felt in no way concerned. Marriage had taken away one wave of children, among them the contortionist. Marriage had also overtaken the elder god, though for some time it had looked as though he might be reprieved. The search among the eligible families had failed to provide someone beautiful and educated and rich enough to satisfy Mrs Tulsi or her daughters, who, notwithstanding the chancy haste of their own marriages, based solely on caste, thought that their brother's bride should be chosen with a more appropriate concern. For a short time afterwards a search was made for an educated, beautiful and rich girl from a caste family who had been converted to Christianity and had lapsed. Finally, it was agreed that any educated, beautiful and rich Indian girl would do, provided she had no Muslim taint. The oil families, whatever their original condition, were too grand. So they searched among the families in soft drinks, the families in ice, the transport families, the cinema families, the families in filling stations. And at last, in a laxly Presbyterian family with one filling station, two lorries, a cinema and some land, they found a girl. Each side patronized the other and neither suspected it was being patronized; after smooth and swift negotiations the marriage took place in a registry office, and the elder god, contrary to Hindu custom and the traditions of his family, did not bring his bride home, but left Hanuman House for good, no longer talking of suicide, to look after the lorries, cinema, land and filling station of his wife's family.

His departure was followed by another. Mrs Tulsi went to live in Port of Spain, not caring for the younger god to be in that city by himself, and not trusting anyone else to look after him. She bought not one house, but three: one to live in, two to rent out. She travelled up to Port of Spain with the god every Sunday evening and came down with him every Friday afternoon.

During her absences the accepted degrees of precedence at Hanuman House lost some of their meaning. Sushila, the widow, was reduced to nonentity. Many sisters attempted to seize power and a number of squabbles ensued. Offended sisters ostentatiously looked after their own families, sometimes even cooking separately for a day or two. Padma, Seth's wife, alone continued to be respected, but she showed no inclination to assert authority. Seth exacted the obedience of everyone; he could not impose harmony. That was re-established every week-end, when Mrs Tulsi and the younger god returned.

And just before the school holidays all quarrels were forgotten. The house was scrubbed and cleaned, the brass polished and the yard tidied, as though to receive passing royalty; and the brothers-in-law vied with one another in laying aside offerings for the god: a Julie mango, a bunch of bananas, an especially large purple-skinned avocado pear.

Mr Biswas brought nothing. Shama complained.

'And what about my son, eh?' Mr Biswas said. 'He lost in the crowd? Who looking after him? He not studying too?'

For, halfway through the term, Anand had begun to go to the mission school. He hated it. He soaked his shoes in water; he was flogged and sent to school in wet shoes. He threw away Captain Cutteridge's *First Primer* and said it had been stolen; he was flogged and given another copy.

'Anand is a coward,' Savi told Mr Biswas. 'He still frightened of school. And you know what Aunt Chinta say to him yesterday? "If you don't look out you will come a grass-cutter just like your father." '

'Grass-cutter! Look, look, Savi. The next time your aunt Chinta open that big mouth' – he broke off, remembering grammar – 'the next time she opens her big mouth –'

Savi smiled.

'– you just ask her whether she has ever read Marcus Aurelius and Epictetus.'

These were household names to Savi.

'Munnih-munnih-munnih,' Mr Biswas muttered.

'Munnih-munnih?'

'Money. Checking munnih-munnih-munnih. That is the only way your mother's family like to get their fat little hands dirty. Look, the next time Chinta or anybody else says I am a grass-cutter, you just tell them that it is better to be a grass-cutter than a crab-catcher. You got that? Better to be a grass-cutter than a crab-catcher.'

And he opened the campaign himself. He had seen some large blue-backed crabs scrambling awkwardly about the black tank in the yard. 'Whoo!' he said in the hall. 'Those are big crabs in the tank. Where did they come from?'

'Govind bought them for Mai and Owad,' Chinta said proudly.

'Bought them?' Mr Biswas said. 'Anybody would say that he caught them.'

When he next went to Hanuman House he found that Savi had delivered all his messages.

Chinta came straight up to him and said, with the mannishness she put on when Mrs Tulsi was away, 'Brother-in-law, I want you to know that until you came to this house there were no crab-catchers here.'

'Eh? No what?'

'Crab-catchers.'

'Crab-catchers? What about crab-catchers? You don't have enough here?'

'Marcus Aurelius-Aurelius,' Chinta said, retreating to the kitchen. 'Shama sister, I don't want to meddle in the way you are bringing up your children, but you are turning them into men and women before their time.'

Mr Biswas winked at Savi.

Presently Chinta came out to the hall again. She had obviously thought of something to say. Sternly and needlessly she rearranged chairs and benches and straightened the photographs of Pundit Tulsi and a huge Chinese calendar which showed a woman of sly beauty against a background of tamed trees and waterfalls. 'Savi,' Chinta said at last, and her voice was gentle, 'you reach first standard at school and you must know the poetry Captain Cutteridge have in that book. I don't think your father know it because I don't think your father reach first standard.'

Mr Biswas had not been brought up on Captain Cutteridge but on the *Royal Reader*. Nevertheless he said, 'First standard? I skipped that one. I went straight from Introductory to second standard.'

'I thought so, brother-in-law. But you, Savi, you know the poetry I mean. The one about *felo-de-se*. The little pigs. You know it?'

'*I* know it! *I* know it!' a boy exclaimed. This was Jai, the expert lace-knotter, fourteen months younger than Savi. He had developed into something of an exhibitionist. He ran to the centre of the hall, held his hands behind his back and said, 'The Three Little Piggies. By Sir Alfred Scott-Gatty.'

> *A jolly old sow once lived in a sty.*
> *And three little piggies had she,*
> *And she waddled about, saying, 'Umph! Umph! Umph!'*
> *While the little ones said, 'Wee! Wee!'*
> *'My dear little brothers,' said one of the brats,*
> *'My dear little piggies,' said he,*
> *'Let us all for the future say, "Umph! Umph! Umph!"*
> *'Tis so childish to say, "Wee! Wee!" '*

While Jai recited Chinta moved her head up and down in time to the rhythm and stared smilingly at Savi.

'So after a time,' Jai went on,

> *So after a time these little pigs died,*
> *They all died of 'felo-de-se',*
> *From trying too hard to say, 'Umph! Umph! Umph!'*
> *When they could only say, 'Wee! Wee!'*

'A moral there is to this little song,' Chinta said, continuing the poem with Jai and wagging her finger at Savi. 'A moral that's easy to see.'

'*Felo-de-se?*' Mr Biswas said. 'Sounds like the name of a crab-catcher to me.'

Chinta stamped, irritated as when she lost at cards, and, looking as though she was about to cry, went back to the kitchen.

'Shama sister,' Mr Biswas heard her say in a breaking voice, 'I want you to ask your husband to stop provoking me. Otherwise I will just have to tell *him*' – her husband, Govind – 'and you know what happened when *he* had a little falling-out with your husband.'

'All right, Chinta sister, I will tell him.'

Shama came out and said, with annoyance, 'Man, stop provoking C. You know she can't take jokes.'

'Jokes? What jokes? Crab-catching is no joke, you hear.'

Chinta had her revenge a few days later.

Mr Biswas arrived at Hanuman House when the evening meal was over and the children were sitting about the hall in groups of three or four, reading primers or pretending to read. One of the economies of the house was that as many children as possible shared a book; and the children were talking among themselves and trying to hide the fact by holding their hands over their mouths and turning pages regularly. When Mr Biswas came they looked at him with amusement and expectancy.

Chinta smiled. 'You have come to see your son, brother-in-law?'

A rustle of turning pages coincided with many muffled titters.

Savi left a group around a book and came to Mr Biswas. She looked unhappy. 'Anand upstairs.' When they were half-way up she whispered, 'He kneeling down.'

In the hall Chinta was singing.

'Kneeling down? What for?'

'He mess up himself at school today and had to leave.'

They went through the Book Room to the long room, which he and Shama had occupied after their marriage. The lotus decorations on the wall were as faded as before; the Demerara window through which he had gargled was propped open with a section of a broomstick.

Anand was kneeling in a corner with his face to the wall.

'He kneeling down since this afternoon,' Savi said.

Mr Biswas didn't feel this was true. Anand had been left to himself, and was now kneeling upright, without a sign of fatigue, as though he had just begun.

'Stop kneeling,' Mr Biswas said.

He was surprised at Anand's outraged and querulous reply. 'They *tell* me to kneel down and I *going* to kneel down.'

It was the first time he had seen Anand in a temper. He looked at the boy's narrow shoulder blades below the thin cotton shirt; the slender neck, the large head; the thin eczema-stained legs in small, loose trousers; the blackened soles – shoes were to be worn only outside the house – and the big toes.

'He was frightened,' Savi said.

'To do what?'

'Frightened to ask Teacher permission to leave the room. And when he leave the room he was frightened again. Frightened to use the school WC.'

'Is a *nasty, stinking* place,' Anand burst out, getting off his knees and turning to face them.

'It really is,' Savi said. 'And then – well –'

Anand cried.

'He went back to the classroom and Teacher ask him to leave.'

Anand looked down at the floor, sniffing and running his fingers along the grooves between the floorboards.

'Well, just then school was over and everybody walk behind Anand. Everybody was laughing.'

'And when I come home Ma beat me,' Anand said. He wasn't complaining. He was angry. 'Ma *beat* me. *She* beat me.' Repeated, the words lost their anger and became pleas for sympathy.

Mr Biswas became the buffoon. He told about his own misadventure at Pundit Jairam's, caricaturing himself, and ridiculing Anand's shame.

Anand didn't look up or smile. But he had ceased to cry. He said, 'I don't want to go back to that school.'

'You want to come with me?'

Anand didn't reply.

They all went down to the hall.

Mr Biswas said, 'Look, Shama, don't make this boy kneel down again, you hear.'

Sushila, the widow, said, 'When we were small Mai used to make us kneel on graters for a thing like that.'

'Well, I don't want my children to grow up like you, that is all.'

Sushila, childless, husbandless and now without the protection of Mrs Tulsi, swept upstairs, complaining that advantage was being taken of her situation.

Chinta said, 'You are taking your son home with you, brother-in-law?'

Shama, noting Mr Biswas's serene mood, said sternly, 'Anand not going anywhere. He got to stay here and go to school.'

'Why?' Chinta asked. 'Brother-in-law could teach him. I sure he know the ABC.'

'A for apple, B for bat, C for crab,' Mr Biswas said.

Anand followed Mr Biswas outside and seemed unwilling to let him leave. He said nothing; he simply hung around the bicycle, occasionally rubbing up against it. Mr Biswas was irritated by his shyness, but he was again touched by the boy's fragility and the carefully ragged 'home clothes' which Anand, like the other children, wore the minute he came from school. Anand's washed-out khaki shorts were spectacularly patched, had slits but no pockets and a gaping empty fob. His shirt was darned and frayed and the collar was chewed; from the crooked stitches, the irregular cut, the weak and absurd decoration on the pocket Mr Biswas could tell that the shirt had been made by Shama.

He asked, 'You want to come with me?'

Anand only smiled and looked down and spun the bicycle pedal with his big toe.

It would soon be dark. Mr Biswas had no lamp (every bicycle lamp and every bicycle pump he bought was promptly stolen) and he could never contrive, as some cyclists did, less to light their way than to appease the police, to ride with a lighted candle in an open paper-bag in one hand.

He cycled down the High Street. Just past the shop with the Red Rose Tea Is Good Tea sign, he looked back. Anand was still under the arcade, next to one of the thick white pillars with the lotus-shaped base; standing and staring like that other boy Mr Biswas had seen outside a low hut at dusk.

When he got to Green Vale it was dark. Under the trees it was night. The sounds from the barracks were assertive and isolated one from the other: snatches of talk, the sound of frying, a shout, the cry of a child: sounds thrown up at the starlit sky from a place that was nowhere, a dot on the map of the island, which was a dot on the map of the world. The dead trees ringed the barracks, a wall of flawless black.

He locked himself in his room.

That week he decided he couldn't wait any longer. Unless he started his house now he never would. His children would stay at Hanuman House, he would remain in the barrack-room, and nothing would arrest his descent into the void. Every night he wound himself up to a panic at his inaction, every morning he reaffirmed his decision, and on Saturday he spoke to Seth about a site.

'Rent you land?' Seth said. 'Rent? Look, man, there is the land. Why don't you just choose a site and build? Don't talk to me about renting.'

The site Mr Biswas had in mind was about two hundred yards from the barracks, screened from it by the trees and separated from it by a shallow damp depression which ran with muddy water after rain. Trees also screened the road. But when he thought of the land as the site of his house, the trees did not seem unfriendly; and he liked to think of the spot as a 'bower', a word that had come to him from Words-worth by way of the *Royal Reader*.

On Sunday morning, after he had had some cocoa, shop bread and red butter, he went to see the builder. The builder lived in a crumbling wooden house in a small Negro settle-ment not far from Arwacas. Just over the gutter a badly-written notice board announced that George Maclean was a carpenter and cabinet-maker; this announcement was choked by much subsidiary information scattered all over the board in small and wavering letters; Mr Maclean was also a black-smith and a painter; he made tin cups and he soldered; he sold fresh eggs; he had a ram for service; and all his prices were keen.

Mr Biswas called, 'Morning!'

From the shack in the hard yellow yard a Negro woman came out, a large calabash full of corn in one hand. Her tight cotton dress imperfectly covered her big body and her kinky hair was in curlers and twists of newspaper.

'The carpenter home?' Mr Biswas asked.

The woman called, 'Georgie!' For a fat woman her voice was surprisingly thin.

Mr Maclean appeared above the half-door at the side of the house. He looked at Mr Biswas suspiciously.

The woman walked to the far end of the yard, scattering corn and clucking loudly, calling the poultry to feed.

Mr Biswas didn't know how to begin. He couldn't just say, 'I want to build a house.' He didn't have all the necessary money and he didn't want to deceive Mr Maclean or expose himself to his scorn. He said shyly, 'I have a little business I want to talk to you about.'

Mr Maclean pushed open the lower half of the door and came down the concrete steps. He was middle-aged, tall and thin; he looked as eager and uncertain as his board. His profession was a frustrating one. The county abounded in work he had not been allowed to finish: exposed and rotting house-frames, houses that had begun with concrete and dressed wood and ended with mud walls and tree branches. Evidence of his compensating activities lay about the yard. In an open shed at the back a half-finished wheel stood amid shavings. Here and there Mr Biswas saw goat droppings.

'What sort of business?' Mr Maclean asked. He reached up and pulled a window open. It rattled and glittered; it was hung on the inside with strings of tin cups.

'Is about a house.'

'Oh. Repairs?'

'Not exactly. It ain't build yet. As a matter of fact —'

'Georgie!' Mrs Maclean shouted. 'Come and see what that damn mongoose do again.'

Mr Maclean went to the back of the house. Mr Biswas heard him mumbling evenly. 'Damn nuisance,' he said, coming back, striking his trousers with a switch. 'So, you want me to build a house for you?'

Mr Biswas mistook his wariness for sarcasm and said defensively, 'Is not a mansion.'

'That is a blessing. Too much people putting up mansion these days. You ever had a close look at the County Road?' He paused. 'Upstairs house?'

Mr Biswas nodded. 'Upstairs house. Small thing. But neat. I don't want too much to make me happy,' he ran on, made uneasy by Mr Maclean. 'I don't see any point in pretending that you have more money than you really have.'

'Naturally,' Mr Maclean said. With the switch he flicked some fowl droppings from the yard into the thick dust under the floor of his own house. Then he drew two equal and adjacent squares on the ground. 'You want two bedrooms.'

'And a drawingroom.'

Mr Maclean added another square of the same size. To this he added half a square and said, 'And a gallery.'

'That's it. Nothing too fancy for me. Small and neat.'

'You want a door from the gallery to the front bedroom. A wood door. And you want another door to the drawing-room. With coloured glass panes.'

'Yes, yes.'

'One side of the gallery you want board up. For the front you would like some fancy rails. You want a nice concrete step with a banister in front.'

'Yes, yes.'

'For the front bedroom you want glass windows, and if you get the money you going to paint them white. The back windows could be pure board. And you want a plain wood staircase at the back, with no banister or anything like that. The kitchen you going to build yourself, somewhere in the yard.'

'Exactly.'

'That's a nice little house you have there. A lot of people would like it. It going to cost you about two hundred and fifty, three hundred dollars. Labour, you know –' He looked at Mr Biswas and slowly rubbed a bare foot over the drawing on the ground. 'I don't know. I busy these days.' He pointed to the unfinished wheel in the shed.

A hen cackled, proclaiming an egg.

'Georgie! Is the Leghorn.'

There was a tremendous squawking and flapping among the poultry.

Mr Maclean said, 'Is a lucky thing. Otherwise she was going straight in the pot.'

'We not bound and 'bliged to build the whole thing right away,' Mr Biswas said. 'Rome wasn't built in a day, you know.'

'So they say. But Rome get build. Anyway, as soon as I get some time I going to come and we could look at the site. You have a site?'

'Yes, yes, man. Have a site.'

'Well, in about two-three days then.'

He came early that afternoon, in hat, shoes and an ironed shirt, and they went to look at the site.

'Is a real little bower,' Mr Biswas said.

'Is a sloping site!' Mr Maclean said in surprise and almost with pleasure. 'You really have to have high pillars.'

'High on one side, low on the other. It could practically be a style. And then I was thinking about a little path down to the road here. Steps. In the ground itself. Garden on both sides. Roses. Exora. Oleanders. Bougainvillaea and poinsettia. And some Queen of Flowers. And a neat little bamboo bridge to the road.'

'It sound nice.'

'I was thinking. About the house. It would be nice to have concrete pillars. Not naked though. I don't think that does look nice. Plastered and smooth.'

'I know what you mean. You think you could give me about a hundred and fifty dollars just to start off with?'

Mr Biswas hesitated.

'You mustn't think I want to meddle in your private affairs. I just wanting to know how much you want to spend right away.'

Mr Biswas walked away from Mr Maclean, among the bushes on the damp site, the weeds and the nettles. 'About a hundred,' he said. 'But at the end of the month I could give you a little bit more.'

'A hundred.'

'All right?'

'Yes, is all right. For a start.'

They went through the weeds and over the leaf-choked gutter to the narrow gravelly road.

'Every month we build a little,' Mr Biswas said. 'Little by little.'

'Yes, little by little.' Mr Maclean wasn't animated, but some of his wariness had gone; he even sounded encouraging. 'I will have to get some labour. Helluva thing these days, getting good labour.' He spoke the word with relish.

And the word pleased Mr Biswas too. 'Yes, you must get labour,' he said, suppressing his astonishment that there were people who depended on Mr Maclean for a living.

'But you better get a few more cents quick.' Mr Maclean said, almost friendly now. 'Otherwise you wouldn't get any concrete pillars.'

'Must have concrete pillars.'

'Then all the house *you* going to build will be a row of concrete pillars with nothing on top of them.'

They walked on.

'A row of coal barrels,' Mr Biswas said.

Mr Maclean didn't intrude.

'Just send me a coal barrel. Yes, you old bitch. Just a coal barrel.'

He decided to borrow the money from Ajodha. He didn't want to ask Seth or Mrs Tulsi. And he couldn't ask Misir: their relationship had cooled since he had borrowed from him to pay Mungroo and Seebaran and Mahmoud. And yet he was unwilling to go to Ajodha. He walked out of the barrackyard but before he reached the main road decided to let the matter rest until the following Sunday. He walked back to his room and put on his bicycle clips, thinking he would spend the afternoon at Hanuman House instead. But he knew so clearly what he would find there that he took off his bicycle clips. Eventually it was the room that drove him out. He caught two buses and was at Pagotes in the late afternoon.

He entered Tara's yard through the wide side gate of unpainted corrugated iron and went down the gravelled way to the garage and the cowpen. Nothing in this part of the yard seemed to have changed since he had first seen it. The plum tree was as desolate as ever; it bore fruit regularly but its grey branches were almost bare and looked dry and stiff and brittle. He no longer wondered what would be done with the heap of scrap metal, and he had given up the hope, which he had had as a boy, of seeing the rusting body of a motorcar reanimated and driven away. The mound of manured grass changed in size but remained where it always had been. For despite the cost and the trouble, and the multiplication of his business interests, Ajodha still kept two or three cows in his yard. They were his pets; he spent most of his free time in the cowpen, which he could never finish improving.

From the cowpen came the hiss of milk in a bucket and the mumble of conversation. It was Sunday; Ajodha would certainly be in the cowpen. Mr Biswas didn't look. He hurried to the back verandah, hoping to see Tara first and to catch her alone.

She was alone, except for the servant girl. She greeted him so warmly that he at once felt ashamed of his mission. His resolve to speak directly came to nothing, for when he asked how she was she replied at length and, instead of asking for money, he had to give sympathy. Indeed, she didn't look well. Her breathing had grown worse and she couldn't move about easily; her body had broadened and become slack; her hair had thinned; her eyes had lost their brightness.

The servant girl brought him a cup of tea and Tara followed the girl back to the kitchen.

The top shelves of the bookcase were still packed with the disintegrating volumes of *The Book of Comprehensive Knowledge*, for which Ajodha had not paid. The lower shelves contained magazines, motor manufacturers' catalogues and illustrated trilingual souvenir booklets of Indian films. The religious pictures on the walls were crowded out by calendars from the distributors of American and English motor vehicles, and an enormous framed photograph of an Indian actress.

Tara came back to the verandah and said that she hoped Mr Biswas would stay to dinner. He had intended to; apart from everything else, he liked their food. She sat down in Ajodha's rockingchair and asked after the children. He told her about the one that was coming. She asked about the Tulsis and he replied as briefly as he could. He knew that, though the two houses had little to do with one another, an antagonism existed between them. The Tulsis, who did *puja* every day and celebrated every Hindu festival, regarded Ajodha as a man who pursued wealth and comfort and modernity and had alienated himself from the faith. Ajodha and Tara simply thought the Tulsis squalid, and had always made it clear that they considered Mr Biswas's marriage into that house a calamity. It was doubly embarrassing to Mr Biswas to discuss the Tulsis with Tara, since despite his concern for his children he found it hard not to agree with her view, particularly when he was in her clean, uncrowded, comfortable house, waiting for a meal he knew would be good.

The cowman came from the pen, called to the girl in the kitchen and passed her the bucket of milk through the window. Then, at the standpipe in the yard he washed his wellingtons, took them off, washed his feet and hands and face.

Mr Biswas felt more and more reluctant to tell Tara what he had come for.

Then it was too late. Rabidat, Bhandat's younger son, came in, and Tara and Mr Biswas fell silent. As far as Tara and Ajodha were concerned, Rabidat was still a bachelor, though it was generally known that, like his brother Jagdat, he was living with a woman of another race and had some children, no one knew how many, by her. He was wearing sandals and brief khaki shorts; his tail-less shirt flapped loose, unbuttoned all the way down, the short sleeves rolled up almost to his armpits. It was as though, unable to hide his prognathous face, he wished to display the rest of himself as well. He had a superb body, well proportioned and well developed and not grossly muscular. He barely nodded to Mr Biswas and ignored Tara. When he sat sprawling on a chair, two thin folds of skin appeared about his middle; they were almost a disfigurement of his neatness. He sucked his teeth, took a film booklet from the bookcase and flicked through it, breathing loudly, his small eyes intent, his prognathous sneer more pronounced. He threw the booklet back on the bookcase and said, 'How is everything, Mohun?' Without waiting for an answer he shouted at the kitchen, 'Food, girl!' and clamped his mouth shut.

'Ooh! The married man!'

It was Ajodha, back from the cowpen.

Rabidat rearranged his legs.

Before Mr Biswas could reply, Ajodha stopped smiling and spoke to Rabidat about the behaviour of a certain lorry.

Rabidat shifted in his chair and sucked his teeth, not looking up.

Ajodha raised his voice querulously.

Rabidat explained awkwardly, sulkily, insolently. He seemed to be trying to bite the inside of his lower lip, and his voice, though deep, was blurred.

Abruptly Ajodha lost interest in the lorry and smiled mischievously at Mr Biswas.

Tara got up from the rockingchair and Ajodha sat in it, fanning his face and opening a shirt button to reveal a grey-haired chest. 'How many children has the married man got now? Seven, eight, a dozen?'

Rabidat smiled uneasily, got up and went to the kitchen.

Mr Biswas thought he would be brave and begin. 'Late last night,' he said, 'some 'larmist bring me a message that my mother was very sick. So I came to see her today and as I was here I thought I would come and see you.'

The servant girl brought a glass of milk for Ajodha. He received it reverentially, holding the glass as though any pressure might cause it to break. He said, 'Bring Mohun some. You know, Mohun, milk is a food in itself, especially when it is fresh like this.'

The milk was brought and drunk. Mr Biswas welcomed the pause. The absurd story he had just made up didn't sound convincing, and he hoped he would be allowed to drop it.

'And how was your mother?' Tara asked. 'I heard nothing.'

'Oh, she. She was all right. It was just some 'larmist, that
was all.'

Ajodha rocked gently. 'What about your job, Mohun?
Somehow I never felt you were made for a job in the fields.
Eh, Tara?'

'Well, as a matter of fact,' Mr Biswas said briskly, 'it was
that I wanted to talk to you about. You see, this is a steady
job –'

Ajodha said, 'Mohun, I don't think you are looking well
at all. Eh, Tara? Look at his face. And, eh –' He broke off with
a giggle and said in English, 'Look, look. He getting a punch.'
He stabbed at Mr Biswas's belly with a long sharp finger, and
when Mr Biswas winced Ajodha gave a little yelping laugh.
'Pap,' he said. 'Your belly soft like pap. Like a woman. All
you young people getting bellies these days.' He winked at
Mr Biswas; then, tilting back his head, he said loudly, 'Even
Rabidat got a punch.'

Tara gave a short, chesty laugh.

Rabidat came out of the kitchen, chewing, his mouth full,
and mumbled incomprehensibly.

Ajodha grimaced, 'Take your face back to the kitchen.
You know you make me ill when you talk with your mouth
full.'

Rabidat swallowed hurriedly. 'Punch?' he said, nibbling at
his lower lip. 'I got a punch?' He pulled his shirt off his shoulders, drew in his breath and the definitions of his abdominal
muscles became sharper. Above his sneering mouth his small
eyes glittered.

Smiling, Ajodha said, 'All right, Rabidat. Go back and eat.
I was only teasing.' The demonstration had pleased him; he
was as proud of Rabidat's body as of his own. 'Good food,'
he told Mr Biswas. 'And lots of exercise.' He threw back his
shoulders, stuck out his stomach, grabbed Mr Biswas's soft
hand with his firm, long fingers and said, 'Feel that. Come on,
feel it.' Mr Biswas didn't respond. Ajodha seized one of Mr
Biswas's fingers and pulled it hard against his stomach. Mr
Biswas felt his finger bend backwards; he wrenched it from
Ajodha's grasp. 'There,' Ajodha said. 'Hard as steel. You still
sleep with a pillow, I imagine?'

Surreptitiously rubbing his paining finger against its neighbour, Mr Biswas nodded.

'I never use a pillow. Nature didn't intend us to use pillows. Train your children from the start, Mohun. Don't let them use pillows. Ooh! *Four* children!' Ajodha gave another little yelp of laughter, jumped out of his chair, walked to the verandah half-wall and shouted irritably to someone outside. He had heard the cowman preparing to leave and was only bidding him good night; that was the voice he always used with his employees. The cowman replied and Ajodha returned to his chair. 'Married man!'

'Well, as I was saying,' Mr Biswas said, 'this job I have is steady. And I am beginning to build a little house.'

'O good, Mohun,' Tara said. 'Very good.'

'I don't know how you managed to live at Hanuman House,' Ajodha said. 'How many people live in that place?'

'About two hundred,' Mr Biswas said, and they all laughed. 'Now, this house is going to be a proper house –'

'You know what you should do, Mohun?' Ajodha said. 'You should take Sanatogen. Not one bottle. Take the full course. You don't get any benefit unless you take the full course.'

Tara nodded.

Rabidat came out of the kitchen again. 'What is this I hear about a house, Mohun? You build a house? Where you get all this money from?'

'He has been saving up,' Ajodha said impatiently. 'Not like you. You are going to end up living in a hole in the ground, Rabidat. I don't know what you do with your money.' It was only indirectly, like this, that Ajodha referred to Rabidat's outside life.

'Look. You!' Rabidat said. 'I wasn't born with money, you hear. And I don't have the scheming mind to make any. My father neither.' He was being provocative, since any mention of his father, like any mention of Mr Biswas's sister, was forbidden.

Ajodha frowned and rocked violently.

And Mr Biswas realized that the time to ask had gone for good.

Ajodha's look wasn't the one he assumed so easily, of worry and petulance, which meant nothing, though it filled his employees with dread. It was a look of anger.

Ignoring Ajodha and smiling at Mr Biswas, Rabidat asked, 'A dirt house?'

'No, man. Concrete pillars. Two bedrooms and a drawing-room. Galvanized roof and everything.'

But Rabidat wasn't listening.

'Tara!' Ajodha said. 'If I didn't take him out of the gutter, where would he be today? If I didn't feed him all that food' – rising so swiftly that the rockingchair shot backwards, he went up to Rabidat and held his biceps – 'do you think he would have these?'

*'Don't touch me!'* Rabidat bawled.

Mr Biswas jumped. Ajodha whipped away his hand.

'Don't touch me!' Tears sprang to Rabidat's small eyes. He closed them tightly, as if in great pain, lifted one foot high and brought it down with all his strength on the floor. 'You didn't make me. If you want to touch children, make them. What you want me to do with the food you feed me? What?'

Tara got up and passed her hand on Rabidat's back. 'All right, all right, Rabidat. It is time for you to go to the theatre.' One of his duties was to go to the cinema twice a day to check the takings.

Breathing hard, almost grunting, and chewing up his words into incomprehensible sounds, he went up the two steps that led from the back verandah to the main section of the house.

Ajodha pulled the rockingchair towards him, sat on it and began to rock briskly.

Tara smiled at Mr Biswas. 'I don't know what to do with them, Mohun.'

'Gratitude!' Ajodha said.

'Tell us about your house, Mohun,' Tara said.

'You take them out of a barrackroom and this is what you get.'

'House?' Mr Biswas said. 'Oh, is nothing really. A small little thing. Is for the children sake that I really building it.'

'We want to build over this house,' Tara said. 'But the trouble! The moment you want to put up anything good, so many forms, so many people's permission. When we built this house we had nothing like that. But I don't imagine you have that worry.'

'O no,' Mr Biswas said. 'No worry about that at all.'

With those light, precise motions on which he prided himself, Ajodha jumped out of his chair and went through the half-door into the yard.

'Those two,' Tara said. 'Always quarrelling. But they don't mean anything. Tomorrow they will be like father and son.'

They heard Ajodha in the cowpen abusing the absent cowman.

Jagdat, Rabidat's elder brother, came in and asked in his cheerful way, 'Something eating your husband, Aunt?' and chuckled.

Whenever Mr Biswas saw Jagdat he felt that Jagdat had just come from a funeral. Not only was his manner breezy; there was also his dress, which had never varied for many years: black shoes, black socks, dark blue serge trousers with a black leather belt, white shirt cuffs turned up above the wrist, and a gaudy tie: so that it seemed he had come back from a funeral, taken off his coat, undone his cuffs, replaced his black tie, and was generally making up for an afternoon of solemnity. His eyes were as small as Rabidat's, but livelier; his face was squarer; he laughed more often, showing rabbitlike teeth. With a hairy ringed hand he slapped Mr Biswas hard on the back, saying, 'The old Mohun, man!'

'The old Jagdat,' Mr Biswas said.

'Mohun is building a house,' Tara said.

'Has he come to invite us to the house-warming? We only see you at Christmas, man. You don't eat the rest of the year? Or is because of all the money you making?' And Jagdat roared with laughter.

Ajodha came back from the cowpen and he and Mr Biswas and Jagdat ate in the verandah. Tara ate by herself in the kitchen. Ajodha was silent and sullen, Jagdat subdued. The food was good but Mr Biswas ate without pleasure.

He had hoped that after the meal he would get Tara alone. But Ajodha remained rocking in the verandah and after a little Mr Biswas thought the time had come to leave. The girl had finished washing up in the kitchen, and the night silence made it seem later than it was.

Tara said he should take back some fruit for the children.

'Vitamin C,' Ajodha said, in his irritable voice. 'Give him lots of vitamin C, Tara.'

She obediently filled a bag with oranges.

Then Ajodha went inside.

As soon as he had gone Tara put some avocado pears into the bag, large purple-skinned ones such as, at Hanuman House, were set aside for Mrs Tulsi and the god. 'They will get ripe soon,' she said. 'The children will like them.'

He didn't want to explain where the children lived and where he lived. But he was glad he hadn't asked her for money.

'I am sorry your uncle was in such a temper,' she said. 'But it doesn't mean anything. The boys are being a little difficult. They want money from him all the time and you can't blame him for getting angry sometimes. They are spreading all sorts of stories about him, too. He doesn't say anything. But he knows.'

Mr Biswas went to say good-bye to Ajodha. His room was in darkness, the door was open, and Ajodha was lying on his pillowless bed with all his clothes on. Mr Biswas knocked lightly and there was no reply. The ledges on the walls were littered with papers. The room had only four pieces of furniture: the bed, a chair, a low chest of drawers and a black iron chest, the top of which was also covered with papers and magazines. Mr Biswas was about to go away when he heard Ajodha say gently, 'I am not asleep, Mohun. But these days I always rest after eating. You mustn't mind if I don't talk or get up.'

On the way to the Main Road to get a bus Mr Biswas was hailed by someone. It was Jagdat. He put his hand on Mr Biswas's shoulder and conspiratorially offered a cigarette. Ajodha forbade smoking and for Jagdat a cigarette was still an excitement.

Jagdat said breezily, 'You come to squeeze something out
of the old man, eh?'

'What? Me? I just come to see the old people, man.'

'That wasn't what the old man tell me.'

Jagdat waited, then clapped Mr Biswas on the back.

'But I didn't tell him anything.'

'The old Mohun, man. Trying out the old diplomatic tactic, eh. The old tic-tac-toe.'

'I wasn't trying out anything.'

'No, no. You mustn't think I look down on you for
trying. What else you think I doing every day? But the old
man sharp, boy. He could smell a thing like that before you
even start thinking about it. So what, eh? You still building
this house for the children sake?'

'You build one for yours?'

There was a sudden abatement of Jagdat's high spirits.
He stopped, half turned, as though about to go back, and
raising his voice, said angrily, 'So they spreading stories
about me, eh? To you?' He bawled, '*O God!* I going to go
back and knock out all their false teeth. *Mohun!* You hearing
me?'

The melodramatic flair seemed to run through the family.
Mr Biswas said, 'They didn't tell me anything. But don't forget that I know you since you was a boy. And if is still the old
Jagdat I imagine you have enough outside children now to
make up your own little school.'

Jagdat, still in the attitude of return, relaxed. They walked
on.

'Just four or five,' Jagdat said.

'How you mean, four or five?'

'Well, four.' Some of Jagdat's bounce had gone and when,
after some time, he spoke again, it was in an elegiac voice.
'Boy, I went to see my father last week. The man living in a
small concrete room in Henry Street in a ramshackle old
house full of creole people. And, and' – his voice was rising
again – 'that son of a bitch' – he was screaming – 'that son of
a bitch not doing a damn thing to help him.'

In lighted windows curtains were raised. Mr Biswas
plucked at Jagdat's sleeve.

Jagdat dropped his voice to one of melancholy piety. 'You remember the old man, Mohun?'

Mr Biswas remembered Bhandat well.

'His face,' Jagdat said, 'come small small.' He half-closed his small eyes and bunched the fingers of one hand raised in a gesture so delicate it might have been made by a pundit at a religious ceremony. 'O yes,' he went on, 'Ajodha always ready to give you vitamin A and vitamin B. But when it come to any real sort of help, don't go to him. Look. He employ a gardener one time. Old man, wearing rags, thin, sick, practically starving. Indian like you and me. Thirty cents a day. *Thirty* cents! Still, poor man can't do better, in all the hot sun the old man working. Doing his little weeding and hoeing. About three o'clock, sun hot like blazes, sweating, back aching as if it want to break, he ask for a cup of tea. Well, they give him a cup of tea. But at the end of the day they dock six cents off his pay.'

Mr Biswas said, 'You think they going to send me a bill for the food they give me?'

'Laugh if you want. But that is the way they treat poor people. My consolation is that they can't bribe God. God is good, boy.'

They were in the Main Road, not far from the shop where Mr Biswas had served under Bhandat. The shop was now owned by a Chinese and a large signboard proclaimed the fact.

The moment came to separate from Jagdat. But Mr Biswas was unwilling to leave him, to be alone, to get on the bus to go back through the night to Green Vale.

Jagdat said, 'The first boy bright like hell, you know.'

It was some seconds before Mr Biswas realized that Jagdat was talking about one of his celebrated illegitimate children. He saw anxiety in Jagdat's broad face, in the bright jumping little eyes.

'I glad,' Mr Biswas said. 'Now you could get him to read *That Body of Yours* to you.'

Jagdat laughed. 'The same old Mohun.'

There was no need to ask where Jagdat was going. He was going to his family. He too, then, lived a divided life.

'She does work in a office,' Jagdat said, anxious again.

Mr Biswas was impressed.

'Spanish,' Jagdat said.

Mr Biswas knew this was a euphemism for a red-skinned Negro. 'Too hot for me, man.'

'But faithful,' Jagdat said.

Knocked about on the wooden seat of the rackety rickety dim-lit bus, going past silent fields and past houses which were lightless and dead or bright and private, Mr Biswas no longer thought of the afternoon's mission, but of the night ahead.

Early next morning Mr Maclean turned up at the barracks and said he had put off other pressing work and was ready to go ahead with Mr Biswas's house. He was in his poor but respectable business clothes. His ironed shirt was darned with almost showy neatness; his khaki trousers were clean and sharply creased, but the khaki was old and would not keep the crease for long.

'You decide how much you want to start off with?'

'A hundred,' Mr Biswas said. 'More at the end of the month. No concrete pillars.'

'Is only a sort of fanciness. You watch. I will get you a crapaud that would last a lifetime. Wouldn't make no difference.'

'Once it neat.'

'Neat and nice,' Mr Maclean said. 'Well, I suppose I better start seeing about materials and labour.'

Materials came that afternoon. The crapaud pillars looked rough; they were not altogether round or altogether straight. But Mr Biswas was delighted by the new scantlings, and the new nails that came in several wrappings of newspaper. He took up handfuls of nails and let them fall again. The sound pleased him. 'Did not know nails was so heavy,' he said.

Mr Maclean had brought a tool-box which had his initials on the cover and was like a large wooden suitcase. It contained a saw with an old handle and a sharp, oiled blade; several chisels and drills; a spirit-level and a T square; a plane; a hammer and a mallet; wedges with smooth, fringed heads; a ball of old, white-stained twine; and a lump of chalk. His tools were like his clothes: old but cared-for. He built a rough work-bench out of the materials and assured Mr Biswas that all the material would be eventually released for the house and would suffer little damage. That was why, he explained in reply to another of Mr Biswas's queries, no nail had been driven right in.

The labour also came. The labour was a labourer named Edgar, a muscular, full-blooded Negro whose short khaki trousers were shaggy with patches, and whose vest, brown with dirt, was full of holes that had been distended by his powerful body into ellipses. Edgar cutlassed the site, leaving it a rich wet green.

When Mr Biswas returned from the fields he found the brushed site marked in white with the plan of the house. Holes for pillars had been indicated and Edgar was digging. Not far off Mr Maclean had constructed a frame which rested level on stones and answered wonderfully to the design he had drawn in his yard.

'Gallery, drawingroom, bedroom, bedroom,' Mr Biswas said, hopping over the spars. 'Gallery, bedroom, bedroom, drawingroom.'

The air smelled of sawdust. Sawdust had spilled rich red and cream on the grass and had been ground into the damp black earth by Edgar's bare feet and Mr Maclean's old, unshining working-boots.

Mr Maclean talked to Mr Biswas about the difficulties of labour.

'I try to get Sam,' he said. 'But he a little too erratic and don't-care. Edgar, now, does do the work of two men. The only trouble is, you got to keep a eye on him all the time. Look at him.'

Edgar was knee-deep in a hole and regularly throwing up spadefuls of black earth.

'You got to tell him to stop,' Mr Maclean said. 'Otherwise, he dig right through till he come out the other side. Well, boss, how about something to wet the job?' He made a drinking gesture. In the early days he had preferred to drink on the completion of a job; now he got his drink as soon as he could.

Mr Biswas nodded and Mr Maclean called, 'Edgar!'

Edgar went on digging.

Mr Maclean tapped his forehead. 'You see what I tell you?' He put two fingers in his mouth and whistled.

Edgar looked up and jumped out of his hole. Mr Maclean asked him to go to the rumshop and buy a nip of rum. Edgar ran to where his belongings were, seized a dusty, squashed and abbreviated felt hat, pressed it on his head and ran off. Some minutes later he came back, still running, one hand holding a bottle, the other holding down his hat.

Mr Maclean opened the bottle, said, 'To you and the house, boss,' and drank. He passed the bottle to Edgar, who said, 'To you and the house, mister boss,' and drank without wiping the bottle.

Mr Maclean required much space when he worked. Next day he built another frame and left it on the ground beside the frame of the floor. The new frame was of the back wall and Mr Biswas recognized the back door and the back window. Edgar finished digging the holes and set up three of the crapaud pillars, making them firm with stones taken from a heap left by the Public Works Department some distance away.

One thing puzzled Mr Biswas. The materials had cost nearly eighty-five dollars. That left fifteen dollars to be divided between Mr Maclean and Edgar for work which, Mr Maclean said, would take from eight to ten days. Yet they were both cheerful; though Mr Maclean had complained, in a whisper, about the cost of labour.

That afternoon, when Mr Maclean and Edgar left, Shama came.

'What is this I hear from Seth?'

He showed her the frames on the ground, the three erect pillars, the mounds of dirt.

'I suppose you use up every cent you had?'

'Every red cent,' Mr Biswas said. 'Gallery, drawingroom, bedroom, bedroom.'

Her pregnancy was beginning to be prominent. She puffed and fanned. 'Is all right for you. But what about me and the children?'

'What you mean? They going to be ashamed because their father building a house?'

'Because their father trying to set himself up in competition with people who have a lot more than him.'

He knew what was upsetting her. He could imagine the whisperings at the monkey house, the puss-puss here, the puss-puss there. He said, 'I know you want to spend all the days of your life in that big coal barrel called Hanuman House. But don't try to keep my children there.'

'Where you going to get the money to finish the house?'

'Don't you worry your head about that. If you did worry a little bit more and a little bit earlier, by now we might have a house.'

'You just gone and throw away your money. You *want* to be a pauper.'

'O God! Stop digging and digging at me like this!'

'Who digging? Look.' She pointed to Edgar's mounds of earth. 'You is the big digger.'

He gave an annoyed little laugh.

For some time they were silent. Then she said, 'You didn't even get a pundit or anything before you plant the first pillar.'

'Look. I get enough good luck the last time Hari come and bless the shop. Remember that.'

'I not going to live in that house or even step inside it if you don't get Hari to come and bless it.'

'If Hari come and bless it, it wouldn't surprise me if nobody at all even get a chance to live in it.'

But she couldn't undo the frames and the pillars, and in the end he agreed. She went back to Hanuman House with an urgent message for Hari, and next morning Mr Biswas told Mr Maclean to wait until Hari had done his business.

Hari came early, neither interested nor antagonistic, just constipatedly apathetic. He came in normal clothes, with his pundit's gear in a small cardboard suitcase. He bathed at one of the barrels behind the barracks, changed into a dhoti in Mr Biswas's room and went to the site with a brass jar, some mango leaves and other equipment.

Mr Maclean had got Edgar to clean out a hole. In his thin voice Hari whined out the prayers. Whining, he sprinkled

water into the hole with a mango leaf and dropped a penny
and some other things wrapped in another mango leaf.
Throughout the ceremony Mr Maclean stood up reverentially, his hat off.

Then Hari went back to the barracks, changed into trousers and shirt, and was off.

Mr Maclean looked surprised. 'That is all?' he asked. 'No
sharing-out of anything – food and thing – as other Indians
does do?'

'When the house finish,' Mr Biswas said.

Mr Maclean bore his disappointment well. 'Naturally. I
was forgetting.'

Edgar was putting a pillar into the consecrated hole.

Mr Biswas said to Mr Maclean, 'Is a waste of a good penny,
if you ask me.'

At the end of the week the house had begun to take shape.
The floor-frame had been put on, and the frames for the
walls; the roof was outlined. On Monday the back staircase
went up after Mr Maclean's work-bench had been dismantled
for its material.

Then Mr Maclean said, 'We going to come back when
you get some more materials.'

Every day Mr Biswas went to the site and examined the
skeleton of the house. The wooden pillars were not as bad as
he had feared. From a distance they looked straight and cylindrical, contrasting with the squareness of the rest of the
frame, and he decided that this was practically a style.

He had to get floorboards; he wanted pitchpine for that,
not the five inch width, which he thought common, but the
two and a half inch, which he had seen in some ceilings. He
had to get boards for the walls, broad boards, with
tongue-and-groove. And he had to get corrugated iron for
the roof, new sheets with blue triangles stamped on the silver,
so that they looked like sheets of an expensive stone rather
than iron.

At the end of the month he set aside fifteen of his twenty-five
dollars for the house. This was extravagant; he was eventually
left with ten.

At the end of the second month he could add only eight dollars.

Then Seth came up with an offer.

'The old lady have some galvanize in Ceylon,' he said. 'From the old brick-factory.'

The factory had been pulled down while Mr Biswas was living at The Chase.

'Five dollars,' Seth said. 'I don't know why I didn't think of it before.'

Mr Biswas went to Hanuman House.

'How is the house, brother-in-law?' Chinta asked.

'Why you asking? Hari bless it, and you know what does happen when Hari bless something.'

Anand and Savi followed Mr Biswas to the back, where everything was gritty with the chaff from the new rice-mill next door, and the iron sheets were stacked like a very old pack of cards against the fence. The sheets were of varying shapes, bent, warped and richly rusted, with corners curled into vicious-looking hooks, corrugations irregularly flattened out, and nail-holes everywhere, dangerous to the touch.

Anand said, 'Pa, you not going to use *that*?'

'You will make the house look like a shack,' Savi said.

'You want something to cover your house,' Seth said. 'When you are sheltering from the rain you don't run outside to look at what is sheltering you. Take it for three dollars.'

Mr Biswas thought again of the price of new corrugated iron, of the exposed frame of his house. 'All right,' he said. 'Send it.'

Anand, who had been displaying more and more energy since his misadventure at school, said, 'All *right*! Go ahead and buy it and put it on your old house. I don't care what it look like now.'

'Another little paddler,' Seth said.

But Mr Biswas felt as Anand. He too didn't care what the house looked like now.

When he got back to Green Vale he found Mr Maclean.

They were both embarrassed.

'I was doing a job in Swampland,' Mr Maclean said. 'I was just passing by here and I thought I would drop in.'

'I was going to come to see you the other day,' Mr Biswas said. 'But you know how it is. I got about eighteen dollars. No, fifteen. I just went to Arwacas to buy some galvanize for the roof.'

'Just in time too, boss. Otherwise all the money you did spend woulda waste.'

'Not new galvanize, you know. I mean, not brand-brand new.'

'The thing about galvanize is that you could always make it look nice. You go be surprised what a little bit of paint could do.'

'They have a few holes here and there. A few. Tiny tiny.'

'We could fix those up easy. Mastic cement. Not expensive, boss.'

Mr Biswas noted the change in Mr Maclean's tone.

'Boss, I know you want pitchpine for the floor. I know pitchpine nice. It does look nice and it does smell nice and it easy to keep clean. But you know it does burn easy. Easy, easy.'

'I was thinking the same thing,' Mr Biswas said. 'At *pujas* we always use pitchpine.' To burn the offerings in a quick, scented flame.

'Boss, I got some cedar planks. A man in Swampland offer me a whole pile of cedar for seven dollars. Seven dollars for a hundred and fifty foot of cedar is a real bargain.'

Mr Biswas hesitated. Of all wood cedar appealed to him least. The colour was pleasing but the smell was acrid and clinging. It was such a soft wood that a fingernail could mark it and splinters could be bitten off with teeth. To be strong it had to be thick; then its thickness made it look ungainly.

'Now, boss, I know they is only rough planks. But you know me. When I finish planing them they would be level level, and when I join them together you wouldn't be able to slip a sheet of bible-paper between them.'

'Seven dollars. That leave eight for you.' Mr Biswas meant it was little to pay for laying a floor and putting on a roof.

But Mr Maclean was offended. 'My labour,' he said.

The corrugated iron came that week-end on a lorry that also brought Anand and Savi and Shama.

Anand said, 'Aunt Sushila bawl off the men when they was loading the galvanize on the lorry.'

'She tell them to throw them down hard, eh?' Mr Biswas said. 'Is that what she tell them? She did want them to dent them up more, eh? Don't frighten to tell me.'

'No, no. She say they wasn't working fast enough.'

Mr Biswas examined the sheets as they were unloaded, looking for bumps and dents he could attribute to Sushila's maliciousness. Whenever he saw a crack in the rust he stopped the loaders.

'Look at this. Which one of you was responsible for this? You know, I mad enough to get Mr Seth to dock your money.' That word 'dock', so official and ominous, he had got from Jagdat.

Stacked on the grass, the sheets made the site look like an abandoned lot. No corrugation of one sheet fitted into the corrugation of any other; the pile rose high and shaky and awkward.

Mr Maclean said, 'I could straighten them out with the hammer. Now, about the rafters, boss.'

Mr Biswas had forgotten about those.

'Now, boss, you must look at it this way. The rafters don't show from the outside. Only from the inside. And even then, when you get a ceiling you could hide the rafters. So I think it would be better and it would cost you nothing if you get tree-branches. When you trim them they does make first-class rafters.'

And when Mr Maclean set to work, he worked alone. Mr Biswas never saw Edgar again and never asked about him.

Mr Maclean went to a ''bandon', brought back tree-branches and trimmed them into rafters. He cut notches in the rafters wherever they were to rest on the main frame, and nailed them on. They looked solid. He used thinner branches, limber, irregular and recalcitrant, for cross-rafters. They looked shaky and reminded Mr Biswas of the rafters of a dirt-and-grass hut.

Then the corrugated iron was nailed on. The sheets were dangerous to handle and the rafters shook under Mr

Maclean's weight and the blows of his hammer. The weeds below and the frame became covered with rust. When Mr Maclean had packed his tools into his wooden suitcase and gone home for the day, it was a pleasure to Mr Biswas to stand below the roof and be in shade where only the day before, only that morning, there had been openness.

As the sheets went up, and they were enough to cover all the rooms except the gallery, the house no longer looked so drab and un-begun. Mr Maclean was right: the sheets did hide the branch-rafters. But every hole in the roof glittered like a star.

Mr Maclean said, 'I did mention a thing called mastic cement. But that was before I did see the galvanize. You would spend as much on mastic cement as on five-six sheets of new galvanize.'

'So what? I just got to sit down in my new house and get wet?'

'Where there's a will there's a way, as the people does say. Pitch. You did think about that? A lot of people does use pitch.'

They got the pitch free, from a neglected part of the road where asphalt was laid on, without gravel, in lavish lumps. Mr Maclean put small stones over the holes in the roof and sealed them down with pitch. He ran sealings of pitch along the edges of the sheets and down the cracks. It was a slow, long job, and when he was finished the roof was curiously patterned in black with many rough lines, straight down, angularly jagged across, and freaked and blobbed and gouted all over with pitch, above the confused red, rust, brown, saffron, grey and silver of the old sheets.

But it worked. When it rained, as it was beginning to do now every afternoon, the ground below the roof remained dry. Poultry from the barrackyard and other places came to shelter and stayed to dig the earth into dust.

The cedar floorboards came, rough and bristly, and impregnated the site with their smell. When Mr Maclean planed them they seemed to acquire a richer colour. He fitted them together as neatly as he had said, nailing them down with headless nails and filling in the holes at the top with wax mixed with sawdust which dried hard and could scarcely be distinguished from the wood. The back bedroom was floored, and part of the drawingroom, so that, with care, it was possible to walk straight up to the bedroom.

Then Mr Maclean said, 'When you get more materials you must let me know.'

He had worked for a fortnight for eight dollars.

Perhaps he didn't pay seven dollars for the cedar, Mr Biswas thought. Only five or six.

The house now became a playground for the children of the barracks. They climbed and they jumped; many took serious falls but, being barrack children, came to little harm. They nailed nails into the crapaud pillars and the cedar floor; they bent nails for no purpose; they flattened them to make knives. They left small muddy footprints on the floor and on the crossbars of the frame; the mud dried and the floor became dusty. The children drove out the poultry and Mr Biswas tried to drive out the children.

'You blasted little bitches! Let me catch one of you and see if I don't cut his foot off.'

As the sugarcane grew taller the dispossessed labourers grew surlier, and Mr Biswas began to receive threats, delivered as friendly warnings.

Seth, who had often spoken of the treachery and dangerousness of the labourers, now only said, 'Don't let them frighten you.'

But Mr Biswas knew of the many killings in Indian districts, so well planned that few reached the courts. He knew of the feuds between villages and between families, conducted with courage, ingenuity and loyalty by those same labourers who, as wage-earners, were obsequious and negligible.

He decided to take precautions. He slept with a cutlass and a *poui* stick, one of his father's, at the side of his bed. And from Mrs Seeung, the Chinese café-owner at Arwacas, he got a puppy, a hairy brown and white thing of indeterminate breed. The first night at the barracks the puppy whined at being left outside, scratched at the door, fell off the step and whined until he was taken in. When Mr Biswas woke up next morning he found the puppy in bed beside him, lying quite still, its eyes open. At Mr Biswas's first gesture, which was one of surprise, the puppy jumped to the floor.

He called the puppy Tarzan, to prepare it for its duties. But Tarzan turned out to be friendly and inquisitive, and a terror only to the poultry. 'The hens stop laying because of your dog,' the poultry owners complained, and it looked true enough, for Tarzan often had pieces of feather stuck in the corners of his mouth, and he was continually bringing trophies of feathers to the room. Then one day Tarzan ate an egg and immediately developed a taste for eggs. The hens laid their eggs in bush, in places which they thought were secret. Tarzan soon got to know these places as well as the owners of the hens and he often came back to the barracks with his mouth yellow and sticky with egg. The owners of the hens took their revenge. One afternoon Mr Biswas found Tarzan's muzzle smeared with fowl droppings, and Tarzan in great misery at this novel and continuing discomfort.

The placards in Mr Biswas's room increased. He worked more slowly on them now, using black and red estate ink and pencils of many colours. He filled the blank space with difficult decorations and his letters became intricate and ornamented.

Thinking it would help him if he read novels, he bought a number of the cheap Reader's Library editions. The covers were dark purple with gold lettering and decorations. In the stall at Arwacas they had looked attractive, but in his room he could scarcely bear to touch them. The gilt stuck to his fingers and the covers reminded him of funeral palls and of those undertakers' horses that were draped with the colours of death every day.

The sun shone and the rain fell. The roof didn't leak. But the asphalt began to melt and hung limply down: a legion of slim, black, growing snakes. Occasionally they fell, and, falling, curled and died.

Late one night, when he had put out the oil lamp and was in bed, he heard footsteps outside his room.

He lay still, listening. Then he jumped out of bed, grabbed his stick and deliberately knocked against the kitchen safe and table and Shama's dressingtable. He stood at the side of the door and violently pushed out the top half, his body protected by the lower half.

He saw nothing but the night, the still, colourless barrack-yard, the dead trees black against the moonlit sky. Two rooms away a light was burning: someone was out, or a child was ill.

Then, making a lapping, happy sound, Tarzan was on the step, wagging his tail so hard it struck against the lower half of the door.

He let him in and stroked him. His coat was damp.

Tarzan, overjoyed at the attention, stuck his muzzle against Mr Biswas's face.

'Egg!'

For a second Tarzan hesitated. No threat appearing, he re-doubled his tail-wagging, continually shifting his hind legs.

Mr Biswas embraced him.

After that he always slept with his oil lamp on.

He began to fear that his house might be burned down. He went to bed with an added anxiety; every morning he opened his side window as soon as he got up, looking past the trees for signs of destruction; in the fields he worried about it. But the house always stood: the variegated roof, the frames, the crapaud pillars, the wooden staircase.

When Shama came he told her of his fears.

She said, 'I don't think they would worry about it.'

And he regretted telling her, for when Seth came he said, 'So you frighten they burn it down, eh? Don't worry. They not so idle.'

Mr Maclean came twice and went away.

And every day the rain fell, the sun blazed, the house became greyer, the sawdust, once fresh and aromatic, became part of the earth, the asphalt snakes hanging from the roof grew longer, and many more died, and Mr Biswas worked more and more elaborate messages of comfort for his walls with a steady, unthinking hand, and a mind in turmoil.

Then one evening a great calm settled on him, and he made a decision. He had for too long regarded situations as temporary; henceforth he would look upon every stretch of time, however short, as precious. Time would never be dismissed again. No action would merely lead to another; every action was a part of his life which could not be recalled; therefore thought had to be given to every action: the opening of a matchbox, the striking of a match. Slowly, then, as though unused to his limbs, and concentrating hard, he had his evening bath, cooked his meal, ate it, washed up, and settled down in his rockingchair to pass – no, to use, to enjoy, to live – the evening. The house was unimportant. The evening, in this room, was all that mattered.

And so great was his assurance that he did something he had not done for weeks. He took down the Reader's Library edition of *The Hunchback of Notre Dame*. He passed his hands over the cover; deliberately he opened the book, broke the spine in a few places, destroying it completely in one place, and, pulling up his legs on to the chair so that he was huddled and cosy, and smacking his lips, which was not one of his habits, he began to read.

His mind was clear. He had pushed everything apart from the Victor Hugo to the boundaries. He had made a clearing in the bush: that was the picture he gave himself of his mind: for his mind had become quite separate from the rest of himself.

The image changed. It was no longer a forest, but a billowing black cloud. Unless he was careful the cloud would funnel into his head. He felt it pressing on his head. He didn't want to look up.

Surely it was only a trick of the oil lamp, which stood directly in front of him on the table?

He huddled a little more on the chair and smacked his lips again.

Then he was so afraid that he almost cried out.

Why should he be afraid? Of whom? Esmeralda? Quasimodo? The goat? The crowd?

People. He could hear them next door and all down the barracks. No road was without them, no house. They were in the newspapers on the wall, in the photographs, in the simple drawings in advertisements. They were in the book he was holding. They were in all books. He tried to think of landscapes without people: sand and sand and sand, without the 'oses' Lal had spoken about; vast white plateaux, with himself safely alone, a speck in the centre.

Was he afraid of real people?

He must experiment. But why? He had spent all his life among people without even thinking that he might be afraid of them. He had faced people across a rumshop counter; he had gone to school; he had walked down crowded main roads on market day.

Why now? Why so suddenly?

His whole past became a miracle of calm and courage.

His fingers were dusted with gilt from the pall-like cover of the book. As he studied them the clearing became over-grown again and the black cloud billowed in. How heavy! How dark!

He put his feet down and sat still, staring at the lamp, seeing nothing. The darkness filled his head. All his life had been good until now. And he had never known. He had spoiled it all by worry and fear. About a rotting house, the threats of illiterate labourers.

Now he would never more be able to go among people.

He surrendered to the darkness.

When he roused himself he opened the top half of the door. He saw no one. The barracks had gone to sleep. He would have to wait until morning to find out whether he was really afraid.

In the morning he had a full minute of lucidity. He re-membered that something had nagged and exhausted him the previous evening. Then, still in bed, he remembered, and the anguish returned. He got up. The bedsheet looked tormented. The mattress was exposed in places and he could smell the dingy old coconut-fibre. Slowly and carefully, like his actions the night before, his thoughts came, and he framed each thought in a complete sentence. He thought: 'The bed is a mess. Therefore I slept badly. I must have been afraid all through the night. Therefore the fear is still with me.'

Outside, beyond the closed window, the light breaking through the chinks and fanning out in dust-shot rays, was the world. Outside there were people.

He spoke aloud some of the words of comfort that hung on the walls. Then, trying to feel them as deeply as he could, he closed his eyes and spoke them again slowly, syllable by syllable. Then he pretended to write the words on his head with his finger.

Then he prayed.

But even in prayer he found images of people, and his prayers were perverted.

He dressed and opened the top half of the door.

Tarzan was waiting.

'You are glad to see me,' he thought. 'You are an animal and think that because I have a head and hands and look as I did yesterday I am a man. I am deceiving you. I am not whole.'

Tarzan wagged his tail.

He opened the lower half of the door.

People!

Fear seized him and hurt like a pain.

Tarzan jumped upon him, egg-stained, shining-eyed.

Grieving, he stroked him. 'I enjoyed this yesterday and the day before. I was whole then.'

Already yesterday, last night, was as remote as childhood. And mixed with his fear was this grief for a happy life never enjoyed and now lost.

He set about doing the things he did every morning. At the beginning of every action he forgot his pain: split seconds of freedom, relished only after they had gone. Breaking the hibiscus twig, for instance, as he did every morning, to brush his teeth with one of the crushed ends, he automatically looked past the trees to see whether his house had been destroyed during the night. Then he remembered how unimportant the house had become.

Bravely, exposing himself to menace, he stripped to bath at the waterbarrel.

The labourers were up. He heard the morning sounds: the hawking, spitting, the fanning of coal-pots, the hissing of fryingpans, the fresh, brisk morning talk. Negligible, nondescript people yesterday, each now had to be considered individually.

He looked at them and checked.

Fear.

The sun was coming up, lighting the dew on the grass, the roof, the trees: a cool sun, a pleasant time of day.

As with actions, so with people. Meeting them, he began to speak as though it was yesterday. Then the questioning came, and the inevitable answer: another relationship spoiled, another piece of the present destroyed.

The day which had begun, for that minute while he was still in bed, as a normal, happy day, was ending with him in an exhausting frenzy of questioning. He looked, he questioned, he was afraid. Then he questioned again. The process was taking a fraction of a second.

By the afternoon, however, he had made some progress. He was not afraid of children. They filled him only with grief. So much that was good and beautiful, from which he was now forever barred, awaited them.

He went to his room, lay down on the bed and forced himself to cry for all his lost happiness.

There was nothing he could do. The questioning went on ceaselessly. One photograph after another, one drawing after another, one story after another. He tried not to look at the newspapers on the wall, but always he had to check, always he was afraid, and then always he became uncertain again.

In the end the futility of lying on the bed caused him to rise and make another of those decisions he had been making all day: decisions to ignore, to behave normally, little decisions, little gestures of defiance that were soon forgotten.

He decided to cycle to Hanuman House.

Every man and woman he saw, even at a distance, gave him a twist of panic. But he had already grown used to that; it had become part of the pain of living. Then, as he cycled, he discovered a new depth to this pain. Every object he had not seen for twenty-four hours was part of his whole and happy past. Everything he now saw became sullied by his fear, every field, every house, every tree, every turn in the road, every bump and subsidence. So that, by merely looking at the

world, he was progressively destroying his present and his
past.

And there were some things he wanted to leave untouched. It was bad enough to deceive Tarzan. He didn't
want to deceive Anand and Savi. He turned and cycled back,
past the fields whose terror was already familiar, to Green Vale.

It occurred to him that by repeating as far as he could all
his actions of the previous night he might somehow exorcize
the thing that had fallen on him. So, with a deliberation that
was like the deliberation of the day before, he bathed,
cooked, ate, then sat down and opened *Notre Dame*.

But the reading only brought back the memory of the previous night, the discovery of fear, and left his hands dusted
with gilt.

Every morning the period of lucidity lessened. The bedsheet, examined every morning, always testified to a tormented night. Between the beginning of a routine action and
the questioning the time of calm grew less. Between the
meeting of a familiar person and the questioning there was
less and less of ease. Until there was no lucidity at all, and all
action was irrelevant and futile.

But it was always better to be out among real people than
to be in his room with the newspapers and his imaginings.
And though he continued to solace himself with visions of
deserted landscapes of sand and snow, his anguish became especially acute on Sunday afternoons, when fields and roads
were empty and everything was still.

Continually he looked for some sign that the corruption
which had come without warning upon him had secretly
gone away again. Examining the bedsheet was one thing.
Looking at his fingernails was the other. They were invariably
bitten down; but sometimes he saw a thin white rim on one
nail, and though these rims never lasted, he took their appearance to mean that release was near.

Then, biting his nails one evening, he broke off a piece of
a tooth. He took the piece out of his mouth and placed it on
his palm. It was yellow and quite dead, quite unimportant: he
could hardly recognize it as part of a tooth: if it were dropped
on the ground it would never be found: a part of himself that

would never grow again. He thought he would keep it. Then he walked to the window and threw it out.

One Saturday Seth said, while they were by the unfinished house, 'What's the matter, Mohun? You are the colour of this.' He placed his large hand on one of the grey uprights.

And Mr Maclean called. Someone he knew had offered him some timber at a bargain price. It would be enough to wall one room.

They went to look at the house. Mr Maclean saw the asphalt hanging from the roof but said nothing about it. The floorboards in the back bedroom had begun to shrink, cracking and cambering. Mr Maclean said, 'The man did say that the wood was cured. But cedar is a damn funny wood. It does never cure at all.'

The new timber was bought. It was cedar.

'No tongue-and-groove,' Mr Maclean said.

Mr Biswas said nothing.

Mr Maclean understood. He had seen this apathy overcome the builders of houses again and again.

The back bedroom was walled. The door to the partially floored drawingroom was built and hung. The door to the non-existent front bedroom was built and nailed into the doorway: 'To prevent accident,' Mr Maclean said, 'in case you want to move in right away.' Mr Biswas had wanted doors with panels; he got planks of cedar nailed to two cross bars. The window was built in the same fashion and hung; the new black bolts gleamed on the new wood.

'It coming along nice,' Mr Maclean said.

Into Mr Biswas's busy, exhausted mind came the thought: 'Hari blessed it. Shama made him bless it. They gave the galvanized iron and they blessed it.'

His sleep was broken by dreams. He was in the Tulsi Store. There were crowds everywhere. Two thick black threads were chasing him. As he cycled to Green Vale the threads lengthened. One thread turned pure white; the black thread became thicker and thicker, purple-black and monstrously long. It was a rubbery black snake; it developed a comic face; it found the chase funny and said so to the white thread, now also a snake.

When he passed the house and saw the black snakes hanging from the roof, he touched a crapaud pillar and said, 'Hari blessed it.' He remembered the suitcase, the whining prayers, the sprinkling with the mango leaf, the dropping of the penny. 'Hari blessed it.'

He was on a hill, a bare, brown-green hill. It was hot but the wind was cool and blew his hair. A woman was at the foot of the hill. She was crying and coming to him for help. He felt her pain but didn't want to be seen. What help could he give? And the woman – Shama, Anand, Savi, his mother – kept coming up the hill. He heard her sobs and wanted to cry to her to go away.

Tarzan was whining outside his door.

One of his paws had been damaged.

'You like eggs too much.'

Then he remembered the dispossessed labourers.

Some nights later he was awakened by barking and shouts.

'Driver! Driver!'

He opened the top half of the door.

'They set fire to Dookinan land,' the watchman said.

He put on his clothes and hurried to the spot, followed by excited labourers.

There was no great danger or damage. Dookinan's plot was small and was separated from the other fields by a trace and a ditch. Mr Biswas ordered the boundary canes of the adjoining fields to be cut, and the labourers, though disappointed at the blaze, which from a distance had promised much, worked with zest. The firelight lit up their bodies and kept away the chill.

The tall red and yellow flames shrank; the trash smouldered, red and black, crackled and collapsed, uncovering the red heart of the fire, quickly cooling to black and grey. Glowing scraps rose, twinkling redly, blackened and diminished. At the roots the canes glowed like charcoal; in places it was as if the earth itself had caught fire. The labourers beat the roots and the trash with sticks; ash floated up; smoke turned from grey to white, and thinned.

Only then, when the danger had disappeared, Mr Biswas realized that for more than an hour he had not questioned himself.

Instantly the questionings, the fear, came.

When the labourers returned to the barracks their chatter lasted a short time, and he was left alone.

But the hour had proved one thing. He was going to get better soon.

It was the first of many disappointments. In time he came to disregard these periods of freedom, just as he no longer expected to wake up one morning and find himself whole again.

At the beginning of the Christmas school holidays, when the sugarcane was in arrow once more and the Christmas shop-signs were going up at Arwacas, Shama sent word by Seth that she was bringing the children to Green Vale for a few days.

Mr Biswas waited for them with dread. On the day they were to arrive he began to wish for some accident that would prevent their coming. But he knew there would be no accident. If anything was to happen he had to act. He decided that he had to get rid of Anand and Savi and himself, in such a way that the children would never know who had killed them. All morning he was possessed of visions in which he cutlassed, poisoned, strangled, burned, Anand and Savi; so that even before they came his relationship with them had been perverted. About Myna and Shama he didn't care; he didn't want to kill them.

They came. At once his designs became insubstantial and absurd. He felt only resignation and a great fatigue. And the deception and especial pain he had wished to avoid began. Even while he allowed himself to be touched and kissed by Anand and Savi he was questioning himself about them, looking for the fear, and wondering whether they had seen the deception and could tell what was going on in his mind.

Of Shama he was not afraid; only envious, for her unthinking assurance. Then almost immediately he began to hate her. Her pregnancy was grotesque; he hated the way she sat down; when she ate he listened for the noises she made; he hated the way she fussed and clucked over the children; he hated it when she puffed and fanned and sweated in her pregnant way; he was nauseated by the frills and embroidery and other ornamentation on her clothes.

Shama, Savi and Myna slept on bedding on the floor. Anand slept with Mr Biswas on the fourposter. Dreading the boy's touch, Mr Biswas built a bank of pillows between Anand and himself.

His fatigue deepened. The next day, Sunday, he scarcely got out of bed. Whereas before he felt he had to be out of the room, now he didn't wish to leave it. He said he was sick and found it easy to simulate the symptoms of malaria.

When Seth came Mr Biswas told him, 'Is ague, I think.'

After a week his fatigue hadn't left him. Sitting up in bed he made kites and toy-carts for Anand and built a chest-of-drawers with matchboxes for Savi. The longer he stayed in the room the less he wanted to leave it. He became constipated. Yet from time to time he had to go outside; then he came back hurriedly, anxiously, relaxing only when he was on the bed again.

He continued to observe Shama closely, with suspicion, hatred and nausea. He never spoke to her directly, but through one of the children; and it was some time before Shama realized this.

As he was lying in bed one morning she came and placed her palm, then the back of her hand, on his forehead. The action offended him, flattered him, and made him uneasy. She had been cutting vegetables and he couldn't bear their smell on her hand.

'No fever,' she said.

She undid his shirt and put her hand, large and dark and foreign, on his pale, soft chest.

He wanted to scream.

He said, 'No, I not fat enough yet. You got to put me back and feed me some more. Here, why don't you just feel my finger?'

She took her hand away. 'Something on your mind, man?'

'Something on your mind?' he mimicked. 'Something in my mind and you know what it is.' He was violently angry; never before had he been so disgusted by her. Yet he wished her to remain there. Half hoping she would take him seriously, half hoping only to amuse and bewilder her, he said in his quick, high-pitched voice, 'Something in my mind all right. Clouds. Lots of little black clouds.'

'What you say?'

'Is a funny thing. You ever notice that when you insult people or tell them the truth they always pretend not to hear you the first time?'

'Is my own fault for meddling in what is not my business. I don't know why I come here for. If it wasn't for the children –'

'So all-you send Hari with his little black box, eh? All-you must think I look like a real fool.'

'Black box?'

'You see what I mean? You didn't hear the first time.'

'Look, I just don't have the time to stand up here talking to you like this, you hear. I wish you had a real fever. That would stop your mouth.'

He was beginning to enjoy the argument. 'I *know* you want me to get a real fever. I know all-you want to see me dead. And then see the old she-fox crying, the little gods laughing, you crying – dressed up like hell to boot. Nice, eh? I *know* that is what all-you want.'

'Dress-up and powder-up? Me? On what you give me?'

Abruptly Mr Biswas went cold with fear.

Seth and the land and the corrugated iron; Hari and the black box; the blessing; and now, since Shama had come, this fatigue.

He was dying.

They were killing him. He would just remain in this room and die.

She was in the kitchen area, cooing to the baby in the hammock.

'Get out!'

Shama looked up.

He jumped out of bed and grabbed the walking-stick. He was cold all over. His heart beat fast and painfully.

Shama climbed up the step to the room.

'Get out! Don't come inside. Don't touch me!'

Myna was crying.

'Man,' Shama said.

'Don't come into this room. Don't set foot in it again.' He waved the stick. He moved to the window and, looking at her, waving the stick, began to draw the bolt. 'Don't touch me,' he bawled, and there were sobs mixed with his words.

She blocked the door.

But he had thought of the window. He pushed it open. It swung out shakily. Light came into the room and fresh air mingled with the musty smell of old boards and newspapers – he had forgotten how musty they smelled. Beyond the flat barrackyard he saw the trees that lined the road and screened his house.

Shama walked towards him.

He began screaming and crying. He pressed his palms on the window-sill and tried to hoist himself up, looking back at her, the stick now useless as a weapon of defence since his hands were occupied.

'What are you doing?' she said in Hindi. 'Look, you will damage yourself.'

He was aware of Tarzan, Savi and Anand below the window. Tarzan was wagging his tail, barking and leaping up against the wall.

Shama came closer.

He was on the sill.

'O God!' he cried, winding his head up and down. 'Go away.'

She was near enough to touch him.

He kicked at her.

She gave a yelp of pain.

He saw, too late, that he had kicked her on the belly.

The women from the barracks rushed up when they heard Shama cry out, and helped her from the room.

Savi and Anand came round to the kitchen area in front. Tarzan ran in puzzlement between them and the women and Mr Biswas.

'Pack up your clothes and go home,' Dookhnee, one of the barrack-women, said. She had often been beaten and had witnessed many wife-beatings; they made all women sisters.

Savi went into the room fearfully and, not looking at her father, started to pack clothes into a suitcase.

Mr Biswas stared and shouted, 'Take your children and go away. Go away!'

Shama, surrounded by the barrack-women, called, 'Anand, pack up your clothes quick.'

Mr Biswas jumped down from the sill.

'*No!*' he said. 'Anand is not going with you. Take your girl children and go.' He didn't know why he had said that. Savi was the only child he knew, yet he had gone out of his way to hurt her; and he didn't know whether he wanted Anand to stay. Perhaps he had spoken only because Shama had mentioned the name.

'Anand,' Shama said, 'Go and pack your clothes.'

Dookhnee said, 'Yes, go and pack your clothes.'

And many of the women said, 'Go, boy.'

'He is not going with you to that house,' Mr Biswas said.

Anand remained where he was, in the kitchen area, stroking Tarzan, not looking at Mr Biswas or the women.

Savi came out of the room with a suitcase and a pair of shoes. She dusted her feet and buckled on a shoe.

Shama, only now beginning to cry, said in Hindi, 'Savi, I have told you many times to wash your feet before putting on your shoes.'

'All right, Ma. I will go and wash them.'

'Don't bother this time,' Dookhnee said.

The women said, 'No, don't bother.'

Savi buckled on the other shoe.

Shama said, 'Anand, do you want to come with me, or do you want to stay with your father?'

Mr Biswas, the stick in his hand, looked at Anand.

Anand continued to stroke Tarzan, whose head was now upturned, his eyes partly closed.

Mr Biswas ran to the green table and awkwardly pulled out the drawer. He took the long box of crayons he used for his placards and held it to Anand. He shook the box; the crayons rattled.

Savi said, 'Come, Anand boy. Go and get your clothes.'

Still stroking Tarzan, Anand said, 'I staying with Pa.' His voice was low and irritable.

'Anand!' Savi said.

'Don't beg him,' Shama said, in control of herself again. 'He is a man and knows what he is doing.'

'Boy,' Dookhnee said. 'Your mother.'

Anand said nothing.

Shama got up and the circle of women around her widened. She took Myna, Savi took the suitcase, and they walked along the path, muddy between sparse and stubborn grass, to the road, scattering the hens and chickens before them. Tarzan followed, and was diverted by the chickens. When he was pecked by an angry hen he looked for Shama and Savi and Myna. They had disappeared. He trotted back to the barracks and Anand.

Mr Biswas opened the box and showed Anand the sharpened crayons. 'Take them. They are yours. You can do what you like with them.'

Anand shook his head.

'You don't want them?'

Tarzan, between Anand's legs, held up his head to be stroked, closing his eyes in anticipation.

'What do you want then?'

Anand shook his head. Tarzan shook his.

'Why did you stay then?'

Anand looked exasperated.

'Why?'

'Because –' The word came out thin, explosive, charged with anger, at himself and his father. 'Because they was going to leave you alone.'

For the rest of that day they hardly spoke.

His instinct had been right. As soon as Shama had gone his fatigue left him. He became restless again, and almost welcomed the familiar constricted turmoil in his mind. He returned to the fields, taking Anand with him on the first day. Anand, dusty, itching, scorched by the sun and cut by sharp grass, refused to go again, and thereafter remained at the barracks with Tarzan.

He made more toys for Anand. A round tin-lid loosely nailed to a rod provided something that rolled when pushed and gave Anand a deep satisfaction. At night they drew imaginary scenes: snow-covered mountains and fir trees, red-hulled yachts in a blue sea below a clear sky, roads winding between well-kept forests to green mountains in the distance. They also talked.

'Who is your father?'

'You.'

'Wrong. I am *not* your father. God is your father.'

'Oh. And what about you?'

'I am just somebody. Nobody at all. I am just a man you know.'

He showed Anand how to mix colours. He taught him that red and yellow made orange, blue and yellow green.

'Oh. That is why the leaves turn yellow?'

'Not exactly.'

'Well, look then. Suppose I take a leaf and wash it and wash it and wash it, it will turn yellow or blue?'

'Not really. The leaf is God's work. You see?'

'No.'

'Your trouble is that you don't really believe. There was a man like you one time. He wanted to mock a man like me. So one day, when the man like me was sleeping, this other man drop an orange in his lap, thinking, "I bet the damn fool going to wake up and say that God drop the orange." So the other man woke up and began eating the orange. And this man come up and say, "I suppose God give you that orange." "Yes," the other man said. "Well, let me tell you. Is not God. Is me." "Well," the other man said, "I prayed for an orange while I was asleep." '

Anand was impressed.

'Now, look,' Mr Biswas said. 'See this matchbox. You see me holding it in my hand. Oops! It fall down. Why?'

'You leggo, that's why.'

'Not that at all. It fall down because of gravity. The law of gravity. They not teaching you children anything at all these days.'

He talked to Anand about people called Coppernickus and Galilyo. And it gave him a thrill to be the first to inform Anand that the world was round and moved about the sun.

'Remember Galilyo. Always stick up for yourself.'

He was glad that Anand was interested. It was the week before Christmas and he was fearing the result of Seth's visit.

He told Anand, 'On Saturday we are going to make a compass.'

And on Saturday Seth said, 'Why you don't come home, Anand boy? Come home and hang up your stocking. What you doing here with your father?'

'He is not my father. It just look to you that he is my father.'

Seth evaded the theological issue. 'They going to make cake and icecream, boy.'

Mr Biswas said, 'Remember Galilyo.'

Anand stayed.

Using the batteries of his electric torch Mr Biswas magnetized a needle and stuck it on a disc of paper; in the centre of the disc he inserted a cap of paper and rested the cap on the head of a pin.

'Where the eye of the needle points, that is north.'

They played with that until the needle lost its magnetism.

Sometimes Mr Biswas said he had ague. Then, wrapped up tightly and shivering, he made Anand recite Hindi hymns after him. And at these times, though nothing was said, Anand became affected by his father's fear and repeated the hymns like charms. The barrackroom, its door and window closed, its edges in darkness, became cavernous and full of menace, and Anand longed for morning.

But there were compensations.

'Today,' Mr Biswas said, 'I am going to show you something about a thing called centrifugal force. Go and get the bucket outside and full it up so high with water.'

Anand brought the water.

'Not enough space here really,' Mr Biswas said.

'Why you don't go outside?'

Mr Biswas didn't listen. 'Got to give it a good swing.' He swung.

The water splashed on the bed, the walls, the floor.

'The bucket was too heavy. Go and get one of the small blue pots from the kitchen. Full that with some water.'

And the second time it worked.

They made an electric buzzer, using the torch batteries, a piece of tin and a nail, a rusty new nail, one of those Mr Maclean had brought in newspaper on the afternoon Edgar had brushed the site for the house.

There were many reasons why Mr Biswas moved from the barracks to the finished room of his house. It was a positive action; it was a confident, defiant gesture; there was his continuing unease at hearing people moving about the barracks. And there was his hope that living in a new house in the new year might bring about a new state of mind. He would not have moved if he had been alone, for he feared solitude more than people. But, with Anand, he had enough company.

Tarzan found a pregnant cat in possession of the empty, dusty room and chased her out.

The room was swept and cleaned. They tried to scrape the asphalt snakes off the floor; but the asphalt, which melted so easily on the corrugated iron, remained hard on the cedar boards. The room was smaller than the barrackroom; the bed, Shama's dressingtable, the green table, the kitchen safe and the rockingchair nearly filled it. 'Got to be careful now,' Mr Biswas said. 'Can't rock too hard.' And there were other inconveniences. There was no kitchen; they had to cook on boxes downstairs, below the room; they both got nausea. The roof had no gutters and water had to be fetched all the way from the barrack barrels. They also had to use the barrack latrine.

And every day Mr Biswas saw the snakes, thin, black, lengthening.

The incompleteness of the house didn't depress him. He saw the rafters, the old corrugated iron, the grey uprights, the cracked boards on the floor and walls, the door to the non-existent bedroom nailed and barred. He knew that they had made him unhappy; but that was at a time so remote he could now scarcely imagine it.

The snakes appeared more often in his dreams. He began to regard them as living, and wondered what it would be like to have one fall and curl on his skin.

The questioning and the fear remained. He hadn't left that at the barracks.

The trees could conceal so much.

And one night Anand was awakened by Mr Biswas jumping out of bed, screaming, tearing at his vest as though he had been attacked by a column of red ants.

A snake had fallen on him. Very thin, and not long.

When they looked up they saw the parent snake, waiting to release some more.

With poles and brooms they tried to pull down the snakes. The asphalt only swung when they hit it. To grab at it was only to pull away a small snake, leaving the pregnant parent above.

He got a cocoa-knife and spent the following evening cutting down the snakes. It was not easy. Below the crust at the roots the asphalt was soft but rubbery. He scraped hard and felt the rust from the roof falling on his face.

By the next afternoon the snakes had begun to grow again.

He said he had another touch of malaria. He wrapped himself in the floursack sheet and rocked in his chair. Tarzan had his tail crushed; he leapt up with a yell, and went out of the room.

'Say *Rama Rama Sita Rama*, and nothing will happen to you,' Mr Biswas said.

Anand repeated the words, faster and faster.

'You don't want to leave me?'

Anand didn't reply.

This had become one of Mr Biswas's fears. By concentrating on it – a power he had in his state – he managed to make it the most oppressive of all his fears: that Anand would leave him and he would be left alone.

Anand was rolling his tin-lid about the yard one afternoon when two men came to the house and asked whether he lived there. Then they asked for the driver.

'He in the fields,' Anand said. 'But he coming back just now.'

Between the trees the road was cool. The men squatted there. They hummed; they talked; they threw pebbles; they chewed blades of grass; they spat. Anand watched them.

One of the men called, 'Boy, come here.' He was fat and yellow-skinned with a black moustache and light eyes.

The other man, who was younger, said, 'We digging for treasure.'

Anand couldn't resist that. Pushing his tin-lid, he went to the road.

'Come on. Dig,' the younger man said.

The fat man cried, 'Yaah!' and pulled out a cent from the gravel.

Anand went to where the fat man was and began scraping

Then the younger man called out, 'Aha!' and took up a penny from the gravel.

Anand ran to him. Then the fat man called out again; he had found another cent.

Anand moved back and forth between the men.

'But I not finding any,' he said.

'Here,' the younger man said. 'Dig here.'

Anand dug and found a penny. 'I could keep it?'

'But is yours,' the younger man said. 'You find it.'

The game went on for some time. Anand found two more cents.

Then the fat man appeared to lose interest. 'The driver taking long,' he said. 'Where your father, boy?'

Anand pointed to the sky and was pleased when the fat man looked puzzled and asked, 'The driver is your father, not so?'

'Well, everybody think he is my father. But he is not my father really. He is just a man I know.'

The men looked at one another. The fat man took up a handful of gravel and made as if to throw it at Anand. 'Run away,' he said. 'Go on, haul your little tail.'

'Is not your road,' Anand said. 'Is the PWD road.'

'So you is a smart man into the bargain? Who the hell you think you talking to?' The fat man rose. 'Since you so smart, give me back my money.'

'Find your own. This is mine.' Anand turned to the younger man. 'You see me find it.'

'Leave the boy,' the younger man said.

'I not going to take cheek from a little boy who rob me of my last few cents,' the fat man said. 'I going to teach him a lesson.' He seized Anand.

'Hit me and I tell my father.'

The fat man hesitated.

'Leave him, Dinnoo,' the younger man said. 'Look, the driver.'

Anand broke away and ran to Mr Biswas. 'That fat man was trying to thief my money.'

'Afternoon, boss,' the fat man said.

'Haul your tail. Who the hell tell you you could lay your hand on my son?'

'Son, boss?'

'He try to thief my money,' Anand said.

'Was a game,' the fat man said.

'Haul off!' Mr Biswas said. 'Job! You not looking for any job. You not getting any either.'

'But, boss,' the younger man said, 'Mr Seth say he did tell you.'

'Didn't tell me nothing.'

'But Mr Seth say –' the fat man said.

'Leave them, Dinnoo,' the younger man said. 'Father and blasted son.'

'Is in the blood,' the fat man said.

'You mind your mouth,' Mr Biswas shouted.

'Tcha!' The man sucked his teeth, backing away.

Anand showed Mr Biswas the coppers he had found.

'The road full of money,' he said. 'They was finding silver. But I didn't find any.'

Mr Biswas was awake and lying in bed when Anand got up. Anand always got up first. Mr Biswas heard him walk along the resounding boards of the unfinished drawingroom floor and step on to the staircase – that was a firmer sound. Then there was a silence, and he heard Anand coming back across the drawingroom.

Anand stood in the doorway. His face was blank. 'Pa.' His voice was weak. His mouth remained half open and quivering.

Mr Biswas threw off the sheet and went to him.

Anand shrugged off his father's hand and pointed across the drawingroom.

Mr Biswas went to look.

On the lowest step he saw Tarzan, dead. The body had been flung down carelessly. The hind quarters were on the step, the muzzle on the ground. The brown and white hair was clotted with black-red blood and stained with dirt; flies were thick about him. The tail was propped up against the second step, erect, the hair ruffled in the light morning breeze, as though it belonged to a living dog. The neck had been cut, the belly ripped open; flies were on his lips and around his eyes, which were mercifully closed.

Mr Biswas felt Anand standing beside him.

'Come. Go inside. I will look after Tarzan.'

He led Anand to the bedroom. Anand walked lightly, very lightly, as though responding only to the pressure of Mr Biswas's fingers. Mr Biswas passed his hand over Anand's hair. Anand angrily shook the hand away. The tight, brittle body quivered and Anand, clutching his shirt with both hands, began dancing on the floor.

It was some seconds before Mr Biswas realized that Anand had drawn a deep breath before screaming. He could do nothing but wait, watching the swollen face, the distended mouth, the narrow eyes. And then it came, a terrible whistle of a shriek that went on and on until it broke up into gurgles and strangulated sounds.

'I don't want to stay here! I want to go!'

'All right,' Mr Biswas said, when Anand sat red-eyed and snuffling on the bed. 'I will take you to Hanuman House. Tomorrow.' It was a plea for time. In the anxiety that palpitated through him he had forgotten the dog, and knew only that he didn't want to be left alone. It was a skill he had acquired: to forget the immediately unpleasant. Nothing could distract him from the deeper pain.

Anand, too, forgot the dog. All he recognized was the plea and his own power. He beat his legs against the side of the rumpled bed and stamped on the floor. 'No! No! I want to go today.'

'All right. I will take you this afternoon.'

Mr Biswas buried Tarzan in the yard, adding another mound to those thrown up by the energetic Edgar and now covered with a skin of vegetation. Tarzan's mound looked raw; but soon the weeds would cover it; like Edgar's mounds it would become part of the shape of the land.

The early morning breeze dropped. It became hazy. The heat rose steadily and no relieving shower came in the early afternoon. Then the haze thickened, clouds turned from white to silver to grey to black and billowed heavily across the sky: a watercolour in black and grey.

It became dark.

Mr Biswas hurried from the fields and said, 'I don't think we can take you to Arwacas today. The rain is going to come any minute.'

Anand was content. Darkness at four o'clock was an event, romantic, to be remembered.

Downstairs, in the makeshift kitchen of boxes, they prepared a meal. Then they went upstairs to wait for the downpour.

Soon it came. Isolated drops, rapping hard on the roof, like a slow roll of drums. The wind freshened, the rain slanted. Every drop that struck the uprights blotted, expanding, into the shape of a spear-head. The rain that struck the dust below the roof rolled itself into dark pellets of dirt, neat and spherical.

They lit the oil lamp. Moths flew to it. Flies, deceived by the darkness, had already settled down for the night; they were thick on the asphalt lengths.

Mr Biswas said, 'If you go to Hanuman House, you have to give me back the colour-pencils.'

The wind blew in gusts, curving the fall of the rain.

'But you did give them to me.'

'Ah. But you didn't take them. Remember? Anyway, I taking them back now.'

'Well, you could take them back. I don't want them.'

'All right, all right. I was only joking. I not taking them back.'

'I don't want them.'

'Take them.'

'No.'

Anand went out to the unfinished drawingroom.

When the real rain came it announced itself seconds in advance by its roar: the roar of wind, of wind through trees, of the deluge on distant trees. Then came a swift crepitation on the roof, instantly lost in a continuous and even hammering, so loud that if Mr Biswas spoke Anand could not have heard.

Here and there Mr Maclean's roof leaked; that added to the cosiness of shelter. Water fell from the corrugations in evenly-spaced streams, enclosing the house. Water flowed down the sloping land below the roof; the pellets of dirt had long disappeared. Water gouged out tortuous channels as it forced its way down to the road and down to the hollow before the barracks. And the rain continued to roar, and the roof resounded.

For several seconds at a time lightning lit up a shining chaotic world. Fresh mud flowed off Tarzan's grave in a thin regular stream. Raindrops glittered as they struck the sodden ground. Then the thunder came, grating and close. Anand thought of a monstrous steam-roller breaking through the sky. The lightning was exciting but it made him feel peculiar. That, and the thunder, sent him back to the bedroom.

He surprised Mr Biswas writing with his finger on his head. Mr Biswas quickly pretended that he was playing with his hair. The flame of the oil lamp, though protected by a glass chimney, wavered; shadows dodged about the room; the shadows of the snakes swung in an ever-changing pattern on the shivering roof.

Still officially annoyed with his father, Anand sat down on the floor, at the foot of the bed, and held his arms over his knees. The din on the roof and the beat of the rain on the trees and earth made him feel chilly. Something fell near him. It was a winged ant, its wings collapsed and now a burden on its wormlike body. These creatures came out only in heavy rain and seldom lived beyond it. When they fell they never rose again. Anand pressed a finger on the broken wing. The ant wriggled, the wing was released; and the ant, suddenly busy, suddenly deceptively whole, moved off towards the dark.

All at once a cycle of heavy rain was over. It still drizzled, and the wind still blew, flinging the drizzle on the roof and walls like showers of sand. It was possible to hear the water from the roof falling to the earth, water gurgling as it ran off in its new channels. The rain had soaked through the gaps between the wall-boards. The edges of the floor were wet.

'Rama Rama Sita Rama, Rama Rama Sita Rama.'

Mr Biswas was lolling on the bed, his legs locked together, his lips moving rapidly. The expression on his face was one of exasperation rather than pain.

Anand thought this was a plea for sympathy and ignored it. He leaned his head on his arms crossed over his knees, and rocked on the floor.

A fresh cycle of rain started. A winged ant dropped on Anand's arm. Hurriedly he brushed it off; where the ant touched him seemed to burn. Then he saw that the room was full of these ants enjoying the last minutes of their short life. Their small wings, strained by large bodies, quickly became useless, and without wings they were without defence. They kept on dropping. Their enemies had already discovered them. On one wall, in the shadow of the reflector of the oil lamp, Anand saw a column of black ants. They were not the crazy ants, thin frivolous creatures who scattered at the slightest disturbance; they were the biting ants, smaller, thicker, neater, purple-black with a dull shine, moving slowly and in strict formation, as solemn and stately as undertakers. Lightning lit up the room again and Anand saw the column of biting ants stretched diagonally across two walls: a roundabout route, but they had their reasons.

'Hear them!'

Anand, watching the ants, his mouth pressed on his goose-fleshed arm, didn't reply.

'Boy!'

The anguish, the loudness of the voice rising above rain and wind made Anand jump. He stood up.

'You hear them?'

Anand listened, trying to pick up the component parts of the din: the rain, the wind, the running of water, the trees, the rain on walls and roof. Talk, indistinct, a bumble, rising and falling.

'You hear them?'

Anything could sound like talk: the gurgle of water, boughs rubbing against one another. Anand opened the door a little way and looked down through the spars of the drawingroom. The ground ran with shining black water. Below the unfloored front bedroom, where the ground was higher and not so wet, two men were squatting before a smoking fire of twigs. Two large heart-shaped leaves of the wild *tannia* were near the men. They must have used the leaves as umbrellas when they had been caught by the heavier shower. The men stared at the fire. One man was smoking a cigarette. In the weak firelight, in the stillness of the scene in the midst of turmoil, this act of smoking, so intense and unruffled, might have been part of an ancient ritual.

'You see them?'

Anand closed the door.

On the floor the winged ants had a new life. They were possessed of scores of black limbs. They were being carted away by the biting ants. They wriggled and squirmed, but did not disturb the even solemnity of their bearers. Bodiless wings were also being carried away.

Lightning obliterated shadows and colour.

The hair on Anand's arms and legs stood straight. His skin tingled.

'You see them?'

Anand thought they might be the men from the day before. But he couldn't be sure.

'Bring the cutlass.'

Anand put the cutlass against the wall near the head of the bed. The wall was running with water.

'And you take the walking-stick.'

Anand would have liked to go to sleep. But he didn't want to get into bed with his father. And with the floor full of ants where it was not wet, he couldn't make up a bed for himself.

*'Rama Rama Sita Rama, Rama Rama Sita Rama.'*

*'Rama Rama Sita Rama,'* Anand repeated.

Then Mr Biswas forgot Anand and began to curse. He cursed Ajodha, Pundit Jairam, Mrs Tulsi, Shama, Seth.

'Say *Rama Rama*, boy.'

*'Rama Rama Sita Rama.'*

The rain abated.

When Anand looked outside, the men under the house had gone with their *tannia* leaves, leaving a dead, hardly-smoking fire.

'You see them?'

The rain came again. Lightning flashed and flashed, thunder exploded and rolled.

The procession of the ants continued. Anand began killing them with the walking-stick. Whenever he crushed a group carrying a living winged ant, the ants broke up, without confusion or haste, re-formed, took away what they could of the crushed body and carried away their dead. Anand struck and struck with his stick. A sharp pain ran up his arm. On his hand he saw an ant, its body raised, its pincers buried in his skin. When he looked at the walking-stick he saw that it was alive with biting ants crawling upwards. He was suddenly terrified of them, their anger, their vindictiveness, their number. He threw the stick away from him. It fell into a puddle.

The roof rose and dropped, grinding and flapping. The house shook.

*'Rama Rama Sita Rama,'* Anand said.

'O God! They coming!'

'They *gone!*' Anand shouted angrily.

Mr Biswas muttered hymns in Hindi and English, left them unfinished, cursed, rolled on the bed, his face still expressing only exasperation.

The flame of the oil lamp swayed, shrank, throwing the room into darkness for seconds, then shone again.

A shaking on the roof, a groan, a prolonged grinding noise, and Anand knew that a sheet of corrugated iron had been torn off. One sheet was left loose. It flapped and jangled continuously. Anand waited for the fall of the sheet that had been blown off.

He never heard it.

Lightning; thunder; the rain on roof and walls; the loose iron sheet; the wind pushing against the house, pausing, and pushing again.

Then there was a roar that overrode them all. When it struck the house the window burst open, the lamp went instantly out, the rain lashed in, the lightning lit up the room and the world outside, and when the lightning went out the room was part of the black void.

Anand began to scream.

He waited for his father to say something, to close the window, light the lamp.

But Mr Biswas only muttered on the bed, and the rain and wind swept through the room with unnecessary strength and forced open the door to the drawingroom, wall-less, floorless, of the house Mr Biswas had built.

Anand screamed and screamed.

Rain and wind smothered his voice, overturned the lamp, made the rockingchair rock and skid, rattled the kitchen safe against the wall, destroyed all smell. Lightning, flashing intermittently, steel-blue exploding into white, showed the ants continually disarrayed, continually re-forming.

Then Anand saw a light swaying in the dark. It was a man, bending forward against the rain, a hurricane lamp in one hand, a cutlass in the other. The living flame was like a miracle.

It was Ramkhilawan from the barracks. He had a jutebag over his head and shoulders like a cape. He was barefooted and his trousers were rolled up above his knees. The hurricane lamp showed glinting streaks of rain, and, as he climbed the slippery steps, his footprints of mud, instantly washed away.

'Oh, my poor little calf!' he called. 'Oh, my poor little calf!'

He closed the drawingroom door. The lamp illuminated a wet chaos. He struggled with the window. As soon as he had pulled it a little way from the wall to which it was pinned, the wind, rising, gave a push, and the window slammed shut, making Ramkhilawan jump back. He took off the dripping jutebag from his head and shoulders; his shirt stuck to his skin.

The oil lamp was not broken. There even remained some oil in it. The chimney was cracked, but still whole.

Ramkhilawan brought out a damp box of matches from his trouser pocket and put a lighted match to the wick. The wick, waterlogged, spluttered; the match burned down; the wick caught.

# 6. A Departure

A MESSAGE had to be sent to Hanuman House. The labourers always responded to the melodramatic and calamitous, and there were many volunteers. Through rain and wind and thunder a messenger went that evening to Arwacas and dramatically unfolded his tale of calamity.

Mrs Tulsi and the younger god were in Port of Spain. Shama was in the Rose Room; the midwife had been attending upon her for two days.

Sisters and their husbands held a council.

'I did always think he was mad,' Chinta said.

Sushila, the childless widow, spoke with her sickroom authority. 'It isn't about Mohun I am worried, but the children.'

Padma, Seth's wife, asked, 'What do you think he is sick with?'

Sumati the flogger said, 'Message only said that he was very sick.'

'And that his house had been practically blown away,' Jai's mother added.

There were some smiles.

'I am sorry to correct you, Sumati sister,' Chinta said. 'But Message said that he wasn't right in his head.'

Seth said, 'I suppose we have to bring the paddler home.'

The men got ready to go to Green Vale; they were as excited as the messenger.

The sisters bustled about, impressing and mystifying the children. Sushila, who occupied the Blue Room when the god was away, cleared it of all personal, womanly things; much of her time was devoted to keeping the mysteries of women from men. She also burned certain evil-smelling herbs to purify and protect the house.

'Savi,' the children said, 'something happen to your pappa.'

And they stuck pins in the wicks of lamps to keep misfortune and death away.

In the verandah and in every bedroom upstairs beds were made earlier than usual, lamps were turned low, and the children fell asleep, lulled by the sound of the rain. Downstairs the sisters sat silently around the long table, their veils pulled close over their heads and shoulders. They played cards and read newspapers. Chinta was reading the *Ramayana*; she continually set herself new ambitions and at the moment wanted to be the first woman in the family to read the epic from beginning to end. Occasionally the card-players chuckled. Chinta was sometimes called to look at the cards one sister had; often the temptation was too great, and Chinta, adopting her frowning card-playing manner, and not saying a word, stayed to play the hand, tapping each card before she played it, throwing down the winning card with the crack she could do so well, then, still silent, going back to the *Ramayana*. The midwife, an old, thin, inscrutable Madrassi, came to the hall and sat on her haunches in a corner, smoking, silent, her eyes bright. Coffee simmered in the kitchen; its smell filled the hall.

When the men returned, dripping, with Anand sleepily and tearfully walking beside them and Govind carrying Mr Biswas in his arms, there was relief, and some disappointment. Mr Biswas was not wild or violent; he made no speeches; he did not pretend he was driving a motorcar or picking cocoa – the two actions popularly associated with insanity. He only looked deeply exasperated and fatigued.

Govind and Mr Biswas had not spoken since their fight. By carrying Mr Biswas in his arms Govind had put himself on the side of authority: he had assumed authority's power to rescue and assist when there was need, authority's impersonal power to forgive.

Recognizing this, Chinta looked solicitously after Anand, drying his hair, taking off his wet clothes and giving him some of Vidiadhar's, giving him food, taking him upstairs and finding a place for him among the sleeping boys.

Mr Biswas was put in the Blue Room, given dry clothes and cautiously offered a cup of hot sweetened milk with nutmeg, brandy and lumps of red butter. He stilled remaining fears by taking the cup without accident, and drinking carefully.

He welcomed the warmth and reassurance of the room. Every wall was solid; the sound of the rain was deadened; the ceiling of two and a half inch pitchpine concealed corrugated iron and asphalt; the jalousied window, set in a deep embrasure, was unrattled by wind and rain.

He knew he was at Hanuman House; but he couldn't assess what had gone before or what was to come. He felt he was continually awakening to a new situation, which was in some way linked to the memories he had, as instantaneous as snapshots, of other happenings that seemed to have spread over an unmeasurable length of time. The rain on the wet bed; the trip in the motorcar; the appearance of Ramkhilawan; the dead dog; the men talking outside; the thunder and lightning; the room suddenly full of Seth and Govind and the others; and now this warm, closed room, yellowly lit by a steady lamp; the dry clothes. As he concentrated, every object acquired a solidity, a permanence. That marble topped table with the china cup and saucer and spoon: no other arrangement of those objects was possible. He knew that this order was threatened; he had a feeling of expectation and unease.

He lay as still as possible. Soon he was asleep. In his last moments of lucidity he thought the sound of the rain, muffled and regular, was comforting.

It was still raining next morning, steadily, but the wind had dropped. It was dark, but there was no lightning and thunder. The gutters around the house were full and muddy. In the High Street the canals overflowed and the road was under water. The children could not go to school. There was excitement among them, not only at the unusual weather and unexpected holiday, but also at the overnight disturbance. Some had memories of being awakened briefly during the night; now Anand was with them and his father was in the Blue Room. Some of the girls pretended to know all that had happened. It was like the morning after a birth in the Rose Room: the mysteries were so well kept and everything carried out so secretly that few of the younger children knew what was afoot until they were told.

'Savi,' the children said, 'your pappa here. In the Blue Room.'

But she didn't want to go to the Blue Room or the Rose Room.

Outside, naked children splashed shrieking in the flooded road and swollen canals, racing paper boats and wooden boats and even sticks.

Towards the middle of the morning the sky lightened and lifted, the rain thinned to a drizzle, then stopped altogether. The clouds rolled back, the sky was suddenly blinding blue and there were shadows on the water. Rapidly, their gurgling soon lost in the awakening every day din, canals subsided, leaving a wash of twigs and dirt on the road. In yards, against fences, there were tidemarks of debris and pebbles which looked as though they had been washed and sifted; around stones dirt had been washed away; green leaves that had been torn down were partly buried in silt. Roads and roofs dried, steaming, areas of dryness spreading out swiftly, like ink on a blotter. And presently roads and yards were dry, except for the depressions where water had collected. Heat nibbled at their edges, until even the depressions failed to reflect the blue sky. And the world was dry again, except for the mud in the shelter of the trees.

The news about Mr Biswas was broken to Shama. She suggested that the furniture from Green Vale should be brought to Hanuman House.

The doctor came, a Roman Catholic Indian, but much respected by the Tulsis for his manners and the extent of his property. He dismissed talk about having Mr Biswas certified and said that Mr Biswas was suffering from nerves and a certain vitamin deficiency. He prescribed a course of Sanatogen, a tonic called Ferrol with reputed iron-giving, body-building qualities, and Ovaltine. He also said that Mr Biswas was to have much rest, and should go to Port of Spain as soon as he was better to see a specialist.

Almost as soon as the doctor had gone the thaumaturge came, an unsuccessful man with a flashy turban and an anxious manner; his fees were low. He purified the Blue Room and erected invisible barriers against evil spirits. He recommended that strips of aloe should be hung in doorways and windows and said that the family ought to have known that they should always have a black doll in the doorway of the hall to divert evil spirits: prevention was better than cure. Then he inquired whether he couldn't prepare a little mixture as well.

The offer was rejected. 'Ovaltine, Ferrol, Sanatogen,' Seth said. 'Give Mohun your mixture and you turn him into a little capsule.'

But they hung the aloe; it was a natural purgative that cost nothing and large quantities were always in the house. And they hung the black doll, one of a small ancient stock in the Tulsi Store, an English line which had not appealed to the people of Arwacas.

That same afternoon a lorry brought the furniture from Green Vale. It was all damp and discoloured. The polish on Shama's dressingtable had turned white. The mattress was soaked and smelly; the coconut fibre had swollen and stained the ticking. The cloth covers of Mr Biswas's books were still sticky, and their colours had run along the edges of the pages, which had wrinkled and stuck together.

The metal sections of the fourposter were left unmounted in that part of the long room which had once been Shama's and Mr Biswas's; the boards and the mattress were put out to dry in the sun. The safe stood in the hall, near the doorway to the kitchen, looking almost new against the sooty green wall. It still exhibited the Japanese coffee-set (the head of a Japanese woman at the bottom of every cup, an embossed dragon breathing fire outside), Seth's wedding present to Shama, never used, only cleaned. The green table was also put in the hall, but in that jumble of unmatching furniture was scarcely noticeable. The rockingchair was taken to the verandah upstairs.

Savi was pained to see the furniture so scattered and disregarded, and angered to see the rockingchair being misused almost at once. At first the children stood on the cane-bottom and rocked violently. From this they evolved a game: four or five climbed into the chair and rocked; another four or five tried to pull them off. They fought over the chair and overturned it: that was the climax of the game. Knowing that to protest was to make herself absurd, Savi went to the Rose Room, with its basins and quaint jugs and tubes and smells, and complained to Shama.

Shama, always gentle with her children when she was alone with them, and especially gentle during her confinements, stroked Savi's hair and told her that she was not to mind, she was being selfish, and if she complained to anybody else she would certainly cause a quarrel. Mr Biswas was sick, Shama said; and she herself was sick. Savi ought not to behave in a way that would annoy anyone.

'And where have they put the bureau?' Shama asked.

'In the long room.'

Shama looked pleased.

Some of Mr Biswas's most elaborate placards had also been brought from Green Vale. They were considered beautiful; though the sentiments, from a man long thought to be an atheist, caused some astonishment. The placards were hung in the hall and the Book Room, and when the children said, 'Savi, your pappa did really paint those signs?' the pain at seeing the furniture scattered was lessened.

The children said, 'Savi, so all-you staying here for good now?'

Lying in the room next to Shama's, perpetually dark, Mr Biswas slept and woke and slept again. The darkness, the silence, the absence of the world enveloped and comforted him. At some far-off time he had suffered great anguish. He had fought against it. Now he had surrendered, and this surrender had brought peace. He had controlled his disgust and fear when the men had come for him. He was glad he had. Surrender had removed the world of damp walls and paper covered walls, of hot sun and driving rain, and had brought him this: this worldless room, this nothingness. As the hours passed he found he could piece together recent happenings, and he marvelled that he had survived the horror. More and more frequently he forgot fear and questioning; sometimes, for as much as a minute or so, he was unable, even when he tried, to re-enter fully the state of mind he had lived through. There remained an unease, which did not seem real or actual and was more like an indistinct, chilling memory of horror.

Further messages had been sent and visitors came. Pratap and Prasad, abashed by the size of the house and conscious of their own condition, felt obliged to be kind to all the children. They began by giving each child a penny; but they had underestimated the number of children; they ended up by giving out halfpennies. They told Mr Biswas exactly what they had been doing when they got Message; it seemed that they both nearly missed Message; they had both, however, had some signs on the night of the storm that something was wrong with Mr Biswas and had told their wives so; they urged Mr Biswas to get confirmation from their wives. Mr Biswas listened with a sense of withdrawal. He asked after their families. Pratap and Prasad construed this as pure politeness, and though there was little to talk about, dismissed their families as worthless of serious consideration. And after making occasional solemn noises, looking down at their hats, examining them from various angles, brushing the bands, they got up to go, sighing.

Ramchand, Mr Biswas's brother-in-law, was less restrained. He had acquired a city brashness that went well with his uniform. He had left the country and the rum-factory years before and was now a warden at the Lunatic Asylum in Port of Spain.

'Don't think I shy of you,' he told Mr Biswas. 'I used to this. This is my work.'

He spoke of himself, his career, the Lunatic Asylum.

'You ain't got a gramophone here?' he asked.

'Gramophone?'

'Music,' Ramchand said. 'We does play music to them all the time.'

He spoke of the perquisites of the job as though the Lunatic Asylum had been organized solely for his benefit.

'Take the canteen now. Everything there five cents and six cents cheaper than outside, you know. But that is because they not running it to make a profit. If you ever want anything you must let me know.'

'Sanatogen?'

'I will see. Look, why you don't leave the country, man, and come to Port of Spain? A man like you shouldn't remain in this backward place. No wonder this thing happen to you. Come up and spend some time with us. Dehuti always talking about you, you know.'

Mr Biswas promised to think it over.

Ramchand walked heavily through the house and when he came into the hall shouted at Sushila, whom he didn't know, 'Everything all right, *maharajin*?'

'He looks like a real *chamar*-caste-type,' Sushila said.

'However much you wash a pig,' Chinta said, 'you can't turn it into a cow.'

That evening Seth went to the Blue Room.

'Well, Mohun. How you feeling?'

'All right, I think.' Mr Biswas spoke with something like his humorous high-pitched voice.

'You thinking of going back to Green Vale?'

To his own surprise, Mr Biswas found himself behaving in the old way. With an expression of mock-horror he said, 'Who? Me?'

'I glad you feel that way. As a matter of fact you can't go back.'

'Look at me. I crying.'

'Guess what happen.'

'All the cane burn down.'

'Wrong. Only your house.'

'Burn down? You mean it insuranburn.'

'No, no. Not insuranburn. It burn fair and square. Green Vale people. Wicked like hell, man, those people.'

Seth saw that Mr Biswas was crying and looked away. But Seth misunderstood.

An immense relief had come upon Mr Biswas. The anxiety, the fear, the anguish which had kept his mind humming and his body taut now ebbed away. He could feel it ebbing; it was a physical sensation; it left him weak and very weary. And he felt an enormous gratitude to Seth. He wanted to embrace him, to promise eternal friendship, to make some vow.

'You mean,' he said at last, 'that after all that rain they burn it down?' And he burst out sobbing.

That night Shama gave birth to her fourth child, another girl.

Mr Biswas's books had been placed among those in the Book Room. Somewhere among them was the *Collins Clear-Type Shakespeare*. No entry was made on its endpaper of this new birth.

The thin, short-winded and repetitive cry of the baby hardly made itself heard outside the Rose Room. The midwife no longer squatted in the hall and smoked. She was busy. She washed, she cleaned, she watched and ruled. After nine days she was paid and dismissed. The sisters told Anand and Savi, 'You have a new sister. Somebody else to get a share of your father's property.' And they told Anand, 'You are lucky. You are still the only boy. But wait. One day you will get a brother, and he will cut off your nose.'

Mr Biswas mixed and drank Sanatogen, drank tablespoonfuls of Ferrol and, in the evenings, glasses of Ovaltine. One day he remembered his fingernails. When he looked he saw they were whole, unbitten. There were still the periods of darkness, the spasms of panic; but now he knew they were not real and because he knew this he overcame them. He remained in the Blue Room, feeling secure to be only a part of Hanuman House, an organism that possessed a life, strength and power to comfort which was quite separate from the individuals who composed it.

'Savi, what you drinking?'
'Ovaltine.'
'Anand, what you drinking?'
'Ovaltine.'
'It nice?'
'Very nice.'
'Ma, Savi and Anand drinking Ovaltine. Their pappa give it to them.'

'Well, let me tell you, eh, boy, your father is not a million-aire to give *you* Ovaltine. You hear?'

And the next day:

'Jai, what you drinking?'

'Ovaltine, like you.'

'Vidiadhar, you drinking Ovaltine too?'

'No. *We* drinking Milo. We like it better.'

Mr Biswas came out from the Blue Room to the drawing-room with the thronelike chairs and the statuary. He felt safe and even a little adventurous. He went through to the wooden house. In the verandah Hari was reading. Instinc-tively Mr Biswas took a step back. Then he remembered there was no need. The two men looked at one another and looked away again.

Leaning on the verandah half-wall, with his back to Hari, Mr Biswas thought about Hari's position in the family. Hari spent all his free time reading. He used this reading for noth-ing; he disliked disputation of any sort. No one was able to check his knowledge of Sanskrit and his scholarship had to be taken on trust. Yet he was respected inside the family and outside it. How did Hari get to that position? Mr Biswas wondered. Where did he start?

What would happen if he, Mr Biswas, made a sudden ap-pearance in the hall in dhoti and beads and sacred thread? Let his top-knot grow again, as it had grown at Pundit Jairam's. Would Hanuman House care to have two sick scholars? But he couldn't see himself as a holy man for long. Sooner or later someone was bound to surprise him, in dhoti, top-knot, sacred thread and caste-marks, reading *The Manxman* or *The Atom*.

Speculating about this, he reviewed his situation. He was the father of four children, and his position was as it had been when he was seventeen, unmarried and ignorant of the Tul-sis. He had no vocation, no reliable means of earning a living. The job at Green Vale was over; he could not rest in the Blue Room forever; soon he would have to make a decision. Yet he felt no anxiety. The second to second agony and despair of those days at Green Vale had given him an experience of unhappiness against which everything had now to be measured. He was more fortunate than most people. His children would never starve; they would always be sheltered and clothed. It didn't matter if he were at Green Vale or Arwacas, if he were alive or dead.

His money dwindled: Ovaltine, Ferrol, Sanatogen; the doctor's fees, the midwife's, the thaumaturge's. And there was no more money to come.

One evening Seth said, 'That tin of Ovaltine could very well be your last, if you don't decide to do something.'

Decide. What was there to decide?

There was room for him at Hanuman House if he stayed. If he left he would not be missed. He had not claimed his children; they avoided him and were embarrassed when they met him.

But it was only when Seth said, 'Mai and Owad are coming home this week-end,' meaning that the Blue Room had to be prepared for Owad, it was only then that Mr Biswas thought of action, unwilling to move to any other part of the house, unwilling to face Mrs Tulsi and the god.

The small brown cardboard suitcase, acquired in exchange for a large number of Anchor Cigarette packets, and decorated on both sides with his monogram, was enough for what he intended to take. He remembered Shama's taunt: 'When you came to us you had no more clothes than you could hang up on a nail.' He still had few clothes; they were all crumpled and dirty. The cork hat he decided to leave; he had always found it absurd, and it belonged to the barracks. He could always send for his books. But he packed his paint-brushes. Through every move they had survived; the soft candle on the bristle of one or two had hardened, cracked and turned to powder.

He wanted to leave early in the morning, to have as much time as possible before it became dark. The crumpled clothes felt loose when he put them on; his trousers sagged; he had grown thinner. He remembered the morning the towel had fallen from him in front of the twelve barrackrooms.

When Savi brought him the cocoa and biscuits and butter he told her, 'I am going away.'

She didn't look surprised or disappointed, and didn't ask where he was going.

He was going out into the world, to test it for its power to frighten. The past was counterfeit, a series of cheating accidents. Real life, and its especial sweetness, awaited; he was still beginning.

He wondered whether he should go to see Shama and the baby. His senses recoiled. As soon as he heard the children leave for school he went downstairs. He was seen, but no one called out to him: the suitcase was not of a significant size.

The High Street was already busy. The market was alive: a high smell of meat and fish, a steady dull roar enlivened by shrieks and the ringing of bells. The haberdashers were coming in, on horse-carts, donkey-carts and ox-carts: ambitious men who set up little boxes and exposed stocks of combs and hairpins and brushes in front of large stores that sold the same things.

The spasms of terror didn't come. The knots of fear were still in his stomach, but they were so subdued he knew he could ignore them. The world had been restored to him. He looked at the nails of his left hand; they were still whole. He tested them against his palm; they were sharp and cutting.

He walked past the Red Rose Tea Is Good Tea sign; past the rumshop with the vast awning; past the Roman Catholic church; the court house; past the police station, primly ochre-and-red, its lawn and hedges trimmed, the drive lined with large whitewashed stones and palm trees which, whitewashed halfway up their trunks, looked like the legs of Pratap and Prasad when, as boys, they returned from the buffalo-pond.

# PART TWO

PART TWO

# 1. 'Amazing Scenes'

TO THE city of Port of Spain, where with one short break he was to spend the rest of his life, and where at Sikkim Street he was to die fifteen years later, Mr Biswas came by accident. When he left Hanuman House and his wife and four children, the last of whom he had not seen, his main concern was to find a place to pass the night. It was still early morning. The sun was rising directly above the High Street in a dazzling haze, against which everyone was silhouetted, outlined in gold, and attached to shadows so elongated that movements appeared uncoordinated and awkward. The buildings on either side were in damp shadow.

At the road junction Mr Biswas had still not decided where to go. Most of the traffic moved north: tarpaulin-covered lorries, taxis, buses. The buses slowed down to pass Mr Biswas, and the conductors, hanging out from the footboard, shouted to him to come aboard. North lay Ajodha and Tara, and his mother. South lay his brothers. None of them could refuse to take him in. But to none of them did he want to go: it was too easy to picture himself among them. Then he remembered that north, too, lay Port of Spain and Ramchand, his brother-in-law. And it was while he was trying to decide whether Ramchand's invitation could be considered genuine that a bus, its engine partially unbonneted, its capless radiator steaming, came to a stop inches away with a squeal of brakes and a racking of its tin and wood body, and the conductor, a young man, almost a boy, bent down and seized Mr Biswas's cardboard suitcase, saying imperiously, impatiently, 'Port of Spain, man, Port of Spain'.

As a conductor of Ajodha's buses Mr Biswas had seized the suitcases of many wayfarers, and he knew that in these circumstances a conductor had to be aggressive to combat any possible annoyance. But now, finding himself suddenly separated from his suitcase and hearing the impatience in the conductor's voice, he was cowed, and nodded. 'Up, up, man,' the conductor said, and Mr Biswas climbed into the vehicle while the conductor stowed away his suitcase.

Whenever the bus stopped to release a passenger or kidnap another, Mr Biswas wondered whether it was too late to get off and make his way south. But the decision had been made, and he was without energy to go back on it; besides, he could get at his suitcase only with the cooperation of the conductor. He fixed his eyes on a house, as small and as neat as a doll's house, on the distant hills of the Northern Range; and as the bus moved north, he allowed himself to be puzzled that the house didn't grow any bigger, and to wonder, as a child might, whether the bus would eventually come to that house.

It was the crop season. In the sugarcane fields, already in parts laid low, cutters and loaders were at work, knee-deep in trash. Along the tracks between fields mudstained, grey-black buffaloes languidly pulled carts carrying high, bristling loads of sugarcane. But soon the land changed and the air was less sticky. Sugarcane gave way to rice-fields, the muddy colour of their water lost in the flawless reflections of the blue sky; there were more trees; and instead of mud huts there were wooden houses, small and old, but finished, painted and jalousied, with fretwork, frequently broken, along the eaves, above doors and windows and around fern-smothered verandahs. The plain fell behind, the mountains grew nearer; but the doll's house remained as small as ever and when the bus turned into the Eastern Main Road Mr Biswas lost sight of it. The road was strung with many wires and looked important; the bus moved westwards through thickening traffic and increasing noise, past one huddled red and ochre settlement after another, until the hills rose directly from the road on the right, and from the left came a smell of swamp and sea, which presently appeared, level, grey and hazy, and they were in Port of Spain, where the stale salt smell of the sea mixed with the sharp sweet smells of cocoa and sugar from the warehouses.

He had feared the moment of arrival and wished that the bus would go on and never stop, but when he got down into the yard next to the railway station his uncertainty at once fell away, and he felt free and excited. It was a day of freedom such as he had had only once before, when one of Ajodha's relations had died and the rumshop had been closed and everybody had gone away. He drank a coconut from a cart in Marine Square. How wonderful to be able to do that in the middle of the morning! He walked on crowded pavements beside the slow, continuous motor traffic, noted the size and number of the stores and cafés and restaurants, the trams, the high standard of the shop signs, the huge cinemas, closed after the pleasures of last night (which he had spent dully at Arwacas), but with posters, still wet with paste, promising fresh gaieties for that afternoon and evening. He comprehended the city whole; he did not isolate the individual, see the man behind the desk or counter, behind the pushcart or the steering-wheel of the bus; he saw only the activity, felt the call to the senses, and knew that below it all there was an excitement, which was hidden, but waiting to be grasped.

It wasn't until four, when stores and offices closed and the cinemas opened, that he thought of making his way to the address Ramchand had given. This was in the Woodbrook area and Mr Biswas, enchanted by the name, was disappointed to find an unfenced lot with two old unpainted wooden houses and many makeshift sheds. It was too late to turn back, to make another decision, another journey; and after making inquiries of a Negro woman who was fanning a coal-pot in one shed, he picked his way past bleaching stones, a slimy open gutter and a low open gutter and a low clotheswire, to the back, where he saw Dehuti fanning a coal-pot in another shed, one wall of which was the corrugated iron fence of the sewer trace.

His disappointment was matched by their surprise when, after the exclamations of greeting, he made it clear that he intended to spend some time with them. But when he announced that he had left Shama, they were welcoming again, their solicitude touched not only with excitement but also with pleasure that in a time of trouble he had come to them.

'You stay here and rest as long as you want,' Ramchand said. 'Look, you have a gramophone. You just stay here and play music to yourself.'

And Dehuti even dropped the sullenness with which she always greeted Mr Biswas, a sullenness which, no longer defensive, held no meaning and was only an attitude fixed by habit, simplifying relationships.

Presently Dehuti's younger son came back from school and Dehuti said sternly, 'Take out your books and let me hear what you learn at school today.'

The boy didn't hesitate. He took out Captain Cutteridge's *Reader*, Standard Four, and read an account of an escape from a German prison camp in 1917.

Mr Biswas congratulated the boy, Dehuti and Ramchand.

'He is a good little reader,' Ramchand said.

'And what is the meaning of "distribute"?' Dehuti asked, still stern.

'Share out,' the boy said.

'I didn't know that at his age,' Mr Biswas said to Ramchand.

'And bring out your copy book and show me what you do in arithmetic today.'

The boy took the book out to her and Dehuti said, 'It look passable. But I don't know anything about arithmetic. Take it to your uncle, let him see.'

Mr Biswas didn't know anything about arithmetic either, but he saw the approving red ticks and again congratulated the boy, Dehuti and Ramchand.

'This education is a helluva thing,' Ramchand said. 'Any little child could pick up. And yet the blasted thing does turn out so damn important later on.'

Dehuti and Ramchand lived in two rooms. One of these Mr Biswas shared with the boy. And though from the outside the unpainted house with its rusting roof and weatherbeaten, broken boards looked about to fall down, the wood inside had kept some of its colour, and the rooms were clean and well kept. The furniture, including the hatrack with the diamond shaped glass, was brilliantly polished. The area between the kitchen shed and the back room was roofed and partly walled; so that the open yard could be forgotten, and there was room and even privacy.

But at night gruff, intimate whispers came through the partitions, reminding Mr Biswas that he lived in a crowded city. The other tenants were all Negroes. Mr Biswas had never lived close to people of this race before, and their proximity added to the strangeness, the adventure of being in the city. They differed from country Negroes in accent, dress and manner. Their food had strange meaty smells, and their lives appeared less organized. Women ruled men. Children were disregarded and fed, it seemed, at random; punishments were frequent and brutal, without any of the ritual that accompanied floggings at Hanuman House. Yet the children all had fine physiques, disfigured only by projecting navels, which were invariably uncovered; for the city children wore trousers and exposed their tops, unlike country children, who wore vests and exposed their bottoms. And unlike country children, who were timid, the city children were half beggars, half bullies.

The organization of the city fascinated Mr Biswas: the street lamps going on at the same time, the streets swept in the middle of the night, the rubbish collected by the scavenging carts early in the morning; the furtive, macabre sounds of the nightsoil removers; the newsboys, really men; the bread van, the milk that came, not from cows, but in rum bottles stopped with brown paper. Mr Biswas was impressed when Dehuti and Ramchand spoke proprietorially of streets and shops, talking with the ease of people who knew their way about the baffling city. Even about Ramchand's going out to work every morning there was something knowing, brave and enviable.

And with Mr Biswas Ramchand was indeed the knowledgeable townsman. He took Mr Biswas to the Botanical Gardens and the Rock Gardens and Government House. They went up Chancellor Hill and looked down at the ships in the harbour. For Mr Biswas this was a moment of deep romance. He had seen the sea, but didn't know that Port of Spain was really a port, at which ocean liners called from all parts of the world.

Mr Biswas was amused by Ramchand's city manners and allowed himself to be patronized by him. Ramchand had in any case always managed to do that, even when he had just stopped being a yard boy at Tara's. Ostracized from the community into which he was born, he had shown the futility of its sanctions. He had simply gone outside it. He had acquired a loudness and heartiness which was alien and which he did not always carry off easily. He spoke English most of the time, but with a rural Indian accent which made his attempts to keep up with the ever-changing Port of Spain slang absurd. And Mr Biswas suffered when, as sometimes happened, Ramchand was rebuffed; when, for instance, partly to impress Mr Biswas, he overdid the heartiness in his relations with the Negroes in the yard and was met with cold surprise.

At the end of a fortnight Ramchand said, 'Don't worry about getting a job yet. You suffering from brain fag, and you got to have lots of rest.'

He spoke without irony, but Mr Biswas, now practically without money, had begun to feel burdened by his freedom. He was no longer content to walk about the city. He wanted to be part of it, to be one of those who stood at the black and yellow bus-stops in the morning, one of those he saw behind the windows of offices, one of those to whom the evenings and week-ends brought relaxation. He thought of taking up sign-writing again. But how was he to go about it? Could he simply put up a sign in front of the house and wait?

Ramchand said, 'Why you don't try to get a job in the Mad House? Good pay, free uniform, and a damn good canteen. Everything there five and six cents cheaper. Ask Dehuti.'

'Yes,' she said, 'Everything there much cheaper.'

Mr Biswas saw himself in the uniform, walking alone through long rooms of howling maniacs.

'Well, why the hell not?' he said. 'Is something to do.'

Ramchand looked slightly offended. He mentioned difficulties; and though he had contacts and influence, he was not sure that it would create a good impression if he made use of them. 'That is the only thing that keeping me back,' he said. 'The *impression*.'

Then one day Mr Biswas was surprised by the spasms of fear. They were weak and intermittent, but they persisted, and reminded him to look at his hands. The nails were all bitten down.

His freedom was over.

And as a last act of this freedom he decided to go to the specialist the Arwacas doctor had recommended. The specialist's office was at the northern end of St Vincent Street, not far from the Savannah. House and grounds suggested whiteness and order. The fence pillars were freshly whitewashed; the brass plaque glittered; the lawn was trimmed; not a piece of earth was out of place on the flower-beds; and on the drive the light-grey gravel, free from impurities, reflected the sunlight.

He went through a white-walled verandah and found himself in a high white room. A Chinese receptionist in a stiff white uniform sat at a desk on which calendar, diary, inkwells, ledgers and lamp were neatly disposed. A fan whirred in one corner. A number of people reclined on low luxurious chairs, reading magazines or talking in whispers. They didn't look sick: there was not a bandage or an oiled face among them, no smell of bay rum or ammonia. This was far removed from Mrs Tulsi's Rose Room; and it was hard to believe that in the same city Ramchand and Dehuti lived in two rooms of a crumbling house. Mr Biswas began to feel that he had come on false pretences; there was nothing wrong with him.

'You have an appointment?' The receptionist spoke with the nasal, elided Chinese highness, and Mr Biswas detected hostility in her manner.

*Fish-face*, he commented mentally.

The receptionist started.

Mr Biswas realized with horror that he had whispered the word; he had not lost the Green Vale habit of speaking his thoughts aloud. 'Appointment?' he said. 'I have a letter.' He took out the small brown envelope which the Arwacas doctor had given him. It was creased, dirty, fuzzy along the edges, the corners curled.

The receptionist deftly slit the envelope open with a tortoiseshell knife. As she read the letter Mr Biswas felt exposed, and more of a fraud than ever. The blunder he had made worried him. He determined to be cautious. He clenched his teeth and tried to imagine whether 'fish-face', heard in a whisper, couldn't be mistaken for something quite different, something even complimentary.

*Fish-face.*

The receptionist looked up.

Mr Biswas smiled.

'You want to make an appointment, or you prefer to wait?' The receptionist was cold.

Mr Biswas decided to wait. He sat on a sofa, sank right into it, fell back and sank further, his knees rising high. He didn't know what to do with his eyes. It was too late to get a magazine. He counted the people in the room. Eight. He had a long time to wait. They probably all had appointments; they were all correctly ill.

A short limping man came in noisily, spoke loudly to the receptionist, stumped over to the sofa, sank into it, breathing hard, and stretched out a short straight leg.

At least there was something wrong with *him*. Mr Biswas eyed the leg and wondered how the man was going to get up again.

The surgery door opened, a man was heard but not seen, a woman came out, and someone else went in.

*A soldier of the legion lay dying in Algiers.*

Mr Biswas felt the lame man's eyes on him.

He thought about money. He had three dollars. A country doctor charged a dollar; but illness was clearly more expensive in this room.

The lame man breathed heavily.

Money was too worrying to think about, *Bell's Standard Elocutionist* too dangerous. His mind wandered and settled on *Tom Sawyer* and *Huckleberry Finn*, which he had read at Ramchand's. He smiled at the memory of Huckleberry Finn, whose trousers 'bagged low and contained nothing', nigger Jim who had seen ghosts and told stories.

He chuckled.

When he looked up he intercepted an exchange of glances between the receptionist and the lame man. He would have left right then, but he was too deeply wedged in his chair; if he attempted to rise he would create a disturbance and draw attention to himself. He became aware of his clothes: the washed-out khaki trousers with the frayed turn-ups, the washed-out blue shirt with the cuffs given one awkward fold backwards (no shirt size fitted him absolutely: collars were too tight or sleeves too long), the little brown hat resting in the valley formed by his thighs and belly. And he had only three dollars.

*You know, I am not a sick man at all.*

The lame man cleared his throat noisily, very noisily for a small man, and agitated his stiff leg.

Mr Biswas watched it.

Suddenly he had levered himself up from the sofa, rocking the lame man violently, and was walking towards the receptionist. Concentrating on his English, he said, 'I have changed my mind. I am feeling much better, thank you.' And, putting on his hat, he went towards the door.

'What about your letter?' the receptionist asked, surprised into her Trinidad accent.

'Keep it,' Mr Biswas said. 'File it. Burn it. Sell it.'

He went through the tiled verandah, crossed the black afternoon shadow on the drive, emerged into the sun, noted a bed of suffering zinnias as he moved briskly down the dazzling gravel to St Vincent Street. The wind from the Savannah was like a blessing. His mind was hot. And now he saw the city as made up of individuals, each of whom had his place in it. The large buildings around the Savannah were white and blank and silent in the heat.

He came to the War Memorial Park, sat on a bench in the shade of a tree and studied the statue of a belligerent soldier. Shadows were black and well-defined and encouraged repose and languor. His stomach was hurting.

His freedom was over, and it had been false. The past could not be ignored; it was never counterfeit; he carried it within himself. If there was a place for him, it was one that had already been hollowed out by time, by everything he had lived through, however imperfect, makeshift and cheating.

He welcomed the stomach pains. They had not occurred for months and it seemed to him that they marked the return of the wholeness of his mind, the restoration of the world; they indicated how far he had lifted himself from the abyss of the past months, and reminded him of the anguish against which everything now had to be measured.

Reluctantly, for it was a pleasure just to sit and let the wind play about his face and neck and down his shirt, he left the park and walked south, away from the Savannah. The quiet, withdrawn houses disappeared; pavements grew narrower and higher and more crowded; there were shops and cafés and buses, cars, trams and bicycles, horns and bells and shouts. He crossed Park Street and continued towards the sea. In the distance, above the roofs at the end of the street, he saw the tops of masts of sloops and schooners at St Vincent Jetty.

He passed the courts and came to the Red House, bulky in red sandstone. Part of the asphalt forecourt was marked off in white and lettered RESERVED FOR JUDGES. He went up the central steps and found himself under a high dome. He saw many green notice-boards and an unplaying fountain. The basin of the fountain was wet, and held many dead leaves and empty cigarette packets.

It was busy under the dome, with messengers in khaki uniforms and clerks in well-ironed clothes carrying buff or green folders, and with people continually passing between St Vincent Street and Woodford Square, where the professional beggars lounged about the bandstand and on benches, so confident of their appearance that they disdained to beg, spending most of their time patching the rags they wore like a uniform, garments thick and shaggy and richly variegated, small rag sewn on to small rag, labours of love. Even about the beggars there was an air of establishment. Woodford Square, cool under the trees and attractively dappled with light, was theirs; they cooked, ate and slept there, disturbed only by occasional political gatherings. They worried no one, and since they all had excellent physiques, and one or two were reputed to be millionaires, no one worried them.

On the green notice-boards, which also served to screen the offices on either side, there were government notices. Mr

Biswas was reading these when he heard someone call out. He turned to see an elderly Negro, respectably dressed, waving to him with a one-armed pair of spectacles.

'You want a certificate?' The Negro's lips snapped ferociously shut between words.

'Certificate?'

'Birth, marriage, death.' The Negro adjusted his mutilated spectacles low over his nose and from a shirt pocket stuffed with paper and pencils he pulled out a sheet of paper and let his pencil circle impatiently above it.

'I don't want any certificate.'

The pencil stopped playing. 'I can't understand it.' The Negro put away paper and pencil, sat down on a long, shiny bench, took off his spectacles, thrust the scratched, white end of the remaining arm into his mouth, and shook his legs. 'Nobody wanting certificates these days. If you ask me, the trouble is that nowadays it just have too damn many searchers. When I sit down on this bench in 1919 I was the onliest searcher. Today every Tom, Dick or Harry running up and down this place' – he jerked his chin towards the fountain – 'calling themself searchers.' His lips snapped ferociously. 'You sure you don't want a certificate? You never know when these things could be useful. I get lots of certificates for Indians, you know. In fact, I prefer getting certificates for Indians. And I could get it for you this afternoon self. I know one of the clerks inside there.' He waved to the office at his back and Mr Biswas saw a high, polished brown counter and pale green walls, lit, on this bright afternoon, by electric light.

'Helluva job,' the Negro said. 'No Christmas and Easter for me, you know. At times like that nobody want any certificate at all. And every day, whether I search for ten or two or no certificates, that damn clerk inside there got to get his twenty cigarettes.'

Mr Biswas began to move away.

'Still, if you know anybody who want a certificate – birth, death, marriage, marriage *in extremis* – send them to me. I come here every morning at eight o'clock sharp. The name is Pastor.'

Mr Biswas left Pastor, overwhelmed by the thought that in the office behind the green notice-board records were kept of every birth and death. And they had nearly missed him! He went down the steps into St Vincent Street and continued south towards the masts. Even Pastor, for all his grumbling, had found his place. What had driven him on a day in 1919 to take a seat outside the Registrar-General's Department and wait for illiterates wanting certificates?

He had thought himself back into the mood he had known at Green Vale, when he couldn't bear to look at the newspapers on the wall. And now he perceived that the starts of apprehension he felt at the sight of every person in the street did not come from fear at all; only from regret, envy, despair.

And, thinking of the newspapers on the barrackroom wall, he was confronted with the newspaper offices: the *Guardian*, the *Gazette*, the *Mirror*, the *Sentinel*, facing each other across the street. Machinery rattled like distant trains; through open windows came the warm smell of oil, ink and paper. The *Sentinel* was the paper for which Misir, the Aryan, was a cent-a-line country correspondent. All the stories Mr Biswas had got by heart from the newspapers in the barrackroom returned to him. *Amazing scenes were witnessed yesterday when . . . Passers-by stopped and stared yesterday when . . .*

He turned down a lane, pushed open a door on the right, and then another. The noise of machinery was louder. An important, urgent noise, but it did not intimidate him. He said to the man behind the high caged desk, 'I want to see the editor.'

*Amazing scenes were witnessed in St Vincent Street yesterday when Mohun Biswas, 31 . . .*

'You got an appointment?'

*. . . assaulted a receptionist.*

'No,' Mr Biswas said irritably.

*In an interview with our reporter . . . In an interview with our special correspondent late last night Mr Biswas said . . .*

'The editor is busy. You better go and see Mr Woodward.'

'You just tell the editor I come all the way from the country to see him.'

*Amazing scenes were witnessed in St Vincent Street yesterday*
*when Biswas, 31, unemployed, of no fixed address, assaulted a re-*
*ceptionist at the offices of the* TRINIDAD SENTINEL. *People*
*ducked behind desks as Biswas, father of four, walked into the build-*
*ing with guns blazing, shot the editor and four reporters dead, and*
*then set fire to the building. Passers-by stopped and stared as the*
*flames rose high, fanned by a strong breeze. Several tons of*
*paper were destroyed and the building itself gutted. In an exclusive*
*interview with our special correspondent late last night Mr Biswas*
*said . . .*

'This way,' the receptionist said, climbing down from his
desk, and led Mr Biswas into a large room which belied the
urgent sounds of typewriters and machinery. Many typewriters were idle, many desks untenanted. A group of men in
shirtsleeves stood around a green water-cooler in one corner;
other groups of two or three were seated on desks; one man
was spinning a swivel-chair with his foot. There was a row of
frosted-glass cubicles along one wall, and the receptionist,
going ahead of Mr Biswas, knocked on one of these, pushed
the door open, allowed Mr Biswas to enter, and closed the
door.

A small fat man, pink and oiled from the heat, half rose
from behind a desk littered with paper. Slabs of lead, edged
with type, served as paperweights. And Mr Biswas was
thrilled to see the proof of an article, headlined and displayed.
It was a glimpse of a secret; isolated on the large white sheet,
the article had an eminence tomorrow's readers would never
see. Mr Biswas's excitement increased. And he liked the man
he saw before him.

'And what is your story?' the editor asked, sitting down.

'I don't have a story. I want a job.'

Mr Biswas saw almost with delight that he had embarrassed
the editor; and he pitied him for not having the decision to
throw him out. The editor went pinker and looked down at
the proof. He was unhappy in the heat and seemed to be
melting. His cheeks flowed into his neck; his neck bulged
over his collar; his round shoulders drooped; his belly
hung over his waistband; and he was damp all over. 'Yes, yes,'
he said. 'Have you worked on a paper before?'

Mr Biswas thought about the articles he had promised to write, but hadn't, for Misir's paper, which had never appeared. 'Once or twice,' he said.

The editor looked at the door, as though for help. 'Do you mean once? Or do you mean twice?'

'I have read a lot.' Mr Biswas said, getting out of dangerous ground.

The editor played with a slab of lead.

'Hall Caine, Marie Corelli, Jacob Boehme, Mark Twain. Hall Caine, Mark Twain,' Mr Biswas repeated. 'Samuel Smiles.'

The editor looked up.

'Marcus Aurelius.'

The editor smiled.

'Epictetus.'

The editor continued to smile, and Mr Biswas smiled back, to let the editor know that he knew he was sounding absurd.

'You read those people just for pleasure, eh?'

Mr Biswas recognized the cruel intent of the question, but he didn't mind. 'No,' he said. 'Just for the encouragement.' All his excitement died.

There was a pause. The editor looked at the proof. Through the frosted glass Mr Biswas saw figures passing in the newsroom. He became aware of the noise again: the traffic in the street, the regular rattle of machinery, the intermittent chatter of typewriters, occasional laughter.

'How old are you?'

'Thirty-one.'

'You have come from the country, you are thirty-one, you have never written, and you want to be a reporter. What do you do?'

Mr Biswas thought of estate-driver, exalted it to overseer, rejected it, rejected shopkeeper, rejected unemployed. He said, 'Sign-painter.'

The editor rose. 'I have just the job for you.'

He led Mr Biswas out of the office, through the newsroom (the group around the water-cooler had broken up), past a machine unrolling sheets of typewritten paper, into a partially dismantled room where carpenters were at work, through more rooms, and then into a yard. Down the lane at one end Mr Biswas could see the street he had left a few minutes before.

The editor walked about the yard, pointing. 'Here and here,' he said. 'And here.'

Mr Biswas was given paint and a brush, and he spent the rest of the afternoon writing signs: No Admittance to Wheeled Vehicles, No Entry, Watch out for Vans, No Hands Wanted.

Around him machinery clattered and hummed; the carpenters beat rhythms on the nails as they drove them in.

*Amazing scenes were witnessed yesterday when . . .*

'Tcha!' he exclaimed angrily.

*Amazing scenes were witnessed yesterday when Mohun Biswas, 31, a sign-painter, set to work on the offices of the* TRINIDAD SENTINEL. *Passers-by stopped and stared as Biswas, father of four, covered the walls with obscene phrases. Women hid their faces in their hands, screamed and fainted. A traffic jam was created in St Vincent Street and police, under Superintendent Grieves, were called in to restore order. Interviewed by our special correspondent late last night, Biswas said . . .*

'Didn't even know who Marcus Aurelius was, the crab-catching son of a bitch.'

*. . . interviewed late last night, Biswas . . . Mr Biswas said, 'The ordinary man cannot be expected to know the meaning of "No Admittance".'*

'What, still here?'

It was the editor. He was less pink, less oiled, and his clothes were dry. He was smoking a short fat cigar; it repeated and emphasized his shape.

The yard was in shadow; the light was going. Machinery clattered more assertively: a series of separate noises; the carpenters' rhythms had ceased. In the street traffic had subsided, footsteps resounded; the passing of a motor, the trilling of a bicycle bell could be heard from afar.

'But that is good,' the editor said. 'Very good indeed.'

You sound surprised, you little chunk of lard. 'I got the letters from a magazine.' You think you are the only one laughing, eh?

'I could eat the Gill Sans R,' the editor said. 'You know, I don't really see why you should want to give up your job.'

'Not enough money.'

'Not much in this either.'

Mr Biswas pointed to a sign. 'No wonder you are doing your best to keep people out.'

'Oh. No Hands Wanted.'

'A nice little sign,' Mr Biswas said.

The editor smiled and then was convulsed with laughter.

And Mr Biswas, the clown again, laughed too.

'That was for carpenters and labourers,' the editor said. 'Come tomorrow, if you are serious. We'll give you a month's trial. But no pay.'

A chance encounter had led him to sign-writing. Sign-writing had taken him to Hanuman House and the Tulsis. Sign-writing found him a place on the *Sentinel*. And neither for the Tulsi Store signs nor for those at the *Sentinel* was he paid.

He worked with enthusiasm. His reading had given him an extravagant vocabulary but Mr Burnett, the editor, was patient. He gave Mr Biswas copies of London papers, and Mr Biswas studied their style until he could turn out presentable imitations. It was not long before he developed a feeling for the shape and scandalizing qualities of every story. To this he added something of his own. And it was part of his sudden good fortune that he was working for the *Sentinel* and not for the *Guardian* or the *Gazette*. For the facetiousness that came to him as soon as he put pen to paper, and the fantasy he had hitherto dissipated in quarrels with Shama and in invective against the Tulsis, were just the things Mr Burnett wanted.

'Let them get their news from the other papers,' he said. 'That is exactly what they are doing at the moment anyway. The only way we can get readers is by shocking them. Get them angry. Frighten them. You just give me one good fright, and the job is yours.'

Next day Mr Biswas turned in a story.

Mr Burnett said, 'You made this one up?'

Mr Biswas nodded.

'Pity.'

The story was headlined:

FOUR CHILDREN ROASTED IN HUT BLAZE
*Mother, Helpless, Watches*

'I liked the last paragraph,' Mr Burnett said.

This read: 'Sightseers are pouring into the stricken village, and we do not feel we are in a position to divulge its name as yet. "In times like this," an old man told me last night, "we want to be left alone." '

Abandoning fiction, Mr Biswas persevered. And Mr Burnett continued to give advice.

'I think you'd better go a little easy on the amazing scenes being witnessed. And how about turning your passers-by into ordinary people every now and then? "Considerably" is a big word meaning "very", which is a pointless word any way. And look. "Several" has seven letters. "Many" has only four and oddly enough has exactly the same meaning. I liked your piece on the Bonny Baby Competition. You made me laugh. But you haven't frightened me yet.'

'Anything funny happen at the Mad House?' Mr Biswas asked Ramchand that evening.

Ramchand looked annoyed.

And Mr Biswas gave up the idea of an exposure piece on the Mad House.

On his way to the *Sentinel* next morning he called at a police station. From there he went to the mortuary, then to the City Council's stable-yard. When he got to the *Sentinel* he sat down at a free desk – no desk was yet his – and wrote in pencil:

Last week the *Sentinel* Bonny Baby Competition was held at Prince's Building. And late last night the body of a dead male baby was found, neatly wrapped in a brown paper parcel, on the rubbish dump at Cocorite.

I have seen the baby and I am in a position to say that it did not win a prize in our Bonny Baby Competition.

Experts are not yet sure whether the baby was specially taken to the rubbish dump, or simply put out with the rubbish in the usual way.

Hezekiah James, 43, unemployed, who discovered the dead baby, told me . . .

'Good, good,' Mr Burnett said. 'But heavy. Heavy. Why not "I am able" instead of "I am in a position"?'

'I got that from the *Daily Express*.'

'All right. Let it pass. But promise me that for a whole week you won't be in a position to do or say anything. It's going to be hard. But try. What sort of baby?'

'Sort?'

'Black, white, green?'

'White. Blueish when I saw it, really. I thought, though, that we didn't mention race, except for Chinese.'

'Listen to the man. If I ran across a black baby on the rubbish dump at Banbury, do you think I would just say a baby?'

And the headlines the next day read:

WHITE BABY FOUND ON RUBBISH DUMP
*In Brown Paper Parcel*
Did Not Win Bonny Baby Competition

'Just one other thing,' Mr Burnett said. 'Lay off babies for a while.'

The job was urgent: the paper had to be printed every evening; by early morning it had to be in every part of the island. This was not the false urgency of writing signs for shops at Christmas or looking after crops. And even after a dozen years Mr Biswas never lost the thrill, which he then felt for the first time, at seeing what he had written the day before appear in print, in the newspaper delivered free.

'You haven't given me a real shock yet,' Mr Burnett said.

And Mr Biswas wanted to shock Mr Burnett. It seemed unlikely that he would ever do so, for in his fourth week he was made shipping reporter, taking the place of a man who had been killed at the docks by a crane load of flour accidentally falling from a great height. It was the tourist season and the harbour was full of ships from America and Europe. Mr Biswas went aboard German ships, was given excellent lighters, saw photographs of Adolf Hitler, and was bewildered by the Heil Hitler salutes.

Excitement!

The ships sailed away with their scorched tourists, distinguished by their tropical clothes, after only a few hours. But they had come from places with famous names. And in the *Sentinel* office news from those places spilled out continually on to spools of paper. Outside was the hot sun, the horse-dunged streets, the choked slums, the rooms where he lived with Ramchand and Dehuti; and, beyond that, the level acres of sugarcane, the sunken ricelands, the repetitive labour of his brothers, the short roads leading from known settlement to known settlement, the Tulsi establishment, the old men who gathered every evening in the arcade of Hanuman House and would travel no more. But within the walls of the office every part of the world was near.

He went aboard American ships on the South American tourist route, interviewed businessmen, had difficulty in understanding the American accent, saw the galleys and marvelled at the quantity and quality of the food thrown away. He copied down passenger lists, was invited by a ship's cook to join a smuggling ring that dealt in camera flash-bulbs, declined and was unable to write the story because it would have incriminated his late predecessor.

He interviewed an English novelist, a man about his own age, but still young, and shining with success. Mr Biswas was impressed. The novelist's name was unknown to him and to the readers of the *Sentinel*, but Mr Biswas had thought of all writers as dead and associated the production of books not only with distant lands, but with distant ages. He visualized headlines – FAMOUS NOVELIST SAYS PORT OF SPAIN WORLD'S THIRD WICKEDEST CITY – and fed the novelist with leading questions. But the novelist considered Mr Biswas's inquiries to have a sinister political motive, and made slow statements about the island's famed beauty and his desire to see as much of it as possible.

I want to see that frighten anybody, Mr Biswas thought.

(Years later Mr Biswas came across the travel-book the novelist had written about the region. He saw himself described as an 'incompetent, aggrieved and fanatical young reporter, who distastefully noted my guarded replies in a laborious longhand'.)

Then a ship called on the way to Brazil.

Within twenty-four hours Mr Biswas was notorious, the *Sentinel*, reviled on every hand, momentarily increased its circulation, and Mr Burnett was jubilant.

He said, 'You have even chilled me.'

The story, the leading one on page three, read:

DADDY COMES HOME IN A COFFIN
*U.S. Explorer's Last Journey*
ON ICE
*by M. Biswas*

Somewhere in America in a neat little red-roofed cottage four children ask their mother every day, 'Mummy, when is Daddy coming home?'

Less than a year ago Daddy – George Elmer Edman, the celebrated traveller and explorer – left home to explore the Amazon.

Well, I have news for you, kiddies.

Daddy is on his way home.

Yesterday he passed through Trinidad. In a coffin.

Mr Biswas was taken on the staff of the *Sentinel* at a salary of fifteen dollars a fortnight.

'The first thing you must do,' Mr Burnett said, 'is to get out and get yourself a suit. I can't have my best reporter running about in those clothes.'

It was Ramchand who brought about the reconciliation between Mr Biswas and the Tulsis; or rather, since the Tulsis had few thoughts on the subject, made it possible for Mr Biswas to recover his family without indignity. Ramchand's task was easy. Mr Biswas's name appeared almost every day in the *Sentinel*, so that it seemed he had suddenly become famous and rich. Mr Biswas, believing himself that this was very nearly so, felt disposed to be charitable.

He was at that time touring the island as the Scarlet Pimpernel, in the hope of having people come up to him and say, 'You are the Scarlet Pimpernel and I claim the *Sentinel* prize.' Every day his photograph appeared in the *Sentinel* together with his report on the previous day's journey and his itinerary for the day.

The photograph was half a column wide and there was no room for his ears; he was frowning, in an unsuccessful attempt to look menacing; his mouth was slightly open and he stared at the camera out of the corners of his eyes, which were shadowed by the low-pulled brim of his hat. As a circulation raiser the Scarlet Pimpernel was a failure. The photograph concealed too much; and he was too well dressed for ordinary people to accost him in a sentence of such length and correctness. The prizes went unclaimed for days and the Scarlet Pimpernel reports became increasingly fantastic. Mr Biswas visited his brother Prasad and readers of the *Sentinel* learned next morning that a peasant in a remote village had rushed up to the Scarlet Pimpernel and said, 'You are the Scarlet Pimpernel and I claim the *Sentinel* prize.' The peasant was then reported as saying that he read the *Sentinel* every day, since no other paper presented the news so fully, so amusingly, and with such balance.

Then Mr Biswas visited his eldest brother Pratap. And there he had a surprise. He found that his mother had been living with Pratap for some weeks. For long Mr Biswas had considered Bipti useless, depressing and obstinate; he wondered how Pratap had managed to communicate with her and persuade her to leave the hut in the back trace at Pagotes. But she had come and she had changed. She was active and lucid; she was a lively and important part of Pratap's household. Mr Biswas felt reproached and anxious. His luck had been too sudden, his purchase on the world too slight. When he got back late that evening to the *Sentinel* office he sat down at a desk, his own (his towel in the bottom drawer), and with memories coming from he knew not where, he wrote:

SCARLET PIMPERNEL SPENDS NIGHT IN A TREE
*Anguish of Six-Hour Vigil*

*Oink! Oink!*
The frogs croaked all around me. Nothing but that and the sound of the rain on trees in the black night.

I was dripping wet. My motorcycle had broken down miles from anywhere. It was midnight and I was alone.

The report then described a sleepless night, encounters with snakes and bats, the two cars that passed in the night, heedless of the Scarlet Pimpernel's cries, the rescue early in the morning by peasants who recognized the Scarlet Pimpernel and claimed their prize.

It was not long after this that Mr Biswas went to Arwacas. He got there in the middle of the morning but did not go to Hanuman House until after four, when he knew the store would be closed, the children back from school and the sisters in the hall and kitchen. His return was as magnificent as he had wished. He was still climbing up the steps from the courtyard when he was greeted by shouts, scampering and laughter.

'You are the Scarlet Pimpernel and I claim the *Sentinel* prize!'

He went around, dropping *Sentinel* dollar-tokens into eager hands.

'Send this in with the coupon from the *Sentinel*. Your money will come the day after tomorrow.'

Savi and Anand at once took possession of him.

Shama, emerging from the black kitchen, said, 'Anand, you will get your father's suit dirty.'

It was as though he had never left. Neither Shama nor the children nor the hall carried any mark of his absence.

Shama dusted a bench at the table and asked whether he had eaten. He didn't reply, but sat where she had dusted. The children asked questions continually, and it was easy not to pay attention to Shama as she brought the food out.

'Uncle Mohun, Uncle Mohun. You really spend a night up a tree?'

'What do you think, Jai?'

'Ma say you make it up. And I don't see how *you* could climb up a tree.'

'I can't tell you how often I fall down.'

It was better than he had imagined to be back in the sooty green hall with the shelflike loft, the long pitchpine table, the unrelated pieces of furniture, the photographs of Pundit Tulsi, the kitchen safe with the Japanese coffee-set.

'Uncle Mohun, that man did really chase you with a cutlass when you try to give a coupon to his wife?'

'Yes.'

'Why you didn't give him one too?'

'Go away. You children getting too smart for me.'

He ate and washed his hands and gargled. Shama urged him to be careful of his tie and jacket: as though they were not new to her, as though she had a wifely interest even in clothes she had not known from the start.

He went up the stairs, past the landing with the broken piano. In the verandah he saw Hari, the holy man, and Hari's wife. They barely greeted him. They both seemed untouched by his new fame or his new suit. Hari, in his pundit's clothes, looked jaundiced and unwell as always; his wife's solemnity was tinged with worry and fatigue. Mr Biswas had often surprised them in similar quiet domestic scenes, withdrawn from the life about them.

He felt he was intruding, and hurried past the door with the coloured glass panes into the Book Room, which smelled mustily of old paper and worm-eaten wood. His books were there with traces of their soaking: bleached covers, stained and crinkled pages. Anand came into the room. His hair was long on his big head; he was in his 'home-clothes'. Mr Biswas held Anand to his leg and Anand rubbed against it. He asked Anand about school and got shy, unintelligible replies. They had little to talk about.

'Exactly when they did start seeing my name in the papers?' Mr Biswas asked.

Anand smiled, raised one foot off the floor, and mumbled.

'Who see it first?'

Anand shook his head.

'And what they say, eh? Not the children, but the big people.'

'Nothing.'

'Nothing? But what about the photo? Coming out every day. What they say when they see *that*?'

'Nothing.'

'Nothing at all?'

'Only Auntie Chinta say you look like a crook.'

'Who is the pretty baby? Tell me, *who* is the pretty baby?'

It was Shama, coming into the room and wandering about it with a baby in her arms.

Mr Biswas had not seen his fourth child. And now he was embarrassed to look.

Shama came closer but did not raise her eyes. 'Who is that man?' she said to the baby. 'Do you *know* that man?'

Mr Biswas did not respond. He felt suffocated, sickened by the picture of mother and child as by the whole furtive domestic scene in this room above the hall: father, mother, children.

'And who is this?' Shama had taken the baby to Anand. 'This is brother.' Anand tickled her chin and the baby gurgled.

'Yes, this is brother. Oh, isn't she a *pretty* baby?'

He noticed that Shama had grown a little plumper.

He relented. He took a step towards Shama and immediately she held up the baby to him.

'Her name is Kamla,' Shama said in Hindi, her eyes still on the baby.

'Nice name,' he said in English. 'Who give it?'

'The pundit.'

'This one register too, I suppose?'

'But you were here when she was born —' And Shama stopped, as though she had ventured on to dangerous ground.

Mr Biswas took the baby.

'Give her back to me,' Shama said after a short time. 'She might get your clothes dirty.'

The reconciliation was soon complete, and on terms that made Mr Biswas feel he had won a victory. It was arranged for him to meet Mrs Tulsi in Port of Spain. She pretended not to know that he had ever left Shama and Hanuman House; he had come to Port of Spain to see the doctor, hadn't he? Mr Biswas said he had. She was glad he was better; Pundit Tulsi always used to say that good health was worth any fortune. She never asked about his job, though she said that she expected much from Mr Biswas and always had; which was why she had been so ready to agree when he came that afternoon to ask for Shama's hand.

Mrs Tulsi proposed that Mr Biswas should move his family to Port of Spain and live with her son and herself. Unless, of course, Mr Biswas was thinking of buying a house of his own; she was only a mother and had no control over Shama's fate. If they came, however, they would have the run of the house, except for those rooms used by Owad and herself. In return they would pay eight dollars a month, Shama would cook, do all the housework and collect the rents from her other two houses: a difficult business: not worth the trouble to get an outsider to do it and she was too old to do it herself.

The offer was stupendous: a house, no less. It was the climax of his current good fortune, which must now, he felt, surely end. To delay acceptance, to cover up his nervousness, he talked about the difficulty of collecting rents. Mrs Tulsi talked about Pundit Tulsi and he listened with solemn sympathy.

They were in the front verandah. Ferns in baskets hung from the eaves, softening the light, cooling the air. Mr Biswas reclined on his morris chair. It was an experience, so new he could not yet savour it, to find himself turned all at once from a visitor into a dweller, in a house that was solid and finished and painted and elegant all over, with a level, gapless floor, straight concrete walls, panelled doors with locks, a complete roof, a ceiling varnished in the drawingroom, painted elsewhere. Finishing details, which up to a few minutes before he had taken for granted, he now noted, one by one, as for the first time. Nothing had to be added, nothing was makeshift; there were no surprises of mud walls or tree-branches, no secret ways of doing anything; everything worked as it was meant to.

The house stood on high pillars and was one of the newest and most imposing in the street. The district had been recently redeveloped and was rising fast, though in every street there were still a number of dwellings of the stubborn poor, unfenced wooden huts which spoke of the time when the district was part of a sugar-estate. The streets were straight; every lot measured one hundred feet by fifty; and a sewerage trace, almost a street itself, ran down the middle of each block, separating back fences. So there was space; space below the floor of the house itself, space at the back, space at the sides, space for a garden at the front.

Could this luck have been more complete?

Ramchand and Dehuti were delighted. The camplife which Mr Biswas's presence enforced on them in their two rooms, though pleasant at first, had begun to be irksome. They were glad, too, that Mr Biswas had been settled. They felt responsible for that as well as the reconciliation. One unexpected result of the negotiations was that Dehuti attached herself to Hanuman House, joining the dozens of strange women who, to Mr Biswas's surprise, were always willing to turn up days before any large function at Hanuman House, abandoning husbands and children, to cook and clean and generally serve, without payment. Dehuti worked hard and was always invited. She often went with the Tulsi sisters to other functions; and at weddings sang the sad songs which had not been sung for her. In time no one thought of her as Mr Biswas's sister, not even Mr Biswas, to whom she became only one of the women attached to the Tulsis.

Once more, then, the furniture moved. And what had choked the barrackroom made little impression on the house at Port of Spain. The fourposter and Shama's dressingtable went into a bedroom; the kitchen safe with the coffee-set remained in the back verandah with the green table. The hatrack and the rockingchair alone had places of honour, in the front verandah; they were put out every morning and brought in every night, to prevent them being stolen. For the rest, the house remained furnished in the manner which Mrs Tulsi had thought appropriate to the city. In the drawing-room four cane-bottomed bentwood chairs stood stiffly around a marble topped three-legged table which carried a potted fern on a crocheted and tasselled white cloth. In the diningroom there was a frigid-looking washstand with a ewer and basin. Mrs Tulsi had brought none of the statuary from Hanuman House but many of the brass vases, which, filled with potted plants, were disposed about the verandah and brought in every night.

Anand and Savi were not easily persuaded to leave Hanuman House. They remained there for some weeks after Shama had left with Myna and Kamla. Then Savi came one Sunday evening with Mrs Tulsi and the god. She saw the street lamps and the lights of the ships in the harbour. Mrs Tulsi took her to the Botanical Gardens; she saw the ponds and grassy slopes of the sunken Rock Gardens; she heard the band play; and she stayed. Anand, however, refused to be allured, until the younger god said, 'They have a new sweet drink in Port of Spain. Something called Coca Cola. The best thing in the world. Come with me to Port of Spain, and I will get your father to buy you a Coca Cola and some real icecream. In cardboard cups. Real icecream. Not homemade.'

To the children of Hanuman House home-made was not a word of commendation. Home-made icecream was the flavourless (officially coconut) congelation churned out by Chinta after lunch on Christmas Day. She used an old, rusted freezer; she said it 'skipped'; and to hasten the freezing she threw lumps of ice into the mixture. The rust from the freezer dripped on the icecream and penetrated it, like a ripple of chocolate.

And it was purely this promise of real icecream and Coca Cola that drew Anand to Port of Spain.

On a Sunday afternoon, when shadows had withdrawn to under the eaves of houses, when the city was hard and bright and empty, with doors closed everywhere, and the glass windows of shops reflected only those opposite, Mr Biswas took Anand on a tour of Port of Spain. They walked with a sense of adventure in the middle of empty streets; they heard their footsteps; like this, the city could be known; it held no threat. They looked at café after café, rejecting, at Anand's insistence, all those which claimed to sell only home-made cakes and icecream. At last they found one which was suitable. On a high red stool, a revelation and luxury in itself, Anand sat at the counter, and the icecream came. In a cardboard tub, frosted, cold to the touch. With a wooden spoon. The cover had to be taken off and licked; the icecream, light pink and spotted with red, steamed: one preparatory delight after another.

'It don't taste like icecream at all,' Anand said. He cleaned the tub, and it was such a perfectly made thing he would have liked to keep it.

When he sipped the Coca Cola he said, 'It is like horse pee.' Which was what some cousin had said of a drink at Hanuman House.

'Anand!' Mr Biswas said, smiling at the man behind the counter. 'You've got to stop talking like that. You are in Port of Spain now.'

The house faced east, and the memories that remained of these first four years in Port of Spain were above all memories of morning. The newspaper, delivered free, still warm, the ink still wet, sprawled on the concrete steps, down which the sun was moving. Dew lay on trees and roofs; the empty street, freshly swept and washed, was in cool shadow, and water ran clear in the gutters whose green bases had been scratched and striped by the sweepers' harsh brooms. Memories of taking the Royal Enfield out from under the house and cycling in a sun still cool along the streets of the awakening city. Stillness at noon: stripping for a short nap: the window of his room open: a square of blue above the unmoving curtain. In the afternoon, the steps in shadow; tea in the back verandah. Then an interview at a hotel, perhaps, and the urgent machinery of the *Sentinel*. The promise of the evening; the expectation of the morning.

With Mrs Tulsi and Owad away on week-ends and during the holidays it was possible at times for Mr Biswas to forget that the house belonged to them. And their presence was hardly a strain. Mrs Tulsi never fainted in Port of Spain, never stuffed soft candle or Vick's Vaporub into her nostrils, never wore bay-rum-soaked bandages around her forehead. She was neither distant nor possessive with the children, and her relations with Mr Biswas became less cautious and formal as his friendship with Owad grew. Owad appreciated Mr Biswas's work and Mr Biswas, flattered to be established as a wit and a madman, developed a respect for the young man who read such big books in foreign languages. They became companions; they went to the cinema and the seaside; and Mr Biswas showed Owad transcripts, which no paper printed, of court proceedings in cases of rape and brothel-keeping.

Mr Biswas ceased to ridicule or resent the excessive care Mrs Tulsi gave to her younger son. Mrs Tulsi believed that prunes, like fish brains, were especially nourishing for people who exercised their brains, and she fed Owad prunes every day. Milk was obtained for him from the Dairies in Phillip Street; it came in proper milk bottles with silver caps; not like the milk Shama got from a man six lots away who, oblivious of the aspirations of the district, kept cows and delivered milk in rum bottles stopped with brown paper.

Though with Owad and Mrs Tulsi Mr Biswas's attitude towards his children was gently deprecatory, he was watching and learning, with an eye on his own household and especially on Anand. Soon, he hoped, Anand would qualify to eat prunes and drink milk from the Dairies.

His household established, Mr Biswas set about establishing his tyrannies.

'Savi!'

No answer.

'Savi! Savi! Oh-Savi-yah! Oh, you there. Why you didn't answer?'

'But I come.'

'Is not enough. You must come *and* answer.'

'All right.'

'All right what?'

'All right, Pa.'

'Good. On that table in the corner you will find cigarettes, matches and a *Sentinel* notebook. Hand them to me.'

'*O God!* That is all you call me for?'

'Yes. That is all. Answer back again, and I make you read out something for me to take down in shorthand.'

Savi ran out of the room.

'Anand! Anand!'

'Yes, Pa.'

'That is better. You are getting a little training now. Sit down there and call out this speech.'

Anand snatched *Bell's Standard Elocutionist* and angrily read out some Macaulay.

'You reading too fast.'

'I thought you was writing shorthand.'

'You answering back too! You see what happen to you children, spending all that time at Hanuman House. Just for that, check while I read back.'

*'O God!'* And Anand stamped, regretting the dying day.

But the checking went on.

Then Mr Biswas said, 'Anand, this is not a punishment. I ask you to do this because I want you to help me.'

He had discovered, with surprise, that this sentence soothed Anand, and he always offered it at the end of these sessions as a consolation.

It was soon established that he did much of his work in bed and was to be expected to call constantly for paper, pencils to be sharpened, matches, cigarettes, ashtrays to be emptied, books to be brought, books to be taken away. It was also established that his sleep was important. He flew into terrible rages when awakened, even at a time he had fixed.

'Savi,' Shama would say, 'go and wake your father.'

'Let Anand go.'

'No, the both of you go.'

To Shama, who began to complain of his 'strictness' – a word which gave him a curious satisfaction – he said, 'It is not strictness. It is training.'

Mrs Tulsi, approving if a little surprised, told tales of the severe training to which Pundit Tulsi had submitted his children.

And whenever Mrs Tulsi was away Shama made claims of her own. She was unable to faint like Mrs Tulsi but she complained of fatigue and liked to be attended by her children. She got Savi and Anand to walk on her and said in Hindi, 'God will bless you,' with such feeling that they considered it a sufficient recompense. Soon, and without this recompense, it became the duty of Savi and Anand to walk on Mr Biswas as well.

Shama herself did not escape training. She had to file all the stories Mr Biswas wrote. Mr Biswas said she did this in-efficiently. He gave her his pay-packet unopened and when she said that the money was insufficient he accused her of incompetence. And so Shama started on her laborious, futile practice of keeping accounts. Every evening she sat down at the green table in the back verandah and noted every penny she had spent during the day, slowly filling both sides of the pages of a bloated, oilstained *Sentinel* notebook with her Mission-school script.

'Your little daily *puja*, eh?' Mr Biswas said.

'No,' she said. 'I only trying to give you a raise.'

Mr Biswas never asked to see Shama's accounts, but she did them partly as a reproach to Mr Biswas and partly because she enjoyed it. Whatever his other qualities, Mr Burnett didn't believe in paying generously and while he edited the *Sentinel* Mr Biswas's salary never rose above fifty dollars a month, money which went almost as soon as it came. Shama's household accounts were complicated by the rents she col-lected. She spent the rent money on the household and then had to make it up with the household money. The figures nearly always came out wrong. And every other week-end Shama's accounting reached a pitch of frenzy, and she was to be seen in the back verandah puzzling over the *Sentinel* note-book, the rent book, the receipt book, doing innumerable little addition and subtraction sums on scraps of paper and occasionally making memoranda. Shama wrote curious memoranda. She wrote as she spoke and once Mr Biswas came on a note that said, 'Old creole woman from 42 owe six dollars.'

'I always did say that you Tulsis were a pack of financial geniuses,' he said.

She said, 'I would like you to know that I used to come first in arithmetic.'

And when Savi and Anand came to her for help with their arithmetic homework she said, 'Go to your father. He was the genius in arithmetic.'

'Know more than you anyway,' he said. 'Savi, ought twos are how much?'

'Two.'

'You are your mother's daughter all right. Anand?'

'One.'

'But what happening these days? They are not teaching as they used to when I was a boy.'

He found fault with all the textbooks.

'Readers by Captain Cutteridge! Listen to this. Page sixty-five, lesson nineteen. Some of Our Animal Friends.' He read in a mincing voice: ' "What should we do without our animal friends? The cow and the goat give us milk and we eat their flesh when they are killed." You hear the savage? And listen. "Many boys and girls have to tie up their goats before going to school in the morning, and help to milk them in the afternoon." Anand, you tie up your goat this morning? Well, you better hurry up. Is nearly milking time. That is the sort of stuff they fulling up the children head with these days. When I was a boy it used to be the *Royal Reader* and *Blackie's Tropical Reader*. *Nesfield's Grammar!*' he exclaimed. 'I used to use Macdougall's.' And he sent Anand hunting for the Macdougall's, a typographical antique, its battered boards hinged with strips of blue tape.

From time to time he called for their exercise books, said he was horrified, and set himself up as their teacher for a few days. He cured Anand of a leaning towards fancy lettering and got him to abridge the convolutions of his C and J and S. With Savi he could do nothing. As a teacher he was exacting and short-tempered, and when Shama went to Hanuman House she was able to tell her sisters with pride, 'The children are afraid of him.'

And, partly to have peace on Sundays, and partly because the combination of the word 'Sunday' with the word 'school' suggested denial and a spoiling of pleasure, he sent Anand and Savi to Sunday school. They loved it. They were given cakes and soft drinks and taught hymns with catchy tunes.

At home one day Anand began singing, 'Jesus loves me, yes I know.'

Mrs Tulsi was offended. 'How do you know that Jesus loves you?'

' 'Cause the Bible tells me so,' Anand said, quoting the next line of the hymn.

Mrs Tulsi took this to mean that, without provocation, Mr Biswas was resuming his religious war.

'Roman cat, your mother,' he told Shama. 'I thought a good Christian hymn would remind her of happy childhood days as a baby Roman kitten.'

But the Sunday school stopped. In its place, and also to counter the influence of Captain Cutteridge, Mr Biswas began reading novels to his children. Anand responded but Savi was again a disappointment.

'I can't see Savi ever eating prunes and drinking milk from the Dairies,' Mr Biswas said. 'Let her go on. All I see her doing is fighting to make up accounts like her mother.'

Unmoved by Mr Biswas's insults, Shama continued to write up her accounts, continued to wrestle once a fortnight with the rent money, and continued to serve eviction notices. Unknown to her family and almost unknown to herself, Shama had become a creature of terror to Mrs Tulsi's tenants. To get the rents she often had to serve eviction notices, particularly on 'old creole woman from 42'. It amused Mr Biswas to read the stern, grammatical injunctions in Shama's placid handwriting, and he said, 'I don't see how that could frighten anybody.'

Shama conducted her exciting operations without any sense that they were exciting. She was unwilling to risk serving notices personally. So late at night, when the tenant was almost certain to be in bed, Shama went out with her notice and pot of glue and pasted the notice on the two leaves of the door, so that the tenant, opening his door in the morning, would tear the notice and would not be able to claim that it had not been served.

Mr Biswas learned shorthand, though of a purely personal sort. He read all the books he could get on journalism, and in his enthusiasm bought an expensive American volume called *Newspaper Management*, which turned out to be an exhortation to newspaper proprietors to invest in modern machinery. He discovered, and became addicted to, the extensive literature aimed at people who want to become writers; again and again he read how manuscripts were to be presented and was warned not to ring up the busy editors of London or New York newspapers. He bought *Short Stories: How to Write Them* by Cecil Hunt and *How to Write a Book*, by the same author.

His salary being increased about this time, he ignored Shama's pleas and bought a secondhand portable typewriter on credit. Then, to make the typewriter pay for itself, he decided to write for English and American periodicals. But he could find nothing to write about. The books he had read didn't help him. And then he saw an advertisement for the Ideal School of Journalism, Edgware Road, London, he filled in and cut out the coupon for the free booklet. The booklet came after two months. Printed sheets of various colours fell from it: initialled testimonials from all over the world. The booklet said that the Ideal School not only taught but also marketed; and it wondered whether Mr Biswas might not find it worth his while to take a course in short story writing as well. The principal of the Ideal School (a bespectacled grandfatherly man, from the spotty photograph) had discovered the secret of every plot in the world and his discovery had been accepted by the British Museum in London and the Bodleian Library in Oxford. Mr Biswas was impressed but couldn't spare the money. There had already been a row with Shama when he had used up the salary increase for a further three months to pay for the first two journalism lessons. In due course the first lesson came.

'Even people with outstanding writing ability say they cannot find subjects. But in reality nothing is easier. You are sitting at your desk.' (Mr Biswas read this in bed.) 'You look through your window. But wait. There is an article in that window. The various types of window, the history of the window, windows famous in history, houses without windows. And the story of glass itself can be fascinating. Already, then, you have subjects for two articles. You look through your window and you see the sky. The weather is always a subject of conversation and there is no reason why you cannot make it the subject of a lively article. The demand for such material is enormous. For your first exercise, then, I want you to write four bright articles on the seasons. You may incorporate as many of these hints as you wish:

'Summer. The crowded trains to the seaside, the chink of ice in a glass, the slap of fish on the fishmonger's slab . . .'

'Slap of fish on the fishmonger's slab,' Mr Biswas said. 'The only fish I see is the fish that does come around every morning in a basket on the old fishwoman head.'

'. . . the tradesmen's blinds, the crack of bat on ball on the village green, the lengthening shadows . . .'

Mr Biswas wrote the article on summer; and with the help of the hints, wrote other articles on spring, winter and autumn.

'Autumn is with us again!' "Season of mist and mellow fruitfulness," as the celebrated poet John Keats puts it so well. We have chopped up logs for the winter. We have gathered in the corn which soon, before a blazing fire in the depths of winter, we shall enjoy, roasted or boiled on the cob . . .'

He received a letter of congratulation from the Ideal School and was told that the articles were being submitted without delay to the English Press. In the meantime he was asked to apply himself to the second lesson and write pieces on Guy Fawkes Night, Some Village Superstitions, The Romance of Place-Names ('Your vicar is likely to prove a mine of colourful information'), Characters at the Local.

He was stumped. No hints were given for these exercises and he wrote nothing. He didn't tell Shama. Not long after he received a heavy envelope from England. It contained his articles on the seasons which he had typed out neatly on *Sentinel* paper and in the manner prescribed by the Ideal School. A printed letter was attached.

'We regret to inform you that your articles have been submitted without success to: *Evening Standard, Evening News, The Times, The Tatler, London Opinion, Geographical Magazine, The Field, Country Life.* At least two editors spoke highly of the work but were forced to reject it through lack of space. We ourselves feel that work of such quality should not be consigned to oblivion. Why not try your local newspaper? That could very well be the beginning of a regular Nature column. Editors are always looking for new ideas, new material, new writers. At any rate let us know what happens. We at the Ideal like to hear of our pupils' successes. In the meantime continue with your exercises.'

'Continue with your exercises!' Mr Biswas said. He thankfully abandoned Guy Fawkes and Characters at the Local, and ignored the expostulations which reached him at regular intervals for the next two years from the Edgware Road.

The typewriter became idle.

'It pay for itself,' Shama said. 'No wonder it now have to rest.'

But soon the machine drew him again; and often, while Shama moved heavily about the back verandah and kitchen, Mr Biswas sat before the typewriter on the green table, inserted a sheet of *Sentinel* paper, typed his name and address at the top righthand corner, as the Ideal School and all the books had recommended, and wrote:

ESCAPE
by M. Biswas

At the age of thirty-three, when he was already the father of four children . . .

Here he often stopped. Sometimes he went on to the end of the page; sometimes, but rarely, he typed frenziedly for page after page. Sometimes his hero had a Hindi name; then he was short and unattractive and poor, and surrounded by ugliness, which was anatomized in bitter detail. Sometimes his hero had a Western name; he was then faceless, but tall and broad-shouldered; he was a reporter and moved in a world derived from the novels Mr Biswas had read and the films he had seen. None of these stories was finished, and their theme was always the same. The hero, trapped into marriage, burdened with a family, his youth gone, meets a young girl. She is slim, almost thin, and dressed in white. She is fresh, tender, unkissed; and she is unable to bear children. Beyond the meeting the stories never went.

Sometimes these stories were inspired by an unknown girl in the advertising department of the *Sentinel.* She often remained unknown. Sometimes Mr Biswas spoke; but whenever the girl accepted his invitation – to lunch, a film, the beach – his passion at once died; he withdrew the invitation and avoided the girl; thus in time creating a legend among the girls of the advertising department, all of whom knew, though he did not suspect, for he kept it as a heavy, shameful secret, that at the age of thirty-three Mohun Biswas was already the father of four children.

Still, at the typewriter, he wrote of his untouched barren heroines. He began these stories with joy; they left him dissatisfied and feeling unclean. Then he went to his room, called for Anand, and to Anand's disgust tried to play with him as with a baby, saying, 'Shompo! Gomp!'

Forgetting that in his strictness, and as part of her training, he had ordered Shama to file all his papers, he thought that these stories were as secret at home as his marriage and four children were at the office. And one Friday, when he found Shama puzzling over her accounts and had scoffed as usual, she said, 'Leave me alone, Mr John Lubbard.'

That was one of the names of his thirty-three-year-old hero.

'Go and take Sybil to the pictures.'

That was from another story. He had got the name from a novel by Warwick Deeping.

'Leave Ratni alone.'

That was the Hindi name he had given to the mother of four in another story. Ratni walked heavily, 'as though perpetually pregnant'; her arms filled the sleeves of her bodice and seemed about to burst them; she sucked in her breath through her teeth while she worked at her accounts, the only reading and writing she did.

Mr Biswas recalled with horror and shame the descriptions of the small tender breasts of his barren heroines.

Shama sucked her teeth loudly.

If she had laughed he would have hit her. But she never looked at him, only at her account books.

He ran to his room, undressed, got his own cigarettes and matches, took down Marcus Aurelius and Epictetus, and got into bed.

It was not long after this that Mr Biswas, painting the kitchen safe and the green table with a tin of yellow paint, yielded to an impulse and painted the typewriter-case and parts of the typewriter as well.

For long the typewriter remained unused, until Anand and Savi began learning to type on it.

But still, in the office, whenever he had cleaned his typewriter or changed the ribbon and wished to test the machine, the sentence he always wrote was: *At the age of thirty-three, when he was already the father of four children . . .*

So used to thinking of the house as his own, and in his new confidence, he made a garden. He planted rose-bushes at the side of the house, and at the front dug a pond for water-lilies, which spread prodigiously. He acquired more possessions, the most massive of which was a combined bookcase and desk, of such weight and sturdiness that three men were required to put it into place in his bedroom, where it stayed until they all moved from Port of Spain to Shorthills. Mice nested in the bookcase, protected and nourished by the mass of paper with which the bookcase was stuffed: newspapers (Mr Biswas insisted that all the newspapers for a month should be kept, and there were quarrels when a particular issue could not be found); every typewritten letter Mr Biswas had received, from the *Sentinel*, the Ideal School, people anxious or grateful for publicity; the rejected articles on the seasons, the unfinished Escape stories (at first shamefully glanced at, though later Mr Biswas read them and regretted he had not taken up short story writing seriously).

Encouraged by Shama, he took an increasing interest in his personal appearance. In his silk suit and tie he had never ceased to surprise her by his elegance and respectability; and whenever she bought him anything, a shirt, cufflinks, a tiepin, he said, 'Going to buy that gold brooch for you, girl! One of these days.' Sometimes, while he was dressing, he would make an inventory of all the things he was wearing and think, with wonder, that he was then worth one hundred and fifty dollars. Once on the bicycle, he was worth about one hundred and eighty. And so he rode to his reporter's job and its curious status: welcomed, even fawned upon, by the greatest in the land, fed as well as anybody and sometimes even better, yet always, finally, rejected.

'A hell of a thing today,' he told Shama. 'As we were leaving Government House H.E. asked me, "Which is your car?" I don't know. I suppose reporters in England must be rich like hell.'

But Shama was impressed. At Hanuman House she started dropping names, and Padma, Seth's wife, traced a tenuous and intricate family relationship between Seth and the man who had driven the Prince of Wales during his visit to Trinidad.

On herself Shama spent little. Unable to buy the best and, like all the Tulsi sisters, having only contempt for the second-rate in cloth and jewellery, she bought nothing at all and made do with the gifts of cloth she received every Christmas from Mrs Tulsi. Her bodices became patched on the breasts and under the arms; and the more Mr Biswas complained the more she patched. But though her indifference to clothes seemed at times almost like inverted pride, she did not wholly lose her concern for appearances. At Hanuman House a wedding invitation to Mrs Tulsi was meant for her daughters as well; and one large gift, invariably part of the Tulsi Store stock, went from the House. But now Shama got invitations in her own right and during the Hindu wedding season she borrowed deeply from the rent money, committing herself to almost inextricable entanglement with her accounts, to buy presents, usually water-sets.

'Forget it this time,' Mr Biswas said. 'They must be so used by now to seeing you with a water-set in your hand that I am sure they would believe that you did carry one.'

'I know what I am doing,' Shama said. 'My children are going to be married one day too.'

'And when they give back all the water-sets poor Savi wouldn't be able to walk, for all the glasses and jugs. If they remember, that is. At least leave it for a few more years.'

But weddings and funerals had become important to Shama. From weddings she returned tired, heavy-lidded and hoarse after the night-long singing, to find a house in confusion: Savi in tears, the kitchen in disorder, Mr Biswas complaining about his indigestion. Pleased at the wedding, the gift that did not disgrace her, the singing, the return home, Shama would say, 'Well, as the saying goes, you never miss the water till the well runs dry.'

And for the following day or two, when she held Mr Biswas and the children absolutely in her power, she would be very gloomy; and it was at these times that she said, 'I tell you, if it wasn't for the children –'

And Mr Biswas would sing, 'Going to buy that gold brooch for you, girl!'

As important as weddings and funerals were to Shama, holiday visits became to the children. They went first of all to Hanuman House. But with every succeeding visit they felt more like strangers. Alliances were harder to take up again. There were new jokes, new games, new stories, new subjects of conversation. Too much had to be explained, and Anand and Savi and Myna often ended by remaining together. As soon as they went back to Port of Spain this unity disappeared. Savi returned to bullying Myna; Anand defended Myna; Savi beat Anand; Anand hit back; and Savi complained.

'What!' Mr Biswas said. 'Hitting your sister! Shama, you see the sort of effect one little trip to the monkey house does have on your children?'

It was a two-fold attack, for the children preferred visiting Mr Biswas's relations. These relations had come as a revelation. Not only were they an untapped source of generosity; Savi and Anand had also felt up to then that Mr Biswas, like all the fathers at Hanuman House, had come from nothing, and the only people who had a proper family were the Tulsis. It was pleasant and novel, too, for Savi and Anand and Myna to find themselves flattered and cajoled and bribed. At Hanuman House they were three children among many; at Ajodha's there were no other children. And Ajodha was rich, as they could tell by the house he was building. He offered them money and was absurdly delighted that they should know its value sufficiently well to take it. Anand got an extra six cents for reading *That Body of Yours*; it would have been worth it for the praise alone. They were fêted at Pratap's; Bipti was embarrassingly devoted and their cousins were shy and admiring and kind. At Prasad's they were again the only children and lived in a mud hut, which they thought quaint: it was like a large doll's house. Prasad didn't give money, but a thick red exercise book, a Shirley Temple fountain pen and a bottle of Waterman's ink. And so, with this encouragement to milk and prunes, the profitable round of holiday visits ended.

Then came the news that Mrs Tulsi had decided to send Owad abroad to study, to become a doctor.

Mr Biswas was overwhelmed. More and more students were going abroad; but they were items of news, remote. He had never thought that anyone so close to him could escape so easily. Concealing his sadness and envy, he made a show of enthusiasm and offered advice about shipping lines. And at Arwacas some of Mrs Tulsi's retainers defected. Forgetting that they were in Trinidad, that they had crossed the black water from India and had thereby lost all caste, they said they could have nothing more to do with a woman who was proposing to send her son across the black water.

'Water on a duck's back,' Mr Biswas said to Shama. 'The number of times that mother of yours has made herself outcast!'

There was talk about the suitability and adequacy of the food Owad would get in England.

'Every morning in England, you know,' Mr Biswas said, 'the scavengers go around picking up the corpses. And you know why? The food there is not cooked by orthodox Roman Catholic Hindus.'

'Suppose Uncle Owad want more,' Anand said. 'You think they will give it to him?'

'Hear the boy,' Mr Biswas said, squeezing Anand's thin arms. 'Let me tell you, eh, boy, that you and Savi come out of the monkey house as going concerns only because of the little Ovaltine you drink.'

'No wonder the others can hold Anand and beat his little tail,' Shama said.

'Your family are *tough*,' Mr Biswas said. He spat the word out and made it an insult. *'Tough,'* he repeated.

'Well, I could say one thing. None of us have calves swinging like hammocks.'

'Of course not. Your calves are *tough*. Anand, look at the back of my hands. No hair. The sign of an advanced race, boy. And look at yours. No hair either. But you never know. With some of your mother's bad blood flowing in your veins you could wake up one morning and find yourself hairy like a monkey.'

Then, after a trip to Hanuman House, Shama reported that the decision to send Owad abroad had reduced Shekhar, the elder god, married man though he was, to tears.

'Send him some rope and soft candle,' Mr Biswas said.

'He never did want to get married,' Shama said.

'Never did want to get married! Never see anybody skip off so smart to check mother-in-law's money.'

'He wanted to go to Cambridge.'

*'Cambridge!'* Mr Biswas exclaimed, startled by the word, startled to hear it coming so easily from Shama. 'Cambridge, eh? Well, why the hell he didn't go? Why the hell the whole pack of you didn't go to Cambridge? Frighten of the bad food?'

'Seth was against it.' Shama's tone was injured and conspiratorial.

Mr Biswas paused. 'Well, you don't say. You *don't* say!'

'I glad it please somebody.'

She could give no more information, and at last said impatiently, 'You getting like a woman.'

She clearly felt that an injustice had been done. And he knew the Tulsis too well to be surprised that the sisters, who never questioned their own neglected education, cat-in-bag marriage and precarious position, should yet feel concerned that Shekhar, whose marriage was happy and whose business was flourishing, had not had all that he might.

Shekhar was coming to spend a week-end in Port of Spain. His family would not be with him and old Mrs Tulsi would be in Arwacas: the brothers were to be boys together for one last week-end. Mr Biswas waited for Shekhar with interest.

He came early on Friday evening. The taxi hooted; Shama switched on the lights in the verandah and the porch; Shekhar ran up the front steps in his white linen suit and breezed through the house on his leather-heeled shoes, charging it with excitement, depositing on the diningtable a bottle of wine, a tin of peanuts, a packet of biscuits, two copies of *Life* and a paper-backed volume of Halévy's *History of the English People*. Shama greeted him with sadness, Mr Biswas with a solemnity which he hoped could be mistaken for sympathy. Shekhar responded with geniality: the absent geniality of the businessman sparing time from his business, the family man away from his family.

Owad's expensive new suitcases were in the back verandah and Mr Biswas was painting Owad's name on them.

'Sort of thing to make you feel *you* want to go away,' Mr Biswas said.

Shekhar wasn't drawn. After the wine and peanuts and biscuits had been shared he showed himself almost paternally preoccupied with the arrangements for Owad's journey, and in spite of Mr Biswas's coaxings never once mentioned Cambridge.

'You and your mouth,' Mr Biswas told Shama.

She had no time for argument. She felt honoured at having to entertain her two brothers at once, on such an important occasion, and was determined to do it well. She had prepared all week for the week-end, and shortly after breakfast that morning had begun to cook.

From time to time Mr Biswas went into the kitchen and whispered, 'Who paying for all this? The old she-fox or you? Not me, you hear. Nobody sending me to Cambridge. Next week, when I eating dry ice, nobody sending me food by parcel post from Hanuman House, you hear.'

It was a Hanuman House festival in miniature, and to the children almost like a game of makebelieve. They had the freedom of the kitchen and nibbled and tasted whenever they could. Shekhar bought sweets for them and on Sunday sent them to the one-thirty children's show at the Roxy. And Mr Biswas got on so well with the brothers that he was invaded by the holiday feeling that they were all men together, and he thought himself privileged to be host to the two sons of the family, one of whom was going abroad to become a doctor. He attempted genuinely to contribute to the enthusiasm, talking again about shipping lines and ships as though he had travelled in them all; he hinted at the write-up he was going to give Owad and flattered him by asking him to refuse to see reporters from the other newspapers; he spoke deprecatingly about Anand's achievements and obtained compliments from Shekhar.

Sunday brought the *Sunday Sentinel* and Mr Biswas's scandalous feature, 'I Am Trinidad's Most Evil Man', one of a series of interviews with Trinidad's richest, poorest, tallest, fattest, thinnest, fastest, strongest men; which was following a series on men with unusual callings: thief, beggar, night-soil remover, mosquito-killer, undertaker, birth-certificate searcher, lunatic-asylum warden; which had followed a series on one-armed, one-legged, one-eyed men; which had come about when, after an M. Biswas interview with a man who had been shot years before in the neck and had to cover up the hole in order to speak, the *Sentinel* office had been crowded with men with interesting mutilations, offering to sell their story.

Mr Biswas's article was hilariously received by Owad and Shekhar, particularly as the most evil man was a wellknown Arwacas character. He had committed one murder under great provocation and after his acquittal had developed into a genial bore. The title of the interview promised for the following week, with Trinidad's maddest man, aroused further laughter.

After breakfast all the men – and this included Anand – went for a bathe at the harbour extension at Docksite. The dredging was incomplete, but the sea-wall had been built and in the early morning parts of the sea provided safe, clean bathing, though at every footstep the mud rose, clouding the water. The reclaimed land, raised to the level of the sea-wall, was not as yet real land, only crusted mud, sharp along the cracks which patterned it like a coral fan.

The sun was not out and the high, stationary clouds were touched with red. Ships were blurred in the distance; the level sea was like dark glass. Anand was left at the edge of the water, near the wall, and the men went ahead, their voices and splashings carrying far in the stillness. All at once the sun came out, the water blazed, and sounds were subdued.

Aware of his unimpressive physique, Mr Biswas began to clown; and, as he did more and more now, he tried to extend his clowning to Anand.

'Duck, boy!' he called. 'Duck and let us see how long you can stay under water.'

'No!' Anand shouted back.

This abrupt denial of his father's authority had become part of the clowning.

'You hear the boy?' Mr Biswas said to Owad and Shekhar. He spoke an obscene Hindi epigram which had always amused them and which they now associated with him.

'You know what I feel like doing?' he said a little later. 'See that rowingboat there, by the wall? Let us untie it. By tomorrow morning it will be in Venezuela.'

'And let us throw you in it,' Shekhar said.

They chased Mr Biswas, caught him, held him above the water while he laughed and squirmed, his calves swinging like hammocks.

'One,' they counted, swinging him. 'Two –'

Suddenly he became affronted and angry.

'Three!'

The smooth water slapped his belly and chest and forehead like something hard and hot. Surfacing, his back to them, he took some time to rearrange his hair, in reality wiping away the tears that had come to his eyes. The pause was long enough to tell Owad and Shekhar that he was angry. They were embarrassed; and he was recognizing the unreasonableness of his anger when Shekhar said, 'Where is Anand?'

Mr Biswas didn't turn. 'The boy is all right. Ducking. His grandfather was a champion diver.'

Owad laughed.

'Ducking, hell!' Shekhar said, and began swimming towards the wall.

There was no sign of Anand. In the shadow of the wall the rowingboat barely rocked above its reflection.

Silently Mr Biswas and Owad watched Shekhar. He dived. Mr Biswas scooped up a handful of water and let it fall on his head. Some of it ran down his face; some of it sprinkled the sea.

Shekhar reappeared near the sea-wall, shook the water from his head and dived again.

Mr Biswas began to wade towards the wall. Owad began to swim. Mr Biswas began to swim.

Shekhar surfaced again, near the rowingboat. There was alarm on his face. He was holding Anand under his left arm and was pulling strongly with his right.

Owad and Mr Biswas moved towards him. He shouted to them to keep away. All at once he stopped pulling with his right hand, stood up, and was only waist-high in water. Behind him, in shadow, the rowingboat barely moved.

They carried Anand to the top of the wall and rolled him. Then Shekhar did some kneading exercises on his thin back. Mr Biswas stood by, noticing only the large safetypin – one of Shama's, doubtless – on Anand's blue striped shirt, which lay in the small heap of his clothes.

Anand spluttered. His expression was one of anger. He said, 'I was walking to the boat.'

'I told you to stay where you were,' Mr Biswas said, angry too.

'And the bottom of the sea drop away.'

'The dredging,' Shekhar said. He had not lost his look of alarm.

'The sea just drop away,' Anand cried, lying on his back, covering his face with a crooked arm. He spoke as one in-sulted.

Owad said, 'Anyway, you've got the record for ducking, Shompo.'

'Shut up!' Anand screamed. He began to cry, rubbing his legs on the hard, cracked ground, then turning over on his belly.

Mr Biswas took up the shirt with the safetypin and handed it to Anand.

Anand snatched the shirt and said, 'Leave me.'

'We shoulda leave you,' Mr Biswas said, 'when you was there, ducking.' As soon as he spoke the last word he regretted it.

'Yes!' Anand screamed. 'You shoulda leave me.' He got up and, going to his heap of clothes, began to dress furiously, forcing his clothes over his wet and gritty skin. 'I am never going to come out with any of you again.' His eyes were small and red, the lids swollen.

He walked away from them, quickly, his small body silhouetted against the sun, across the weed-ridden mud flat. Unused, his towel remained rolled, a large bundle below his arm.

'Well,' Mr Biswas said. 'Back for a little duck?'

Owad and Shekhar smiled. Then, slowly, they all dressed.

'I never thought the day would come when I would be glad that I was a sea scout,' Shekhar said. 'It was just like a hole in the sea, you know. And there was a helluva pull. By tomorrow little Anand would really have been in Venezuela.'

They found Shama anxious to know why Anand had been sent back. He had said nothing and had locked himself in his room.

Savi and Myna burst into tears when they heard.

The lunch was the climax of the week-end festivities, but Anand did not come out of his room. He ate only a slice of water melon which Savi took to him.

Later that afternoon, after Shekhar had left, Shama gave vent to her annoyance. Anand had spoiled the week-end for everybody and she was going to flog him. She was dissuaded only by Owad's pleas.

'My children! My children!' Shama said. 'Well, the example set. They just following.'

The next day Mr Biswas wrote an angry article about the lack of warning notices at Docksite. In the afternoon Anand came home from school a little more composed and, extraordinarily, without being asked, took out a copy book from his bag and handed it to Mr Biswas, who was in the hammock in the back verandah. Then Anand went to change.

The copy book contained Anand's English compositions, which reflected the vocabulary and ideals of Anand's teacher as well as Anand's obsession with the stylistic device of the noun followed by a dash, an adjective and the noun again: for example, 'the robbers – the ruthless robbers'.

The last composition was headed 'A Day by the Seaside'. Below that the phrases supplied by the teacher had been copied down: project a visit – feverish preparations – eager anticipation – laden hampers – wind blowing through open car – spirits overflowing into song – graceful curve of coconut trees – arc of golden sand – crystalline water – pounding surf – majestic rollers – energetically battling the waves – cries of delirious joy – grateful shade of coconut trees – glorious sunset – sad to leave – memory to be cherished in future days – looking forward in eager anticipation to paying a return visit.

Mr Biswas was familiar with the clarity and optimism of the teacher's vision, and he expected Anand to write: 'With anticipation – eager anticipation – we projected a visit to the seaside and we made preparations – feverish preparations – and then on the appointed morning we struggled with hampers – laden hampers – into the motorcar.' For in these compositions Anand and his fellows knew nothing but luxury.

But in this last composition there were no dashes and repetitions; no hampers, no motorcar, no golden arcs of sand; only a walk to Docksite, a concrete sea-wall and liners in the distance. Mr Biswas read on, anxious to share the pain of the previous day. 'I raised my hand but I did not know if it got to the top. I opened my mouth to cry for help. Water filled it. I thought I was going to die and I closed my eyes because I did not want to look at the water.' The composition ended with a denunciation of the sea.

None of the teacher's phrases had been used but the composition had been given twelve marks out of ten.

Anand had come back to the verandah and was having his tea at the table.

Mr Biswas wished to be close to him. He would have done anything to make up for the solitude of the previous day. He said, 'Come and sit down here and go through the composition with me.'

Anand became impatient. He was pleased by the marks but was fed up with the composition and even a little ashamed of it. He had been made to read it out to the class, and the confession that he had not struggled with laden hampers into a car and driven to palm-fringed beaches but had walked to common Docksite had caused some laughter. So had the sentences: 'I opened my mouth to cry for help. Water filled it.'

'Come,' Mr Biswas said, making room in the hammock.

'No!' Anand shouted.

But there was no one to laugh.

Mr Biswas's hurt turned to anger. 'Go and cut me a whip,' he said, getting out of the hammock. 'Go on. Quick sharp.'

Anand stamped down the back stairs. From the neem tree that grew at the edge of the lot and hung over into the sewerage trace he cut a thick rod, far thicker than those he normally cut. His purpose was to insult Mr Biswas. Mr Biswas recognized the insult and was further enraged. He seized the rod and beat Anand savagely. In the end Shama had to intervene.

'I can't stand this,' Savi cried. 'I can't stand you people. I am going back to Hanuman House.'

Myna was crying as well.

Shama said to Anand, 'You see what you cause?'

He said nothing.

'Good!' Savi said. 'All this shouting and screaming make this house sound like every other house in the street. I hope the low minds of some people are satisfied.'

'Yes,' Mr Biswas said calmly. 'Some people are satisfied.'

His smile drove Savi to fresh tears.

But Anand had his revenge that evening.

Now that there were only a few days left to Owad in Trinidad, and very few before the family came to Port of Spain for the farewell, Mr Biswas and Anand ate as many meals as possible with him. They ate formally, in the dining-room. And that evening, just before Mr Biswas sat at the table, Anand pulled the chair from under him, and Mr Biswas fell noisily to the floor.

'Shompo! Lompo! Gomp!' Owad said, roaring with laughter.

Savi said, 'Well, some people are satisfied.'

Mr Biswas didn't talk during the meal. Afterwards he went for a walk. When he came back he went directly to his room and never once called to anyone to get his cigarettes or matches or books.

It was his habit to walk through the house at six in the morning, rustling the newspaper and getting everyone up. Then he himself went back to bed: he had the gift of enjoying sleep in snatches. He woke no one the next morning and didn't show himself while the children were getting ready for school.

But before Anand left, Shama gave him a six-cents piece.

'From your Father. For milk from the Dairies.'

At three that afternoon, when school was over, Anand walked down Victoria Avenue, past the racketing wheels and straps of the Government Printery, crossed Tragarete Road for the shade of the ivory-covered walls of Lapeyrouse Cemetery, and turned into Phillip Street where, in the cigarette factory, was the source of the sweet smell of tobacco which hung over the district. The Dairies looked expensive and forbidding in white and pale green. Anand tiptoed to the caged desk, said to the woman, 'A small bottle of milk, please,' paid, got his voucher, and sat on a tall pale green stool at the milky-smelling bar. The white-capped barman tried to stab off the silver top a little too nonchalantly and, failing twice, pressed it out with a large thumb. Anand didn't care for the ice-cold milk and the cloying sweetness it left at the back of his throat; it also seemed to have the tobacco smell, which he associated with the cemetery.

When he got home Shama gave him a small brown paper parcel. It contained prunes. They were his, to eat as and when he pleased.

Both he and Savi were told to keep the milk and the prunes secret, lest Owad should hear of it and laugh at them for their presumptuousness.

And almost immediately Anand began to pay the price of the milk and prunes. Mr Biswas went to the school and saw the headmaster and the teacher whose vocabulary he knew so well. They agreed that Anand could win an exhibition if he worked, and Mr Biswas made arrangements for Anand to be given private lessons after school, after milk. To balance this, Mr Biswas also arranged for Anand to have unlimited credit at the school shop; thus deranging Shama's accounts further.

Savi's heart went out to Anand.

'I am too glad,' she said, 'that God didn't give me a brain.'

In the week before Owad's departure the house filled up with sisters, husbands, children and those of Mrs Tulsi's retainers who remained faithful. The women came in their brightest clothes and best jewellery and, though only twenty miles from their villages, looked exotic. Heedless of stares, they stared; and made comments in Hindi, unusually loud, unusually ribald, because in the city Hindi was a secret language, and they were in holiday mood. A tent covered the back of the yard where Anand and Owad had sometimes played cricket. Fire-holes had been dug on the pitch itself, and over these food was always being cooked in large black cauldrons specially brought from Hanuman House. The visitors had come with musical instruments. They played and sang late into the night, and neighbours, too fascinated to object, peeped through holes in the corrugated iron fences.

Few of the visitors knew Mr Biswas or knew the position he held in the house. And all at once this position became uncertain. He found himself squeezed into one room, and for periods lost track of Shama and his children. 'Eight dollars,' he whispered to Shama. 'That is the rent I pay every month. I have my rights.'

The rose-bushes and the lily-pond suffered.

'Set up trip-wires,' he told Shama. 'Then let them carry on. "*Aré*, what have we here?"' He imitated an old woman talking Hindi. 'Then, oops! Trip! Bam! Fall. All the pretty clothes get dirty like hell. Face wet with mud. Let that happen a few times. Then they will learn that flowers don't just grow like that.'

After two days he gave up his flowers as lost. He went for long walks in the evening and stayed out as late as possible, calling at various police stations on the chance of picking up a story. One night he stayed out until the street dogs began their round, futile creatures that hunted in packs, fled at the sound of a human foot and left a trail of overturned dustbins and sifted garbage. The house was alive but subdued when he got back. He found four children on his bed. They were not his. Thereafter he occupied his room early in the evening, bolted the door and refused to answer knocks, calls, scratches and cries.

And all at once, too, the bond between Owad and himself seemed to have evaporated. Owad was out for much of the time making farewell calls; when he came to the house he was immediately besieged by friends and relations who gazed on him and wept and offered advice which they later discussed among themselves, to prove their concern: advice about money, the weather, food, alcohol, women.

The time came for photographs. Husbands, children and friends watched as Owad posed with Shekhar, with Mrs Tulsi, with Shekhar and Mrs Tulsi, with Shekhar, Mrs Tulsi and the whole array of the sisters who, because the occasion was sad, ignored the pleas of the Chinese photographer and scowled at the camera.

On the last day Seth arrived. He wore his khaki uniform; his bluchers rang on the floor; he dominated, imposing formality wherever he went. His absence had been noted, and now everyone was expectant. But after the final family council Owad, Shekhar, Mrs Tulsi and Seth looked only solemn, which could have been a sign of disagreement, or sorrow.

Mr Biswas achieved a minor notoriety when he brought the *Sentinel* photographer to the house, cleared the drawing-room and did his best to appear to be directing both Owad and the photographer. But on the following morning the story, on page three – TRINIDAD MAN OFF TO U.K. FOR MEDICAL STUDIES – was given little attention, for those who were not occupied with dressing their children for the wharf or getting wharf passes were at the service Hari was conducting in the tent.

Finally they went to the wharf. Only new-born babies and their mothers stayed behind. The Tulsi contingent stared at the ship; and the ship's rails were presently lined with in-transit passengers and members of the ship's company, getting an unusually exotic glimpse of Port of Spain harbour. The word went around that well-wishers could go aboard and in a matter of minutes the Tulsis and their friends had overrun the ship. They stared at officers and passengers and the photographs of Adolf Hitler, and listened attentively to the guttural language around them, to mimic it later. The older women kicked at decks and rails and the sides of the ship, testing its seaworthiness. Some of the more susceptible took it in turns to sit on Owad's bunk and weep. The men were shyer, and more respectful before the might of the ship; they wandered about silently with their hats in their hands. Whatever doubts remained about ship and crew vanished when an officer began giving out presents: lighters to the men, dolls in country dress to the women. And all the time, unnoticed by those he was seeking to impress, Mr Biswas scurried knowingly about the ship, talking to the foreigners and writing in his notebook.

They came out of the ship and massed formally in front of a magenta-coloured shed with French and English notices forbidding smoking. From somewhere a chair had been obtained and Mrs Tulsi sat on it, her veil pulled low over her forehead, a handkerchief crushed in one hand, with Sushila, the sickroom widow, at her side.

Owad started to kiss, strangers first. But they were too many; soon he abandoned them and concentrated on the family. He kissed each sister into a spurt of tears; he shook the men by the hand, and when it was Mr Biswas's turn he smiled and said, 'No more ducking.'

Mr Biswas was unaccountably moved. His legs shook; he felt unsteady. He said, 'I hope war doesn't break out –' Tears rushed to his eyes, he choked and could say no more.

Owad had passed on. He embraced the children; then Shekhar; then Seth, who cried copiously; and finally Mrs Tulsi, who didn't cry at all.

He went into the ship. Presently he appeared at the rails and waved. A passenger joined him; they began to talk.

The passengers' gangway was drawn up. Then there were shouts, raucous, unsustained singing, and three Germans with bruised faces and torn and dirty clothes came staggering along the wharf, comically supporting one another, drunk.

Someone from the ship called to them harshly; they shouted back and, drunk and collapsing though they were, and without touching the rope-rail, they walked up the narrow gang-board at the stern. All the doubts about the ship were re-excited.

Whistles: waves from ship, from shore: the ship edging away: the dock less protected, the dark, dirty water surfaced with litter. And soon they stood quite exposed in front of the customs shed, staring at the ship, staring at the gap it had left.

The weakness that had come to him at the touch of Owad's hands remained with Mr Biswas. There was a hole in his stomach. He wanted to climb mountains, to exhaust himself, to walk and walk and never return to the house, to the empty tent, the dead fire-holes, the disarrayed furniture. He left the wharves with Anand and they walked aimlessly through the city. They stopped at a café and Mr Biswas bought Anand icecream in a tub and a Coca Cola.

The paper would sprawl on the sunny steps in the morning; there would be stillness at noon and shadow in the afternoon. But it would be a different day.

# 2. The New Régime

HAVING NO further business in Port of Spain, Mrs Tulsi returned to Arwacas. The tent was taken down and after a few days the house was cleared of stragglers. Mr Biswas set about restoring his rose-beds and the lily-pond, whose edges had collapsed, turning the water into bubbling mud. He worked without heart, feeling the emptiness of the house and not knowing how much longer he would be allowed to stay there. None of Mrs Tulsi's furniture had been removed: the house there seemed to be awaiting change. Some of the savour went out of his job at the *Sentinel*. He needed to address his work mentally to someone. At first this had been Mr Burnett; then it had been Owad. Now there was only Shama. She seldom read his articles; when he read them aloud to her she showed neither interest nor amusement and made no comments. Once he gave her the typescript of an article and she infuriated him by turning over the last page and looking for more. 'No more, no more,' he said. 'I don't want to strain you.'

And from Hanuman House came more reports of disturbance. Govind, the eager, the loyal, was discontented; Shama reported his seditious sayings. Nothing had outwardly changed, but Mrs Tulsi no longer directed and her influence was beginning to be felt more and more as only that of a cantankerous invalid. With her two sons settled, she appeared to have lost interest in the family. She spent much of her time in the Rose Room, acquiring illnesses, grieving for Owad. As for Seth, he still controlled; but his control was superficial. Though nothing had been said openly, Shekhar's reported displeasure, uncontradicted, lay against him and made him suspect to the sisters. When all was said and done Seth was not of the family and he alone could not maintain its harmony, as had been shown by his helplessness when squabbles had arisen between sisters during Mrs Tulsi's absences in Port of Spain. Seth ruled effectively only in association with Mrs Tulsi and through her affection and trust. That trust, not officially withdrawn, was no longer so fully displayed; and Seth was even beginning to be resented as an outsider.

Then came rumours that Seth had been inspecting properties.

'Buying it for Mai, you think?' Mr Biswas asked.

Shama said, 'I glad it make somebody happy.'

And Mr Biswas was soon to regret his jubilation. The Christmas school holidays came and Shama took the children to Hanuman House. By now they were complete strangers there. The old crêpe paper decorations and the goods in the dark, choked Tulsi Store were petty country things after the displays in the Port of Spain shops, and Savi felt pity for the people of Arwacas, who had to take them seriously. At last on Christmas Eve the store was closed and the uncles went away. Savi, Anand, Myna and Kamla hunted for stockings and hung them up. And got nothing. There was no one to complain to. Some of the sisters had secretly provided gifts for their children; and on Christmas morning in the hall, where Mrs Tulsi was not waiting to be kissed, the gifts were displayed and compared. With Owad in England, Mrs Tulsi in her room, all the uncles away, and Shekhar spending the day with his wife's family, there was no one to organize games, to give a lead to the gaiety. And Christmas was reduced to lunch and Chinta's icecream, as tasteless and rust-rippled as ever. The sisters were sullen; the children quarrelled, and some were even flogged.

Shekhar came on the morning of Boxing Day with a large bag of imported sweets. He went up to Mrs Tulsi's room, had lunch in the hall, and then went away again. When Mr Biswas arrived later that afternoon he found that the talk among the sisters was not of Seth, but of Shekhar and his wife. The sisters felt that Shekhar had abandoned them. Yet no one blamed him. He was under the influence of his wife, and the fault was wholly hers.

Relations between the sisters and Shekhar's wife had never been easy. Despite the untraditional organization of Hanuman House, where married daughters lived with their mother, the sisters were alert to certain of the conventions of Hindu family relationships: mothers-in-law, for example, were expected to be hard on daughters-in-law, sisters-in-law were to be despised. But Shekhar's wife had from the first met Tulsi patronage with arrogant Presbyterian modernity. She flaunted her education. She called herself Dorothy, without shame or apology. She wore short frocks and didn't care that they made her look lewd and absurd: she was a big woman who had grown fat after the birth of her first child, and her dresses hung from her high, shelflike hips as from a hoop. Her voice was deep, her manner hearty; once, when she had damaged her ankle, she used a stick, and Chinta remarked that it suited her. Added to all this she sometimes sold the tickets at her cinema; which was disgraceful, besides being immoral. So far, however, from making any impression on Dorothy, the sisters continually found themselves defeated. They had said she wouldn't be able to keep a house: she turned out to be maddeningly house-proud. They had said she was barren: she was bearing a child every two years. Her children were all girls, but this was scarcely a triumph for the sisters. Dorothy's daughters were of exceptional beauty and the sisters could complain only that the Hindi names Dorothy had chosen – Mira, Leela, Lena – were meant to pass as Western ones.

And now old charges were made again and for the benefit of Shama and other attentive visiting sisters fresh details added. As the talk scratched back and forth over the same topic these details became increasingly gross: Dorothy, like all Christians, used her right hand for unclean purposes, her sexual appetite was insatiable, her daughters already had the eyes of whores. Over and over the sisters concluded that Shekhar was to be pitied, because he had not gone to Cambridge and had instead been married against his will to a wife who was shameless. Padma, Seth's wife, was present, and Seth's behaviour could not be discussed. Whenever Cambridge was mentioned looks and intonation made it clear to Padma that she was excluded from this implied criticism of her husband, that she, like Shekhar, was to be pitied for having such a spouse. And Mr Biswas marvelled again at the depth of Tulsi family feeling.

Mr Biswas had always got on well with Dorothy; he was attracted by her loudness and gaiety and regarded her as an ally against the sisters. But on that hot still afternoon, when a holiday staleness lay over Arwacas, the hall, with its confused furniture, its dark loft and sooty green walls, with flies buzzing in and out of the white sunny spots on the long table, seemed abandoned, deprived of animation; and Mr Biswas, feeling Shekhar's absence as a betrayal, could sympathize with the sisters.

Savi said, 'This is the last Christmas I spend at Hanuman House.'

Change followed change. At Pagotes Tara and Ajodha were decorating their new house. In Port of Spain new lamp-posts, painted silver, went up in the main streets and there was talk of replacing the diesel buses by trolley-buses. Owad's old room was let to a middle-aged childless coloured couple. And at the *Sentinel* there were rumours.

Under Mr Burnett's direction the *Sentinel* had overtaken the *Gazette* and, though some distance behind the *Guardian*, it had become successful enough for its frivolity to be an embarrassment to the owners. Mr Burnett had been under pressure for some time. That Mr Biswas knew, but he had no head for intrigue and did not know the source of this pressure. Some of the staff became openly contemptuous and spoke of Mr Burnett as uneducated; a joke went around the office that he had applied from the Argentine for a job as a sub-editor and his letter had been misunderstood. As if in reply to all this Mr Burnett became increasingly perverse. 'Let's face it,' he said. 'Editorials from Port of Spain didn't have much effect in Spain. They are not going to stop Hitler either.' The *Guardian* responded to the war by starting a fighter fund: in a box on the front page twelve aeroplanes were outlined, and as the fund rose the outlines were filled in. Right up to the end the *Sentinel* had been headlining the West Indian cricket tour of England, and when the tour was abandoned it printed a drawing of Hitler which, when cut out and folded along certain dotted lines, became a drawing of a pig.

Early in the new year the blow fell. Mr Biswas was lunching with Mr Burnett in a Chinese restaurant, in one of those cubicles weakly lit by a low-hanging naked bulb, with lengths of flex loosely attached to the flyblown, grimy celotex partitions, when Mr Burnett said, 'Amazing scenes are going to be witnessed soon. I'm leaving.' He paused. 'Sacked.' As if divining Mr Biswas's thoughts, he added, 'Nothing for you to worry about, though.' Then, in quick succession, he displayed a number of conflicting moods. He was gay; he was depressed; he was glad to leave; he was sorry to go; he didn't want to talk about it; he talked about it; he wasn't going to talk any more about himself; he talked about himself. He ate in spasms, attacking the food as though it had done him some injury. 'Shoots? Is that what they call this? There'll be damned little bamboo left in China at this rate.' He pressed the bell, which lay at the centre of a roughly circular patch of grime on the wall. They heard it ring in some distant cavern, above a multitude of other bells, the pattering of waitresses' feet and talk in adjacent cubicles.

The harassed waitress came and Mr Burnett said, 'Shoots? This is just plain bamboo. What do you think I have inside here?' He tapped his belly. 'A paper factory?'

'That was one portion,' the waitress said.

'That was one bamboo.'

He ordered more lager and the waitress sucked her teeth and went out, leaving the swing door swinging rapidly to and fro.

'One portion,' Mr Burnett said. 'They make it sound like hay. And this damned room is like a stall. I'm not worried. I've got other strings to my bow. You too. You could go back to your sign-writing. I leave, you leave. Let's all leave.'

They laughed.

Mr Biswas returned to the office in a state of great agitation. He had been associated, and zestfully, with some of the most frivolous excesses of the *Sentinel*. Now at the thought of each he felt a stab of guilt and panic. He was expecting to be summoned to mysterious rooms and told by their secure occupants that his services were no longer required. He sat at his desk – but it belonged to him no more than the columns of

the *Sentinel* he filled – and listened to the noises made by the
carpenters. Those were the noises he had heard on his first
day in the office; building and rebuilding had gone on without interruption ever since. The newsroom came to its afternoon life. Reporters arrived, took off their jackets, opened
notebooks and typed; groups gathered at the green water-
cooler and broke up again; at some desks proofs were being
corrected, the inner pages laid out. For more than four years
he had been part of this excitement. Now, waiting for the
summons, he could only observe it.

Getting to believe that by staying in the office he was increasing the risk of dismissal, he left early and cycled home.
Fear led to fear. Suppose he had to send the children back to
Hanuman House, would there be anyone to receive them?
Suppose Mrs Tulsi gave him notice – as Shama did so often
to the tenement people – where would he go? How would
he live?

The years stretched ahead, dark.

When he got home he mixed and drank some Maclean's
Brand Stomach Powder, undressed, got into bed and began
to read Epictetus.

But the days went by and no summons came. And at last
it was time for Mr Burnett to leave. Mr Biswas wanted to
make some gesture to show his gratitude and sympathy, but
he could think of nothing. And after all Mr Burnett was escaping; he was staying behind. The *Sentinel* reported Mr Burnett's departure on the society page. There was an unkind
photograph of Mr Burnett looking uncomfortable in a dinner
jacket, his small eyes popping in the flash of the camera, a
cigar stuck in his mouth as if for comic effect. He was reported as being sorry to leave; he had to take up an appointment in America; he had learned much from his association
with Trinidad and the *Sentinel*, and he would take a great
interest in the progress of both; he thought the standards of
local journalism 'surprisingly high'. It was left to the other
newspapers to reveal the other strings to his bow that Mr
Burnett had spoken about. They reported that an Indian
troupe, made up of dancers, a fire-walker, a snake-charmer
and a man who could rest on a bed of nails, was accom-

panying Mr Burnett, a former editor of a local newspaper, on his travels to America. One headline was THE CIRCUS MOVES ON.

And the new régime started at the *Sentinel*. The day after Mr Burnett's departure the newsroom was hung with posters which said DON'T BE BRIGHT, JUST GET IT RIGHT and NEWS NOT VIEWS and FACTS? IF NOT AXE and CHECK IT OR CHUCK IT. Mr Biswas regarded them all as aimed at himself alone, and their whimsicality scared him. The office was subdued and everyone wore a look of earnestness, those who had gone up, those who had gone down. Mr Burnett's news editor had been made a sub-editor. His bright reporters had been variously scattered. One went to Today's Arrangements, Invalids and The Weather, one to Shipping, one to Diana's Diary on the society page, one to Classified Advertisements. Mr Biswas joined Court Shorts.

'Write?' he said to Shama. 'I don't call that writing. Is more like filling up a form. X, aged so much, was yesterday fined so much by Mr Y at this court for doing that. The prosecution alleged. Electing to conduct his own defence, X said. The magistrate, passing sentence, said.'

But Shama approved of the new régime. She said, 'It will teach you to have some respect for people and the truth.'

'Hear you. Hear you! But you don't surprise me. I *expect* you to talk like that. But let them wait. New régime, eh. Just see the circulation drop now.'

It was only to Shama that Mr Biswas spoke about the changes. At the office the subject was never mentioned. Mr Burnett's favourites avoided one another and, fearing intrigue, mixed with no one else. Apart from the posters there had been no directive, but they had all, so far as their new duties permitted writing, changed their styles. They wrote longer paragraphs of complete sentences with bigger words.

Presently the directives came, in a booklet called *Rules for Reporters*; and it was in keeping with the aloof severity of the new authorities that the booklets should have appeared on every desk one morning without explanation, with only the name of the reporter, preceded by a 'Mr', in the top right-hand corner.

'He must have got up early this morning,' Mr Biswas said to Shama.

The booklet contained rules about language, dress, behaviour, and at the bottom of every page there was a slogan. On the front cover was printed 'THE RIGHTEST NEWS IS THE BRIGHTEST NEWS', the inverted commas suggesting that the statement was historical, witty and wise. The back cover said: REPORT NOT DISTORT.

'Report not distort,' Mr Biswas said to Shama. 'That is all the son of a bitch doing now, you know, and drawing a fat salary for it too. Making up those slogans. Rules for Reporters. *Rules!*'

A few days later he came home and said, 'Guess what? Editor peeing in a special place now, you know. "Excuse me. But I must go and pee – alone." Everybody peeing in the same place for years. What happen? He taking a course of Dodd's Kidney Pills and peeing blue or something?'

In Shama's accounts Maclean's Brand Stomach Powder appeared more often, always written out in full.

'Just watch and see,' Mr Biswas said. 'Everybody going to leave. People not going to put up with this sort of treatment, I tell you.'

'When you leaving?' Shama asked.

And worse was to come.

'I don't know,' he said. 'I suppose they just want to frighten me. I will henceforward – henceforward: you hear the sort of words that son of a bitch using – I will henceforward spend my afternoons at the cemeteries of Port of Spain. Just hand me that yellow book. Rules for Reporters! Let me see. Anything about funerals? By God! They damn well have it in! "The *Sentinel* reporter should be soberly dressed on these occasions, that is, in a dark suit." Dark suit! The man must think I haven't got a wife and four children. He must think he paying me a fortune every fortnight. "Neither by his demeanour nor by his dress should the reporter offend the mourners, since this will certainly lose the paper much goodwill. The *Sentinel* reporter should remember that he represents the *Sentinel*. He should encourage trust. It cannot be stressed too often that the reporter should get every name right. A name incorrectly spelt is offensive. All orders and decorations should be mentioned, but the reporter should use his discretion in making inquiries about these. To be ignorant of an individual's decorations is almost certain to offend him. To ask an OBE whether he is an MBE is equally likely to offend. Far better, in this hypothetical case, to make inquiries on the assumption that the individual is a CBE. After the immediate family, the names of all mourners should be set out in alphabetical order."

'God! *God!* Isn't this just the sort of arseness to make you go and dance on the grave afterwards? You know, I could turn the funeral column into a bright little feature. Yesterday's Undertakings. By Gravedigger. Just next to Today's Arrangements. Or set it next to Invalids. Heading: Going Going, Gone. How about this? Photo of weeping widow at graveside. Later, photo of widow hearing about will and laughing. Caption: "Smiling, Mrs X? We thought so. Where there's a will there *is* a way." Two photos side by side.'

In the meantime he bought a dark serge suit on credit. And while Anand walked beside the wall of Lapeyrouse Cemetery on his way to the Dairies in the afternoon, Mr Biswas was often inside the cemetery, moving solemnly among the tombstones and making discreet inquiries about names and decorations. He came home tired, complaining of headaches, his stomach rising.

'A capitalist rag,' he began to say. 'Just another capitalist rag.'

Anand remarked that his name no longer appeared in it.

'Glad like hell,' Mr Biswas said.

And on four Saturdays in succession he was sent to unimportant cricket matches, just to get the scores. The game of cricket meant nothing to him, but he was made to understand that the assignment was part of his retraining and he cycled from fourth-class match to fourth-class match, copying symbols and scores he did not understand, enjoying only the brief esteem of surprised and thrilled players under trees. Most of the matches finished at half past five and it was impossible to be at all the grounds at the same time. It sometimes happened that when he got to a ground there was no one there. Then secretaries had to be hunted out and there was more cycling. In this way those Saturday afternoons and evenings were ruined, and often Sunday as well, for many of the scores he had gathered were not printed.

He began to echo phrases from the prospectus of the Ideal School of Journalism. 'I can make a living by my pen,' he said. 'Let them go ahead. Just let them push me too far.' At this period one-man magazines, nearly all run by Indians, were continually springing up. 'Start my own magazine,' Mr Biswas said. 'Go around like Bissessar, selling them myself. He tell me he does sell his paper like hot cakes. Like hot cakes, man!'

He abandoned his own régime of strictness at home and instead spoke so long of various members of the *Sentinel* staff that Shama and the children got to feel that they knew them well. From time to time he indulged in a tiny rebellion.

'Anand, on your way to school stop at the café and telephone the *Sentinel*. Tell them I don't feel like coming to work today.'

'Why you don't telephone them yourself? You know I don't like telephoning.'

'We can't always do what we like, boy.'

'And you want me to say that you just don't feel like going out to work today.'

'Tell them I'm sick. Cold, headache, fever. You know.'

When Anand left, Mr Biswas would say, 'Let them sack me. Let them sack me like hell. Think I care? I *want* them to sack me.'

'Yes,' Shama said. 'You want them to sack you.'

But he was careful to space out these days.

He made himself unpopular among the boys and young men of the street who played cricket on the pavement in the afternoons and chattered under the lamp-post at night. He shouted at them from his window and, because of his suit, his job, the house he lived in, his connexion with Owad, his influence with the police, they were cowed. Sometimes he ostentatiously went to the café and telephoned the local police sergeant, whom he had known well in happier days. And he rejoiced in the glares and the mutterings of the players

when, soberly dressed, unlikely to offend mourners, he
cycled out to his funerals in the afternoon.

He read political books. They gave him phrases which he
could only speak to himself and use on Shama. They also revealed one region after another of misery and injustice and
left him feeling more helpless and more isolated than ever.
Then it was that he discovered the solace of Dickens. Without difficulty he transferred characters and settings to people
and places he knew. In the grotesques of Dickens everything
he feared and suffered from was ridiculed and diminished, so
that his own anger, his own contempt became unnecessary,
and he was given strength to bear with the most difficult part
of his day: dressing in the morning, that daily affirmation of
faith in oneself, which at times was for him almost like an act
of sacrifice. He shared his discovery with Anand; and though
he abstracted some of the pleasure of Dickens by making
Anand write out and learn the meanings of difficult words, he
did this not out of his strictness or as part of Anand's training.
He said, 'I don't want you to be like me.'

Anand understood. Father and son, each saw the other as
weak and vulnerable, and each felt a responsibility for the
other, a responsibility which, in times of particular pain, was
disguised by exaggerated authority on the one side, exaggerated respect on the other.

Suddenly the pressure ceased at the *Sentinel*. Mr Biswas
was taken off court shorts, funerals and cricket matches, and
put into the Sunday Magazine, to do a weekly feature.

'If they did just push me so much farther,' he told Shama,
'I would have resigned.'

'Yes. You would have resigned.'

'Sometimes I don't know why the hell I ever bother to
talk to you.'

He had in fact mentally composed many sonorous letters
of resignation, varying from the abusive to the dignified to
the humorous and even to the charitable (these ended with
his best wishes for the continued success of the *Sentinel*).

But the features he now wrote were not the features he
wrote for Mr Burnett. He didn't write scandalous interviews

with one-eyed men: he wrote serious surveys of the work done by the Institute for the Blind. He didn't write 'I Am Trinidad's Maddest Man': he wrote about the splendid work of the Lunatic Asylum. It was his duty to praise, to look always beyond the facts to the official figures; for it was part of the *Sentinel*'s new policy of sobriety that this was the best of all worlds and Trinidad's official institutions its most magnificent aspects. He had not so much to distort as to ignore: to forget the bare, toughened feet of the children in an orphanage, the sullen looks of dread, the shameful uniforms; to accept a temporary shaming eminence and walk through workshops and vegetable gardens, noting industry, rehabilitation and discipline; to have lemonade and a cigarette in the director's office, and get the figures; to put himself on the side of the grotesques.

These features were not easy to write. In the days of Mr Burnett once he had got a slant and an opening sentence, everything followed. Sentence generated sentence, paragraph led to paragraph, and his articles had a flow and a unity. Now, writing words he did not feel, he was cramped, and the time came when he was not sure what he did feel. He had to note down ideas and juggle them into place. He wrote and rewrote, working extremely slowly, nagged by continual headaches, completing his articles only to meet the Thursday dead-line. The results were laboured, dead, incapable of giving pleasure except to the people written about. He didn't look forward to Sunday. He was up early as usual, but the paper remained on the front steps until Shama or one of the children brought it in. He avoided turning to his article for as long as possible. It was always a surprise, when he did turn to it, to see how photographs and lay-out concealed the dullness of the matter. Even then he did not read through what he had written, but glanced at odd paragraphs, looking for cuts and changes that would indicate editorial disapproval. He said nothing to Shama, but he lived now in constant expectation of the sack. He knew his work was not good.

At the office the authorities remained aloof. There was no criticism, but no reassurance. The new régime was still a forbidden subject and reporters still did not mix easily. Of Mr

Burnett's favourites only the former news editor was generally accepted; he had, indeed, become an office character. He had grown haggard with worry. He lived in Barataria and came up every morning by bus through the packed, narrow and dangerous Eastern Main Road. He had developed a fear that he would die in a road accident and leave his wife and baby daughter unprovided for. All travel terrified him; morning and evening he had to travel; and every day he laid out stories of accidents, with photographs of 'the twisted wreckage'. He spoke continually of his fear, ridiculed it and allowed himself to be ridiculed. But as the afternoon wore on his agitation became more marked, and at the end he was quite frantic, anxious to go home, yet fearing to leave the office, the only place where he felt safe.

Untended, the rose trees grew straggly and hard. A blight made their stems white and gave them sickly, ill-formed leaves. The buds opened slowly to reveal blanched, tattered blooms covered with minute insects; other insects built bright brown domes on the stems. The lily-pond collapsed again and the lily-roots rose brown and shaggy out of the thick, muddy water, which was white with bubbles. The children's interest in the garden was spasmodic, and Shama, claiming that she had learned not to interfere with anything of Mr Biswas's, planted some zinnias and marigolds of her own, the only things, apart from an oleander tree and some cactus, that had flourished in the garden of Hanuman House.

The war was beginning to have its effects. Prices were rising everywhere. Mr Biswas's salary was increased, but the increases were promptly absorbed. And when his salary reached thirty-seven dollars and fifty cents a fortnight the *Sentinel* started giving COLA, a cost-of-living allowance. Henceforth it was COLA that went up; the salary remained stationary.

'Psychology,' Mr Biswas said. 'They make it sound like a tea party at the orphanage, eh?' He raised his voice. 'All right, kiddies? Got your cake? Got your icecream? Got your cola?'

The shorter the money became, the worse the food, the more meticulously Shama kept her accounts, filling reporter's notebook after reporter's notebook. These she never threw away; they lay in a swollen, grubby pile on the kitchen shelf.

There were fights in shops for hoarded, weevil-ridden flour. The police kept a sharp eye on stall holders in markets, and a number of vegetable growers and small farmers were fined and imprisoned for selling above the scheduled price. Flour continued to be scarce and full of weevils; and Shama's food became worse.

To Mr Biswas's complaints she said, 'I walk miles every Saturday to save a cent here and a cent there.'

And soon, food forgotten, they were quarrelling. Their quarrels lasted from day to day, from week to week, quarrels differing only in words from those they had had at The Chase.

'Trapped!' Mr Biswas would say. 'You and your family have got me trapped in this hole.'

'Yes,' Shama would say. 'I suppose if it wasn't for my family you would have a grass roof over your head.'

'Family! Family! Put me in one poky little barrackroom and pay me twenty dollars a month. Don't talk to me about your family.'

'I tell you, if it wasn't for the children —'

And often, in the end, Mr Biswas would leave the house and go for a long night walk through the city, stopping at some empty shack of a café to eat a tin of salmon, trying to stifle the pain in his stomach and only making it worse; while below the weak electric bulb the sleepy-eyed Chinese shopkeeper picked and sucked his teeth, his slack, bare arms resting on a glasscase in which flies slept on stale cakes. Up to this time the city had been new and held an expectation which not even the deadest two o'clock sun could destroy. Anything could happen: he might meet his barren heroine, the past could be undone, he would be remade. But now not even the thought of the *Sentinel*'s presses, rolling out at that moment reports of speeches, banquets, funerals (with all names and decorations carefully checked), could keep him from seeing that the city was no more than a repetition of this: this dark, dingy café, the chipped counter, the flies thick on the electric flex, the empty Coca Cola cases stacked in a corner, the cracked glasscase, the shopkeeper picking his teeth, waiting to close.

And in the house, while he was out, the children would come out of bed and go to Shama. She would take down her bloated reporter's notebooks and try to explain how she had spent the money given her.

At school one day Anand asked the boy who shared his desk, 'Your father and mother does quarrel?'

'What about?'

'Oh, about anything. About food, for instance.'

'Nah. But suppose he ask her to go to town and buy something. And suppose she don't buy it. Boy!'

One evening, after a quarrel had flared up and died without being concluded, Anand went to Mr Biswas's room and said, 'I have a story to tell you.'

Something in his manner warned Mr Biswas. He put down his book, settled a pillow against the head of the bed and smiled.

'Once upon a time there was a man —' Anand's voice broke.

'Yes?' Mr Biswas said, in a mocking friendly voice, still smiling, scraping his lower lip with his teeth.

'Once upon a time there was a man who —' His voice broke again, his father's smile confused him, he forgot what he had planned to say and abandoning grammar, added quickly, 'Who, whatever you do for him, wasn't satisfied.'

Mr Biswas burst out laughing, and Anand ran out of the room, trembling with rage and humiliation, to the kitchen, where Shama comforted him.

For many days Anand didn't speak to Mr Biswas and, in secret revenge, didn't drink milk at the Dairies, but iced coffee. Mr Biswas was effusive towards Savi and Myna and Kamla, and relaxed with Shama. The atmosphere in the house was less heavy and Shama, now Anand's defender, took much pleasure in urging Anand to speak to his father.

'Leave him, leave him,' Mr Biswas said. 'Leave the story-teller.'

Anand became steadily more morose. When he came home after private lessons one afternoon he refused to eat or talk. He went to his room, lay down on the bed and, despite Shama's coaxings, stayed there.

Mr Biswas came in and presently walked into the room, saying in his rallying voice, 'Well, well. What happen to our Hans Andersen?'

'Eat some prunes, son,' Shama said, taking out the little brown paper-bag from the table drawer.

Mr Biswas saw the distress on Anand's face and his manner changed. 'What's the matter?'

Anand said, 'The boys laugh at me.'

'He who laughs last laughs best,' Shama said.

'Lawrence say that his father is your boss.'

There was silence.

Mr Biswas sat on the bed and said, 'Lawrence is the night editor. Nothing to do with me.'

'He say they have you like an office boy in the office.'

'You know I write features.'

'And he say that when you go to his father house you have to go to the back door.'

Mr Biswas stood up. His linen suit was crumpled, the jacket pulled out of shape by the notebooks in the pockets, the tops of which were dirty and a little frayed.

'You never went to his father house?'

'Why should he go to Lawrence's house?' Shama said.

'And you never went to the back door?'

Mr Biswas walked to the window. It was dark; his back was to them.

'Let me put on the light,' Shama said briskly. Her footsteps were heavy. The light went on. Anand covered his face with his arm. 'Is that all that's been upsetting you?' Shama asked. 'Your father has nothing to do with Lawrence. You heard what he said.'

Mr Biswas went out of the room.

Shama said, 'You shouldn't have told him that, you know, son.'

For the rest of that evening Shama walked and talked and did everything as noisily as she could.

The next morning, with his books and lunch parcel in his bag and the six cents for milk in his pocket, Anand was kissing

Shama in the back verandah when Mr Biswas came to him
and said, 'I don't depend on them for a job. You know that.
We could go back any time to Hanuman House. All of us.
You know that.'

On Saturday he took the children on a surprise visit to
Ajodha's. Tara and Ajodha were as delighted as the children,
and the visit lasted till Sunday. There was much to look at in
the new house. It was a grand two-storeyed concrete house
built and decorated and furnished in the modern manner.
The concrete blocks looked like rough-hewn stone; there
was no dust-collecting fretwork hanging from the eaves;
doors and windows were varnished, not painted, and closed
and opened in interesting ways; chairs were upholstered and
vast, not small and cane-bottomed; floors were stained and
polished; the lavatory flushes were chainless. In the drawingroom they studied Tara's photographs of the dead; they saw
Raghu in his flower-strewn coffin surrounded by his thin,
big-eyed children. The kitchen was enormous and abounded
in modern contrivances; Tara, old, slow and oldfashioned,
seemed out of place in it. When they were tired of the house
they wandered about the yard, which had not changed. They
talked to the cowman and the gardener, examined the various
people who called, and played among the abandoned frames
of motor vehicles. After lunch on Saturday they went to the
cinema, and on Sunday Ajodha arranged an excursion.

The following week-end they went again, and the week-
end after that; and soon this week-end visit was established.
They travelled up on Saturday morning, since that was the
only time it was reasonably easy to get a bus out of Port of
Spain. As soon as they got on the bus in the George Street
station Mr Biswas changed, dropping his week-day morose-
ness and becoming gay and even impish. The mood lasted
until Sunday evening; then they were all silent as they got
nearer the city, the house, Shama, Monday morning. For a
day or two afterwards the house in Port of Spain seemed dark
and clumsy.

Shama went on only one of these visits, and that she almost
ruined. The old, unspoken antagonism between the families

still existed and she was not eager to go. There had been a minor quarrel just before they went through the gate, and Shama was sullen when she stepped into Tara's house. Then, either from pride, or because she was made uneasy by the grandeur of the house, or because she was unable to make the effort, she remained sullen throughout the week-end. She said afterwards that she had known all along that Ajodha and Tara did not care for her; and she never went again.

She was often alone in Port of Spain. The children were not anxious to go with her to Hanuman House, and as dissension there increased she went less often herself, regretting the old warmth, fearing to be involved in new quarrels. She had hardly moved outside her own family and did not know how to get on with strangers. She was shy of people of another race, religion or way of life. Her shyness had got her a reputation for hardness among the tenants, and she had done little to get to know the woman who lived in Owad's old room. But now, alone at the week-ends, she felt the need of company and sought out the woman, who not only responded, but showed herself exceedingly curious. And Shama took down her account books and explained.

So the house became Shama's, the place where she stayed, the place to which Mr Biswas and the children returned with sadness after the week-end.

And during the week Anand's life was a misery. While Mr Biswas struggled with features on the splendid work of the Chacachacare Leper Settlement (with a photograph of lepers at prayer) and the Young Offenders' Detention Institution (with a photograph of young offenders at prayer), Anand wrote down and learned by heart copious notes on geography and English. Textbooks were discarded; only the notes of the teacher mattered; any deviation was instantly and severely punished; and there was not a day when some boy was not flogged and put to stand behind the blackboard. For this was the exhibition class, where no learning mattered except that which led to good examination results; and the teacher knew his job. At home Mr Biswas read Anand *Self-Help* and on his birthday gave him *Duty*, adding as a pure frivolity a school edition of Lamb's *Tales from Shakespeare*. Childhood, as a time of gaiety and irresponsibility, was for these exhibition pupils only one of the myths of English Composition. Only in compositions did they give delirious shouts of joy and their spirits overflowed into song; only there did they indulge in what the composition notes called 'schoolboy's pranks'.

Anand, following the example of those Samuel Smiles heroes who had in youth concealed the brilliance of their later years, did what he could to avoid school. He pretended to be ill; he played truant, forged excuses, was found out and flogged; he destroyed his shoes. He abandoned private lessons one afternoon, telling the teacher that he was wanted at home for a Hindu prayer ceremony which could take place only at half past three that afternoon, and telling his parents that the teacher's mother had died and the teacher had gone to the funeral. Mr Biswas, anxious to remain in the teacher's favour, cycled to the school the next day to offer his condolences. Anand was called a young scamp (the teacher sank in his estimation for using a word that sounded so slangy), flogged and left behind the blackboard. At home Mr Biswas said, 'Those private lessons are costing me money, you know.' 'Pranks' were permitted only in English Composition.

Most of his male cousins had undergone the brahminical initiation, and though Anand shared Mr Biswas's distaste for religious ritual, he was immediately attracted by this ceremony. His cousins had had their heads shaved, they were invested with the sacred thread, told the secret verses, given little bundles and sent off to Benares to study. This last was only a piece of play-acting. The attraction of the ceremony lay in the shaving of the head: no boy with a shaved head could go to a predominantly Christian school. Anand began a strong campaign for initiation. But he knew Mr Biswas's prejudices and worked subtly. He told Mr Biswas one evening that he was unable to offer up the usual prayers with sincerity, since the words had become meaningless. He needed an original prayer, so that he could think of each word. He wanted Mr Biswas to write this prayer for him, though he made it clear that, unlike Mr Biswas, he wanted no east-west compromise: he wanted a specifically Hindu prayer. The prayer was written. And Anand got Shama to bring a coloured print of the goddess Lakshmi from Hanuman House. He hung the print on the wall above his table and objected when lights were turned on in the evening before he had said his prayer to Lakshmi. Shama was delighted at this example of blood triumphing over environment; and Mr Biswas, despite his Aryan aversion to Sanatanist, Tulsi-like idol worship, could not hide the honour he felt at being asked to write Anand's prayer. After some time Anand complained that the whole procedure was improper, a mockery, and would continue to be so until he had been initiated.

Shama was thrilled.

But Mr Biswas said, 'Wait till the long holidays.'

And so, during the long holidays, when Savi and Myna and Kamla were making their round of holiday visits, including a fortnight at a beach house Ajodha had rented, Anand, shaved and thoroughly brahmin, but ashamed of showing his bald head, stayed in Port of Spain and Mr Biswas gave him portions of *Macdougall's Grammar* to learn and listened to him recite his geography and English notes. The evening worship of Lakshmi stopped.

Towards the end of that year a letter came to Mr Biswas from Chicago. The stamp was cancelled: REPORT OBSCENE MAIL TO YOUR POSTMASTER. Though the envelope was long the letter was short, a third of the paper being taken up by the florid, raised red and black letterhead of a newspaper. The letter was from Mr Burnett.

Dear Mohun, As you can see, I have left my little circus and am back in the old business. As a matter of fact I didn't leave the circus. It left me. Perhaps fire in Trinidad is different. But when that boy from St James was given one small American fire to walk through, he just ran. Away. My guess is that he is somewhere on Ellis Island, with nobody to claim him. The snake-charmer was all right until his snake bit him. We gave him a good funeral. I hunted high and low to get a Hindu priest to say the last few words, but no luck. I was going to do the job myself, but I couldn't dress the part, not being able to tie the headpiece or the tailpiece. Now and then I see a copy of the *Sentinel*. Why don't you give America a try?

Though the letter was a joke and nothing in it was to be taken seriously, Mr Biswas was moved that Mr Burnett had written at all. He immediately began to reply, and went on for pages, writing detailed denigrations of the new members of the staff. He thought he was being light and detached, but when at lunchtime he re-read what he had written he saw how bitter he appeared, how much he had revealed of himself. He tore the letter up. From time to time, until he died, he thought of writing. But he never wrote. And Mr Burnett never wrote again.

The school term ended and the children, forgetting the disappointment of the previous year, talked excitedly of going to Hanuman House for Christmas. Shama spent hours in the back verandah sewing clothes on an old hand machine which, mysteriously, was hers, how or since when no one knew. The broken wooden handle was swathed in red cotton and looked as though it had bled profusely from a deep wound; the chest, waist, rump and hind quarters of the animal-like machine, and its wooden stall, were black with oil and smelled of oil; and it was a wonder that cloth emerged clean and unmangled from the clanking, champing and chattering which Shama called forth from the creature by the touch of a finger on its bloody bandaged tail. The back verandah smelled of machine oil and new cloth and became dangerous with pins on the floor and pins between floorboards. Anand marvelled at the delight of his sisters in the tedious operations, and marvelled at their ability to put on dresses bristling with pins and not be pricked. Shama made him two shirts with long tails, the fashion among the boys at school (even exhibition pupils have their unscholarly moments) being for billowing shirts, barely tucked into the trousers.

But none of the clothes Shama made then were worn at Hanuman House.

One afternoon Mr Biswas came back from the *Sentinel* and as soon as he pushed his cycle through the front gate he saw that the rose garden at the side of the house had been destroyed and the ground levelled, red earth mingling with the black. The plants were in a bundle against the corrugated iron fence. The stems, hard and stained and blighted on the outside, yet showed white and wet and full of promise where they had been cleanly gashed; their illformed leaves had not begun to quail; they still looked alive.

He threw his bicycle against the concrete steps.

'Shama!'

He walked briskly, his footsteps resounding, through the drawingroom to the back verandah. The floor was littered with scraps of cloth and tangles of thread.

'Shama!'

She came out of the kitchen, her face taut. Her eyes sought to still his voice.

He took in the table and the sewingmachine, the scraps of cloth, the thread, the pins, the kitchen safe, the rails, the banister. Below, in the yard, standing in a group against the fence, he saw the children. They were looking up at him. Then he saw the back of a lorry, a pile of old corrugated iron sheets, a heap of new scantlings, two Negro labourers with dusty heads, faces and backs. And Seth. Rough and managerial in his khaki uniform and heavy bruised bluchers, the ivory cigarette holder held down in one shirt pocket by the buttoned flap.

He saw it clearly. For what seemed a long time he contemplated it. Then he was running down the back steps; Seth looked up, surprised; the labourers, stooping on the lorry, looked up; and he was fumbling among the scantlings. He tried to take one up, had misjudged its size, abandoned it, Shama saying from the verandah, 'No, no,' picked up a large stained wet stone from the bleaching-bed and 'Who tell you you could come and cut down my rose trees? Who?' Scraping the words out of his throat so that they didn't seem to come from where he stood, but from someone just behind him. A labourer jumped down from the lorry, there was surprise and even dread in Seth's eyes. 'Pa!' one girl cried, and he hoisted

his arm, Shama saying 'Man, man.' His wrist was seized, roughly, by large hot gritty fingers. The stone fell to the ground.

Disarmed, he was without words. Beside the three men he
felt his frailty, his baggy linen suit beside Seth's tight khaki
clothes and the labourers' working rags. The cuffs of his
jacket bore the imprints of dirty fingers; his wrist burned
where it had been held.

Seth said, 'You see. You make your children frighten like
hell.' And to the loaders, 'All right, all right.'

The unloading continued.

'Rose trees?' Seth said. 'They did just look like black sage
bush to me.'

'Yes,' Mr Biswas said. 'Yes! I know they just look like bush
to you. Tough!' he added. 'Tough!' As he turned he stumbled
against the bed of bleaching stones.

'Oops!' Seth said.

'Tough!' Mr Biswas repeated, walking away.

Shama followed him.

Heads were withdrawn from the fence on either side.
Curtains dropped back into place.

'Thug!' Mr Biswas said, going up the steps.

'Eh, eh,' Seth said, smiling at the children. 'Helluva temper, man. But my lorries can't sleep in the road.'

From the verandah Mr Biswas, unseen, said, 'This is not
the end of this. The old lady will have something to say about
this, I guarantee you. And Shekhar.'

Seth laughed. 'The old hen and the big god, eh?' He
looked up at the verandah and said in Hindi, 'Too many
people have the idea that everything belongs to the Tulsis.
How do you think this house was bought?'

Mr Biswas appeared at the banister of the verandah.

Anand looked away.

'You will be hearing from my solicitor,' Mr Biswas said.
'And those two *rakshas* you have with you. They too.' He
disappeared again.

The labourers, unaware of their identification with Hindu
mythological forces of evil, unloaded.

Seth winked at the children. 'Your father is a damn funny
sort of man. Behaving as though he own the place. Let me tell

you that when you children born your father couldn't feed
you. Ask him. And see the gratitude I get? Everybody defying
me these days. Or you don't know?'

'Savi! Myna! Kamla! Anand!' Shama called.

'You know what your father was doing when I pick him
up and marry him to your mother? You know? He tell you?
He wasn't even catching crab. He was just catching flies.'

'Savi! Anand!'

They hesitated, afraid of Seth, afraid of the house and Mr
Biswas.

'Today, look! White suit, collar and tie. And me. Still in
the same dirty clothes you see me with since you born. Gratitude, eh? But I will tell you children that if I leave them
today, all of them – your father, mother and all – all of them
start catching crab tomorrow, *I* guarantee you.'

From somewhere in the house Mr Biswas's voice came,
raised, indistinct, heated.

Seth moved to the lorry.

'Eh, Ewart?' he said gently to one of the loaders. 'They was
nice roses, eh?'

Ewart smiled, his tongue over his top lip, and made sounds
which committed him in no way.

Seth jerked his chin toward the house, still the source
of angry, indistinct words. He smiled. Then he stopped smiling and said, 'We mustn't pay any mind to these damn
jackasses.'

The children moved to the foot of the back steps, where
they were hidden from Seth and the loaders.

Mr Biswas's mutterings died away.

Suddenly an obscenity cracked out from the house. The
children were quite still. There was silence, even from the
lorry. Anand could have wept. Then the corrugated iron
sheets jangled again.

A series of resonant crashes came from the kitchen.

'Cut down the rose trees,' Mr Biswas was shouting. 'Cut
them down. Break up everything else.'

The children, now below the house, heard his footsteps on
the floor above as he went from room to room, pulling things
down.

Anand walked under the house to the front, past Mr Biswas's abandoned bicycle. The fence cast a shadow over the pavement and part of the road. Anand leaned against the fence and envied the calm of the other houses in the street, the group of boys and young men, the cricket players, the night chatterers, around the lamp-post.

Fresh noises came from the yard. It was not Mr Biswas pulling things down, but Seth and Ewart and Ewart's colleague putting up a shed for Seth's lorries at the side of the house, over Mr Biswas's garden.

On the road the shadows of houses and trees quickly lengthened, were distorted, became unrecognizable and finally dissolved into darkness.

Mr Biswas came down the front steps.

'Come with me for a walk.'

Anand would have liked to go, if only because he didn't want to hurt by refusing. But he wanted more to inspect the damage and comfort Shama.

The damage was slight. Mr Biswas had ordered his destruction with economy. The mirror of Shama's dressingtable had been unhinged and thrown on the bed, where it lay intact, reflecting the ceiling. The books had been knocked about a good deal; *Selections from Sankaracharya* had suffered especially. Mrs Tulsi's marble topped tables had all been overturned; the marble tops, crashing, must have been responsible for some of the more frightening noises. Many of the brass vases had been dented, and two potted palms had lost their pots without in any way losing their shape. The hatrack was in a semi-recumbent position against the half-wall of the front verandah, but it had been thrown there gently: a few hooks had snapped, but the glass was whole. In the kitchen no glass or china had been thrown, only noisy things like pots and pans and enamel plates.

When Mr Biswas returned his mood had changed.

'Shama, *how* did those marble tops break?' he asked, mimicking Mrs Tulsi. Then he acted himself. 'Break, Mai? What break? Oh, marble top. Yes, Mai. It really break. It *look* as if it break. Now I wonder how that happened.' He examined the broken hooks of the hatrack. 'Didn't know metal was such a funny thing. Come and look, Savi. Is not smooth inside, you know. Is more like packed sand.' As for the re-diffusion set, which he had kicked from room to room and disembowelled, he said, 'I wanted to do that for a long time. The company always saying that they replace sets free.'

When the engineers saw the battered box and asked what had happened, he said, 'I feel we listen to it too hard.' They left a brand-new set in exchange, of the latest design.

Every night Seth's lorries rested in the shed at the side of the house. Mr Biswas had never thought of Tulsi property as belonging to any particular person. Everything, the land at Green Vale, the shop at The Chase, belonged simply to the House. But the lorries were Seth's.

# 3. The Shorthills Adventure

DESPITE THE solidity of their establishment the Tulsis had never considered themselves settled in Arwacas or even Trinidad. It was no more than a stage in the journey that had begun when Pundit Tulsi left India. Only the death of Pundit Tulsi had prevented them from going back to India; and ever since they had talked, though less often than the old men who gathered in the arcade every evening, of moving on, to India, Demerara, Surinam. Mr Biswas didn't take such talk seriously. The old men would never see India again. And he could not imagine the Tulsis anywhere else except at Arwacas. Separate from their house, and lands, they would be separate from the labourers, tenants and friends who respected them for their piety and the memory of Pundit Tulsi; their Hindu status would be worthless and, as had happened during their descent on the house in Port of Spain, they would be only exotic.

But when Shama went hurrying to Arwacas to give her news of Seth's blasphemies, she found Hanuman House in commotion. The Tulsis had decided to move on. The clay-brick house was to be abandoned, and everyone was full of talk of the new estate at Shorthills, to the northeast of Port of Spain, among the mountains of the Northern Range.

The High Street was bright and noisy as always at the Christmas season, though because of the war there were few imported goods in the shops. In the Tulsi Store there were no Christmas goods except for the antique black dolls, and no decorations except Mr Biswas's faded, peeling signs. Many shelves were empty; everything that could be of use at Shorthills had been packed.

And Shama's news was stale. The disagreement between Seth and the rest of the family had already turned to open war. He and his wife and children had left Hanuman House

and were living in a back street not far away; they were taking
no part in the move to Shorthills. The cause of the quarrel
remained obscure, each side accusing the other of ingratitude
and treachery, and Seth abusing Shekhar in particular.
Neither Mrs Tulsi nor Shekhar had made any statement.
Shekhar, besides, was seldom in Arwacas, and it was the sisters
who carried on the quarrel. They had forbidden their
children to speak to Seth's children; Seth had forbidden
his children to speak to the Tulsi children. Only Padma,
Seth's wife, was welcome, as Mrs Tulsi's sister, at Hanuman
House; she could not be blamed for her marriage and continued
to be respected for her age. Since the breach she had paid one
clandestine visit to Hanuman House. The sisters regarded her
loyalty as a tribute to the rightness of their cause; that she had
had to come secretly was proof of Seth's brutality.

The crop season was at hand and the sugarcane fields,
managerless, were open to the malice of those who bore the
Tulsis grudges. Two fires had already been started and there
were rumours that Seth was stirring up fresh trouble, claiming
Tulsi property as his own. The husbands of some sisters said
they had been threatened.

Yet the talk was less of Seth than of the new estate. Shama
heard its glories listed again and again. In the grounds of the
estate house there was a cricket field and a swimming pool;
the drive was lined with orange trees and gri-gri palms with
slender white trunks, red berries and dark green leaves. The
land itself was a wonder. The saman trees had lianas so strong
and supple that one could swing on them. All day the immortelle trees dropped their red and yellow bird-shaped flowers
through which one could whistle like a bird. Cocoa trees
grew in the shade of the immortelles, coffee in the shade of
the cocoa, and the hills were covered with tonka bean. Fruit
trees, mango, orange, avocado pear, were so plentiful as to
seem wild. And there were nutmeg trees, as well as cedar,
*poui*, and the *bois-canot* which was light yet so springy and
strong it made you a better cricket bat than the willow. The
sisters spoke of the hills, the sweet springs and hidden waterfalls with all the excitement of people who had known only
the hot, open plain, the flat acres of sugarcane and the muddy

ricelands. Even if one didn't have a way with land, as they had, if one did nothing, life could be rich at Shorthills. There was talk of dairy farming; there was talk of growing grapefruit. More particularly, there was talk of rearing sheep, and of an idyllic project of giving one sheep to every child as his very own, the foundation, it was made to appear, of fabulous wealth. And there were horses on the estate: the children would learn to ride.

Though it was never clear afterwards why this large decision had been taken so suddenly, and puzzling that the last corporate effort of the Tulsis should have been directed towards this uprooting, Shama left for Port of Spain full of enthusiasm. She wanted to be part of her family again, to share the adventure.

'Horses?' Mr Biswas said. 'I bet you when you go there all you find is one old monkey swinging from the liana on the saman tree. I can't understand this craziness that possess your family.'

Shama spoke about the sheep.

'Sheep?' Mr Biswas said. 'To ride?'

She said that Seth was no longer part of the family and that two husbands who had left Hanuman House after disagreements with Seth had rejoined the family for the move to Shorthills.

Mr Biswas didn't listen. 'About those sheep. Savi get one, Anand get one, Myna get one, Kamla get one. Make four in all. What are we going to do with four sheep. Breed more? To sell and kill? Hindus, eh? Feeding and fattening just in order to kill. Or you see the six of us sitting down and making wool from four sheep? You know how to make wool? Any of your family know how to make wool?'

The children did not want to move to a place they didn't know, and they were a little frightened of living with the Tulsis again. Above all, they did not want to be referred to as 'country pupils' at school; the advantages – being released fifteen minutes earlier in the afternoon – could not make up for the shame. And Mr Biswas turned Shama's propaganda into a joke. He read out 'The Emperor's New Clothes' from

*Bell's Standard Elocutionist*; he drove imaginary flocks of sheep through the drawingroom, making bleating noises. As always during the holidays, he announced his arrival by ringing his bicycle bell from the road; then the children walked out in single file to meet him, staggering under imaginary loads. 'Watch it, Savi!' he would call. 'Those tonka beans are heavy like hell, you know.' Later he would ask, 'Make a lot of wool today?' And once, when Anand came into the drawingroom just as the lavatory chain was pulled, Mr Biswas said, 'Walking back? What's the matter? Forgot your horse at the waterfall?'

Shama sulked.

'Going to buy that gold brooch for you, girl! Anand, Savi, Myna! Come and sing a Christmas carol for your mother.'

They sang 'While Shepherds Watched their Flocks by Night'.

Shama's gloom, persisting, defeated them all. And that Christmas, the first they spent by themselves, was made more memorable by Shama's gloom. She could not make icecream because she didn't have a freezer, but she did what she could to turn the day into a miniature Hanuman House Christmas. She got up early and waited to be kissed, like Mrs Tulsi. She spread a white cloth on the table and put out nuts and dates and red apples; she cooked an extravagant meal. She did everything punctiliously, but as one martyred. 'Anybody would think you were making another baby,' Mr Biswas said. And in his diary, a *Sentinel* reporter's notebook which he had begun to fill at Mr Biswas's suggestion, as an additional exercise in English Composition and as practice in natural writing, Anand wrote, 'This is the worst Christmas Day I have ever spent;' and, not forgetting the literary purpose of the diary, added, 'I feel like Oliver Twist in the workhouse.'

But Shama never relented.

Soon she received impressive assistance. The house became full of sisters and husbands on their way to and from Shorthills. The fine dresses, veils and jewellery of the sisters contrasted with their mood, which they seemed to get from Shama. They fixed Mr Biswas with injured, helpless, accusing woman's looks which he found difficult to ignore. The jokes about sheep and waterfalls and tonka beans stopped; he locked himself in his room. Sometimes Shama, after much coaxing from her sisters, dressed and went to Shorthills with them. She came back gloomier than ever, and when Mr Biswas said, 'Well, tell me, girl, tell me,' she did not reply and only cried silently. When Mrs Tulsi came Shama cried all the time.

Since the quarrel with Seth Mrs Tulsi had ceased to be an invalid. She had left the Rose Room to direct the move from Arwacas and was, indeed, the source of the new enthusiasm. She tried to persuade Mr Biswas to join the move, and Mr Biswas, flattered at this attention, listened sympathetically. There would be no Seth, Mrs Tulsi said; one could live for nothing at Shorthills; Mr Biswas would be able to save his salary; there were many good sites for houses, and with timber from the estate Mr Biswas might even build himself a little house.

'Leave him, leave him,' Shama said. 'All this talk about house was only to spite me.'

'But if I keep my job in Port of Spain I don't see how I would be able to do anything on the estate,' Mr Biswas said.

'Never mind,' Mrs Tulsi said.

He wasn't sure whether she wanted him to move for Shama's sake; or whether, without Seth, she needed as many men as possible around her; or whether she wanted no one, by his coolness, to make her question her own enthusiasm. And he agreed to go to Shorthills with her one morning, to have a look at the estate.

He made Anand telephone the *Sentinel* and went with Mrs Tulsi to the bus stop. There he suffered some moments of anxiety, for with her long white skirt, her veil, her arms braceleted from wrist to elbow and a thick gold yoke around her neck, Mrs Tulsi was noticeable in any Port of Spain street, and Mr Biswas feared he would be spotted by someone from the office. He leaned against the lamp-post, hiding his face.

'Regular bus service,' he said after a time.

'From Shorthills, the buses always leave on the dot.'

'Instead of giving every child a sheep, better to give them a horse. Ride to school. Ride back.'

At last the bus came, empty except for the driver and the conductor. The body had been made locally, a crude jangling box of wood and tin and felt and large naked bolts. Mr Biswas bumped exaggeratedly up and down on the rough wooden seat. 'Just practising,' he said.

The city ended abruptly at the Maraval terminus. The road climbed and dipped; hills intermittently shut out the view. After half an hour Mr Biswas pointed to the bush on a roundabout. 'Estate?' They went past a puzzling huddle of three crumbling shacks. Two black water barrels stood in the hard yellow yard. 'Cricket field?' Mr Biswas said. 'Swimming pool?'

After many curves and climbs the road straightened out and ran steadily down into a widening valley. The hills looked wild, the tops of trees rising one behind the other: a coagulation of greenery. But here and there the faded thatch of a lean-to, warm against the still, dark green, showed that the wilderness had been charted. Houses and huts appeared on either side of the road, widely separated and so hidden by green that, from the bus, Shorthills was only flitting patches of colour: the rust of a roof, the pink or ochre of a wall.

'Next bus to Port of Spain in ten minutes,' the conductor said conversationally. Mr Biswas got up. Mrs Tulsi pulled him down. 'They like to reverse first.' The bus reversed in a dirt lane and came to rest on the verge, under an avocado pear tree.

The driver and conductor squatted under the tree, smoking. Across the road and next to the lane in which the bus had reversed Mr Biswas saw an open square of ground, mounds and faded wreaths alone indicating its purpose.

Mr Biswas waved at the forlorn little cemetery and the dirt lane which, past a few tumbledown houses, disappeared behind bush and apparently led only to more bush and the mountain which rose at the end. 'Estate?' he asked.

Mrs Tulsi smiled. 'And on this side.' She waved at the other side of the road.

Beyond a deep gully, whose sides were sheer, whose bed was strewn with boulders, stones and pebbles, perfectly graded, Mr Biswas saw more bush, more mountains. 'A lot of bamboo,' he said. 'You could start a paper factory.'

It was easy to see just how far the buses went. Up to the dirt lane the road was smooth, its centre black and dully shining. Past that the road narrowed, was gravelly and dusty, its edges obscured by the untended verge.

'I suppose we go along there,' Mr Biswas said.

They began walking.

Mrs Tulsi bent down and tore up a plant from the verge. 'Rabbit meat,' she said. 'Best food for rabbits. In Arwacas you have to buy it.'

Below the overarching trees the road was in soft shadow. Sunlight spotted the gravel in white blurs, spotted the wet green verges, the dark ridged trunks of trees. It was cool. And then Mr Biswas began seeing the fruit trees. Avocado pear trees grew at the side of the road as casually as any bush; their fruit, only just out of flower, were tiny but already perfectly shaped, with a shine they would soon lose. The land between the road and the gully widened; the gully grew shallower. Beyond it Mr Biswas saw the tall immortelles and their red and yellow flowers. And then the untrodden road blazed with the flowers. Mr Biswas picked one up, put it between his lips, tasted the nectar, blew, and the bird-shaped flower whistled. Even as they stood flowers fell on them. Under the immortelles he saw the cocoa trees, stunted, their branches black and dry, the cocoa pods gleaming with all the colours between yellow and red and crimson and purple, not like things that had grown, but like varnished wax models stuck on to dead branches. Then there were orange trees, heavy with leaf and fruit. And always they walked between two hills. The road narrowed; they heard no sound except that of their feet on the loose gravel. Then, far away, they heard the bus starting on its journey back to bustling, barren, concrete and timber Port of Spain. Impossible that it was less than an hour away!

The gully grew shallower and shallower, and then it was only a depression carpeted with a soft vine of a tender green.

Mrs Tulsi bent down and disturbed it. A vine hung from her fingers; it had a faint smell of mint.

'Old man's beard,' she said. 'In Arwacas they grow it in baskets.'

The house was partly hidden by a large, branching, towering saman tree. Swollen parasite vines veined its branches and massive trunk; wild pines sprouted like coarse hair from every crotch; and it was hung with lianas. Below the tree, beside the gully, there was a short walk lined with orange trees, and around the trunk there was a clump of wild tannia, pale green, four feet tall, nothing but stem and giant heart-shaped leaves, cool with quick beads of dew.

An old signpost stood slightly askew in the gully. The letters were bleached and faint: *Christopher Columbus Road.* It was fitting. The land, though fruitful from a former cultivation, felt new.

'This used to be the old road,' Mrs Tulsi said.

And Mr Biswas found it easy to imagine the other race of Indians moving about this road before the world grew dark for them.

Nothing in Shama's accounts had prepared him for the view of the house from the gully, at the end of the tree-lined drive. It was a two-storeyed house with a long verandah on the lower floor; it stood far from the road on an escarpment on the hill, above a broad flight of concrete steps, white against the surrounding green.

And everything was as Shama had said. On one side of the drive there was a cricket field; the pitch was red and broken: obviously the village team did not use matting. On the other side, beyond the saman tree, the lianas, the wild tannia, there was a swimming pool, empty, cracked, sandy, plants pushing up through the concrete, but it was easy to see it mended and filled with clear water; and beyond that, on an artificial mound, a cherry tree, its thick branches trimmed level at the bottom above a wrought-iron seat. And in the drive the grigri palms, with their white trunks, red berries and dark green leaves; though they were perhaps too old: they had grown so tall they could not be seen whole, and could even be missed.

Then at the far end of the cricket ground Mr Biswas saw a mule. It looked old and dispirited. Untethered, it remained still, against a camouflage of cocoa-trees.

'Ah!' Mr Biswas said, breaking the silence. 'Horses.'

'That's not a horse,' Mrs Tulsi said.

They left the drive and stood among the wild tannia under the saman tree. Mrs Tulsi held a liana and offered it to Mr Biswas. While he felt it, she held a thinner liana and pulled it down. 'As strong as rope,' she said. 'The children could skip with this.'

They walked along the weed-ridden drive. The narrow canal at one side was silted with fine, rippled sand. 'You could just sell the sand from this place,' Mrs Tulsi said. They came to the broad flight of shallow concrete steps. Mr Biswas went up slowly: impossible not to feel regal ascending steps like these.

On either side of the house there was an abandoned garden, flowerless except for some stray marigolds; but through the bush it was possible to see the pattern of the beds, edged with concrete and the stunted shrubs called 'green tea' and 'red tea'. At the end of one garden a Julie mango tree stood on a concrete-walled circular bed more than three feet high.

'Just the spot for a temple,' Mrs Tulsi whispered.

The house was of timber, but the timber had been painted to look like blocks of granite: grey, flecked with black, red, white and blue, and marked with thin white lines. A folding screen separated the regal drawingroom from the regal dining-room; and there was a multiplicity of rooms whose purposes were uncertain. The house had its own electricity plant; not working at the moment, Mrs Tulsi said, but it could be fixed. There was a garage, servants' quarters, an outdoor bathroom with a deep concrete tub. The kitchen, linked to the house by a roofed way, was vast, with a brick oven. The hill rose directly behind the kitchen; the view through the back window was of the green hillside just a few feet away. And tonka beans grew on the hill.

'Who owned the house before?' Mr Biswas asked.

'Some French people.'

This, allied to a brief acquaintance during his Aryan days with the writings of Romain Rolland, gave Mr Biswas a respect for the French.

They walked and looked. The silence, the solitude, the fruitful bush in a broken landscape: it was an enchantment.

They heard the bus in the distance.

'Well,' he said. 'I suppose it is time to go home now.'

'Home?' said Mrs Tulsi. 'Isn't this your home now?'

So the Tulsis left Arwacas. The lands were rented out and it fell to the tenants to contend with Seth's claims. The Tulsi Store was leased to a firm of Port of Spain merchants. At Port of Spain one of the tenements was sold and Shama relieved of her rent-collecting duties. It was only then that Shama, still sulking after her victory, disclosed that Mrs Tulsi had decided to raise the rent of the Port of Spain house. Mr Biswas was shocked, and to shock him further Shama brought down her account books and showed how his salary went to the grocer almost as soon as it came, how her debts were rising.

The solitude and silence of Shorthills was violated. The villagers bore the invasion without protest and almost with indifference. They were an attractive mixture of French and Spanish and Negro and, though they lived so near to Port of Spain, formed a closed, distinctive community. They had a rural slowness and civility, and spoke English with an accent derived from the French patois they spoke among themselves. They appeared to exercise some rights on the grounds of the house. They played cricket on the cricket field most afternoons and there was a match every Sunday, when the grounds were virtually taken over by the villagers. For some time after the coming of the Tulsis courting couples strolled about the orange walks and the drive in the afternoon, disappearing from time to time into the cocoa woods. But this custom soon ceased. The couples, finding themselves surprised at every turn by a Tulsi, moved further up the gully.

Mr Biswas's first impression on moving to Shorthills was that the Tulsi family had increased. Seth and his family were absent; but those sisters who for one reason and another had lived away from Hanuman House had brought their families;

and there were many married grandchildren as well, and their families.

Mr Biswas was given a room on the upper floor, one of six rooms of equal size about a central corridor. It was a hotel-like arrangement, with a couple in each room, and widows and children moving about the common area downstairs. Mr Biswas's room became the headquarters of his family; it was there that Anand did his homework, there that the children came to complain, there that Mr Biswas gave them delicacies to eat in private. The fourposter, Shama's dressingtable, the bookcase and desk and the table were in this room; the rest of his furniture, rockingchair, hatrack, kitchen safe, was disposed, like his children at night, about the house.

The drawingroom furnishings of Hanuman House had been similarly scattered. There could be no division of this house into the used and the unused, and the thronelike chairs, the statuary and the vases were left in the drawingroom, which in appearance and purpose presently became the equivalent of the Hanuman House hall.

A certain unpleasantness was added to Mr Biswas's situation by the presence directly across the corridor of a brother-in-law he had never seen at Hanuman House, a tall, contemptuous man who had taken an immediate dislike to him and expressed this dislike by a quivering of the nostrils.

Anand said, 'Prakash say his pappa got more books than you.'

Mr Biswas sent Anand to find out what books Prakash's father had.

Anand reported, 'All the books exactly the same size. On the cover they have a green shield marked "Boots". And they are all by a man called W. C. Tuttle.'

'Trash,' Mr Biswas said.

'Trash,' Anand told Prakash.

'You call my books trash?' Prakash's father asked Mr Biswas some mornings later, when they opened their doors at the same time.

'I didn't call your books trash.'

The nostrils quivered. 'What about your Epictetus and *Manxman* and Samuel Smiles?'

'How do you know about my Epictetus?'

'How do you know about my books?'

Thereafter Mr Biswas locked his room whenever he left it. The news spread and there were comments.

'So you start up already?' Shama said.

And having got to Shorthills, everyone waited, for the sheep, the horses, for the swimming pool to be repaired, the drive weeded, the gardens cleaned, the electricity plant fixed, the house repainted.

Waiting, the children stripped the saman tree of its lianas. But there was no use to which they could put these improbable and pleasing growths; they were not good for skipping, as Mrs Tulsi had said: the thin ones frayed easily, the fat ones were unwieldy. Hari cut down the Julie mango tree on the raised bed at the end of the garden and built a small, kennel-like box-board hut; this was the temple. The reader of W. C. Tuttle put up a large framed print of the goddess Lakshmi in the drawingroom and offered up his own prayers before it every evening; Prakash said his father knew more of these matters than Hari. The brick oven in the kitchen was levelled; the roofed way between the house and kitchen was pulled down and the open area roofed with old corrugated iron and tree-branches from the hillside at the back.

Anand's patience broke. Spreading a rumour among the children that the house was going to be repainted right away but that the old paint had to be scraped off first, he soon had more than a dozen helpers working on the granite blocks. They made many pink and cream scars on the grey verandah walls before they were noticed; and this effort to force improvements ended in a mass flogging.

Mr Biswas, too, was waiting for improvements. But he did not greatly care about them. For him Shorthills was an adventure, an interlude. His job made him independent of the Tulsis; and Shorthills was an insurance against the sack. It also provided an opportunity to save, an opportunity to plunder. And secretly he was plundering: half a dozen oranges at a time, half a dozen avocado pears or grapefruit or lemons, sold to a café keeper in St Vincent Street with some story about the variety of fruit trees he had in his backyard. The money was little but regular, the thrill of plundering delicious. Plunder! The very sound of the word excited Mr Biswas. Cycling to work in the cool of the morning and whistling in his way, he would suddenly jump off his bicycle, look right, look left, pull down oranges or avocado pears, drop them into his saddlebag, hop on to his saddle and cycle measuredly away, whistling.

He came back one afternoon to find the cherry tree cut down, the artificial mound partly dug up, the swimming pool partly filled in. By the end of the week the mound was a flat black patch and the swimming pool did not exist. A tent was put up over the area occupied by the pool and sisters and husbands remarked again and again that it was wonderful not only to have so much bamboo so near but not to have to pay for it either, as they had had to at Arwacas.

The tent was for wedding guests. It appeared that a whole wave of Shama's nieces was to be married off. One marriage had been arranged before the move, and during the idle weeks at Shorthills the idea had grown. Action was swift and sudden. Details – the bridegrooms and dowries – had been easily settled, and now the puzzling estate was forgotten and all energy went to preparing for the weddings. Days before the ceremony guests and retainers and dancers, singers and musicians came from Arwacas. They slept in the tent, the verandah, the garage, the covered space between the kitchen and house, and by day wandered through the grounds and woods, plundering.

Much bamboo was used in the decorations. The drive and walks were lined with bamboo poles placed horizontally on vertical bamboo poles; every horizontal section was filled with oil and fitted with a wick. On the night of the weddings many small flickering flames seemed to be suspended in the darkness; trees, outlined, not illuminated, looked solid; and the grounds felt protected, a warm cave in the night. The seven bridegrooms came in seven cavalcades with seven teams of drummers, followed by the stupefied villagers. At the foot of the concrete steps there were seven ceremonies of welcome, and in the wedding-tent, built over one of the

gardens flattened for the purpose, the seven wedding ceremonies went on all night, while in the tent over the swimming pool there was singing, dancing and feasting.

When the weddings were over, the population of the
house temporarily reduced by seven, the guests gone away,
and the tents over the ruined garden and swimming pool
taken down, everyone began waiting again, for the small
cricket pavilion to be restored, the drive cleaned, its culverts
mended, the canal cleared of silt, for the evergreen hedges at
the bottom of the hill to be trimmed, for the unruined garden
to be replanted. Unasked, the children did what they could,
but their scattered efforts made no impression on the grounds.
They collected tonka beans from the hillside and, not knowing what to do with them, left them in the garage, where they
presently rotted and smelled.

Then suddenly some sheep appeared. Half a dozen scrag-
gy, bare, bewildered sheep. The children had been promised
sheep, but they had expected fleecy things, and there was no
rush to claim these. The sheep remained nibbling in the
cricket field, offending the children and the cricketers.

Nothing was done to the cocoa trees or the orange trees.
Week by week the bush advanced and the estate, from looking neglected, began to look abandoned. There was still no
one to plan or direct. As suddenly as she had emerged from
her sickroom to supervise the move, so Mrs Tulsi had now
withdrawn. She had a small room on the lower floor, overlooking the ruined garden and Hari's box-board temple. But
her window was closed, the room was sealed against light and
air, and there, in an ammoniac darkness, she spent much of
the day, looked after by Sushila and Miss Blackie. It was as
though her energy had been stimulated only by the quarrel
with Seth and, ebbing, had depressed her further into exhaustion and grief.

Govind tore down the cricket pavilion one day. A rough
cowshed went up in its place, and Mr Biswas heard, with
astonishment, that his cow was to be stabled there.

'Cow? *My* cow?'

It turned out that the cow, whose name was Mutri, was
one of Shama's secret possessions, like her sewingmachine.

Mutri had been kept on the estate at Arwacas with all the other Tulsi cows. She was an old black cow, tired, with short bruised horns.

'What about the milk?' Mr Biswas asked. 'The calves?'

'What about the grass?' Shama replied. 'The water? The feed?'

Govind looked after the cows and for that reason alone Mr Biswas made no further inquiries. Govind was becoming increasingly surly. He scarcely spoke to anyone, and worked off his rages on the cows. He beat them with thick lengths of wood and at milking time the slightest misdemeanour threw him into a rage. The animals didn't moan or wince or show anger; they only tried to move away. No one protested; there was no one to complain to.

Mr Biswas said, 'Poor Mutri.'

Before cows and sheep the cricketers retreated. The cricket field turned to mud and manure, and someone planted a pumpkin vine at the edge of it.

Then the tree-cutting began. In less than a morning the reader of W. C. Tuttle cut down the gri-gri palms along the drive. He came back sweating to the house and, since none of the watertaps worked, had a bath at a waterbarrel. Mrs Tulsi ate the hearts of the trees, which had been recommended to her by one of her Arwacas friends, and the children consoled themselves with the red berries. Govind, asserting himself, then cut down the orange trees: they were blighted, encouraged snakes, and could conceal thieves.

'Damn stupid thieves if they think they could find anything in this place,' Mr Biswas said. 'They cut down the trees only to make it easier to pick the oranges, that is all.'

The oranges were collected by Govind and Chinta and their children, put into sacks and sent to Port of Spain by bus. Everyone wondered who took the money. The trees were chopped into logs and burned in the kitchen, the moss-covered barks making excellent kindling.

The children lost heart. They now had to be compelled to gather tonka beans, to pick oranges and avocado pears to be sent to Port of Spain. On some Saturdays they pulled up weeds from the drive, urged on by the adults to hollow competitions to see who could amass the highest pile of weeds. The plumbing remained unrepaired. Some lesser husbands built a latrine on the hillside. The house toilet, unused, became a sewingroom.

In place of the orange trees and the palm trees seedlings were planted along the drive and hedged around with bamboo stakes. The cows broke down the cricket field fence. The sheep, escaping, broke down the bamboo stakes and stripped the seedlings clean. The silt rose in the canal at the side of the drive. Weeds grew from the cracks in the concrete culvert and up the wide, shallow steps.

Every morning Hari said his prayers and rang his bell and beat his gong in his boxboard kennel in the ruined garden; and every evening the man Mr Biswas now thought of as W. C. Tuttle said his prayers before the framed print in the drawingroom. The rubbish heap started by the Tulsis at the foot of the hill grew higher and wider. The sheep, neglected, unfruitful, survived. The cows were milked. The pumpkin vine spread rapidly in the manured mud and broke into frail yellow flower. The first pumpkin, the first Tulsi fruit, was welcomed with enthusiasm; and since, because of a Hindu taboo no one could explain, women were forbidden to cut pumpkins open, a man was invited to do so. And the man was W. C. Tuttle.

It was W. C. Tuttle who dismantled the electricity plant and melted down the lead to make dumb-bells. And it was W. C. Tuttle who announced that a furniture factory was to be started. Scores of cedar trees were cut down, sawed and stacked in the garage, and W. C. Tuttle sent to his own village for a Negro called Théophile. Théophile was a blacksmith whose trade had declined with the coming of the motorcar. He was lodged in a small room below the drawingroom, fed three times a day and turned loose among the cedar planks. He made many benches; gaining confidence, he put together a vast, irregularly oval table; then a number of wardrobes like sentry-boxes. No joint was clean; no door fitted; and the soft wood showed many little clusters of hammer indentations. It was stated by W. C. Tuttle, his wife, his chil-

dren and Théophile himself that stain and varnish would hide
these flaws. And, Tulsi excitement mounting, Théophile
went to work on morris chairs. W. C. Tuttle ordered a
bookcase. Mr Biswas ordered a bookcase. The doors of Mr
Biswas's bookcase sloped at the top and would have formed a
peak if they could meet: Théophile said it was a style. By this
time the planks on the oval table had shrunk, the joints were
loose and the wax had dropped out, and the wardrobe doors
could never close. Théophile worked with saw and hammer
and nails on the table and wardrobes; then the chairs and
bookcases needed attention; then the wardrobes gave trouble
again. Théophile was dismissed to his village, and there was
no further talk about the furniture factory. The morris chairs
fell apart and were used as firewood; some of the more adventurous children slept on the table at night. W. C. Tuttle, acting as Mrs Tulsi's agent, sold the cedar planks in the garage.
Shortly afterwards he bought a lorry, and hired it out to the
Americans.

Then the Americans came to the village. They had decided to build a post somewhere in the mountains, and day
and night army lorries rolled through the village on skid
chains. The lane next to the cemetery was widened and on
the dark green mountains in the distance a thin dirt-red line
zigzagged upwards. The Tulsi widows got together, built a
shack at the corner of the lane and stocked it with Coca Cola,
cakes, oranges and avocado pears. The American lorries
didn't stop. The widows spent some money on a liquor
licence and, with great trepidation, spent more money on
cases of rum. The lorries didn't stop. One night a lorry
crashed into the shack. The widows retreated.

Though surrounded by devastation, Mr Biswas remained
detached. He paid no rent; he spent nothing on food; he was
saving most of his salary. For the first time he had money, and
every fortnight it was increasing. He closed his heart to sorrow and anger at a dereliction he was powerless to prevent;
and, recognizing with a thrill that it was now every man for
himself – the phrase gave him much pleasure – he continued
to plunder, enjoying the feeling that in the midst of chaos he
was calmly going about his own devilish plans.

Then the news of the ravages of W. C. Tuttle and Govind was whispered through the house. W. C. Tuttle had been selling whole cedar trees. Govind had been selling lorry loads of oranges and papaws and avocado pears and limes and grapefruit and cocoa and tonka beans. Mr Biswas felt exceedingly foolish next morning when he dropped half a dozen oranges into his bag. He wondered, too, how it was possible for someone to steal a cedar tree without being noticed. Shama, outraged like most of the sisters, explained the trees had been sold on the ground, for very little. The buyers' lorries had come to the estate from the north, taking the roundabout, dangerous and virtually unused road over the mountains. Nothing would have been known had not the clearing on the hillside grown too large and attracted the attention of the estate overseer, a sad worried man who had come with the estate, like the mule, and without knowing what his duties were, had to look occupied to keep his job.

Govind and Chinta ignored the whispers and silence. W. C. Tuttle replied to them by scowling and exercising with his dumb-bells. His wife looked offended. The nine little Tuttles refused to speak to the other children.

The villagers at last banded against the Tulsis. Many of the Tulsi children were going to schools in Port of Spain and they filled the seven o'clock bus at the terminus near the graveyard. The villagers, who had hitherto found the hourly bus service to Port of Spain quite adequate, began to board the bus just before it reached the graveyard, paying the extra penny to be sure of their seat to Port of Spain. And the children found that the seven o'clock bus came in nearly full, and no one got out. There was no great competition for the vacant seats, and for many days most of the children did not go to school, until W. C. Tuttle, frowningly forgiving, offered, for no more than the bus fare, to take the children to school on his lorry.

The lorry had to be at the American base at six in the morning. Therefore the children could not be deposited at school much after half past five. To do this they had to leave Shorthills at a quarter to five. So they had to be up at four. It was still night when, sitting close together on planks fixed to the tray of the lorry, their teeth chattering, they drove through the chilly hills below the low dripping trees; and the street lamps were still on when they got to Port of Spain. They were put down outside their schools before newsboys delivered papers, before servants were up, before the school gates opened. They remained on the pavement and played hopscotch in the pre-dawn light. The caretaker of the girls' school rose at six and dressed hurriedly and let them in, asking them not to make too much noise and disturb his wife, who was still asleep. The caretaker's house was small, with only two rooms and a tiny, partly-exposed kitchen; and the caretaker had a numerous family. They had been used to wandering about the school yard in the early mornings dressed as they pleased; they brushed their teeth and spat in the sandy yard; they quarrelled; they slipped naked from house to outdoor bathroom and towelled themselves in the open; they cooked and ate under the tamarind tree; they hung up intimate washing. Now correctness was imposed on them from dawn. While the caretaker and his family breakfasted, in silence, the children became hungry again and ate the lunches which had been prepared from them three hours before. It was the best time to eat the lunches, for by midday the curry was beginning to go red and smell. The children who kept their food till lunchtime often gave it away then in exchange for things like bread and cheese; and, the reputation of Indian food surviving even Tulsi cooking, both sides thought they were getting the better bargain.

The return to Shorthills had its own problems. The children left school at three. The lorry left the American base at six. It was therefore out of the question if the children were to get home before eight. And the bus service from Port of Spain became more difficult from week to week. Because of wartime shortages and restrictions there were fewer city buses, and the Shorthills bus was used by people who didn't go all the way. To get the bus the children had to walk nearly three miles to the terminus at the railway station. The last uncrowded bus was the two-thirty; to get this meant leaving school shortly after lunch. The child who hoped to get the

three-thirty left school at half past two, walked to the terminus and joined the waiting crowd. There was no queue
and the bus on its arrival became the object of an immediate
scrimmage. People scrambled through the open windows,
climbing up on tyres and the cap of the petrol tank, and burst
through the emergency exit at the back; so that even if a child
managed to squeeze in first through the door he found the
seats taken. So the children walked until they could be taken
on by the bus when it was less full, or by the lorry returning
from the American base. Mrs Tulsi sent word from her room
that the children could lessen the fatigue of walking in the
afternoon if they all sang; if the girls were molested they were
to take off their shoes (they wore crêpe soles) and strike the
molester on the head.

Eventually, however, a car was bought, and one of the
sons-in-law drove it to Port of Spain with the children and
the oranges. It was a Ford V-8 of the early nineteen-thirties,
not inelegant, and it might have performed less erratically if it
carried a lighter load. Under the weight of children and oranges it sank low on the rear springs, the bonnet was slightly
uptilted, and for the steeper climbs the children had to get off.
Often the car broke down and then the driver, who knew
nothing about cars, asked the children to push. Like ants
around a dead cockroach the children surrounded the car (the
girls in their dark blue uniforms) and pushed and pulled.
Sometimes they pushed for more than a mile. Sometimes
they pushed the car to the top of a hill, jumped aside as it
rolled down, heard it start, raced after it, the driver urging
them to hurry, sprang inside three at a time. Then the engine
stalled; and they sat, crouched or half-stood, suffocated and
silent, waiting for the fruitless, scraping whine of the starter.
Sometimes the car got into Port of Spain with one side of the
bonnet up and a child on the wing, operating a pump of some
sort. Sometimes the car didn't get to Port of Spain at all. This
pleased the children more than the driver; he had no packed
lunch. Sometimes the car was laid up for days. Then the
children went to Port of Spain by lorry; or they surprised
the villagers, who had relaxed their precautions, by taking the
seven o'clock bus.

The Ford V-8 was finally abandoned when some of the lesser sons-in-law, not profiting by the experience of the children, went in it one evening to a film-show in Port of Spain. The house blazed with lights all night; and the sisters concerned, armed with sticks to daunt molesters, made frequent sallies along the Port of Spain road. The men returned just before dawn, pushing. The children went to school by lorry. The car was pushed from the road into the gully and up to the clump of wild tannia under the saman tree, where, being presently stripped by an unknown person of its saleable parts, it remained, a plaything for the children.

Another car was bought, another Ford V-8, but a sports model with a dicky seat. And into this, miraculously, all the children were squeezed, standing in the dicky seat like stemmed flowers in a vase. A second trip was made for the oranges. While they were in the country the children could pretend to be on the top of a stage-coach, but when they got to Port of Spain they attracted derisive attention and missed the shelter of the saloon.

So for the children Shorthills became a nightmare. Daylight was nearly always gone when they returned, and there was little to return to. The food grew rougher and rougher and was eaten more casually, in the kitchen itself, where the brick floor had been topped with mud, or in the covered space between the kitchen and the house. No child knew from one night to the next where he was going to sleep; beds were made anywhere and at any time. On Saturdays the children pulled up weeds; on Sundays they collected oranges or other fruit.

At week-ends the children submitted to the laws of the family. But during the week, when they spent so much time away from the house, they formed a community of their own, outside family laws. No one ruled; there were only the weak and the strong. Affection between brother and sister was despised. No alliance was stable. Only enmities were lasting, and the hot afternoon walks which Mrs Tulsi had seen lightened by song were often broken by bitter fights of pure hate.

Mr Biswas scarcely saw his children, and they became separated from one another. Anand felt disgraced by his sisters. They were all among the weak. Myna had developed a bad bladder; every journey with her involved shame. Sometimes the car stopped, sometimes it didn't. Kamla walked in her sleep; but this was a novelty and was thought endearing, especially in one so young. Savi was unnoticed until she had been chosen to sing at a school concert organized by the distributors of a face lotion called Limacol. She had never used Limacol but agreed with the master of ceremonies that the slogan, 'The Freshness of a Breeze in a Bottle', was just. Then in a high voice and with many quaverings she sang 'Some Sunday Morning' and was given a miniature Limacol bottle. The Tulsi sisters were shocked. They spoke of Savi almost as of a public entertainer, and lectured their children. Thereafter Savi was mocked and ridiculed. She drew maps with minutely indented coastlines, on the basis of her observations at beaches. She had attempted to propagate this method and had some disciples; but now one of Govind's daughters said that these indentations were as stupid and conceited as the quavers with which Savi had sung 'Some Sunday Morning', and Savi's disciples recanted. When one evening she was put off the bus because she had lost her fare, and had to walk all the way to Shorthills, arriving after nightfall, ill with fright and fatigue, and having to be massaged by Shama, it was felt that justice had been done. The news of the massage in the room on the upper floor, Savi's tears, Mr Biswas's rage when he returned, quickly went round the house. Kamla, the petted sleep-walker, was pumped for details, and Kamla gave them, pleased to excite so much interest and amusement.

Though no one recognized his strength, Anand was among the strong. His satirical sense kept him aloof. At first this was only a pose, and imitation of his father. But satire led to contempt, and at Shorthills contempt, quick, deep, inclusive, became part of his nature. It led to inadequacies, to self-awareness and a lasting loneliness. But it made him unassailable.

The children were ready to go to school one morning. Their lunches, wrapped in brown paper, were stuffed in their bags, and the car was waiting on the road. Quickly the chil-

dren filled the car. They squashed in. They wedged themselves in. They screwed themselves in. A door was slammed.
Anand, somewhere in the dicky seat, heard a shriek and a
groan. They came from Savi. The children, always breathless
and bad-tempered when the car was stationary, shouted for
the car to drive off. But someone cried, 'Quick! Open the
door. Her hand.'

Anand laughed. No one joined him. The car emptied and
he saw Savi sitting on the wet rabbit-grass of the verge. He
could not bear to look at her hand.

Shama and Mr Biswas and some of the sisters came out to
the road.

Myna said, 'Anand laugh, Pa.'

Mr Biswas slapped Anand hard.

And Mr Biswas decided that the time had come for him to
withdraw from the Shorthills adventure. A return to Port of
Spain was impossible. When he went for walks about the
estate he kept his eye open for a suitable site.

Then, in quick succession, a number of deaths occurred.

Sharma, the son-in-law who collected oranges and drove
the children to school, slipped off a mossy orange branch one
rainy morning and broke his neck. He died almost at once.
The children did not go to school that day. Sharma's widow
tried to turn the holiday into a day of mourning. She sobbed
and wailed and embraced everyone who went near her and
asked for messages to be sent. Messages were sent and Sharma's relations turned up in the afternoon, nondescript people,
not able even in their sorrow to drown their shyness. They
put Sharma in a plain coffin and carried him to the graveyard,
where the village had assembled to see the Hindu rites. Hari,
in white jacket and beads, whined over the grave and sprinkled water over it with a mango leaf.

'Same thing he did to my house,' Mr Biswas said to Anand.

Sharma's widow shrieked, fainted, revived and tried to
fling herself into the grave. The villagers watched with interest. Some of the knowing whispered about *suttee*.

W. C. Tuttle took over the job of driving the children to
school. He placed all his children in the front seat next to

himself and stuffed the others into the dicky seat. He complained about the behaviour of the car and attributed all its
faults to Sharma. Soon there was talk that W. C. Tuttle was
using the car to transport his subsidiary plunder. He threatened not to drive the car if the talk didn't stop. There was no
one else who could drive, apart from the surly Govind, and
the talk stopped.

Despite W. C. Tuttle's abuse Sharma was speedily forgotten. And one hot Sunday afternoon, when nearly everyone
was out of doors, Anand came upon Hari and his wife sitting
alone in the diningroom, at one end of the vast cedar table that
had been made by W. C. Tuttle's blacksmith. They made a sad
couple. Hari's wife had tears in her eyes, and Hari's expressionless face was yellow. Anand, wishing to animate them and
to show off a new accomplishment, offered to recite a poem
to them. He had just mastered all the gestures illustrated on the
frontispiece of *Bell's Standard Elocutionist*. Hari and his wife
looked moved; they smiled and asked Anand to recite.

Anand drew his feet together, bowed, and said, 'Bingen on
the Rhine.' He joined his palms, rested his head on them, and
recited:

'*A soldier of the legion lay dying in Algiers.*'

He was pleased to see that the smiles of Hari and his wife
had been replaced by looks of the utmost solemnity.

'*There was lack of woman's nursing, there was dearth of woman's
tears.*

'*But a comrade stood beside him while his life blood ebbed away.*'

Anand's voice quavered with emotion. Hari stared at the
floor. His wife fixed her large eyes on a spot somewhere
above Anand's shoulder. Anand had not expected such a full
and immediate response. He increased the pathos in his voice,
spoke more slowly and exaggerated his gestures. With both
hands on his left breast he acted out the last words of the
dying legionnaire.

'*Tell her the last night of my life, for ere this moon be risen,*

'*My body will be out of pain, my soul be out of prison.*'

Hari's wife burst out crying. Hari put his hand on hers. In
this way they listened to the end; and Anand, after being
given a six-cents piece, left them shaken.

Less than a week later Hari died. It was only then that Anand learned that Hari had known for some time that he was going to die soon. W. C. Tuttle, ferociously brahminical in an embroidered silk jacket, did the last rites. The house went into mourning for Hari; no one used sugar or salt. He was one of those men who, by a negativeness that amounts to charity, are thought of kindly by everyone. He had taken part in no disputes; his goodness, like his scholarship, was a family tradition. Everyone had been used to seeing Hari as the officiating pundit at religious ceremonies; everyone had been used to receiving the consecrated foods from him every morning. Hari, in dhoti, his forehead marked with sandalwood paste; Hari doing morning and evening *puja*; Hari with his religious texts on the elaborately carved bookrest: these had been fixed sights in the Tulsi house. There had been no one to take Seth's place. There was no one to take Hari's.

The duty of the *puja* was shared by many of the men and boys. Sometimes even Anand had to do it. Untutored in the prayers, he could only go through the motions of the ritual. He washed the images, placed fresh flowers on the shrine, diverted himself by trying to stick the stem of a flower in the crook of a god's arm or between the god's chin and chest. He put fresh sandalwood paste on the foreheads of the gods, on the smooth black and rose and yellow pebbles, and on his own forehead; lit the camphor, circled the flame about the shrine with his right hand while with his left he tried to ring the bell; blew at the conch shell, emitting a sound like that of a heavy wardrobe scraping on a wooden floor; then, his cheeks aching from the effort of blowing the conch shell, he hurried out to eat, first making the round of the house to offer the milk and tulsi leaves which, unbelievably, he had consecrated. When he dressed for school he brushed the caked sandalwood marks from his forehead.

About a fortnight after Hari died news came from Arwacas of another death. Anand was working at the table in the room on the upper floor one evening, and Mr Biswas was reading in bed, when the door was thrown open and Savi ran in and said, 'Great Aunt Padma is dead!'

Mr Biswas closed his eyes and put his hand on his heart.

Anand screamed, 'Savi!'

She stood still, her eyes shining.

From downstairs a deep-drawn lamentation burst out and spread through the house, rising, falling, relayed from one sister to the other and back again, like the barking of dogs at night.

Sharma's death had done little more than upset routine. Hari's had saddened. Padma's terrified. She was Mrs Tulsi's sister: death had come closer to them all. She had known them all their lives; she had died away from them. The sisters said these things over and over as they embraced each other and embraced their children. The house shook with footsteps, shrieks, wails and the crying of frightened children. Mrs Tulsi was reported to be out of her mind; there were rumours that she too was dying. The children stuck pins into lamp wicks and murmured incantations to keep off fresh disaster. They heard Mrs Tulsi clamouring to be taken to the body of her sister. The cry was taken up by some of the sisters, and despite the hour and despite the quarrel with Seth, preparations were made and the lorry and sports car set off for Arwacas, and only men and children were left in the house.

The women returned the following afternoon, with more than their grief. For most of them it had been their first visit to Arwacas since the move, their first glimpse of Seth. They had not spoken to him, but the truce had enabled them to inspect the property which Seth, still vigorously pursuing the quarrel, had bought on the High Street not far from Hanuman House, a first step, they had been told, to his buying over of Hanuman House itself. It was a grocery and it was large enough and new enough and well enough stocked to alarm the sisters. But there could be no talk of Seth just then.

Padma appeared in many dreams that night. In the morning every dream was recounted and it was agreed that Padma's spirit had come to the house in Shorthills, which she had never visited while she lived. This was confirmed by the experience of one sister. In the middle of the night she had heard footsteps in the road. She recognized them as Padma's. There was silence as Padma had crossed the gully, footsteps again as Padma came up the sandy drive and up the concrete steps. Padma had then made a tour of the house, sat down on the back steps and wept. Many people saw Padma after that. Much attention was given to the story of one of the Tuttle children. In broad daylight he had seen a woman in white walking from the graveyard towards the house. He caught up with her and said, 'Aunt.' She turned. It wasn't an aunt. It was Padma; she was crying. Before he could speak she pulled her veil over her face, and he had run. When he looked back he saw no one.

Yet it was some time before the sisters realized that Padma appeared so often because she had a message. They then decided that anyone who saw her should ask what her message was. The messages varied. At first Padma merely asked after certain people and said she wished she were alive and with them; sometimes she also said she had died of a broken heart. But Padma's later messages, when whispered from sister to sister, from child to child, caused consternation. She said Seth had driven her to take poison; she said Seth had poisoned her; she said Seth had beaten her to death and bribed the doctor not to have a post mortem.

'Don't tell Mai,' the sisters said.

Anger overrode their grief. Every sister cursed Seth and vowed never to speak to him again.

Mrs Tulsi kept to the room with the closed windows. Sushila and Miss Blackie made brandy poultices for her eyelids, as before, and massaged her head with bay rum. But in the box-board temple at the end of the ruined, overgrown garden there was no Hari to say prayers for her and the house. Bells were rung and gongs were struck, but the luck, the virtue had gone out of the family.

And two of the sheep died. The canal at the side of the drive was at last completely silted over and the rain, which ran down the hillside in torrents after the briefest shower, flooded the flat land. The gully, no longer supported by the roots, began to be eaten away. The old man's beard was deprived of a footing; its thin tangled roots hung over the banks like a threadbare carpet. The gully bed, washed clean of black soil and the plants that grew on it, showed sandy, then pebbly, then rocky. It could no longer be forded by the car, and the car stayed on the road. The sisters were puzzled by the erosion, which seemed to them sudden; but they accepted it as part of their new fate.

Govind stopped looking after the cows. He bought a secondhand motorcar and operated it as a taxi in Port of Spain. W. C. Tuttle opened a quarry on the estate. His enterprise aroused envy. He had been the first to sell estate trees; now that there were few trees to sell he was selling the very earth. Mr Biswas continued to transport his plunder of oranges and avocado pears in the saddlebag of his bicycle.

For nearly all the sisters still with husbands Shorthills had become only an interlude. For the widows there was only Shorthills, and land they did not understand. It was not riceland or caneland. But the widows united, and after much whispered discussion and ostentatious silence when other sisters, husbands or their children were near, the widows announced that they were going to start a chicken farm. To feed the chickens they needed maize. They cut down a hillside, burned it, and planted maize. Then they bought some chickens and set them loose. At first the chickens stayed close to the house and sometimes inside it, leaving their droppings everywhere. Presently snakes and mongooses attacked the chickens. Those that survived took to the bush, learned to fly high, and laid their eggs where the widows couldn't get them. In the meantime the maize was reaped and husked. The widows and their children ate much corn, boiled and roasted. The remainder was heaped in the verandah; there were no chickens to give it to. The corn turned from pale yellow to hard bright orange. Intermittently the widows and their children shelled the cobs on graters. There was talk of selling maize flour; with the continuing shortage of wheat flour the prospects were considered bright. The widows invested in a mill: two circular slabs of toothed stone resting one on the other. After some time and much labour a little flour was ground, but there was not the demand for it that the widows had expected. The maize remained in the verandah; weevils and other insects burrowed neatly through the golden cobs.

Mrs Tulsi remained in her dark room, devising economies and issuing directives about food. She had heard that the Chinese, an ancient race, ate bamboo shoots. The estate abounded in bamboo; Mrs Tulsi ordered that bamboo shoots were to be eaten. But what were bamboo shoots? Were they the neat little green buds at the joints of the bamboo trunks? Were they the very young bamboo stalks? Were they the very young bamboo leaves? No one knew. Buds, stalks and leaves were collected, washed, chopped, boiled, and curried with tomatoes. No one could eat it. The leaves of the shining bush, a prolific shrub that grew even in sand, had been used in the house to make a mildly purgative brew that was not unpleasant and was reputedly good for colds, coughs and fevers. Mrs Tulsi directed that tea should no longer be bought: the shining bush was to be used instead. Already the widows and their children were making coffee and chocolate from the beans on the estate. Now maize flour was to be used instead of wheat flour, and coconut oil was to be made, not bought. No one had thought of growing vegetables and, since they too could not be bought, efforts were made to find vegetable substitutes: hard coconut, green papaw, green mango, green *pomme cithère*, and almost any green fruit. But when Mrs Tulsi ordered the widows to experiment with birds' nests, which the Chinese ate, and the widows looked at the long stockinglike corn-bird nests of dry twigs hanging from the saman tree, there was such an outcry that the idea was dropped.

It was W. C. Tuttle's duty, after taking the children to school, to bring back stale cakes for the cows. To prevent them being stolen, the cakes were heaped in the verandah next to the widows' dry corn. The widows' children, foraging among the stale cakes, came upon some that were still edible. The news was reported to Mrs Tulsi; thereafter stale cakes were shared between the cows and the widows. In this period of experiment many new foods were discovered. The children discovered that brown sugar in a dry pancake made a better lunch than curried bamboo, which could not be exchanged for anything at school. Someone hit upon the idea of dipping sardines in condensed milk, and someone else made the accidental discovery that condensed milk burned in the tin had an original and pleasing flavour.

Economy went further. Directing that no tins were to be thrown away, Mrs Tulsi summoned a tinker from Arwacas. For a fortnight he shared the household food, slept in the verandah, and made tin cups and tin plates; from a sardine tin he made a whistle. Ink was no longer bought; a violet liquid, faint but unwashable, was extracted from the small berries of the black sage. Mrs Tulsi, hearing that coconut husks were being thrown away, decided that mattresses and cushions were to be made, and possibly sold. The widows and their children soaked and pounded and stretched and shredded the coconut husks, washed the fibre and dried it. Then Mrs Tulsi sent for the mattress-maker from Arwacas. He came and made mattresses and cushions for a month.

Sisters with husbands fed their children secretly. And when it was learned that some of the widows' sons had killed a sheep, roasted it in the woods and eaten it, W. C. Tuttle expressed his outrage at this un-Hindu act, refused to eat any more from the common kitchen and made his wife cook separately. One of his sons reported that W. C. Tuttle's brahmin mouth had burst into sores the day the sheep was eaten. Mr Biswas, though unable to produce W. C. Tuttle's spectacular symptoms, made Shama cook separately as well. Touched by the prevailing obsession with food, Mr Biswas had been making experiments of his own. He had decided that the gospo, a mixture of the orange and the lemon, and the shadduck, which no one ate, had extraordinary virtues. There was one gospo tree on the estate, and the fruit had been used by the children to play cricket (using bats of *bois-canot*). Mr Biswas put an end to that. He drank a glass of the unpleasant gospo juice every morning and made his children do the same, until the gospo tree, which stood at one corner of the cricket field, collapsed into the gully after a flood, still laden with its hybrid fruit.

With the disappearance of the gospo tree the cricket field shrank rapidly. After every shower part of it was carved away, leaving a grass-covered overhang which collapsed in a day or two and was carried off by the next downpour. The drive became tall with weeds, and through the weeds a narrow, curiously wavering path led to the concrete steps, now cracked and sagging and bursting into vegetation at every crack. The evergreen hedge was a tangle of small trees, and whenever it rained the grounds smelled fresh, as of fish, telling that snakes were about.

No one had time to fight the bush. The widows, when not cooking or washing or cleaning or looking after the cows, were making coffee or chocolate or coconut oil or grinding maize. Their clothes became patched, their arms hard. They looked like labourers, and they had to bear with the exulting comments Seth sent through common friends. He had given his life to the family; then he had been rejected and slandered. Their punishment was only beginning. Had he not said that when he left them they would all start catching crabs?

And the widows worked like men. When the gully became a gorge they threw a bridge of coconut trunks across it. The gorge widened; the trunks collapsed. The widows built another bridge; that collapsed too. The widows prevailed on Mrs Tulsi to buy lengths of rail. The rails were laid across the gorge, coconut trunks laid across the rails, and for a time this structure survived, shaky, slippery, with gaps through which a child might fall to the rocks below.

Mr Biswas could no longer ignore the dereliction about him; yet when he spoke about moving, Shama, though excluded from the councils of the widows and the confidences of the other sisters, became sullen and sometimes cried.

Then came the scandal of the eighty dollars.

Chinta announced one day that someone had stolen eighty dollars from her room. It was an astonishing announcement, not only because an accusation of theft had never been made in the family before, but also because no one knew that Chinta and Govind had so much money. Chinta told again and again of the last time she had checked the money, and of the accident that had led her to find out that the money was missing. She said she knew who had stolen the money, but was waiting for the thief to trip himself up.

After a few days the thief had not tripped himself up, and Chinta went on searching, drawing crowds wherever she went. Sometimes she spoke Hindi incantations; sometimes she searched with a candle in one hand and a crucifix in the other; sometimes she spat on her left palm, struck the spittle with a finger, and searched in the direction indicated by the flight of the spittle. Finally she decided to hold a trial by Bible and key.

'The old Roman cat and kitten,' Mr Biswas said to Shama. 'Like mother, like daughter. But look, eh, I don't want my children meddling in that sort of tomfoolery.'

This was repeated throughout the house.

Chinta said, 'I don't blame him.'

The Bible-and-key trial lasted the whole of one afternoon. Chinta invoked the names of Saints Peter and Paul and spoke the accusations; Miss Blackie, invoking the same names, defended; and the innocence of everyone except Mr Biswas and his family was established.

Mr Biswas refused to have his room searched and ignored Shama's pleas that he should allow the children to be tried. 'She is a Roman cat,' he said. 'So what? I look like a Hindu mouse?' For some time he and Govind had not spoken; now he and Chinta did not speak. Shama attempted to maintain relations with Chinta, but was rebuffed.

'I am not blaming anybody,' Chinta said. 'I am only blaming the man who set the example.'

Then the whisperings began.

'Don't talk to them. But watch them.'

'Vidiadhar! Quick! I left my purse on the table in the diningroom.'

'Anand likes his nose to run. He swallows the snot. It is like condensed milk to him.'

'Savi does eat the scabs of sores.'

'You ever see Kamla's head? Crawling with lice. But she is like a monkey. She eats them.'

And the girls begged Mr Biswas to move.

He had found a site such as he always wanted, isolated, unused and full of possibilities. It was some way from the estate house, on a low hill buried in bush and well back from the road. The house was begun and, unblessed, completed in less than a month. Its pattern was precisely that of the house he had attempted in Green Vale, precisely that of thousands of houses in rural Trinidad. It had a verandah, two bedrooms and a drawingroom, and stood on tall pillars. Estate trees provided the timber; he had to pay only for the sawing. He bought corrugated iron for the roof, plain glass and frosted glass for the windows, coloured glass for the drawingroom door, and cement for the pillars.

The speed with which the house went up took him by surprise. The builders had given him no opportunity to withdraw, and at the end he found that his savings were nearly all gone. He felt uneasy. His circumstances had changed; but his ambition had remained steady, and now seemed only idyllic and absurd. He had built his own house, in a place as wild and out-of-the-way as he could have wished. But Shama had to walk a mile to the village to do her shopping, water had to be brought up the hill from a spring in the cocoa woods. And there was the problem of transport. He had to cycle long distances every day, and though he had cut himself off from the family, his children had to go to school in the family car.

After he had bought a Slumberking bed (delivered by two Port of Spain vanmen who swore as they made their various trips up and down the improperly cleared and precipitous path) his money was exhausted. The house was not painted. It stood red-raw in its unregulated green setting, not seeming to invite habitation so much as decay.

Shama, though pained by the quarrel with Chinta, did not approve of the move. She regarded it as provocative, and like the children, she had watched the house rise and wished it not to be completed. The children wanted to go back to Port of Spain, to the life they had had before Shorthills. They knew about the housing shortage but blamed Mr Biswas for not trying hard enough. The new house imprisoned them in silence and bush. They had no pleasures, no cinema shows, no walks, no games even, for the land around the house still smelled of snakes. The nights seemed longer and blacker. The girls stayed close to Shama, as though frightened to be by themselves; and in her shanty kitchen Shama sang sad Hindi songs.

Late one afternoon, not long after they had moved, Anand found himself alone in the house. Mr Biswas was out, the girls were in the kitchen with Shama. The house felt bare, unused and still exposed; corners held no secrets; none of the furniture seemed to have found its place. Moved by boredom more than curiosity, Anand opened the bottom drawer of Shama's dressingtable. In an envelope he found his parents' marriage certificate and the birth certificates of his sisters and himself. On a birth certificate, which he did not at first recognize as Savi's, he saw a name, Basso, which he had never heard used. He saw Mr Biswas's harsh scrawl: *Real calling name: Lakshmi*. In the column headed 'Father's Occupation' *labourer* had been energetically scratched out and *proprietor* written in. No other birth certificate had been so scribbled over. Some photographs were wrapped in crinkled brown paper. One was of the Tulsi sisters standing in a straight line and scowling; the others were of the entire Tulsi family, of Hanuman House, of Pundit Tulsi, of Pundit Tulsi in Hanuman House.

In the kitchen Shama was singing her doleful song and slapping dough between her palms.

Anand came upon a bundle of letters. They were all still in their envelopes. The stamps were English and bore the head of George V. From one envelope fell small brown photographs of an English girl, a dog, a house with a faded X on a window; in another envelope there was a newspaper clipping with one name underlined in ink in a long paragraph of names. The letters were neatly written and said little at great length. They spoke about letters received, about school, about holidays; they thanked for photographs. Abruptly they were touched with feeling; they expressed surprise that arrangements for marriage had been made so soon; they attempted to soften surprise with congratulation. Then there were no more letters.

Anand closed the drawer and went to the drawingroom. He rested his elbows on the window-sill and looked out. The sun had just set and the bush was turning black against a sky that was still clear. Smoke came through the kitchen door and window and Anand listened to Shama singing. Darkness filled the valley.

That evening Shama discovered the ransacked drawer. 'Thief!' she said. 'Some thief was in the house.'

Refusing to yield to the gloom of his family and his own feeling that he had been rash, Mr Biswas set about clearing the land. He spared only the *poui* trees, for their branches and their yellow flowers, which came out bright and pure for one week in the year. The integrity of living bush was replaced by a brown chaos of collapsed and dying trees. Through this Mr Biswas made a winding path from the house down to the road, cutting steps into the earth and shoring them with bamboo. The debris could not be immediately fired, for though the leaves were dead and brittle the wood was green. Waiting, Mr Biswas cut *poui* sticks and roasted them in bonfires. And he was reminded of a duty.

He sent for his mother. He had for so long been telling her – ever since he was a boy in the back trace – that she was to come to stay with him when he had built his own house, that he now doubted whether she would come. But she came, for a fortnight. Her feelings could not be read. He was at first extravagantly affectionate. But Bipti remained calm, and Mr Biswas followed her example. It was as if the relationship between them had been granted without their asking, and had only to be accepted.

Though the children understood Hindi they could no longer speak it, and this limited communication between them and Bipti. From the start, however, Shama and Bipti got on well. Shama gave not a hint of the sullenness she used with Bipti's sister Tara; to Mr Biswas's surprise and pleasure, she treated Bipti with all the respect of a Hindu daughter-in-law. She had touched Bipti's feet with her fingers when Bipti came, and she never appeared before Bipti with her head uncovered.

Bipti helped with the housework and on the land. When, after Bipti's death, Mr Biswas wished to be reminded of her, he thought less of his childhood and the back trace than of this fortnight at Shorthills. He thought of one moment in particular. The ground in front of the house had been only partly cleared, and one afternoon, when he had pushed his bicycle up the earth steps to the top of the hill, he saw that part of the ground, which he had left that morning cumbered and unbroken, had been cleared and levelled and forked. The black earth was soft and stoneless; the spade had cut cleanly into it, leaving damp walls as smooth as mason's work. Here and there the prongs of the fork had left shallow parallel indentations on the upturned earth. In the setting sun, the sad dusk, with Bipti working in a garden that looked, for a moment, like a garden he had known a dark time ages ago, the intervening years fell away. Thereafter the marks of a fork in earth made him think of that moment at the top of the hill, and of Bipti.

The children looked forward to the firing of the land as to a celebration. The Civil Defence authorities had given them a taste for large conflagrations, and now they were to have a hill on fire in their own backyard. It would be almost as good as the mock air-raid on the Port of Spain race course. Of course there would be no dummy houses to burn, no ambulances, no nurses attending to people groaning at mock wounds, no Boy Scouts on motor bicycles dashing about through the thick smoke with dummy dispatches; but at the same time there would be none of those eager firefighters who, in spite of the public outcry, had rescued some of the dummy buildings before they were even scorched.

Mr Biswas, displaying manual skills which his children secretly distrusted, dug trenches and prepared little nests of twigs and leaves at what he called strategic points. On Saturday afternoon he summoned the children, soaked a brand in pitch-oil, set it alight, and ran from nest to nest, poking the brand in and jumping back, as though he had touched off an explosion. A leaf caught here and a twig there, blazed, shrank, smouldered, died. Mr Biswas didn't wait to see. Ignoring the cries of the children, he ran on, leaving a trail of subsiding wisps of dark smoke.

'Is all right,' he said, coming down the hillside, the brand dripping fire. 'Is all right. Fire is a funny thing. You think it out, but it blazing like hell underground.'

One of the smoke wisps shrank like a failing fountain.

'That one take your advice and gone underground,' Savi said.

'I don't know,' he said, rubbing one itching ankle against the other. 'Perhaps it is a little too green. Perhaps we should wait until next week.'

There were protests.

Savi put her hand to her face and backed away.

'What's the matter?'

'The heat,' Savi said.

'You just carry on. See if you don't get hot somewhere else. Clowns. That's what I'm raising. A pack of clowns.'

From the kitchen Shama shouted, 'Hurry up, all-you. The sun going down.'

They went to examine the nests Mr Biswas had fired. They found them collapsed, reduced: shallow heaps of grey leaves and black twigs. Only one had caught, and from it the fire proceeded unspectacularly, avoiding thick branches and nibbling at lesser ones, making the bark curl, attacking the green wood with a great deal of smoke, staining it, then retreating to run up a twig with a businesslike air, scorching the brown leaves, creating a brief blaze, then halting. On the gound there were a few isolated flames, none higher than an inch.

'Fireworks,' Savi said.

'Well, do it yourself.'

The children ran to the kitchen and seized the pitch-oil Shama had bought for the lamps. They poured the pitch-oil haphazardly on the bush and set it alight. In minutes the bush blazed and became a restless sea of yellow, red, blue and green. They exchanged theories about the various colours; they listened with pleasure to the chatter and crackle of the quick fire. Too soon the tall flames contracted. The sun set. Charred leaves rose in the air. After dinner they had the sad task of beating down the fire at the edge of the trench. The brown sea had turned black, with red glitters and twinkles.

'All right,' Mr Biswas said. '*Puja* over. Books now.'

They retired to the bare drawingroom. From time to time they went to the window. The hill was black against a lighter sky. Here and there it showed red and occasionally burst into yellow flame, which seemed unsupported, dancing in the air.

Anand was in a bus, one of those dilapidated, crowded buses that ran between Shorthills and Port of Spain. Something was wrong. He was lying on the floor of the bus and people were looking down at him and chattering. The bus must have been running over a newly-repaired road: the wheels were kicking up pebbles against the wings.

Myna and Kamla stood over him, and he was being shaken by Savi. He lay on his bedding in the drawingroom.

'Fire!' Savi said.

'What o'clock it is?'

'Two or three. Get up. Quick.'

The chattering, the pebbles against the wings, was the noise of the fire. Through the window he saw that the hill had turned red, and the land was red in places where no fire had been intended.

'Pa? Ma?' he asked.

'Outside. We have to go to the big house to tell them.'

The house appeared to be encircled by the red, unblazing bush. The heat made breathing painful. Anand looked for the two *poui* trees at the top of the hill. They were black and leafless against the sky.

Hurriedly he dressed.

'Don't leave us,' Myna said.

He heard Mr Biswas shouting outside, 'Just beat it back. Just beat it back from the kitchen. House safe. No bush around it. Just keep it back from the kitchen.'

'Savi!' Shama called. 'Anand wake?'

'Don't leave us,' Kamla cried.

All four children left the house and walked past the newly-forked land in front to the path that led to the road. Just below the brow of the hill they were surprised by an absolute darkness. Between the path and the road there was no fire.

Myna and Kamla began to cry, afraid of the darkness before them, the fire behind them.

'Leave them,' Shama called. 'And hurry up.'

THE SHORTHILLS ADVENTURE 413

Savi and Anand picked their way down the earth steps they couldn't see.

'You can hold my hand,' Anand said.

They held hands and worked their way down the hill, into the gully, up the gully and into the road. Trees vaulted the blackness. The blackness was like a weight; it was as if they wore hats that came down to their eyebrows. They didn't look up, not willing to be reminded that darkness lay above them and behind them as well as in front of them. They fixed their eyes on the road and kicked the loose gravel for the noise. It was chilly.

'Say *Rama Rama*,' Savi said. 'It will keep away anything.'

They said *Rama Rama*.

'Is Pa to blame for this,' Savi said suddenly.

The repetition of *Rama Rama* comforted them. They became used to the darkness. They could distinguish trees a few yards ahead. The squat concrete box, where behind a steel door estate explosives were kept, was a reassuring white blur on the roadside.

At last they came to the bridge of coconut trunks. The white fretwork along the eaves of the house were visible. In Mrs Tulsi's room, as always at night, a light burned. They made their way across the dangerous bridge and emerged into the open, grateful at that moment for the tree-cutting of Govind and W. C. Tuttle. The tall wet weeds on the drive stroked their bare legs. They sniffed, alert for the smell of snakes.

They heard a heavy breathing. They could not tell from which direction it came. They stopped muttering *Rama Rama*, came close together and began to run towards the concrete steps, a distant grey glow. The breathing followed, and a dull, unhurried tramp.

Glancing to his left, Anand saw the mule in the cricket field. It was following them, moving along the snarled fence-wires. They reached the end of the drive. The mule reached the corner of the field and stopped.

They ran up the concrete steps, avoiding the overhanging nutmeg tree. They fumbled with the bolt on the verandah gate and the noise frightened them. They scratched at doors and windows, tapped the wall of Mrs Tulsi's room, rattled the tall drawingroom doors. They called. There was no reply. Every noise they made seemed to them an explosion. But in the silence and blackness they were only whispering. Their footsteps, their knockings, Anand's stumbling among the stale cakes and the widow's corn, sounded only like the scuttling of rats.

Then they heard voices: low and alarmed: one aunt whispering to another, Mrs Tulsi calling for Sushila.

Anand shouted: 'Aunt!'

The voices were silenced. Then they were raised again, this time defiantly. Anand knocked hard on a window.

A woman's voice said, 'Two of the little people!'

There was an exclamation.

They were thought to be the spirits of Hari and Padma.

Mrs Tulsi groaned and spoke a Hindi exorcism. Inside, doors were opened, the floor pounded. There was loud aggressive talk about sticks, cutlasses and God, while Sushila, the sickroom widow, an expert on the supernatural, asked in a sweet conciliatory voice, 'Poor little people, what can we do for you?'

'Fire!' Anand cried.

'Fire,' Savi said.

'Our house on fire!'

And Sushila, though she had taken part in the whisperings against Savi and Mr Biswas, found herself obliged to continue talking sweetly to Savi and Anand.

The apprehension of the house turned to joyous energy at the news of the fire.

'But really,' Chinta said, as she happily got ready, 'what fool doesn't know that to set fire to land in the night is to ask for trouble?'

Lights went on everywhere. Babies squealed, were hushed. Mrs Tuttle was heard to say, 'Put something on your head, man. This dew isn't good for anyone.' 'A cutlass, a cutlass,' Sharma's widow called. And the children excitedly relayed the news: 'Uncle Mohun's house is burning down!' Some thrilled alarmists feared that the fire might spread through the woods to the big house itself; and there was speculation about the effects of the fire on the explosives.

The journey to the fire was like an excursion. Once there, the Tulsi party fell to work with a will, cutting, clearing, beating. It became a celebration. Shama, host for the second time to her family, prepared coffee in the kitchen, which was untouched. And Mr Biswas, forgetful of animosities, shouted to everyone, 'Is all right. Is all right. Everything under control.'

Some eggs were discovered, burnt black, and dry inside. Whether they were snakes' eggs or the eggs of the widows' errant hens no one knew. A snake was found burnt to death less than twenty yards from the kitchen. 'The hand of God,' Mr Biswas said. 'Burning the bitch up before it bite me.'

Morning revealed the house, still red and raw, in a charred and smoking desolation. Villagers came running to see, and were confirmed in their belief that their village had been taken over by vandals.

'Charcoal, charcoal,' Mr Biswas called to them. 'Anybody want charcoal?'

For days afterwards the valley darkened with ash whenever the wind blew. Ash dusted the plot Bipti had forked.

'Best thing for the land,' Mr Biswas said. 'Best sort of fertilizer.'

# 4. Among the Readers and Learners

HE COULD not simply leave the house in Shorthills. He had to be released from it. And presently this happened. Transport became impossible. The bus service deteriorated; the sports car began to give as much trouble as its predecessor and had to be sold. And just about this time Mrs Tulsi's house in Port of Spain fell vacant. Mr Biswas was offered two rooms in it, and he immediately accepted.

He considered himself lucky. The housing shortage in Port of Spain had been aggravated by the steady arrival of illegal immigrants from the other islands in search of work with the Americans. A whole shanty town had sprung up at the east end of the city; and even to buy a house was not to assure yourself of a room, for there were now laws against the indiscriminate eviction Shama had so coolly practised.

He put up a sign in the midst of the desolation he had created: HOUSE FOR RENT OR SALE, and moved to Port of Spain. The Shorthills adventure was over. From it he had gained only two pieces of furniture: the Slumberking bed and Théophile's bookcase. And when he moved back to the house in Port of Spain, he did not move alone.

The Tuttles came, Govind and Chinta and their children came, and Basdai, a widow. The Tuttles occupied most of the house. They occupied the drawingroom, the diningroom, a bedroom, the kitchen, the bathroom; this gave them effective control of both the front and back verandahs, for which they paid no rent. Govind and Chinta had only one room. Chinta hinted that they could afford more, but were saving and planning for better things; and, as if in promise of this, Govind suddenly gave up wearing rough clothes, and for six successive days, during which he smiled maniacally at everyone, appeared in a different threepiece suit. Every morning Chinta hung out five of Govind's suits in the sun, and brushed them.

She cooked below the tall-pillared house, and her children slept below the house, on long cedar benches which Théophile had made at Shorthills. Basdai, the widow, lived in the servantroom, which stood by itself in the yard.

Mr Biswas's two rooms could be entered only through the front verandah, which was Tuttle territory. At first Mr Biswas slept in the inner room. Light and noise from the Tuttles' drawingroom came through the ventilation gaps at the top of the partition and drove him to the front room, where he was enraged by the constant passage of Shama and the children to and from the inner room. Shama, like Chinta, cooked below the house; and when Mr Biswas shouted for his food or his Maclean's Brand Stomach Powder, it had to be taken to him up the front steps, in full view of the street.

The house was never quiet, and became almost unbearable when W. C. Tuttle bought a gramophone. He played one record over and over:

> *One night when the moon was so mellow*
> *Rosita met young man Wellow.*
> *He held her like this, his loveliness,*
> *And stole a kiss, this fellow.*
> *Tippy-tippy-tum tippy-tum*

– and here W. C. Tuttle always joined in, whistling, singing, drumming; so that whenever the record came on, Mr Biswas was compelled to listen, waiting for W. C. Tuttle's accompaniment to:

> *Tippy-tippy-tum tippy-tum*
> *Tippy-tippy-teeeee pi-tum-tum tum.*

A dispute also arose between W. C. Tuttle and Govind. They both parked their vehicles in the garage at the side of the house, and in the morning one was invariably in the way of the other. They conducted this quarrel without ever speaking to one another. W. C. Tuttle told Mrs Tuttle that her brothers-in-law were unlettered, Govind grunted at Chinta, and both wives listened penitentially. And now, away from Mrs Tulsi, the sisters also had daily squabbles of their own, about whose children had dirtied the washing, whose children had left the wc filthy. Basdai, the widow, often mediated, and sometimes there were maudlin reconciliations in the Tuttles' back verandah. It was Chinta who remarked that these reconciliations had the habit of taking place after the Tuttles had acquired some new item of furniture or clothing.

Despite the strict brahminical régime of his household, W. C. Tuttle was all for modernity. In addition to the gramophone he possessed a radio, a number of dainty tables, a morris suite; and he created a sensation when he bought a four foot high statue of a naked woman holding a torch. An especially long truce followed the arrival of the torchbearer, and Myna, wandering about the Tuttles' establishment one day, accidentally broke off the torchbearing arm. The Tuttles sealed their frontiers again. Myna, in response to wordless pressure, was flogged, and a frostiness came once more into the relations between the Tuttles and the Biswases. Matters were not helped when Shama announced that she had ordered a glass cabinet from the joiner in the next street.

The glass cabinet came.

Chinta shouted to her children in English. 'Vidiadhar and Shivadhar! Stay away from the front gate. I don't want you to go breaking other people things and have other people saying that is because I jealous.'

As the elegant cabinet was being taken up the front steps one of the glass doors swung open, struck the steps and broke. This was observed by the Tuttles, imperfectly concealed behind the jalousies on either side of the drawingroom door.

'Oh! Oh!' Mr Biswas said that evening. 'Glass cabinet come, Shama. Glass cabinet come, girl. The only thing you have to do now is to get something to put inside it.'

She spread out the Japanese coffee-set on one shelf. The other shelves remained empty, and the glass cabinet, for which she had committed herself to many months of debt, became another of her possessions which were regarded as jokes, like her sewingmachine, her cow, the coffee-set. It was placed in the front room, which was already choked with the Slumberking, Théophile's bookcase, the hatrack, the kitchen table and the rockingchair. Mr Biswas said, 'You know, Shama girl, what we want to put these rooms really straight is another bed.'

In the house the crowding became worse. Basdai, the widow, who had occupied the servantroom as a base for a financial assault on the city, gave up that plan and decided instead to take in boarders and lodgers from Shorthills. The widows were now almost frantic to have their children educated. There was no longer a Hanuman House to protect them; everyone had to fight for himself in a new world, the world Owad and Shekhar had entered, where education was the only protection. As fast as the children graduated from the infant school at Shorthills they were sent to Port of Spain. Basdai boarded them.

Between her small servantroom and the back fence Basdai built an additional room of galvanized iron. Here she cooked. The boarders ate on the steps of the servantroom, in the yard, and below the main house. The girls slept in the servantroom with Basdai; the boys slept below the house, with Govind's children.

Sometimes, driven out by the crowd and the noise, Mr Biswas took Anand for long night walks in the quieter districts of Port of Spain. 'Even the streets here are cleaner than that house,' he said. 'Let the sanitary inspector pay just one visit there, and everybody going to land up in jail. Boarders, lodgers and all. I mad to lay a report myself.'

The house, pouring out a stream of scholars every morning and receiving a returning stream in the afternoon, soon attracted the attention of the street. And whether it was this, or whether a sanitary inspector had indeed made a threat, news came from Shorthills that Mrs Tulsi had decided to do something. There was talk of flooring and walling the space below the house, talk of partitions and rooms, of lattice work above brick walls. The outer pillars were linked by a half-wall of hollow clay bricks, partly plastered, never painted; there was no sign of lattice work. Instead, to screen the house, the wire fence was pulled down and replaced by a tall brick wall; and this was plastered, this was painted; and the people in the street could only make surmises about the arrangements for the feeding and lodging of the childish multitude who, in the afternoons and evenings and early mornings, buzzed like a school.

The children were divided into residents and boarders, and subdivided into family groups. Clashes were frequent. The boarders also brought quarrels from Shorthills and settled them in Port of Spain. And all evening, above the buzzing, there were sounds of flogging (Basdai had flogging powers over her boarders as well), and Basdai cried, 'Read! Learn! Learn! Read!'

And every morning, his hair neatly brushed, his shirt clean, his tie carefully knotted, Mr Biswas left this hell and cycled to the spacious, well-lit, well-ventilated office of the *Sentinel*.

Now when he said to Shama: 'Hole! That's what your family has got me in. This hole!' his words had an unpleasant relevance. For whereas before he had spoken of his house in the country and his mother-in-law's estate, now he kept his address as secret as an animal keeps its hole. And his hole was not a haven. His indigestion returned, virulently; and he saw his children increasingly riddled with nervous afflictions. Savi suffered from a skin rash, and Anand suddenly developed asthma, which laid him in bed for three days at a time, choking, having his chest scorched and peeled by the futile applications of a medicated wadding.

Still the boarders came. The education frenzy had spread to Mrs Tulsi's friends and retainers at Arwacas. They all wanted their children to go to Port of Spain schools, and Mrs Tulsi, fulfilling a duty that had been imposed in a different age, had to take them in. And Basdai boarded them. The floggings and the rows increased. The cries of 'Read! Learn!' increased; and every morning, not long after the babbling children had streamed through the narrow gateway between the high walls, Mr Biswas emerged, neatly dressed, and cycled to the *Sentinel*.

Despite his duties and despite the fear of the sack, which he had never quite lost, even during the adventure at Shorthills, the office now became the haven to which he escaped every morning; and like Mr Burnett's news editor, he dreaded leaving it. It was only at midday, when the readers and learners were at school and W. C. Tuttle and Govind were at work, that he found the house bearable. He gave himself a longer midday break and stayed later in the office in the afternoons.

Then once more Shama started to bring out her account books, and once more she showed how impossible it was for them to live on what he earned. Self-disgust led to anger, shouts, tears, something to add to the concentrated hubbub of the evening, the nerve-torn helplessness. In daylight, in a *Sentinel* motorcar and with a *Sentinel* photographer, he drove through the open plain to call on Indian farmers to get material for his feature on Prospects for This Year's Rice Crop. They, illiterate, not knowing to what he would return that evening, treated him as an incredibly superior being. And these same men who, like his brothers, had started on the estates and saved and bought land of their own, were building mansions; they were sending their sons to America and Canada to become doctors and dentists. There was money in the island. It showed in the suits of Govind, who drove the Americans in his taxi; in the possessions of W. C. Tuttle, who hired out his lorry to them; in the new cars; the new buildings. And from this money, despite Marcus Aurelius and Epictetus, despite Samuel Smiles, Mr Biswas found himself barred.

It was now that he began to speak to his children of his childhood. He told them of the hut, the men digging in the garden at night; he told them of the oil that was later found on the land. What fortune might have been theirs, if only his father had not died, if only he had stuck to the land like his brothers, if he had not gone to Pagotes, not become a sign-writer, not gone to Hanuman House, not married! If only so many things had not happened!

He blamed his father; he blamed his mother; he blamed the Tulsis; he blamed Shama. Blame succeeded blame confusedly in his mind; but more and more he blamed the *Sentinel*, and hinted savagely to Shama, almost as if she were on the board of the paper, that he was going to keep his eye open for another job, and that if the worst came to the worst he would get a job as a labourer with the Americans.

'Labourer!' Shama said. 'With those hammocks you have for muscles, I would like to see how long you would last.'

Which either made him angry, or reduced him to an absurd puckishness. Then, lying on the Slumberking in vest and pants, as was his wont when he indulged in speculations about the future, he would lift up one leg and prod the slack calf with a finger, or make it swing, as he had done when they were newly married, in the long room at Hanuman House. These were the times (for the children were not excluded from this talk about money) when Mr Biswas delivered insincere homilies on the honest manner of his livelihood, and told his children that he had nothing to leave them but good education and a sound training.

It was at one of these sessions that Anand told how at school boys were being challenged to say what their fathers did. This, a new school game, had spread even to the exhibition class. The most assiduous challengers came from the most harassed and insecure strata, and their aggressive manner suggested that they were neither harassed nor insecure themselves. Anand, who had read in an American newspaper that 'journalist' was a pompous word, had said that his father was a reporter; which, though not grand, was unimpeachable. Vidiadhar, Govind's son, had said that his father worked for the Americans. 'That is what all of them are saying these days,' Anand said. 'Why didn't Vidiadhar say that his father was a taxi-driver?'

Mr Biswas didn't smile. Govind had six suits, Govind was making money, Govind would soon have his own house. Vidiadhar would be sent abroad to get a profession. And what awaited Anand? A job in the customs, a clerkship in the civil service: intrigue, humiliation, dependence.

Anand felt his joke going bad. And a few days later, when a new quiz was going round the school – what did the boys call their parents? – Anand, wishing only to debase himself, lied and said, 'Bap and Mai,' and was duly derided; while Vidiadhar, shrewd despite his short stay at the school, unhesitatingly said, 'Mummy and Daddy.' For these boys, who called their parents Ma and Pa, who all came from homes where the sudden flow of American dollars had unleashed ambition, push and uncertainty, these boys had begun to take their English compositions very seriously: their Daddies worked in offices, and at week-ends Daddy and Mummy took them in cars to the seaside, with laden hampers.

Mr Biswas knew that for all his talk he would never leave the *Sentinel* to go to work for the Americans as labourer, clerk or taxi-driver. He lacked the taxi-driver's personality, the labourer's muscles; and he was frightened of throwing up his job: the Americans would not be in the island forever. But as a gesture of protest against the *Sentinel*, he enrolled all his children in the Tinymites League of the *Guardian*, the rival paper; and in the *Junior Guardian*, for years thereafter, Mr Biswas's children were greeted on their birthdays. The pleasure he got from this was enhanced when W. C. Tuttle, imitating, enrolled his children among the Tinymites as well.

The *Sentinel* had its revenge. A small but steady decline in circulation hinted to the directors that there might be something wrong with their policy that conditions in the colony could not be better; they began to admit that readers might occasionally want views instead of news, and that news was not necessarily bright if right. For not only was the *Guardian* winning over *Sentinel* readers, the *Guardian* was also getting people who had never read newspapers. So the *Sentinel* started the Deserving Destitutes Fund, the name suggesting that there was not a necessary inconsistency between the fund and the leaders which spoke of the unemployed as the unemployable. The Deserving Destitutes Fund was an answer to the *Guardian*'s Neediest Cases Fund; but while the Neediest Cases Fund was a Christmas affair, the Deserving Destitutes Fund was to be permanent.

Mr Biswas was appointed investigator. It was his duty to read the applications from destitutes, reject the undeserving, visit the others to see how deserving or desperate they were, and then, if the circumstances warranted it, to write harrowing accounts of their plight, harrowing enough to encourage contributions for the fund. He had to find one deserving destitute a day.

'Deserving Destitute number one,' he told Shama. 'M. Biswas. Occupation: investigator of Deserving Destitutes.'

The *Sentinel* could not have chosen a better way of terrifying Mr Biswas, of reviving his dread of the sack, illness or sudden disaster. Day after day he visited the mutilated, the defeated, the futile and the insane living in conditions not far removed from his own: in suffocating rotting wooden kennels, in sheds of box-board, canvas and tin, in dark and sweating concrete caverns. Day after day he visited the eastern sections of the city where the narrow houses pressed their scabbed and blistered façades together and hid the horrors that lay behind them: the constricted, undrained backyards, coated with green slime, in the perpetual shadow of adjacent houses and the tall rubble-stone fences against which additional sheds had been built: yards choked with flimsy cooking sheds, crowded fowl-coops of wire-netting, bleaching stones spread with sour washing: smell upon smell, but none overcoming the stench of cesspits and overloaded septic tanks: horror increased by the litters of children, most of them illegitimate, with navels projecting inches out of their bellies, as though they had been delivered with haste and disgust. Yet occasionally there was the neat room, its major piece of furniture, a table, a chair, polished to brilliance; giving no hint of the squalor it erupted into the yard. Day after day he came upon people so broken, so listless, it would have required the devotion of a lifetime to restore them. But he could only lift his trouser turn-ups, pick his way through mud and slime, investigate, write, move on.

He was treated with respect by most of the DDS or Deserving Destees, as, in order to lessen the dread they inspired, he had begun to call them. But sometimes a destitute turned sullen and, suddenly annoyed by Mr Biswas's probings, refused to divulge the harrowing details Mr Biswas needed for his copy. On these occasions Mr Biswas was accused of being in league with the rich, the laughing, the government. Sometimes he was threatened with violence. Then forgetting shoes and trouser turn-ups, he retreated hastily to the street, pursued by words, his undignified movements followed with idle interest by several dozen people, all destitute, all perhaps deserving. 'Deserving Destitute Turns Desperate,' he thought, visualizing the morning's headline. (Though that would never have done: the *Sentinel* wanted only the harrowing details, the grovelling gratitude.)

His bicycle suffered. First the valve-caps were stolen; then the rubber handlegrips; then the bell; then the saddlebag in which he had transported his plunder from Shorthills; and one day the saddle itself. It was a pre-war Brooks saddle, highly desirable, new ones being unobtainable. Cycling that afternoon from the east end of the city to the west end, continually bobbing up and down, unable to sit, had been fatiguing and, judging by the stares, spectacular.

There were other dangers. He was sometimes accosted by burly Negroes, pictures of health and strength; 'Indian, give me some money.' Occasionally exact sums were demanded: 'Indian, give me a shilling.' He had been used to such threatening requests from healthy Negroes outside the larger cinemas, but there the bright lights and the watchful police had given him the confidence to refuse. In the east end the lights were not bright and there were few policemen; and, not wishing to antagonize destitutes any more than was necessary, he took the precaution of going on his investigations with coppers distributed about his pockets. These he gave, and later recovered from the *Sentinel* as expenses.

And other dangers. Once, climbing up a short flight of steps and pushing past the obstructing lace curtain in a room of exceptional cleanliness, he found himself confronted by a woman of robust appearance. Her large lips were grotesquely painted; rouge flared on her black cheeks. 'You from the paper?' she asked. He nodded. 'Give me some money,' she said, as roughly as any man. He gave her a penny. His promptness surprised her. She gazed at the coin with awe, then kissed it. 'You don't know what a thing it is, when a man *give* you money.' His experience on 'Court Shorts' enabling him to recognize a piece of the prostitute's lore, he made perfunctory inquiries and prepared to go. 'Where my money?' the woman said. She followed him to the door, shouting, 'The man – me right here, behind this curtain, and now he don't want to pay.' She called the women and children of the yard and the yards on either side to witness her injury; and Mr Biswas, feeling that his suit, his air of respectability, and the time of day gave some weight to the accusation, hurried guiltily away.

It was some time before he could distinguish the applications of the fraudulent: people who merely wanted the publicity, those who wanted to work off grudges, those who had wanted merely to write, and an astonishing number of well-to-do shopkeepers, clerks and taxi-drivers who wanted money and publicity, and offered to share what money they got with Mr Biswas. Many of his early visits were wasted, and since he had to provide a convincing destitute every morning he had sometimes had to take a mediocre destitute and exaggerate his situation.

The authorities at the *Sentinel* continued neither to comment on his work nor to interfere; and this policy, which he had at first regarded as sinister, now made his position one of responsibility and power. His recommendations were the only things that mattered; his decision was final. He was given a by-line and described as 'Our Special Investigator', which won Anand some respect at school. And for the first time in his life Mr Biswas was offered bribes. It was a mark of status. But, largely through a distrust of the Deserving Destitutes, he accepted nothing, though he did allow a crippled Negro joiner to make him a diningtable at a low price.

He wished he hadn't, for when the table came it made the congestion in his rooms absolute. Shama's glass cabinet was taken to the inner room, and the table placed in his, parallel to the bed and separated from it by a way so narrow that, after bending down to put on his shoes, for instance, he often knocked his head when he straightened up; and if, having put his shoes on, he stood up too quickly, he struck the top of his hip-bone against the table. The generous joiner had made the table six feet long and nearly four feet wide, wide enough to make shutting and opening the side window possible only if you climbed on to the table. On his restless nights Mr Biswas had been in the habit of relegating Anand to the foot of the Slumberking; now when this happened Anand left the bed in a huff and spent the rest of the night on the table, an arrange-

ment Mr Biswas tried to make permanent. The window had
to remain open: the room would have been stifling otherwise. The afternoon rain came swiftly and violently. Shama
could never mount the table quickly enough; and presently
that part of the table directly below the window acquired a
grey, black-spotted bloom which defied all Shama's stainings,
varnishings and polishings. 'First and last diningtable *I* buy,'
Mr Biswas said.

He was lying in vest and pants on the Slumberking one
evening, reading, trying to ignore the buzzing and shrieks of
the readers and learners, and W. C. Tuttle's new gramophone
record of a boy American called Bobby Breen singing 'When
There's a Rainbow on the River'. Someone came into the
room and Mr Biswas, his back to the door, added to the pan-
demonium by wondering aloud who the hell was standing in
his light.

It was Shama. 'Hurry up and get some clothes on,' she said
excitedly. 'Some people have come to see you.'

He had a moment of panic. He had kept his address secret,
yet since he had become investigator of destitutes he had been
repeatedly traced. Once, indeed, he had been accosted by a
destitute just as he was wheeling his bicycle between the high
walls. He had pretended that he was investigating a deserving
case, and as this had looked likely, he had managed to get rid
of the man by taking down his particulars there and then,
standing on the pavement, and promising to investigate him
as soon as possible.

Now he twisted his head and saw that Shama was smiling.
Her excitement contained much self-satisfaction.

'Who?' he asked, jumping out of bed, striking the top of
his hip-bone against the diningtable. Standing between the
table and the bed, it was impossible for him to bend down to
get his shoes. He sat down carefully on the bed again and
fished out a shoe.

Shama said it was the widows from Shorthills.

He relaxed. 'I can't see them outside?'

'Is private.'

'But how the hell I can see them inside here?' It was a
problem. The widows would have to stand just inside the

door, in the narrow area between the bed and the partition; and he would have to stand between the bed and the table. However, it was evening. He took the cotton sheet from below the pillow and threw it over himself.

Shama went out to summon the widows, and the five widows entered almost at once, in their best white clothes and veils, their faces roughened by sun and rain, their demeanour grave and conspiratorial as it always was whenever they were hatching one of their disastrous schemes: poultry farming, dairy farming, sheep raising, vegetable growing.

Mr Biswas, the sheet pulled halfway up his chest, scratched his bare, slack arms. 'Can't ask you to sit down,' he said. 'Nowhere to sit down. Except the table.'

The widows didn't smile. Their solemnity affected Mr Biswas. He stopped scratching his arms and pulled the sheet up to his armpits. Only Shama, already conspicuous in her patched and dirty home-clothes, continued to smile.

Sushila, the senior widow, came to the foot of the bed and spoke.

Could they be considered Deserving Destitutes?

She spoke in a steady, considered way.

Mr Biswas was too embarrassed to reply.

Of course, Sushila said, they couldn't *all* be Deserving Destitutes. But couldn't one?

It was impossible. However destitute they might be, they were relations. But they had put on their best clothes and jewellery and come all the way from Shorthills, and he could not reject them at once. 'What about the name?' he asked.

That had occurred to them. The Tulsi name need not be mentioned. Their husbands' names could be used.

Mr Biswas thought rapidly. 'But what about the children at school?'

They had thought of that too. Sushila had no children. And as for the photograph: with veil, glasses and a few pieces of facial jewellery she could be effectively disguised.

Mr Biswas could think of no other delaying objection. He scratched his arms slowly.

The widows gazed solemnly, then accusingly at him. As his silence lengthened, Shama's smile turned to a look of annoyance; in the end she, too, was accusing.

Mr Biswas slapped his left arm. 'I would lose my job.'

'But that time,' Sushila said, 'when you were the Scarlet Pimpernel, you went around dropping tokens-okens to your mother, your brothers and all the children.'

'That was different,' Mr Biswas said. 'I am sorry. Really.'

The five widows were silent. For some time they remained immobile, staring at Mr Biswas until their eyes went blank. He avoided their eyes, felt for cigarettes, and patted the bed until the matchbox rattled.

Sushila started on a deep sigh, and one by one the widows, staring at Mr Biswas's forehead, sighed and shook their heads. Shama gave Mr Biswas a look of perfect fury. Then she and the widows trooped out of the door.

A child was being flogged downstairs. W. C. Tuttle's gramophone was playing 'One Night When the Moon Was so Mellow'.

'I am sorry,' Mr Biswas said, to the back of the last widow. 'But I would lose my job. Sorry.'

And really he was sorry. But even if they were not relations, he could not have made their case convincing. How could one speak of a woman as destitute when she lived on her mother's estate, in one of her mother's three houses; when her brother was studying medicine in the United Kingdom; and when another brother was a figure of growing importance in the South, his name all over the paper, in the gossip columns, in the news columns for his business deals and political statements, in his own stylish advertisements ('Tulsi Theatres Trinidad proudly present . . .')?

It was not long after this that Mr Biswas had another request which disturbed him. It came from Bhandat, Ajodha's ostracized brother. Mr Biswas had never seen Bhandat since Bhandat had left the rumshop in Pagotes for his Chinese mistress in Port of Spain; he had only heard from Jagdat, Bhandat's son, that Bhandat was living in a poverty which he bore with fortitude. Mr Biswas could do nothing for Bhandat. They were related, and again it would have been impossible to make a case for a man whose brother was known to be one of the wealthiest men in the colony.

Bhandat had given an address in the city centre which might have led someone without a knowledge of the city's slums to believe that Bhandat was a dealer in cocoa or sugar, an import-and-export king. In fact he lived in a tenement that lay between an importer of eastern goods and an exporter of sugar and copra. It was an old, Spanish style building. The flat façade, diversified by irregular areas of missing plaster, small windows with broken shutters, and two rusty iron balconies, rose directly from the pavement.

From the exporter came the rancid smell of copra and the heavy smell of sacked sugar, a smell quite different from the fetid, sweet smell of the sugar factories and buffalo ponds Mr Biswas remembered from his boyhood. From the importer came the many-accented smell of pungent spices. From the road came the smell of dust, straw, the urine and droppings of horses, donkeys and mules. At every impediment the gutters had developed a wrinkled film of scum, as white as the skin on boiled milk, with a piercing, acrid smell, which, blended and heated by the afternoon sun, rose suffocatingly from the road and pursued Mr Biswas as he turned off into the sudden black shadow of an archway between the tenement and the exporter's. He leaned his bicycle against the cool wall, fought off the bees from the exporter's sugar, and made his way down a cobbled lane along which ran a shallow green and black gutter, glittering in the gloom. The lane opened out into a paved yard which was only slightly wider. On one side was the high blank wall of the exporter's; on the other was the wall of the tenement, with windows that gaped black above dingy curtains. A leaning standpipe dripped on a mossy base and fed the gutter; at the end of the yard, their doors open, were a newspaper-littered lavatory and a roofless bathroom. Above was the sky, bright blue. Sunlight struck diagonally across the top of the exporter's wall.

Beyond the standpipe Mr Biswas turned into a passage. He was passing a curtained doorway when a shrill voice cried out, almost gaily, 'Mohun!'

He felt he had become a boy again. All the sense of weakness and shame returned.

It was a low, windowless room, lit only by the light from the passage. A folding screen barred off one corner. In another corner there was a bed, and from it came gurgling happy sounds. Bhandat was not decrepit. Mr Biswas, who had feared to find him shrunken to a melodramatic Indian decrepitude, was relieved. The face was thinner; but the bumps on the top lip were the same; the eyebrows, still those of a worrying man, bunched over eyes that were still bright.

Bhandat raised thin arms. 'You are my child, Mohun. Come.' The shrillness in the voice was new.

'How are you, Uncle?'

Bhandat didn't seem to hear. 'Come, come. You may think you are a big man, but to me you are still my child. Come, let me kiss you.'

Mr Biswas stood on the sugarsack rug and bent over the stale-smelling bed. He was at once pulled vigorously down. He saw that the distempered ceiling and walls were coated with dust and soot, felt Bhandat's unshaven chin scraping against his neck, felt Bhandat's dry lips on his cheek. Then he cried out. Bhandat had pulled sharply at his hair. He jumped back and Bhandat hooted.

Waiting for Bhandat to calm down, Mr Biswas looked around the room. Clothes hung on one wall from nails that had been driven into the mortar between the stones. On the gritty concrete floor what had at first looked like bundles of clothes turned out to be stacks of newspapers. Next to the screen there was a small table with more newspapers, a cheap writingpad, a bottle of ink and a chewed pen: it was at that table, no doubt, that Bhandat had written his letter.

'You are examining my mansion, Mohun?'

Mr Biswas refused to be moved. 'I don't know. It seems to me that you are all right here. You should see how some people live.' And he nearly added, 'You should see how I live.'

'I am an old man,' Bhandat said, in his new, hooting voice. His eyes became wet, and a small, unreliable smile appeared on his lips.

Mr Biswas edged further away from the bed.

Sounds came from behind the dingy cotton-print screen: a clink of a coal-pot ring, the striking of a match, brisk fanning. The Chinese woman. A thrill of curiosity ran through Mr Biswas. White charcoal smoke rose above the screen, coiled about the room and escaped, racing, through the door.

'Why do you use Lux Toilet Soap?'

Mr Biswas saw that Bhandat was staring at him earnestly. 'Lux Toilet? I think we use Palmolive. A green thing –'

Bhandat said in English, 'I use Lux Toilet Soap because it is the soap used by lovely film stars.'

Mr Biswas was disturbed.

Bhandat turned on his side and began to rummage among the newspapers on the floor. 'None of my worthless sons ever come to see me. You are the only one, Mohun. But you were always like that.' He frowned at a newspaper. 'No. This one is over. Fernandes Rum. The perfect round in every circle. That is the sort of thing they want. Rum, Mohun. Remember? Ah! Yes, this is the one.' He handed Mr Biswas a newspaper and Mr Biswas read the details of the Lux slogan competition. 'Help an old man, Mohun. Tell me why you use Lux Toilet Soap.'

Mr Biswas said, 'I use Lux Toilet Soap because it is antiseptic, refreshing, fragrant and inexpensive.'

Bhandat frowned. The words had made no impression on him. And Mr Biswas knew for sure then, what he had intuited and dismissed: Bhandat was deaf.

'Write it down, Mohun,' Bhandat cried. 'Write it down before I forget it. I don't have any luck with these things. Crosswords. Missing Ball competitions. Slogans. They are all the same.'

While Mr Biswas wrote, Bhandat began on an account of his life. His deafness must have occurred some time ago: he spoke in complete sentences, which gave his talk a literary quality. It was a familiar story of jobs acquired and lost, great enterprises which had failed, wonderful opportunities Bhandat had not taken because of his own honesty or the dishonesty of his associates, all of whom were now famous and rich.

He liked the slogan. 'This is bound to win, Mohun. Now, what about the crosswords, Mohun. Couldn't you make me win just one?'

Mr Biswas was saved from replying, for just then the woman came from behind the screen. She moved briskly, furtively, setting an enamel plate with small yellow cakes on the table, pulling out the chair, placing it next to where Mr Biswas stood, then hurrying behind the screen again. She was middle-aged, very thin, with a long neck and a small face. She gave an impression of perpendicularity: her unwashed black hair hung straight, her washed-out blue cotton dress dropped straight, her thin legs were straight.

Mr Biswas looked at Bhandat for signs of embarrassment. But Bhandat went on talking undisturbed about the competitions he had entered and lost.

The woman came out again with two tall enamel cups of tea. She put a cup on the table and pushed the plate of cakes towards Mr Biswas, who was now seated on the chair she had pulled out. She gave the other cup to Bhandat, who sat up to receive it, handing her the sheet of paper on which Mr Biswas had written the slogan.

Bhandat sipped his tea, and for a moment he could have been Ajodha. The gesture was the same: the slow bringing of the cup to the lips, the half-closing of the eyes, the lips resting on the brim, the blowing at the tea. Then came the sip with closed eyes, as though the drink had been consecrated; and peace spread across the tormented face.

He opened his eyes: torment returned. 'It good, eh?' he said to the woman in English. She glanced hastily at Mr Biswas. She seemed anxious to return behind her screen.

'He is a big man now,' Bhandat said. 'But you know, I did know him when he was a boy so high.' He gave a hoot. 'Yes, so high.'

Mr Biswas tried to avoid Bhandat's gaze by taking one of the yellow cakes and biting at it.

'Since he was a boy so high. He is a big man now. But I used to put the licks on him good too, you know. Eh, Mohun? Yes, man.' Bhandat held the cup in his left hand and whipped his right forefinger against his thumb.

This was the moment Mr Biswas had feared. But now that it had come, he found only that he was relieved. Bhandat had not revived the shame: he had removed it.

The cup trembled in Bhandat's hand. The woman ran to the bed and opened her mouth wide. No words came out of that mouth: only a clacking of the tongue that erupted, at the end, into a shrill croak.

The tea had spilled on the bed, on Bhandat. And Mr Biswas, thinking of deafness, dumbness, insanity, the horror of the sexual act in that grimy room, felt the yellow cake turn to a sweet slippery paste in his mouth. He could neither chew nor swallow. On the bed Bhandat was in a paroxysm of rage, cursing in Hindi, while the woman, unheeding, took the cup from his hand, ran behind the screen and brought out a floursack rag, burned in places, and began rubbing briskly on the sheet and Bhandat's vest.

'You awkward barren cow!' Bhandat screamed in Hindi. 'Always full to the brim! Always full to the brim!'

As she rubbed, her thin dress shook, revealing the thick coarse hair under her arms, the shape of her graceless body, the outline of one of her undergarments. Mr Biswas forced himself to swallow the paste in his mouth and washed it down with the strong sweet tea. He was glad when the woman rolled up the floursack rag, put it under Bhandat's vest, and went behind the screen.

Bhandat calmed down at once. He smiled impishly at Mr Biswas and said, 'She doesn't understand Hindi.'

Mr Biswas rose to go.

The woman appeared again, and croaked at Bhandat.

'Stay and eat a proper meal, Mohun,' Bhandat said. 'I am not so poor that I can't afford to feed my child.'

Mr Biswas shook his head and tapped the notebook in his jacket pocket.

The woman withdrew.

'Antiseptic, fragrant, refreshing and inexpensive, eh? God will thank you for this, Mohun. As for those worthless sons of mine –' Bhandat smiled. 'Come and let me kiss you before you go, Mohun.'

Mr Biswas smiled, left Bhandat hooting, and went behind the screen to say good-bye to the woman. A lighted coal-pot stood on a box; on another box there were vegetables and plates. A basin of dirty water rested on the wet, black floor.

He said, 'I'll see what I can do. But I can't promise anything.'

The woman nodded.

'Is his back, really.'

The words were low but clear. She was not dumb!

He did not wait for an explanation. He hurried out of the room into the lane. It was chokingly warm. Once more he received the shock of the street's hot smells. The bees, honeymakers, buzzed around the exporters' sweating sugarsacks. Bits of the coarse cake were still between his teeth. He swallowed. Instantly his mouth filled with saliva again.

As soon as he got to the house he went to the old bookcase, dug past his newspaper clippings, his correspondence from the Ideal School, a nest of pink blind baby mice, and took out his unfinished *Escape* stories, the dreams of the barren heroine. He took the stories to the lavatory in the yard and stayed there for some time, creating a din of his own, pulling the chain again and again. When he came out there was a little queue of readers and learners, impatient but interested.

On Sundays the din of the readers and learners was at its peak, and Mr Biswas started once more to take his children on visits to Pagotes. But now he spent little time with them when they got there. Jagdat, like a vicious schoolboy eager to corrupt, was always anxious to get Mr Biswas out of the house, and Mr Biswas was always willing. Between Jagdat and Mr Biswas there had developed an easy, relaxing relationship. They had never quarrelled; they could never be friends; yet each was always pleased to see the other. Neither believed or was interested in what the other said, and did not feel obliged even to listen. Mr Biswas liked, too, to be with Jagdat in Pagotes, for once outside the house Jagdat was a person of importance, Ajodha's heir, and his manner was that of someone used to obedience and affection. Despite his age, his family, his premature, attractive grey hair, Jagdat was still treated as the young man for whom allowances had to be made. His main pleasure lay in breaking Ajodha's rules, and for a few hours Mr Biswas had to pretend that these rules applied to him as well. Smoking was forbidden: they began to smoke as soon as they were in the road. Drinking was forbidden, and on Sunday mornings rumshops were closed by law: therefore they drank. Jagdat had an arrangement with a rumshop-keeper who, in return for free petrol from Ajodha's pumps, offered the use of his drawingroom for this Sunday morning drinking. In this drawingroom, which was strangely respectable, with four highly polished morris chairs around a small table, Mr Biswas and Jagdat drank whisky and soda. In the beginning they were young men, for whom the world was still new, and neither mentioned the affections to which he had that day to return. But there always came a time when, after a silence, with each willing the talk to continue as before, anxieties and affections returned. Jagdat mentioned his family; he spoke their names: they became individuals. Mr Biswas spoke about the *Sentinel*, about Anand and the exhibition. And always at the end the talk turned to Ajodha. Mr Biswas heard old and new stories of Ajodha's selfishness and cruelty; again and again he heard how it was Bhandat who had made Ajodha's early success possible. Distrustful of the family, despite the drink, Mr Biswas listened and made no comments, only squeezing in words about the Tulsis from time to time, half-heartedly trying to suggest that he had suffered as grand a betrayal as Bhandat. One Sunday morning he told Jagdat about his visit to Bhandat.

'Ah! So you see the old man then, Mohun? How he keeping? Tell me, he say anything about that bloodsucking hog?'

This was clearly Ajodha. Mr Biswas, looking down at his glass as though deeply moved, shook his head.

'You see the sort of man he is, Mohun. No malice.'

Mr Biswas drank some whisky. 'He tell me that none of you does go to see him or give him a little help or anything.'

After a pause Jagdat said, 'Son of a bitch lying like hell. That old bitch he living with smart too, you know. She always putting him up to something or the other.'

Thereafter Jagdat never spoke of Bhandat, and Mr Biswas resolved only to listen.

At these sessions Jagdat gave every indication of growing drunk. Mr Biswas nearly always became drunk, and when they left the rumshop-keeper's drawingroom they sometimes decided to break more rules. They went to Ajodha's garage, filled one of Ajodha's vans or lorries with Ajodha's petrol and drove to the river or the beach. Jagdat drove very fast, but with acute judgement; and it was a recurring mortification to Mr Biswas to find that as soon as they got back to Ajodha's Jagdat became quite sober. He said that he had been out on some business, described conversations and incidents with an abundance of inconsequential, credible detail, and talked happily all through lunch. Mr Biswas said little and moved with a slow precision. His children noted his bloodshot eyes and wondered what had happened to subdue the vivacity he had shown earlier that morning in the bus-station in Port of Spain.

At lunch Ajodha invariably spoke to Mr Biswas of his business problems. 'They didn't give me that contract, you know, Mohun. I think you should write an article about these Local Road Board contracts.' And: 'Mohun, they are not giving me a permit to import diesel lorries. Can you find out why? Will you write them a letter for me? I am sure the oil companies are behind it. Why don't you write an article about it, Mohun?' And there and then followed the looking at official forms, correspondence, illustrated booklets from American firms, with Mr Biswas adopting a side-sitting attitude, breathing away from Ajodha, mumbling inanities through half-closed lips about the war and restrictions.

When the children asked Mr Biswas what was wrong he complained of his indigestion; and sometimes he slept through the afternoon. He did get indigestion too: his increased consumption of Maclean's Brand Stomach Powder, his silence, his unquenchable thirst were symptoms which Shama came to understand, to her shame.

So the children often found themselves on their own at Pagotes. There was only Tara to welcome them, and she was now crippled by asthma. In the large, well-equipped, empty house only the antagonism between Ajodha and his nephews could be felt. Anything could lead to a quarrel: the pronunciation of 'Iraq', a discussion of the merits of the Buick. As quarrels became more frequent they became shorter, but so violent and obscene it seemed impossible that uncle and nephews could ever speak to one another again. Yet in a few minutes Ajodha would come out of his room, his glasses on, papers in his hand, and there would be normal talk and even laughter. Ajodha was bound to his nephews, and they to him. Ajodha needed his nephews in his business, since he distrusted strangers; he needed them more in his house, since he feared to be alone. And Jagdat and Rabidat, with large unacknowledged families, with no money, no gifts, and no status except that they derived from Ajodha's protection, knew that they were tied to Ajodha for as long as he lived. Rabidat, of the beautiful, exposed body, seemed to have his prognathous mouth perpetually set for a snarl. Jagdat's giggles could turn in a moment to screams and tears. In Ajodha's presence he was always on the verge of hysteria: it showed in his small unsteady eyes, which always belied his hearty, back-slapping manner.

More and more the children felt like intruders. They became aware of their status. And they were eventually humiliated.

In response to a plea from Aunt Juanita of the *Guardian* Tinymites League, Anand had gone around with a blue card collecting money for Polish refugee children. He had collected from teachers, the school caretaker, shop-keepers, and even from W. C. Tuttle. The cashier at the Dairies in Port of Spain had given six cents and congratulated him for undertaking good works while yet so young. And in the back verandah at Pagotes one Sunday morning, after he had read out an article on the importance of breathing, he presented the blue card to Ajodha and asked for a contribution.

Ajodha bunched his eyebrows and looked offended.

'You are a funny sort of family,' Ajodha said. 'Father collecting money for destitutes. You collecting for Polish refugees. Who collecting for you?'

It was a long time before Anand went back to Ajodha's. He collected no more money for Polish refugees, tore up the card. The money he had collected melted away, and for some months he lived in the dread of being summoned by Aunt Juanita to account for it. The kindness he received every afternoon from the woman in the Dairies was like a pain.

These Sunday excursions, mornings of makebelieve, afternoons and evenings of distress, grew less frequent, and Mr Biswas found himself more fully occupied with his campaigns at home.

To combat W. C. Tuttle's gramophone Chinta and Govind had been giving a series of pious singings from the *Ramayana*. The study of the *Ramayana*, which Chinta had started many years before, while Mr Biswas still lived at Green Vale, was now apparently complete; she sang very well. Govind sang less mellifluously: he partly whined and partly grunted, from his habit of singing while lying on his belly. Caught in this crossfire of song, which sometimes lasted a whole evening, Mr Biswas, listening, listening, would on a sudden rush in pants and vest to the inner room and bang on the partition of Govind's room and bang on the partition of W. C. Tuttle's drawingroom.

The Tuttles never replied. Chinta sang with added zest. Govind sometimes only chuckled between couplets, making it appear to be part of his song: the *Ramayana* singer is free to add his own rubric in sound between couplets. Sometimes, however, he interrupted his singing to shout insulting things through the partition. Mr Biswas shouted back, and then Shama had to run upstairs to silence Mr Biswas.

Govind had become the terror of the house. It was as if his long spells in his taxi with his back to his passengers had turned him into a complete misanthrope, as if his threepiece suits had buttoned up whatever remained of his eagerness and loyalty and turned it into a brooding which was liable to periodic sour eruptions. He had suffered a corresponding physical change. His weak handsome face had become gross and unreadable, and since he had taken to driving a taxi his body had lost its hardness and broadened into the sort of body that needs a waistcoat to give it dignity, to suggest that the swelling flesh is under control. His behaviour was odd and unpredictable. The *Ramayana* singing had taken nearly everyone by surprise, and would have been amusing if it hadn't coincided with several displays of violence. For days he noticed nobody; then, without provocation, he fastened his attention on someone and pursued him with childish taunts and a frightening smile. He insulted Shama and the children; Shama, appreciating the limitations of Mr Biswas's hammock-like muscles, bore these insults in silence. He made a number of surprise assaults on Basdai's readers and learners and generally terrorized them. Appeals to Chinta were useless; the fear Govind inspired was to her a source of pride. The story how Govind had once thrashed Mr Biswas she passed on to her children, and they passed it on to the readers and learners, terrifying them utterly.

A quarrel between Govind and Mr Biswas upstairs was invariably accompanied by a quarrel between their children downstairs.

Once Savi said, 'I wonder why Pa doesn't buy a house.'

Govind's eldest daughter replied, 'If some people could put money where their mouth is they would be living in palaces.'

'Some people only have mouth and belly.'

'Some people at least have a belly. Other people have nothing at all.'

Savi took these defeats badly. As soon as the quarrel upstairs subsided she went to the inner room and lay down on the fourposter. Not wishing to hurt herself again or to hurt her father, she could not tell him what had happened; and he was the only person who could have comforted her.

In the circumstances W. C. Tuttle came to be regarded as a useful ally. His physical strength matched Govind's (though this was denied by Govind's children), and their dispute about the garage still stood. It helped, too, that W. C. Tuttle and Mr Biswas had something in common: they both felt that by

marrying into the Tulsis they had fallen among barbarians.
W. C. Tuttle regarded himself as one of the last defenders of
brahmin culture in Trinidad; at the same time he considered
he had yielded gracefully to the finer products of Western
civilization: its literature, its music, its art. He behaved at all
times with a suitable dignity. He exchanged angry words with
no one, contenting himself with silent contempt, a quivering
of his longhaired nostrils.

And, indeed, apart from the unpleasantness caused by the
gramophone, there was between Mr Biswas and W. C. Tuttle
only that rivalry which had been touched off when Myna
broke the torchbearer's torchbearing arm and Shama bought
a glass cabinet. The battle of possessions Mr Biswas lost by
default. After the acquisition of the glass cabinet (its broken
door unrepaired, its lower shelves filled with schoolbooks and
newspapers) and the grateful destitute's diningtable, Mr Biswas had no more room. W. C. Tuttle had the whole of the
front verandah: he bought two morris rockingchairs, a standard lamp, a rolltop desk and a bookcase with sliding glass
doors. Mr Biswas had gained a slight advantage by being the
first to enrol his children in the *Guardian* Tinymites League;
but he had squandered this by imitating W. C. Tuttle's khaki
shorts. W. C. Tuttle's shorts were proper shorts, and he had
the figure for them. Mr Biswas lacked this figure, and his
khaki shorts were only long khaki trousers which Shama,
against her judgement, had amputated, and hemmed on her
machine with a wavering line of white cotton. Mr Biswas
suffered a further setback when the Tuttle children revealed
that their father had taken out a life insurance policy. 'Take
out one too?' Mr Biswas said to Myna and Kamla. 'If I start
paying insurance every month, you think any of you would
live to draw it?'

The picture war started when Mr Biswas bought two
drawings from an Indian bookshop and framed them in passepartout. He found he liked framing pictures. He liked playing
with clean cardboard and sharp knives; he liked experiment-
ing with the colours and shapes of mounts. He saw the glass
cut to his measurements, he cycled tremulously home with it,
and a whole evening was transformed. Framing a picture was

like writing a sign: it required neatness and precision; he could concentrate on what his hands did, forget the house, subdue his irritations. Soon his two rooms were as hung with pictures as the barrackroom in Green Vale had been with religious quotations.

W. C. Tuttle began with a series of photographs, in large wooden frames, of himself. In one photograph W. C. Tuttle, naked except for dhoti, sacred thread and caste-marks, head shown except for the top-knot, sat crosslegged, fingers bunched delicately on his upturned soles, and meditated with closed eyes. Next to this W. C. Tuttle stood in jacket, trousers, collar, tie, hat, one well-shod foot on the running-board of a motorcar, laughing, his gold tooth brilliantly revealed. There were photographs of his father, his mother, their house; his brothers, in a group and singly; his sisters, in a group and singly. There were photographs of W. C. Tuttle in various transitory phases: W. C. Tuttle with beard, whiskers and moustache, W. C. Tuttle with beard alone, moustache alone; W. C. Tuttle as weight-lifter (in bathing trunks, glaring at the camera, holding aloft the weights he had made from the lead of the dismantled electricity plant at Shorthills); W. C. Tuttle in Indian court dress; W. C. Tuttle in full pundit's regalia, turban, dhoti, white jacket, beads, standing with a brass jar in one hand, laughing again (a number of blurred, awestruck faces in the background). In between there were pictures of the English countryside in spring, a view of the Matterhorn, a photograph of Mahatma Gandhi, and a picture entitled 'When Did You Last See Your Father?' It was W. C. Tuttle's way of blending East and West.

But Govind, taxi-driving, *Ramayana*-grunting, remained untouched by this or any other rivalry and continued as menacing and offensive as before. The readers and learners openly wished that he would be maimed or killed in a motor accident. Instead, he won a safety award and had his hand shaken by the mayor of Port of Spain. This appeared to free him of all inhibitions, and both Basdai and Mr Biswas began to talk of calling in the police.

But the police were never called. For, quite suddenly, Govind ceased to be a problem.

An abrupt, stunning silence fell on the house one evening. The learners and readers stopped buzzing. W. C. Tuttle's gramophone went dead. The *Ramayana* singing broke off in mid-couplet. And from Govind's room came a series of grunts, thumps, cracks and crashes.

Anand came running on tiptoe into Mr Biswas's room and whispered joyfully, 'Daddy is beating Mummy.'

Mr Biswas sat up and listened. It sounded true. Vidiadhar's Daddy was beating Vidiadhar's Mummy.

The whole house listened. And when the noises from Govind's room died down, and Govind resumed whining out the *Ramayana*, the buzzing downstairs built up again, a new, satisfied sound, and W. C. Tuttle's gramophone played, music of celebration.

So it was whenever Chinta was beaten by Govind. Which was often. The readers and learners recovered from their terror, for having found this outlet, Govind sought no other. Her beatings gave Chinta a matriarchal dignity and, curiously, gained her a respect she had never had before. They had the subsidiary effects of quelling her children, killing her song, and rousing her to cultural rivalry.

Vidiadhar was also in the exhibition class. He was not in the star section, like Anand; but Chinta put this down only to bribery and corruption. And one afternoon, while Anand was sitting on the end stool at the bar in the Dairies, an Indian boy came in. It was Vidiadhar. Anand was surprised. Vidiadhar looked surprised as well. And in their surprise, neither boy spoke to the other. Vidiadhar walked past Anand to the stool at the other end of the bar and asked for a half-pint of milk. Anand was pleased to see him making this mistake: money was first paid at the desk, and the receipt presented to the barman. So Vidiadhar had to walk past the whole row of high stools again, get his receipt from the cashier, and walk past the stools once more to the end he had chosen. Without looking at one another, they drank their milk, slowly, each unwilling to be the first to leave. Neither had intended to cut the other; the cutting had simply happened. But each boy considered he had been cut; and never again, until they were men, did they speak. In the shifting, tangled, multifarious relationships in that crowded house, this silence remained constant. It became historic. Then Vidiadhar said that he had done the cutting that afternoon, and Anand said that *he* had done it. And every afternoon, at five minutes past three, the people in the Dairies saw two Indian boys sitting at opposite ends of the milk bar, drinking half-pints of milk through straws, not looking at one another, never speaking.

Myna and Kamla, resenting the challenge of Vidiadhar, who was now openly eating prunes, began to claim astounding scholastic achievements for Anand.

'My brother read more books than all of all-you put together.'

'Hear you. But all right. If Anand read so much, let him tell me who is the author of *Singing Guns*.' This from a young Tuttle.

'Tell him, Anand. Tell him who is the author of *Singing Guns*.'

'I don't know.'

'Ah-ah-ah!'

'But how you could expect him to know that?' Myna said. 'He does only read books of common sense.'

'Okay. Anand does read a lot of books. But my brother *write* a book. A *whole* book. And he writing another right now.'

The writer had indeed done that. He was the eldest Tuttle boy. He had impressed his parents by a constant demand for exercise books and by a continuous show of writing. He said he was making notes. In fact, he had copied out every word of *Nelson's West Indian Geography*, by Captain Cutteridge, Director of Education, author of *Nelson's West Indian Readers* and *Nelson's West Indian Arithmetics*. He had completed the *Geography* in more than a dozen exercise books, and was at the moment engaged on the first volume of *Nelson's West Indian History*, by Captain Daniel, Assistant Director of Education.

With the exhibition examination less than two months away, Anand lived a life of pure work. Private lessons were given in the morning for half an hour before school; private lessons were given in the afternoon for an hour after school;

private lessons were given for the whole of Saturday morning. Then in addition to all these private lessons from his class teacher, Anand began to take private lessons from the head-master, at the headmaster's house, from five to six. He went from school to the Dairies to school again; then he went to the headmaster's, where Savi waited for him with sand-wiches and lukewarm Ovaltine. Leaving home at seven in the morning, he returned at half past six. He ate. Then he did his school homework; then he prepared for all his private lessons.

All the boys in the star section of the exhibition class en-dured almost similar privation, but they strove to maintain the fiction that they were schoolboys given to pranks, enjoying the most carefree days of their lives. There were a few anxious boys who talked of nothing but work. But most talked of the football season just beginning, the Santa Rosa race meeting just concluded, giving one another to under-stand that their Daddies had taken them to the races in cars with laden hampers and that they had proceeded to bet, and lose, vast sums on the pari mutuel. They discussed the pros-pects of Brown Bomber and Jetsam at the Christmas meeting (the examination was in early November and this was a means of looking beyond it). Anand was not the most backward in these conversations. Though horseracing bored him to a de-gree, he had made it his special subject. He knew, for example, that Jetsam was by Flotsam out of Hope of the Val-ley; he claimed to have seen all three horses and spread a race-track story that the young Jetsam used to eat clothes left out to dry. Retailing some more racetrack gossip, he maintained (and began to be known for this) that, in spite of a career of almost unmitigated disaster, Whitstable was the finest horse in the colony; it was a pity he was so erratic, but then these greys were temperamental.

The talk turned one Monday lunchtime to films, and it appeared that nearly every boy who lived in Port of Spain had been to see the double programme at the London Theatre over the week-end: *Jesse James* and *The Return of Frank James.*

'What a double!' the boys exclaimed. 'A major double!'

Anand, whose championship of Whitstable had established him as the holder of the perverse opinion, said he didn't care for it.

The boys rounded on him.

Anand, who had not seen the double, repeated that he didn't care for it. 'Give me *When the Daltons Rode* and *The Daltons Ride Again*. Any day, old man.'

It was just his luck for one boy to say then, 'I bet you he didn't go to see it! You could see that old crammer going to a theatre?'

'You are a hypocritical little thug,' Anand said, using two words he had got from his father. 'You are a bigger crammer than me.'

The boy wished to shift the conversation: he was a tremendous crammer. He repeated, less warmly, 'I bet you didn't go.' By now, however, the other boys had prepared to listen, and the accuser, gaining confidence, said, 'All right-all right. He went. Just let him tell me what happened when Henry Fonda –'

Anand said, 'I don't like Henry Fonda.'

This created a minor diversion.

'How you mean, you don't like Fonda. Anybody would think that you never see Fonda walk.'

'*That* is walk, old man.'

'All right-all right,' the accuser went on. 'What happened when Henry Fonda and Brian Donlevy –'

'I don't like him either,' Anand said. And, to his great relief, the bell rang.

He could tell from the annoyance of his accuser that the cross-examination would be continued. He went straight after school to the Dairies; when he came back it was time for private lessons; and after private lessons he managed to slip away to the headmaster's. When he got home he said he could do no work that evening and wanted to go to the London Theatre, to give his brain a rest.

'I have no money,' Shama said. 'You will have to ask your father.'

Mr Biswas said, 'When you get to my age you wouldn't care for Westerns.'

Anand lost his temper. 'When I get to your age I don't want to be like you.'

He regretted what he had said. He was, indeed, fatigued; and Mr Biswas's dismissing manner had seemed to him callous. But he made no apology. He talked instead about the headaches he was getting and said he was sure he was suffering from brainfag and brainfever, crammer's afflictions, which his rivals at school had often prophesied for him.

Mr Biswas said, 'I haven't got a red cent on me. I don't get pay till the day after tomorrow. Right now I am dipping into the Deserving Destees' petty cash at the office. Go and ask your mother.'

As usual, it turned out that she did have some money. 'How much you want?'

Anand calculated. Adult, twelve cents, children, half price. Just to make sure, however, he said, 'Thirty-six cents.' He would return the change afterwards.

'Thirty-six cents. Well, boy, you clean me out. Look.'

All he saw in her purse were a few coppers. But she always managed. And pay day was the day after tomorrow.

The evening show began at half past eight. Mr Biswas and Anand left the house at about eight. Not far from the cinema there was a Chinese café. Something had to be bought there; it was part of the cinema ritual. They had eighteen cents to spend. They bought peanuts, *channa* and some mint sweets, six cents in all.

The entrance to the London pit was through a narrow tunnel, as to a dungeon of romance. It allowed not more than one person to advance at a time and enabled the ticket-collector, who sat at the end with a stout stick laid across the arms of his chair, to repel gate-crashers. Mr Biswas and Anand arrived to find the mouth of the tunnel blocked by a turbulent, unaccommodating mob. They stood hesitantly at the edge of the mob, and in an instant, driven from behind, found themselves part of it. They lost control of their hands and feet. Anand, wedged between tall men, shut off from light and air, could only allow himself to be carried along. Cries of frustration and anguish ran through the mob: the film had started: they could hear the opening music. The pressure on Anand increased; he feared he would be crushed against the angle of wall and tunnel; Mr Biswas called to him in a voice that seemed to come from far; he could not answer; he could not look up or down. There was only the thought that at the end of this lay Henry Fonda and Brian Donlevy and Tyrone Power, all of whom, despite what he had said at school, commanded Anand's highest esteem. He heard men crying for tickets; they were getting near. Through a small, semi-circular, lighted hole in the wall of the tunnel money was being pushed in, tickets out, and the hands of the ticketseller occasionally flashed: a woman's hands, fat and cool.

It was Mr Biswas's turn. Struggling to remain in front of the hole, to prevent himself being swept down, ticketless, to the ticket-collector with the stick, he placed a shilling on the smooth, shining wood. 'One and a half.'

A woman's voice said, 'Half price only at matinée.' The hands, about to tear a ticket from the reel, waited.

'Two, then.'

Two green tickets were pushed towards him, and he and Anand yielded gratefully to the pressure at their backs.

'Hey, you!' the woman's voice called from the hole.

Selling had stopped, and the clamour redoubled all down the tunnel.

'You!'

Mr Biswas went back to the lighted hole.

'What you mean, giving me only a shilling?' The coin lay on her palm.

'Two twelves.'

'Two twenties. Sixteen cents more.'

Anand stood where he was. The turmoil and the shouting became remote.

The soundtrack indicated that a fire was in progress. People who had seen the film before recognized the sound; it wound them up to a frenzy.

How could he have forgotten that there was half price only at matinées? How could he have forgotten that on Mondays as on Saturdays and Sundays, the price was not twelve cents, but twenty?

Mr Biswas put the two green tickets down. One was torn off and given back to him, with four cents.

They stood against the wall next to the ticket-collector, while the men who had been behind them hurried past, re-arranging their disordered clothes.

'You go,' Mr Biswas said.

Anand's cheeks bulged over the mint sweet. He had stopped sucking it; it felt cold and wet. He shook his head. Shock had taken away all desire to see the films; if he stayed he would have to walk home alone at midnight.

They were continually jostled. They were in the way.

Mr Biswas said, 'I'll come back for you.'

Anand hesitated. But at that moment there was a new scramble up the tunnel; someone shouted, 'Why the hell you don't go if you going?'; the ticket-collector said, 'Make up your mind. You blocking the way.' And Anand said to Mr Biswas, 'You go,' and Mr Biswas, appearing to obey instantly, vanished behind many backs and was propelled into the cinema to see films he hadn't wanted to see.

Anand stayed in the tunnel, pressed flat against the wall, while people passed inside. Presently, with the film well advanced, the tunnel was empty. The distempered ochre walls were rubbed shiny. In the lighted hole the hands were knitting.

He walked past the Woodbrook Market Square, the Chinese café, the Murray Street playground. The house, when he returned to it, was humming. But no one saw him. He went straight to the front room, took off his shoes and lay down on the Slumberking.

There Shama found him when she came upstairs and turned on the light.

'Boy! You had me frightened. You didn't go to the theatre?'

'Yes. But I had a headache.'

'And your father?'

'He is there.'

The front gate clicked, and someone came up the concrete steps. The door opened and they saw Mr Biswas.

'Well!' Shama said. 'You had a headache too?'

He didn't answer. He worked his way between table and bed, and sat on the bed.

'I can't understand the pair of you,' Shama said. She went into the inner room, came out with some sewing and went downstairs.

Mr Biswas said, 'Boy, get me the *Collins Clear-Type Shakespeare*. And my pen.'

Anand climbed over the head of the bed and got the book and the pen.

For some time Mr Biswas wrote.

'Blasted thing blot like hell. But, still, read it.'

On the fly-leaf, below the four masculine names that had been chosen for Savi before she was born, Anand read: *'I, Mohun Biswas, do hereby promise my son Anand Biswas that in the event of his winning a College Exhibition, I will buy him a bicycle.'* Signature and date followed.

Mr Biswas said, 'I think you'd better witness it.'

Anand wrote the latest version of his signature and added 'witness' in brackets.

'All fair and square now,' Mr Biswas said. 'Just a minute though. Let me see the book again. I think I left out something.'

He took the *Collins Clear-Type Shakespeare*, changed the full stop of his declaration into a comma and added, *war conditions permitting*.

In the house the eruptions of sound had ceased. The humming had subsided to a low, steady burr. It was late. Shama and Savi came up and went to the inner room, where Myna and Kamla were already asleep. Anand lay down on the Slumberking, separated from Mr Biswas by a bank of pillows. He pulled the cotton sheet over his face to keep out the light, and soon fell asleep. Mr Biswas stayed awake for some time, reading. Then he got up, turned off the light, and felt his way back to the bed.

He awoke, as nearly always now, when it was still night. He never wished to know the time: it would be too early or too late. The house was full of sound: with renters, readers and learners upstairs and downstairs, the house snored. The world was without colour; it awaited no one's awakening. Through the open window, above the silhouette of trees and the roof of the house next door, he could see the deep starlit sky. It magnified his distress. Anguish quickened to panic, the familiar knot in his stomach.

He slept late next morning; bathed in the open-air bathroom, ate in the sunny front room, put on yesterday's shirt (he wore one shirt for two days), wrist-watch, tie, jacket, hat; and, respectably attired, cycled out to interview destitutes.

And at school, when confronted by his accuser, Anand said, 'Of course I went. But I hated it so much I left before it began.'

It was agreed that it was a characteristic remark.

Anand's attacks of asthma occurred at intervals of four weeks or less, and Mr Biswas and Shama feared that he might get one during the week of the exhibition examination. But the attack came in the week before, ran for its three days, and then, his chest discoloured and peeling from the medicated wadding, Anand was free to attend to his last, intensive private lessons. His labours were increased when Mr Biswas, determined to leave as little as possible to chance, wrote essays on the Grow More Food Campaign and the Red Cross and made Anand commit them to memory, Mr Biswas flattering himself that he had concealed his own personality in these essays and made them the work, not of a dissident adult, but of a brilliant and loyal schoolboy. They were as full of noble sentiments as a *Sentinel* leader; they appealed urgently for support for campaign and society; they said that the war had to be won, to preserve those free institutions which Anand dearly loved.

The examination was on a Saturday. On Friday evening Shama laid out Anand's speechday clothes and all his equipment. Anand, objecting to the clothes, said it was like preparing for a *puja*. And Chinta, who had kept her plans secret, did have a little *puja* for Vidiadhar. A pundit came up from Arwacas on his motorbike on Friday evening and spent the night among the readers and learners below the house. On Saturday morning, while Anand was doing a last-minute revision, Vidiadhar bathed in consecrated water, put on a dhoti and faced the pundit across a sacrificial fire. He listened to the pundit's prayers, burned some ghee and chipped coconut and brown sugar, and the readers and learners rang bells and struck gongs.

Anand did not escape ritual himself. He had to wear the dark-blue serge shorts, the white shirt, the unchewed school tie; and Shama, braving his anger, sprinkled his shirt with lavender water when he wasn't looking. He said he was willing to rely on the clock in the school hall, but he was given Mr Biswas's Cyma wrist-watch; it hung on his wrist like a loose bracelet and had to be pulled down to his forearm. He was given Mr Biswas's pen, in case his own should fail. He was given a large new bottle of ink, in case the examiners didn't provide enough. He was given many blotters, many *Sentinel* pencils, a pencil sharpener, a ruler, and two erasers, one for pencil, one for ink. He said, 'Anybody would believe I am going to this place to get married.' Lastly, Shama gave him two shillings. She didn't say what this was a precaution against, and he didn't ask.

Similar attentions were being bestowed on a simpering, lip-licking Vidiadhar; he was also provided by Chinta with many charms, which were put on under the pundit's supervision and with ostentatious secrecy, after much shooing away of curious readers and learners. At last the boys left for the school, both smelling of lavender, Vidiadhar going in his father's taxi, Anand walking, accompanied by Mr Biswas, who wheeled his Royal Enfield bicycle. Halfway down the street Anand put his hand in his trousers pocket and felt something soft, small and round. It was a dry lime. It must have been put there by Shama, to cut bad luck. He threw it into the gutter.

It was as Anand feared. The exhibition candidates, prepared for years for the sacrificial day, had all come dressed for the sacrifice. They all wore serge shorts, white shirts and school ties, and Anand could only guess at what charms these clothes concealed. Their pockets were stuffed with pens and pencils. In their hands they carried blotters, rulers, erasers and new pots of ink; some carried complete cases of mathematical instruments; many wore wrist-watches. The schoolyard was full of Daddies, the heroes of so many English compositions;

they seemed to have dressed with as much care as their sons. The boys looked at the Daddies; and the Daddies, wrist-watchless, eyed each other, breeders of rivals. There were few cars outside the school and Vidiadhar had achieved a temporary glory when he arrived in his father's car. But Govind hadn't left quickly enough and the boys, skilled in noticing such things, saw the H on the number plate which indicated that the car was for hire. Altogether it was a dreadful day, a day of reckoning, with Daddies exposed to scrutiny on every side, and the examination to follow.

Anand wanted Mr Biswas to go at once. Not that Mr Biswas couldn't withstand scrutiny; but no boy with an anxious father at his side could pretend that he didn't care about the examination, and Anand wanted passionately to give that impression. Mr Biswas submitted and left, thinking about the ingratitude and callousness of children. Anand joined the fatherless boys who, for the benefit of the Daddies, were making an exaggerated show of being schoolboys: they shouted, bullied the bullied, called each other by nicknames, and laughed noisily at stale, but private, classroom jokes. Loudly they discussed the football match that was to take place that afternoon in the Savannah, just at the end of the street; many said they were going to watch it. One brave soul talked about the film he had seen the night before. They talked, their sweating hands staining blotters, rulers, and slipping over ink-bottles; and they waited.

When the bell rang the schoolyard was instantly stilled. Shouts were suspended, sentences hung unfinished. The traffic on Tragarete Road could be heard, the din from the kitchens of the Queen's Park Hotel. A fluttering of white shirts; newly polished shoes pattering on the asphalt quadrangle and grating up the concrete steps; a wavering line of blue serge at every door; unemphatic footsteps in the hall; here and there a defiant banging of a desk-lid. Then silence. And the Daddies, alone in the schoolyard, looked at the hall doors.

Slowly they dispersed. Three hours later they began to reassemble, their clothes hanging a little more loosely, their faces shining. Many carried oilstained paper parcels. They

stood in the shade of buildings and trees and stared at the
hall doors. A self-possessed invigilator in shirtsleeves
walked slowly up and down, sheets of paper in his hand; from
time to time he coughed noiselessly into a loosely-clenched
fist. A car stopped not far from the school gates; the middle-
aged driver lounged in the angle of seat and door,
rested a newspaper on the steering-wheel and read, picking
his nose.

Then a hamper appeared. A wicker basket with the edges
of an ironed white napkin peeping out below the flaps. A
uniformed maid held the hamper in the crook of her arm and
waited in the shade of the tree next to the caretaker's house,
ignoring the glances of the Daddies with oilstained paper parcels.

More cars came. Mr Biswas, fresh from writing up the sensational decline and fall of a destitute for the *Sunday Sentinel*,
arrived on his Royal Enfield. Yielding to a habit he had
formed since frequenting destitutes, he chained the bicycle to
the school rails. He walked into the schoolyard with his bicycle clips still on: they gave him an urgent, athletic air.

Two more hampers came. Their carriers, one in uniform,
one in a black cotton frock, stood next to the other hamper
carrier.

Govind came. His mood had changed since the morning.
He slammed the door of his taxi hard and paced up and down
outside the school gates, smiling at the pavement, humming,
his hands behind his back.

A flutter as of pigeons in the hall: papers being collected.
A steady and prolonged banging of desk-lids, a shuffling and
a scraping, footsteps more assertive than in the morning, a
disorderly rash of white shirts, many broken lines of blue
serge: as though the disciplined battalion of a few hours before had been routed and were retreating hurriedly, their
equipment abandoned. And the Daddies advanced, like
people welcoming a train, some purposefully, claiming their
own, some getting lost in the eddies of white and dark blue,
and hesitating.

Even in this disorder the hampers were noted, and two
provided surprises, for their recipients were mild mannered

and insignificant; they were now being bullied by maids and led to classrooms.

Everywhere Daddies were getting reports. Question papers were displayed, inkstained fingers pointed. Already, too, backs were being turned, and brown paper parcels and white paper parcels unwrapped and furtively explored.

Mr Biswas saw Vidiadhar first: running down the steps, a lime bulging clearly in each trouser pocket, clothes a little battered, but a face as gay and as fresh and as unstained as when he went in. The little thug. He joined a group of fatherless who had gathered around the class-teacher. No longer posing for the Daddies or one another, they were anxious, excited and shrill.

Anand avoided them when he came out. The pen Mr Biswas had lent him, just in case, had leaked in his shirt pocket and left a large wet stain: it was as though his heart had bled ink. His hair was disordered, his lips black and moustached with ink, his cheeks and forehead smudged. His face was drawn; he looked dejected, exhausted and irritable.

'Well,' Mr Biswas said, smiling, his heart sinking. 'It went all right?'

'Take your bicycle clips off!'

Stunned by the boy's vehemence, Mr Biswas obeyed.

Anand handed him the question papers, clumsily folded, already dirty. Mr Biswas began opening them.

'Oh, put it in your pocket,' Anand said, and Mr Biswas obeyed again.

A worried Chinese boy, looking irreparably scruffy, with over-broad and over-long serge trousers flapping below thin knees, left the group around the teacher and came up to them. In one small hand he unashamedly held a large cheese sandwich, far too thick, it would have seemed, for his narrow mouth; but one end of the sandwich was already irregularly pinked. In the other hand he had a bottle of aerated water. His shrunken face was distorted with anxiety: sandwich and aerated water were irrelevant.

'Biswas,' he said, paying no attention to Mr Biswas. 'That sum about the cyclist –'

'Oh, don't bother me,' Anand said.

Mr Biswas smiled apologetically at the boy, but the boy didn't notice. Daddyless, he wandered off, alone with his anxieties, no one to assure him that his answer was right, the teacher's wrong.

'You shouldn't behave like that,' Mr Biswas said.

'Here. Take back your pen.'

Mr Biswas took back his pen. It dripped with ink.

'And your wrist-watch.' Anand was anxious to get rid of every reminder of the morning's preparations.

Govind and Vidiadhar had gone. So had the other cars. The yard was less noisy. Mr Biswas took Anand to the Dairies for lunch. Crowded with boys and their fathers, it had become an unfamiliar place. As a treat Anand had a chocolate drink instead of milk; but he didn't enjoy that or anything else: it was only part of the day's sacrificial ritual.

The schoolyard filled again. Cars came back, deposited boys, and left. The hampers and the maids left. When the bell rang there was not the instant and complete silence of the morning: there was chatter, shuffling and banging, dwindling to silence.

Mr Biswas opened Anand's question papers. The arithmetic paper was filled in its margins with crabbed and frantic figures: fractions being reduced, and many little multiplications, some completed, some abandoned. Mr Biswas didn't like the look of them. Then he saw that on the geography paper Anand had written his initials elaborately, outlining them in pencil, shading them in pencil; and this dismayed him entirely.

The afternoon session was shorter, and at the end of it few Daddies were in the schoolyard. Only one car came. The drama of the day was over. There was no rush out of the hall. The boys took off their ties, folded them and put them in their shirt pockets with the broad end hanging out (a recent fashion). An invigilator, in a dingy jacket and bicycle clips, brought his rickety bicycle down the steps: no longer remote and awesome, only a man going home after work.

Anand, his tie in his shirt pocket, his collar turned up, ran smiling to Mr Biswas. 'Look!' he said, showing the English paper.

One of the essay subjects was the Grow More Food Campaign.

They smiled at each other, conspirators.

'Biswas!' a boy called. 'You coming to the Savannah?'

'Yes, man!'

He ran to join the boys; and Mr Biswas, loaded with the pen and pencils, the ruler and erasers and bottle of ink, cycled home.

It was strange that, having talked about football and racing all through the term, the boys should now, watching an important football match, talk about nothing but the examination.

Anand returned home shortly after nightfall. His serge trousers were dusty, his shirt wet with perspiration, and he was very gloomy.

'I've failed,' he said.

'What happened?' Mr Biswas asked.

'In the spelling paper. The synonyms and homonyms. They were so easy I thought I'd leave them for last. Then I just didn't do them.'

'You mean you left out a whole question?'

'I realized it in the Savannah.'

The gloom spread to Savi and Myna and Kamla and Shama, and was deepened by the joy of Vidiadhar's brothers and sisters. Vidiadhar had been untouched by the day's events, and was at that moment in the Roxy Theatre, seeing the complete serial of *Daredevils of the Red Circle*. He had brought home question papers that were quite clean except for gay ticks at the side of those questions he had answered. His arithmetic answers, neatly written on a strip of paper, were all correct. He had known the meanings of all the difficult words; he had spotted the synonyms and had not been fooled by one homonym. And he had not had private lessons. He had not had private lessons after private lessons. No one had taken him Ovaltine and sandwiches at five. He had not been going for very long to a Port of Spain school; he had drunk little milk and eaten few prunes.

'I always say,' Shama said, though she had never said anything of the sort, 'I always say that carelessness was going to
be your downfall.'

'In a few years you will look back on this and laugh,' Mr
Biswas said. 'You did your best. And no true effort is ever
wasted. Remember that.'

'What about you?' Anand said.

And though they slept on the same bed, neither spoke to
the other for the rest of the evening.

Anand had no more work to do that year and no more
milk to drink, but on Monday he went to school. All Saturday's candidates were there. They had become a superior,
leisured caste. A few boys did spend the day writing the
examination as nearly as possible as they had done on Saturday. (The Chinese boy, with a mortification that amounted
almost to terror, got the correct answer to the sum about the
cyclist.) The others flaunted their idleness. At first they were
content to be in the classroom and not of the class, seeing the
exhibition discipline enforced on next year's candidates. But
this soon palled, and they wandered out into the yard. Their
attitude to the examination had changed since Saturday afternoon: they all now had tales of disaster. Anand, believing
none of them, magnified his own blunder. In the end they
were all boasting of how badly they had done; and apparently
none of them really cared. Time hung heavily on their hands,
and the afternoon was only partially enlivened by a packet of
cigarettes: disappointing, but a prank, at last. For the first time
for many years Anand was free to go home as soon as
the afternoon bell rang. Up to last week this had seemed
the supreme freedom. But now he dreaded leaving the
boys, dreaded going back to the house. He did not get home
till six.

Unusually, Mr Biswas was below the house, in that section
of it which Shama used as a kitchen. He was in his working
clothes, and tired, but very gay.

'Ah, the young man himself,' he greeted Anand. 'I've been
waiting for you. I've got something for you, young man.' He
took out an envelope from his jacket pocket.

It was a letter from an English judge. He said he had been following Mr Biswas's work in the *Sentinel*, admired it, and would like to meet Mr Biswas, to try and persuade him to join a literary group he had formed.

'What about me, eh. What about me. I tell you, man, no true effort is wasted. Not that I expect to get anything from that blasted paper. Or from you.'

Mr Biswas's elation was extravagant. Anand thought he knew why. But he was in no mood to give comfort, to associate himself with weakness. He handed back the letter to Mr Biswas without a word.

Mr Biswas took the letter absently, told Shama to send up his food, and went to the front room. He was alone, too, when he awoke in the night to the snoring house, Anand asleep beside him, and looked through the window at the clear, dead sky.

He saw the judge the next day, and went to the meeting of the literary group on Friday evening. He was especially glad to be out of the house then, for on Friday evenings the widows came up from Shorthills and spent the night below the house. Encouraged by the success of Indian shirtmakers, the widows had decided to go into the clothesmaking business. Since none of the five could sew at all well, they had decided to learn, and every Friday they went to the sewing classes at the Royal Victoria Institute, each widow specializing in a different aspect of the craft. They came in the late afternoon, they were rapturously welcomed by the readers and learners, and Basdai fed them. The readers and learners, not subject to Basdai's floggings while their mothers were present, were unusually vociferous; there was an air of festival.

Mr Biswas found himself a little out of his depth in the literary group. Apart from the poems in the *Royal Reader* and *Bell's Standard Elocutionist*, the only poems he knew were those of Ella Wheeler Wilcox and Edward Carpenter; and at the judge's the emphasis was on poetry. But there was much to drink, and it was late when Mr Biswas came back and wheeled his bicycle below the house, his head ringing with the names of Lorca and Eliot and Auden. The readers and learners were asleep on benches and tables. The widows, dressed in white and singing softly, sat below a weak bulb, playing cards, drinking coffee, and handling pieces of sewing which had grown grubby over the weeks of tuition. He went up the dark front stairs and turned the light on in his room. Anand sprawled on the bed behind the bank of pillows. He undressed and squeezed himself between the diningtable and the bed. Shama came from the inner room, in answer to the light, and noted those symptoms, of slowness, precision and silence, which she associated with his Sunday excursions to Pagotes.

As a condition of his acceptance by the group he had to read something of his own. He didn't know what to offer them. He couldn't write poetry, and he had thrown away the 'Escape' stories. He knew that story well, however; it could be written again. He still could think of no satisfactory end, but he had read enough of modern prose to know that a neat end might offend the group. He couldn't make his hero the faceless 'John Lubbard', who was 'tall, broad-shouldered, handsome'; he would be laughed down. He had to be ruthless. His hero would be Gopi, a country shopkeeper, 'small, spare and shrunken'. He took a *Sentinel* pad, got into bed and, neatly, began to write the familiar words: *At the age of thirty-three, when he was already the father of four children* . . .

Those words were never read to the group. This story, like the others, was never finished. For, even before Gopi could meet his barren heroine, news came that Bipti, Mr Biswas's mother, had died.

He called the children away from school and they went with Shama to Pratap's. From the road the open verandah and steps, thick with mourners, appeared to be draped with white. He had not expected such a crowd. Tara was there, and Ajodha, looking annoyed. But most of the mourners he didn't know: the families of his sister-in-law, his brother's friends, Bipti's friends. He might have been attending the funeral of a stranger. The body laid out in a coffin on the verandah belonged more to them. He longed to feel grief. He was surprised only by jealousy.

Shama did her duty and wept. Dehuti, who had been ostracized since her marriage, sat halfway up the steps, shrieking at new mourners and grabbing at their feet, as if anxious to trip them up, to prevent them going any further. The mourners, finding their trousers or skirts clutched to a wet face, stroked Dehuti's covered head and at the same time tried to shake their garments free. No one made any effort to move Dehuti. Her story was known, and it was felt that she was doing a penance which it would have been improper to interrupt. Ramchand was more controlled but equally impressive. He occupied himself with the funeral arrangements, and behaved with such authority that no one would have guessed that he had not spoken to Bipti or Mr Biswas's brothers.

Mr Biswas went past Dehuti to look at the body. Then he did not wish to see it again. But always, as he wandered about the yard among the mourners, he was aware of the body. He was oppressed by a sense of loss: not of present loss, but of something missed in the past. He would have liked to be alone, to commune with this feeling. But time was short, and always there was the sight of Shama and the children, alien growths, alien affections, which fed on him and called him away from that part of him which yet remained purely himself, that part which had for long been submerged and was now to disappear.

The children did not go to the burial ground. They strayed about Pratap's large yard, eyed other groups of children, town children versus country children. Anand, in his exhibition clothes, led his sisters through the vegetable garden to the cowpen. They examined a broken cartwheel. Behind the pen they surprised a hen and its brood scratching a dung heap. Girls and chickens fled in opposite directions, and the country children tittered.

Back in Port of Spain, they noticed Mr Biswas's stillness, his silence, his withdrawal. He did not complain about the noise; he discouraged, but gently, all efforts to engage him in conversation; he went alone for long night walks. He summoned no one to get his matches or cigarettes or books. And he wrote. He told no one what he was writing. He wrote with energy but without enthusiasm, doggedly, destroying sheet after sheet. He ate little, but his indigestion had gone. Shama bought him tinned salmon, his favourite food; she had the girls clean his bicycle and made Anand pump the tyres every morning. But he did not appear to notice these attentions.

She went to the front room one evening and stood at the head of the bed. He was writing; his back was to her. She was in his light, but he did not shout.

'What's the matter, man?'

He said in an expressionless voice, 'You are blocking the light.' He laid down paper and pencil.

She worked her way between the table and bed and sat on the edge of the bed, near his head. Her weight created a minor disturbance. The pillow tilted and his head slipped off it, falling almost into her lap. He tried to move his head, but when she held it he remained still.

'You don't look well,' she said.

He accepted her caresses. She stroked his hair, remarked on its fine quality, said it was going thin, but not, thank God, going grey like hers. She pulled out a hair from her head and laid it across his chest. 'Look,' she said, 'completely grey,' laughing.

'Grey all right.'

She looked over his chest to the sheets he had put down. She saw *My Dear Doctor*, with the *My* crossed out and written in again.

'Who you writing to?'

She couldn't read more, for beyond the first line the handwriting had deteriorated into a racing scrawl.

He didn't reply.

For some time, until the position became uncomfortable for Shama, they remained like that, silent. She stroked his head, looked from him to the open window, heard the buzz and shrieks upstairs and downstairs. He closed his eyes and opened them under her stroking.

'Which doctor?' Though there had been a long silence, there seemed to be no break between her questions.

He was silent.

Then he said, 'Doctor Rameshwar.'

'The one who . . .'

'Yes. The one who signed my mother's death certificate.'

She went on stroking his head, and, slowly, he began to speak.

There had been some trouble about the certificate. No, it wasn't really trouble. Pratap had first dispatched messages; Prasad had come and they had both gone, with urgent grief, to the doctor's. It was midday, hot; the body would not last. They had been made to wait for very long in the doctor's verandah; they had complained, and the doctor had damned them and damned their mother. His bad temper continued all the way to the house; with anger and disrespect he had examined Bipti's body, signed the certificate, demanded his fee and left. This had been told to Mr Biswas by his brothers, not in anger; they told it simply as part of the tribulations of the day: the death, the sending of messages, the arrangements.

'And why didn't you tell me?' Shama asked in Hindi.

He didn't say. It was something that concerned him alone. By speaking of it he would have exposed himself to the disregard of Shama and the children; he would also have involved them in his own humiliation.

Shama's solace was a surprise. She spoke to the children, and he was further strengthened when they expressed, not hurt, but anger.

He became almost gay, and addressed himself to the letter now with something like zest. He read out to Anand the drafts he had made and asked for comments. The drafts were hysterical and libellous. But in his new mood, and after many re-writings, the letter developed into a broad philosophical essay on the nature of man. Both he and Anand thought it humorous, charitable and in parts correctly condescending; and it thrilled them to think of the doctor's surprise at receiving such a letter from the relation of someone he had thought to be only a peasant. Mr Biswas introduced himself as the son of the woman whose death the doctor had so rudely certified. He compared the doctor to an angry hero of a Hindu epic, and asked to be forgiven for mentioning the Hindu epics to an Indian who had abandoned his religion for a recent superstition that was being exported wholesale to savages all over the world (the doctor was a Christian). Perhaps the doctor had done so for political reasons or social reasons, or simply to escape from his caste; but no one could escape from what he was. This theme was developed and the letter concluded that no one could deny his humanity and keep his selfrespect. Mr Biswas and Anand hunted through the *Collins Clear-Type Shakespeare* and found the play of *Measure for Measure* rich in things that could be quoted. They also quoted from the New Testament and the *Gita*. The letter ran to eight pages. It was typed on the yellow typewriter and posted; and Mr Biswas, exhilarated by his fortnight's work, said to Anand, 'How about a few more letters before Christmas? One to a business man. To fix up Shekhar. One to an editor. Fix up the *Sentinel*. Publish them as a booklet. Dedicate it to you.'

But the wound was still there, too deep for anger or thoughts of retribution. What had happened was locked away in time. But it was an error, not a part of truth. He wished this stated; and he wanted to do something that would be a defiance of what had happened. The body, lying in earth, was unhallowed, and he owed it honour: the mother who had remained unknown and whom he had never loved. Waking in the night, he felt exposed and vulnerable. He longed for hands to cover him all over, and he could only fall asleep again with his hands over his navel, unable to bear the feel of any alien object, however slight, on that part of his body.

To do honour he had no gifts. He had no words to say what he wanted to say, the poet's words, which held more than the sum of their meanings. But awake one night, looking at the sky through the window, he got out of bed, worked his way to the light switch, turned it on, got paper and pencil, and began to write. He addressed his mother. He did not think of rhythm; he used no cheating abstract words. He wrote of coming up to the brow of the hill, seeing the black, forked earth, the marks of the spade, the indentations of the fork prongs. He wrote of a journey he had made a long time before. He was tired; she made him rest. He was hungry; she gave him food. He had nowhere to go; she welcomed him. The writing excited, relieved him; so much so that he was able to look at Anand, asleep beside him, and think, 'Poor boy. Failed his exam.'

The poem written, his selfconsciousness violated, he was whole again. And when on Friday the five widows arrived in Port of Spain for their sewing lessons at the Royal Victoria Institute, and the house resounded with clatter and chatter and shrieks and singing and the radio and the gramophone, Mr Biswas went to the meeting of his literary group and announced that he was going to read his offering at last.

'It is a poem,' he said. 'In prose.'

Everything glowed richly in the judge's dimly-lit verandah. On the table there were bottles of whisky and rum, ginger and soda water, and a bowl of crushed ice.

Mr Biswas sat in the chair below the reading light and sipped his whisky and soda. 'There is no title,' he said. And, as he had expected, this was received with satisfaction.

Then he disgraced himself. Thinking himself free of what he had written, he ventured on his poem boldly, and even with a touch of selfmockery. But as he read, his hands began to shake, the paper rustled; and when he spoke of the journey his voice failed. It cracked and kept on cracking; his eyes tickled. But he went on, and his emotion was such that at the end no one said a word. He folded the paper and put it in his jacket pocket. Someone filled his glass. He stared down at his lap, as if angry, as if he had been completely alone. He said nothing for the rest of the evening, and in his shame and confusion drank much. When he went home the widows were singing softly, the children were asleep, and he shamed Shama by being noisily sick in the outdoor lavatory.

Whatever happened, Anand would go to college. So Mr Biswas and Shama decided. It wouldn't be easy, but it would be cruel and foolish to give the boy nothing more than an elementary school education. The girls agreed. They had not had any milk and prunes, and their chances of going to high schools were slight; but they did badly in their classes and did not consider themselves worthy. Myna and Kamla insisted that Mr Biswas should make a public declaration that Anand was going to the college, for Vidiadhar was behaving as though he had already won the exhibition and was openly learning Latin and French and algebra and geometry, the wonderful subjects taught at the college.

The declaration was made, though neither Mr Biswas nor Shama could say where the money was going to come from.

Shama talked of recovering her cow Mutri from Shorthills.

'Where you going to keep it?' Mr Biswas asked. 'With the boarders downstairs?'

'Milk selling at ten and twelve cents a bottle,' Shama said.

'What about grass, eh? You think you could just tie out Mutri in Adam Smith Square or the Murray Street playground? You've been reading too much Captain Cutteridge. And how much milk you think poor old Mutri going to give after living all those years with your family?'

Commercial ventures were running high in Shama's mind since one of the widows, despairing of any but long-term returns from the clothesmaking scheme, had brought up a bag of oranges from Shorthills one Friday. She was exceptionally grave. She called one of her sons aside and ordered him to place the oranges on a tray, the tray on a box, and the box on the pavement. Then she went to the Royal Victoria Institute. The widow's idea was simplicity itself: it required little effort and no outlay. There was much agitated discussion among the sisters that evening; many plans were adumbrated, and futures tremulously envisaged. The widow herself said nothing, and continued as grave and mournful as before, sucking thread, threading needles, and sewing.

The appearance of a shallow heap of oranges on a tray outside the tall blank walls of the house created a small sensation in the residential street. And it increased Mr Biswas's dread of being traced to his home by impatient destitutes.

With the exhibition examination and the death of his mother he had been neglecting the destitutes. Correspondence had accumulated, and as he was sitting in the *Sentinel* office one morning and typing for the tenth time, *Dear Sir, Your letter awaited me on my return from holiday . . .*, a reporter came to his desk and said, 'Congrats, old man.'

It was the *Sentinel's* education correspondent. He held some typewritten sheets. They were the exhibition results.

In a page of names the name stood out.

Anand had been placed third, had got one of the twelve exhibitions.

As bewitching as the news was the generosity with which it was welcomed by the older members of the staff. The very young, who had sat the examination not many years before, were aloof and unimpressed.

But third! Third in the island! It was fantastic. Only two boys more intelligent! It couldn't be grasped right away.

Recovering, Mr Biswas attempted to deflect some of the praise. 'Mark you, the teacher knows his stuff.' But he couldn't keep this up. 'Careless boy, too, you know. Left out one whole question. In the spelling paper. Synonyms and homonyms.'

He began to lose his audience.

'He knew them. Thought they were easy.'

Reporters returned to their desks.

'And then didn't do them at all. Left them out. A whole question.'

After a light-hearted morning in which he investigated the circumstances of two destitutes with a good humour which offended those people, he returned to the office and invited the education correspondent and Mr Burnett's news editor to have beers with him at the café on the corner. There, surrounded by flamboyant murals of revelry on tropical beaches, they drank: three men, none over forty, who considered their careers closed and rested their ambitions on the achievements of their children. The success of the son of one gave the others hope. They shared Mr Biswas's joy; they could not achieve his delirium.

'You could leave old Mutri to die in peace,' he said to Shama when he got back to the quiet house at midday; and his gaiety had her guessing. 'What about oranges? Want to go in the selling business? Join the widows? The five financial wizards.'

The orange venture had in fact failed. Three oranges had been sold to a stray American soldier for a penny; the others had gone bad in the sun. The failure was put down to the unsuitability of the site and the snobbishness and jealousy of the neighbours who, to spite the widow, had preferred to go all the way to the city market to buy their oranges at a higher price. The widow's son was also blamed for his lack of enthusiasm and his false pride: he had stood some distance from the tray of oranges and tried to pretend that they had nothing to do with him.

When Mr Biswas broke the news of the exhibition, Shama set about defending the widows, and she and Mr Biswas had a long and friendly squabble about the Tulsi family. It was like old times, and Mr Biswas, the victor as always, solaced Shama by saying, what he had forgotten for some time, 'Going to buy that gold brooch for you, girl! One of these days.'

'I suppose it would look nice in my coffin.'

The school had taken the first four places and won seven of the twelve exhibitions. The teacher's notes and private lessons, legendarily virtuous, had triumphed once again. Five of the exhibitions went to known crammers like Anand and the Chinese boy and aroused little comment. The sixth went to one of the mild, hamper-fed boys; he was now considered sly. But the biggest surprise was provided by the boy who had come first. He was a Negro boy of astonishing size. He was a year younger than Anand but looked incomparably older. His forearms were already veined, and his chin and cheeks were dotted with little springs of hair. He had been loud in his denunciation of crammers; he had taken a leading part in discussions about films and sport; he had a phenomenal knowledge of English county cricket scores throughout the nineteen-thirties; and he had introduced the topic of sex. He claimed to have had many sexual encounters and his talk encouraged the belief that when he left school after private lessons, his satchel bouncing off his high bottom, it was not to do homework but to indulge in sexual intrigue and, joyously, to be pursued by older women. He displayed a convincing knowledge of the female body and its functions; and the conception of his life away from school as one of indifference to books and notes and homework was reinforced by his passionate devotion to the novels of P. G. Wodehouse, whose style he successfully imitated in his English compositions. His popularity was at its lowest that morning; his success cast doubt on all his tales of sexual adventure. He protested that he had not worked, that he had done no more than a hasty last-minute revision, and that the result had surprised him more than anyone else. But he protested in vain.

Photographers from the newspapers came. The exhibitioners straightened their ties and were photographed. Then they were free. They had ceased to be members of the school. School and teacher dwindled, and the boys were anxious to be out of the yard. None dared say he wanted to go home to break the news; besides, none wanted to put an end to the day.

The city was black and white in the sun. Trees were still, the sky high. They walked up to the Savannah, sat and looked at the people going in and out of the Queen's Park Hotel. In the whitewashed bays on either side of the hotel entrance two doorkeepers of a rare blackness stood in stiff snow-white tunics. The effect was severe but picturesque. The boys wondered aloud what made the hotel get the blackest men in the island for that job, and what made the men take the job. Then they had a long discussion whether, given such a blackness, they would take the job themselves. The taxi-drivers, squatting on the asphalt pavement, chuckled; and the doorkeepers, compelled because of the constant coming and going to maintain their statuesque pose, could only make furtive threatening gestures and open their mouths to frame silent, hurried obscenities. The boys laughed and retreated. They walked along the Savannah, always in the shade of large trees. At Queen's Park West they came on a mobile stall selling syrupy ice shavings in two colours. They bought; they sucked; they stained hands, faces, shirts. Then the Negro boy, anxious to regain his character, suggested that they should go to the Botanical Gardens to look for copulating couples. They went, they looked. Deployed by the Negro boy, they surprised one couple into a hasty show of decency. The second time they were chased by an enraged American sailor. They retreated to the Rock Gardens, and walked past the architectural marvels of Maraval Road. They walked past the Scottish baronial castle, the Moorish mansion, the semi-Oriental palace, the Bishop's Spanish Colonial residence, and came to the blue and red Italianate college, empty now, though there were two cars below a pillared and balustraded balcony. They were proud and a little frightened. Kings for half a day, they would soon be new boys here, and nothing. The clock struck three. They looked up at the tower. The dial would be seen for weeks and months and years; those chimes would become familiar. They would warn of many things; they would mark many beginnings and ends. Now they said that the half-holiday was over. 'See you next term,' the boys said, and went their separate ways.

That evening, while Mr Biswas and the parents of the other exhibitioners beat their way to the teacher's door with gifts of rum and whisky, trussed fowls and hobbled goats, the Tuttle children were set to their books with a new rigidity, although Christmas was not far off and the school term nearly ended. The writer, encouraged, completed the first volume of Captain Daniel's *West Indian History*. For Vidiadhar it was an unhappy evening. He was given no food. For he had not won an exhibition, Vidiadhar who had brought home clean question papers with ticks beside the questions he had done and a neat list of correct answers to the arithmetic sums, who had begun to learn Latin and French, who had gone to the intercollegiate football match and uttered partisan cries. Now, deprived of his Latin and French books, he was made to sit up late before his exhibition notes, and was repeatedly flogged by Chinta.

The newspapers next morning carried photographs of Anand and the other exhibitioners. There were also columns of fine print containing the names of the many hundred who had only passed the examination. The readers and learners searched among these for Vidiadhar's name. They didn't find it. Always on the winning side, the readers and learners turned over the page and pretended to look there, and then they pretended to go through the classified advertisements, which were in the same small type. Having no flogging powers over the readers and learners, and unable now to threaten them with Govind, Chinta could only abuse them. She abused them individually; she abused Shama; she abused W. C. Tuttle; she abused Anand and his sisters; she accused Mr Biswas of bribing the examiners; she brought up the theft of the eighty dollars. Her voice was a grating whine; her eyes were red, her whole face inflamed. The readers and learners giggled. Vidiadhar, enjoying the holiday granted to the school for its exhibition successes, was set to his exhibition notes again. From time to time Chinta interrupted her abuse to scream at him. 'Watch me! Give me that knife and see if I don't cut his little tongue.' And: 'You are going to live on bread and water from now on. That is the only thing that will satisfy some people in this house.' Sometimes she fell silent and ran, literally ran, to the table where he sat and twisted his ears as if she were winding up an alarm clock, until, like an alarm, Vidiadhar went off. Then she slapped him and cuffed him, pulled his hair and pressed her fingers around his throat. Stupefied, Vidiadhar filled page after page with meaningless notes in his crapaud-foot handwriting; and his sisters and brothers scowled at everyone as though they were all responsible for Vidiadhar's failure and punishment.

All day and all evening Chinta kept it up, her shrill voice part of the background noise of the house, until even W. C. Tuttle was driven to comment, in his pure Hindi, in a voice loud enough to penetrate the partition of Mr Biswas's inner room, whence the comment was reported to Mr Biswas in the front room, preparing the way for a reconciliation between the two men, which was completed when W. C. Tuttle's second eldest boy, due to write the exhibition examination next year, came down to ask Anand to be his tutor.

And it was from the Tuttles that Anand got the only presents he had for winning the exhibition: a copy of *The Talisman* from W. C. Tuttle, which he found unreadable, and a dollar from Mrs Tuttle, which he gave to Shama. Mr Biswas was ashamed to mention the promise in the *Collins Clear-Type Shakespeare*, and Anand didn't remind him: he was content to assume that war conditions did not permit the buying of a bicycle. There was no prize from the school either. Again war conditions did not permit; and as 'a war measure' Anand was given a certificate printed by the Government Printery at the bottom of the street, 'in lieu of' the leather-bound, gilt-edged book stamped with the school crest.

It had been a year of scarcity, of rising prices and fights in shops for hoarded flour. But at Christmas the pavements were crowded with overdressed shoppers from the country, the streets choked with slow but strident traffic. The stores had only clumsy local toys of wood, but the signs were bright as always with rosy-cheeked Santa Clauses, prancing reindeer, holly and berries and snow-capped letters. Never were destitutes more deserving, and Mr Biswas worked harder than ever. But everything – shops, signs, crowds, noise, busyness – generated the urgent gaiety that belonged to the season. The year was ending well.

And it was to end even better.

One morning early in Christmas week, when Mr Biswas was looking through applications in the hope of finding a destitute carpenter for Christmas Eve, a well-dressed middle-aged man whom he did not know came straight to his desk, handed him an envelope with a stiff gesture, and, without a word, turned and walked briskly out of the newsroom.

Mr Biswas opened the envelope. Then he pushed back his chair and ran outside. The man was in a car and already driving away.

'You didn't see him?' the receptionist asked. 'He did ask for you. Doctor feller. Rameshwar.'

He had returned the letter. The error had been acknowledged.

'What about it, boy?' he said to Anand later that day. 'Series of letters. To a doctor. A judge. Businessman, editor. Brother-in-law, mother-in-law. *Twelve Open Letters*, by M. Biswas. What about it?'

# 5. The Void

THE COLLEGE had no keener parent than Mr Biswas. He delighted in all its rules, ceremonies and customs. He loved the textbooks it prescribed, and reserved to himself the pleasure of taking Anand's exhibitioner's form to Muir Marshall's in Marine Square and bringing home a parcel of books, free. He papered the covers and lettered the spines. On the front and back endpapers of each book he wrote Anand's name, form, the name of the college, and the date. Anand was put to much trouble to conceal this from the other boys at school who wrote their own names and were free to desecrate their books in whatever way they chose. Though it concerned neither Anand nor himself, Mr Biswas went to the college speech day. He insisted, too, on going to the Science Exhibition, and spoiled it for Anand; for while the Negro boy ran to the parentless, saying, 'Look, man, a snail can screw itself,' Anand had to remain with Mr Biswas who, dutifully beginning at the beginning, looked long and carefully at the electrical exhibits and got no further than the microscopes. 'Stand up here,' he told Anand. 'Hide me while I pull out this slide. Just going to cough and spit on it. Then we could both have a look.' 'Yes, *Daddy*,' Anand said. 'Of course, *Daddy*.' But they didn't see the snails. When, as an experiment, each boy was given a homework book which parents or guardians were supposed to fill in and sign every day, Mr Biswas filled in and signed punctiliously. Few other parents did; and the homework books were soon abandoned, Mr Biswas filling in and signing to the last. He had no doubt that his interest in Anand was shared by the entire college; and when Anand went back to classes after one of his asthmatic attacks, Mr Biswas always asked in the afternoon, 'Well, what did they say, eh?' as though Anand's absence had dislocated the running of the school.

In October Myna was put on milk and prunes. She had unexpectedly been chosen to sit the exhibition examination in November. Mr Biswas and Anand went with her to the examination hall, Anand condescending, revisiting the scenes of his childhood. He saw his name painted on the board in the headmaster's room, and was touched at this effort of the school to claim him. When Myna came out at lunchtime she was very cheerful, but under Anand's severe questioning she had grown dazed and unhappy, had admitted mistakes and tried to show how other mistakes could be construed as accurate. Then they took her to the Dairies, all three feeling that money was being wasted. When the results came out no one congratulated Mr Biswas, for Myna's name was lost in the columns of fine print, among those who had only passed.

Change had come over him without his knowing. There had been no precise point at which the city had lost its romance and promise, no point at which he had begun to consider himself old, his career closed, and his visions of the future became only visions of Anand's future. Each realization had been delayed and had come, not as a surprise, but as a statement of a condition long accepted.

But it was not so when, waking up one night, he saw that he had for some time grown to accept his circumstances as unalterable: the buzzing house, the kitchen downstairs, the food being brought up the front steps, the growing children and Shama and himself squeezed into two rooms. He had grown to look upon houses – the bright drawingrooms through open doors, the chink of cutlery from diningrooms at eight, when he was on the way to a cinema, the garages, the hose-sprayed gardens in the afternoons, the barelegged lounging groups in verandahs on Sunday mornings – he had grown to look upon houses as things that concerned other people, like churches, butchers' stalls, cricket matches and football matches. They had ceased to rouse ambition or misery. He had lost the vision of the house.

He sank into despair as into the void which, in his imagining, had always stood for the life he had yet to live. Night after night he sank. But there was now no quickening panic, no knot of anguish. He discovered in himself only a great unwillingness, and that part of his mind which feared the consequences of such a withdrawal was increasingly stilled. Destitutes were investigated and the deserving written about. The truce with W. C. Tuttle was broken, patched up and broken again. The readers and learners read and learned. Anand and Vidiadhar continued not to speak, and this silence between the cousins was beginning to be known at the college, which Vidiadhar had also managed to enter, though at a suitably low form. Govind beat Chinta, wore his threepiece suits and drove his taxi. The widows stopped taking sewing lessons at the Royal Victoria Institute, gave up the clothes-making scheme and all other schemes. One came and camped, roomless, under the house, threatened to take a stall in the George Street Market, was dissuaded, and returned to Shorthills. W. C. Tuttle acquired a gramophone record of a fifteen-year-old American called Gloria Warren singing 'You Are Always in My Heart'. And every morning, after the readers and learners had streamed out of the house, Mr Biswas escaped to the *Sentinel* office.

Suddenly, quite suddenly, he was revivified.

It happened during Anand's second year at the college. Because of his unrivalled experience of destitutes Mr Biswas had become the *Sentinel*'s expert on matters of social welfare. His subsidiary duties had included interviewing the organizers of charities and eating many dinners. One morning he found a note on his desk requesting him to interview the newly arrived head of the Community Welfare Department. This was a government department that had not yet begun to function. Mr Biswas knew that it was part of the plan for postwar development, but he did not know what the department intended to do. He sent for the file. It was not helpful. Most of it he had written himself, and forgotten. He telephoned, arranged for an interview that morning, and went. When, an hour later, he walked down the Red House steps into the asphalt court, he was thinking, not of his copy, but of his letter of resignation to the *Sentinel*. He had been offered, and had accepted, a job as Community Welfare

Officer, at a salary fifty dollars a month higher than the one he was getting from the *Sentinel*. And he still had no clear idea of the aims of the department. He believed it was to organize village life; why and how village life was to be organized he didn't know.

He had been immediately attracted by Miss Logie, the head of the department. She was a tall, energetic woman in late middle age. She was not pompous or aggressive, as he had found women in authority inclined to be. She had the graces, and even before there was talk of the job he had found himself attempting to please. She also had the attraction of novelty. He had known no Indian woman of her age as alert and intelligent and inquiring. And when the matter of the job was raised he had no hesitation. He rejected Miss Logie's offer of time to think it over; he feared all delay.

He walked light-heartedly down St Vincent Street back to the office. What had just happened was unexpected in every way. He had stopped thinking of a new job. He had paid no more than a journalist's attention to all the talk of postwar development, since he did not see how it involved him and his family. And now, on a Monday morning, he had walked into a new job, and his job made him part of the new era. And it was a job with the government! He thought with pleasure of all the jokes he had heard about civil servants, and felt the full weight of the fears that had been with him since Mr Burnett had left. He could have been sacked from the *Sentinel* at any moment; there was nothing or no one to protect him. But in the Service no one could be sacked just like that. There were things like Whitley Councils, he believed. The matter would have to go through all sorts of channels – that was the delicious word – and this, he understood, was such a complicated proceeding that few civil servants ever did get the sack. What was that story about the messenger who had stolen and sold all a department's typewriters? Didn't they just say, 'Put that man in a department where there are no typewriters'?

How many letters of resignation he had mentally addressed to the *Sentinel*! Yet when, letters having passed between the Secretariat and himself, the moment came and he sat up in the

Slumberking to write to the *Sentinel*, he used none of the phrases and sentences he had polished over the years. Instead, to his surprise, he found himself grateful to the paper for employing him for so long, for giving him a start in the city, equipping him for the Service.

He felt a fool when he received the editor's reply. In five lines he was thanked for his letter, his services were acknowledged, regret was expressed, and he was wished luck in his new job. The letter was typed by a secretary, whose smart lowercase initials were in the bottom left corner.

Working out his notice, he let the Destees slide, and prepared zestfully for his new job. He borrowed books from the Central Library and from the department's small collection. He began with books on sociology and immediately came to grief: he could not understand their charts or their language. He moved on to simpler paperbacked books about village reconstruction in India. These were more amusing: they gave pictures of village drains before and after, showed how chimneys could be built at no cost, how wells could be dug. They stimulated Mr Biswas to such a degree that for a few days he wondered whether he oughtn't to practise on the little community in his own house. A number of books laid a puzzling stress on the need for folk dances and folk singing during the carrying out of cooperative undertakings; some gave examples of songs. Mr Biswas saw himself leading a singing village as they cooperatively mended roads, cooperatively put up superhuts, cooperatively dug wells; singing, they harvested one another's fields. The picture didn't convince: he knew Indian villagers too well. Govind, for instance, sang, and W. C. Tuttle liked music; but Mr Biswas couldn't see himself leading them and the singing readers and learners to reconcrete the floor under the house, to plaster the half-walls, to build another bathroom or lavatory. He doubted whether he could even get them to sing. He read of cottage industries: romantic words, suggesting neatly clad peasants with grave classical features sitting at spinning wheels in cooperatively built superhuts and turning out yards and yards of cloth before going on to the folk singing and dancing under the village tree in the evening, by the light of flambeaux. But he knew what the villages were by night, when the rumshop emptied. He saw himself instead in a large timbered hall, walking up and down between lines of disciplined peasants making baskets. From cottage industries he was diverted by juvenile delinquency, which he found more appealing than adult delinquency. He particularly liked the photographs of the hardened delinquents: stunted, smoking, supercilious, and very attractive. He saw himself winning their confidence and then their eternal devotion. He read books on psychology and learned some technical words for the behaviour of Chinta when she flogged Vidiadhar.

Miss Logie, who had at first encouraged his enthusiasm, now attempted to control it. He saw her often during the month, and their relationship grew even better. Whenever she introduced him to anyone she spoke of him as her colleague, a graciousness he had never before experienced; and from being relaxed with her he became debonair.

Then he had a fright.

Miss Logie said she would like to meet his family.

Readers! Learners! Govind! Chinta! The Slumberking bed and the destitute's diningtable! And perhaps some widow might want to try again, and there would be a little tray of oranges or avocado pears outside the gate.

'Mumps,' he said.

It was partly true. The contagion had struck down Basdai's readers and learners wholesale, had attacked a little Tuttle; but it had not yet got to Mr Biswas's children.

'They are all down with mumps, I fear.'

And when later Miss Logie asked after the children, Mr Biswas had to say they had recovered, though they had in fact just succumbed.

Promptly at the end of the month the free delivery of the *Sentinel* stopped.

'Don't you think a little holiday before you begin would be refreshing?' Miss Logie said.

'I was thinking of that.' The words came out easily; they were in keeping with his new manner. And he saw himself condemned to a pay-less week among the readers and learners. 'Yes, a little holiday would be most refreshing.'

'Sans Souci would be very nice.'

Sans Souci was in the northeast of the island. Miss Logie, a newcomer, had been there; he had not.

'Yes,' he said. 'Sans Souci would be nice. Or Mayaro,' he added, trying to take an independent line by mentioning a resort in the southeast.

'I am sure your family would enjoy it.'

'You know, I believe they would.' Family again! He waited. And it came. She still wanted to meet them.

Poise deserted him. What could he suggest? Bringing them to the Red House one by one?

Miss Logie came to his rescue. She wondered whether they couldn't all go to Sans Souci on Sunday.

That at least was safer. 'Of course, of course,' he said. 'My wife can cook something. Where shall we meet?'

'I'll come and pick you up.'

He was caught.

'As a matter of fact I have taken a house in Sans Souci,' Miss Logie said. And then her plan came out. She wanted Mr Biswas to take his family there for a week. Transport was difficult, but the car would come for them at the end of the week. If Mr Biswas didn't go, the house would be empty, and that would be a waste.

He was overwhelmed. He had regarded his holidays simply as days on which he did not go to work; he had never thought that he might use the time to take his family to some resort: the thing was beyond ambition. Few people went on such holidays. There were no boarding-houses or hotels, only beach houses, and these he had always imagined to be expensive. And now this! After all those letters to destitutes beginning, *Dear Sir, Your letter awaited me on my return from holiday* . . .

He made objections, but Miss Logie was firm. He thought it better not to make a fuss, for he did not wish to give the impression that he was making the thing bigger than it was. Miss Logie had made the offer out of friendship; he would accept as a friend. He warned her, however, that he would have to consult Shama, and Miss Logie said she understood.

But he felt that he had been found out, that he had revealed more of himself to Miss Logie than he had thought; and this feeling was especially oppressive on the following morning when, after his bath in the outdoor bathroom, he stood before Shama's dressingtable in the inner room. In moods of self-disgust he hated dressing, and this morning he saw that his comb, which he had repeatedly insisted was his and his alone, was webbed with woman's hair. He broke the comb, broke another, and used language which went neither with his clothes nor with the manner he assumed when he put them on.

He reported to Miss Logie that Shama was delighted, and self-reproach was quickly forgotten when he and Shama began to prepare for the holiday. They were like conspirators. They had decided on secrecy. There was no reason for this except that it was one of the rules of the house: the Tuttles, for instance, had been unusually aloof just before the arrival of the naked torchbearer, and Chinta had been almost mournful before Govind had gone into threepiece suits.

On Saturday Shama began packing a hamper.

The secret could no longer be kept from the children. The laden hamper, the car, the drive to the seaside: it was something they knew too well. 'Vidiadhar and Shivadhar!' Chinta called. 'You just keep your little tails here, eh, and read your books, you hear. Your father is not in any position to take *you* for excursion, you hear. He not drawing money regular from the government, let me tell you.' The readers and learners stood around Shama while she packed the hamper. Shama, uncharacteristically stern and preoccupied, ignored them. Her manner suggested that the whole affair – as indeed she said to Basdai, the widow, who had come to watch and offer advice – was very troublesome, and she was going through with it simply to please the children and their father.

Their destination and length of the holiday had been disclosed. The manner of transportation was still kept secret: it was to be the final surprise. It also caused Mr Biswas much anxiety. All week he had been dreading the arrival of Miss Logie in her brand-new Buick. He intended the gap between her arrival and their departure to be as brief as possible. Under

no circumstances was she to be allowed to get out of the car.
For then she might go through the gate and get a glimpse of
what went on below the house; she might even go there. Or
she might go up the steps and knock on the front door; W. C.
Tuttle would come out, and heaven knows what pose he
would be in that morning: yogi, weight-lifter, pundit, lorry-
driver at rest. At all costs she had to be prevented from entering the front room and seeing the Slumberking where Mr
Biswas had lain and written his formal acceptance of the post
of Community Welfare Officer, seeing the destitute's diningtable still stacked with books on sociology, village reconstruction in India, cottage industries and juvenile delinquency.

Accordingly, although Miss Logie had said she would arrive at nine, the children were fed and dressed by eight, and
set up as sentinels by the gate. From time to time they
deserted their posts; then, after agitated search, they were ex-
tricated from groups of readers and learners or hurried out of
the lavatory. Shama was finding she had forgotten all sorts of
things: toothbrushes, towels, bottle-opener. Mr Biswas himself could not decide what book to take, and was in and out
of the front room. Eventually all was ready and they stood
strung out on the front steps, waiting to pounce. Mr Biswas
was dressed as for holiday: tieless, with Saturday's shirt bearing the impress of Saturday's tie, his coat over his arm and his
book in his hand. Shama was in her ornate visiting clothes;
she might have been going to a wedding.

Waiting, they were infiltrated by readers and learners.
'Haul your little tail,' Mr Biswas whispered savagely. 'Get
back inside. Go and comb your hair. And you, go and put on
some shoes.' A few of the younger were cowed; the older,
knowing that Mr Biswas had no rights, flogging or ordering,
over them, were openly contemptuous and, to Mr Biswas's
dismay, some went out on to the pavement, where they stood
like storks, jamming the sole of one foot against the smudged
and streaked pink-washed wall. The gramophone was playing
an Indian film song; Govind was whining out the *Ramayana*;
Chinta's scraping voice was raised querulously; Basdai was
shrilling after some of her girls to come and help with the
lunch.

Then the cries came. A green Buick had turned the corner. Mr Biswas and his family were down the steps with suitcases and hampers, Mr Biswas shouting angrily now to the readers and learners to get away.

When the car stopped, Mr Biswas and his family were standing right on the edge of the pavement. Miss Logie, sitting next to the chauffeur, smiled and gave a little wave, using fingers alone. She appeared to recognize what was required of her and did not get out of the car. Expressionlessly the chauffeur opened doors and stowed away suitcases and hampers in the boot.

W. C. Tuttle came out to the verandah, the lorry-driver at rest. His khaki shorts revealed round sturdy legs, and his white vest showed off a broad chest and large flabby arms. Leaning over the half-wall of the verandah, under the hanging ferns, he put a long finger delicately to one quivering nostril and, with a brief explosive noise, emitted some snot from the other nostril.

Mr Biswas chattered on in a daze, to divert attention from the readers and learners and W. C. Tuttle, to drown the noises from the house, the sudden piercing cry from Chinta, as from someone in agony: 'Vidiadhar and Shivadhar! Come back here this minute, if you don't want me to break your foot.'

Shy, interested readers and learners streamed steadily through the gate.

'There's lots of room,' Miss Logie said, smiling. 'It won't be a squeeze for long. I shan't be going all the way to Sans Souci. I don't feel very well and a day at the beach would be too much for me.'

Mr Biswas understood. 'Only these four,' he said. 'Only these four.' He kicked backwards in the direction of the readers and learners. The circle merely widened.

'Orphans,' Mr Biswas said.

Then mercifully they were off, some of the orphans racing the Buick a little way down the street.

They commiserated with Miss Logie on her indisposition and begged her to change her mind; there would be no pleasure for them if she did not come. She said she hadn't intended to go bathing at all; she had intended to come with them only for the ride. But presently, when it was established without doubt that there were only four children in the car and that there would be no stops for more, her resolution weakened and she said the fresh air had revived her a little and she would come with them after all.

When people stared from the road the children didn't know whether to smile, frown or look away; those who were near the straps held on to them. Never, as from the windows of that Buick, did North Trinidad look so beautiful. They noted, as though they had never seen it before from a bus, how the landscape changed, from marsh just outside Port of Spain, to straggling suburb, to hilly country, to country village, to country town, to rice fields and sugarcane fields, with the Northern Range always on their left. They drove along the smooth new American highway, were checked on entering and leaving the American army post by soldiers with helmets and rifles. Then they drove along a winding road overarched by cool trees to Arima, which welcomed careful drivers; and on to Valencia, where the road ran straight for miles, with untouched bush on either side.

They were, Anand reflected, driving with hampers – laden hampers – to the sea. The English composition had come true.

Mr Biswas was worried about Shama. Sitting plumply next to Miss Logie on the front seat, her elaborate georgette veil over her hair, Shama was showing herself self-possessed and even garrulous. She was throwing off opinions about the new constitution, federation, immigration, India, the future of Hinduism, the education of women. Mr Biswas listened to the flow with surprise and acute anxiety. He had never imagined that Shama was so well-informed and had such violent prejudices; and he suffered whenever she made a grammatical mistake.

They stopped at Balandra, and walked to the dangerous part of the bay where the waves were five feet high and a sign warned against bathing. Never had water seemed so blue; never had sand shone so golden; never had bay curved so beautifully, waves broken so neatly. It was a perfect world, the curve of the coconut trees repeated in the curve of the bay, the curl of the waves, the arc of the horizon. Already they could taste the salt on their lips. The fresh wind blew; the trousers of Mr Biswas and the chauffeur sausaged out; the women and girls held down their skirts.

They bathed where it was safe.

(And later Anand pointed out to Mr Biswas that in spite of what she had said Miss Logie had brought her bathing suit.)

They opened the hampers and ate on the dry sand in the dangerous shade of coconut trees ('Over a million coconuts will fall on the East Coast today,' had been the hollow bright opening of a feature he had written for the *Sentinel* on the copra industry).

Then they drove to Sans Souci, through narrow, ill-tended roads darkened by bush on both sides. Small villages surprised them here and there, lost and lonely. And now the sea was always with them. Unseen, it thundered continuously. The wind never ceased to rage through the trees; above the swaying bush, the dancing plumes of green, the sky was high and open. From time to time they had glimpses of the sea: so near, so unending, so alive, so impersonal. What would happen if, by some accident, they should drive off the road into it?

In a dream that night this accident was to happen, and Kamla was to wake gratefully, yet to find herself in a new dread, for she had forgotten the room where they had all gone to sleep, in the large bare house at the top of the hill, impenetrably black all round, with the sea beating a little distance away and the coconut trees groaning in the perpetual wind.

They had arrived in the late afternoon and had not had much time to explore. Miss Logie, the chauffeur and the Buick had gone back; and finding themselves alone, in a large house, on holiday, they had all grown shy with one another. Night brought an additional uneasiness. In the strange, musty, blank-walled drawingroom they sat around an oil lamp, the contents of the hamper gone stale and unappetizing, the cream cheese, bought from the Dairies the day before, already gone bad. The house was large enough for them to have had one room each; but the noise, the loneliness, the unknown surrounding blackness had kept them all in one room.

Wind and sea welcomed them in the morning. Light showed them where they were. The wind and the sea raged all night, but now they were both fresh, heralds of the new day. The children walked about the shining wet grass on the top of the hill; the sea, glimpsed through the tormented coconut trees, lay below them; their hands and faces became sticky with salt.

Their shyness slowly wore away. They went to deserted beaches, where lay the partly buried wrecks of strange trees brought across the sea. Beyond the wavering tidewrack the dimpled sand was pitted with the holes of sand crabs, small, nervous creatures the colour of sand. They made excursions to the places with French names: Blanchisseuse, Matelot; and to Toco and Salybia Bay. They picked almonds, sucked them, crushed the seeds; in land so wild and remote it was inconceivable that anything was owned by anyone. From trees that bordered the road they picked bright red cashew nuts, sucked the fruit and took the nuts to the house and roasted them. The days were long. Once they came upon a group of fishermen who were talking a French patois; once they met a group of well-dressed, noisy Indian youths, one of whom asked Myna what Savi's name was, and Mr Biswas saw that as a father he now had fresh responsibilities. In the evenings, with the noise of sea and wind, comforting now, around them, they played cards: they had found four packs in the house.

Another discovery, in a cupboard full of tinned food, was Cerebos Salt. They had never seen salt in tins. The shop salt they knew was coarse and damp; this was fine and dry, and ran as easily as the drawing on the tin showed.

They forgot the house in Port of Spain and spread themselves about the house on the hill. It seemed there was no one in the world but themselves, nothing alive but themselves and the sea and the wind. They had been told that on a clear day they could see Tobago; but that never happened.

And then the Buick came for them.

As they drove back to Port of Spain the new shy pleasure they had found in being alone was forgotten. They were preparing for the two rooms, the city pavements, the badly concreted floor under the house, the noise, the quarrels. On the way out they had feared arrival, a casting off into the unknown; now they dreaded returning to what they knew. But they spoke of other things. Shama spoke about the evening meal, remembered she had nothing. The car stopped at a shop in the Eastern Main Road and they enjoyed a brief distinction as the occupants of a chauffeur-driven car.

There was no reception for them in Port of Spain. It was evening. The readers and learners were reading and learning. Everything was as they had left it: the weak light bulbs, the long tables, the chanting of some readers as they attempted to learn lessons by heart. Only, the house seemed lower, darker, suffocating. At first they were ignored. But presently the questioning began, the prying to see whether any disaster had befallen, for the sadness with which they had returned had already made them irritable and short-tempered.

Did the wilderness really exist? Was the house still at the top of the hill? Was the wind still making the coconut trees groan? Did the sea beat on those empty beaches? Was it at that moment of night bringing to shore those black berries, branches and strands of seaweed from miles and thoughtless miles away?

They fell asleep with the roar of wind and sea in their heads. In the morning they woke to the humming house.

Mr Biswas did not immediately superintend lines of peasants making baskets. No one sang for him. And he encouraged no one to build better huts or to take up cottage industries. He began to survey an area, and went from house to house filling in questionnaires prepared by Miss Logie. Most of the people he interviewed were flattered. Some were puzzled: 'Who send you? Government? Think they really care?' Some were more than puzzled: 'You mean they paying you for this? Just to find out how we does live. But I could tell them for nothing, man.' Mr Biswas hinted that there was more to the survey than they thought; pressed, he had to bluff. It was like interviewing destitutes; only there was no money for anyone except himself at the end. And he was doing well. In addition to his salary he could claim subsistence and travel allowances; and on many evenings he had to lay aside his books and work out his claims. He filled in a form, submitted it, and after a few days got a voucher. He took the voucher to the Treasury and exchanged it with a man behind a zoo-like cage for another voucher which was limp with handling and ticked, initialled, signed and stamped in various colours. This he exchanged at another cage, this time for real money. It took time, but these trips to the Treasury made him feel that he was at last getting at the wealth of the colony.

He found that the extra money could be spent in any of a number of new ways, and he did not save as much as he had hoped. Savi had to be sent to a better school; their food had to be improved; something had to be done about Anand's asthma. And he decided, and Shama agreed, that it was time he got himself some new suits, to go with his new job.

Apart from the serge suit in which he had gone to funerals, he had never had a proper suit, only cheap things of silk and linen; and he ordered his new suits with love. He discovered he was a dandy. He fussed about the quality and tone of the cloth, the cut of the suits. He enjoyed fittings: the baked smell of the white-tacked cloth, the tailor's continual reverential destruction of his own work. When the first suit was ready he decided to wear it right away. It pricked his calves unpleasantly; it had a new smell; and when he looked down at himself the cascade of brown appeared grotesque and alarming. But the mirror reassured him, and he felt the need to show off the suit without delay. There was an inter-colonial cricket match at the Oval. He did not understand the game, but he knew that there was always a crowd at these matches, that shops and schools closed for them.

It was the fashion at the time for men to appear on sporting occasions with a round tin of fifty English cigarettes and a plain box of matches held in one hand, the forefinger pressing the matchbox to the top of the tin. Mr Biswas had the matches; he used half a day's subsistence allowance to buy the cigarettes. Not wishing to derange the hang of his jacket, he cycled to the Oval with the tin in his hand.

As he came along Tragarete Road he heard faint scattered applause. It was just before lunch, too early for the crowds; it would have been better after tea. Nevertheless he cycled round to the stands side of the Oval, leaned his bicycle against the peeling corrugated iron fence, chained it, removed the clips from his carefully folded trousers, shook down the trousers, smoothed out the pleats, straightened the prickly jacket over his shoulders. There was no queue. He paid a dollar for his ticket and, holding his tin of cigarettes and box of matches, walked up the stairs to the stand. It was less than a quarter full. Most of the people were at the front. He spied an empty seat in the middle of one of the few packed rows.

'Excuse me,' he said, and started on a slow progress down the row, people rising before him, people rising in the row behind, people settling down again in his wake, and 'Excuse me,' he kept on saying, quite urbane, unaware of the disturbance. At last he came to his seat, dusted it with a handkerchief, stooping slightly in response to a request from someone behind. While he unbuttoned his jacket a burst of applause came from all. Absently casting a glance at the cricket field, Mr Biswas applauded. He sat down, hitched up his trousers, crossed his legs, operated the cutter on the lid of the cigarette tin, extracted a cigarette and lit it. There was a tremendous burst of applause. Everyone in the stand stood up. Chairs scraped backwards, some overturned. Mr Biswas rose and clapped with the others. What crowd there was had advanced on to the field; the cricketers were racing away, flitting blobs of white. The stumps had disappeared; the umpires, separated by the crowd, were walking sedately to the pavilion. The match was over. Mr Biswas did not inspect the pitch. He went outside, unlocked his bicycle and cycled home, holding the tin of cigarettes in his hand.

His one suit, hanging out to sun on Shama's line in the backyard, did not make much of a showing against Govind's five threepiece suits on Chinta's line, which had to be supported by two pronged poles. But it was a beginning.

The interviews completed, it was Mr Biswas's duty to analyze the information he had gathered. And here he floundered. He had investigated two hundred households; but after every classification he could never, on adding, get two hundred, and then he had to go through all the questionnaires again. He was dealing with a society that had no rules and patterns, and classifications were a chaotic business. He covered many sheets with long, snakelike addition sums, and the Slumberking was spread with his questionnaires. He pressed Shama and the children into service, damned them for their incompetence, dismissed them, and worked late into the night, squatting on a chair before the diningtable. The table was too high; sitting on pillows had proved unsatisfactory; so he squatted. Sometimes he threatened to cut down the legs of the diningtable by half and cursed the destitute who had made it.

'This blasted thing is getting me sick,' he shouted, whenever Shama and Anand tried to get him to go to bed. 'Getting me sick, I tell you. *Sick*. I don't know why the hell I didn't stay with my little destitutes.'

'Everywhere you go, is the same,' Shama said.

He did not tell her of his deeper fears. Already the department was under attack. Citizen, Taxpayer, Pro Bono Publico and others had written to the newspapers to ask exactly what the department was doing and to protest against the waste of taxpayers' money. The party of Southern businessmen to which Shekhar belonged had started a campaign for the abolition of the department: a distinguishing cause, long sought, for no party had a programme, though all had the same objective: to make everyone in the colony rich and equal.

This was Mr Biswas's first experience of public attack, and it did not console him that such letters had always been written, that the government in all its departments was being continually criticized by all the island's parties. He dreaded opening the newspapers. Pro Bono Publico had been particularly nasty: he had written the same letter to all three papers, and there was a whole fortnight between the letter's first appearance and its last. Nor did it console Mr Biswas that no one else appeared to be worried. Shama considered the government unshakable; but she was Shama. Miss Logie could always go back to where she came from. The other officers had been seconded from various government departments and they could go back to where they came from. He could only go back to the *Sentinel* and fifty dollars a month less.

He was glad he had written a mild letter of resignation. And, preparing for misfortune, he took to dropping in at the *Sentinel* office. The newspaper atmosphere never failed to excite him, and the welcome he received stilled his fears: he was regarded as one who had escaped and made good. Yet with every improvement in his condition, every saving, he felt more vulnerable: it was too good to last.

In time he completed his charts (to display the classifications clearly he joined three double foolscap sheets and produced a scroll nearly five feet long, which made Miss Logie roar with laughter); and he wrote his report. Charts and report were typed and duplicated and, he was told, sent to various parts of the world. Then he was at last free to get villagers to sing or to take up cottage industries. He was given an area. And a memorandum informed him that, to enable him to move easily about his area, he was to be given a car, on a painless government loan.

The rule of the house was followed again. The children were sworn to secrecy. Mr Biswas brought home glossy booklets which had the aromatic smell of rich art paper and seemed to hold the smell of the new car. Secretly he took driving lessons and obtained a driving licence. Then, on a perfectly ordinary Saturday morning, he drove to the house in a brand-new Prefect, parked it casually before the gate, not quite parallel to the pavement, and walked up the front steps, ignoring the excitement that had broken out.

'Vidiadhar! Come back here this minute, if you don't want me to break your hand and your foot.'

When Govind arrived at lunchtime he found his parking space occupied. His Chevrolet was larger, but old and unwashed; the mudguards had been dented, cut, welded; one door had been ducoed in a lustreless colour that did not exactly match; there was the H – for hire – on the number plate; and the windscreen was made ugly by various stickers and a circular plaque which carried Govind's photograph and taxi-driver's permit.

'Matchbox,' Govind muttered. 'Who leave this matchbox here?'

He did not impress the orphans, and he did not diminish the energy of Mr Biswas's children who, ever since the car had been so carelessly parked by Mr Biswas, had been wiping away dust and saying crossly how a new car collected dust. They found dust everywhere: on the body, the springs, the underside of the mudguards. They wiped and polished and discovered, with distress, that they were leaving scratches on the paintwork, very slight, but visible from certain angles. Myna reported this to Mr Biswas.

He was lying on the Slumberking, surrounded by many glossy booklets. He asked, 'You hear anything? What they saying, eh?'

'Govind say it is a matchbox.'

'Matchbox, eh. English car, you know. Would last for years and still be running when his Chevrolet is on the rubbish dump.'

He returned to studying an intricate drawing in red and black which explained the wiring of the car. He could not fully understand it, but it was his habit whenever he bought anything new, whether a pair of shoes or a bottle of patent medicine, to read all the literature provided.

Kamla came into the room and said that the orphans had been fingering the car and blurring the shine.

Mr Biswas knelt on the bed and advanced on his knees to the front window. He lifted the curtain and, pushing a vested chest outside, shouted, 'You! Boy! Leave the car alone! You think is a taxi?'

The orphans scattered.

'I coming to break the hands of some of you,' Basdai, the guardian widow, called. News of her advance and her pause to break a whip from the neem tree at the side of the yard was relayed by hoots and shouts and giggles. Some orphans, disdaining to run, were flogged on the pavement. There was crying, and Basdai said, 'Well, *some* people satisfy now.'

Shama stayed under the house and did not go out to see the car. And when Suniti, the former contortionist, now baby-swollen, who often stopped at the house on her way to and from Shorthills after quarrels and reconciliations with her husband, and attempted to shock by talk of getting a divorce, and wore ugly and unsuitable frocks as a mark of her modernity, when Suniti came to Shama and said, 'So, Aunt, you come a big-shot now. Car and thing, man!' Shama said, 'Yes, my child,' as though the car was another of Mr Biswas's humiliating excesses. But she had begun to prepare another hamper.

There was no need for Mr Biswas to ask where they wanted to go. They all wanted to go to Balandra, to repeat the experience of delight: the drive in the private car, the hampers, the beach.

They went to Balandra, but it was a different experience. They did not attend to the landscape. They savoured the smell of new leather, the sweet smell of a new car. They listened to the soft, steady beat of the engine and compared it with the grinding and pounding of the vehicles they met. And they listened acutely for wrong noises. The grilled cover of an ashtray on one door did not sit properly and tinkled distractingly; they attempted to stop it with a matchstick. The ignition key had already been provided by Mr Biswas with a chain. The chain struck the dashboard. That distracted them too. At one moment it looked as though it might rain; a few drops flecked the windshield. Anand promptly put the wiper on. 'You'll scratch the glass!' Mr Biswas cried. They worried about putting their shoes on the floormats. They consulted the dashboard clock constantly, comparing it with those they saw on the road. They marvelled at the working of the speedometer.

'Man was telling me,' Mr Biswas said, 'that these Prefect clocks go wrong in no time.'

And they decided to call in on Ajodha.

They parked the car in the road and walked around the house to the back verandah. Tara was in the kitchen. Ajodha was reading the *Sunday Guardian*. Mr Biswas said they were going to the beach and had just dropped in for a minute. There was a pause, and each of them wondered whether they should tell.

Ajodha commented on the sickliness of them all, pinched Anand's arms and laughed when the boy winced.

Then, as though to cure them at once, he made them drink glasses of fresh milk and had the servant girl peel some oranges from the bag in the corner of the verandah.

Jagdat came in, his funeral clothes relieved by his broad, bright tie, his unbuttoned cuffs folded back above hairy wrists. He asked jocularly, 'Is your car outside, Mohun?'

The children studied their glasses of milk.

Mr Biswas said gently, 'Yes, man.'

Jagdat roared as at a good joke. 'The old Mohun, man!'

'Car?' Ajodha said, puzzled, petulant. 'Mohun?'

'A little Prefect,' Mr Biswas said.

'Some of those pre-war English cars can be very good,' Ajodha said.

'This is a new one,' Mr Biswas said. 'Got it yesterday.'

'Cardboard.' Ajodha bunched his fingers. 'It will mash like cardboard.'

'A drive, man, Mohun!' Jagdat said.

The children, Shama, were alarmed. They looked at Mr Biswas, Jagdat smiling, slapping his hands together.

Mr Biswas was aware of their alarm.

'You are right, Mohun,' Ajodha said. 'He will lick it up.'

'It isn't that,' Mr Biswas said. 'Seaside.' He looked at his Cyma watch. Then, noticing that Jagdat had stopped smiling, he added, 'Running in, you know.'

'I run in more cars than you,' Jagdat said angrily. 'Bigger and better.'

'He will lick it up,' Ajodha repeated.

'It isn't that,' Mr Biswas said again.

'Hear him,' Jagdat said. 'But don't give me that, eh, man. Listen. I was driving motorcars before you even learn to drive a donkey-cart. Look at me. You think I pining to drive in your sardine can? You think that?'

Mr Biswas looked embarrassed.

The children didn't mind. The car was safe.

*'Mohun! You think that?'*

At Jagdat's scream the children jumped.

'Jagdat,' Tara said.

He strode out of the verandah into the yard, cursing.

'I know what it is, Mohun,' Ajodha said. 'The first time you get a car is always the same.' He waved at his yard, the graveyard of many vehicles.

He went out with them to the road. When he saw the Prefect he hooted.

'Six horse power?' he said. 'Eight?'

'Ten,' Anand said, pointing to the red disc below the bonnet.

'Yes, ten.' He turned to Shama. 'Well, niece, where are you going in your new car?'

'Balandra.'

'I hope the wind doesn't blow too hard.'

'Wind, Uncle?'

'Or you will never get there. Poof! Blow you off the road, man.'

They continued in gloom for some way.

'Wanting to drive my car,' Mr Biswas said. 'As if I would let him. I know the way he does drive cars. Lick them up in no time at all. No respect for them. And getting vexed into the bargain, I ask you.'

'I always say you have some low people in your family,' Shama said.

'Another man wouldn't even ask a thing like that,' Mr Biswas said. '*I* wouldn't ask it. Feel how the car sitting nice on the road? Feel it, Anand? Savi?'

'Yes, Pa.'

'Poof! Blow me off the road. You wouldn't expect an old man like that to be jealous, eh? But that is exactly what he is. Jealous.'

Yet whenever they saw another Prefect on the road they could not help noticing how small and fussy it looked; and this was strange, for their own car enclosed them securely and did not feel small in any way. They continued to listen for noises. Anand held the chain of the ignition key to keep it from striking the dashboard. When they stopped at Balandra they made sure the car was parked away from coconut trees; and they worried about the effect of the salt air on the body.

Disaster came when they were leaving. The rear wheels sank into the hot loose sand. They watched the wheels spinning futilely, kicking up sand, and felt that the car had been irremediably damaged. They pushed coconut branches and coconut shells and bits of driftwood under the wheels and at last got the car out. Shama said she was convinced that the car now leaned to one side; the whole body, she said, had been strained.

On Monday Anand cycled to school on the Royal Enfield, and the promise in the *Collins Clear-Type Shakespeare* was thereby partly fulfilled. War conditions had at last permitted; in fact, the war had been over for some time.

And during all this time W. C. Tuttle had remained quiet. He had not attempted to reply to Mr Biswas's new suits, the new car, the holiday; so that it seemed that these reverses, coming one after the other, had been too much for him. But when the glory of the Prefect began to fade, when it was accepted that floormats became dirty, when washing the car became a chore and was delegated by the children to Shama, when the dashboard clock stopped and no one noticed the tinkle of the ashtray lid, W. C. Tuttle with one stroke wiped out all Mr Biswas's advantages, and killed the rivalry by rising above it.

Through Basdai, the widow, he announced that he had bought a house in Woodbrook.

Mr Biswas took the news badly. He neglected Shama's consolations and picked quarrels with her. ' "What is for you is for you",' he mocked. 'So that is your philosophy, eh? I'll tell you what your philosophy is. Catch him. Marry him. Throw him in a coal barrel. That is the philosophy of your family. Catch him and throw him in a coal barrel.' He became acutely sensitive to criticism of the Community Welfare Department. The books on social work and juvenile delinquency gathered dust on the diningtable, and he returned to his philosophers. The Tuttles' gramophone played with infuriating gaiety, and he banged on the partition and shouted, 'Some people still living here, you know.'

Philosophically, he attempted to look on the brighter side. The garage problem would be simplified: with three vehicles the position had become impossible, and he had often had to leave his car on the road. There would be no gramophone. And he might even rent the rooms the Tuttles were vacating.

But the days passed and the Tuttles didn't move.

'Why the hell doesn't he take up his gramophone and naked woman and clear out?' Mr Biswas asked Shama. '*If* he got this house.'

Basdai came up with fresh information. The house was full of tenants, and W. C. Tuttle, for all his calm, was at that moment engaged in tortuous litigation to get them out.

'Oh,' Mr Biswas said. 'Is *that* sort of house.' He imagined one of those rotting warrens he had visited when investigating destitutes. And now at one moment Mr Biswas wished W. C. Tuttle out of the house immediately and at another moment wanted him to fail in his litigation. 'Throwing those poor people out. Where they going to live, eh? But your family don't care about things like that.'

One morning Mr Biswas saw W. C. Tuttle leaving the house in a suit, tie and hat. And that afternoon Basdai reported that litigation had failed.

'I thought he was going to Ace Studios to take out another photo,' Mr Biswas said.

Overjoyed, he did what he had so far resisted doing: he drove to see the house. To his disappointment he found that it was in a good area, on a whole lot: a sound, oldfashioned timber building that needed only a coat of paint.

Not long after Basdai reported that the tenants were leaving. W. C. Tuttle had persuaded the City Council that the house was dangerous and had to be repaired, if not pulled down altogether.

'Any old trick to throw the poor people out,' Mr Biswas said. 'Though I suppose with ten fat Tuttles jumping about no house could be safe. Repairs, eh? Just drive the old lorry down to Shorthills and cut down a few more trees, I suppose.'

'That is exactly what he is doing,' Shama said, affronted at the piracy.

'You want to know why I can't get on in this place? That is why.' And even as he spoke he recognized that he was sounding like Bhandat in the concrete room.

The Tuttles left without ceremony. Only Mrs Tuttle, braving the general antagonism, kissed her sisters and those of the children she found in the way. She was sad but stern, and her manner suggested that though she had nothing to do with it, her husband's piracy was justified and she was ready for trouble. Cowed, the sisters could only be sad in their turn, and the leave-taking was as tearful as if Mrs Tuttle had just been married.

Mr Biswas's hopes of renting the rooms the Tuttles had vacated were dashed when it was announced that Mrs Tulsi was coming from Shorthills to take them over. The news cast a gloom over the whole house. Her daughters now accepted that Mrs Tulsi's active life was finished, that only death awaited her. But she still controlled them all in varying ways, and her caprices had to be endured. Miserable herself, Basdai made the readers and learners miserable by threats of what Mrs Tulsi would do to them.

She came with Sushila, the sickroom widow, and Miss Blackie; and at once the house became quieter. The readers and learners were quelled, but Mrs Tulsi's presence brought them an unexpected advantage: they knew that if they howled loud enough beforehand they would be spared floggings.

Mrs Tulsi had no precise illness. She was simply ill. Her eyes ached; her heart was bad; her head always hurt; her stomach was fastidious; her legs were unreliable; and every other day she had a temperature. Her head had continually to be soaked in bay rum; she had to be massaged once a day; she needed poultices of various sorts. Her nostrils were stuffed with soft candle or Vick's Vaporub; she wore dark glasses; and she was seldom without a bandage around her forehead. Sushila was kept on the go all day. At Hanuman House Sushila had sought to gain power by being Mrs Tulsi's nurse; now that the organization of the house had been broken up, the position carried no power, but Sushila was bound to it, and she had no children to rescue her.

Time hung heavily on Mrs Tulsi's hands. She did not read. The radio offended her. She was never well enough to go

out. She moved from her room to the lavatory to the front
verandah to her room. Her only solace was talk. Daughters
were always at hand, but talk with them seemed only to en-
rage her; and as her body decayed so her command of invective and obscenity developed. Her rages fell oftenest on
Sushila, whom she ordered out of the house once a week. She
cried out that her daughters were all waiting for her to die,
that they were sucking her blood; she pronounced curses on
them and their children, and threatened to expel them from
the family.

'I have no luck with my family,' she told Miss Blackie. 'I
have no luck with my race.'

And it was Miss Blackie who received her confidences,
Miss Blackie who reported and comforted. And there was the
Jewish refugee doctor. He came once a week and listened.
The house was always specially prepared for him, and Mrs
Tulsi treated him with love. He resurrected all that remained
of her softness and humour. When he left, she said to Miss
Blackie, 'Never trust your race, Black. Never trust them.'
And Miss Blackie said, 'No'm.' Gifts of fruit were sent regu-
larly to the doctor and sometimes Mrs Tulsi would suddenly
order Basdai and Sushila to prepare an elaborate meal and take
it to the doctor's house, treating the matter as one of urgency,
as though she was satisfying some craving of her own.

Still her daughters came to the house. They knew they all
had some small hold on her: they knew that she feared loneliness and never wished to push them beyond her reach; they
knew they could hurt her by staying away. If Miss Blackie
reported that one daughter had been particularly upset, then
Mrs Tulsi made overtures, and made promises. In such moods
she might give a piece of jewellery, she might take off a ring
or a bracelet and give it. So the daughters came, and none was
willing to let Mrs Tulsi be alone with any other. The visits of
Mrs Tuttle were especially distrusted. She bore abuse with
unexampled patience and was able at the end to suggest that
Mrs Tulsi should look at plants, because green nourished the
eyes and soothed the nerves.

Though she abused her daughters, she took care not to
offend her sons-in-law. She greeted Mr Biswas briefly but

politely. And she never attempted to remonstrate with Govind, who continued to behave as before. He beat Chinta when the mood took him, and, ignoring pleas for silence for Mrs Tulsi's headaches, sang from the *Ramayana*. It was left to the sisters to comment on Govind's behaviour.

There were times when she wished to have children about her. Then she summoned the readers and learners to scrub the floor of the drawingroom and verandah, or she made them sing Hindi hymns. Her mood changed without warning, and the readers and learners were perpetually apprehensive, never knowing whether they were required to be solemn or amusing. Sometimes she stood them in lines in her room and made them recite arithmetic tables, flogging the inaccurate with as much vigour as her arms would allow, flabby, muscleless arms, broad and loose towards the armpit, and swinging like dead flesh. Miss Blackie burst into squelchy laughter when a child made a stupid mistake or when Mrs Tulsi made a witticism; and Mrs Tulsi, her eyes masked by dark glasses, would give a pleased, crooked smile. In sterner moments Miss Blackie grew stern as well and moved her jaws up and down quickly, saying 'Mm!' at every blow Mrs Tulsi gave.

Another trial for the readers and learners was Mrs Tulsi's concern for their health. Every five Saturdays or so she called them to her room and dosed them with Epsom salts; and between these gloomy, wasted week-ends she listened for coughs and sneezes. There was no escaping her. She had learned to recognize every voice, every laugh, every footstep, every cough and almost every sneeze. She took a special interest in Anand's wheeze and doglike cough. She bought him some poisonous herb cigarettes; when these had no effect she prescribed brandy and water and gave him a bottle of brandy. Anand, while hating the brandy and water, drank it for its literary associations: he had read of the mixture in Dickens.

Sometimes she sent for old friends from Arwacas. They came and camped for a week or so, and listened to Mrs Tulsi. She, refreshed, talked all day and late into the night, while the friends, lying on bedding on the floor, made drowsy mechanical affirmations: 'Yes, Mother. Yes, Mother.' Some visits were cut short by illness, some by carefully documented dreams of bad omen; those visitors who stayed to the end went away fatigued, doped, bleary-eyed.

Regularly too, she had *pujas*, austere rites aimed at God alone, without the feasting and gaiety of the Hanuman House ceremonies. The pundit came and Mrs Tulsi sat before him; he read from the scriptures, took his money, changed in the bathroom and left. More and more prayer flags went up in the yard, the white and red pennants fluttering until they were ragged, the bamboo poles going yellow, brown, grey. For every *puja* Mrs Tulsi tried a different pundit, since no pundit could please her as well as Hari. And, no pundit pleasing her, her faith yielded. She sent Sushila to burn candles in the Roman Catholic church; she put a crucifix in her room; and she had Pundit Tulsi's grave cleaned for All Saints' Day.

The more she was recommended not to exert herself the less she was able to exert herself, until she appeared to live only for her illness. She became obsessed with the decay of her body, and finally wanted the girls to search her head for lice. No louse could have survived the hourly dousing with bay rum which her head received, but she was enraged when the girls found nothing. She called them liars, pinched them, pulled their hair. Sometimes she was only hurt; then she shuffled out to the verandah and sat, taking her veil to her lips, feeding her eyes on the green, as Mrs Tuttle had recommended. She would speak to no one, refuse to eat, reject all care. She would sit, feeding her eyes on the green, the tears running down her slack cheeks below her dark glasses.

Of all hands she liked Myna's best. She wanted Myna to search her head for lice, wanted Myna to kill them, wanted to hear them being squashed between Myna's fingernails. This preference created some jealousy, upset Myna, annoyed Mr Biswas.

'Don't go and pick her damn lice,' Mr Biswas said.

'Don't worry with your father,' Shama said, unwilling to lose this unexpected hold over Mrs Tulsi.

And Myna went and spent hours in Mrs Tulsi's room, her slender fingers exploring every strand of Mrs Tulsi's thin, grey, bay-rum-scented hair. From time to time, to satisfy Mrs

Tulsi, Myna clicked her fingernails, and Mrs Tulsi swallowed
and said, 'Ah,' pleased that one of her lice had been caught.

An additional constraint came upon the house when
Shekhar and his family paid one of their visits to Mrs Tulsi. If
Shekhar had come alone he would have been more warmly
welcomed by his sisters. But the antagonism between them
and Shekhar's Presbyterian wife Dorothy had deepened as
Shekhar had prospered and Dorothy's Presbyterianism had
become more assertive and excluding. There had almost been
an open quarrel when Shekhar, approached by the widows
for a loan to start a mobile restaurant, had offered them jobs
in his cinemas instead. They regarded this as an insult and saw
in it the hand of Dorothy. Of course they refused: they did
not care to be employed by Dorothy and they would never
work in a place of public entertainment.

Shekhar could never appear as more than a visitor. He
came in his car, led his wife and five elegant daughters
upstairs, and for a long time nothing was heard except occasional footsteps and Mrs Tulsi's low voice going evenly on.
Then Shekhar came downstairs by himself, forbiddingly correct in white short sleeved sports shirt and white slacks. Having listened to his mother, he now listened to his sisters,
staring them in the eye and saying, 'Hm – hm,' his top lip
hanging over his lower lip and almost concealing it. He spoke
little, as though unwilling to disturb the set of his mouth. His
words came out abruptly, his expression never changed, and
everything he said seemed to have an edge. When he tried to
be friendly with the readers and learners he only frightened
them. Yet he never appeared unkind; only preoccupied.

After lunch, prepared by Basdai and Sushila and eaten upstairs, Dorothy and her daughters passed downstairs, Dorothy
booming out her greetings, her daughters remaining close
together and speaking in fine, almost inaudible voices. Then
Dorothy would look at her watch and say, '*Caramba! Ya son
las tres. Dónde está tu Padre? Lena, va a llamarle. Vamos, vamos.
Es demasiado tarde.* Well, all right, people,' she would say,
turning to the outraged sisters and the wondering readers and
learners, 'we got to go.' Since they had taken to spending
holidays in Venezuela and Colombia, Dorothy used Spanish

when she spoke to her children or to Shekhar in the presence
of her sisters-in-law. Later the sisters agreed that Shekhar was
to be pitied; they had all noted his unhappiness.

Before they left, Shekhar and Dorothy always called on Mr
Biswas. Mr Biswas did not relish these calls. It wasn't only that
Shekhar's party was campaigning against the Community
Welfare Department. Shekhar had never forgotten that Mr
Biswas was a clown, and whenever they met he tried to provoke an act of clowning. He made a belittling remark, and Mr
Biswas was expected to extend this remark wittily and fanci-
fully. To Mr Biswas's fury, Dorothy had also adopted this
attitude; and from this relationship there was no escape, since
anger and retaliation were counted parts of the game. Shekhar
came into the front room and asked in his brusque, humour-
less manner, 'Is the welfare officer still well-fed?' Then he
hoisted himself on to the destitute's diningtable and threatened Mr Biswas with the destruction of the department and
joblessness. For a time Mr Biswas responded in his old way.
He told stories about civil servants, spoke of the trouble he
had making up his expense sheets, the work he had looking
for work. But soon he made his annoyance plain. 'You take
these things too personally,' Shekhar said, still playing the
game. 'Our differences are only political. You've got to be a
little more sophisticated, man.' 'Be a little more sophisticated,' Mr Biswas said, when Shekhar left. 'On a hungry belly?
The old scorpion. Wouldn't care a damn if I lose my job
tomorrow.'

For some time there had been rumours. And now at last
the news was given out: Owad, Mrs Tulsi's younger son, was
returning from England. Everyone was excited. Sisters came
up from Shorthills in their best clothes to talk over the news.
Owad was the adventurer of the family. Absence had turned
him into a legend, and his glory was undiminished by the
numbers of students who were leaving the colony every week
to study medicine in England, America, Canada and India.
His exact attainments were not known, but were felt by all to
be extraordinary and almost beyond comprehension. He was
a doctor, a professional man, with letters after his name! And

he belonged to them! They could no longer claim Shekhar.
But every sister had a story which proved how close she had
been to Owad, what regard he had had for her.

Mr Biswas felt as proprietary as the sisters towards Owad
and shared their excitement. But he was uneasy. Once, many
years before, he had felt that he had to leave Hanuman House
before Owad and Mrs Tulsi returned to it. Now he experienced the same unease: the same sense of threat, the same
need to leave before it was too late. Over and over he
checked the money he had saved, the money he was going to
save. His additions appeared on cigarette packets, in the margins of newspapers, on the backs of buff government folders.
The sum never varied: he had six hundred and twenty dollars;
by the end of the year he would have seven hundred. It was
a staggering sum, more than he had ever possessed all at once.
But it couldn't attract a loan to buy any house other than one
of those wooden tenements that awaited condemnation. At
two thousand dollars or so they were bargains, but only for
speculators who could take the tenants to court, rebuild, or
wait for the site to rise in value. Now, his anxiety growing
with the excitement about him, Mr Biswas scanned agents'
lists every morning and drove about the city looking for
places to rent. When for one whole week the City Council bought pages and pages in the newspapers to serialize the
list of houses it was putting up for auction because their rates
had not been paid, Mr Biswas turned up at the Town Hall
with all the city's estate agents; but he lacked the confidence
to bid.

He could not avoid Mrs Tulsi when he returned to the
house. She sat in the verandah, feeding her eyes on the green,
patting her lips with her veil.

And though he had nerved himself for the blow, he grew
frantic when it came.

It was Shama who brought the message.

'The old bitch can't throw me out like that,' Mr Biswas
said. 'I still have some rights. She has got to provide me with
alternative accommodation.' And: 'Die, you bitch!' he hissed
towards the verandah. 'Die!'

'Man!'

'Die! Sending poor little Myna to pick her lice. That did you any good? Eh? Think she would throw out the little god like that? O no. The god must have a room to himself. You and me and my children can sleep in sugarsacks. The Tulsi sleeping-bag. Patents applied for. Die, you old bitch!'

They heard Mrs Tulsi mumbling placidly to Sushila.

'I have my rights,' Mr Biswas said. 'This is not like the old days. You can't just stick a piece of paper on my door and throw me out. Alternative accommodation, if you please.'

But Mrs Tulsi had provided alternative accommodation: a room in one of the tenements whose rents Shama had collected years before. The wooden walls were unpainted, grey-black, rotting; at every step on the patched, shaky floor wood dust excavated by woodlice showered down; there was no ceiling and the naked galvanized roof was fluffy with soot; there was no electricity. Where would the furniture go? Where would they sleep, cook, wash? Where would the children study?

He vowed never to talk to Mrs Tulsi again; and she, as though sensing his resolve, did not speak to him. Morning after morning he went from house to house, looking for rooms to rent, until he was exhausted, and exhaustion burned out his anger. Then in the afternoons he drove to his area, where he stayed until evening.

Returning late one night to the house, which seemed to him more and more ordered and sheltering, he saw Mrs Tulsi sitting in the verandah in the dark. She was humming a hymn, softly, as though she were alone, removed from the world. He did not greet her, and was passing into his room when she spoke.

'Mohun?' Her voice was groping, amiable.

He stopped.

'Mohun?'

'Yes, Mother.'

'How is Anand? I haven't heard his cough these last few days.'

'He's all right.'

'Children, children. Trouble, trouble. But do you remember how Owad used to work? Eating and reading. Helping in the store and reading. Checking money and reading. Helping head and head with everybody else, and still reading. You remember Hanuman House, Mohun?'

He recognized her mood, and did not wish to be seduced by it. 'It was a big house. Bigger than the place we are going to.'

She was unruffled. 'Did they show you Owad's letter?'

Those of Owad's letters which went the rounds were mainly about English flowers and the English weather. They were semi-literary, and were in a large handwriting with big spaces between the words and big gaps between the lines. 'The February fogs have at last gone,' Owad used to write, 'depositing a thick coating of black on every window-sill. The snowdrops have come and gone, but the daffodils will be here soon. I planted six daffodils in my tiny front garden. Five have grown. The sixth appears to be a failure. My only hope is that they will not turn out to be blind, as they were last year.'

'He never took much interest in flowers when he was a boy,' Mrs Tulsi said.

'I suppose he was too busy reading.'

'He always liked you, Mohun. I suppose that was because you were a big reader yourself. I don't know. Perhaps I should have married all my daughters to big readers. Owad always said that. But Seth, you know –' She stopped; it was the first time he had heard her speak the name for years. 'The old ways have become oldfashioned so quickly, Mohun. I hear that you are looking for a house.'

'I have my eye on something.'

'I am sorry about the inconvenience. But we have to get the house ready for Owad. It isn't his father's house, Mohun. Wouldn't it be nice if he could come back to his father's house?'

'Very nice.'

'You wouldn't like the smell of paint. And it's dangerous too. We are putting up some awnings and louvres here and there. Modern things.'

'It sounds very nice.'

'Really for Owad. Though I suppose it would be nice for you to come back to.'

'Come back to?'

'Aren't you coming back?'

'But yes,' he said, and couldn't keep the eagerness out of his voice. 'Yes, of course. Louvres would be very nice.'

Shama was elated at the news.

'I never did believe,' she said, 'that Ma did want us to stay away for good.' She spoke of Mrs Tulsi's regard for Myna, her gift of brandy to Anand.

'God!' Mr Biswas said, suddenly offended. 'So you've got the reward for lice-picking? You're sending back Myna to pick some more, eh? God! God! Cat and mouse! Cat and mouse!'

It sickened him that he had fallen into Mrs Tulsi's trap and shown himself grateful to her. She was keeping him, like her daughters, within her reach. And he was in her power, as he had been ever since he had gone to the Tulsi Store and seen Shama behind the counter.

'Cat and mouse!'

At any moment she might change her mind. Even if she didn't, to what would they be allowed to come back? Two rooms, one room, or only a camping place below the house? She had shown how she could use her power; and now she had to be courted and pacified. When she was nostalgic he had to share her nostalgia; when she was abusive he had to forget.

To escape, he had only six hundred dollars. He belonged to the Community Welfare Department: he was an unestablished civil servant. Should the department be destroyed, so would he.

'Trap!' he accused Shama. 'Trap!'

He sought quarrels with her and the children.

'Sell the damn car!' he shouted. And knowing how this humiliated Shama, he said it downstairs, where it was heard by sisters and the readers and learners.

He became surly, constantly in pain. He threw things in his room. He pulled down the pictures he had framed and broke them. He threw a glass of milk at Anand and cut him above the eye. He slapped Shama downstairs. So that to the house he became, like Govind, an object of contempt and ridicule. Beside him, the Community Welfare Officer, the absent Owad shone with virtue, success and the regard of everyone.

They moved the glass cabinet, Shama's dressingtable, Théophile's bookcase, the hatrack and the Slumberking to the tenement. The iron fourposter was dismantled and taken downstairs with the destitute's diningtable and the rocking-chair, whose rockers splintered on the rough, uneven concrete. Life became nightmarish, divided between the tenement room and the area below the house. Shama continued to cook below the house. Sometimes the children slept there with the readers and learners; sometimes they slept with Mr Biswas in the tenement.

And every afternoon Mr Biswas drove to his area to spread knowledge of the finer things in life. He distributed booklets; he lectured; he formed organizations and became involved in the complicated politics of small villages; and late at night he drove back to Port of Spain, to the tenement which was far worse than any of the houses he had visited during the day. The Prefect became coated with dust which rain had hardened and dappled; the floormats were dirty; the back seat was dusty and covered with folders and old, brown newspapers.

His duties then took him to Arwacas, where he was organizing a 'leadership' course. And, to avoid the long late drive to Port of Spain, to avoid the tenement and his family, he decided to spend the time at Hanuman House. The back house had been vacant for some time, and no one lived there except a widow who, pursuing an undisclosed business scheme, had stolen back from Shorthills, trusting to her insignificance to escape Seth's notice. There was little need for her to worry. For some time after the death of his wife Seth had acted wildly. He had been charged with wounding and using insulting behaviour, and had lost much local support. His skills appeared to have left him as well. He had tried to insuranburn one of his old lorries and had been caught and charged with conspiracy. He had been acquitted but it had cost much money; and he had thereafter grown quiescent. He looked after his dingy foodshop, sent no threats, and no longer spoke of buying over Hanuman House. The family quarrel, never bursting into incident, had become history; neither Seth nor the Tulsis were as important in Arwacas as they had been.

In the store the Tulsi name had been replaced by the Scottish name of a Port of Spain firm, and this name had been spoken for so long that it now fully belonged and no one was aware of any incongruity. A large red advertisement for Bata shoes hung below the statue of Hanuman, and the store was bright and busy. But at the back the house was dead. The courtyard was littered with packing cases, straw, large sheets of stiff brown paper, and cheap untreated kitchen furniture. In the wooden house the doorway between the kitchen and hall had been boarded over and the hall used as a storeroom for paddy, which sent its musty smell and warm tickling dust everywhere. The loft at one side was as dark and jumbled as before. The tank was still in the yard but there were no fish in it; the black paint was blistered and flaked, and the brackish rainwater, with iridescent streaks as of oil on its surface, jumped with mosquito larvae. The almond tree was still sparse-leaved, as though it had been stripped by a storm in the night; the ground below was dry and fibrous. In the garden the Queen of Flowers had become a tree; the oleander had grown until its virtue had been exhausted and it was flowerless; the zinnias and marigolds were lost in bush. All day the Sindhis who had taken over the shop next door played mournful Indian film songs on their gramophone; and their food had strange smells. Yet there were times when the wooden house appeared to be awaiting reanimation: when, in the still hot afternoons, from yards away came the thoughtful cackling of fowls, the sounds of dull activity; when in the evenings oil lamps were lit, and conversation was heard, and laughter, a dog being called, a child being flogged. But Hanuman House was silent. No one stayed when the store closed; and the Sindhis next door slept early.

The widow occupied the Book Room. This large room had always been bare. Stripped of its stacks of printed sheets, surrounded by emptiness, the muted sounds of life from neighbouring houses, the paddy rising high in the hall downstairs, it seemed more desolate than ever. A cot was in one corner; religious and comforting pictures hung low on the walls about it; next to it was a small chest in which the widow kept her belongings.

The widow, pursuing her business, visiting, was seldom in. Mr Biswas welcomed the silence, the stillness. He requisitioned a desk and swivel-chair from government stores (strange, such proofs of power), and turned the long room into an office. In this room, where the lotuses still bloomed on the wall, he had lived with Shama. Through the Demerara window he had tried to spit on Owad and flung the plateful of food on him. In this room he had been beaten by Govind, had kicked *Bell's Standard Elocutionist* and given it the dent on the cover. Here, claimed by no one, he had reflected on the unreality of his life, and had wished to make a mark on the wall as proof of his existence. Now he needed no such proof. Relationships had been created where none existed; he stood at their centre. In that very unreality had lain freedom. Now he was encumbered, and it was at Hanuman House that he tried to forget the encumbrance: the children, the scattered furniture, the dark tenement room, and Shama, as helpless as he was and now, what he had longed for, dependent on him.

On the baize-covered desk in the long room there were glasses and spoons stained white with Maclean's Brand Stomach Powder, sheafs and sheafs of paper connected with his duties as Community Welfare Officer, and the long, half-used pad in which he noted his expenses for the Prefect, parked in the grounds of the court house.

The redecoration of the house in Port of Spain proceeded slowly. Frightened by the price, Mrs Tulsi had not handed over the job to a contractor. Instead, she employed individual workmen, whom she regularly abused and dismissed. She had no experience of city workpeople and could not understand why they were unwilling to work for food and a little pocketmoney. Miss Blackie blamed the Americans and said that rapaciousness was one of her people's faults. Even after wages had been agreed Mrs Tulsi was never willing to pay fully. Once, after he had worked for a fortnight, a burly mason, insulted by the two women, left the house in tears, threatening to go to the police. 'My people, mum,' Miss Blackie said apologetically.

It was nearly three months before the work was done. The house was painted upstairs and downstairs, inside and out. Striped awnings hung over the windows; and glass louvres, looking fragile and out of place in that clumsy, heavy house, darkened the verandahs.

And Mr Biswas's nightmare came to an end. He was invited to return from the tenement. He did not return to his two rooms but, as he had feared, to one, at the back. The rooms he had surrendered were reserved for Owad. Govind and Chinta moved into Basdai's room, and Basdai, able now only to board, moved under the house with her readers and learners. In his one room Mr Biswas fitted his two beds, Théophile's bookcase and Shama's dressingtable. The destitute's diningtable remained downstairs. There was no room for Shama's glass cabinet, but Mrs Tulsi offered to lodge it in her diningroom. It was safe there and made a pleasing, modern show. Sometimes the children slept in the room; sometimes they slept downstairs. Nothing was fixed. Yet after the tenement the new arrangement seemed ordered and was a relief.

And now Mr Biswas began to make fresh calculations, working out over and over the number of years that separated each of his children from adulthood. Savi was indeed a grown person. Concentrating on Anand, he had not observed her with attention. And she herself had grown reserved and grave; she no longer quarrelled with her cousins, though she could still be sharp; and she never cried. Anand was more than halfway through college. Soon, Mr Biswas thought, his responsibilities would be over. The older would look after the younger. Somehow, as Mrs Tulsi had said in the hall of Hanuman House when Savi was born, they would survive: they couldn't be killed. Then he thought: 'I have missed their childhoods.'

# 6. The Revolution

A LETTER from London. A postcard from Vigo. Mrs Tulsi ceased to be ill and irritable, and spent most of her day in the front verandah, waiting. The house began to fill with sisters, their children and grandchildren, and shook with squeals and thumps. A huge tent was put up in the yard. The bamboo poles were fringed with coconut branches which curved to form arches, and a cluster of fruit hung from every arch. Cooking went on late into the night, and singing; and everyone slept where he could find a place. It was like an old Hanuman House festival. There had been nothing like it since Owad had gone away.

A cable from Barbados threw the house into a frenzy. Mrs Tulsi became gay. 'Your heart, mum,' Miss Blackie said. But Mrs Tulsi couldn't sit still. She insisted on being taken downstairs; she inspected, she joked; she went upstairs and came downstairs again; she went a dozen times to the rooms reserved for Owad. And in the confusion a messenger was sent to summon the pundit even after the pundit had come, a self-effacing man who, in trousers and shirt, had passed unnoticed in the growing crowd.

The sisters announced their intention of staying awake all that night. There was so much cooking to do, they said. The children fell asleep. The group of men around the pundit thinned; the pundit fell asleep. The sisters cooked and joyously complained of overwork; they sang sad wedding songs; they made pots of coffee; they played cards. Some sisters disappeared for an hour or so, but none admitted she had gone to sleep, and Chinta boasted that she could stay awake for seventy-two hours, boasting as though Govind was still the devoted son of the family, as though his brutalities had not occurred, as though time had not passed and they were still sisters in the hall of Hanuman House.

They grew lethargic just before dawn, but the morning light kindled them into fresh, over-energetic activity. Children were washed and fed and dressed before the street awoke; the house was swept and cleaned. Mrs Tulsi was bathed and dressed by Sushila; on her smooth skin there were small beads of perspiration, although the sun had not yet come out and she seldom perspired. Presently the visitors started arriving, many of them only tenuously related to the house, and not a few – the relations, say, of a grandchild's in-laws – unknown. The street was choked with cars and bright with the dresses of women and girls. Shekhar and Dorothy and their five daughters came. Everyone fussed about something: children, food, wharf-passes, transport. Continually cars drove off with an important noise. Their drivers, returning, showed passes and told of encounters with startled harbour officials.

For Mr Biswas it had been a difficult night. And the morning began badly. When he asked Anand to bring him the *Guardian* Anand reported that the paper had been appropriated by the pundit and had disappeared. Then he was turned out of the room while Shama and the girls dressed. Downstairs was chaos. He took one look at the bathroom and decided not to use it that day. When he went back to the room it was filled with the slight but offensive smell of face powder and there were clothes everywhere. Miserably, he dressed. 'The wreck of the blasted Hesperus,' he said, using a comb to clean his brush of woman's hair, sniffing as the dust rose visibly in the sunlight that slanted in below the striped awning. Shama noted his irritability but did not comment upon it; this enraged him further. The house, upstairs and down, resounded with impatient footsteps, shouts and shrieks.

The cavalcade left the house in sections. Mrs Tulsi travelled in Shekhar's car. Mr Biswas went in his Prefect; but his family had split up and gone in other cars, and he was obliged to take some people he didn't know.

The liner, white and reposed, lay at anchor in the gulf. A chair was found for Mrs Tulsi and set against the dull magenta wall of the customs shed. She was dressed in white, her veil pulled over her forehead. She pressed her lips together from time to time and crumpled a handkerchief in one hand. She was flanked by Miss Blackie, in her churchgoing clothes and a straw hat with a red ribbon, and by Sushila, who carried a large bag with an assortment of medicines.

A tug hooted. The liner was being towed in. Some of the children, those who had learnt at school that one proof of the roundness of the earth was the way ships disappeared beyond the horizon, exaggerated the distance between ship and wharf. Many said the ship would come alongside in two to three hours. Shivadhar, Chinta's younger son, said it wouldn't do so until the evening of the following day.

But the adults were concerned with something else.

'Don't tell Mai,' the sisters whispered.

Seth was on the wharf. He stood two customs sheds away. He was in a cheap suit of an atrocious brown, and to anyone who remembered him in his khaki uniform and heavy bluchers he looked like a labourer in his Sunday suit.

Mr Biswas glanced at Shekhar. He and Dorothy were staring resolutely at the approaching ship.

Seth was uncomfortable. He fidgeted. He took out his long cigarette holder from his breast pocket and, concentrating, fixed a cigarette into it. With that suit, and with such uncertain gestures, the cigarette holder was an absurd affectation, and appeared so to the children who could not remember him. As soon as he had lighted the cigarette a khaki-uniformed official pounced and pointed to the large white notices in English and French on the customs sheds. Seth ejected the cigarette and crushed it with the sole of an unshining brown shoe. He replaced the holder in his breast pocket and clasped his hands behind his back.

Soon, too soon for some of the children, the ship was alongside. The tugs hooted, retrieved their ropes. Ropes were flung from ship to wharf, which now, in the shadow of the white hull, was sheltered and almost roomlike.

Then they saw him. He was wearing a suit they had never known, and he had a Robert Taylor moustache. His jacket was open, his hands in his trouser pockets. His shoulders had broadened and he had grown altogether bigger. His face was fuller, almost fat, with enormous round cheeks; if he wasn't tall he would have looked gross.

'Is the cold in England,' someone said, explaining the cheeks.

Mrs Tulsi, Miss Blackie, the sisters, Shekhar, Dorothy and every granddaughter who had borne a child began to cry silently.

A young white woman joined Owad behind the rails. They laughed and talked.

'Aré bap!' one of Mrs Tulsi's woman friends cried out through her tears.

But it was only a passing alarm.

The gangway was laid down. The children went to the edge of the quay and examined the mooring ropes and tried to look through the lighted portholes. Someone started a discussion about anchors.

And then he was down. His eyes were wet.

Mrs Tulsi, sitting on her chair, all her effervescence gone, lifted her face to him as he stooped to kiss her. Then she held him round the legs. Sushila, in tears, opened her bag and held a bright blue bottle of smellig-salts at the ready. Miss Blackie wept with Mrs Tulsi, and every time Mrs Tulsi sniffed, Miss Blackie said, 'Hm-mm. Hm. Mm.' Children, ungreeted, stared. The brothers shook hands, like men, and smiled at one another. Then it was the turn of the sisters. They were kissed; they burst into new tears and feverishly attempted to introduce those of their children who had been born in the intervening years. Owad, kissing, crying, went through them quickly. Then it was the turn of the eight surviving husbands. Govind, who had known Owad well, was not there, but W. C. Tuttle, who had scarcely known him, was. Long brahminical hairs sprouted out of his ears, and he drew further attention to himself by closing his eyes, neatly shaking away tears, putting a hand on Owad's head and speaking a Hindi benediction. As his turn came nearer Mr Biswas felt himself weakening, and when he offered his hand he was ready to weep. But Owad, though taking the hand, suddenly grew distant.

Seth was advancing towards Owad. He was smiling, tears in his eyes, raising his hands as he approached.

In that moment it was clear that despite his age, despite Shekhar, Owad was the new head of the family. Everyone looked at him. If he gave the sign, there was to be a reconciliation.

'Son, son,' Seth said in Hindi.

The sound of his voice, which they had not heard for years, thrilled them all.

Owad still held Mr Biswas's hand.

Mr Biswas noted Seth's cheap, flapping brown jacket, the stained cigarette holder. Seth held out his hands and nearly touched Owad.

Owad turned and said in English, 'I think I'd better go and see about the baggage.' He released Mr Biswas's hand and walked briskly away, his jacket swinging.

Seth stood still. The tears suddenly stopped. But the smile remained.

The Tulsi crowd became agitated, drowning their relief in noise.

He could have turned away before, Mr Biswas kept on thinking. He could have turned away before.

Seth's hands dropped slowly. The smile died. One hand went up to the cigarette holder and he held his head to one side as though he was going to say something. But he only jiggled the cigarette holder, turned and walked firmly away between two customs sheds towards the main gates.

Owad came back to the group.

'With mother? With brother? With father? Or with all of all-you?' someone asked, and Mr Biswas recognized the sardonic voice of the *Sentinel* photographer.

The photographer nodded and smiled at Mr Biswas, as though he had found Mr Biswas out.

'By himself,' Mrs Tulsi said. 'Just by himself.'

Owad threw back his shoulders and laughed. His teeth showed; his moustache widened; his cheeks, shining and perfectly round, rose and rested against his nose.

'Thank you,' the photographer said.

A young reporter, whom Mr Biswas didn't know, came up with a notebook and pencil, and from the way he handled

these implements Mr Biswas could tell that he was inexperienced, as inexperienced as he himself had been when he interviewed the English novelist and tried to get him to say
sensational things about Port of Spain.

Many emotions came to him and, saying good-bye to no
one, he left the crowd and got into the Prefect, oven-hot
with the windows closed, and drove to his area.

'Tulips and daffodils!' he muttered, remembering Owad's
horticultural letters as he drove along the Churchill-Roose-
velt Highway, past the swamplands, the crumbling huts, the
rice fields.

It was just after ten when he got back to Port of Spain. The
house was silent and upstairs was in darkness: Owad had gone
to bed. But downstairs and in the tent lights blazed. Only the
younger children were asleep; for everyone else, including
those of the morning's visitors who had decided to stay the
night, the excitement of the day still lingered. Some were
eating, some were playing cards; many were talking in whispers; and a surprising number were reading newspapers.
Anand and Savi and Myna ran to Mr Biswas as soon as they
saw him and breathlessly began telling of Owad's adventures
in England: his firefighting during the war, the rescues he had
conducted, his narrow escapes; the operations he had been
called in to perform at the last minute on famous men, the
jobs that had been offered to him as a result, the seat in par-
liament; the distinguished men he had known and sometimes
defeated in public debate: Russell, Joad, Radhakrishnan,
Laski, Menon: these had already become household names.
The whole house had fallen under Owad's spell, and everywhere in the tent little groups were going over Owad's tales.
Chinta had already worked up a great antipathy for Krishna
Menon, whom Owad particularly disliked. And in one afternoon the family reverence for India had been shattered:
Owad disliked all Indians from India. They were a disgrace to
Trinidad Indians; they were arrogant, sly and lecherous; they
pronounced English in a peculiar way; they were slow and
unintelligent and were given degrees only out of charity; they
were unreliable with money; in England they went around

with nurses and other women of the lower classes and were frequently involved in scandals; they cooked Indian food badly (the only true Indian meals Owad had in England were the meals he had cooked himself); their Hindi was strange (Owad had repeatedly caught them out in solecisms); their ritual was debased; the moment they got to England they ate meat and drank to prove their modernity (a brahmin boy had offered Owad curried corn beef for lunch); and, incomprehensibly, they looked down on colonial Indians. The sisters said they had never really been fooled by Indians from India; they spoke of the behaviour of the missionaries, merchants, doctors and politicians they had known; and they grew grave as they realized their responsibilities as the last representatives of Hindu culture.

The pundit, in dhoti, vest, sacred thread, caste-marks and wrist-watch, reclined on a blanket spread on the swept and flattened earth. He was reading a paper Mr Biswas had never seen before. And Mr Biswas saw then that the many other newspapers in the tent were similar to the pundit's. It was the *Soviet Weekly*.

It was past midnight before Mr Biswas, moving from group to group, decided he had heard enough; and when Anand tried to tell of Owad's meeting with Molotov, of the achievements of the Red Army and the glories of Russia, Mr Biswas said it was time for them to go to sleep. He went up to his room, leaving Anand and Savi in the festival atmosphere downstairs. His head rang with the great names the children and the sisters had spoken so casually. To think that the man who had met those people was sleeping under the same roof! There, where Owad had been, was surely where life was to be found.

For a full week the festival continued. Visitors left; fresh ones arrived. Perfect strangers – the ice-man, the salted-peanuts-man, the postman, the beggars, the street-sweepers, many stray children – were called in and fed. The food was supplied by Mrs Tulsi and there was communal cooking, as in the old days, which seemed to have returned with Owad. The fruit hanging from the coconut-frond arches in the tent disappeared; the fronds became yellow. But Owad was still followed by admiring eyes, it was still an honour to be spoken to by him, and everything he had said was to be repeated. At any time and to anyone Owad might start on a new tale; then a crowd instantly collected. Regularly in the evening there were gatherings in the drawingroom or, when Owad was tired, in his bedroom. Mr Biswas attended as often as he could. Mrs Tulsi, forgetting her own illnesses and anxious instead to nurse, held Owad's hand or head while he spoke.

He had canvassed for the Labour Party in 1945 and was considered by Kingsley Martin to be one of the architects of the Labour victory. In fact Kingsley Martin had pressed him to join the *New Statesman and Nation*; but he, laughing as at a private joke, said he had told Kingsley no. He had earned the bitter hatred of the Conservative Party by his scathing denunciations of Winston Churchill's Fulton speech. Scathing was one of his favourite words, and the person he had handled most scathingly was Krishna Menon. He didn't say, but it appeared from his talk that he had been gratuitously insulted by Menon at a public meeting. He had collected funds for Maurice Thorez and had discussed Party strategy in France with him. He spoke familiarly of Russian generals and their battles. He pronounced Russian names impressively.

'Those Russian names are ugly like hell,' Mr Biswas ventured one evening.

The sisters looked at Mr Biswas, then looked at Owad.

'Beauty is in the eye of the beholder,' Owad said. 'Biswas is a funny name, if you say it in a certain way.'

The sisters looked at Mr Biswas.

'Rokossovsky and Coca-cola-kowsky,' Mr Biswas said, a little annoyed. 'Ugly like hell.'

'Ugly? Vyacheslav Molotov. Does that sound ugly to you, Ma?'

'No, son.'

'Joseph Dugashvili,' Owad said.

'That's the one I had in mind,' Mr Biswas said. 'Don't say you think *that* pretty.'

Owad replied scathingly, '*I* think so.'

The sisters smiled.

'Gawgle,' Owad said, raising his chin (he was lying in bed) and making a strangulated noise.

Mrs Tulsi passed her hand from his chin to his Adam's apple.

'What was that?' Mr Biswas asked.

'Gogol,' Owad said. 'The world's greatest comic writer.'

'It sounded like a gargle.' Mr Biswas waited for the applause, but Shama only looked warningly at him.

'You couldn't say that in Russia,' Chinta said.

This led Owad from the beauty of Russian names to Russia itself. 'There is work for everyone and everyone must work. It is distinctly written in the Soviet Constitution – Basdai, pass me that little book there – that he who does not work shall not eat.'

'That is fair,' Chinta said, taking the copy of the Soviet Constitution from Owad, opening it, looking at the title page, closing it, passing it on. 'Is exactly the sort of law we want in Trinidad.'

'He who does not work shall not eat,' Mrs Tulsi repeated slowly.

'I just wish they could send some of *my* people to Russia,' Miss Blackie said, sucking her teeth, shaking her skirt and shifting in her chair to express the despair to which her people reduced her.

Mr Biswas said, 'How can he, who does not eat, work?'

Owad paid no attention. 'In Russia, you know, Ma' – it was his habit to address many of his sentences to her – 'they grow cotton of different colours. Red and blue and green and white cotton.'

'Just growing like that?' Shama asked, making up for Mr Biswas's irreverence.

'Just growing like that. And you,' Owad said, speaking to a widow who had been trying without success to grow an acre of rice at Shorthills, 'you know the labour it is to plant rice. Bending down, up to your knees in muddy water, sun blazing, day in, day out.'

'The backache,' the widow said, arching her back and putting her hand where she ached. 'You don't have to tell me. Just planting that one acre, and I feel like going to hospital.'

'None of that in Russia,' Owad said. 'No backache and bending down. In Russia, you know how they plant rice?'

They shook their heads.

'Shoot it from an aeroplane. Not shooting bullets. Shooting rice.'

'From an aeroplane?' the rice-planting widow said.

'From an aeroplane. You could plant your field in a few seconds.'

'Take care you don't miss,' Mr Biswas said.

'And you,' Owad said to Sushila. 'You should really be a doctor. Your bent is that way.'

'I've been telling her so,' Mrs Tulsi said.

Sushila, who had had enough of nursing Mrs Tulsi, hated the smell of medicines and asked for nothing more than a quiet dry goods shop to support her old age, nevertheless agreed.

'In Russia you *would* be a doctor. Free.'

'Doctor like you?' Sushila asked.

'Just like me. No difference between the sexes. None of this nonsense about educating the boys and throwing the girls aside.'

Chinta said, 'Vidiadhar always keep on telling me that he want to be a aeronautical engineer.'

This was a lie. Vidiadhar didn't even know the meaning of the words. He just liked their sound.

'He would be an aeronautical engineer,' Owad said.

'To take out the rice grains from the aeroplane gas-tank,' Mr Biswas said. 'But what about me?'

'You, Mohun Biswas. Welfare Officer. After they have broken people's lives, deprived them of opportunity, sending you around like a scavenger to pick the pieces up. A typical capitalist trick, Ma.'

'Yes, son.'

'M-m-m-m.' It was Miss Blackie, purring.

'Using you like a tool. You have given us five hundred dollars profit. Here, we give you five dollars charity.'

The sisters nodded.

O God, Mr Biswas thought, another scorpion trying to do me out of a job.

'But you are not really a capitalist lackey,' Owad said.

'Not really,' Mr Biswas said.

'You are not really a bureaucrat. You are a journalist, a writer, a man of letters.'

'Yes, I suppose so. Yes, man.'

'In Russia, they see you are a journalist and a writer, they give you a house, give you food and money and tell you, "Go ahead and write." '

'Really really?' Mr Biswas said. 'A house, just like that?'

'Writers get them all the time. A dacha, a house in the country.'

'Why,' asked Mrs Tulsi, 'don't we all go to Russia?'

'Ah,' Owad said. 'They fought for it. You should hear what they did to the Czar.'

'M-m-m-m.' Miss Blackie said, and the sisters nodded gravely.

'You,' Mr Biswas said, now full of respect, 'are you a member of the Communist Party?'

Owad only smiled.

And his reaction was equally cryptic when Anand asked how, as a communist working for the revolution, he could take a job in the government medical service. 'The Russians have a proverb,' Owad said. 'A tortoise can pull in its head and go through a cesspit and remain clean.'

By the end of the week the house was in a ferment. Everyone was waiting for the revolution. The Soviet Constitution and the *Soviet Weekly* were read more thoroughly than the *Sentinel* or the *Guardian*. Every received idea was shaken. The readers and learners, happy to think themselves in a society that was soon to be utterly destroyed, relaxed their efforts to read and learn and began to despise their teachers, whom they had previously reverenced, as ill-informed stooges.

And Owad was an all-rounder. He not only had views on politics and military strategy; he not only was knowledgeable about cricket and football; he lifted weights, he swam, he rowed; and he had strong opinions about artists and writers.

'Eliot,' he told Anand. 'Used to see him a lot. American, you know. *The Waste Land. The Song of J. Alfred Prufrock.* Let us go then, you and I. Eliot is a man I simply loathe.'

And at school Anand said, 'Eliot is a man I simply loathe';
and added, 'I know someone who knows him.'

While they waited for the revolution, life had to be lived.
The tent was taken down. Sisters and married granddaughters
left. Visitors no longer came in great numbers. Owad took up
his duties at the Colonial Hospital and for a time the house
had to be content with stories of the operations he had carried
out. The refugee doctor was dismissed and Owad looked after
Mrs Tulsi himself. She improved spectacularly. 'These doctors stopped learning twenty years ago,' Owad said. 'They
don't even bother to keep up with the journals.' Journals had
been coming to him by almost every post from England, and
drug samples, which he displayed proudly, though sometimes
with scathing comments.

Communal cooking had stopped, but communal life continued. Sisters and granddaughters often came to spend a
night or a week-end. They brought all their illnesses to him
and he attended to them without charge, giving injections
wholesale with new miracle drugs which he said were as yet
unknown in the colony. Later the sisters worked out what
they would have had to pay another doctor, and there was a
gentle rivalry as to who had been favoured with the most
expensive treatment.

And Owad's success grew. For long the emphasis in the
house had been on reading and learning, which many of the
readers and learners couldn't do well and approached reluctantly. Now Owad said that this emphasis was wrong.
Everyone had something to offer. Physical strength and manual skills were as important as academic success, and he spoke
of the equality in Russia of peasants, workers and intellectuals. He organized swimming parties, boating expeditions,
ping-pong tournaments; and such was the admiration and respect felt for him that even enemies came together. Anand
and Vidiadhar played some ping-pong sets and, though not
speaking a word to one another before or after, were scrupu-
lously polite during the game, saying 'Good shot!' and 'Bad
luck!' at the least opportunity. Vidiadhar, who had developed
into a games-playing thug, more keen than competent and

never picked for any college side, excelled in these family games and was the house champion.

'I can't tell you,' Chinta said to Owad, 'how Vidiadhar got me worried. That boy does sweat so much. You can't get him to stick in a corner with some old book. He always exercising or playing some rough game or other. He done break a hand, a foot and some ribs. I does keep on trying to stop him. But he don't listen. And he does sweat so much.'

'Nothing to worry about there,' Owad said, the doctor now. 'That is quite normal.'

'You take a weight off my mind,' Chinta said, disappointed, for she believed that profuse sweating was a sign of exceptional virility and had hoped to be told so. 'He *does* sweat so much.'

Regularly Shekhar, Dorothy and their five daughters came to the house, and these visits gave the sisters a sweet revenge. They treated Shekhar with the respect due to him, but they made their contempt for Dorothy plain. 'I am sorry,' Chinta said to her one Sunday. 'I cannot understand you. I only speak Spanish.' Dorothy had not spoken Spanish since Owad's arrival and the sisters felt that they were at last making her boil down. But their behaviour had an unexpected result. For Owad, taking his cue from the sisters, spoke rallyingly to Dorothy; she responded with rough good humour and soon a familiarity grew up between them; and one Sunday, to the dismay of the sisters, Dorothy came with her cousin, a handsome young woman who had graduated from McGill University and had all the elegance of the Indian girl from South Trinidad. When they had gone Owad calmed the sisters' fears by deriding the girl's Canadian degree, her slight Canadian accent and her musical skills. 'She went all the way to Canada to learn to play the violin,' he said. 'I hope she doesn't want to play to me. I'll break the bow on her parents' heads. People starving, not getting enough to eat in Trinidad, and she playing the violin in Canada!'

And though he spent more and more time with his friends and colleagues and often went south to Shekhar's, and though when his friends called the house had to be silent and the sisters and the readers and learners hidden, the sisters continued to feel safe. For after every journey, every meeting, Owad related his adventures to them. His appetite for talk was insatiable, his dramatic gifts never failed, and the comments he made on the people he had met were invariably scathing.

The sisters now sought audience with him singly or in small groups. They came to the house, waited up for him, and when he returned they fell to talking, under the house, so as not to disturb Mrs Tulsi's sleep. In time each sister felt she had a special hold on him; and having received his confidences, offered hers. At first the sisters spoke of their financial difficulties. But Owad was unwilling to anticipate the revolution. Then the sisters complained. They complained about the teachers who were keeping their children back at school; they complained about Dorothy, about Shekhar, about their husbands; they complained about absent sisters. Every scandal was gone over, every petty dispute, every resentment. And Owad listened. The children listened as well, kept awake by the sisters' bumbling and their frequent hawking and spitting (a sign of intimacy: the warmer the feeling, the noisier the hawk, the longer the period of speaking through the spittle). In the morning the sisters who had talked late into the night were brisk and exceptionally friendly towards the people they had criticized, exceptionally proprietary towards Owad.

The house was always full of sisters on Sunday, when there was communal cooking. Sometimes Shekhar came by himself and then before lunch there were discussions between the brothers and Mrs Tulsi. The sisters did not feel threatened by these discussions as they had done when Shekhar and Dorothy and Mrs Tulsi talked. They did not feel excluded. For, with Owad there, these discussions were like the old Hanuman House family councils. So the sisters cooked below the house and sang and were gay. They were even anxious to exaggerate the difference between their brothers and themselves. It was as if by doing so they paid their brothers a correct reverence, a reverence which comforted and protected the sisters by assigning them a place again. They spoke no Hindi, used the grossest English dialect and the coarsest expressions and vied with one another in doing menial jobs and getting themselves dirty. In this way they sealed the family bond for the day.

It was the custom on these Sunday mornings, after the discussions and before lunch, which came before the trip to the sea, for the men to play bridge.

And on this morning Shekhar, despite Anand's pleas for sophistication, showed his disrelish of Owad's talk about the extermination of capitalists and what the Russians had done to the Czar, and tried to turn the conversation. It turned, oddly, to modern art.

'I can't make head or tail of this Picasso,' Shekhar said.

'Picasso is a man I loathe,' Owad said.

'But isn't he a comrade?' Anand said.

Owad frowned. 'And as for Chagall and Rouault and Braque –'

'What do you think of Matisse?' Shekhar asked, using a name he had got from *Life* and putting a stop to the flow of names he didn't know.

'*He's* all right,' Owad said. 'Delicious colour.'

This was unfamiliar language to Shekhar. He said, 'That was a nice picture they made. Didn't do too well, though. *The Moon and Sixpence*. With George Sanders.'

Owad, concentrating on his cards, didn't reply.

'These artists are funny fellers,' Shekhar said.

They were playing for matches. Anand scattered his heap and said, 'Portrait by Picasso.'

Everyone laughed, except Owad.

'Is a long time now I want to read the book,' Shekhar said. 'Isn't it by Somerset Morgue-hum?'

Anand scattered his matches again.

Owad said, 'Why don't you look in the mirror if you want to see a portrait by Picasso?'

This was clearly one of Owad's scathing comments. Shekhar smiled and grunted. The watching sisters and their children roared with laughter. Owad acknowledged their approval by smiling at his cards.

Anand felt betrayed. He had adopted all of Owad's political and artistic views; he had announced himself as a communist at school, he had stated that Eliot was a man he loathed. It was his turn to deal. In his confusion he dealt to himself first. 'Sorry, sorry,' he said, looking down and trying to inject a laugh into his voice.

'There is no need to apologize for that,' Owad said sternly. 'It is simply a sign of your conceited selfishness and egocentricity.'

The watchers held their breath.

Joviality fled from the table, Shekhar studied his cards. Owad frowned at his. His foot was tapping on the concrete floor. More watchers came.

Anand felt his ears burning. He looked hard at his cards, feeling the silence that had spread to all parts of the house. He was aware of watchers coming, Savi, Myna, Kamla. He was aware of Shama.

Owad breathed heavily and swallowed noisily.

When Shekhar bid his voice was low, as though he wished to take no part in the struggle. Vidiadhar, Shekhar's partner, bid in a voice choked by saliva; but there was no mistaking the voice of the free, unoffending man.

Anand bid stupidly.

Owad pressed his teeth far below his lower lip, shook his head slowly, tapped his feet, and breathed more loudly. When he bid, his voice, full of anger now, suggested that he was trying to redeem a hopeless situation.

The game dragged on. Anand played worse and worse. Shekhar, as though doing it against his will, gathered in trick after trick.

Owad's breathing and swallowing made Anand feel choked. His back was cold: his shirt was wet with perspiration.

At last the game was over. Neatly, deliberately, Shekhar noted the score. They waited for Owad to speak. Shuffling the cards, though it was not his turn, breathing heavily, he said, 'That's what we get from your genius.'

The tears rushed to Anand's eyes. He jumped up, throwing his chair backwards, and shouted, 'I didn't tell you I was any blasted genius.'

*Slap!* His right cheek burned; then trembled, even after Owad's hand was removed, as though the cheek had had to wait before registering the blow. And Owad was standing and Shekhar was bending down, picking up the cards from the dusty floor. And *slap!* his left cheek burned and trembled heavily. He forgot the watchers, concentrating only on the breathing before, the rising of the white-shirted chest. Owad's chair was overthrown. And Shekhar, leaning awkwardly on the table, his chair pushed back, was looking at the cards as he let them fall from one palm to another, his brow furrowed, his top lip swelling over the lower.

The table was jerked aside. Anand found himself standing ridiculously upright, half blinded by the shaming tears. Owad was striding energetically to the front steps. And then Anand had time to take in the thrill, the satisfaction of the watchers, the silence of the house, with Govind's singing in the background, the noise of some children in the street, the roll of a car from the main road.

Shekhar still sat at the table, playing with the cards.

A mumble came from the watchers.

'You!' Anand turned to them. 'What the hell are you standing up there for? Puss-puss, puss-puss all the blasted night, talk-talk-talk.'

The effect was unexpected and humiliating. They laughed. Even Shekhar lifted his head and gave his grunting laugh, shaking his shoulders.

Shama's gravity made her almost absurd.

The watchers broke up. Everyone went back to his task. A lightness that was like gaiety spread through the house.

Shekhar stacked the cards neatly on the table, rose, put his hands on Anand's shoulders, sighed, and went upstairs.

They heard Owad moving about from room to room.

Anand found Mr Biswas lying in vest and pants on the bed, his back to the door, papers on his drawn-up knees. He said without turning, 'You, boy? Here, see if you can work out these blasted travelling expenses right.' He passed the pad. 'What's the matter, boy?'

'Nothing, nothing.'

'All right, just work those figures out. Everybody else making a fortune out of their cars. I sure I losing.'

'Pa.'

'Just a minute, boy. Ought oughts are ought. Two fives are ten. Put down ought. Carry one.' Mr Biswas was relaxed, and even clowning: he knew that his method of multiplying always amused.

'Pa. We must move.'

Mr Biswas turned.

'We must move. I can't bear to live here another day.'

Mr Biswas heard the distress in Anand's voice. But he was unwilling to explore it. 'Move? All in good time. All in good time. Just waiting for the revolution and my dacha.'

These happy moods of his father were getting rare. And Anand said nothing more.

He did the complicated sums for the travelling expenses. Presently he heard the dry, crisp sounds of the ping-pong ball, the exclamations of Owad and Vidiadhar and Shekhar and the others.

He did not go down to have the lunch to which he had looked forward; and when Shama brought it up he could not eat or drink. Mr Biswas, his clowning mood persisting, squatted on the chair and pretended to spit on his food, to save it from Anand's gluttony. He knew this trick infuriated Anand. But Anand did not respond.

Downstairs the men were getting ready to go to the sea. Sons asked their mothers for towels, mothers urged their sons to be careful.

'Not going with them?'

Anand didn't reply.

Mr Biswas had withdrawn from these excursions. They were far too energetic, and the example of Owad led to dangerous competitive feats. Instead, after lunch he went for a walk by himself, looking at houses, occasionally making inquiries, but mostly simply looking.

The brightness of their aunts and cousins, their new and excluding chumminess, drove Savi and Kamla and Myna to join Anand in their room, where they lay on the bed, for want of places to sit, and made disjointed, selfconscious conversation.

Anand sipped his orange juice. The ice had melted, the juice gone flat and warm. The girls went for a walk to the

Botanical Gardens. Shama had her bath: Anand heard her singing in the open-air bathroom and washing clothes. When she came up her hair was wet and straight, her fingers pinched, but for all her songs her anxiety had not gone.

She said in Hindi, 'Go and apologize to your uncle.'

'No!' It was the first word he had spoken for a long time.

She petted him. 'For my sake.'

'The revolution,' he said.

'You wouldn't lose anything. He is older than you. And your uncle.'

'Not my uncle. Shooting rice from aeroplanes!'

Shama began to sing softly. She flung her hair down over her face and beat it with a stretched towel. The noises were like muffled sneezes.

The girls came back from their walk. They were brighter and talked more easily.

Then they were silent.

The men had returned. They heard their loud talk, their footsteps; Owad's voice raised in friendliness, breaking into laughter; the light inquiries from aunts; Shekhar's goodbyes, his car driving off.

Savi asked Shama in a whisper, 'What happened?'

'Nothing has happened,' Shama said coaxingly, not replying to Savi, but repeating her plea to Anand. 'He will just go and apologize to your uncle, and that is all. Nothing at all.'

The girls did not want to desert Anand, and they feared going downstairs.

'Remember,' Shama said. 'Not a word to your father. You know what he is like.'

She left the room. They heard her talking normally, even jestingly, with one of the aunts, and they admired her for her courage. Then the girls also went down, to face the righteousness of the unpersecuted.

The shower upstairs was going. Owad was in the bathroom, singing a song from an old Indian film. This was part of his virtue: it showed how untainted he had been by England and flattered everyone. For the virtue with which everyone had endowed him in his absence was now found in the smallest things: Anand remembered one sister saying that

Owad had brought back from England the shoes and shirts and underclothes he had taken from Trinidad.

'Same shoes after eight years,' Anand muttered. 'Blasted liar.'

The bathroom went silent.

Shama came to the room. 'Quick. Before they go to the theatre.'

Anand knew the Sunday routine: the bridge, the ping-pong, lunch, the sea, the shower, dinner, then the evening show.

The cousins could be heard assembling in the dining-room. Owad's voice, smothered by a towel, came from his bedroom.

Anand walked down the back stairs and up the stairs to the back verandah, the same verandah to which he had returned after he had nearly been drowned at Docksite. From the verandah he had a glimpse of the diningroom, where he had pulled the chair from under his father in the presence of Owad.

The cousins saw him. Some aunts saw him. The talk stopped. Faces were turned down, though the aunts continued to look solemn and offended and judicial. Then the talk broke out again. The cousins were playing with cards, idly, waiting for dinner. Vidiadhar, the sweater, was smiling down at the table, licking his lips.

Anand had to wait in the verandah for some time before Owad came out from the bedroom. He came out with his usual heavy brisk steps. As soon as he saw Anand he became stern. And there was silence.

Anand went in, held his hands behind his back.

'I apologize,' Anand said.

Owad continued to look stern.

At last he said, 'All right.'

Anand didn't know what to do. He remained where he was, so that it seemed he was waiting for an invitation to dinner and the theatre. But there was no word. He turned and walked slowly out of the room to the back verandah. As he went down the steps he heard the talk break out, heard the conscientious bustling of the aunts in the kitchen.

Shama was waiting for him in their room. He knew that her pain was as great as his, possibly greater, and he did not wish to increase it. She waited for him to do or say something, so that she could apply the soothing words. But he said nothing.

'You will eat something now?'

He shook his head. How ridiculous were the attentions the weak paid one another in the shadow of the strong!

She went downstairs.

When Owad and the cousins left she came back. He was willing to eat then.

Shortly after, Mr Biswas returned from his walk. His mood had changed. His face was twisted with pain and Anand had to mix him some stomach powder. He was tired after his walk and wanted to go to bed. He could sleep early on Sundays; on other evenings he came back late from his area.

The light from the diningroom came through the tall ventilation gaps at the top of the partition. He called Shama and told her, 'Go and get them to take off that light.'

It was an awkward request at the best of times, though before Owad's return Shama had sometimes made it successfully. Now she could do nothing.

Mr Biswas lost his temper. He ordered Shama and Anand to get sheets of cardboard, and with these he tried to block the gaps at the top of the partition, jumping from the bed to the ledge on the partition. Of the three sections he put up two fell down almost at once.

'Uncle Podger,' Savi said.

He was about to lose his temper with her as well; but, as if in answer to the commotion, the light in the dining-room went out. He lay down on the bed in the dark and was soon asleep, grinding his teeth, and making strange contented smacking sounds with his mouth.

Anand sat in the darkness. Shama came to the room and got into the fourposter. Anand did not want to go downstairs. He lay on the bed beside his father and remained quite still.

He was disturbed by chatter and heavy footsteps, and made wide awake by the light coming in through the two open sections above the partition. Some aunts who had been waiting up below the house were now heard moving about the kitchen. The chatter continued, and laughter.

Mr Biswas stirred and groaned. 'Good *God!*'

Anand felt Shama awake and anxious. Listened to in this way, the chatter was as unbearable as the dripping of a water-tap.

'*God!*' Mr Biswas cried.

There was a moment's silence in the diningroom.

'Other people in this house,' Mr Biswas shouted.

The visiting sisters and the readers and learners could be heard awakening downstairs.

Softly, as though speaking only to the people with him, Owad said, 'Don't we all know it, old man.' There were giggles.

The giggles maddened Mr Biswas. 'Go to France!' he cried.

'And you can go to hell.' It was Mrs Tulsi. Her words, evenly spaced, were cold and firm and clear.

'Ma!' Owad said.

Mr Biswas didn't know what to say. Surprise was followed by shock, shock by anger.

Shama got up from the fourposter and said, 'Man, man.'

'Let him go to hell,' Mrs Tulsi said, almost conversationally. Her voice was followed by a groan, a creaking of a bedspring and a shuffling on the floor.

Lights went on downstairs, lit up the yard and reflected through the jalousied door into Mr Biswas's room.

'Go to hell?' Mr Biswas said. 'Go to hell? To prepare the way for you? Praying to God, eh? Cleaning up the old man's grave.'

'For God's sake, Biswas,' Owad called, 'hold your damned tongue.'

'You don't talk to me about God. Red and blue cotton! Shooting rice from aeroplanes!'

The girls came into the room.

Savi said, 'Pa, stop being stupid. For God's sake, stop it.'

Anand was standing between the two beds. The room was like a cage.

'Let him go to hell,' Mrs Tulsi sobbed. 'Let him get out.'

'Neighbour! Neighbour!' a woman cried shrilly from next door. 'Anything wrong, neighbour?'

'I can't *stand* this,' Owad shouted. 'I can't stand it. I don't know what I've come back to.' His footsteps were heard pounding across the drawingroom. He mumbled loudly, angrily, indistinctly.

'Son, son,' Mrs Tulsi said.

They heard him going down the steps, heard the gate click and shiver.

Mrs Tulsi began to wail.

'Neighbour! Neighbour!'

A wonderful sentence formed in Mr Biswas's mind, and he said, 'Communism, like charity, should begin at home.'

Mr Biswas's door was pushed open, fresh light and shadows confused the patterns on the walls, and Govind came into the room, his trousers unbelted, his shirt unbuttoned.

'Mohun!'

His voice was kind. Mr Biswas was overwhelmed to tears. 'Communism, like charity,' he said to Govind, 'should begin at home.'

'We know, we know,' Govind said.

Sushila was comforting Mrs Tulsi. Her wail broke up into sobs.

'I am giving you notice,' Mr Biswas shouted. 'I curse the day I step into your house.'

'Man, man.'

'You curse the day,' Mrs Tulsi said. 'Coming to us with no more clothes than you could hang on a nail.'

This wounded Mr Biswas. He could not reply at once. 'I am giving you notice,' he repeated at last.

'*I* am giving *you* notice,' Mrs Tulsi said.

'I gave it to you first.'

There was an abrupt silence. Then in the drawingroom there was an outburst of low, amused chatter, and downstairs the readers and learners, who had kept silent all along, were whispering.

'Cha!' the woman next door said. 'Bother with people business.'

Govind patted Mr Biswas on the shoulder, gave a little
laugh and left the room.

The whispers downstairs subsided. The light which came
through the jalousies from the yard and striped the room was
extinguished. The laughter in the drawingroom died away.
Throats were cleared with faint satiric intonations, and there
were muted apprehensive chuckles. There were shuffles on
the floor, and whispers. Then the light went out and the
room was in darkness and the house was absolutely silent.

They remained appalled in the room, not daring to move,
to break the silence, unable in the dark and the stillness to
believe fully in what had just happened.

Presently, exhausted by their inactivity, the children went
downstairs.

Morning would show the full horror of the past few
minutes.

They awoke with a sense of unease. Almost at once they
remembered. They avoided one another. They listened,
above the hawking and spitting, the running taps, the continuous scuffling, the fanning of coal-pots, the metallic hiss of
the lavatory flush, for the footsteps and voices of Mrs Tulsi
and Owad. But the house was quiet upstairs. Then they
learned that Owad had left early that morning for a week's
tour of Tobago. The instinct of Mr Biswas's children was to
get away at once, to escape from the house to the separate
reality of the streets and school.

Mr Biswas's anger had gone stale; it burdened him. Now
there was also shame at his behaviour, shame at the whole
gross scene. But the uncertainty that had been with him ever
since he heard that Owad was returning from England had
disappeared. He found it easy to ignore his fears; and after he
had had his bath he felt energetic and even light-headed. He
too was anxious to get out of the house. And as he left it his
sympathy went out to Shama, who had to remain.

The sisters looked chastened. Unpersecuted, they believed
in their righteousness; and though Owad's departure, in
anger, as was reported, involved them all in disgrace and
threatened them all, every sister was sure of her own hold on

Owad, and her attitude to Shama was one of blame and re-coil.

'So, Aunt,' Suniti, the former contortionist, said, 'I hear you moving to a new house, man.'

'Yes, my dear,' Shama said.

At school Anand defended Eliot, Picasso, Braque, Chagall. He who had been leaving copies of the *Soviet Weekly* in the readingroom between the pages of *Punch* and *The Illustrated London News* now announced that he frowned upon com-munism. The phrase was thought odd; but the action, coin-ciding with the widespread renunciation of communism by distinguished intellectuals in Europe and America, caused little comment.

Shortly after he had been taken on the *Sentinel* Mr Biswas went late one night to the city centre to interview the home-less people, whose families among them, who regularly slept in Marine Square. 'That conundrum – the housing question –' he had begun his article; and though the words were ex-cised by Mr Burnett, Mr Biswas was taken by their rhythm and had never forgotten them. They drummed in his head that morning; he spoke them and sang them under his breath; and throughout the Monday conference at the office he was exceptionally lively and garrulous. When the conference was over he went down St Vincent Street to the café with the gay murals and sat at the bar, waiting for people he knew.

'Got notice to quit, man,' he said.

He spoke lightly, expecting solicitude, but his lightness was met with lightness.

'I expect I will be joining you in Marine Square,' a *Guard-ian* reporter said.

'Hell of a thing, though. Married with four children and nowhere to go. Know any places for rent?'

'If I know one I would be there right now.'

'Ah, well. I suppose it will be the square.'

'It look so.'

The café, close to newspaper offices, government offices and the courts, was frequented by newspapermen and civil servants; by people who came in for a drink before their cases were called and then disappeared, sometimes for months; by solicitors' clerks and by junior clerks who spent days of te-dium tracing titles at the polished desks in the outer room of the Registrar-General's Department.

It was a title-tracer who said, 'If Billy was still here I woulda tell you to go and see Billy. All-you remember Billy?

'Billy used to promise them that he wasn't only going to get them a house, but that he was going to move them free into the bargain. Everybody rushing to get this free move – you know black people – and paying Billy deposit. When he pick up a good few deposit Billy decide it was time to put a end to this stupidness and to make tracks for the States.

'But listen. The day before he leave, Billy plan leak out. But Billy get to know that the plan leak out. So the next day, Billy ship waiting in the harbour, Billy hire a lorry, put on his khaki working-clothes and went around to all the people he take money from. Everybody so surprise they forgetting they vex. All of them telling Billy how they call police and they saying, "But, Billy, we hear that you was leaving today." And Billy saying, "I don't know where you get the niggergram from. I not leaving. *You* leaving. I come to move you. You got everything pack?" None of them had anything pack, and Billy start getting into one big temper, saying how they make him waste his time, and he was mad not to move them at all. And they calm him down by saying if he pass back in the afternoon they would have everything pack and ready to move. So Billy leave and the people pack and wait for Billy. They still waiting.'

The laughter broke, but Mr Biswas could take no part in it. Outside it had grown dark. There was a blue instant of lightning, a crack and roll of thunder. The thought of driving to his area with the windows closed was not appealing. He had drunk many lagers and they had steadily reduced him to silence and stillness. He did not want to go to the country; he did not want to stay in the café. But the rain, which had begun to fall in heavy drops that blotted on the pave-ment and presently had it wet and running, encouraged him to stay, silent and unlistening on a tall stool, drinking

lager, staring at the crude bright murals, surrendering to the
gloom.

He felt a hand on his shoulder and turned to see a very tall,
thin coloured man. He had occasionally seen this man about
St Vincent Street and knew him to be a solicitor's clerk. In
the past year or two they had been nodding to one another
but they had never spoken.

'Is true?' the man asked.

Mr Biswas noted the man's size, the concern in his voice
and in his young-old face. 'Yes, man.'

'You really got notice?'

Mr Biswas responded to this sympathy by pursing his lips,
looking down at his glass and nodding.

'Hell of a thing. How long?'

'Notice. A month, I suppose.'

'Hell of a thing. Married? Children?'

'Four.'

'God! You try the government? You in the Service now,
not so? And ain't they have some sort of housing loans
scheme?'

'Only for established people.'

'You can't get a good place to rent for all the tea in China,'
the man said. He edged his way around Mr Biswas, cutting
him off from the talkers, some of whom were beginning to
eat, at the bar, at tables. 'Much easier to buy a house really. In
the long run. What you drinking? Lager? Two lagers, miss. A
hell of a thing, man.'

The lagers came.

'I know,' the man said. 'I was in the same position not so
long ago. I only had my mother. But even that was hell, I
could tell you. Is like being sick.'

'Sick?'

'When you sick you forget what it is to be well. And when
you well you don't really know what it is to be sick. Is the
same with not having a place to go back to every afternoon.'

Lights were turned on in the café. People stood silently in
every doorway, looking out at the rain. From the dark street
came the hiss of wet tyres and the beat of the rain, drowning
the scrape of knives and forks on plates, the chatter.

'I don't know,' the man said. 'But look. What you doing now?'

'I got to go to the country. But with all this rain –'

'You know what? You better come and have some lunch with me. No, not here.' He looked around the café, and in his look Mr Biswas saw the chatterers rebuked for their callousness.

They went outside and hurried through the rain, brushing against people who stood close to walls. They turned into a side street and entered the grimy green hall of a Chinese restaurant. The coconut-fibre mat was damp and black, the floor wet. They went up bare steps and the solicitor's clerk seemed to be continually meeting people he knew. To all of them he said, patting Mr Biswas on the shoulder, 'Hell of a thing here, man. The man got notice. And he got nowhere to go.' People looked at Mr Biswas, made sympathetic sounds, and Mr Biswas, muddled by the lager, the strange faces and the unexpected interest, became very tragic.

They went to a celotex-partitioned cubicle and the solicitor's clerk ordered food.

'I don't know,' he said. 'But look. My position is this. I living with my mother in a two-storey house in St James. But she a lil old now, you know –'

'My mother dead,' Mr Biswas said, finding himself, to his surprise, eating. 'Blasted doctor didn't want to give a death certificate. Write him a letter, though. A long one –'

'Hell of a thing, man. But the position is this. The old queen have a lil heart trouble. Can't climb steps and that sort of thing. It does strain the heart, you know.' The solicitor's clerk put his hand on his chest and his shoulders see-sawed. 'And right at this moment I have a offer of a house in Mucurapo which would suit the old lady right down to the ground. Trouble is, I can't buy it unless somebody buy mine.'

'And you want me buy yours.'

'In a sort of way. I could help you and you could help me. And the old queen.'

'Upstairs house, you say.'

'All modern conveniences and full and immediate vacant possession.'

'I wish I had that sort of money, old man.'

'Wait until you see it.'

And before the meal was over Mr Biswas had agreed to go to see the house. He knew what he was doing. He knew that he had no more than eight hundred dollars and was only wasting the clerk's time and his own. But courtesy demanded no less.

'You would be doing me a favour,' the solicitor's clerk said. 'And you would be doing the old queen a favour.'

So in the pouring rain, the windscreen wiper occasionally sticking, they drove down St Vincent Street and around Marine Square and along Wrightson Road – settled by secure people – and across Woodbrook to the Western Main Road, past the vast grounds and the saman-lined drive of the Police Barracks, and turned into Sikkim Street.

It was still raining when the car stopped outside the house. The fence, half concrete, with lead pipes running between square concrete pillars, was covered with the vines of the Morning Glory spattered with small red flowers drooping in the rain. The height of the house, the cream and grey walls, the white frames of doors and windows, the red brick sections with white pointing: all these things Mr Biswas took in at once, and knew that the house was not for him.

When, racing into the house out of the rain, he met the old queen, not as old as the solicitor's clerk had made out, he was overwhelmed by her courtesy. Continually, with his suit and tie and shining shoes and Prefect car, he felt he was deceiving the public. Here, in this house in Sikkim Street, so desirable, so inaccessible, deception was especially painful. He tried to respond to the old queen's civility with equal civility; he tried not to think of his crowded room, his eight hundred dollars. Slowly and carefully, aware now of the lager, he sipped tea and smoked a cigarette. Hesitantly, fearing a frank appraisal would be rude, he took in the distempered walls, the washed celotex ceiling with strips of wood painted chocolate and looking brand-new, frosted-glass windows and frosted-glass doors with white woodwork, white lattice work, a polished floor, a polished morris suite. And when the solicitor's clerk, frank and trusting, ignorant of the eight hundred dollars, insisted that Mr Biswas should see the rooms upstairs, Mr Biswas went round quickly, seeing a bathroom with a toilet bowl and – luxury! – a porcelain wash-basin, two bed-rooms with green walls, a verandah, so cool without the sun, the Morning Glory on the fence below, his Prefect in the road, and just for a moment he thought of the house as his own, and the thought was so heady he rejected it at once and hurried downstairs.

The old queen, whose heart had not permitted her to climb the steps, greeted him as though he had returned from a long journey.

He sat in one of the morris chairs and drank more tea and took another cigarette.

Not a word had been said so far about the price. Mr Biswas kept on fixing it in his mind at something high and impossible which would relieve him of responsibility and regret. He thought of eight thousand, nine thousand. So near the busy Main Road: an ideal site for a shop. And yet so quiet in the rain!

'Not bad for six thousand,' the solicitor's clerk said.

Mr Biswas smoked and said nothing.

The old queen came out from the kitchen with a plate of cakes. The solicitor's clerk insisted that Mr Biswas should try one. The old queen had made them herself.

Mr Biswas took a cake. The old queen smiled at him, and he smiled back.

'Well, to be honest. We both want to make a sale in a hurry. So let's say five five.'

Once Mr Biswas had read a story by a French writer about a woman who worked for twenty years to pay off a debt on an imitation necklace. He had never been able to understand why it was considered a comic story. Debt was a fearful thing; and with all its ifs and might-have-beens the story came too near the truth: hope followed by blight, the passing of the years, the passing of life itself, and then the revelation of waste: Oh, my poor Matilda! But they were false! Now, sit-ting in the clerk's morris chair, Mr Biswas knew he was close to such a debt, a similar blight, a similar waste: and he was again lying awake at night, hearing the snores of the crowded house, looking through the window at the empty sky swept by silent searchlights.

'Five five and we will throw in this morris suite.' The clerk gave a little laugh. 'I always hear that Indians was sharp bargainers, but I never know till now just how sharp they was.'

The old queen smiled as charitably as ever.

'I will have to think about it.'

The old queen smiled.

On the way back Mr Biswas decided to be aggressive.

'You so anxious to sell your house I don't understand why you don't go to an agent.'

'Me? You mean you didn't hear what those people was saying in the café. Those agents are just a bunch of crooks, man.'

He felt he had seen the last of the house. He did not know then that, in the five years of life left to him, that drive along the Western Main Road, through Woodbrook to Wrightson Road and South Quay was to become familiar and even boring.

Alone once more, his depression, his panic returned. But when he got back to the house he assumed an air of confidence and sternness and said loudly to Shama, who was surprised to see him back so soon. 'Didn't go to the country today. Been looking at some properties.'

The headache which had been nagging him, which he had put down to his uneasiness, now defined itself as the alcoholic headache he always had when he drank in the day. He went up to the room, stripped to pants and vest, tried to read Marcus Aurelius, failed, and soon fell asleep, to the astonishment of his children, who wondered how in a crisis which affected them all their father could find time for sleep so early in the afternoon.

He had seen the house like a guest under heavy obligation to his host. If it had not been raining he might have walked around the small yard and seen the absurd shape of the house. He would have seen where the celotex panels on the eaves had fallen away, providing unrestricted entry to the bats of the neighbourhood. He would have seen the staircase that hung at the back, open, with only a banister, and sheltered by

unpainted corrugated iron. He would not have been deceived
into cosiness by the thick curtain over the back doorway on
the lower floor. He would have seen that the house had no
back door at all. If he had not had to rush out of the rain he
might have noticed the street lamp just outside the house; he
would have known that a street lamp, so near the main road,
attracted idlers like moths. But he saw none of these things.
He had only a picture of a house cosy in the rain, with a
polished floor, and an old lady who baked cakes in the kitchen.

If he had not been disturbed he might have queried the
clerk's eagerness more impolitely. But events were too rapid,
too neat. A quarrel in the night, the offer of a house with
immediate possession the very next afternoon. And before
the evening was out the sum of five thousand five hundred
dollars had become less inaccessible.

'Somebody come for you,' Shama was saying.

He awoke and was puzzled to find it was evening.

'Another destee?' His fame had survived his resignation
from the *Sentinel*; destitutes still occasionally sought him out.

'I don't know. I don't think so.'

He dressed, his head humming, walked through the house
downstairs to the foot of the front steps and surprised the visitor, a respectably dressed Negro of the artisan class, who was
waiting for him at the top of the steps.

'Good night,' the Negro said. His accent betrayed him as
an illegal immigrant from one of the smaller islands. 'Is about
the house I come. I want to buy it.'

Everybody wanted to buy or sell houses that day. 'I ain't
even pay down for it yet,' Mr Biswas said.

'The house in Shorthills?'

'Oh, that. That. But I can't sell that. The land isn't mine.
I don't even rent it.'

'I know. If I buy the house I would take it away.' He went
on to explain. He had bought a lot in Petit Valley. He wanted
to build his own house, but building materials were scarce
and expensive and he was offering to buy Mr Biswas's house,
not as a house, but for the materials. He said he was not pre-

pared to haggle. He had studied the building carefully and was prepared to offer four hundred dollars.

And when Mr Biswas went back to the room with the rumpled beds, the disarrayed furniture, the chaos on Shama's dressingtable, he had twenty twenty-dollar bills in his pocket.

'You don't believe in God,' he said to Anand. 'But look.'

Between eight hundred dollars and one thousand two hundred dollars there is a great difference. Eight hundred dollars are petty savings. One thousand two hundred dollars stand for real money. The difference between eight hundred and five thousand is immense. The difference between one thousand two hundred and five thousand is negotiable.

A week before Mr Biswas would have dismissed any thought of buying a house for five thousand dollars. He wanted one at three thousand or three thousand five hundred; he never looked at any above four thousand. And the strange thing now was that, having raised his sights, it did not occur to him to look at other five-thousand-dollar houses.

He sought out the solicitor's clerk the next day, paid him a deposit of one hundred dollars, and was shrewd enough to ask for a stamped receipt.

'I going to take this money and pay down right away on the house I want to buy,' the solicitor's clerk said. 'Wait until the old queen hear. She going to be so glad.'

When Shama heard she burst into tears.

'Ah!' Mr Biswas said. 'Swelling up. Vexed. You could only be happy if we just keep on living with your mother and the rest of your big, happy family, eh?'

'I don't think anything. *You* have the money, *you* want to buy house, and *I* don't have to think anything.'

And that was when Shama, leaving the room, encountered Suniti, and Suniti said, 'I hear that you come like a big-shot. Buying house and thing.'

'Yes, child.'

'Shama!' Mr Biswas called. 'Tell that girl to go back and help that worthless husband of hers to look after their goats at Pokima Halt.'

The goats were an invention of Mr Biswas which never failed to irritate Suniti. 'Goats,' she said to the yard, sucking her teeth. 'Well, some people at least have goats. That is more than I could say for some other people.'

Mr Biswas had divined only part of Shama's motives. She knew that the time had come for them to move. But she did not want this to happen after a quarrel and a humiliation. She hoped that the estrangement between her mother and herself would disappear; and she regarded Mr Biswas's action as rash and provocative.

He released the tremendous details one by one.

'Five thousand five hundred,' he said.

He had his effect.

'O God!' Shama said. 'You mad! You mad! You hanging a millstone around my neck.'

'A necklace.'

Her despair frightened him. But it made him stiffer: he mortified himself to inflict pain on her.

'Well, we still paying for the car. And you don't know how long this job with the government going to last.'

'Your brother hoping it won't last at all. Tell me, eh. Deep down in your heart you really believe that this job I am doing is nothing, eh? Deep down you really believe that. Eh?'

'If you think so,' she cried, and went down the steps to the kitchen below the house, to the readers and learners and sisters and married nieces, working and talking in the light of weak, flyblown bulbs. She was surrounded by security; yet disaster was coming upon her and she was quite alone.

She went back up to the room.

'How you going to get the money?'

'You don't worry about that.'

'If you start throwing away your money I could always help you. Tomorrow I going to go to de Lima's and buy that brooch you always talking about.'

He sniggered.

As soon as she went out of the room he was seized by panic. He left the house and went for a walk around the Savannah, along the wide, silent, grass-lined streets of St Clair, where open doors revealed softly lit, opulent, undisturbed interiors.

Having committed himself, he lacked the courage to go back yet found the energy to go ahead. He was encouraged by the gloom of Shama and strengthened by the enthusiasm of the children. He avoided questioning himself; and, dreading the return of Owad, he developed the anxiety that he might not after all be good enough for the house of the solicitor's clerk and the old queen who baked cakes and served them with such grace.

It was this anxiety which made him drive on Thursday afternoon to Ajodha's and tell Tara as soon as he saw her that he had come to borrow four thousand dollars to buy a house. She took it well; she said she was glad that he was at last going to be free of the Tulsis. And when Ajodha came in, fanning himself with his hat, Mr Biswas was equally forthright and Ajodha treated the matter as a petty business transaction. Four thousand five hundred dollars at eight per cent, to be repaid in five years.

Mr Biswas stayed to have a meal with them, and continued to be blunt and loud and full of bounce. It was only when he drove away that his exhilaration left him and he saw that he had involved himself not only in debt but also in deception. Ajodha did not know that the car had not yet been paid for; Ajodha did not know that he was only an unestablished civil servant. And the loan could not be repaid in five years: the interest alone would come to thirty dollars a month.

Still there were occasions he could have withdrawn. When, for instance, they went to see the house on Friday evening.

Anxious to show himself worthy of the house, he insisted that the children should put on their best clothes, and urged Shama to say as little as possible when they got there.

'Leave me behind. Leave me behind,' Shama said. 'I have no shame for you and I will shame you in front of your high and mighty house-seller.'

And all the way she kept it up until, just before they turned into Sikkim Street, Mr Biswas lost his temper and said, 'Yes. You damn well will shame me. Stay and live with your family and leave me alone. I don't want you to come in with me.'

She looked surprised. But there was no time for the quarrel to subside. They were in Sikkim Street. He drove the car past the house, parked it some distance away, called to the children to come with him if they wanted to or stay with their mother and continue living with the Tulsis if they wanted to do that, slammed the door and walked away. The children got out and followed him.

So that the one glimpse Shama had of the house before it was bought was from the moving Prefect. She saw concrete walls softly coloured in the light of the street lamp, with romantic shadows thrown by the trees next door. And she, who might have noticed the grossness of the staircase, the dangerous curve of the beams, the lack of finish in the lattice work and in all the woodwork, she who might have noticed the absence of a back door, the absence of a hundred small but important touches, sat in the car overcome by anger and dread.

While the children, on their best behaviour, made conversation with the old queen and were pleased by the interest she showed in them and her approval of nearly everything they said. They saw the polished floor, the rich curtains, the celotex ceiling, the morris suite, and they wanted to see little more. They drank tea and ate cakes; while Mr Biswas, not at all displeased by the success of his children, smoked cigarettes and drank whisky with the solicitor's clerk. When they went upstairs, the solicitor's clerk went first. It was dark. They did not note the absence of a light on the staircase; the darkness masked the crudity of the construction. Used for so long to the makeshift and the oldfashioned, dazzled by what they had seen, and in the position of guests, they didn't stop to inquire; and once they had got to the top they were too taken by the bathroom and the green bedrooms and the verandah and the rediffusion set.

'A radio!' they cried. They had forgotten what it was like to have one.

'I will leave it here if you want it,' the solicitor's clerk said, as if offering to pay the rental of the set.

'Well, you like it?' Mr Biswas asked, when they left.

There was no doubt that they did. Something so new, so clean, so modern, so polished. They were anxious to win Shama over to it, to get her to see it herself. But in the face of Mr Biswas's gaiety and triumph Shama was firm. She said she had no intention of shaming Mr Biswas or his children.

During the week Mrs Tulsi had been ill but placid. With Owad's return she became maudlin. She spent most of the day in her room, asking for her hair to be soaked in bay rum, and listening for Owad's footsteps. She sought to win him back by talking about his boyhood and Pundit Tulsi. Abusing no one, raging against no one, the tears flowing from the wells, as it seemed, of her dark glasses, she wove a lengthy tale of injustice, neglect and ingratitude. Her daughters came to listen. They came bowed and penitent and respected their brother's silence by showing themselves solemn and correct. They spoke Hindi; they did not debase themselves; they all tried to look as though they had offended. But Owad's mood did not break. He did not relate his adventures in Tobago; and the sisters directed their own silent accusations at Shama. Owad spent more time away from home. He mixed with his medical colleagues, a new caste separate from the society from which it had been released. He went south to Shekhar's. He played tennis at the India Club. And, almost as suddenly as it had started, talk of the revolution ended.

# 7. The House

THE SOLICITOR's clerk was as good as his word, and as soon as the transaction was completed he and the old queen hurriedly abandoned the house. On Monday night Mr Biswas made his final decision. On Thursday the house awaited him. Late on Thursday afternoon they went in the Prefect to Sikkim Street. The sun came through the open windows on the ground floor and struck the kitchen wall. Woodwork and frosted glass were hot to the touch. The inside of the brick wall was warm. The sun went through the house and laid dazzling stripes on the exposed staircase. Only the kitchen escaped the sun; everywhere else, despite the lattice work and open windows, was airlessness, a concentration of heat and light which hurt their eyes and made them sweat.

Without curtains, empty except for the morris suite, with the hot floor no longer shining and polished, the sun showing only grit and scratches and dusty footprints, the house seemed smaller than the children remembered and had lost the cosiness they had noted at night, in the soft lights, with thick curtains keeping out the world. Undraped by curtains, the large areas of lattice work left the house open, to the green of the breadfruit tree next door, the bleedingheart vine thick and tendrilled on the rotting fence, the decaying slum house at the back, the noises of the street.

They discovered the staircase: unhidden by curtains, it was too plain. Mr Biswas discovered the absence of a back door. Shama discovered that two of the wooden pillars supporting the staircase landing were rotten, whittled away towards the bottom and green with damp. They all discovered that the staircase was dangerous. At every step it shook, and at the lightest breeze the sloping corrugated iron sheets rose in the middle and gave snaps which were like metallic sighs.

Shama did not complain. She only said, 'It look as though we will have to do a few repairs before we move.'

In the days that followed they made more discoveries. The landing pillars had rotted because they stood next to a tap which emerged from the back wall of the house. The water from the tap simply ran into the ground. Shama spoke about the possibility of subsidence. Then they discovered that the yard had no drainage of any sort. When it rained the water from the pyramidal roof fell directly to the ground, turned the yard into mud and spattered walls and doors, the bottoms of which appeared to have been sprayed with wet soot.

They discovered that none of the windows downstairs would close. Some grated on the concrete sill; others had been so warped by the sun that their bolts could no longer make contact with the grooves. They discovered that the front door, elegant with white woodwork and frosted panes and with herringbone lattice work on either side, flew open in a strong wind even when locked and bolted. The other drawingroom door could not open at all: it was pinned to the wall by two floorboards which had risen, pressing against each other, to make a miniature and even mountain range.

'Jerry-builder,' Mr Biswas said.

They discovered that nothing was faced and that the lattice work was everywhere uneven, and split in many places by nails which showed their large heads.

'Tout! Crook!'

They discovered that upstairs no door resembled any other, in shape, structure, colour or hinging. None fitted. One stood six inches off the floor, like the swingdoor of a bar.

'Nazi and blasted communist!'

The upper floor curved towards the centre and from downstairs they noted a corresponding bend in the two main beams. Shama thought that the floor curved because the inner verandah wall it supported was made of brick.

'We'll knock it down,' Shama said, 'and put a wood parti-tion.'

'Knock it down!' Mr Biswas said. 'Be careful you don't knock down the house. For all we know it is that same wall which is keeping the whole damned thing standing.'

Anand suggested a pillar rising from the drawingroom downstairs to support the sagging beams.

Soon they began to keep their discoveries secret. Anand discovered that the square pillars of the front fence, so pretty with Morning Glory, were made of hollow bricks that rested on no foundation. The pillars rocked at the push of a finger. He said nothing, and only suggested that the mason might have a look at the fence when he came.

The mason came to build a concrete drain around the house and a low sink below the tap at the back. He was a squat Negro with catlike whiskers and he sang continually:

> *There was a man called Michael Finnegan*
> *Who grew whiskers on his chin again.*

His gaiety depressed them all.

Daily they moved between the hostile Tulsi house and Sikkim Street. They became short-tempered. They took little joy in the morris suite or the rediffusion set.

' "I will leave the rediffusion set for you." ' Mr Biswas said, mimicking the solicitor's clerk. 'You old crook. If I don't see you roasting in hell!'

The rental of the rediffusion set was two dollars a month. Landrent was ten dollars a month, six dollars more than he paid for his room. Rates, which had always seemed as remote as fog or snow, now had a meaning. Landrent, rediffusion set, rates, interest, repairs, debt: he was discovering commitments almost as fast as he discovered the house.

Then the painters came, two tall sad Negroes who had been out of work for some time and were glad to get a job at the very low wages Mr Biswas had to borrow to pay them. They came with their ladders and planks and buckets and brushes and when Anand heard them jumping about on the top floor he became anxious and went up to reassure himself that the house was not falling down. The painters did not share Anand's concern. They continued to jump from plank to floor and he was too ashamed to tell them anything. He stayed to watch. The fresh distemper made the long, ominous crack in the verandah wall clearer and more ominous. While the rediffusion set filled the hot empty house with light music and bright commercials, the painters talked, sometimes of women, but mostly of money. When, from the rediffusion set, a woman sang, as from some near but inaccessible city of velvet, glass and gold where all was bright and secure and even sadness was beautiful:

> *They see me night and day time*
> *Having such a gay time.*
> *They don't know what I go through –*

one painter said, 'That's me, boy. Laughing on the outside, crying on the inside.' Yet he had never laughed or smiled. And for Anand the songs that came over and over from the rediffusion set into the hollow, distemper-smelling house were forever after tinged with uncertainty, threat and emptiness, and their words acquired a facile symbolism which would survive age and taste: 'Laughing on the Outside', 'To Each His Own', 'Till Then', 'The Things We Did Last Summer'.

And more expense was to come. Sewer pipes had not been laid down in this part of the city and the house had a septic tank. Before the painters left, the septic tank became choked. The lavatory bowl filled and bubbled; the yard bubbled; the street smelled. Sanitary engineers had to be called in, and a new septic tank built. By this time the money Mr Biswas had borrowed had run out altogether, and Shama had to borrow two hundred dollars from Basdai, the widow who took in boarders.

But at last they could leave the Tulsi house. A lorry was hired – more expense – and all the furniture packed into it. And it was astonishing how the furniture, to which they had grown accustomed, suddenly, exposed on the tray of the lorry in the street, became unfamiliar and shabby and shameful. About to be moved for the last time: the gatherings of a lifetime: the kitchen safe (encrusted with varnish, layer after layer of it, and paint of various colours, the wire-netting broken and clogged), the yellow kitchen table, the hatrack with the futile glass and broken hooks, the rockingchair, the fourposter (dismantled and unnoticeable), Shama's dressingtable (standing against the cab, without its mirror, with all the drawers taken out, showing the unstained, unpolished wood inside, still, after all these years, so raw, so new), the bookcase and desk, Théophile's bookcase, the Slumberking (a pink, intimate rose on the headrest), the glass cabinet (rescued from Mrs Tulsi's drawingroom), the destitute's diningtable (on its back, its legs roped around, loaded with drawers and boxes), the typewriter (still a brilliant yellow, on which Mr Biswas was going to write articles for the English and American Press, on which he had written his articles for the Ideal School, the letter to the doctor): the gatherings of a lifetime for so long scattered and even unnoticed, now all together on the tray of the lorry. Shama and Anand rode with the lorry. Mr Biswas drove the girls; they carried dresses which would have been damaged by packing.

They could only unpack that evening. A rough meal was prepared in the kitchen and they ate in the chaotic diningroom. They said little. Only Shama moved and spoke without constraint. The beds were mounted upstairs. Anand slept in the verandah. He could feel the floor curving below him towards the offending brick wall. He placed his hand on the wall, as if that might give him some idea of its weight. At every footstep, particularly Shama's, he could feel the floor shake. When he closed his eyes he experienced a spinning, swaying sensation. Hurriedly he opened them again to reassure himself that the floor had not sunk further, that the house still stood.

Every afternoon they had seen an elderly Indian rocking contentedly in the verandah of the house next door. He had a square, heavy-lidded face that was almost Chinese; he always looked impassive and sleepy. Yet when Mr Biswas, pursuing his policy of getting on good terms with the neighbours, greeted him, the man brightened at once, sat forward in his rockingchair and said, 'You have been doing a lot of repairs.'

Mr Biswas took the man's words as an invitation to his verandah. His house was new and well-built; the walls were solid, the floor even and firm, the woodwork everywhere neat and finished. There was no fence; and a shed of rusted corrugated iron and grey-black boards abutted at the back of the house.

'Nice house you have here,' Mr Biswas said.

'With the help of God and the boys we manage to build it. Still have to put up a fence and build a kitchen, as you see. But that could wait for the time being. You had to do a lot of repairs.'

'A few things here and there. Sorry about the septic tank.'

'You don't have to be sorry about that. I did expect it to happen even before. He build it himself.'

'Who? The man?'

'And not only that. He build the whole house himself. Working on Saturday and Sunday and in the afternoons. It was like a hobby with him. If he employ a carpenter I didn't see it. And I better warn you. He do all the wiring too. The man was a joke, man. I don't know how the City Council pass a house like that. The man used to bring all sort of tree-trunk and tree-branch to use as rafters and beams.'

He was an old man, pleased that after a lifetime, with the help of his sons, he had built a solid, well-made house. The past lay in the shed at the back of his house, in the ruinous wooden houses still in the street. He spoke only out of a sense of achievement, without malice.

'A strong little house, though,' Mr Biswas said, looking at it from the old man's verandah. And he saw how the old man's breadfruit tree framed the house to advantage, how elegant the lattice work looked through the bleeding-heart vine, its lack of finish unimportant at this distance. But he noticed how pronounced the crack was that spread from the brick wall in the verandah. And it was only then that he noticed how many of the celotex panels had fallen from the eaves; and even as he looked bats flew in and out. 'Strong little house. That is the main thing.'

The old man continued to talk, no hint of argument in his voice. 'And those pillars at the four corners. Anybody else woulda make them of concrete. You know what he make them of? Just those clay bricks. Hollow inside.'

Mr Biswas could not hide his alarm and the old man smiled benevolently, pleased to see his information having such an effect.

'The man was a joke, man,' he went on. 'As I say, it was like a hobby to him. Picking up window frames here and there, from the American base and where not. Picking up a door here and another one there and bringing them here. A real disgrace. I don't know how the City Council pass the place.'

'I don't suppose,' Mr Biswas said, 'that the City Council woulda pass it if it *wasn't* strong.'

The old man paid no attention. 'A spec'lator, that's what he was. A real spec'lator. This ain't the first house he built like this, you know. He build two-three in Belmont, one in Woodbrook, this one, and right now he building one in Morvant. Building it and living in it at the same time.' The old man rocked and chuckled. 'But he get stick with this one.'

'He live in it a long time,' Mr Biswas said.

'Couldn't get anybody to buy it. Is a good little site, mark you. But he was asking too much. Four five.'

'Four five!'

'If you please. And look. Look at that little house down the road.' He pointed to a new neat bungalow, which Mr Biswas, with his newly acquired eye for carpentry, had recognized as of good design and workmanship. 'Small, but very nice. *That* sell this year for four five.'

A Tuttle boy, the writer, came unexpectedly to the house one afternoon, talked of this and that and then, casually, as if delivering a message he had forgotten, said that his parents were going to call that evening, because Mrs Tuttle wanted to ask Shama's advice about something.

Rapidly, they made ready. The floor was polished and walking on it was forbidden. Curtains were rearranged, and the morris suite and the glass cabinet and the bookcase pushed into new positions. The curtains masked the staircase; the bookcase and the glass cabinet hid part of the lattice work, which was also draped with curtains. The door that couldn't close was left wide open and curtains hung over the doorway. The door that couldn't open was left shut; and a curtain hung over that. The windows that couldn't close were left open and curtains hung over them as well. And when the Tuttles came they were greeted by an enclosed, shining, softly-lit house, the morris chairs and the small palm in the brass pot reflecting on the polished floor. Shama seated them on the morris chairs, left them to marvel in silence for a minute or so, and, as cosily as the old queen herself, made tea in the kitchen and offered that and biscuits.

And the Tuttles were taken in! Shama could tell from the hardening of Mrs Tuttle's expression into one of outrage and self-pity, from the nervous little chuckles of W. C. Tuttle who sat with a mixture of Eastern and Western elegance on his morris chair, rubbing one hand over the ankle that rested on his left knee, twirling the long hairs in his nose with the other hand.

Mrs Tuttle said to Myna, who had amputated the torch-bearer's torchbearing arm, 'Hello, Myna girl. You forget your aunt these days. I don't suppose you want to come round to my old house after this.'

Myna smiled, as though Mrs Tuttle had hit on an embarrassing truth.

Mrs Tuttle said to Shama in Hindi, 'Well, it is old. But it is full of room.' She pressed her elbows to her side to show the constriction she felt in Shama's house. 'And we didn't want to get into debt or anything like that.'

W. C. Tuttle played with the hairs in his nose and smiled.

'I don't want anything bigger,' Shama said. 'This is just right for me. Something small and nice.'

'Yes,' W. C. Tuttle said. 'Something nice and small.'

And they had a moment of panic when he jumped up from his chair and, going to the wall with the lattice work, began measuring it by extending his fingers, gathering them up again and extending them once more. But it was only the length of the wall, not the quality of the work, that interested him. He measured, gave a little laugh and said, 'Twelve by twenty.'

'Fifteen by twenty-five,' Shama said.

'Nice and small,' W. C. Tuttle said. 'That, to me, is the beauty of it.'

And Shama had another uneasy moment when W. C. Tuttle asked to be shown upstairs. But it was night. They had enclosed the staircase with lattice work from banister to roof, with strips of wood from banister to steps, and it had all been painted. A weak bulb lit up the landing, threw the yard into darkness, and the effect of cosiness was maintained.

And how quickly they forgot the inconveniences of the house and saw it with the eyes of the visitors! What could not be hidden, by bookcase, glass cabinet or curtains, they accommodated themselves to. They mended the fence and made a new gate. They put up a garage. They bought rose trees and planted a garden. They began to grow orchids and Mr Biswas had the exciting idea of attaching them to dead coconut trunks buried in the ground. At the side of the house, in the shade of the breadfruit tree, they had a bed of anthurium lilies. To keep the lilies cool they surrounded them with damp, rotting immortelle wood which they got from Shorthills. And it was on a visit to Shorthills that they saw the concrete pillars rising out of tall bush on the hill where Mr Biswas had once built a house.

Soon it seemed to the children that they had never lived anywhere but in the tall square house in Sikkim Street. From now their lives would be ordered, their memories coherent. The mind, while it is sound, is merciful. And rapidly the memories of Hanuman House, The Chase, Green Vale, Shorthills, the Tulsi house in Port of Spain would become jumbled, blurred; events would be telescoped, many forgotten. Occasionally a nerve of memory would be touched – a puddle reflecting the blue sky after rain, a pack of thumbed cards, the fumbling with a shoelace, the smell of a new car, the sound of a stiff wind through trees, the smells and colours of a toyshop, the taste of milk and prunes – and a fragment of forgotten experience would be dislodged, isolated, puzzling. In a northern land, in a time of new separations and yearnings, in a library grown suddenly dark, the hailstones beating against the windows, the marbled endpaper of a dusty leatherbound book would disturb: and it would be the hot noisy week before Christmas in the Tulsi Store: the marbled patterns of oldfashioned balloons powdered with a rubbery dust in a shallow white box that was not to be touched. So later, and very slowly, in securer times of different stresses, when the memories had lost the power to hurt, with pain or joy, they would fall into place and give back the past.

Though Mr Biswas had mentally devised many tortures to which he was going to put the solicitor's clerk, he took care to avoid the café with the gay murals. And it was with surprise and embarrassment that he came back one afternoon, less than five months after he had moved, to find the solicitor's clerk, a cigarette hanging from his lips, pacing with some method about the lot next to his house.

The clerk was unabashed. 'How, man? How the wife? And the children? Still getting on all right with their studies?'

Instead of replying, what he felt, 'Stop asking about my children and their studies, you nasty old crooked communist tout!' Mr Biswas said that they were all well and asked, 'How the old queen?'

'Half and half. The old heart still playing the fool.'

The lot next door was practically empty. At the far end it contained only a neat two-roomed building, the office of a friendly society; so that Mr Biswas had no neighbours on one side. Mr Biswas did not like the clerk's concentration. But he decided to keep cool.

'You happy in Mucurapo?' he asked. 'Eh, but what I saying? Is Morvant, not so?'

'The old queen don't care for the area. Damp, you know.'

'And the mosquitoes. I can imagine. I hear that is bad for the heart.'

'Still,' the clerk said. 'We got to keep on trying.'

'You sell the Morvant house yet?'

'Not yet. But I have a lot of offers.'

'And you thinking of building here again.'

'Want to put up a lil house like yours. Two-storey.'

'You not putting up any damn two-storey house here, you old jerry-building tout!'

The clerk stopped pacing and came to the fence, scarlet and green with a bougainvillaea Mr Biswas had planted. Over the bougainvillaea he wagged a long finger in Mr Biswas's face and said, 'Mind your mouth! Mind your mouth! You say enough to spend a nice lil time in jail. Mind your mouth! It look like you don't know the law.'

'The City Council not going to pass this one. I pay rates and I have my rights.'

'Don't say I didn't warn you. You just mind your mouth, you hear.'

When the solicitor's clerk left, Mr Biswas walked about the yard, trying to imagine the effect in the street of two tall boxes side by side. He walked and looked and pondered and gauged. Then, before the sun went down, he called out, 'Shama! Shama! Bring a ruler or your tape measure.'

She brought a ruler and Mr Biswas began measuring the width of his lot foot by foot, starting from the half-empty lot and working towards the house of the old Indian, who had observed everything, rocking, his Chinese face wrinkled with smiles.

'He come to build another one, eh?' he called out, when Mr Biswas was near enough. 'That don't surprise me at all.'

'He going to build it over my dead body,' Mr Biswas called back, measuring.

The old man rocked, greatly amused.

'Aha!' Mr Biswas said, when he got to the end of the lot. 'Aha! I always suspected.' He stooped and started to measure back to the half-empty lot, while the old man rocked and chuckled.

'Shama!' Mr Biswas said, running to the kitchen. 'Where you have the deed for the house?'

'In the bureau.'

She went up to get it. She brought it down and Mr Biswas read.

'Aha! The old tout! Shama, we going to get a bigger yard.'

By accident or design the fence the solicitor's clerk had put up was a full twelve feet inside the boundary indicated in the deed.

'I always thought,' Shama said, 'that we didn't have a fifty-foot frontage.'

'Frontage, eh?' Mr Biswas said. 'Nice word, Shama. But you're picking up a lot of nice words in your old age, you know.'

And the solicitor's clerk appeared in the street no more.

'So you catch him then,' the old man said. 'But you must say this for him. He was a sharp fellow.'

'Didn't fool me,' Mr Biswas said.

In the extra space Mr Biswas planted a laburnum tree. It grew rapidly. It gave the house a romantic aspect, softened the tall graceless lines, and provided some shelter from the afternoon sun. Its flowers were sweet, and in the still hot evenings their smell filled the house.

# Epilogue

BEFORE THE end of the year Owad left Port of Spain. After
his marriage to Dorothy's cousin, the Presbyterian violinist,
he left the Colonial Hospital and moved to San Fernando,
where he set up in private practice. And at the end of the year
the Community Welfare Department was abolished. It was
not because of Shekhar's party; that had disintegrated even
before, when all four of its candidates were defeated in the
colony's first general election, encouraging Shekhar ('The
Poor Man's Friend', according to his posters) to withdraw
from public life and concentrate on his cinemas. The department was abolished because it had grown archaic. Thirty,
twenty or even ten years before, there would have been
people to support it. But the war, the American bases, an
awareness of America had given everyone the urge, and many
the means, to self-improvement. The encouragement and
guidance of the department were not needed. And when the
department was attacked, no one, not even those who had
enjoyed its 'leadership' courses, knew how to defend it. And
Miss Logie, like Mr Burnett, left.

Mr Biswas slipped from his low eminence as a civil servant
and returned to the *Sentinel*. The car was now his own; but
he was getting less than those who had stayed with the paper.
He had paid five hundred dollars of the debt; now he could
hardly pay the interest. He wanted to sell the car, and an Englishman came to the house one day to look it over. Shama was
exceedingly rude, and the Englishman, finding himself in the
centre of a family quarrel, withdrew. Mr Biswas gave in.
Shama had never reproached him for the house, and he had
begun to credit her with great powers of judgement. Again
and again she said she was not worried, that the debt would
settle itself; and though Mr Biswas felt that her words were
hollow, he did get comfort from them.

But the debt remained. At nights, with a clear view of the sky through the slightly crooked window frames on the top floor, he felt the time flying by, the five years shrinking to four, to three, bringing disaster closer, devouring his life. In the morning the sun struck through the lattice work on the landing and below the bar-room door into his bedroom, and calmness returned. The children would see about the debt.

But the debt remained. Four thousand dollars. Like a buffer at the end of a track, frustrating energy and ambition. Beyond the *Sentinel* there was nothing. And though he had at first found the newspaper office stimulating, with its urgency, the daily miracle of seeing what he had written in the afternoon transformed into solid print read by thousands the next morning, his enthusiasm, unsupported by ambition, faded. His work became painstaking and laboured: the zest went out of his articles as it had gone out of himself. He grew dull and querulous and ugly. Living had always been a preparation, a waiting. And so the years had passed; and now there was nothing to wait for.

Except the children. Suddenly the world opened for them. Savi got a scholarship and went abroad. Two years later Anand got a scholarship and went to England. The prospects of repaying the debt receded. But Mr Biswas felt he could wait; at the end of five years he could make other arrangements.

He missed Anand and worried about him. Anand's letters, at first rare, became more and more frequent. They were gloomy, self-pitying; then they were tinged with a hysteria which Mr Biswas immediately understood. He wrote Anand long humorous letters; he wrote about the garden; he gave religious advice; at great expense he sent by air mail a book called *Outwitting Our Nerves* by two American women psychologists. Anand's letters grew rare again. There was nothing Mr Biswas could do but wait. Wait for Anand. Wait for Savi. Wait for the five years to come to an end. Wait. Wait.

They sent a message to Shama one afternoon and she packed Mr Biswas's pyjamas and hurried to the Colonial

Hospital. He had collapsed in the *Sentinel* office. It was not the stomach which was at fault, the stomach which he had so often said he would like to cut out of himself and have a good look at, to see exactly what was playing the fool. It was the heart, about which he had never complained.

He spent a month in hospital. When he came home he found that Shama and Kamla and Myna had distempered the walls downstairs. The floor had been freshly stained and polished. The garden was blooming. He was moved. He wrote to Anand that he hadn't realized until then what a nice little house it was. But writing to Anand was like taking a blind man to see a view.

Forbidden to climb staircases, Mr Biswas lived downstairs; and this was a recurring humiliation, for the lavatory was upstairs. The afternoon sun made it hard to be downstairs all day; even when Shama put up an awning over the windows the glare remained and the heat was stifling. Knowing his heart was unreliable, he was afraid. He feared for his heart. He feared for Anand. He feared for the end of the five years. He continued to write cheerful letters to Anand. At long intervals the replies came, impersonal, brief, empty, constrained.

Then the *Sentinel* put Mr Biswas on half-pay. Within a month he was back at work, climbing the steps to the *Sentinel* office, climbing the steps to his bedroom, driving the Prefect, now old and troublesome, to all parts of the island, in all weathers; then sweating over his articles, injecting what gaiety he could into dull subjects. These articles he sent to Anand, but they were seldom acknowledged, and, as if ashamed of them, he ceased to send them. A lethargy fell over him. His face grew puffy. His complexion grew dark; not the darkness of a naturally dark skin, not the darkness of sunburn: this was a darkness that seemed to come from within, as though the skin was a murky but transparent film and the flesh below it had been bruised and become diseased and its corruption was rising.

Then Shama got another message one day, and when she went to the hospital she found it was much more serious. His face held a pain she could scarcely bear to watch; he was not able to talk.

She wrote to Anand and Savi. Savi answered in about a fortnight. She was returning as soon as possible. Anand wrote a strange, maudlin, useless letter.

Mr Biswas came home after six weeks. Again he lived downstairs. Everyone was now adjusted to his condition and no preparations had been made to welcome him as before. The distemper was still new; the curtains remained unchanged. He had stopped smoking altogether; his appetite returned and he fancied he had made a significant discovery. He wrote Anand warning him against cigarettes and continued to talk about the garden and the growth of his shade tree, which they all called his 'shade'. His face grew puffier, even gross; it grew darker; and he began to put on weight. Waiting for Savi, waiting for Anand, waiting for the end of the five years, he became more and more irritable.

Then the *Sentinel* sacked him. It gave him three months' notice. And now Mr Biswas needed his son's interest and anger. In all the world there was no one else to whom he could complain. And at last, forgetting Anand's own pain, he wrote on the yellow typewriter a hysterical, complaining, despairing letter, with not a mention of the shade or the roses or the orchids or the anthurium lilies.

When, after three weeks, he had received no reply from Anand, he wrote to the Colonial Office. This elicited a brief letter from Anand. Anand said he wanted to come home. At once the debt, the heart, the sack, the five years became less important. He was prepared to take on a further debt to get Anand home. But the plan fell through; Anand changed his mind. And Mr Biswas never complained again. In his letters he once again became the comforter. The time for his last paypacket from the *Sentinel* drew near, and not far behind that the end of the five years.

And right at the end everything seemed to grow bright. Savi returned and Mr Biswas welcomed her as though she were herself and Anand combined. Savi got a job, at a bigger salary than Mr Biswas could ever have got; and events organized themselves so neatly that Savi began to work as soon as Mr Biswas ceased to be paid. Mr Biswas wrote to Anand: 'How can you not believe in God after this?' It was a letter

full of delights. He was enjoying Savi's company; she had
learned to drive and they went on little excursions; it was
wonderful how intelligent she had grown. He had got a But-
terfly orchid. The shade was flowering again; wasn't it strange
that a tree which grew so quickly could produce flowers with
such a sweet scent?

One of the first stories Mr Biswas had written for the *Sentinel* had been about a dead explorer. The *Sentinel* was then a
boisterous paper and he had written a grotesque story, which
he had often later regretted. He had tried to lessen his guilt by
thinking that the explorer's relations were unlikely to read the
*Sentinel*. He had also said that when his own death was reported he would like the headline to be ROVING REPORTER
PASSES ON. But the *Sentinel* had changed, and the headline
he got was JOURNALIST DIES SUDDENLY. No other paper
carried the news. An announcement came over twice on rediffusion sets all over the island. But that was paid for.

Her sisters did not fail Shama. They all came. For them it
was an occasion of reunion, no longer so frequent, for they
had all moved to their own houses, some in the town, some
in the country.

Downstairs the doors of the house were open. The door
that couldn't open had been made to, and its hinges dislocated. The furniture was pushed to the walls. All that day
and evening well-dressed mourners, men, women and children, passed through the house. The polished floor became
scratched and dusty; the staircase shivered continually; the top
floor resounded with the steady shuffle. And the house did
not fall.

The cremation, one of the few permitted by the Health
Department, was conducted on the banks of a muddy stream
and attracted spectators of various races. Afterwards the sisters
returned to their respective homes and Shama and the children went back in the Prefect to the empty house.

# A Bend in the River

# Contents

# O N E

## The Second Rebellion

### 1

The world is what it is; men who are nothing, who allow themselves to become nothing, have no place in it.

Nazruddin, who had sold me the shop cheap, didn't think I would have it easy when I took over. The country, like others in Africa, had had its troubles after independence. The town in the interior, at the bend in the great river, had almost ceased to exist; and Nazruddin said I would have to start from the beginning.

I drove up from the coast in my Peugeot. That isn't the kind of drive you can do nowadays in Africa—from the east coast right through to the centre. Too many of the places on the way have closed down or are full of blood. And even at that time, when the roads were more or less open, the drive took me over a week.

It wasn't only the sand drifts and the mud and the narrow, winding, broken roads up in the mountains. There was all that business at the frontier posts, all that haggling in the forest outside wooden huts that flew strange flags. I had to talk myself and my Peugeot past the men with guns—just to drive through bush and more bush. And then I had to talk even harder, and shed a few more bank notes and give away more of my tinned food, to get myself—and the Peugeot—out of the places I had talked us into.

Some of these palavers could take half a day. The top man would ask for something quite ridiculous—two or three thousand dollars. I would say no. He would go into his hut, as though there was nothing more to say; I would hang around outside, because there was nothing else for me to do. Then after an hour or two I would go inside the hut, or he would come outside, and we would settle for two or three dollars. It was as Nazruddin had said, when I asked him about visas and he had said that bank notes were better. "You can always get into those places. What is hard is to get out. That is a private fight. Everybody has to find his own way."

As I got deeper into Africa—the scrub, the desert, the rocky climb up to the mountains, the lakes, the rain in the afternoons, the mud, and then, on the other, wetter side of the mountains, the fern forests and the gorilla forests—as I got deeper I thought: But this is madness. I am going in the wrong direction. There can't be a new life at the end of this.

But I drove on. Each day's drive was like an achievement; each day's achievement made it harder for me to turn back. And I couldn't help thinking that that was how it was in the old days with the slaves. They had made the same journey, but of course on foot and in the opposite direction, from the centre of the continent to the east coast. The further away they got from the centre and their tribal area, the less likely they were to cut loose from the caravans and run back home, the more nervous they became of the strange Africans they saw about them, until at the end, on the coast, they were no trouble at all, and were positively anxious to step into the boats and be taken to safe homes across the sea. Like the slave far from home, I became anxious only to arrive. The greater the discouragements of the journey, the keener I was to press on and embrace my new life.

When I arrived I found that Nazruddin hadn't lied. The place had had its troubles: the town at the bend in the river was more than half destroyed. What had been the European suburb near the rapids had been burnt down, and bush had grown over the ruins; it was hard to distinguish what had been gardens from what had been streets. The official and commercial area near the dock and customs house survived, and some residential streets in the centre. But there wasn't much else. Even the African cités were inhabited only in corners, and in decay elsewhere, with many of the low, box-like concrete houses in pale blue or pale green abandoned, hung with quick-growing, quick-dying tropical vines, mattings of brown and green.

Nazruddin's shop was in a market square in the commercial

area. It smelt of rats and was full of dung, but it was intact. I had bought Nazruddin's stock—but there was none of that. I had also bought the goodwill—but that was meaningless, because so many of the Africans had gone back to the bush, to the safety of their villages, which lay up hidden and difficult creeks. After my anxiety to arrive, there was little for me to do. But I was not alone. There were other traders, other foreigners; some of them had been there right through the troubles. I waited with them. The peace held. People began coming back to the town; the *cité* yards filled up. People began needing the goods which we could supply. And slowly business started up again.

Zabeth was among the earliest of my regular customers. She was a *marchande*—not a market woman, but a retailer in a small way. She belonged to a fishing community, almost a little tribe, and every month or so she came from her village to the town to buy her goods wholesale.

From me she bought pencils and copybooks, razor blades, syringes, soap and toothpaste and toothbrushes, cloth, plastic toys, iron pots and aluminum pans, enamel plates and basins. These were some of the simple things Zabeth's fisherfolk needed from the outside world, and had been doing without during the troubles. Not essentials, not luxuries; but things that made ordinary life easier. The people here had many skills; they could get by on their own. They tanned leather, wove cloth, worked iron; they hollowed out large tree trunks into boats and smaller ones into kitchen mortars. But to people looking for a large vessel that wouldn't taint water and food, and wouldn't leak, imagine what a blessing an enamel basin was!

Zabeth knew exactly what the people of her village needed and how much they would be able or willing to pay for it. Traders on the coast (including my own father) used to say—especially when they were consoling themselves for some bad purchase—that everything eventually had its buyer. That wasn't so here. People were interested in new things—like the syringes, which were a surprise to me—and even modern things; but their tastes had set around the first examples of these things that they had accepted. They trusted a particular design, a particular trade-mark. It was useless for me to try to "sell" anything to Zabeth; I had to stick as far as possible to familiar stock. It made for dull business, but it avoided complications. And it helped to make Zabeth the good and direct businesswoman that, unusually for an African, she was.

She didn't know how to read and write. She carried her complicated shopping list in her head and she remembered what she had paid for things on previous occasions. She never asked for credit—she hated the idea. She paid in cash, taking the money out from the vanity case she brought to town with her. Every trader knew about Zabeth's vanity case. It wasn't that she distrusted banks; she didn't understand them.

I would say to her, in that mixed river language we used, "One day, Beth, somebody will snatch your case. It isn't safe to travel about with money like that."

"The day that happens, Mis' Salim, I will know the time has come to stay home."

It was a strange way of thinking. But she was a strange woman.

"Mis'," as used by Zabeth and others, was short for "mister." I was mister because I was a foreigner, someone from the far-off coast, and an English-speaker; and I was mister in order to be distinguished from the other resident foreigners, who were *monsieur*. That was, of course, before the Big Man came along and made us all *citoyens* and *citoyennes*. Which was all right for a while, until the lies he started making us all live made the people confused and frightened, and when a fetish stronger than his was found, made them decide to put an end to it all and go back again to the beginning.

Zabeth's village was only about sixty miles away. But it was some distance off the road, which was little more than a track; and it was some miles in from the main river. By land or by water it was a difficult journey, and took two days. By land during the rainy season it could take three. In the beginning Zabeth came by the land way, trekking with her women assistants to the road and waiting there for a van or truck or bus.

When the steamers started up again, Zabeth always used the river; and that wasn't much easier.

The secret channels from the villages were shallow, full of snags, humming with mosquitoes. Down these channels Zabeth and her women poled and often pushed their dugouts to the main river. There, close to the bank, they waited for the steamer, the dugouts full of goods—usually food—to be sold to people on the steamer and the barge the steamer towed. The food was mainly fish or monkey, fresh or *boucané*—smoked in the way of the country, with a thick black crust. Sometimes there was a smoked snake or a smoked small crocodile, a black hunk barely recognizable for what it had been—but with white or pale pink flesh below the charred crust.

When the steamer appeared, with its passenger barge in tow, Zabeth and her women poled or paddled out to the middle of the river and stood at the edge of the steamer channel, drifting down with the current. The steamer passed; the dugouts rocked in the swell; and then came the critical moment when the dugouts and the barge came close together. Zabeth and her women threw ropes onto the lower steel deck of the barge, where there were always hands to grab the ropes and tie them to some bulkhead; and the dugouts, from drifting downstream and against the side of the barge, began moving in the other direction, while people on the barge threw down pieces of paper or cloth on the fish or the monkey they wanted to buy.

This attaching of dugouts to the moving steamer or barge was a recognized river practice, but it was dangerous. Almost every trip the steamer made there was a report of a dugout being overturned somewhere along the thousand-mile route and of people being drowned. But the risk was worth taking: afterwards, without labour, as a *marchande* selling goods, Zabeth was towed up the river to the very edge of the town, uncoupling her dugouts by the ruins of the cathedral, a little before the docks, to avoid the officials there, who were always anxious to claim some tax. What a journey! Such trouble and danger to sell simple village things, and to take other goods back to the people of her village.

For a day or two before the steamer came there was a market

and a camp in the open space outside the dock gate. Zabeth became part of this camp while she was in the town. If it rained she slept in the verandah of a grocery or a bar; at a later date she put up in an African lodging house, but in the beginning such places didn't exist. When she came to the shop there was nothing in her appearance that spoke of her difficult journey or her nights in the open. She was formally dressed, wrapped in her cotton in the African style that by folds and drapes emphasized the bigness of her bottom. She wore a turban—a piece of downriver style; and she had her vanity case with the creased notes she had got from people in her village and people on the steamer and barge. She shopped, she paid; and some hours before the steamer sailed again her women—thin, short, bald-looking, and in ragged working clothes—came to take the goods away.

This was a quicker journey, downriver. But it was just as dangerous, with the same coupling and uncoupling of the dugouts and the barge. In those days the steamer left the town at four in the afternoon; so it was deep night when Zabeth and her women came to where they had to cast off from the steamer. Zabeth took care then not to give away the entrance to her village. She cast off; she waited for the steamer and the barge and the lights to disappear. Then she and her women poled back up or drifted down to their secret channel, and their nighttime labour of poling and pushing below the overhanging trees.

Going home at night! It wasn't often that I was on the river at night. I never liked it. I never felt in control. In the darkness of river and forest you could be sure only of what you could see— and even on a moonlight night you couldn't see much. When you made a noise—dipped a paddle in the water—you heard yourself as though you were another person. The river and the forest were like presences, and much more powerful than you. You felt unprotected, an intruder.

In the daylight—though the colours could be very pale and ghostly, with the heat mist at times suggesting a colder climate— you could imagine the town being rebuilt and spreading. You could imagine the forests being uprooted, the roads being laid across creeks and swamps. You could imagine the land being made part of the present: that was how the Big Man put it later, offering us the vision of a two-hundred-mile "industrial park" along the river. (But he didn't mean it really; it was only his wish to appear a greater magician than any the place had ever known.) In daylight, though, you could believe in that vision of the future. You could imagine the land being made ordinary, fit for men like yourself, as small parts of it had been made ordinary for a short while before independence—the very parts that were now in ruins.

But at night, if you were on the river, it was another thing. You felt the land taking you back to something that was familiar, something you had known at some time but had forgotten or ignored, but which was always there. You felt the land taking you back to what was there a hundred years ago, to what had been there always.

What journeys Zabeth made! It was as though she came out each time from her hidden place to snatch from the present (or the future) some precious cargo to take back to her people— those razor blades, for instance, to be taken out from their packets and sold one by one, miracles of metal—cargo that became more precious the further she got from the town, the nearer she got to her fishing village, the true, safe world, protected from other men by forest and clogged-up waterways. And protected in other ways as well. Every man here knew that he was watched from above by his ancestors, living forever in a higher sphere, their passage on earth not forgotten, but essentially preserved, part of the presence of the forest. In the deepest forest was the greatest security. That was the security that Zabeth left behind, to get her precious cargo; that was the security to which she returned.

No one liked going outside his territory. But Zabeth travelled without fear; she came and went with her vanity case and no one molested her. She was not an ordinary person. In appearance she was not at all like the people of our region. They were small and slight and very black. Zabeth was a big woman with a coppery complexion; there were times when this copper glow, especially on her cheekbones, looked like a kind of make-up. There was something else about Zabeth. She had a special smell. It was strong and unpleasant, and at first I thought—because she came from a fishing village—that it was an old and deep smell of fish. Then I thought it had to do with her restricted village diet. But the people of Zabeth's tribe whom I met didn't smell like Zabeth. Africans noticed her smell. If they came into the shop when Zabeth was there they wrinkled their noses and sometimes they went away.

Metty, the half-African boy who had grown up in my family's house on the coast and had come to join me, Metty said that Zabeth's smell was strong enough to keep mosquitoes away. I thought myself that it was this smell that kept men away from Zabeth, in spite of her fleshiness (which the men here liked) and in spite of her vanity case—because Zabeth wasn't married and, so far as I knew, lived with no man.

But the smell was meant to keep people at a distance. It was Metty—learning local customs fast—who told me that Zabeth was a magician, and was known in our region as a magician. Her smell was the smell of her protecting ointments. Other women used perfumes and scents to attract; Zabeth's ointments repelled and warned. She was protected. She knew it, and other people knew it.

I had treated Zabeth so far as a *marchande* and a good customer. Now that I knew that in our region she was a person of power, a prophetess, I could never forget it. So the charm worked on me as well.

# 2

Africa was my home, had been the home of my family for centuries. But we came from the east coast, and that made the difference. The coast was not truly African. It was an Arab-Indian-Persian-Portuguese place, and we who lived there were really people of the Indian Ocean. True Africa was at our back. Many miles of scrub or desert separated us from the upcountry

people; we looked east to the lands with which we traded—
Arabia, India, Persia. These were also the lands of our ancestors.
But we could no longer say that we were Arabians or Indians or
Persians; when we compared ourselves with these people, we felt
like people of Africa.

My family was Muslim. But we were a special group. We were
distinct from the Arabs and other Muslims of the coast; in our
customs and attitudes we were closer to the Hindus of north-
western India, from which we had originally come. When we had
come no one could tell me. We were not that kind of people. We
simply lived; we did what was expected of us, what we had seen
the previous generation do. We never asked why; we never recorded. We felt in our bones that we were a very old people; but
we seemed to have no means of gauging the passing of time.
Neither my father nor my grandfather could put dates to their
stories. Not because they had forgotten or were confused; the
past was simply the past.

I remember hearing from my grandfather that he had once
shipped a boatful of slaves as a cargo of rubber. He couldn't tell
me when he had done this. It was just there in his memory,
floating around, without date or other association, as an unusual
event in an uneventful life. He didn't tell it as a piece of wickedness or trickery or as a joke; he just told it as something unusual
that he had done—not shipping the slaves, but describing them
as rubber. And without my own memory of the old man's story I
suppose that would have been a piece of history lost forever. I
believe, from my later reading, that the idea of rubber would
have occurred to my grandfather at the time, before the First
World War, when rubber became big business—and later a big
scandal—in central Africa. So that facts are known to me which
remained hidden or uninteresting to my grandfather.

Of that whole period of upheaval in Africa—the expulsion of
the Arabs, the expansion of Europe, the parcelling out of the
continent—that is the only family story I have. That was the sort
of people we were. All that I know of our history and the history
of the Indian Ocean I have got from books written by Europeans. If I say that our Arabs in their time were great adven-

turers and writers; that our sailors gave the Mediterranean the lateen sail that made the discovery of the Americas possible; that an Indian pilot led Vasco da Gama from East Africa to Calicut; that the very word *cheque* was first used by our Persian merchants—if I say these things it is because I have got them from European books. They formed no part of our knowledge or pride. Without Europeans, I feel, all our past would have been washed away, like the scuff marks of fishermen on the beach outside our town.

There was a stockade on this beach. The walls were of brick. It was a ruin when I was a boy, and in tropical Africa, land of impermanent building, it was like a rare piece of history. It was in this stockade that the slaves were kept after they had been marched down from the interior in the caravans; there they waited for the dhows to take them across the sea. But if you didn't know, then the place was nothing, just four crumbling walls in a picture-postcard setting of beach and coconut trees.

Once the Arabs had ruled here; then the Europeans had come; now the Europeans were about to go away. But little had changed in the manners or minds of men. The fishermen's boats on that beach were still painted with large eyes on the bows for good luck; and the fishermen could get very angry, even murderous, if some visitor tried to photograph them—tried to rob them of their souls. People lived as they had always done; there was no break between past and present. All that had happened in the past was washed away; there was always only the present. It was as though, as a result of some disturbance in the heavens, the early morning light was always receding into the darkness, and men lived in a perpetual dawn.

The slavery of the east coast was not like the slavery of the west coast. No one was shipped off to plantations. Most of the people who left our coast went to Arabian homes as domestic servants. Some became members of the family they had joined; a few became powerful in their own right. To an African, a child of the forest, who had marched down hundreds of miles from the interior and was far from his village and tribe, the protection of a foreign family was preferable to being alone among strange and unfriendly Africans. This was one reason why the trade went on long after it had been outlawed by the European powers; and why, at the time when the Europeans were dealing in one kind of rubber, my grandfather could still occasionally deal in another. This was also the reason why a secret slavery continued on the coast until the other day. The slaves, or the people who might be considered slaves, wanted to remain as they were.

In my family's compound there were two slave families, and they had been there for at least three generations. The last thing they wanted to hear was that they had to go. Officially these people were only servants. But they wanted it known—to other Africans, and to poor Arabs and Indians—that they were really slaves. It wasn't that they were proud of slavery as a condition; what they were fierce about was their special connection with a family of repute. They could be very rough with people they considered smaller fry than the family.

When I was young I would be taken for walks in the narrow white-walled lanes of the old part of the town, which was where our house was. I would be bathed and dressed; they would put kohl on my eyes and hang a good-luck charm around my neck; and then Mustafa, one of our old men, would hoist me on his shoulders. That was how I took my walk: Mustafa displaying me on his shoulders, displaying the worth of our family, and at the same time displaying his own trusted position in our family. There were some boys who made a point of taunting us. Mustafa, when we ran into these boys, would set me down, encourage me to speak insults, would add to these insults himself, would encourage me to fight, and then, when things became too hot for me, would lift me out of reach of the boys' feet and fists and place me again on his shoulders. And we would continue our walk.

This talk of Mustafa and Arabia and dhows and slaves might sound like something out of the *Arabian Nights*. But when I think of Mustafa, and even when I hear the word "slave," I think of the squalor of our family compound, a mixture of school yard and back yard: all those people, someone always shrieking, quantities of clothes hanging on the lines or spread out on the bleaching stones, the sour smell of those stones running into the smell of the latrine and the barred-off urinal corner, piles of dirty enamel and brass dishes on the washing-up stand in the middle of the yard, children running about everywhere, endless cooking in the blackened kitchen building. I think of a hubbub of women and children, of my sisters and their families, the servant women and their families, both sides apparently in constant competition; I think of quarrels in the family rooms, competitive quarrels in the servants' quarters. There were too many of us in that small compound. We didn't want all those people in the servants' quarters. But they weren't ordinary servants, and there was no question of getting rid of them. We were stuck with them.

That was how it was on the east coast. The slaves could take over, and in more than one way. The people in our servant houses were no longer pure African. It wasn't acknowledged by the family, but somewhere along the line, or at many places along the line, the blood of Asia had been added to those people. Mustafa had the blood of Gujarat in his veins; so had Metty, the boy who later came all the way across the continent to join me. This, though, was a transferring of blood from master to slave. With the Arabs on our coast the process had worked the other way. The slaves had swamped the masters; the Arabian race of the master had virtually disappeared.

Once, great explorers and warriors, the Arabs had ruled. They had pushed far into the interior and had built towns and planted orchards in the forest. Then their power had been broken by Europe. Their towns and orchards disappeared, swallowed up in bush. They ceased to be driven on by their idea of their position in the world, and their energy was lost; they forgot who they were and where they had come from. They knew only that they were Muslims; and in the Muslim way they needed wives and more wives. But they were cut off from their roots in Arabia and could only find their wives among the African women who had once been their slaves. Soon, therefore, the Arabs, or the people who called themselves Arabs, had become indistinguishable from Africans. They barely had an idea of their original civilization. They had the Koran and its laws; they stuck to certain fashions in dress, wore a certain kind of cap, had a special cut of beard; and that was all. They had little idea of what their ancestors had done in Africa. They had only the habit of authority, without the energy or the education to back up that authority. The authority of the Arabs—which was real enough when I was a boy—was only a matter of custom. It could be blown away at any time. The world is what it is.

I was worried for the Arabs. I was also worried for us. Because, so far as power went, there was no difference between the Arabs and ourselves. We were both small groups living under a European flag at the edge of the continent. In our family house when I was a child I never heard a discussion about our future or the future of the coast. The assumption seemed to be that things would continue, that marriages would continue to be arranged between approved parties, that trade and business would go on, that Africa would be for us as it had been.

My sisters married in the traditional way; it was assumed that I, too, would marry when the time came and extend the life of our family house. But it came to me while I was quite young, still at school, that our way of life was antiquated and almost at an end.

Small things can start us off in new ways of thinking, and I was started off by the postage stamps of our area. The British administration gave us beautiful stamps. These stamps depicted local scenes and local things; there was one called "Arab Dhow." It was as though, in those stamps, a foreigner had said, "This is what is most striking about this place." Without that stamp of the dhow I might have taken the dhows for granted. As it was, I learned to look at them. Whenever I saw them tied up at the waterfront I thought of them as something peculiar to our region, quaint, something the foreigner would remark on, something not quite modern, and certainly nothing like the liners and cargo ships that berthed in our own modern docks.

So from an early age I developed the habit of looking, detaching myself from a familiar scene and trying to consider it as from a distance. It was from this habit of looking that the idea came to me that as a community we had fallen behind. And that was the beginning of my insecurity.

I used to think of this feeling of insecurity as a weakness, a failing of my own temperament, and I would have been ashamed if anyone had found out about it. I kept my ideas about the future to myself, and that was easy enough in our house, where, as I have said, there was never anything like a political discussion. My family were not fools. My father and his brothers were traders, businessmen; in their own way they had to keep up with the times. They could assess situations; they took risks and sometimes they could be very bold. But they were buried so deep in their lives that they were not able to stand back and consider the nature of their lives. They did what they had to do. When things went wrong they had the consolations of religion. This wasn't just a readiness to accept Fate; this was a quiet and profound conviction about the vanity of all human endeavour.

I could never rise so high. My own pessimism, my insecurity, was a more terrestrial affair. I was without the religious sense of my family. The insecurity I felt was due to my lack of true religion, and was like the small change of the exalted pessimism of our faith, the pessimism that can drive men on to do wonders. It was the price for my more materialist attitude, my seeking to occupy the middle ground, between absorption in life and soaring above the cares of the earth.

If the insecurity I felt about our position on the coast was due to my temperament, then little occurred to calm me down. Events in this part of Africa began to move fast. To the north there was a bloody rebellion of an upcountry tribe which the British seemed unable to put down; and there were explosions of disobedience and rage in other places as well. Even hypochondriacs sometimes have real illnesses, and I don't think it was my nervousness alone that made me feel that the political system we had known was coming to an end, and that what was going to replace it wasn't going to be pleasant. I feared the lies—black men assuming the lies of white men.

If it was Europe that gave us on the coast some idea of our history, it was Europe, I feel, that also introduced us to the lie.

Those of us who had been in that part of Africa before the Europeans had never lied about ourselves. Not because we were more moral. We didn't lie because we never assessed ourselves and didn't think there was anything for us to lie about; we were people who simply did what we did. But the Europeans could do one thing and say something quite different; and they could act in this way because they had an idea of what they owed to their civilization. It was their great advantage over us. The Europeans wanted gold and slaves, like everybody else; but at the same time they wanted statues put up to themselves as people who had done good things for the slaves. Being an intelligent and energetic people, and at the peak of their powers, they could express both sides of their civilization; and they got both the slaves and the statues.

Because they could assess themselves, the Europeans were better equipped to cope with changes than we were. And I saw, when I compared the Europeans with ourselves, that we had ceased to count in Africa, that really we no longer had anything to offer. The Europeans were preparing to get out, or to fight, or to meet the Africans halfway. We continued to live as we had always done, blindly. Even at this late stage there was never anything like a political discussion in our house or in the houses of families I knew. The subject was avoided. I found myself avoiding it.

I used to go twice a week to play squash in the squash court of my friend Indar. His grandfather had come from the Punjab in India to work on the railway as a contract labourer. The old Punjabi had done well. When he had worked out his contract he had settled on the coast and become a market money-lender, lending twenty or thirty shillings a time to stall-keepers in the market who ran short and depended on these small loans to buy their goods. For ten shillings lent this week twelve or fifteen had to be returned the next. Not the best kind of business; but an active man (and a tough man) could increase his capital many times over in a year. Well, it was a service, and a living. And more than a living. The family had become very grand. They had become merchant bankers in an unofficial way, staking small prospecting companies, staking trading ventures to India and Arabia and the Persian Gulf (still in the Arab dhows of the postage stamp).

The family lived in a big compound in an asphalted yard. The main house was at the far end; there were smaller houses at the side for members of the family who wished to live by themselves, other houses for the servants (proper servants, hire-and-fire people, not limpets like ours); and there was the squash court. Everything was surrounded by a high ochre-washed wall, and there was a main gate with a watchman. The compound was in a newer part of the town; I didn't think it was possible to be more exclusive or protected.

Rich people never forget they are rich, and I looked upon Indar as a good son of his money-lending or banking family. He was handsome, careful of his appearance, and slightly effeminate, with something buttoned up in his expression. I put that expression down to his regard for his own wealth and also to his sexual anxieties. I thought he was a great brothel man on the sly and lived in fear of being exposed or catching some disease.

We were having cold orange juice and hot black tea after our game (Indar was already concerned about his weight), when he told me he was leaving. He was going away, going to England to a famous university to do a three-year course. It was like Indar, and his family, to announce important news in this casual way. The news depressed me a little. Indar could do what he was doing not only because he was rich (I associated going abroad to study with great wealth), but also because he had gone right through our local English-language college until he was eighteen. I had left when I was sixteen. Not because I wasn't bright or didn't have the inclination, but because no one in our family had stayed at school after sixteen.

We were sitting on the steps of the squash court, in the shade. Indar said in his quiet way, "We're washed up here, you know. To be in Africa you have to be strong. We're not strong. We don't even have a flag."

He had mentioned the unmentionable. And as soon as he spoke I saw the wall of his compound as useless. Two generations had built what I saw; and I mourned for that lost labour. As soon as Indar spoke I felt I could enter his mind and see what he saw—the mocking quality of the grandeur, the gate and the watchman that wouldn't be able to keep out the true danger.

But I gave no sign that I understood what he was talking about. I behaved like the others who had infuriated and saddened me by refusing to acknowledge that change was coming to our part of the world. And when Indar went on to ask, "What are you going to do?" I said, as though I didn't see any problem, "I'll stay. I'll go into the business."

It wasn't true at all. It was the opposite of what I felt. But I found that I was unwilling—as soon as the question had been put to me—to acknowledge my helplessness. I instinctively fell into the attitudes of my family. But with me the fatalism was bogus; I cared very much about the world and wished to renounce nothing. All I could do was to hide from the truth. And that discovery about myself made the walk back through the hot town very disturbing.

The afternoon sun fell on the soft black asphalt road and the tall hibiscus hedges. It was all so ordinary. There was as yet no danger in the crowds, the broken-down streets, the blank-walled lanes. But the place was poisoned for me.

I had an upstairs room in our family house. It was still light when I got back. I looked out over our compound, saw the trees and greenery of the neighbouring yards and open spaces. My aunt was calling to one of her daughters: some old brass vases that had been taken out to the yard to be scoured with limes hadn't been taken back in. I looked at that devout woman, sheltered behind her wall, and saw how petty her concern with the brass vases was. The thin whitewashed wall (thinner than the wall of the slave stockade on the beach) protected her so little. She was so vulnerable—her person, her religion, her customs, her way of life. The squalling yard had contained its own life, had been its own complete world, for so long. How could anyone not take it for granted? How could anyone stop to ask what it was that had really protected us?

I remembered the look of contempt and irritation Indar had

given me. And the decision I came to then was this. I had to break away. I couldn't protect anyone; no one could protect me. We couldn't protect ourselves; we could only in various ways hide from the truth. I had to break away from our family compound and our community. To stay with my community, to pretend that I had simply to travel along with them, was to be taken with them to destruction. I could be master of my fate only if I stood alone. One tide of history—forgotten by us, living only in books by Europeans that I was yet to read—had brought us here. We had lived our lives in our way, done what we had to do, worshipped God and obeyed his commandments. Now—to echo Indar's words—another tide of history was coming to wash us away.

I could no longer submit to Fate. My wish was not to be good, in the way of our tradition, but to make good. But how? What did I have to offer? What talent, what skill, apart from the African trading skills of our family? This anxiety began to eat away at me. And that was why, when Nazruddin made his offer, of a shop and business in a far-off country that was still in Africa, I clutched at it.

Nazruddin was an exotic in our community. He was a man of my father's age, but he looked much younger and was altogether more a man of the world. He played tennis, drank wine, spoke French, wore dark glasses and suits (with very wide lapels, the tips of which curled down). He was known among us (and slightly mocked behind his back) for his European manners, which he had picked up not from Europe (he had never been there), but from a town in the centre of Africa where he lived and had his business.

Many years before, following some fancy of his own, Nazruddin had cut down on his business on the coast and begun to move inland. The colonial boundaries of Africa gave an international flavour to his operations. But Nazruddin was doing no more than following the old Arab trading routes to the interior; and he had fetched up in the centre of the continent, at the bend in the great river.

That was as far as the Arabs had got in the last century. There they had met Europe, advancing from the other direction. For Europe it was one little probe. For the Arabs of central Africa it was their all; the Arabian energy that had pushed them into Africa had died down at its source, and their power was like the light of a star that travels on after the star itself has become dead. Arab power had vanished; at the bend in the river there had grown up a European, and not an Arab, town. And it was from that town that Nazruddin, reappearing among us from time to time, brought back his exotic manners and tastes and his tales of commercial success.

Nazruddin was an exotic, but he remained bound to our community because he needed husbands and wives for his children. I always knew that in me he saw the prospective husband of one of his daughters; but I had lived with this knowledge for so long that it didn't embarrass me. I liked Nazruddin. I welcomed his visits, his talk, his very alienness as he sat downstairs in our drawing room or verandah and spoke of the excitements of his far-off world.

He was a man of enthusiasms. He relished everything he did. He liked the houses he bought (always bargains), the restaurants he chose, the dishes he had ordered. Everything worked out well for him, and his tales of unfailing luck would have made him intolerable if he didn't have the gift of describing things so well. He made me long to do what he had done, to be where he had been. In some ways he became my model.

He was something of a palmist, in addition to everything else, and his readings were valued because he could do them only when the mood took him. When I was ten or twelve he had given me a reading and had seen great things in my hand. So I respected his judgment. He added to that reading from time to time. I remember one occasion especially. He was on the bentwood rocker, rocking unsteadily from the edge of the carpet onto the concrete floor. He broke off what he was saying and asked to see my hand. He felt the tips of my fingers, bent my fingers, looked briefly at my palm, and then let my hand go. He thought for a little about what he had seen—it was his way, thinking about what he had seen rather than looking at the hand all the time—and he said, "You are the most faithful man I know." This didn't please me; it seemed to me he was offering me no life at all. I said, "Can you read your own hand? Do you know what's in store for you?" He said, "Don't I know, don't I know." The tone of his voice was different then, and I saw that this man, for whom (according to his talk) everything worked out beautifully, really lived with a vision of things turning out badly. I thought: This is how a man should behave; and I felt close to him after that, closer than I did to members of my own family.

Then came the crash which some people had been quietly prophesying for this successful and talkative man. Nazruddin's adopted country became independent, quite suddenly, and the news from that place for weeks and months was of wars and killings. From the way some people talked you might have believed that if Nazruddin had been another kind of person, if he had boasted less of his success, drunk less wine and been more seemly in his behaviour, events would have taken another turn. We heard that he had fled with his family to Uganda. There was a report that they had driven through the bush for days on the back of a truck and had turned up panic-stricken and destitute at the border town of Kisoro.

At least he was safe. In due course he came to the coast. People looking for a broken man were disappointed. Nazruddin was as sprightly as ever, still with his dark glasses and suit. The disaster appeared not to have touched him at all.

Usually when Nazruddin came to visit, efforts were made to receive him well. The drawing room was given a special cleaning, and the brass vases with the hunting scenes were polished up. But this time, because of the belief that he was a man in trouble, and therefore ordinary again, just like us, no one had tried hard. The drawing room was in its usual state of mess and we sat out on the verandah facing the yard.

My mother brought tea, offering it not in the usual way, as the shamefaced hospitality of simple folk, but behaving as though she was performing some necessary final rite. When she put the tray down she seemed about to burst into tears. My brothers-in-

law gathered around with concerned faces. But from Nazruddin
—in spite of that tale about the long-distance ride on the back of
a truck—there came no stories of disaster, only stories of continuing luck and success. He had seen the trouble coming; he had
pulled out months before it came.

Nazruddin said: "It wasn't the Africans who made me nervous. It was the Europeans and the others. Just before a crash
people go crazy. We had a fantastic property boom. Everybody
was only talking about money. A piece of bush costing nothing
today was selling for half a million francs tomorrow. It was like
magic, but with real money. I got caught up in it myself, and
nearly got trapped.

"One Sunday morning I went out to the development where I
had bought a few lots. The weather was bad. Hot and heavy. The
sky was dark but it wasn't going to rain; it was just going to stay
like that. The lightning was far away—it was raining somewhere
else in the forest. I thought: What a place to live in! I could hear
the river—the development wasn't too far from the rapids. I
listened to the river and looked up at that sky and I thought:
This isn't property. This is just bush. This has always been bush.
I could scarcely wait for Monday morning after that. I put everything up for sale. Lower than the going price, but I asked to be
paid in Europe. I sent the family to Uganda.

"Do you know Uganda? A lovely country. Cool, three to four
thousand feet up, and people say it's like Scotland, with the hills.
The British have given the place the finest administration you
could ask for. Very simple, very efficient. Wonderful roads. And
the Bantu people there are pretty bright."

That was Nazruddin. We had imagined him done for. Instead,
he was trying to excite us with his enthusiasm for his new country, and asking us to contemplate his luck yet again. The
patronage, in fact, was all on his side. Though he never said
anything openly, he saw us on the coast as threatened, and he
had come that day to make me an offer.

He still had interests in his old country—a shop, a few agencies. He had thought it prudent to keep the shop on, while he was
transferring his assets out of the country, to prevent people look-

ing at his affairs too closely. And it was this shop and those agencies that he now offered me.

"They aren't worth anything now. But they will be again. I really should be giving it to you for nothing. But that would be bad for you and for me. You must always know when to pull out. A businessman isn't a mathematician. Remember that. Never become hypnotized by the beauty of numbers. A businessman is someone who buys at ten and is happy to get out at twelve. The other kind of man buys at ten, sees it rise to eighteen and does nothing. He is waiting for it to get to twenty. The beauty of numbers. When it drops to ten again he waits for it to get back to eighteen. When it drops to two he waits for it to get back to ten. Well, it gets back there. But he has wasted a quarter of his life. And all he's got out of his money is a little mathematical excitement."

I said, "This shop: assuming you bought at ten, what would you say you were selling it to me for?"

"Two. In three or four years it will climb up to six. Business never dies in Africa; it is only interrupted. For me it is a waste of time to see that two get up to six. There is more for me in cotton in Uganda. But for you it will be a trebling of your capital. What you must always know is when to get out."

Nazruddin had seen faithfulness in my hand. But he had read me wrong. Because when I accepted his offer I was in an important way breaking faith with him. I had accepted his offer because I wanted to break away. To break away from my family and community also meant breaking away from my unspoken commitment to Nazruddin and his daughter.

She was a lovely girl. Once a year, for a few weeks, she came to the coast to stay with her father's sister. She was better educated than I was; there was some talk of her going in for accountancy or law. She would have been a very nice girl to marry, but I admired her as I would have admired a girl of my own family. Nothing would have been easier than to marry Nazruddin's daughter. Nothing, to me, would have been more stifling. And it was from that stifling as well as from everything else that I drove away, when I left the coast in the Peugeot.

I was breaking faith with Nazruddin. Yet he—a relisher of life, a seeker after experience—had been my exemplar; and it was to his town that I drove. All that I knew of the town at the bend of the river I had got from Nazruddin's stories. Ridiculous things can work on us at moments of strain; and towards the end of that hard drive what was often in my head was what Nazruddin had said about the restaurants of the town, about the food of Europe and the wine. "The wines are Saccone and Speed," he had said. It was a merchant's observation. He had meant that even there, in the centre of Africa, the wine had come from the shippers on our east coast, and not from the people on the other side. But in my imagination I allowed the words to stand for pure bliss.

I had never been to a real European restaurant or tasted wine —forbidden to us—with any pleasure; and I knew that the life Nazruddin had described had come to an end. But I drove through Africa to Nazruddin's town as to a place where this life might be re-created for me.

When I arrived I found that the town from which Nazruddin had brought back his tales had been destroyed, had returned to the bush he had had a vision of when he had decided to sell. In spite of myself, in spite of all that I had been told about recent events, I felt shocked, let down. My faithlessness hardly seemed to matter.

Wine! It was hard to get the simplest food; and if you wanted vegetables you either got them out of an old—and expensive— tin, or you grew them yourself. The Africans who had abandoned the town and gone back to their villages were better off; they at least had gone back to their traditional life and were more or less self-sufficient. But for the rest of us in the town, who needed shops and services—a few Belgians, some Greeks and Italians, a handful of Indians—it was a stripped, Robinson Crusoe kind of existence. We had cars and we lived in proper houses—I had bought a flat over an empty warehouse for almost nothing. But if we had worn skins and lived in thatched huts it wouldn't have been too inappropriate. The shops were empty; water was a problem; electricity was erratic; and petrol was often short.

Once for some weeks we were without kerosene. Two empty oil barges had been shanghaied by people downriver, towed as river spoil to a hidden creek, and converted into living quarters. The people here liked to scrape their yards down to the red earth, to keep away snakes; and the steel decks of the barges provided an ideal living surface.

On those keroseneless mornings I had to boil my water on an English-made cast-iron charcoal brazier—part of my shop stock, intended for sale to village Africans. I took the brazier to the landing of the external staircase at the back of the house, squatted and fanned. All around me people were doing the same; the place was blue with smoke.

And there were the ruins. *Miscerique probat populos et foedera jungi.* These Latin words, whose meaning I didn't know, were all that remained of a monument outside the dock gates. I knew the words by heart; I gave them my own pronunciation, and they ran like a nonsense jingle in my head. The words were carved at the top of a block of granite, and the rest of the granite was now bare. The bronze sculpture below the words had been torn away; the jagged little bits of bronze that remained anchored in the granite suggested that the sculptor had done banana leaves or palm branches at the top, to frame his composition. I was told that the monument had been put up only a few years before, almost at the end of the colonial time, to mark sixty years of the steamer service from the capital.

So almost as soon as it had been put up—no doubt with speeches about a further sixty years of service—the steamer monument had been knocked down. With all the other colonial statues and monuments. Pedestals had been defaced, protective railings flattened, floodlights smashed and left to rust. Ruins had been left as ruins; no attempt had been made to tidy up. The names of all the main streets had been changed. Rough boards carried the new, roughly lettered names. No one used the new names, because no one particularly cared about them. The wish had only been to get rid of the old, to wipe out the memory of the intruder. It was unnerving, the depth of that African rage, the wish to destroy, regardless of the consequences.

But more unnerving than anything else was the ruined suburb near the rapids. Valuable real estate for a while, and now bush again, common ground, according to African practice. The houses had been set alight one by one. They had been stripped— before or afterwards—only of those things that the local people needed: sheets of tin, lengths of pipe, bathtubs and sinks and lavatory bowls (impermeable vessels, useful for soaking cassava in). The big lawns and gardens had returned to bush; the streets had disappeared; vines and creepers had grown over broken, bleached walls of concrete or hollow clay brick. Here and there in the bush could still be seen the concrete shells of what had been restaurants (Saccone and Speed wines) and nightclubs. One nightclub had been called "Napoli"; the now meaningless name, painted on the concrete wall, was almost bleached away.

Sun and rain and bush had made the site look old, like the site of a dead civilization. The ruins, spreading over so many acres, seemed to speak of a final catastrophe. But the civilization wasn't dead. It was the civilization I existed in and in fact was still working towards. And that could make for an odd feeling: to be among the ruins was to have your time-sense unsettled. You felt like a ghost, not from the past, but from the future. You felt that your life and ambition had already been lived out for you and you were looking at the relics of that life. You were in a place where the future had come and gone.

With its ruins and its deprivations, Nazruddin's town was a ghost town. And for me, as a newcomer, there was nothing like a social life. The expatriates weren't welcoming. They had been through a lot; they still didn't know how things were going to turn out; and they were very nervous. The Belgians, especially the younger ones, were full of resentments and a sense of injustice. The Greeks, great family men, with the aggressiveness and frustrations of family men, kept to their families and their immediate friends. There were three houses that I visited, visiting them in turn on weekdays for lunch, which had become my main meal. They were all Asian or Indian houses.

There was a couple from India. They lived in a small flat that smelled of asafoetida and was decorated with paper flowers and brightly coloured religious prints. He was a United Nations expert of some sort who hadn't wanted to go back to India and had stayed on doing odd jobs after his contract had expired. They were a hospitable couple and they made a point (I feel for religious reasons) of offering hospitality to frightened or stranded foreigners. They spoilt their hospitality by talking a little too much about it. Their food was too liquid and peppery for me, and I didn't like the way the man ate. He bent his head low over his food, keeping his nose an inch or two away from his plate, and he ate noisily, slapping his lips together. While he ate like this his wife fanned him, never taking her eyes off his plate, fanning with her right hand, resting her chin on the palm of her left hand. Still, I went there twice a week, more for the sake of having somewhere to go than for the food.

The other place I went to was a rough, ranch-like house that belonged to an elderly Indian couple whose family had all gone away during the troubles. The yard was big and dusty, full of abandoned cars and trucks, the relics of a transport business in colonial days. This old couple didn't seem to know where they were. The bush of Africa was outside their yard; but they spoke no French, no African language, and from the way they behaved you would have thought that the river just down the road was the Ganges, with temples and holy men and bathing steps. But it was soothing to be with them. They didn't look for conversation, and were quite happy if you said nothing, if you ate and ran.

Shoba and Mahesh were the people I felt closest to, and I soon thought of them as friends. They had a shop in what ought to have been a prime commercial position, opposite the van der Weyden Hotel. Like me, they were migrants from the east and refugees from their own community. They were an extraordinarily good-looking couple; it was strange, in our town, to find people so careful of their dress and appearance. But they had lived too long apart from their fellows and had forgotten how to be curious about them. Like many isolated people, they were wrapped up in themselves and not too interested in the world outside. And this beautiful couple had their days of tension. Shoba, the lady, was vain and neurotic. Mahesh, the simpler partner, could be in a state of anxiety about her.

That was my life in Nazruddin's town. I had wanted to break away and make a fresh start. But there are degrees in everything, and I felt burdened by the bareness of my days. My life was unconstricted, but narrower than it had ever been; the solitude of my evenings was like an ache. I didn't think I had the resources to last. My comfort was that I had lost little, except time; I could always move on—though where, I didn't yet know. And then I found I couldn't move. I had to stay.

What I had feared would happen on the coast came to pass. There was an uprising; and the Arabs—men almost as African as their servants—had been finally laid low.

I first heard the news from my friends Shoba and Mahesh, who had got it from the radio—that expatriate habit of listening to the BBC news was something I had not yet got into. We treated the news as a secret, as something that had to be kept from the local people; this was one occasion when we were glad there was no local newspaper.

Then newspapers from Europe and the United States came to various people in the town and were passed around; and it was extraordinary to me that some of the newspapers could have found good words for the butchery on the coast. But people are like that about places in which they aren't really interested and where they don't have to live. Some papers spoke of the end of feudalism and the dawn of a new age. But what had happened was not new. People who had grown feeble had been physically destroyed. That, in Africa, was not new; it was the oldest law of the land.

Letters eventually came from the coast—in a batch—from members of my family. They were cautiously written, but their message was plain. There was no place for us on the coast; our life there was over. The family was scattering. Only old people would stay on in our family compound—a quieter life there, at last. The family servants, burdensome to the end, refusing to go away, insisting on their slave status even at this time of revolution, were being split up among the family. And one of the points of the letters was that I had to take my share.

It was not for me to choose whom I wanted; apparently I had

already been chosen by someone. One of the boys or young men from the servant houses wanted to get as far away from the coast as possible, and he had been firm about being sent "to stay with Salim." The boy said he had always had "a special liking for Salim," and he had made such a fuss that they had decided to send him to me. I could imagine the scene. I could imagine the screaming and the stamping and the sulking. That was how the servants got their way in our house; they could be worse than children. My father, not realising what other people in the family had written, simply said in his letter that he and my mother had decided to send someone to look after me—he meant, of course, that he was sending me a boy to look after and feed.

I couldn't say no: the boy was on his way. That this boy had "a special liking" for me was news to me. A better reason for his choice of me was that I was just three or four years older than he was, unmarried, and more likely to put up with his wandering ways. He had always been a wanderer. We had sent him to the Koranic school when he was small, but he was always running off somewhere else, in spite of beatings by his mother. (And how he screamed in the quarters, and how his mother shouted—both of them overdoing the drama, trying to get as much attention as possible from the rest of the compound!) He was nobody's idea of a house servant. With bed and board always provided, he was more a man about town, friendly and unreliable and full of friends, always willing, always offering to help, and never doing a quarter of what he promised.

He turned up at the flat one evening in one of Daulat's trucks, not long after I had got the letters saying that he had been sent. And my heart went out to him: he looked so altered, so tired and frightened. He was still living with the shock of events on the coast; and he hadn't liked the journey across Africa at all.

He had done the first half of the journey by the railway, which travelled at an average speed of ten miles an hour. Then he had transferred to buses and finally to Daulat's trucks: in spite of wars, bad roads and worn-out vehicles, Daulat, a man of our community, maintained a trucking service between our town and the eastern frontier. Daulat's drivers helped the boy past the various officials. But the mixed-race man about town from the coast was still African enough to be unsettled by his passage through the strange tribes of the interior. He couldn't bring himself to eat their food, and he hadn't eaten for days. Without knowing it, he had made in reverse the journey which some of his ancestors had made a century or more before.

He threw himself into my arms, converting the Muslim embrace into a child's clinging. I patted him on the back, and he took this as a signal to scream the place down. Right away, between screams and bawls, he began telling me about the killings he had seen in the market at home.

I didn't take in all that he was saying. I was worried about the neighbours, and trying to get him to tone down the screaming, trying to get him to understand that that kind of showing-off slave behaviour (which it partly was) was all right on the coast, but that people here wouldn't understand. He was beginning to go on a little bit, too, about the savagery of the *kafar*, the Africans, behaving as though my flat was the family compound and he could shout anything he wanted about people outside. And all the time Daulat's friendly African loader was coming up the external staircase with luggage—not much, but in many small, awkward pieces: a few bundles, a wickerwork laundry basket, some cardboard boxes.

I broke away from the bawling boy—to pay attention was to encourage him—and I dealt with the loader, walking out with him to the street to tip him. The bawling in the flat upstairs died down, as I had expected; solitude and the strangeness of the flat were having their effect; and when I went back up I refused to hear any more from the boy until he had had something to eat.

He became quiet and correct, and while I prepared some baked beans and cheese on toast he brought out, from his bundles and boxes, the things that had been sent me by my family. Ginger and sauces and spices from my mother. Two family photographs from my father, and a wall print on cheap paper of one of our holy places in Gujarat, showing it as a modern place, though: the artist had put in motorcars and motorbikes and bicycles and even trains pell-mell in the surrounding streets. It was my father's way of saying that, modern as I was, I would return to the faith.

"I was in the market, Salim," the boy said, after he had eaten. "At first I thought it was just a quarrel around Mian's stall. I couldn't believe what I was seeing. They were behaving as though knives didn't cut, as though people weren't made of flesh. I couldn't believe it. At the end it was as if a pack of dogs had got into a butcher's stall. I saw arms and legs bleeding and lying about. Just like that. They were still there the next day, those arms and legs."

I tried to stop him. I didn't want to hear more. But it wasn't easy to stop him. He went on about those cut-off arms and legs that belonged to people we had known since we were children. It was terrible, what he had seen. But I was also beginning to feel that he was trying to excite himself to cry a little bit more after he had stopped wanting to cry. I felt that it worried him to find that from time to time he was forgetting, and thinking of other things. He seemed to be wanting to thrill himself again and again; and this disturbed me.

In a few days, though, he thawed out. And the events of the coast were never spoken of again. He settled down more easily than I expected. I had expected him to go sulky and withdrawn; I had thought, especially after his unhappy journey, that he would have hated our backward town. But he liked it; and he liked it because he was himself liked, in a way he hadn't been before.

Physically he was quite different from the local people. He was taller, more muscular, looser and more energetic in his movements. He was admired. The local women, with their usual free ways, made no secret of finding him desirable—calling out to him in the street, and stopping and staring with wicked, half-smiling (and slightly crossed) eyes that appeared to say: "Consider this a joke, and laugh. Or take it seriously." My own way of looking at him changed. He ceased to be one of the boys from the servant houses. I saw what the local people saw; in my own eyes he became more handsome and distinctive. To the local people he wasn't quite an African, and he aroused no tribal uneasiness; he was an exotic with African connections whom they wanted to claim. He flourished. He picked up the local language fast, and he even got a new name.

At home we had called him Ali or—when we wanted to suggest the special wild and unreliable nature of this Ali—Ali-wa ("Ali! Ali! But where is this Ali-wa?"). He rejected his name now. He preferred to be called Metty, which was what the local people called him. It was some time before I understood that it wasn't a real name, that it was just the French word *métis*, someone of mixed race. But that wasn't how I used it. To me it was only a name: Metty.

Here, as on the coast, Metty was a wanderer. He had the bedroom just across the passage from the kitchen; it was the first door on the right as you came in from the landing of the external staircase. I often heard him coming in late at night. That was the freedom he had come to me for. But the Metty who enjoyed that freedom was a different person from the boy who had arrived bawling and screaming, with the manners of the servant house. He had quickly shed those manners; he had developed a new idea of his worth. He became useful in the shop; and in the flat, his wandering habits—which I had dreaded—kept his presence light. But he was always there, and in the town he was like one of my own. He lessened my solitude and made the empty months more bearable—months of waiting for trade to start up again. As, very slowly, it was beginning to do.

We fell into the routine of morning coffee at the flat, shop, separate lunches, shop, separate evenings. Man and master sometimes met, as equals with equal needs, in the dark little bars that began to appear in our town, signs of reawakening life: rough little cells with roofs of corrugated iron, no ceilings, concrete walls painted dark blue or green, red concrete floors.

In one such place Metty put the seal on our new relationship one evening. When I entered I saw him dancing fantastically— slim-waisted, narrow-hipped, wonderfully made. He stopped as soon as he saw me—his servant's instinct. But then he bowed and made a show of welcoming me as though he owned the place. He said, in the French accent he had picked up, "I must do nothing indecent in front of the *patron*." And that was precisely what he went on to do.

So he learned to assert himself. But there were no strains between us. And he became, increasingly, an asset. He became my customs clerk. He was always good with the customers and won me and the shop much goodwill. As an exotic, a licensed man, he was the only person in the town who would risk making a joke with Zabeth, the *marchande* who was also a sorceress.

That was how it was with us, as the town came to life again, as the steamers started to come up again from the capital, once a week, then twice a week, as people began coming back from the villages to the *cités* in the town, as trade grew and my business, which had stood for so long at zero, climbed (to use Nazruddin's scale of ten) back up to two, and even gave me glimpses of four.

# 3

Zabeth, as a magician or sorceress, kept herself from men. But it hadn't always been so; Zabeth hadn't always been a magician. She had a son. She spoke of him sometimes to me, but she spoke of him as part of a life she had put behind her. She made that son seem so far away that I thought the boy might be dead. Then one day she brought him to the shop.

He was about fifteen or sixteen, and already quite big, taller and heavier than the men of our region, whose average height was about five feet. His skin was perfectly black, with nothing of his mother's copper colour; his face was longer and more firmly modelled; and from what Zabeth said I gathered that the boy's father came from one of the tribes of the south.

The boy's father was a trader. As a trader, he had travelled about the country during the miraculous peace of the colonial time, when men could, if they wished, pay little attention to tribal boundaries. That was how, during his travels, he and Zabeth had met; it was from this trader that Zabeth had picked up her trading skills. At independence, tribal boundaries had become important again, and travel was not as safe as it had been. The man from the south had gone back to his tribal land, taking the son he had had by Zabeth. A father could always claim his child; there were any number of folk sayings that expressed this almost universal African law. And Ferdinand—that was the name of the boy—had spent the last few years away from his mother. He had gone to school in the south, in one of the mining towns, and had been there through all the troubles that had come after independence, especially the long secessionist war.

Now for some reason—perhaps because the father had died, or had married again and wished to get rid of Ferdinand, or simply because Zabeth had wished it—Ferdinand had been sent back to his mother. He was a stranger in the land. But no one here could be without a tribe; and Ferdinand, again according to tribal custom, had been received into his mother's tribe.

Zabeth had decided to send Ferdinand to the lycée in our town. That had been cleaned up and got going again. It was a solid two-story, two-courtyard stone building in the colonial-official style, with wide verandahs upstairs and downstairs. Squatters had taken over the downstairs part, cooking on fire stones in the verandah and throwing out their rubbish onto the courtyards and grounds. Strange rubbish, not the tins and paper and boxes and other containers you would expect in a town, but a finer kind of waste—shells and bones and ashes, burnt sacking —which made the middens look like grey-black mounds of sifted earth.

The lawns and gardens had been scuffed away. But the bougainvillaea had grown wild, choking the tall palmiste trees, tumbling over the lycée wall, and climbing up the square pillars of the main gate to twine about the decorative metal arch where, in letters of metal, was still the lycée motto: *Semper Aliquid Novi*. The squatters, timid and half-starved, had moved out as soon as they had been asked. Some doors and windows and shutters had been replaced, the plumbing repaired, the place painted, the rubbish on the grounds carted away, the grounds asphalted over; and in the building which I had thought of as a ruin there had begun to appear the white faces of the teachers.

It was as a lycée boy that Ferdinand came to the shop. He

wore the regulation white shirt and short white trousers. It was a simple but distinctive costume; and—though the short trousers were a little absurd on someone so big—the costume was important both to Ferdinand and to Zabeth. Zabeth lived a purely African life; for her only Africa was real. But for Ferdinand she wished something else. I saw no contradiction; it seemed to me natural that someone like Zabeth, living such a hard life, should want something better for her son. This better life lay outside the timeless ways of village and river. It lay in education and the acquiring of new skills; and for Zabeth, as for many Africans of her generation, education was something only foreigners could give.

Ferdinand was to be a boarder at the lycée. Zabeth had brought him to the shop that morning to introduce him to me. She wanted me to keep an eye on him in the strange town and take him under my protection. If Zabeth chose me for this job, it wasn't only because I was a business associate she had grown to trust. It was also because I was a foreigner, and English-speaking as well, someone from whom Ferdinand could learn manners and the ways of the outside world. I was someone with whom Ferdinand could practise.

The tall boy was quiet and respectful. But I had the feeling that that would last only while his mother was around. There was something distant and slightly mocking in his eyes. He seemed to be humouring the mother he had only just got to know. She was a village woman; and he, after all, had lived in a mining town in the south, where he must have seen foreigners a good deal more stylish than myself. I didn't imagine him having the respect for my shop that his mother had. It was a concrete barn, with the shoddy goods spread all over the floor (but I knew where everything was). No one could think of it as a modern place; and it wasn't as brightly painted as some of the Greek shops.

I said, for Ferdinand's benefit as well as Zabeth's, "Ferdinand's a big boy, Beth. He can look after himself without me."

"No, no, Mis' Salim. Fer'nand will come to you. You beat him whenever you want."

There was little likelihood of that. But it was only a way of speaking. I smiled at Ferdinand and he smiled at me, pulling back the corners of his mouth. The smile made me notice the neatness of his mouth and the sharp-cut quality of the rest of his features. In his face I felt I could see the starting point of certain kinds of African masks, in which features were simplified and strengthened; and, with memories of those masks, I thought I saw a special distinction in his features. The idea came to me that I was looking at Ferdinand with the eyes of an African, and that was how I always looked at him. It was the effect on me of his face, which I saw then and later as one of great power.

I wasn't happy about Zabeth's request. But it had to be assented to. And when I swung my head slowly from side to side, to let them both know that Ferdinand was to look upon me as a friend, Ferdinand began to go down on one knee. But then he stopped. He didn't complete the reverence; he pretended that something had itched him on that leg, and he scratched the back of the knee he had bent. Against the white trousers his skin was black and healthy, with a slight shine.

This going down on one knee was a traditional reverence. It was what children of the bush did to show their respect for an older person. It was like a reflex, and done with no particular ceremony. Outside the town you might see children break off what they were doing and suddenly, as though they had been frightened by a snake, race to the adults they had just seen, kneel, get their little unconsidered pats on the head, and then, as though nothing had happened, run back to what they were doing. It was a custom that had spread from the forest kingdoms to the east. But it was a custom of the bush. It couldn't transfer to the town; and for someone like Ferdinand, especially after his time in the southern mining town, the child's gesture of respect would have seemed old-fashioned and subservient.

I had already been disturbed by his face. Now I thought: There's going to be trouble here.

The lycée wasn't far from the shop, an easy walk if the sun wasn't too hot or if it wasn't raining—rain flooded the streets in no time. Ferdinand came once a week to the shop to see me. He came at about half past three on Friday afternoon, or he came on Saturday morning. He was always dressed as the lycée boy, in white; and sometimes, in spite of the heat, he wore the lycée blazer, which had the *Semper Aliquid Novi* motto in a scroll on the breast pocket.

We exchanged greetings, and in the African way we could make that take time. It was hard to go on after we had finished with the greetings. He offered me nothing in the way of news; he left it to me to ask questions. And when I asked—for the sake of asking—some question like "What did you do at school today?" or "Does Father Huismans take any of your classes?" he gave me short and precise answers that left me wondering what to ask next.

The trouble was that I was unwilling—and very soon unable —to chat with him as I would have done with another African. I felt that with him I had to make a special effort, and I didn't know what I could do. He was a boy from the bush; when the holidays came he would be going back to his mother's village. But at the lycée he was learning things I knew nothing about. I couldn't talk to him about his school work; the advantage there was on his side. And there was his face. I thought there was a lot going on behind that face that I couldn't know about. I felt there was a solidity and self-possession there, and that as a guardian and educator I was being seen through.

Perhaps, with nothing to keep them going, our meetings would have come to an end. But in the shop there was an attraction: there was Metty. Metty got on with everybody. He didn't have the problems I had with Ferdinand; and it was for Metty that Ferdinand soon began to come, to the shop and then to the flat as well. After his stiff conversation in English or French with me, Ferdinand would, with Metty, switch to the local patois. He would appear then to undergo a character change, rattling away in a high-pitched voice, his laughter sounding like part of his speech. And Metty could match him; Metty had absorbed many of the intonations of the local language, and the mannerisms that went with the language.

From Ferdinand's point of view Metty was a better guide to the town than I was. And for these two unattached young men the pleasures of the town were what you would expect—beer, bars, women.

Beer was part of people's food here; children drank it; people began drinking from early in the morning. We had no local brewery, and a lot of the cargo brought up by the steamers was that weak lager the people here loved. At many points along the river, village dugouts took on cases from the moving steamer; and the steamer, on the way back to the capital, received the empties.

About women, the attitude was just as matter-of-fact. Shortly after I arrived, my friend Mahesh told me that women slept with men whenever they were asked; a man could knock on any woman's door and sleep with her. Mahesh didn't tell me this with any excitement or approval—he was wrapped up in his own beautiful Shoba. To Mahesh the sexual casualness was part of the chaos and corruption of the place.

That was how—after early delight—I had begun to feel myself. But I couldn't speak out against pleasures which were also my own. I couldn't warn Metty or Ferdinand against going to places I went to myself. The restraint, in fact, worked the other way. In spite of the changes that had come to Metty, I still regarded him as a member of my family; and I had to be careful not to do anything to wound him or anything which, when reported back, would wound other members of the family. I had, specifically, not to be seen with African women. And I was proud that, difficult though it was, I never gave cause for offence.

Ferdinand and Metty could drink in the little bars and openly pick up women or drop in at the houses of women they had got to know. It was I—as master of one man and guardian of the other—who had to hide.

What could Ferdinand learn from me? I had heard it said on the coast—and the foreigners I met here said it as well—that Africans didn't know how to "live." By that was meant that Africans didn't know how to spend money sensibly or how to keep a house. Well! My circumstances were unusual, but what would Ferdinand see when he considered my establishment?

My shop was a shambles. I had bolts of cloth and oilcloth on the shelves, but most of the stock was spread out on the concrete floor. I sat on a desk in the middle of my concrete barn, facing the door, with a concrete pillar next to the desk giving me some feeling of being anchored in that sea of junk—big enamel basins, white and blue-rimmed, or blue-rimmed with floral patterns; stacks of white enamel plates with squares of coarse, mud-coloured paper between the plates; enamel cups and iron pots and charcoal braziers and iron bedsteads and buckets in zinc or plastic and bicycle tires and torchlights and oil lamps in green or pink or amber glass.

That was the kind of junk I dealt in. I dealt in it respectfully because it was my livelihood, my means of raising two to four. But it was antiquated junk, specially made for shops like mine; and I doubt whether the workmen who made the stuff—in Europe and the United States and perhaps nowadays Japan—had any idea of what their products were used for. The smaller basins, for instance, were in demand because they were good for keeping grubs alive in, packed in damp fibre and marsh earth. The larger basins—a big purchase: a villager expected to buy no more than two or three in a lifetime—were used for soaking cassava in, to get rid of the poison.

That was my commercial setting. There was a similar rough-and-ready quality about my flat. The unmarried Belgian lady who had lived there before had been something of an artist. To her "studio" atmosphere I had added a genuine untidiness—it was like something beyond my control. Metty had taken over the kitchen and it was in a terrible state. I don't believe he ever cleaned the kerosene stove; with his servant-house background, he would have considered that woman's work. And it didn't help if I cleaned the stove. Metty wasn't shamed: the stove soon began to smell again and became sticky with all kinds of substances. The whole kitchen smelled, though it was used just for making morning coffee, mainly. I could scarcely bear to go into the kitchen. But Metty didn't mind, though his bedroom was just across the passage from the kitchen.

You entered this passage directly from the landing of the external staircase, which hung at the back of the building. As soon as you opened the landing door you got the warmed-up, shut-in smell of rust and oil and kerosene, dirty clothes and old paint and old timber. And the place smelled like that because you couldn't leave any window open. The town, run down as it was, crawled with thieves, and they seemed able to wriggle through any little opening. To the right was Metty's bedroom: one look showed you that Metty had turned it into a proper little servant's room, with his cot, his bedding rolls and his various bundles, his cardboard boxes, his clothes hanging on nails and window catches. A little way down the passage, to the left, after the kitchen, was the sitting room.

It was a large room, and the Belgian lady had painted it white all over, ceiling, walls, windows, and even window panes. In this white room with bare floorboards there was a couch upholstered in a coarse-weave, dark-blue material; and, to complete the studio–sitting room effect, there was an unpainted trestle table as big as a Ping-Pong table. That had been spread over with my own junk—old magazines, paperbacks, letters, shoes, rackets and spanners, shoe boxes and shirt boxes in which at different times I had tried to sort things. One corner of the table was kept clear, and this was perpetually covered by a scorched white cloth: it was where Metty did his ironing, sometimes with the electric iron (on the table, always), sometimes (when the electricity failed) with the old solid flatiron, a piece of shop stock.

On the white wall at the end of the room was a large oil painting of a European port, done in reds and yellows and blues. It was in slapdash modern style; the lady had painted it herself and signed it. She had given it pride of place in her main room. Yet she hadn't thought it worth the trouble of taking away. On the floor, leaning against the walls, were other paintings I had inherited from the lady. It was as if the lady had lost faith in her own junk, and when the independence crisis came, had been glad to go.

The bedroom was at the end of the passage. It was for me a place of special desolation, with its big fitted cupboards and its very big foam bed. What anticipations that bed had given me, as it had no doubt given the lady! Such anticipations, such an assurance of my own freedom; such letdowns, such a sense of shame. How many African women were hustled away at difficult hours—before Metty came in, or before Metty woke up! Many times on that bed I waited for morning to cleanse me of memory; and often, thinking of Nazruddin's daughter and the faith of that man in my own faithfulness, I promised to be good. In time that was to change; the bed and the room were to have other associations for me. But until then I knew only what I knew.

The Belgian lady had attempted to introduce a touch of Europe and home and art, another kind of life, to this land of rain and heat and big-leaved trees—always visible, if blurred, through the white-painted window panes. She would have had a high idea of herself; but judged on its own, what she had tried to do wasn't of much value. And I felt that Ferdinand, when he looked at my shop and flat, would come to the same conclusion about me. It would be hard for him to see any great difference between my life and the life he knew. This added to my nighttime glooms. I wondered about the nature of my aspirations, the very supports of my existence; and I began to feel that any life I might have anywhere—however rich and successful and better furnished—would only be a version of the life I lived now.

These thoughts could take me into places I didn't want to be. It was partly the effect of my isolation: I knew that. I knew there was more to me than my setting and routine showed. I knew there was something that separated me from Ferdinand and the life of the bush about me. And it was because I had no means in my day-to-day life of asserting this difference, of exhibiting my true self, that I fell into the stupidity of exhibiting my things.

I showed Ferdinand my things. I racked my brains wondering what to show him next. He was very cool, as though he had seen it all before. It was only his manner, the dead tone of voice he used when he spoke to me. But it irritated me.

I wanted to say to him: "Look at these magazines. Nobody pays me to read them. I read them because I am the kind of person I am, because I take an interest in things, because I want to know about the world. Look at those paintings. The lady took a lot of trouble over them. She wanted to make something beautiful to hang in her house. She didn't hang it there because it was a piece of magic."

I said it in the end, though not in those words. Ferdinand didn't respond. And the paintings were junk—the lady didn't know how to fill the canvas and hoped to get away with the rough strokes of colour. And the books and magazines were junk—especially the pornographic ones, which could depress me and embarrass me but which I didn't throw away because there were times when I needed them.

Ferdinand misunderstood my irritation.

He said one day, "You don't have to show me anything, Salim."

He had stopped calling me mister, following Metty's lead. Metty had taken to calling me *patron*, and in the presence of a third person, could make it sound ironical. Metty was there that day; but Ferdinand, when he told me I wasn't to show him anything, wasn't speaking ironically. He never spoke ironically.

I was reading a magazine when Ferdinand came to the shop one afternoon. I greeted him and went on with the magazine. It .was a magazine of popular science, the kind of reading I had become addicted to. I liked receiving these little bits of knowledge; and I often thought, while I read, that the particular science or field I was reading about was the thing to which I should have given my days and nights, adding knowledge to knowledge, making discoveries, making something of myself, using all my faculties. It was a good feeling; from my point of view, it was as good as the life of knowledge itself.

Metty was at the customs that afternoon, clearing some goods that had arrived by the steamer a fortnight before—that was the pace at which things moved here. Ferdinand hung about the shop for a while. I had felt rebuked by what he had said about not showing him things, and I wasn't going to take the lead in conversation. At last he came to the desk and said, "What are you reading, Salim?"

I couldn't help myself: the teacher and the guardian in me came out. I said, "You should look at this. They're working on a new kind of telephone. It works by light impulses rather than an electric current."

I never really believed in these new wonder things I read about. I never thought I would come across them in my own life. But that was the attraction of reading about them: you could read article after article about these things you hadn't yet begun to use.

Ferdinand said, "Who are they?"

"What do you mean?"

"Who are the 'they' who are working on the new telephone?"

I thought: We are here already, after only a few months at the lycée. He's just out of the bush; I know his mother; I treat him like a friend; and already we're getting this political nonsense. I didn't give the answer I thought he was expecting. I didn't say, "The white men." Though with half of myself I felt like saying it, to put him in his place.

I said instead, "The scientists."

He said no more. I said no more, and deliberately went back to reading. That was the end of that little passage between us. It was also, as it turned out, the end of my attempts to be a teacher, to show myself and my things to Ferdinand.

Because I thought a lot about my refusal to say "the white men" when Ferdinand asked me to define the "they" who were working on the new telephone. And I saw that, in my wish not to give him political satisfaction, I had indeed said what I intended to say. I didn't mean the white men. I didn't mean, I couldn't mean, people like those I knew in our town, the people who had stayed behind after independence. I really did mean the scientists; I meant people far away from us in every sense.

They! When we wanted to speak politically, when we wanted to abuse or praise politically, we said "the Americans," "the Europeans," "the white people," "the Belgians." When we wanted to speak of the doers and makers and the inventors, we all—whatever our race—said "they." We separated these men from their groups and countries and in this way attached them to ourselves. "They're making cars that will run on water." "They're making television sets as small as a matchbox." The "they" we spoke of in this way were very far away, so far away as to be hardly white. They were impartial, up in the clouds, like good gods. We waited for their blessings, and showed off those blessings—as I had shown off my cheap binoculars and my fancy camera to Ferdinand—as though we had been responsible for them.

I had shown Ferdinand my things as though I had been letting him into the deeper secrets of my existence, the true nature of my life below the insipidity of my days and nights. In fact, I—and all the others like me in our town, Asian, Belgian, Greek—were as far away from "they" as he was.

That was the end of my attempts to be a teacher to Ferdinand. I decided now simply to let him be, as before. I felt that by giving him the run of the shop and the flat I was keeping my promise to his mother.

The rainy-season school holidays came, and Zabeth came to town to do her shopping and to take Ferdinand back with her. She seemed pleased with his progress. And he didn't seem to mind exchanging the lycée and the bars of the town for Zabeth's village. So he went home for the holidays. I thought of the journey downriver by steamer and dugout. I thought of rain on the river; Zabeth's women poling through the unlit waterways to the hidden village; the black nights and the empty days.

The sky seldom cleared now. At most it turned from grey or dark grey to hot silver. It lightened and thundered much of the time, sometimes far away over the forest, sometimes directly overhead. From the shop I would see the rain beating down the flamboyant trees in the market square. Rain like that killed the vendors' trade; it blew all around the wooden stalls and drove people to shelter under the awnings of the shops around the square. Everyone became a watcher of the rain; a lot of beer was drunk. The unsurfaced streets ran red with mud; red was the colour of the earth on which all the bush grew.

But sometimes a day of rain ended with a glorious clouded sunset. I liked to watch that from the viewing spot near the rapids. Once that spot had been a little park, with amenities; but all that remained of the park was a stretch of concrete river wall and a wide cleared area, muddy in rain. Fishermen's nets hung on great stripped tree trunks buried among the rocks at the edge of the river (rocks like those that, in the river, created the rapids). At one end of the cleared area were thatched huts; the place had become a fishing village again. The sinking sun shot through layers of grey cloud; the water turned from brown to gold to red to violet. And always there was the steady noise of the rapids, innumerable little cascades of water over rock. The darkness came; and sometimes the rain came as well, and to the sound of the rapids was added the sound of rain on water.

Always, sailing up from the south, from beyond the bend in the river, were clumps of water hyacinths, dark floating islands on the dark river, bobbing over the rapids. It was as if rain and river were tearing away bush from the heart of the continent and floating it down to the ocean, incalculable miles away. But the water hyacinth was the fruit of the river alone. The tall lilac-coloured flower had appeared only a few years before, and in the local language there was no word for it. The people still called it "the new thing" or "the new thing in the river," and to them it was another enemy. Its rubbery vines and leaves formed thick tangles of vegetation that adhered to the river banks and clogged up waterways. It grew fast, faster than men could destroy it with the tools they had. The channels to the villages had to be constantly cleared. Night and day the water hyacinth floated up from the south, seeding itself as it travelled.

I had decided to let Ferdinand be. But in the new term I noticed a change in his attitude to me. He was less distant with me, and when he came to the shop he wasn't so anxious to leave me for Metty. I thought that his mother might have given him a talking to. I thought also that though he had been cool when he had gone to his mother's village for the holidays, he had probably been shocked by his time there—how, I wondered, had he spent the days?—and no longer took the town, and the life of the town, for granted.

The truth was simpler. Ferdinand had begun to grow up, and he was finding himself a little bit at sea. He was of mixed tribal heritage, and in this part of the country he was a stranger. He had no group that was really his own, and he had no one to model himself on. He didn't know what was expected of him. He wanted to find out, and he needed me to practise on.

I could see him now trying on various characters, attempting different kinds of manners. His range was limited. For a few days after Zabeth came to town for her goods, he might be the son of his mother, the *marchande*. He would pretend to be my business associate, my equal, might make inquiries about sales and prices. Then he might become the young African on the way up, the lycée student, modern, go-ahead. In this character he liked to wear the blazer with the *Semper Aliquid Novi* motto; no doubt he felt it helped him carry off the mannerisms he had picked up from some of his European teachers. Copying one teacher, he might, in the flat, stand with crossed legs against the white studio wall and, fixed in that position, attempt to conduct a whole conversation. Or, copying another teacher, he might walk around the trestle table, lifting things, looking at them, and then dropping them, while he talked.

He made an effort now to talk to me. Not in the way he talked to Metty; with me he attempted a special kind of serious conversation. Whereas before he had waited for me to ask questions, now it was he who put up little ideas, little debating points, as though he wanted to get a discussion going. It was part of the new lycée character he was working on, and he was practising, treating me almost as a language teacher. But I was interested. I began to get some idea of what was talked about at the lycée—and I wanted to know about that.

He said to me one day, "Salim, what do you think of the future of Africa?"

I didn't say; I wanted to know what he thought. I wondered whether, in spite of his mixed ancestry and his travels, he really had an idea of Africa; or whether the idea of Africa had come to him, and his friends at school, from the atlas. Wasn't Ferdinand still—like Metty, during his journey from the coast—the kind of man who, among strange tribes, would starve rather than eat their strange food? Did Ferdinand have a much larger idea of

Africa than Zabeth, who moved with assurance from her village
to the town only because she knew she was especially protected?

Ferdinand could only tell me that the world outside Africa
was going down and Africa was rising. When I asked in what way
the world outside was going down, he couldn't say. And when I
pushed him past the stage where he could repeat bits of what he
had heard at the lycée, I found that the ideas of the school discussion had in his mind become jumbled and simplified. Ideas of
the past were confused with ideas of the present. In his lycée
blazer, Ferdinand saw himself as evolved and important, as in
the colonial days. At the same time he saw himself as a new man
of Africa, and important for that reason. Out of this staggering
idea of his own importance, he had reduced Africa to himself;
and the future of Africa was nothing more than the job he might
do later on.

The conversations that Ferdinand, in this character, attempted
with me had a serial quality, because he wasn't always well
briefed. He took a discussion up to a certain point and then
dropped it without embarrassment, as though it had been a language exercise in which he would do better next time. Then,
returning to old ways, he would look for Metty and leave me.

Though I was learning more of what went on in the lycée (so
quickly colonial-snobbish again), and what went on in the mind
of Ferdinand, I didn't feel I was getting closer to him. When I
had considered him a mystery, distant and mocking behind his
mask-like face, I had seen him as a solid person. Now I felt that
his affectations were more than affectations, that his personality
had become fluid. I began to feel that there was nothing there,
and the thought of a lycée full of Ferdinands made me nervous.

Yet there was the idea of his importance. It unsettled me—
there wasn't going to be security for anyone in the country—and
it unsettled Metty. When you get away from the chiefs and the
politicians there is a simple democracy about Africa: everyone is
a villager. Metty was a shop assistant and a kind of servant;
Ferdinand was a lycée boy with a future; yet the friendship between the two men was like the friendship between equals. That
friendship continued. But Metty, as a servant in our family

house, had seen playmates grow into masters; and he must have felt himself—with his new idea of his worth—being left behind again.

I was in the flat one day when I heard them come in. Metty was explaining his connection with me and the shop, explaining his journey from the coast.

Metty said: "My family used to know his family. They used to call me Billy. I was studying bookkeeping. I'm not staying here, you know. I am going to Canada. I've got my papers and everything. I'm just waiting for my medical."

Billy! Well, it was close to Ali. Canada—that was where one of my brothers-in-law had gone; in a letter I received shortly after Metty joined me I had heard about the anxiety of the family about that brother-in-law's "medical." That was no doubt where Metty had picked up the talk about Canada.

I made a noise to let them know I was in the flat, and when they came into the sitting room I pretended I had heard nothing.

Not long after this, on an afternoon of settled rain, Ferdinand came to the shop and abruptly, wet and dripping as he was, said, "Salim, you must send me away to America to study."

He spoke like a desperate man. The idea had burst inside him; and he clearly had felt that if he didn't act right away, he might never act. He had come through the heavy rain and the flooded streets; his clothes were soaked. I was surprised by the abruptness and the desperation, and by the bigness of his request. To me, going abroad to study was something rare and expensive, something beyond the means of my own family.

I said, "Why should I send you to America? Why should I spend money on you?"

He had nothing to say. After the desperation and the trip through the rain, the whole thing might just have been another attempt at conversation.

Was it only his simplicity? I felt my temper rising—the rain and the lightning and the unnatural darkness of the afternoon had something to do with that.

I said, "Why do you think I have obligations to you? What have you done for me?"

And that was true. His attitude, since he had begun to feel towards a character, was that I owed him something, simply because I seemed willing to help.

He went blank. He stood still in the darkness of the shop and looked at me without resentment, as though he had expected me to behave in the way I was behaving, and had to see it through. For a while his eyes held mine. Then his gaze shifted, and I knew he was going to change the subject.

He pulled the wet white shirt—with the lycée monogram embroidered on the pocket—away from his skin, and he said, "My shirt is wet." When I didn't reply, he pulled the shirt away in one or two other places and said, "I walked through the rain."

Still I didn't reply. He let the shirt go and looked away to the flooded street. It was his way of recovering from a false start: his attempts at conversation could end with these short sentences, irritating observations about what he or I was doing. So now he looked out at the rain and spoke scattered sentences about what he saw. He was pleading to be released.

I said, "Metty is in the storeroom. He will give you a towel. And ask him to make some tea."

That was not the end of the business, though. With Ferdinand now, things seldom ended neatly.

Twice a week I had lunch with my friends Shoba and Mahesh in their flat. Their flat was gaudy and in some ways like themselves. They were a beautiful couple, certainly the most beautiful people in our town. They had no competition, yet they were always slightly overdressed. So, in their flat, to the true beauty of old Persian and Kashmiri carpets and old brassware they had added many flimsy, glittery things—crudely worked modern Moradabad brass, machine-turned wall plaques of Hindu gods, shiny three-pronged wall lights. There was also a heavy carving in glass of a naked woman. This was a touch of art, but it was also a reminder of the beauty of women, the beauty of Shoba— personal beauty being the obsession and theme of that couple, like money for rich people.

At lunch one day Mahesh said, "What's got into that boy of yours? He's getting *malin* like the others."

"Metty?"

"He came to see me the other day. He pretended he had known me a long time. He was showing off to the African boy he had with him. He said he was bringing me a customer. He said the African boy was Zabeth's son and a good friend of yours."

"I don't know about good friend. What did he want?"

"Metty ran away just when I was beginning to get angry, and left the boy with me. The boy said he wanted a camera, but I don't think he wanted anything at all. He just wanted to talk."

I said, "I hope he showed you his money."

"I didn't have any cameras to show him. That was a bad business, Salim. Commission, commission all the way. You hardly get your money back in the end."

The cameras were one of Mahesh's ideas that had gone wrong. Mahesh was like that, always looking for the good business idea, and full of little ideas he quickly gave up. He had thought that the tourist trade was about to start again, with our town being the base for the game parks in the east. But the tourist trade existed only in the posters printed in Europe for the government in the capital. The game parks had gone back to nature, in a way never meant. The roads and rest houses, always rudimentary, had gone; the tourists (foreigners who might be interested in cut-price photographic equipment) hadn't come. Mahesh had had to send his cameras east, using the staging posts that were still maintained by people like ourselves for the transport (legal or otherwise) of goods in any direction.

Mahesh said, "The boy said you were sending him to America or Canada to do his studies."

"What am I sending him to study?"

"Business administration. So he can take over his mother's business. Build it up."

"Build it up! Buying a gross of razor blades and selling them one by one to fishermen."

"I knew he was only trying to compromise you with your friends."

Simple magic: if you say something about a man to his friends, you might get the man to do what you say he is going to do.

I said, "Ferdinand's an African."

When I next saw Ferdinand I said, "My friend Mahesh has been telling me that you are going to America to study business administration. Have you told your mother?"

He didn't understand irony. This version of the story caught him unprepared, and he had nothing to say.

I said, "Ferdinand, you mustn't go around telling people things that aren't true. What do you mean by business administration?"

He said, "Bookkeeping, typing, shorthand. What you do."

"I don't do shorthand. And that's not business administration. That's a secretarial course. You don't have to go to America or Canada to do that. You can do that right here. I am sure there are places in the capital. And when the time comes you'll find you want to do more than that."

He didn't like what I said. His eyes began to go bright with humiliation and anger. But I didn't stay for that. It was with Metty, and not me, that he had to settle accounts, if there were accounts to be settled.

He had found me as I was leaving to play squash at the Hellenic Club. Canvas shoes, shorts, racket, towel around my neck—it was like old times on the coast. I left the sitting room and stood in the passage, to give him the chance to leave, so that I could lock up. But he stayed in the sitting room, doubtless waiting for Metty.

I went out to the staircase landing. It was one of our days without electricity. The smoke from charcoal braziers and other open fires rose blue among the imported ornamental trees—cassia, breadfruit, frangipani, flamboyant—and gave a touch of the forest village to a residential area where, as I had heard, in the old days neither Africans nor Asians were permitted to live. I knew the trees from the coast. I suppose they had been imported there as well; but I associated them with the coast and home, another life. The same trees here looked artificial to me, like the town itself. They were familiar, but they reminded me where I was.

I heard no more about Ferdinand's studies abroad, and soon he even dropped the bright-young-lycée-man pose. He began trying out something new. There was no more of that standing against the wall with crossed legs, no more walking around the trestle table and lifting and dropping things, no more of that serious conversation.

He came in now with a set face, his expression stern and closed. He held his head up and moved slowly. When he sat on the couch in the sitting room, he slumped so far down that sometimes his back was on the seat of the coach. He was languid, bored. He looked without seeing; he was ready to listen, but couldn't be bothered to talk himself—that was the impression he tried to give. I didn't know what to make of this new character of Ferdinand's, and it was only from certain things that Metty said that I understood what Ferdinand was aiming at.

During the course of the term there had come to the lycée some boys from the warrior tribes to the east. They were an immensely tall people; and, as Metty told me with awe, they were used to being carried around on litters by their slaves, who were of a smaller, squatter race. For these tall men of the forest there had always been European admiration. Ever since I could remember there had been articles about them in the magazines— these Africans who cared nothing about planting or trade and looked down, almost as much as Europeans, on other Africans. This European admiration still existed; articles and photographs continued to appear in magazines, in spite of the changes that had come to Africa. In fact, there were now Africans who felt as the Europeans did, and saw the warrior people as the highest kind of African.

At the lycée, still so colonial in spite of everything, the new boys had created a stir. Ferdinand, both of whose parents were traders, had decided to try out the role of the indolent forest warrior. He couldn't slump around at the lycée and pretend he was used to being waited on by slaves. But he thought he could practise on me.

I knew other things about the forest kingdom, though. I knew that the slave people were in revolt and were being butchered back into submission. But Africa was big. The bush muffled the sound of murder, and the muddy rivers and lakes washed the blood away.

Metty said, "We must go there, *patron*. I hear it is the last good place in Africa. *Y a encore bien, bien des blancs côté-qui-là*. It have a lot of white people up there still. They tell me that in Bujumbura it is like a little Paris."

If I believed that Metty understood a quarter of the things he said—if I believed, for instance, that he really longed for the white company at Bujumbura, or knew where or what Canada was—I would have worried about him. But I knew him better; I knew when his chat was just chat. Still, what chat! The white people had been driven out from our town, and their monuments destroyed. But there were a lot of white people up there, in another town, and warriors and slaves. And that was glamour for the warrior boys, glamour for Metty, and glamour for Ferdinand.

I began to understand how simple and uncomplicated the world was for me. For people like myself and Mahesh, and the uneducated Greeks and Italians in our town, the world was really quite a simple place. We could understand it, and if too many obstacles weren't put in our way we could master it. It didn't matter that we were far away from our civilization, far away from the doers and makers. It didn't matter that we couldn't make the things we liked to use, and as individuals were even without the technical skills of primitive people. In fact, the less educated we were, the more at peace we were, the more easily we were carried along by our civilization or civilizations.

For Ferdinand there was no such possibility. He could never be simple. The more he tried, the more confused he became. His mind wasn't empty, as I had begun to think. It was a jumble, full of all kinds of junk.

With the arrival of the warrior boys, boasting had begun at the lycée, and I began to feel that Ferdinand—or somebody—had been boasting about me too. Or what had been got out of me. The word definitely appeared to have got around that term that I was interested in the education and welfare of young Africans.

Young men, not all of them from the lycée, took to turning up at the shop, sometimes with books in their hands, sometimes with an obviously borrowed *Semper Aliquid Novi* blazer. They wanted money. They said they were poor and wanted money to continue their studies. Some of these beggars were bold, coming straight to me and reciting their requests; the shy ones hung around until there was no one else in the shop. Only a few had bothered to prepare stories, and these stories were like Ferdinand's: a father dead or far away, a mother in a village, an unprotected boy full of ambition.

I was amazed by the stupidity, then irritated, then unsettled. None of these people seemed to mind being rebuffed or being hustled out of the shop by Metty; some of them came again. It was as if none of them cared about my reactions, as if somewhere out there in the town I had been given a special "character," and what I thought of myself was of no importance. That was what was unsettling. The guilelessness, the innocence that wasn't innocence—I thought it could be traced back to Ferdinand, his interpretation of our relationship and his idea of what I could be used for.

I had said to Mahesh, lightly, simplifying matters for the benefit of a prejudiced man: "Ferdinand's an African." Ferdinand had perhaps done the same for me with his friends, explaining away his relationship with me. And I felt now that out of his lies and exaggerations, and the character he had given me, a web was being spun around me. I had become prey.

Perhaps that was true of all of us who were not of the country. Recent events had shown our helplessness. There was a kind of peace now; but we all—Asians, Greeks and other Europeans—remained prey, to be stalked in different ways. Some men were to be feared, and stalked cautiously; it was necessary to be servile with some; others were to be approached the way I was approached. It was in the history of the land: here men had always been prey. You don't feel malice towards your prey. You set a trap for him. It fails ten times; but it is always the same trap you set.

Shortly after I had arrived Mahesh had said to me of the local Africans: "You must never forget, Salim, that they are *malins*." He had used the French word, because the English words he

might have used—"wicked," "mischievous," "bad-minded"—
were not right. The people here were *malins* the way a dog chasing a lizard was *malin*, or a cat chasing a bird. The people were *malins* because they lived with the knowledge of men as prey.

They were not a sturdy people. They were very small and slightly built. Yet, as though to make up for their puniness in that immensity of river and forest, they liked to wound with their hands. They didn't use their fists. They used the flat of the hand; they liked to push, shove, slap. More than once, at night, outside a bar or little dance hall, I saw what looked like a drunken pushing and shoving, a brawl with slaps, turn to methodical murder, as though the first wound and the first spurt of blood had made the victim something less than a man, and compelled the wounder to take the act of destruction to the end.

I was unprotected. I had no family, no flag, no fetish. Was it something like this that Ferdinand had told his friends? I felt that the time had come for me to straighten things out with Ferdinand, and give him another idea of myself.

I soon had my chance, as I thought. A well-dressed young man came into the shop one morning with what looked like a business ledger in his hand. He was one of the shy ones. He hung around, waiting for people to go away, and when he came to me I saw that the ledger was less businesslike than it looked. The spine, in the middle, was black and worn from being held. And I saw too that the man's shirt, though obviously his best, wasn't as clean as I had thought. It was the good shirt he wore on special occasions and then took off and hung up on a nail and wore again on another special occasion. The collar was yellow-black on the inside.

He said, "Mis' Salim."

I took the ledger, and he looked away, puckering up his brows.

The ledger belonged to the lycée, and it was old. It was something from near the end of the colonial time: a subscription list for a gymnasium the lycée had been planning to build. On the inside of the cover was the lycée label, with the coat of arms and the motto. Opposite that was the principal's appeal, in the stiff and angular European handwriting style which had been passed down to some of the Africans here. The first subscriber was the governor of the province, and he had signed royally, on a whole page. I turned the pages, studying the confident signatures of officials and merchants. It was all so recent, but it seemed to belong to another century.

I saw, with especial interest, the signature of a man of our community about whom Nazruddin had talked a great deal. That man had had old-fashioned ideas about money and security; he had used his wealth to build a palace, which he had had to abandon after independence. The mercenaries who had restored the authority of the central government had been quartered there; now the palace was an army barracks. He had subscribed for an enormous amount. I saw Nazruddin's signature—I was surprised: I had forgotten that he might be here, among these dead colonial names.

The gymnasium hadn't been built. All these demonstrations of loyalty and faith in the future and civic pride had gone for nothing. Yet the book had survived. Now it had been stolen, its money-attracting properties recognized. The date had been altered, very obviously; and Father Huismans's name had been written over the signature of the earlier principal.

I said to the man before me, "I will keep this book. I will give it back to the people to whom it belongs. Who gave you the book? Ferdinand?"

He looked helpless. Sweat was beginning to run down his puckered forehead, and he was blinking it away. He said, "Mis' Salim."

"You've done your job. You've given me the book. Now go."

And he obeyed.

Ferdinand came that afternoon. I knew he would—he would want to look at my face, and find out about his book. He said, "Salim?" I didn't acknowledge him. I let him stand. But he didn't have to stand about for long.

Metty was in the storeroom, and Metty must have heard him. Metty called out: "Oo-oo!" Ferdinand called back, and went to the storeroom. He and Metty began to chat in the patois. My temper rose as I heard that contented, rippling, high-pitched sound. I took the gymnasium book from the drawer of my desk and went to the storeroom.

The room, with one small barred window set high, was half in darkness. Metty was on a ladder, checking stock on the shelves on one wall. Ferdinand was leaning against the shelves on another wall, just below the window. It was hard to see his face.

I stood in the doorway. I made a gesture towards Ferdinand with the book and I said, "You are going to get into trouble."

He said, "What trouble?"

He spoke in his flat, dead way. He didn't mean to be sarcastic; he really was asking what I was talking about. But it was hard for me to see his face. I saw the whites of his eyes, and I thought I saw the corners of his mouth pulling back in a smile. That face, that reminder of frightening masks! And I thought: Yes—what trouble?

To talk of trouble was to pretend there were laws and regulations that everyone could acknowledge. Here there was nothing. There had been order once, but that order had had its own dishonesties and cruelties—that was why the town had been wrecked. We lived in that wreckage. Instead of regulations there were now only officials who could always prove you wrong, until you paid up. All that could be said to Ferdinand was: "Don't harm me, boy, because I can do you greater harm."

I began to see his face more clearly.

I said, "You will take this book back to Father Huismans. If you don't, I will take it back myself. And I will see that he sends you home for good."

He looked blank, as though he had been attacked. Then I noticed Metty on the ladder. Metty was nervous, tense; his eyes betrayed him. And I knew I had made a mistake, saving up all my anger for Ferdinand.

Ferdinand's eyes went bright, and the whites showed clearly. So that, at this terrible moment, he seemed like a comic in an old-time film. He appeared to lean forward, to be about to lose his balance. He took a deep breath. His eyes never left my face. He was spitting with rage; his sense of injury had driven him mad. His arms hung straight and loose at his sides, so that they seemed longer than usual. His hands curled without clenching. His mouth was open. But what I had thought was a smile was no smile at all. If the light had been better I would have seen that at the beginning.

He was frightening, and the thought came to me: This is how he will look when he sees his victim's blood, when he watches his enemy being killed. And climbing on that thought was another: "This is the rage that flattened the town."

I could have pushed harder, and turned that high rage into tears. But I didn't push. I thought I had given them both a new idea of the kind of man I was, and I left them in the storeroom to cool down. After some time I heard them talking, but softly.

At four o'clock, closing time, I shouted to Metty. And he, glad of the chance to come out and be active, said, "*Patron,*" and frowned to show how seriously he took the business of closing up the shop.

Ferdinand came out, quite calm, walking with a light step. He said, "Salim?" I said, "I will take the book back." And I watched him walk up the red street, tall and sad and slow below the leafless flamboyants, past the rough market shacks of his town.

# 4

Father Huismans wasn't in when I went to the lycée with the book. There was a young Belgian in the outer office, and he told me that Father Huismans liked to go away for a few days from time to time. Where did he go? "He goes into the bush. He goes to all those villages," the young man—secretary or teacher—said, with irritation. And he became more irritated when I gave him the gymnasium book.

He said, "They come and beg to be admitted to the lycée. As soon as you take them in they start stealing. They would carry away the whole school if you let them. They come and beg you to look after their children. Yet in the streets they jostle you to show you they don't care for you." He didn't look well. He was pale, but the skin below his eyes was dark, and he sweated as he talked. He said, "I'm sorry. It would be better for you to talk to Father Huismans. You must understand that it isn't easy for me here. I've been living on honey cake and eggs." It sounded as though he had been put on an especially rich diet. Then I understood that he was really telling me he was starving.

He said, "Father Huismans had the idea this term of giving the boys African food. Well, that seemed all right. There's an African lady in the capital who does wonderful things with prawns and shellfish. But here it was caterpillars and spinach in tomato sauce. Or what looked like tomato sauce. The first day! Of course, it was only for the boys, but the sight of it turned my stomach. I couldn't stay in the hall and watch them chew. I can't bring myself to eat anything from the kitchens now. I don't have cooking facilities in my room, and at the van der Weyden there's this sewer smell from the patio. I'm leaving. I've got to go. It's all right for Huismans. He's a priest. I'm not a priest. He goes into the bush. I don't want to go into the bush."

I couldn't help him. Food was a problem for everybody here. My own arrangements were not of the happiest; I had had lunch that day with the couple from India, in a smell of asafoetida and oilcloth.

When, a week or so later, I went back to the lycée I heard that just two days after our meeting the young Belgian had taken the steamer and gone away. It was Father Huismans who gave me the news; and Father Huismans, sunburnt and healthy after his own trip, didn't seem put out by the loss of one of his teachers. He said he was glad to have the gymnasium book back. It was part of the history of the town; the boys who had stolen the book would recognize that one day themselves.

Father Huismans was in his forties. He wasn't dressed like a priest, but even in ordinary trousers and shirt there was something about him of the man apart. He had the "unfinished" face which I have noticed that certain Europeans—but never Arabs or Persians or Indians—have. In these faces there is a baby-like quality about the cut of the lips and the jut of the forehead. It might be that these people were born prematurely; they seem to have passed through some very early disturbance, way back. Some of these people are as fragile as they look; some are very tough. Father Huismans was tough. The impression he gave was of incompleteness, fragility, and toughness.

He had been out on the river, visiting some villages he knew, and he had brought back two pieces—a mask and an oldish wood carving. It was about these finds that he wanted to talk, rather than about the teacher who had gone away or the gymnasium book.

The carving was extraordinary. It was about five feet high, a very thin human figure, just limbs and trunk and head, absolutely basic, carved out of a piece of wood no more than six to eight inches in diameter. I knew about carving—it was one of the things we dealt in on the coast; we gave employment to a couple of carving families from a tribe who were gifted that way. But Father Huismans dismissed this information when I gave it to him, and talked instead of what he saw in the figure he had picked up. To me it was an exaggerated and crude piece, a carver's joke (the carvers we employed did things like that sometimes). But Father Huismans knew what the thin figure was about, and to him it was imaginative and full of meaning.

I listened, and at the end he said with a smile, "*Semper aliquid novi.*" He had used the lycée motto to make a joke. The words were old, he told me, two thousand years old, and referred to Africa. An ancient Roman writer had written that out of Africa there was "always something new"—*semper aliquid novi*. And when it came to masks and carvings, the words were still literally true. Every carving, every mask, served a specific religious purpose, and could only be made once. Copies were copies; there was no magical feeling or power in them; and in such copies Father Huismans was not interested. He looked in masks and carvings for a religious quality; without that quality the things were dead and without beauty.

That was strange, that a Christian priest should have had such regard for African beliefs, to which on the coast we had paid no attention. And yet, though Father Huismans knew so much about African religion and went to such trouble to collect his pieces, I never felt that he was concerned about Africans in any other way; he seemed indifferent to the state of the country. I envied him that indifference; and I thought, after I left him that day, that his Africa, of bush and river, was different from mine. His Africa was a wonderful place, full of new things.

He was a priest, half a man. He lived by vows I couldn't make; and I had approached him with the respect that people of my background feel for holy men. But I began to think of him as something more. I began to think of him as a pure man. His presence in our town comforted me. His attitudes, his interests, his knowledge, added something to the place, made it less barren. It didn't worry me that he was self-absorbed, that he had been indifferent to the breakdown of one of his teachers, or that he scarcely seemed to take me in while he was talking to me. To me that was part of his particular religious nature. I sought him out and tried to understand his interests. He was always willing to talk (always looking away slightly) and to show his new finds. He came a few times to the shop and ordered things for the lycée. But the shyness—that wasn't really shyness—never left him. I was never easy with him. He remained a man apart.

He explained the second motto of the town for me—the Latin words carved on the ruined monument near the dock gates: *Miscerique probat populos et foedera jungi.* "He approves of the mingling of the peoples and their bonds of union": that was what the words meant, and again they were very old words, from the days of ancient Rome. They came from a poem about the founding of Rome. The very first Roman hero, travelling to Italy to found his city, lands on the coast of Africa. The local queen falls in love with him, and it seems that the journey to Italy might be called off. But then the watching gods take a hand; and one of them says that the great Roman god might not approve of a settlement in Africa, of a mingling of peoples there, of treaties of union between Africans and Romans. That was how the words occurred in the old Latin poem. In the motto, though, three words were altered to reverse the meaning. According to the motto, the words carved in granite outside our dock gates, a settlement in Africa raises no doubts: the great Roman god approves of the mingling of peoples and the making of treaties in Africa. *Miscerique probat populos et foedera jungi.*

I was staggered. Twisting two-thousand-year-old words to celebrate sixty years of the steamer service from the capital! Rome was Rome. What was this place? To carve the words on a monument beside this African river was surely to invite the destruction of the town. Wasn't there some little anxiety, as in the original line in the poem? And almost as soon as it had been put up the monument had been destroyed, leaving only bits of bronze and the mocking words, gibberish to the people who now used the open space in front as a market and bivouac, with their goats and crated hens and tethered monkeys (food, like the goats and hens), for the two days or so before the steamer sailed.

But I was glad I didn't speak, because to Father Huismans the words were not vainglorious. They were words that helped him to see himself in Africa. He didn't simply see himself in a place in the bush; he saw himself as part of an immense flow of history. He was of Europe; he took the Latin words to refer to himself. It didn't matter that the Europeans in our town were uneducated, or that there was such a difference between what he stood for in his own life and what the ruined suburb near the rapids had stood for. He had his own idea of Europe, his own idea of his civilization. It was that that lay between us. Nothing like that came between me and the people I met at the Hellenic Club. And yet Father Huismans stressed his Europeanness and his separateness from Africans less than those people did. In every way he was more secure.

He wasn't resentful, as some of his countrymen were, of what had happened to the European town. He wasn't wounded by the insults that had been offered to the monuments and the statues. It wasn't because he was more ready to forgive, or had a better understanding of what had been done to the Africans. For him the destruction of the European town, the town that his countrymen had built, was only a temporary setback. Such things happened when something big and new was being set up, when the course of history was being altered.

There would always have been a settlement at that bend in the river, he said. It was a natural meeting place. The tribes would have changed, power would have shifted, but men would always have returned there to meet and trade. The Arab town would have been only a little more substantial than the African settlements, and technologically not much more advanced. The Arabs, so far in the interior, would have had to build with the products of the forest; life in their town wouldn't have been much more than a kind of forest life. The Arabs had only prepared the way for the mighty civilization of Europe.

For everything connected with the European colonization, the opening up of the river, Father Huismans had a reverence which would have surprised those people in the town who gave him the reputation of being a lover of Africa and therefore, in their way of thinking, a man who rejected the colonial past. That past had been bitter, but Father Huismans appeared to take the bitterness for granted; he saw beyond it. From the ship-repair yard near the customs, long neglected and full of junk and rust, he had taken away pieces of old steamers and bits of disused machinery from the late 1890s and laid them—like relics of an early civilization —in the inner courtyard of the lycée. He was especially pleased with a piece that carried, on an oval steel plate, the name of the makers in the town of Seraing in Belgium.

Out of simple events beside that wide muddy river, out of the mingling of peoples, great things were to come one day. We were just at the beginning. And to Father Huismans colonial relics were as precious as the things of Africa. True Africa he saw as dying or about to die. That was why it was so necessary, while that Africa still lived, to understand and collect and preserve its things.

What he had collected from that dying Africa lay in the gun room of the lycée, where the antiquated rifles of the school cadet corps used to be kept in the old days. The room was as big as a classroom and from the outside looked like one. But there were no windows, only tall panelled doors on two sides; and the only light was from a bare bulb hanging on a long cord.

When Father Huismans first opened the door of that room for

me, and I got the warm smell of grass and earth and old fat, and had a confused impression of masks lying in rows on slatted shelves, I thought: This is Zabeth's world. This is the world to which she returns when she leaves my shop. But Zabeth's world was living, and this was dead. That was the effect of those masks lying flat on the shelves, looking up not at forest or sky but at the underside of other shelves. They were masks that had been laid low, in more than one way, and had lost their power.

That was the impression only of a moment, though. Because in that dark, hot room, with the mask smells growing stronger, my own feeling of awe grew, my sense of what lay all around us outside. It was like being on the river at night. The bush was full of spirits; in the bush hovered all the protecting presences of a man's ancestors; and in this room all the spirits of those dead masks, the powers they invoked, all the religious dread of simple men, seemed to have been concentrated.

The masks and carvings looked old. They could have been any age, a hundred years old, a thousand years old. But they were dated; Father Huismans had dated them. They were all quite new. I thought: But this one's only 1940. I was born in that year. Or: This is 1963. That was when I came here. While this was being made I was probably having lunch with Shoba and Mahesh.

So old, so new. And out of his stupendous idea of his civilization, his stupendous idea of the future, Father Huismans saw himself at the end of it all, the last, lucky witness.

## 5

Most of us knew only the river and the damaged roads and what lay beside them. Beyond that was the unknown; it could surprise us. We seldom went to places off the established ways. In fact, we seldom travelled. It was as though, having come so far, we didn't want to move about too much. We kept to what we knew—flat, shop, club, bar, the river embankment at sunset.

Sometimes we made a weekend excursion to the hippopotamus island in the river, above the rapids. But there were no people there, just the hippopotamuses—seven of them when I first used to go, three now.

We knew the hidden villages mainly by what we saw of the villagers when they came to the town. They looked exhausted and ragged after their years of isolation and want, and seemed glad to be able to move about freely again. From the shop I used to see them idling about the market stalls in the square, gazing at the displays of cloth and ready-made clothes, and wandering back to the food stalls: little oily heaps of fried flying ants (expensive, and sold by the spoonful) laid out on scraps of newspaper; hairy orange-coloured caterpillars with protuberant eyes wriggling in enamel basins; fat white grubs kept moist and soft in little bags of damp earth, five or six grubs to a bag—these grubs, absorbent in body and of neutral taste, being an all-purpose fatty food, sweet with sweet things, savory with savory things. These were all forest foods, but the villages had been cleaned out of them (the grubs came from the heart of a palm tree); and no one wanted to go foraging too far in the forest.

More and more of the villagers who came as visitors remained to camp in the town. At night there was cooking in the streets and the squares. On the pavements below shop awnings, symbolic walls were put up around sleeping spaces—low fences of cardboard held between stones or bricks, or lengths of string tied (like the ropes of a miniature boxing ring) to sticks kept upright by cairns of stones.

From being abandoned, the town began to feel crowded. It seemed that nothing could stop the movement of people from the villages. Then, from the great unknown outside the town, came the rumour of a war.

And it was the old war, the one we were still recovering from, the semi-tribal war that had broken out at independence and shattered and emptied the town. We had thought it over and done with, the passions burnt out. There was nothing to make us think otherwise. Even local Africans had begun to talk of that time as a time of madness. And madness was the word. From

Mahesh and Shoba I had heard dreadful stories of that time, of casual killings over many months by soldiers and rebels and mercenaries, of people trussed up in disgusting ways and being made to sing certain songs while they were beaten to death in the streets. None of the people who came in from the villages seemed ready for that kind of horror. Yet now it was all starting up again.

At independence the people of our region had gone mad with anger and fear—all the accumulated anger of the colonial period, and every kind of reawakened tribal fear. The people of our region had been much abused, not only by Europeans and Arabs, but also by other Africans; and at independence they had refused to be ruled by the new government in the capital. It was an instinctive uprising, without leaders or a manifesto. If the movement had been more reasoned, had been less a movement of simple rejection, the people of our region might have seen that the town at the bend in the river was theirs, the capital of any state they might set up. But they had hated the town for the intruders who had ruled in it and from it; and they had preferred to destroy the town rather than take it over.

Having destroyed their town, they had grieved for it. They had wished to see it a living place again. And seeing it come to a kind of life again, they had grown afraid once more.

They were like people who didn't know their own mind. They had suffered so much; they had brought so much suffering on themselves. They looked so feeble and crazed when they came out of their villages and wandered about the town. They looked so much like people needing the food and the peace that the town offered. But it was people like them, going back to their villages, who wished to lay the town low again. Such rage! Like a forest fire that goes underground and burns unseen along the roots of trees it has already destroyed and then erupts in scorched land where it has little to feed on, so in the middle of destruction and want the wish to destroy flared up again.

And the war, which we had thought dead, was all at once around us. We heard of ambushes on roads we knew, of villages attacked, of headmen and officials killed.

It was at this time that Mahesh said something which I remembered. It wasn't the kind of thing I was expecting from him—so careful of his looks and clothes, so spoiled, so obsessed with his lovely wife.

Mahesh said to me: "What do you do? You live here, and you ask that? You do what we all do. You carry on."

We had the army in our town. They came from a warrior tribe who had served the Arabs as slave-hunters in the region, and had later, with one or two nasty mutinies, served the colonial government as soldiers. So the pattern of policing was old.

But slaves were no longer required, and in post-colonial Africa everybody could get guns; every tribe could be a warrior tribe. So the army was discreet. Sometimes there were trucks with soldiers in the streets—but the soldiers never showed their weapons. Sometimes there was a ceremonial coming and going at the barracks—the palace built by the great man of our community, which now had women's washing hung out in the partitioned verandahs upstairs and downstairs (a Greek had the laundry contract for the soldiers' uniforms). The army was seldom more provocative than that. They couldn't afford to be. They were among their traditional enemies, their former slave prey; and though they were paid regularly and lived well, they were kept short of equipment. We had a new President, an army man. This was his way of policing the country and controlling his difficult army.

It made for a balance in the town. And a well-paid, domesticated army was good for trade. The soldiers spent. They bought furniture, and they loved carpets—that was a taste they had inherited from the Arabs. But now the balance in our town was threatened. The army had a real war to fight; and no one could say whether those men, given modern weapons again and orders to kill, wouldn't fall into the ways of their slave-hunting ancestors and break up into marauding bands, as they had done at independence, with the collapse of all authority.

No, in this war I was neutral. I was frightened of both sides. I didn't want to see the army on the loose. And though I felt sympathy for the people of our region, I didn't want to see the town destroyed again. I didn't want anybody to win; I wanted the old balance to be maintained.

One night I had a premonition that the war had come close. I woke up and heard the sound of a truck far away. It could have been any truck; it could even have been one of Daulat's, near the end of its hard run from the east. But I thought: That is the sound of war. That sound of a steady, grinding machine made me think of guns; and then I thought of the crazed and half-starved village people against whom the guns were going to be used, people whose rags were already the colour of ashes. This was the anxiety of a moment of wakefulness; I fell asleep again.

When Metty brought me coffee in the morning he said, "The soldiers are running back. They came to a bridge. And when they got to that bridge their guns began to bend."

"Metty!"

"I am telling you, *patron.*"

That was bad. If it was true that the army was retreating, it was bad; I didn't want to see that army in retreat. If it wasn't true, it was still bad. Metty had picked up the local rumours; and what he said about the bending guns meant that the rebels, the men in rags, had been made to believe that bullets couldn't kill them, that all the spirits of the forest and the river were on their side. And that meant that at any moment, as soon as someone gave the correct call, there could be an uprising in the town itself.

It was bad, and there was nothing I could do. The stock of the shop—there was no means of protecting that. What other things of value did I have? There were two or three kilos of gold I had picked up in various little deals; there were my documents—my birth certificate and my British passport; there was the camera I had shown Ferdinand, but didn't want to tempt anyone with now. I put these things in a wooden crate. I also put in the wall print of the holy place my father had sent me by Metty, and I got Metty to put in his passport and money as well. Metty had become the family servant again, anxious, for the sake of prestige, even at this moment, to behave just like me. I had to stop him from throwing in all kinds of rubbish. We dug a hole in the yard just at the bottom of the external staircase—it was easy: no stones in the red earth—and buried the crate there.

It was early morning. Our back yard was so drab, so ordinary with sunlight and the smell of the neighbours' chickens, so ordinary with red dust and dead leaves and the morning shadows of trees I knew at home on the coast, that I thought: This is too stupid. A little later I thought: I've made a mistake. Metty knows that everything of value that I possess is in that box. I've put myself in his hands.

We went and opened the shop; I was carrying on. We did a little business in the first hour. But then the market square began to empty and the town began to go silent. The sun was bright and hot, and I studied the contracting shadows of trees and market stalls and buildings around the square.

Sometimes I thought I could hear the noise of the rapids. It was the eternal noise at that bend in the river, but on a normal day it couldn't be heard here. Now it seemed to come and go on the wind. At midday, when we shut the shop for lunch, and I drove through the streets, it was only the river, glittering in the hard light, that seemed alive. No dugouts, though; only the water hyacinths travelling up from the south, and floating away to the west, clump after clump, with the thick-stalked lilac flowers like masts.

I was taking lunch that day with the old Asian couple—they had had a transport business until independence, when business just stopped, and the rest of the family went away. Nothing had changed there since I had made the arrangement to have lunch with them twice a week. They were people almost without news, and we still had very little conversation. The view, from the verandah of the rough, ranch-like house, was still of abandoned motor vehicles, relics of the old business, rotting away in the yard. I would have minded that view, if it had been my business. But the old people didn't seem to mind or know that they had lost a lot. They seemed content just to live out their lives. They had done all that their religion and family customs had required them to do; and they felt—like the older people of my own family—that they had lived good and complete lives.

On the coast I used to grieve for people of our community who were like that, indifferent to what lay around them. I wanted to shake them up and alert them to danger. But it was soothing now to be with these calm old people; and it would have been nice, on a day like this, not to have to leave that house, to be a child again, protected by the wisdom of the old, and to believe that what they saw was true.

Who wanted philosophy or faith for the good times? We could all cope with the good times. It was for the bad that we had to be equipped. And here in Africa none of us were as well equipped as the Africans. The Africans had called up this war; they would suffer dreadfully, more than anybody else; but they could cope. Even the raggedest of them had their villages and tribes, things that were absolutely theirs. They could run away again to their secret worlds and become lost in those worlds, as they had done before. And even if terrible things happened to them they would die with the comfort of knowing that their ancestors were gazing down approvingly at them.

But this was not true of Ferdinand. With his mixed parentage, he was almost as much a stranger in the town as I was. He came to the flat in the afternoon, and he was wild, close to hysteria, possessed by all the African terror of strange Africans.

Classes had been suspended at the lycée; thoughts there were of the safety of the boys and the teachers. Ferdinand had decided that the lycée wasn't safe; he thought it would be one of the first places to be attacked if there was an uprising in the town. He had dropped all his characters, all his poses. The blazer, which he had once worn with pride as a young man of new Africa, he had discarded as dangerous, something that made him more a man apart; and he was wearing long khaki trousers, not the white shorts of the school uniform. He talked in a frantic way of returning to the south, to his father's people. But that was impossible—he knew it was impossible; and there was no question either of sending him downriver to his mother's village.

The big boy, almost a man, sobbed, "I didn't want to come here. I don't know anyone here. My mother wanted me to come. I didn't want to be in the town or go to the lycée. Why did she send me to the lycée?"

It was a comfort to us, Metty and myself, to have someone to comfort. We decided that Ferdinand was to sleep in Metty's room, and we dug out some bedding for him. The attention calmed Ferdinand down. We ate early, while it was still light. Ferdinand was silent then. But later, when we were in our different rooms, he and Metty talked.

I heard Metty say: "They came to a bridge. And all the trucks stalled and the guns began to bend."

Metty's voice was high-pitched and excited. That wasn't the voice he had used when he had given me the news in the morning. He was talking now like the local Africans, from whom he had got the story.

In the morning the market square outside the shop didn't come to life at all. The town remained empty. The squatters and campers in the street seemed to have gone into hiding.

When I went to Shoba and Mahesh's flat for lunch I noticed that their better carpets had disappeared, and some of the finer glassware and silver, and the crystal figure of the nude woman. Shoba looked strained, especially around her eyes, and Mahesh seemed more nervous of her than of anything else. Shoba's mood always dictated the mood of our lunch, and she seemed that day to want to punish us for the good lunch she had prepared. We ate for some time in silence, Shoba looking down at the table with her tired eyes, Mahesh constantly looking at her.

Shoba said, "I should have been at home this week. My father is sick. Did I tell you, Salim? I should have been with him. And it is his birthday."

Mahesh's eyes hopped about the table. Spoiling the effect of the words that I had found so wise, he said, "We'll carry on. It will be all right. The new President's not a fool. He isn't just going to stay in his house like the last man, and do nothing."

She said, "Carry on, carry on. That's all I've been doing. That's how I've spent my life. That's how I've lived in this place, among Africans. Is that a life, Salim?"

She looked at her plate, not at me. And I said nothing.

Shoba said, "I've wasted my life, Salim. You don't know how

I've wasted my life. You don't know how I live in fear in this place. You don't know how frightened I was when I heard about you, when I heard that a stranger had come to the town. I've got to be frightened of everybody, you know." Her eyes twitched. She stopped eating, and pressed her cheekbones with the tips of her fingers, as though pressing away a nervous pain. "I come from a well-to-do family, a rich family. You know that. My family had plans for me. But then I met Mahesh. He used to own a motorcycle shop. Something terrible happened. I slept with him almost as soon as I met him. You know us and our ways well enough to know that that was a terrible thing for me to do. But it was terrible for me in another way as well. I didn't want to get to know anybody else after that. That has been my curse. Why aren't you eating, Salim? Eat, eat. We must carry on."

Mahesh's lips came together nervously, and he looked a little foolish. At the same time his eyes brightened at the praise contained in the complaining words; yet he and Shoba had been together for nearly ten years.

"My family beat up Mahesh terribly. But that just made me more determined. My brothers threatened to throw acid on me. They were serious. They also threatened to kill Mahesh. That was why we came here. I watched for my brothers every day. I still do. I wait for them. You know that with families like ours certain things are no joke. And then, Salim, while we were here, something worse happened. Mahesh said one day that I was stupid to be watching out for my brothers. He said, 'Your brothers wouldn't come all the way here. They'll send somebody else.' "

Mahesh said, "That was a joke."

"No, that wasn't a joke. That was true. Anybody could come here—they could send anybody. It doesn't have to be an Asian. It could be a Belgian or a Greek or any European. It could be an African. How am I to know?"

She did all the talking at lunch, and Mahesh let her; he seemed to have handled this kind of situation before. Afterwards I drove him back to the centre of the town—he said he didn't want to take his car in. His nervousness disappeared as soon as we left

Shoba. He didn't seem embarrassed by what Shoba had said about their life together, and made no comment about it.

He said, as we drove through the dusty red streets, "Shoba exaggerates. Things are not as bad as she believes. The new man's no fool. The steamer came in this morning with the white men. You didn't know? Go across to the van der Weyden and you'll see a few of them. The new man might be a maid's son. But he's going to hold it together. He's going to use this to put a lot of people in their place. Go to the van der Weyden. It will give you an idea of what things were like after independence."

Mahesh was right. The steamer had arrived; I had a glimpse of it when we drove by the docks. It hadn't hooted and I hadn't looked for it earlier. Low-decked, flat-bottomed, it was almost hidden by the customs sheds, all but the top of the superstructure at the rear. And when I stopped outside Mahesh's shop, which was opposite the van der Weyden, I saw a number of army vehicles, and some civilian trucks and taxis that had been commandeered.

Mahesh said, "It's a good thing Africans have short memories. Go and have a look at the people who've come to save them from suicide."

The van der Weyden was a modern building, four stories high, concrete and straight lines, part of the pre-independence boom; and in spite of all that it had gone through, it still pretended to be a modern hotel. It had many glass doors at pavement level; the lobby had a mosaic floor; there were lifts (not reliable now); there was a reception desk with a pre-independence airline advertisement and a permanent *Hôtel Complet* ("No Vacancies") sign—which hadn't been true for some years.

I had expected a crowd in the lobby, noise, rowdiness. I found the place looking emptier than usual, and it was almost hushed. But the hotel had guests: on the mosaic floor there were about twenty or thirty suitcases with identical blue tie-on labels printed *Hazel's Travels*. The lifts weren't working, and a single hotel boy—a small old man wearing the servant costume of the colonial time: short khaki trousers, short-sleeved shirt, and a large, coarse white apron over that—had the job of taking the suitcases up the terrazzo steps at the side of the lift. He was working under the direct supervision of the big-bellied African (from downriver somewhere) who normally stood behind the reception desk cleaning his teeth with a toothpick and being rude to everybody, but was now standing by the suitcases and trying to look busy and serious.

Some of the hotel's new guests were in the patio bar, where there were a few green palms and creepers in concrete pots. The terrazzo floor here sloped from all sides to a central grille, and from this grille there always came, but especially after rain, a smell of the sewer. In this smell—not particularly bad now: it was dry and hot, a triangle of sunlight dazzled on one wall—the white men sat, eating the van der Weyden's sandwiches and drinking lager.

They wore civilian clothes, but they would have been a noticeable crowd anywhere. An ordinary bar crowd would have had some flabby types and would have been more mixed in age. These men were all in fine physical condition, and even the few grey-haired ones among them didn't look over forty; they could have passed as some kind of sports team. They sat in two distinct groups. One group was rougher-looking, noisier, with a few flashy dressers; two or three very young men in this group were pretending to be drunk, and clowning. The men in the other group were graver, cleaner-shaved, more educated in face, more conscious of their appearance. And you might have thought the two groups had accidentally come together in the bar, until you saw that they were all wearing the same kind of heavy brown boots.

Normally at the van der Weyden the hotel boys drooped around. The old ones, with their squashed and sour little faces, sat on their stools and expected only to be tipped, wearing their shorts and very big aprons like a pensioner's uniform (and sometimes, in their great stillness, hiding their arms below their aprons and looking like men at the barber's); the younger, post-independence boys wore their own clothes and chatted behind the counter as though they were customers. Now they were all alert and jumping about.

I asked for a cup of coffee, and no cup of coffee ever came to me more quickly at the van der Weyden. It was a tiny old man who served me. And I thought, not for the first time, that in colonial days the hotel boys had been chosen for their small size, and the ease with which they could be manhandled. That was no doubt why the region had provided so many slaves in the old days: slave peoples are physically wretched, half-men in everything except in their capacity to breed the next generation.

The coffee came fast, but the stainless steel jug the old man brought me had only a stale-looking trickle of powdered milk. I lifted the jug. The old man saw before I could show him, and he looked so terrified that I put the jug down and sipped the awful coffee by itself.

The men in the bar had come to do a job. They—or their fellows—had probably already begun. They knew they were dramatic figures. They knew I had come to see what they looked like; they knew the boys were terrified of them. Until this morning those hotel servants had been telling one another stories about the invincibility of their people in the forest; and those hotel servants were men who, given an uprising in the town, would have done terrible things with their small hands. Now, so quickly, they had become abject. In one way it was good; in another way it was pitiful. This was how the place worked on you: you never knew what to think or feel. Fear or shame—there seemed to be nothing in between.

I went back to the shop. It was a way of carrying on, and a way of passing the time. The flamboyant trees were in new leaf, feathery, a delicate green. The light changed; shadows began to angle across the red streets. On another day at this time I would have been starting to think of tea at the flat, squash at the Hellenic Club, with cold drinks afterwards in the rough little bar, sitting at the metal tables and watching the light go.

When Metty came in, just before four, closing time, he said, "The white men came this morning. Some of them went to the barracks and some of them went to the hydro." This was the hydroelectric station, some miles upriver from the town. "The first thing they did at the barracks was to shoot Colonel Yenyi. It was what the President asked them to do. He doesn't play, this new President. Colonel Yenyi was running out to meet them. They didn't let him talk. They shot him in front of the women and everybody. And Iyanda, the sergeant—he bought that bolt of curtain material with the apple pattern—they shot him too, and a few other soldiers as well."

I remembered Iyanda with his overstarched uniform, his broad face, and his smiling, small, malicious eyes. I remembered the way he had rubbed the palm of his hand over the cloth with the big red apples, the proud way he had pulled out the rolled-up notes to pay—such a small sum, really. Curtain material! The news of his execution would have pleased the local people. Not that he was a wicked man; but he belonged to that detested slave-hunting tribe, like the rest of the army, like his colonel.

The President had sent terror to our town and region. But at the same time, by terrorizing the army as well, he was making a gesture to the local people. The news of the executions would have spread fast, and people would already have become confused and nervous. They would have felt—as I began to feel— that for the first time since independence there was some guiding intelligence in the capital, and that the free-for-all of independence had come to an end.

I could see the change in Metty. He had brought quite bloody news. Yet he seemed calmer than in the morning; and he made Ferdinand calmer. Late in the afternoon we began to hear guns. In the morning that sound would have panicked us all. Now we were almost relieved—the guns were far away, and the noise was a good deal less loud than thunder, to which we were accustomed. The dogs were disturbed by the strange noise, though, and set up a barking that rolled back and forth, at times drowning the sound of the guns. Late sunlight, trees, cooking smoke: that was all we could see when we went out to the landing of the external staircase to look.

No lights came on at sunset. There was no electricity. The machinery had failed again, or the power had been deliberately turned off, or the power station had been captured by the rebels. But it wasn't bad to be without lights now; it meant that at least there would be no uprising during the night. People here didn't like the dark, and some could sleep only with lights in their rooms or huts. And none of us—neither Metty nor Ferdinand nor myself—believed that the station had been captured by the rebels. We had faith in the President's white men. The situation, so confused for us in the morning, had become as simple as that now.

I stayed in the sitting room and read old magazines by an oil lamp. In their room Metty and Ferdinand talked. They didn't use their daytime voices or the voices they might have used in electric light. They both sounded slow, contemplative, old; they talked like old men. When I went out to the passage I saw, through the open door, Metty sitting on his cot in undershirt and pants, and Ferdinand, also in undershirt and pants, lying on his bedding on the floor, one raised foot pressed against the wall. In lamplight it was like the interior of a hut; their leisurely, soft talk, full of pauses and silences, matched their postures. For the first time in days they were relaxed, and they felt so far from danger now that they began to talk of danger, war and armies.

Metty said he had seen the white men in the morning.

Ferdinand said, "There were a lot of white soldiers in the south. That was a real war."

"You should have seen them this morning. They just raced to the barracks and they were pointing their guns at everybody. I never saw soldiers like that before."

Ferdinand said, "I saw soldiers for the first time when I was very young. It was just after the Europeans went away. It was in my mother's village, before I went to stay with my father. These soldiers came to the village. They had no officers and they began to behave badly."

"Did they have guns?"

"Of course they had guns. They were looking for white people to kill. They said we were hiding white people. But I think they only wanted to make trouble. Then my mother spoke to them and they went away. They just took a few women."

"What did she say to them?"

"I don't know. But they became frightened. My mother has powers."

Metty said, "That was like the man we had on the coast. He

came from somewhere near here. He was the man who made the people kill the Arabs. It began in the market. I was there. You should have seen it, Ferdinand. The arms and legs lying about in the streets."

"Why did he kill the Arabs?"

"He said he was obeying the god of Africans."

Metty had never told me about that. Perhaps he hadn't thought it important; perhaps it had frightened him. But he had remembered.

They went silent for a while; I had the feeling that Ferdinand was examining what he had heard. When they spoke again it was of other things.

The gunfire went on. But it came no nearer. It was the sound of the weapons of the President's white men, the promise of order and continuity; and it was oddly comforting, like the sound of rain in the night. All that was threatening, in that great unknown outside, was being held in check. And it was a relief, after all the anxiety, to sit in the lamplit flat and watch the shadows that electric lights never made; and to hear Ferdinand and Metty talk in their leisurely old men's voices in that room which they had turned into a warm little cavern. It was a little like being transported to the hidden forest villages, to the protection and secrecy of the huts at night—everything outside shut out, kept beyond some magical protecting line; and I thought, as I had thought when I had had lunch with the old couple, how nice it would be if it were true. If in the morning we could wake up and find that the world had shrunken only to what we knew and what was safe.

In the morning there came the fighter plane. Almost as soon as you heard it, before you had time to go out and look for it, it was overhead, flying low, and screaming at such a pitch that you barely felt yourself in possession of your body; you were close to a cutting-out of the senses. A jet fighter flying low, so low that you clearly see its triangular silver underside, is a killing thing. Then it was gone, and was soon hardly visible in the sky, white with the heat of the day that had just begun. It made a few more passes over the town, that one plane, like a vicious bird that wouldn't go away. Then it flew over the bush. At last it lifted, and just a little while later, at some distance, the missiles it had released exploded in the bush. And that was like the thunder we were used to.

It came back more than once during the week, that single plane, to fly low over the town and the bush and to drop its explosives at random in the bush. But the war was over that first day. Though it was a month before the army began to come back from the bush, and a full two months before the van der Weyden began to lose its new guests.

In the beginning, before the arrival of the white men, I had considered myself neutral. I had wanted neither side to win, neither the army nor the rebels. As it turned out, both sides lost.

Many of the soldiers—from the famous warrior tribe—were killed. And afterwards many more lost their guns and over-starched uniforms and the quarters they had spent so much of their money furnishing. The army was reorganized by the President, far away in the capital; in our town the army became more mixed, with men from many tribes and different regions. The men of the warrior tribe were turned out unprotected into the town. There were dreadful scenes at the barracks; the women wailed in the forest way, lifting their bellies and letting them drop heavily again. A famous tribe, now helpless among their traditional prey: it was as though some old law of the forest, something that came from Nature itself, had been overturned.

As for the starveling rebels of our region, they soon began to reappear in the town, more starved and abject, their blackened rags hanging on them, men who only a few weeks before had thought they had found a fetish powerful enough to cause the guns of their enemies to bend and to turn bullets to water. There was bitterness in their wasted faces, and for a little while they were withdrawn, like people slightly crazed. But they needed the town they had wanted to destroy; as Mahesh said, they had been saved from suicide. They recognized the new intelligence that ran the country from afar, and they returned to their old habit of obedience.

For the first time since I had arrived there was something like life at the van der Weyden. The steamers brought up not only supplies for the President's white men, but also very plump and fantastically dressed women from the downriver peoples, beside whom the women of our region, polers of dugouts and carriers of loads, looked like bony boys.

Eventually we were allowed to drive out to the dam and the hydroelectric station, near where there had been fighting. The installations were untouched; but we had lost one of our new nightclubs. It had been started by a refugee from the Portuguese territory to the south (a man avoiding conscription), and it was beautifully sited, on a cliff overlooking the river. It was a place to which we had just begun to get accustomed. The trees were hung with small coloured bulbs and we sat out at metal tables and drank light Portuguese white wine and looked at the gorge and the floodlit dam; it was like luxury to us, and made us feel stylish. That place had been captured by the rebels and pillaged. The main building was basic and very ordinary—walls of concrete blocks around an unroofed dance floor with a covered bar at one side. The walls still stood (though they had tried to set the concrete alight: there were fire marks in many places); but all the fittings had been destroyed. The rage of the rebels was like a rage against metal, machinery, wires, everything that was not of the forest and Africa.

There were signs of that rage in other places as well. After the earlier war a United Nations agency had repaired the power station and the causeway at the top of the dam. A metal plaque set on a small stone pyramid, some distance from the dam itself, recorded this fact. That plaque had been defaced, battered with some heavy metal piece, individual letters filed away. At the beginning of the causeway old cast-iron lamp standards from Europe had been placed as a decorative feature—old lamps at a site of new power. A pretty idea; but the lamp standards had also received a battering, and again attempts had been made to file away the lettering—the name of the nineteenth-century makers in Paris.

It was the rage that made an impression—the rage of simple men tearing at metal with their hands. And already, after only a few weeks of peace, with so many people from the villages hungry and scrounging in the town, it seemed far away, hard to imagine.

It was during these early days of the peace that Father Huismans went out on one of his trips and was killed. His death need never have been discovered; he could easily have been buried somewhere in the bush. But the people who killed him wanted the fact to be known. His body was put in a dugout, and the dugout drifted down the main river until it caught against the bank in a tangle of water hyacinths. His body had been mutilated, his head cut off and spiked. He was buried quickly, with the minimum of ceremony.

It was terrible. His death made his life seem such a waste. So much of his knowledge was buried with him, and what to me was more than knowledge—his attitudes, his relish for Africa, his feeling for the beliefs of the forest. A little bit of the world was lost with him.

I had admired him for his purity, but now I had to ask whether in the end it had been of value. A death like that makes us question everything. But we are men; regardless of the deaths around us we continue to be flesh and blood and mind, and we cannot stay with that questioning mood for long. When the mood went away I felt—what deep down, as a life-loving man, I had never doubted—that he had passed his time better than most of us. The idea Father Huismans had of his civilization had made him live his particular kind of dedicated life. It had sent him looking, inquiring; it had made him find human richness where the rest of us saw bush or had stopped seeing anything at all. But his idea of his civilization was also like his vanity. It had made him read too much in that mingling of peoples by our river; and he had paid for it.

Little was said about the way he had died. But the body had floated down the main river in a dugout and must have been seen by many people. Word got around the lycée. In our town Father Huismans had the reputation—though most people were rather vague about him—of being a lover of Africa; and some of the boys at the lycée were embarrassed and ashamed. Some were aggressive. Ferdinand—recovered from the days of fright, his wish to be back in his father's or mother's village—was one of the aggressive ones. I wasn't surprised.

Ferdinand said, "It is a thing of Europeans, a museum. Here it is going against the god of Africans. We have masks in our houses and we know what they are there for. We don't have to go to Huismans's museum."

"The god of Africans"—the words were Metty's, and Metty had got them from the leader of the uprising against the Arabs on the coast. I had heard the words for the first time that night when we heard the gunfire from the hydroelectric station and knew that we were safe. The words, occurring when they did, seemed to have released certain things in Ferdinand. Those days in the flat had been days of special crisis for Ferdinand, and he had ever since been settling into a new character. This one fitted, or made more sense. He was no longer concerned about being a particular kind of African; he was simply an African, himself, ready to acknowledge all sides of his character.

It didn't make him easier. He abandoned politeness; he became aggressive and perverse, over a secret nervousness. He began to stay away from the shop and flat. I expected that; it was his way of demonstrating, after the great fright of the rebellion, that he could do without me. But then one day Metty brought me a letter from Ferdinand, and the letter moved me. It was a one-sentence letter written in very big letters on a lined sheet roughly torn out from an exercise book, and sent without an envelope, the sheet just folded small and tight. "Salim! You took me in that time and treated me as a member of your own family. F."

It was his letter of thanks. I had given him shelter under my own roof, and to him, as an African, that hospitality was extraordinary and had to be acknowledged. But he didn't want to appear fawning or weak, and everything in the letter was deliberately crude—no envelope, the lined paper torn down one side, the very big and careless handwriting, the absence of the direct word of thanks, the "Salim!" and not "Dear Salim," the "F." and not "Ferdinand."

I found it funny and moving. Yet there was something ironical about the whole thing. The action which had drawn that softness from Ferdinand was the simple gesture of a man from the coast whose family had lived close, too close, to their servants, once their slaves, descendants of people snatched from this part of Africa. Ferdinand would have been outraged if he knew. Still, the letter, and his unapologetic new character, showed how far, as a man, he had rounded out. And that was what his mother, Zabeth, had had in mind when she brought him to the shop and asked me to look after him.

What Ferdinand had said about Father Huismans's collection, other people began to say. While he lived, Father Huismans, collecting the things of Africa, had been thought a friend of Africa. But now that changed. It was felt that the collection was an affront to African religion, and no one at the lycée took it over. Perhaps there was no one there with the knowledge and the eye that were required.

Visitors were sometimes shown the collection. The wooden carvings remained as they were; but in the unventilated gun room the masks began to deteriorate and the smell became more unpleasant. The masks themselves, crumbling on the slatted shelves, seemed to lose the religious power Father Huismans had taught me to see in them; without him, they simply became extravagant objects.

In the long peace that now settled on the town, we began to receive visitors from a dozen countries, teachers, students, helpers in this and that, people who behaved like discoverers of Africa, were happy with everything they found, and looked down quite a bit on foreigners like ourselves who had been living there. The collection began to be pillaged. Who more African than the young American who appeared among us, who more ready to put on African clothes and dance African dances? He left suddenly by the steamer one day; and it was discovered afterwards that the bulk of the collection in the gun room had been crated and shipped back with his belongings to the United States, no doubt to be the nucleus of the gallery of primitive art he often spoke of starting. The richest products of the forest.

# The New Domain

## 6

If you look at a column of ants on the march you will see that there are some who are stragglers or have lost their way. The column has no time for them; it goes on. Sometimes the stragglers die. But even this has no effect on the column. There is a little disturbance around the corpse, which is eventually carried off—and then it appears so light. And all the time the great busyness continues, and that apparent sociability, that rite of meeting and greeting which ants travelling in opposite directions, to and from their nest, perform without fail.

So it was after the death of Father Huismans. In the old days his death would have caused anger, and people would have wanted to go out to look for his killers. But now we who remained—outsiders, but neither settlers nor visitors, just people with nowhere better to go—put our heads down and got on with our business.

The only message of his death was that we had to be careful ourselves and remember where we were. And oddly enough, by acting as we did, by putting our heads down and getting on with our work, we helped to bring about what he had prophesied for our town. He had said that our town would suffer setbacks but that they would be temporary. After each setback, the civilization of Europe would become a little more secure at the bend in the river; the town would always start up again, and would grow a little more each time. In the peace that we now had, the town wasn't only re-established; it grew. And the rebellion and Father Huismans's death receded fast.

We didn't have Father Huismans's big views. Some of us had our own clear ideas about Africans and their future. But it occurred to me that we did really share his faith in the future.

Unless we believed that change was coming to our part of Africa, we couldn't have done our business. There would have been no point. And—in spite of appearances—we also had the attitude to ourselves that he had to himself. He saw himself as part of a great historical process; he would have seen his own death as unimportant, hardly a disturbance. We felt like that too, but from a different angle.

We were simple men with civilizations but without other homes. Whenever we were allowed to, we did the complicated things we had to do, like the ants. We had the occasional comfort of reward, but in good times or bad we lived with the knowledge that we were expendable, that our labour might at any moment go to waste, that we ourselves might be smashed up; and that others would replace us. To us that was the painful part, that others would come at the better time. But we were like the ants; we kept on.

People in our position move rapidly from depression to optimism and back down again. Now we were in a period of boom. We felt the new ruling intelligence—and energy—from the capital; there was a lot of copper money around; and these two things—order and money—were enough to give us confidence. A little of that went a long way with us. It released our energy; and energy, rather than quickness or great capital, was what we possessed.

All kinds of projects were started. Various government departments came to life again; and the town at last became a place that could be made to work. We already had the steamer service; now the airfield was recommissioned and extended, to take the jets from the capital (and to fly in soldiers). The *cités* filled up, and new ones were built, though nothing that was done could cope with the movement of people from the villages; we never lost the squatters and campers in our central streets and squares. But there were buses now, and many more taxis. We even began to get a new telephone system. It was far too elaborate for our needs, but it was what the Big Man in the capital wanted for us.

The growth of the population could be gauged by the growth

of the rubbish heaps in the *cités*. They didn't burn their rubbish in oil drums, as we did; they just threw it out on the broken streets—that sifted, ashy African rubbish. Those mounds of rubbish, though constantly flattened by rain, grew month by month into increasingly solid little hills, and the hills literally became as high as the box-like concrete houses of the *cités*.

Nobody wanted to move that rubbish. But the taxis stank of disinfectant; the officials of our health department were fierce about taxis. And for this reason. In the colonial days public vehicles had by law to be disinfected once a year by the health department. The disinfectors were entitled to a personal fee. That custom had been remembered. Any number of people wanted to be disinfectors; and now taxis and trucks weren't disinfected just once a year; they were disinfected whenever they were caught. The fee had to be paid each time; and disinfectors in their official jeeps played hide and seek with taxis and trucks among the hills of rubbish. The red dirt roads of our town, neglected for years, had quickly become corrugated with the new traffic we had; and these disinfectant chases were in a curious kind of slow motion, with the vehicles of hunters and hunted pitching up and down the corrugations like launches in a heavy sea.

All the people—like the health officials—who performed services for ready money were energetic, or could be made so: the customs people, the police, and even the army. The administration, however hollow, was fuller; there were people you could appeal to. You could get things done, if you knew how to go about it.

And the town at the bend in the river became again what Father Huismans had said it had always been, long before the peoples of the Indian Ocean or Europe came to it. It became the trading centre for the region, which was vast. *Marchands* came in now from very far away, making journeys much more difficult than Zabeth's; some of those journeys took a week. The steamer didn't go beyond our town; above the rapids there were only dugouts (some with outboard motors) and a few launches. Our town became a goods depot, and I acquired a number of agencies (re-assuming some that Nazruddin had had) for things that until then I had more or less been selling retail.

There was money in agencies. The simpler the product, the simpler and better the business. It was a different kind of business from the retail trade. Electric batteries, for instance—I bought and sold quantities long before they arrived; I didn't have to handle them physically or even see them. It was like dealing in words alone, ideas on paper; it was like a form of play—until one day you were notified that the batteries had arrived, and you went to the customs warehouse and saw that they existed, that workmen somewhere had actually made the things. Such useful things, such necessary things—they would have been acceptable in a plain brown-paper casing; but the people who had made them had gone to the extra trouble of giving them pretty labels, with tempting slogans. Trade, goods! What a mystery! We couldn't make the things we dealt in; we hardly understood their principles. Money alone had brought these magical things to us deep in the bush, and we dealt in them so casually!

Salesmen from the capital, Europeans most of them, preferring to fly up now rather than spend seven days on the steamer coming up and five going down, began to stay at the van der Weyden, and they gave a little variety to our social life. In the Hellenic Club, in the bars, they brought at last that touch of Europe and the big city—the atmosphere in which, from his stories, I had imagined Nazruddin living here.

Mahesh, with his shop just across the road from the van der Weyden, saw the comings and goings, and his excitement led him into a series of little business ventures. It was strange about Mahesh. He was always on the lookout for the big break, but he could spend weeks on things that were quite petty.

He acquired at one time a machine for cutting out or engraving letters and numbers, and he acquired a stack of the very tough plastic plates on which the numbers or letters were to be engraved. His idea was to supply nameplates to the town. He practised at home; Shoba said the noise was terrible. Mahesh, in his flat and in his shop, showed off the practice nameplates as though it was he, rather than the machine, that had made the beautiful letters. The modernity and precision—and, above all, the "manufactured" look of the plates—really excited him, and he was sure it would excite everybody else as well.

He had bought the equipment from a salesman who had stayed at the van der Weyden. And it was typical of Mahesh's casual approach to business that when it came to getting engraving orders, he could only think of crossing the road back to the van der Weyden—reversing the trip of the salesman who had sold him the equipment. He had pinned all his hopes on the van der Weyden. He was going to redo the room numbers, all the *Hommes* and *Dames* signs, and he was going to affix descriptive plates on almost every door downstairs. The van der Weyden alone was going to keep him busy for weeks and pay back for the machine. But the van der Weyden owners (a middle-aged Italian couple who kept themselves in the background and hid behind their African front men) didn't want to play. And not many of us felt the need to have our names on triangular sections of wood on our desks. So that idea was dropped; that tool was forgotten.

Mahesh, broaching a new idea, liked to be mysterious. The time, for instance, he wanted to import a machine from Japan for cutting little flat wood sticks and spoons for ice cream, he didn't say so right out. He began by offering me a sample spoon in a paper wrapper which the salesman had given him. I looked at the little shoe-shaped spoon. What was there to say? He asked me to smell the spoon and then to taste it; and while I did so he looked at me in a way that made me feel that I was going to be surprised. There was no surprise: he was just demonstrating to me—something I must say I had never stopped to think about—that ice cream spoons and sticks shouldn't taste or smell.

He wanted to know whether there was a local wood which was like that nice Japanese wood. To import the wood from Japan with the machine would be too complicated, and might make the sticks and spoons cost more than the ice cream. So for some weeks we thought and talked about wood. The idea interested me; I got taken up with it, and began to look at trees in a different way. We had tasting sessions, smelling and tasting different kinds of wood, including some varieties that Daulat, the man with the trucks, picked up for us on his runs east. But then it occurred to me that it was important to find out—before the spoon-making machine came down—whether the local people, with their own tastes in food, were ready for ice cream. Perhaps there was a good reason why the ice cream idea hadn't occurred to anybody else; and we had Italians in the town, after all. And how was the ice cream going to be made? Where were the milk and the eggs?

Mahesh said, "Do you need eggs to make ice cream?"

I said, "I don't know. I was asking you."

It wasn't the ice cream that attracted Mahesh. It was the idea of that simple machine, or rather the idea of being the only man in the town to own such a machine. When Shoba had met him he had been a motorcycle repairman; and he had been so flattered by her devotion that he had not risen above that kind of person. He remained the man who loved little machines and electrical tools and saw them as magical means of making a living.

I knew a number of men like that on the coast, men of our community; and I believe people like that exist wherever machines are not made. These men are good with their hands and gifted in their own way. They are dazzled by the machines they import. That is part of their intelligence; but they soon start behaving as though they don't just own the machines, but the patents as well; they would like to be the only men in the world with such magical instruments. Mahesh was looking for the wonderful imported thing which he would own exclusively, the simple thing which would provide a short-cut to power and money. So that in this respect Mahesh was only a notch or two above the *marchands* who came to the town to buy modern goods to take back to their villages.

I used to wonder how someone like Mahesh had survived all that he had survived in our town. There was a kind of quiet wisdom or canniness there, no doubt of that. But I also began to feel that he had survived because he was casual, without doubts or deep anxieties, and—in spite of his talk of getting out to a better country (standard talk among us)—without deeper ambitions. He suited the place; he would have found it hard to survive anywhere else.

Shoba was his life. She told him—or by her devotion showed him—how fine he was; and I believe he saw himself as she saw him. Outside that, he took things as they came. And now in the most casual way, with almost no attempt at secrecy or guile, he became involved in "business" deals that frightened me when he told me about them. He seemed unable to resist anything that might be described as a business offer. And most of those business offers came to him now from the army.

I wasn't too happy with our new army. I preferred the men from the warrior tribe, for all their roughness. I understood their tribal pride and—always making allowance for that—I had found them straight. The officers of the new army were a different breed. No warrior code there; no code. They were all in varying ways like Ferdinand, and they were often as young as Ferdinand. They were as aggressive, but without Ferdinand's underlying graciousness.

They wore their uniforms the way Ferdinand had at one time worn his lycée blazer: they saw themselves both as the new men of Africa and the men of the new Africa. They made such play with the national flag and the portrait of the President—the two now always going together—that in the beginning I thought, after all that the country had gone through, and all that had happened to them, the officers, all the lucky accidents that had taken them where they had got, in the beginning I thought these new officers stood for a new, constructive pride. But they were simpler. The flag and the President's portrait were only like their fetishes, the sources of their authority. They didn't see, these young men, that there was anything to build in their country. As far as they were concerned, it was all there already. They had only to take. They believed that, by being what they were, they had earned the right to take; and the higher the officer, the greater the crookedness—if that word had any meaning.

With their guns and jeeps, these men were poachers of ivory and thieves of gold. Ivory, gold—add slaves, and it would have been like being back in oldest Africa. And these men would have dealt in slaves, if there was still a market. It was to the traders in the town that the army turned when they wished to clear their gold or, more especially, the ivory they had poached. Officials

and governments right across the continent were engaged in this
ivory trade which they themselves had declared illegal. It made
smuggling easy; but I was nervous of getting involved, because a
government that breaks its own laws can also easily break you.
Your business associate today can be your jailer or worse tomorrow.

But Mahesh didn't mind. Like a child, as it seemed to me, he
accepted all the poisoned sweets that were offered him. But he
wasn't a child; he knew the sweets were poisoned.

He said, "Oh, they will let you down. But if they let you down,
you pay up. That is all. In your costing you make allowances for
that. You just pay. I don't think you understand, Salim. And it
isn't an easy thing to understand. It isn't that there's no right and
wrong here. There's no right."

Twice, miraculously interpreting a nonsense telephone call
from him as an appeal for help, I had to take away things from
his flat.

The first time, one afternoon, after some inconsequential talk
from him about tennis and the shoes I had asked for, I drove to
his flat and blew my horn. He didn't come down. He opened a
window of his sitting room and shouted down to me in the street,
"I'm sending the boy down with the tennis shoes for you. Right,
Salim!" And, still standing before the window, he turned and
shouted in patois to someone inside. "'Phonse! Aoutchikong
pour Mis' Salim!"—aoutchikong, from caoutchouc, the French
word for rubber, being patois for canvas shoes. With many people looking on, the boy Ildephonse brought down something
roughly wrapped in newspaper. I threw it on the back seat and
drove off without hanging around. It turned out, when I examined it later, to be a bundle of foreign bank notes; and it went, as
soon as it was dark, into the hole in the ground at the foot of my
external staircase. To help Mahesh like this, though, was only to
encourage him. The next time I had to bury some ivory. Burying
ivory! What age were we living in? What did people want ivory
for, apart from carving it—and not too well these days—into
cigarette holders and figurines and junk like that?

Still, these deals made Mahesh money, and he acknowledged

my help and put me in the way of adding to my little store of gold. He had said that there was no right. It was hard for me to adapt to that; but he managed it beautifully. He was always cool and casual, never ruffled. I had to admire him for it. Though the casualness could lead him into situations that were quite ridiculous.

He said to me one day, with the mysterious, over-innocent manner he put on when he was about to tell about some deal: "You read the foreign papers, Salim. Are you keeping an eye on the copper market? What's it like?" Well, copper was high. We all knew that; copper was at the bottom of our little boom. He said, "It's that war the Americans are fighting. I hear they've used up more copper in the last two years than the world has used in the last two centuries." This was boom talk, salesmen's chat from the van der Weyden. Mahesh, just across the road, picked up a fair amount of that chat; without it, he might have had less idea than he had of what was happening in the world.

From copper he turned to the other metals, and we talked for a while, quite ignorantly, about the prospects for tin and lead. Then he said, "Uranium—what about that? What are they quoting that at now?"

I said, "I don't think they quote that."

He gave me his innocent look. "But it must be pretty high? A chap here wants to sell a piece."

"Do they sell uranium in pieces? What does it look like?"

"I haven't seen it. But the chap wants to sell it for a million dollars."

That was what we were like. One day grubbing for food, opening rusty tins, cooking on charcoal braziers and over holes in the ground; and now talking of a million dollars as though we had talked of millions all our lives.

Mahesh said, "I told the general it could be sold only to a foreign power, and he told me to go ahead. You know old Mancini. He is consul for quite a few countries here—that's a nice line of business, I always think. I went to see him. I told him straight out, but he wasn't interested. In fact, Mancini went crazy. He ran to the door and closed it and stood with his back

against it and told me to get out. His face was red, red. Everybody's frightened of the Big Man in the capital. What do you
think I should tell the general, Salim? He's frightened too. He
told me he stole it from some top-security place. I wouldn't like
to make an enemy of the general. I wouldn't like him to think I
hadn't tried. What do you think I should tell him? Seriously,
seriously."

"You say he's frightened?"

"Very frightened."

"Then tell him he's being watched and he mustn't come to see
you again."

I looked in my science magazines and children's encyclopaedia parts (I had grown to love those) and read up on
uranium. Uranium is one of those things we all hear about but
not many of us know about. Like oil. I used to think, from
hearing and reading about oil reservoirs, that oil ran in trapped
underground streams. It was my encyclopaedia parts which told
me that oil reservoirs were of stone and could even be of marble,
with the oil in tiny pockets. It was in just such a way, I suppose,
that the general, hearing of the immense value of uranium, had
thought of it as a kind of super-precious metal, a kind of gold
nugget. Mancini the consul, must have thought so too. My reading told me of tons and tons of ore that had to be processed and
reduced—but reduced to hefty blocks.

The general, offering a "piece," might have been duped himself. But for some reason—Mahesh might have told him he was
being watched—he never troubled Mahesh again. And not long
afterwards he was posted away from our town. It was the method
of the new President: he gave his men power and authority, but
he never allowed them to settle in anywhere and become local
kings. He saved us a lot of trouble.

Mahesh went on as coolly as before. The only man who had
had a fright was Mancini, the consul.

That was what we were like in those days. We felt that there
was treasure around us, waiting to be picked up. It was the bush
that gave us this feeling. During the empty, idle time, we had

been indifferent to the bush; during the days of the rebellion it had depressed us. Now it excited us—the unused earth, with the promise of the unused. We forgot that others had been here before us, and had felt like us.

I shared in the boom. I was energetic in my own modest way. But I was also restless. You so quickly get used to peace. It is like being well—you take it for granted, and forget that when you were ill, to be well again had seemed everything. And with peace and the boom I began to see the town as ordinary, for the first time.

The flat, the shop, the market outside the shop, the Hellenic Club, the bars, the life of the river, the dugouts, the water hyacinths—I knew it so well. And especially on hot sunny afternoons—that hard light, those black shadows, that feeling of stillness—it seemed without further human promise.

I didn't see myself spending the rest of my days at that bend in the river, like Mahesh and the others. In my own mind I separated myself from them. I still thought of myself as a man just passing through. But where was the good place? I couldn't say. I never thought constructively about it. I was waiting for some illumination to come to me, to guide me to the good place and the "life" I was still waiting for.

From time to time now letters from my father on the coast reminded me of his wish to see me settled—married to Nazruddin's daughter: that was almost like a family commitment. But I was less prepared than ever for that. Though it was a comfort on occasion to play with the idea that outside this place a whole life waited for me, all the relationships that bind a man to the earth and give him a feeling of having a place. But I knew that it wasn't like that really. I knew that for us the world was no longer as safe as that.

And again events caught up with my anxieties. There was trouble in Uganda, where Nazruddin had a cotton-ginning business. Uganda up till then had been the secure and well-run country Nazruddin had tried to excite us about, the country which received refugees from neighbouring countries. Now in Uganda itself a king was overthrown and forced to flee; Daulat brought back stories of yet another army on the loose. Nazruddin, as I remembered, lived with the knowledge that, after all his luck, things were going to end badly for him; and I thought that his luck had run out now. But I was wrong; Nazruddin's luck was still with him. The trouble in Uganda didn't last; only the king suffered. Life there went back to normal. But I began to fear for Nazruddin and his family, and the idea of marriage to his daughter ceased to be the idea of a correct family duty. It became a more oppressive kind of responsibility, and I pushed it to the back of my mind as something I would face when I absolutely had to.

So in the midst of the boom I had my anxieties and became almost as dissatisfied and restless as I had been at the beginning. It wasn't only outside pressures, or my solitude and my temperament. It also had to do with the place itself, the way it had altered with the peace. It was nobody's fault. It was something that had just happened. During the days of the rebellion I had had the sharpest sense of the beauty of the river and the forest, and had promised myself that when the peace came I would expose myself to it, learn it, possess that beauty. I had done nothing of the sort; when the peace came I had simply stopped looking about me. And now I felt that the mystery and the magic of the place had gone.

In those days of fear I felt we had been in touch, through the Africans, with the spirits of the river and forest; and that everything had been full of tension. But all the spirits seemed now to have left the place, as, after Father Huismans's death, the spirits appeared to have left his masks. We had been so nervous of the Africans during those days; we hadn't taken any man for granted. We had been the intruders, the ordinary men, they the inspired ones. Now the spirits had left them; they were ordinary, squalid, poor. Without effort we had become, in a real way, the masters, with the gifts and skills they needed. And we were so simple. On the land now ordinary again we had arranged such ordinary lives for ourselves—in the bars and brothels, the night-clubs. Oh, it was unsatisfactory. Yet what else could we do? We

did only what we could do. We followed Mahesh's motto: we
carried on.

Mahesh did more than that. He pulled off a coup. He continued to consult catalogues, fill in coupons, write off for further
information; and at last he found the package he had been looking for, the thing he could import whole and use as a short-cut to
business and money. He got the Bigburger franchise for our
town.

It wasn't what I was expecting. He had been running an odd
little shop that dealt in ironmongery of various sorts, electrical
goods, cameras, binoculars, lots of little gadgets. Hamburgers—
Bigburgers—didn't seem to be his thing. I wasn't even sure that
the town would go for Bigburgers. But he had no doubts.

He said, "They've done their market research and they've decided to make a big push in Africa. They have an area office now
in one of the French places on the west coast. The chap came the
other day and measured up and everything. They don't just send
you the sauce, you know, Salim. They send you the whole shop."

And that was what they did. The crates that came up on the
steamer in a couple of months did contain the whole shop: the
stoves, the milk-shake machines, the coffee machine, the cups
and plates, the tables and chairs, the made-to-measure counter,
the stools, the made-to-measure wall panelling with the Bigburger design. And after all this serious stuff there were the toys:
the Bigburger cruets, the Bigburger ketchup containers, the
Bigburger menus and menu holders, and the lovely advertisements: "Bigburgers—The Big One—The Bigwonderful One,"
with pictures of different kinds of Bigburgers.

I thought the Bigburger pictures looked like smooth white lips
of bread over mangled black tongues of meat. But Mahesh didn't
like it when I told him, and I decided not to say anything dis-
respectful about Bigburgers again. Mahesh had been full of
jokes about the project; but as soon as the stuff arrived he became deadly serious—he had become Bigburger.

Mahesh's shop was structurally quite simple, the standard
concrete box of our town; and in no time the local Italian builder

had cleared it of Mahesh's shelves, rewired, put in new plumbing, and fitted up a dazzling snack bar that seemed to have been imported from the United States. The whole prefabricated business did work; and it was great fun to be in Bigburger, to leave the sewer smells of the street, and the dust and the rubbish, and to step into this modern interior, with the advertisements and everything. So Mahesh did, after all, pull it off.

The prettiness had an effect on Shoba too. It made her energetic and brought out something of her family business talents. She organized the place and soon had it running smoothly. She arranged for the deliveries of meat from our new supermarket (the meat came from South Africa, like our eggs now) and she arranged with an Italian for the loaves. She trained the boys and worked out their schedules.

Ildephonse, the houseboy, was taken from the flat and given a Bigburger chef's cap and a yellow Bigburger jacket and put behind the counter. It was Mahesh's idea to give Ildephonse a label for his jacket with his name and the designation—in English, for the extra style—Manager. Mahesh did little things like that sometimes which showed you that, casual as he was, he knew instinctively how to operate in our town. He said he called Ildephonse the manager to ward off African resentment of the new, rich-looking place, and also to attract African customers. And he made a point of leaving Ildephonse in charge for some hours every day.

It was strange about Ildephonse, though. He loved his Bigburger costume and he loved his new job. No one was quicker and more friendly and more anxious to please than he was, when Shoba or Mahesh was around. They trusted Ildephonse; they boasted of their trust in him, in his presence. Yet as soon as he was left alone he became a different person. He went vacant. Not rude, just vacant. I noticed this alteration in the African staff in other places as well. It made you feel that while they did their jobs in their various glossy settings, they were only acting for the people who employed them; that the job itself was meaningless to them; and that they had the gift—when they were left alone, and had no one to act for—of separating themselves in spirit from their setting, their job, their uniform.

Bigburger was a success. The van der Weyden, across the road, was content to make money from its beds and rooms. The service and the kitchens there drove people out to look for food, and Bigburger was perfectly placed to capture that refugee trade. Bigburger attracted a lot of African officials and army people as well—they liked the décor and the modernity. So that Mahesh, from running a nondescript little hardware shop, found himself at the centre of things in our town.

All this happened quickly, in less than a year. Everything happened quickly now. It was as though everyone felt he had to make up for the lost years, or as though everyone felt that time was short, that the place might close down at any moment again.

Mahesh said to me one day, "Noimon offered me two million. But you know Noimon. When he offers two, you know it's worth four."

Noimon was one of our local big Greeks. The new furniture shop—doing fantastic business—was just one of his ventures. The two million he offered were local francs, which were thirty-six to the dollar.

Mahesh said, "I suppose your place is worth a lot now. Nazruddin offered it to me, you know. A hundred and fifty thousand. What do you think you'll get for it now?"

You heard that kind of property talk everywhere now. Everyone was totting up how much he had gained with the boom, how much he was worth. People learned to speak huge figures calmly.

There had been a boom before, just at the end of the colonial period, and the ruined suburb near the rapids was what it had left behind. Nazruddin had told a story about that. He had gone out there one Sunday morning, had thought that the place was bush rather than real estate, and had decided to sell. Lucky for him then; but now that dead suburb was being rehabilitated. That development or redevelopment had become the most important feature of our boom. And it had caused the big recent rise in property values in the town.

The bush near the rapids was being cleared. The ruins which had seemed permanent were being levelled by bulldozers; new avenues were being laid out. It was the Big Man's doing. The government had taken over all that area and decreed it the Domain of the State, and the Big Man was building what looked like a little town there. It was happening very fast. The copper money was pouring in, pushing up prices in our town. The deep, earth-shaking burr of bulldozers competed with the sound of the rapids. Every steamer brought up European builders and artisans, every airplane. The van der Weyden seldom had rooms to spare.

Everything the President did had a reason. As a ruler in what was potentially hostile territory, he was creating an area where he and his flag were supreme. As an African, he was building a new town on the site of what had been a rich European suburb —but what he was building was meant to be grander. In the town the only "designed" modern building was the van der Weyden; and to us the larger buildings of the Domain were startling—concrete louvres, pierced concrete blocks of great size, tinted glass. The smaller buildings—houses and bungalows —were more like what we were used to. But even they were on the large side and, with air conditioners sticking out in many places like building blocks that had slipped, looked extravagant.

No one was sure, even after some of the houses were furnished, what the Domain was to be used for. There were stories of a great new model farm and agricultural college; a conference hall to serve the continent; holiday houses for loyal citizens. From the President himself there came no statement. We watched and wondered while the buildings were run up. And then we began to understand that what the President was attempting was so stupendous in his own eyes that even he would not have wanted to proclaim it. He was creating modern Africa. He was creating a miracle that would astound the rest of the world. He was by-passing real Africa, the difficult Africa of bush and villages, and creating something that would match anything that existed in other countries.

Photographs of this State Domain—and of others like it in other parts of the country—began to appear in those magazines about Africa that were published in Europe but subsidized by governments like ours. In these photographs the message of the

Domain was simple. Under the rule of our new President the miracle had occurred: Africans had become modern men who built in concrete and glass and sat in cushioned chairs covered in imitation velvet. It was like a curious fulfilment of Father Huismans's prophecy about the retreat of African Africa, and the success of the European graft.

Visitors were encouraged, from the *cités* and shanty towns, from the surrounding villages. On Sundays there were buses and army trucks to take people there, and soldiers acted as guides, taking people along one-way paths marked with directional arrows, showing the people who had recently wished to destroy the town what their President had done for Africa. Such shoddy buildings, after you got used to the shapes; such flashy furniture —Noimon was making a fortune with his furniture shop. All around, the life of dugout and creek and village continued; in the bars in the town the foreign builders and artisans drank and made easy jokes about the country. It was painful and it was sad.

The President had wished to show us a new Africa. And I saw Africa in a way I had never seen it before, saw the defeats and humiliations which until then I had regarded as just a fact of life. And I felt like that—full of tenderness for the Big Man, for the ragged villagers walking around the Domain, and the soldiers showing them the shabby sights—until some soldier played the fool with me or some official at the customs was difficult, and then I fell into the old way of feeling, the easier attitudes of the foreigners in the bars. Old Africa, which seemed to absorb everything, was simple; this place kept you tense. What a strain it was, picking your way through stupidity and aggressiveness and pride and hurt!

But what was the Domain to be used for? The buildings gave pride, or were meant to; they satisfied some personal need of the President's. Was that all they were for? But they had consumed millions. The farm didn't materialize. The Chinese or the Taiwanese didn't turn up to till the land of the new model African farm; the six tractors that some foreign government had given remained in a neat line in the open and rusted, and the grass grew high about them. The big swimming pool near the building that was said to be a conference hall developed leaks and remained empty, with a wide-meshed rope net at the top. The Domain had been built fast, and in the sun and the rain decay also came fast. After the first rainy season many of the young trees that had been planted beside the wide main avenue died, their roots waterlogged and rotted.

But for the President in the capital the Domain remained a living thing. Statues were added, and lamp standards. The Sunday visits went on; the photographs continued to appear in the subsidized magazines that specialized in Africa. And then at last a use was found for the buildings.

The Domain became a university city and a research centre. The conference-hall building was turned into a polytechnic for people of the region, and other buildings were turned into dormitories and staff quarters. Lecturers and professors began to come from the capital, and soon from other countries; a parallel life developed there, of which we in the town knew little. And it was to the polytechnic there—on the site of the dead European suburb that to me, when I first came, had suggested the ruins of a civilization that had come and gone—that Ferdinand was sent on a government scholarship, when he had finished at the lycée.

The Domain was some miles away from the town. There was a bus service, but it was irregular. I hadn't been seeing much of Ferdinand, and now I saw even less of him. Metty lost a friend. That move of Ferdinand's finally made the difference between the two men clear, and I thought that Metty suffered.

My own feelings were more complicated. I saw a disordered future for the country. No one was going to be secure here; no man of the country was to be envied. Yet I couldn't help thinking how lucky Ferdinand was, how easy it had been made for him. You took a boy out of the bush and you taught him to read and write; you levelled the bush and built a polytechnic and you sent him there. It seemed as easy as that, if you came late to the world and found ready-made those things that other countries and peoples had taken so long to arrive at—writing, printing, universities, books, knowledge. The rest of us had to take things in stages. I thought of my own family, Nazruddin, myself—we were so clogged by what the centuries had deposited in our minds and hearts. Ferdinand, starting from nothing, had with one step made himself free, and was ready to race ahead of us.

The Domain, with its shoddy grandeur, was a hoax. Neither the President who had called it into being nor the foreigners who had made a fortune building it had faith in what they were creating. But had there been greater faith before? *Miscerique probat populos et foedera jungi*: Father Huismans had explained the arrogance of that motto. He had believed in its truth. But how many of the builders of the earlier city would have agreed with him? Yet that earlier hoax had helped to make men of the country in a certain way; and men would also be made by this new hoax. Ferdinand took the polytechnic seriously; it was going to lead him to an administrative cadetship and eventually to a position of authority. To him the Domain was fine, as it should be. He was as glamorous to himself at the polytechnic as he had been at the lycée.

It was absurd to be jealous of Ferdinand, who still after all went home to the bush. But I wasn't jealous of him only because I felt that he was about to race ahead of me in knowledge and enter realms I would never enter. I was jealous more of that idea he had always had of his own importance, his own glamour. We lived on the same patch of earth; we looked at the same views. Yet to him the world was new and getting newer. For me that same world was drab, without possibilities.

I grew to detest the physical feel of the place. My flat remained as it had always been. I had changed nothing there, because I lived with the idea that at a moment's notice I had to consider it all as lost—the bedroom with the white-painted window panes and the big bed with the foam mattress, the roughly made cupboards with my smelly clothes and shoes, the kitchen with its smell of kerosene and frying oil and rust and dirt and cockroaches, the empty white studio–sitting room. Always there, never really mine, reminding me now only of the passing of time.

I detested the imported ornamental trees, the trees of my childhood, so unnatural here, with the red dust of the streets that turned to mud in rain, the overcast sky that meant only more heat, the clear sky that meant a sun that hurt, the rain that seldom cooled and made for a general clamminess, the brown river with the lilac-coloured flowers on rubbery green vines that floated on and on, night and day.

Ferdinand had moved only a few miles away. And I, so recently his senior, felt jealous and deserted.

Metty, too, was like a man with preoccupations. Freedom had its price. Once he had had the slave's security. Here he had gained an idea of himself as a man to be measured against other men. That had so far brought him only pleasure. But now it seemed to have brought him a little bitterness as well. He seemed to be staying away from his friends.

He was full of friends, and all kinds of people came to the shop and the flat to ask about him. Or sometimes they sent others to ask about him. One such messenger I grew to recognize. She was like a very thin boy, the kind of girl you would see poling the dugouts, someone regarded by her people just as labour, a pair of hands. Hard work and bad food appeared to have neutered her, worn away her feminine characteristics, and left her almost bald.

She used to come for Metty at the shop, hanging around outside. Sometimes he spoke to her; sometimes he was rough with her. Sometimes he made as if to chase her away, bending down to pick up an imaginary stone, the way people did here when they wanted to frighten away a pariah dog. No one like the slave for spotting the slave, or knowing how to deal with the slave. This girl was among the lowest of the low; her status, in whatever African household she was, would have been close to that of a slave.

Metty succeeded in driving her away from the shop. But one afternoon, when I went to the flat after closing the shop, I saw her on the pavement outside, standing among the dusty hummocks of wild grass near the side entrance to our back yard. An ashy, unwashed cotton smock, wide-sleeved and wide-necked, hung loosely from her bony shoulders and showed she was wearing nothing else below. Her hair was so sparse her head looked shaved. Her thin little face was set in a frown which wasn't a frown but was only meant to say she wasn't looking at me.

She was still there when, after making myself some tea, and changing, I went down again. I was going to the Hellenic Club for my afternoon squash. It was my rule: whatever the circumstances, however unwilling the spirit, never give up the day's exercise. Afterwards I drove out to the dam, to the Portuguese nightclub on the cliff, now got going again, and had some fried fish there—I am sure they did it better in Portugal. It was too early for the band and the town crowd, but the dam was floodlit, and they turned on the coloured lights on the trees for me.

The girl was still on the pavement when I went back to the flat. This time she spoke to me. She said, "*Metty-ki là?*"

She had only a few words of the local patois, but she could understand it when it was spoken, and when I asked her what she wanted she said, "*Popo malade. Dis-li Metty.*"

*Popo* was "baby." Metty had a baby somewhere in the town, and the baby was sick. Metty had a whole life out there, separate from his life with me in the flat, separate from his bringing me coffee in the mornings, separate from the shop.

I was shocked. I felt betrayed. If we had been living in our compound on the coast, he would have lived his own life, but there would have been no secrets. I would have known who his woman was; I would have known when his baby was born. I had lost Metty to this part of Africa. He had come to the place that was partly his home, and I had lost him. I felt desolate. I had been hating the place, hating the flat; yet now I saw the life I had made for myself in that flat as something good, which I had lost.

Like the girl outside, like so many other people, I waited for Metty. And when, very late, he came in, I began to speak at once.

"Oh, Metty, why didn't you tell me? Why did you do this to me?" Then I called him by the name we called him at home.

"Ali, Ali-wa! We lived together. I took you under my roof and treated you as a member of my own family. And now you do this."

Dutifully, like the servant of the old days, he tried to match his mood to mine, tried to look as though he suffered with me.

"I will leave her, *patron*. She's an animal."

"How can you leave her? You've done it. You can't go back on that. You've got that child out there. Oh, Ali, what have you done? Don't you think it's disgusting to have a little African child running about in somebody's yard, with its *toto* swinging from side to side? Aren't you ashamed, a boy like you?"

"It is disgusting, Salim." He came and put his hand on my shoulder. "And I am very ashamed. She's only an African woman. I will leave her."

"How can you leave her? That is now your life. Didn't you know it was going to be like that? We sent you to school, we had the mullahs teach you. And now you do this."

I was acting. But there are times when we act out what we really feel, times when we cannot cope with certain emotions, and it is easier to act. And Metty was acting too, being loyal, reminding me of the past, of other places, reminding me of things I could scarcely bear that night. When I said, acting, "Why didn't you tell me, Metty?" he acted back for my sake. He said, "How could I tell you, Salim? I knew you were going to get on like this."

How did he know?

I said, "You know, Metty, the first day you went to school, I went with you. You cried all the time. You began to cry as soon as we left the house."

He liked being reminded of this, being remembered from so far back. He said, almost smiling, "I cried a lot? I made a lot of noise?"

"Ali, you screamed the place down. You had your white cap on, and you went down the little alley at the side of Gokool's house, and you were bawling. I couldn't see where you had gone. I just heard you bawling. I couldn't stand it. I thought they were doing terrible things to you, and I begged for you not to go to school. Then the trouble was to get you to come back home. You've forgotten, and why should you remember? I've been noticing you since you've been here. You've been very much getting on as though you're your own man."

"Oh, Salim! You mustn't say that. I always show you respect."

That was true. But he had returned home; he had found his new life. However much he wished it, he couldn't go back. He had shed the past. His hand on my shoulder—what good was that now?

I thought: Nothing stands still. Everything changes. I will inherit no house, and no house that I build will now pass to my children. That way of life has gone. I have lost my twenties, and what I have been looking for since I left home hasn't come to me. I have only been waiting. I will wait for the rest of my life. When I came here, this flat was still the Belgian lady's flat. It wasn't my home; it was like a camp. Then that camp became mine. Now it has changed again.

Later, I woke to the solitude of my bedroom, in the unfriendly world. I felt all the child's heartache at being in a strange place. Through the white-painted window I saw the trees outside—not their shadows, but the suggestion of their forms. I was homesick, had been homesick for months. But home was hardly a place I could return to. Home was something in my head. It was something I had lost. And in that I was like the ragged Africans who were so abject in the town we serviced.

# 7

Discovering the ways of pain, the aging that it brings, I wasn't surprised that Metty and myself should have been so close just at that moment when we understood that we had to go our separate ways. What had given the illusion of closeness that evening was only our regret for the past, our sadness that the world doesn't stand still.

Our life together didn't change. He continued to live in his room in the flat, and he continued to bring me coffee in the mornings. But now it was understood that he had a whole life outside. He altered. He lost the brightness and gaiety of the servant who knows that he will be looked after, that others will decide for him; and he lost what went with that brightness—the indifference to what had just happened, the ability to forget, the readiness for every new day. He seemed to go a little sour inside. Responsibility was new to him; and with that he must also have discovered solitude, in spite of his friends and his new family life.

I, too, breaking out of old ways, had discovered solitude and the melancholy which is at the basis of religion. Religion turns that melancholy into uplifting fear and hope. But I had rejected the ways and comforts of religion; I couldn't turn to them again, just like that. That melancholy about the world remained something I had to put up with on my own. At some times it was sharp; at some times it wasn't there.

And just when I had digested that sadness about Metty and the past, someone from the past turned up. He walked into the shop one morning, Metty leading him in, Metty calling out in high excitement, "Salim! Salim!"

It was Indar, the man who had first brought out my panic on the coast, confronted me—after that game of squash in the squash court of his big house—with my own fears about our future, and had sent me away from his house with a vision of disaster. He had given me the idea of flight. He had gone to England, to his university; I had fled here.

And I felt now, as Metty led him in, that he had caught me out again, sitting at my desk in the shop, with my goods spread out on the floor, as they had always been, and with my shelves full of cheap cloth and oilcloth and batteries and exercise books.

He said, "I heard some years ago in London that you were here. I wondered what you were doing." His expression was cool, balanced between irritation and a sneer, and it seemed to say that he didn't have to ask now, and that he wasn't surprised by what he had found.

It had happened so quickly. When Metty came running in

saying, "Salim! Salim! Guess who's here," I had at once had an idea that it would be someone we had both known in the old days. I thought it would be Nazruddin, or some member of my family, some brother-in-law or nephew. And I had thought: But I can't cope. The life here is no longer the old life. I cannot accept this responsibility. I don't want to run a hospital.

Expecting, then, someone who was about to make a claim on me in the name of family and community and religion, and preparing a face and an attitude for that person, I was dismayed to find Metty leading Indar into the shop, Metty beside himself with joy, not pretending now, but for that moment delighted to re-create something of the old days, being the man in touch with great families. And from being myself the man full of complaint, the man who was going to pour out his melancholy in harsh advice to a new arrival who was perhaps already half crushed— "There is no place for you here. There is no place here for the homeless. Find somewhere else"—from being that kind of man, I had to be the opposite. I had to be the man who was doing well and more than well, the man whose drab shop concealed some bigger operation that made millions. I had to be the man who had planned it all, who had come to the destroyed town at the bend in the river because he had foreseen the rich future.

I couldn't be any other way with Indar. He had always made me feel so backward. His family, though new on the coast, had outstripped us all; and even their low beginnings—the grandfather who was a railway labourer, then a market money-lender —had become (from the way people spoke) a little sacred, part of their wonderful story. They invested adventurously and spent money well; their way of living was much finer than ours; and there was their unusual passion for games and physical exercise. I had always thought of them as "modern" people, with a style quite different from ours. You get used to differences like that; they can even begin to appear natural.

When we had played squash that afternoon, and Indar had told me he was going to England to a university, I hadn't felt resentful or jealous of him for what he was doing. Going abroad, the university—that was part of his style, what might have been expected. My unhappiness was the unhappiness of a man who felt left behind, unprepared for what was coming. And my resentment of him had to do with the insecurity he had made me feel. He had said, "We're washed up here, you know." The words were true; I knew they were true. But I disliked him for speaking them: he had spoken as someone who had foreseen it all and had made his dispositions.

Eight years had passed since that day. What he had said would happen had happened. His family had lost a lot; they had lost their house; they (who had added the name of the town on the coast to their family name) had scattered, like my own family. Yet now, as he came into the shop, it seemed that the distance between us had remained the same.

There was London in his clothes, the trousers, the striped cotton shirt, the way his hair was cut, his shoes (oxblood in colour, thin-soled but sturdy, a little too narrow at the toes). And I—well, I was in my shop, with the red dirt road and the market square outside. I had waited so long, endured so much, changed; yet to him I hadn't changed at all.

So far I had remained sitting. As I stood up I had a little twinge of fear. It came to me that he had reappeared only to bring me bad news. And all I could find to say was: "What brings you to the back of beyond?"

He said, "I wouldn't say that. You are where it's at."

" 'Where it's at'?"

"Where big things are happening. Otherwise I wouldn't be here."

That was a relief. At least he wasn't giving me my marching orders again, without telling me where to go.

Metty all this while was smiling at Indar and swinging his head from side to side, saying, "Indar! Indar!" And it was Metty who remembered our duty as hosts. He said, "You would like some coffee, Indar?" As though we were on the coast, in the family shop, and he just had to step down the lane to Noor's stall and bring back the little brass cups of sweet and muddy coffee on a heavy brass tray. No coffee like that here; only Nescafé, made in the Ivory Coast, and served in big china cups. Not the same kind of drink: you couldn't chat over it, sighing at each hot sweet sip.

Indar said, "That would be very nice, Ali."

I said, "His name here is Metty. It means 'half-caste.' "

"You let them call you that, Ali?"

"African people, Indar. *Kafar*. You know what they give."

I said, "Don't believe him. He loves it. It makes him a great hit with the girls. Ali's a big family man now. He's lost."

Metty, going to the storeroom to boil the water for the Nescafé, said, "Salim, Salim. Don't let me down too much."

Indar said, "He was lost a long time ago. Have you heard from Nazruddin? I saw him in Uganda a few weeks ago."

"What's it like out there now?"

"Settling down. For how long is another matter. Not one bloody paper has spoken up for the king. Did you know that? When it comes to Africa, people don't want to know or they have their principles. Nobody cares a damn about the people who live in the place."

"But you do a lot of travelling."

"It's my business. How are things with you here?"

"It's been very good since the rebellion. The place is booming. Property is fantastic. Land is two hundred francs a square foot in some parts now."

Indar didn't look impressed—but the shop wasn't an impressive place. I felt, too, I had run on a little bit and was doing the opposite of what I intended to do with Indar. Wishing to let him know that his assumptions about me were wrong, I was in fact acting out the character he saw me as. I was talking the way I had heard traders in the town talk, and even saying the things they said.

I said, attempting another kind of language, "It's a specialized business. A sophisticated market would be easier in some ways. But here you can't follow your personal likes and dislikes. You have to know exactly what is needed. And of course there are the agencies. That's where the real money is."

Indar said, "Yes, yes. The agencies. It's like old times for you, Salim."

I let that pass. But I decided to tone the whole thing down. I said, "I don't know how long it's going to last, though."

"It will last as long as your President wants it to last. And no one can tell how long that will be. He's a strange man. He seems to be doing nothing at all, and then he can act like a surgeon. Cutting away some part he doesn't like."

"That's how he settled the old army. It was terrible, Indar. He sent a message to Colonel Yenyi telling him to stay at the barracks and to welcome the commander of the mercenaries. So he stayed on the steps in full uniform, and when they arrived he began to walk to the gate. They shot him as he walked. And everybody with him."

"It saved your bacon, though. I have something for you, by the way. I went to see your father and mother before I came here."

"You went home?" But I dreaded hearing about it from him.

He said, "Oh, I've been there a few times since the great events. It isn't so bad. You remember our house? They've painted it in the party colours. It's some kind of party building now. Your mother gave me a bottle of coconut chutney. It isn't for you alone. It is for Ali and you. She made that clear." And to Metty, coming back then with the jug of hot water and the cups and the tin of Nescafé and the condensed milk, he said, "Ma sent you some coconut chutney, Ali."

Metty said, "Chutney, coconut chutney. The food here is *horrible*, Indar."

We sat all three around the desk, stirring coffee and water and condensed milk together.

Indar said, "I didn't want to go back. Not the first time. I didn't think my heart could stand it. But the airplane is a wonderful thing. You are still in one place when you arrive at the other. The airplane is faster than the heart. You arrive quickly and you leave quickly. You don't grieve too much. And there is something else about the airplane. You can go back many times to the same place. And something strange happens if you go back often enough. You stop grieving for the past. You see that the past is something in your mind alone, that it doesn't exist in real life. You trample on the past, you crush it. In the beginning it is like trampling on a garden. In the end you are just walking on ground. That is the way we have to learn to live now. The past is here." He touched his heart. "It isn't there." And he pointed at the dusty road.

I felt he had spoken the words before, or had gone over them in his mind. I thought: He fights to keep his style. He's probably suffered more than the rest of us.

We sat, the three of us, drinking Nescafé. And I thought the moment beautiful.

Still, the conversation had so far been one-sided. He knew everything about me; I knew nothing about his recent life. When I had first arrived in the town I had noticed that for most people conversation meant answering questions about themselves; they seldom asked you about yourself; they had been cut off for too long. I didn't want Indar to feel that way about me. And I really wanted to know about him. So, a little awkwardly, I began to ask.

He said he had been in the town for a couple of days and was going to stay for a few months. Had he come up by the steamer? He said, "You're crazy. Cooped up with river Africans for seven days? I flew up."

Metty said, "I wouldn't go anywhere by the steamer. They tell me it's horrible. And it's even worse on the barge, with the latrines and the people cooking and eating everywhere. It's horrible-horrible, they tell me."

I asked Indar where he was staying: it had occurred to me that I should make the gesture of offering him hospitality. Was he staying at the van der Weyden?

This was the question he was waiting to be asked. He said in a soft and unassuming voice, "I'm staying at the State Domain. I have a house there. I'm a guest of the government."

And Metty behaved more graciously than I. Metty slapped the desk and said, "Indar!"

I said, "The Big Man invited you?"

He began to scale it down. "Not exactly. I have my own outfit. I am attached to the polytechnic for a term. Do you know it?"

"I know someone there. A student."

Indar behaved as though I had interrupted him; as though—

although I lived in the place, and he had just arrived—I was trespassing, and had no right to know a student at the polytechnic.

I said, "His mother's a *marchande*, one of my customers."

That was better. He said, "You must come and meet some of the other people there. You may not like what's going on. But you mustn't pretend it isn't happening. You mustn't make that mistake again."

I wanted to say: "I live here. I have lived through quite a lot in the last six years." But I didn't say that. I played up to his vanity. He had his own idea of the kind of man I was—and indeed he had caught me in my shop, at my ancestral business. He had his own idea of who he was and what he had done, the distance he had put between himself and the rest of us.

His vanity didn't irritate me. I found I was relishing it, in the way that years before, on the coast, as a child, I had relished Nazruddin's stories of his luck and of the delights of life here, in the colonial town. I hadn't slapped the desk like Metty, but I was impressed by what I saw of Indar. And it was a relief to put aside the dissatisfactions he made me feel, to forget about being caught out, and to give him a straight admiration for what he had made of himself—for his London clothes and the privilege they spoke of, his travelling, his house in the Domain, his position at the polytechnic.

To give him admiration, to appear not to be competing or resisting, was to put him at his ease. As we chatted over our Nescafé, as Metty exclaimed from time to time, expressing in his servant's manner the admiration which his master also felt, Indar's edginess wore off. He became gentle, full of manners, concerned. At the end of the morning I felt I had at last made a friend of my kind. And I badly needed such a friend.

And far from being his host and guide, I became the man who was led about. It wasn't all that absurd. I had so little to show him. All the key points of the town I knew could be shown in a couple of hours, as I discovered when I drove him around later that morning.

There was the river, with a stretch of broken promenade near the docks. There were the docks themselves; the repair yards with open corrugated-iron sheds full of rusting pieces of machinery; and some way downriver the ruined cathedral, beautifully overgrown and looking antique, like something in Europe —but you could only look from the road, because the bush was too thick and the site was famous for its snakes. There were the scuffed squares with their defaced and statueless pedestals; the official buildings from the colonial time in avenues lined with palmiste trees; the lycée, with the decaying masks in the gun room (but that bored Indar); the van der Weyden and Mahesh's Bigburger place, which were hardly things to show to a man who had been to Europe.

There were the *cités* and the squatters' settlements (some of them I was driving into for the first time) with their hills of rubbish, their corrugated dusty lanes, and a lot of old tires lying in the dust. To me the rubbish hills and the tires were features of the *cités* and shanty towns. The spidery little children that we had here did wonderful somersaults off those tires, running, jumping on the tires, and then springing high in the air. But it was nearly noon. There were no children doing somersaults when we drove by; and I realized that (after a monument with nothing on it, and pedestals without statues) I was literally just showing Indar a lot of rubbish. I cut short the tour at that point. The rapids and the fishermen's village—that had been incorporated into the State Domain; that he had already seen.

As we drove to the Domain—the intervening area, once empty, now filling up with the shacks of new arrivals from the villages: shacks which, in Indar's company, I seemed to be seeing for the first time: the red ground between the shacks stained with rivulets of black or grey-green filth, maize and cassava planted in every free space—as we drove, Indar said, "How long did you say you've been living here?"

"Six years."

"And you've shown me everything?"

What hadn't I shown him? A few interiors of shops and houses and flats, the Hellenic Club—and the bars. But I wouldn't have shown him the bars. And really, looking at the place with his eyes, I was amazed at the little I had been living with. And I had stopped seeing so much. In spite of everything, I had thought of the town as a real town; I saw it now as an agglomeration of shack settlements. I thought I had been resisting the place. But I had only been living blind—like the people I knew, from whom in my heart of hearts I had thought myself different.

I hadn't liked it when Indar had suggested that I was living like our community in the old days, not paying attention to what was going on. But he wasn't so far wrong. He was talking about the Domain; and for us in the town the Domain had remained only a source of contracts. We knew little of the life there, and we hadn't wanted to find out. We saw the Domain as part of the waste and foolishness of the country. But more importantly, we saw it as part of the President's politics; and we didn't want to become entangled with that.

We were aware of the new foreigners on the periphery of our town. They were not like the engineers and salesmen and arti-sans we knew, and we were a little nervous of them. The Domain people were like tourists, but they were not spenders—every-thing was found for them on the Domain. They were not inter-ested in us; and we, thinking of them as protected people, looked upon them as people separate from the true life of the place, and for this reason not quite real, not as real as ourselves.

Without knowing it, and thinking all the time that we were keeping our heads down and being wise and protecting our in-terests, we had become like the Africans the President ruled. We were people who felt only the weight of the President's power. The Domain had been created by the President; for reasons of his own he had called certain foreigners to live there. For us that was enough; it wasn't for us to question or look too closely.

Sometimes, after Ferdinand had come to the town to see his mother during one of her shopping trips, I had driven him back to his hostel in the Domain. What I saw then was all that I knew, until Indar became my guide.

It was as Indar had said. He had a house in the Domain and he was a guest of the government. His house was carpeted and furnished showroom style—twelve hand-carved dining chairs, upholstered chairs in fringed synthetic velvet in two colours in the sitting room, lamps, tables, air conditioners everywhere. The air conditioners were necessary. The Domain houses, naked in levelled land, were like grander concrete boxes, with roofs that didn't project at all, so that at any hour of a bright day one wall, or two, got the full force of the sun. With the house there was also a boy, in the Domain servant costume—white shorts, white shirt and a white *jacket de boy* (instead of the apron of colonial days). It was the Domain style for people in Indar's position. The style was the President's. It was he who had decided on the costumes for the boys.

And in the strange world of the Domain Indar appeared to be well regarded. Part of this regard was due to the "outfit" to which he belonged. He couldn't quite explain to me what the outfit was that sent him on African tours—or I might have been too naïve to understand. But a number of people on the Domain seemed to belong to outfits that were as mysterious; and they looked upon Indar not as a man of our community or a refugee from the coast, but as one of themselves. It was all a little extraordinary to me.

These were the new-style foreigners whom we, in the town, had seen arriving for some time past. We had seen them putting on African clothes; we had noticed their gaiety, so unlike our own caution; their happiness with everything they found. And we had considered them parasites and half dangerous, serving some hidden cause of the President's, people we had to be careful with.

But now, being with them in the Domain, which in every way was their resort, and being admitted so easily to their life, their world of bungalows and air conditioners and holiday ease, catching in their educated talk the names of famous cities, I swung the other way and began to see how shut in and shabby and stagnant we in the town would have seemed to them. I began to get some sense of the social excitements of life on the Domain, of people associating in a new way, being more open, less concerned with enemies and danger, more ready to be interested and entertained, looking for the human worth of the other man. On the

Domain they had their own way of talking about people and events; they were in touch with the world. To be with them was to have a sense of adventure.

I thought of my own life and Metty's; of Shoba and Mahesh and their overheated privacy; of the Italians and Greeks—especially the Greeks—bottled up and tense with their family concerns and their nervousness of Africa and Africans. There was hardly anything new there. So to travel those few miles between the town and the Domain was always to make some adjustment, to assume a new attitude, and each time almost to see another country. I was ashamed of myself for the new judgments I found myself making on my friends Shoba and Mahesh, who had done so much for me for so many years, and with whom I had felt so safe. But I couldn't help those thoughts. I was tilting the other way, to the life of the Domain, as I saw it in the company of Indar.

I was aware, in the Domain, that I belonged to the other world. When I met people with Indar I found I had little to say. There were times when I thought that I might be letting him down. But there seemed to be no such thought in his head. He introduced me round as a friend of his family's from the coast, a member of his community. He didn't only want me to witness his success with the people of the Domain; he seemed to want me to share it as well. It was his way of rewarding me for my admiration, and I saw a delicacy in him that I had never seen on the coast. His manners were like a form of consideration; and however small the occasion, his manners never failed. They were the manners of an impresario, a little bit. But it was also his old family style; it was as though he had needed security and admiration to bring it out again. In the artificiality of the Domain he had found his perfect setting.

We in the town could offer Indar nothing like the regard and the social excitements he enjoyed at the Domain; we could scarcely appreciate what he enjoyed there. With our cynicism, created by years of insecurity, how did we look on men? We judged the salesmen in the van der Weyden by the companies they represented, their ability to offer us concessions. Knowing such men, having access to the services they offered, and being flattered by them that we were not ordinary customers paying the full price or having to take our place in the queue, we thought we had mastered the world; and we saw those salesmen and representatives as men of power who had to be courted. We judged traders by their coups, the contracts they landed, the agencies they picked up.

It was the same with Africans. We judged them by their ability, as army men or officials in the customs or policemen, to do us services; and that was how they also judged themselves. You could spot the powerful in Mahesh's Bigburger place. They, sharing in our boom, and no longer as shoddy as they once were, wore gold as much as possible—gold-rimmed glasses, gold rings, gold pen-and-pencil sets, gold watches with solid gold wristlets. Among ourselves we scoffed at the vulgarity and pathos of that African lust for gold. Gold—how could it alter the man, who was only an African? But we wanted gold ourselves; and we regularly paid tribute to the Africans who wore gold.

Our ideas of men were simple; Africa was a place where we had to survive. But in the Domain it was different. There they could scoff at trade and gold, because in the magical atmosphere of the Domain, among the avenues and new houses, another Africa had been created. In the Domain, Africans—the young men at the polytechnic—were romantic. They were not always present at the parties or gatherings; but the whole life of the Domain was built around them. In the town "African" could be a word of abuse or disregard; in the Domain it was a bigger word. An "African" there was a new man whom everybody was busy making, a man about to inherit—the important man that years before, at the lycée, Ferdinand had seen himself as.

In the town, when they were at the lycée, Ferdinand and his friends—certainly his friends—were still close to village ways. When they were off duty, not at the lycée or with people like myself, they had merged into the African life of the town. Ferdinand and Metty—or Ferdinand and any African boy—could become friends because they had so much in common. But in the Domain there was no question of confusing Ferdinand and his friends with the white-uniformed servants.

Ferdinand and his friends had a clear idea of who they were

and what was expected of them. They were young men on government scholarships; they would soon become administrative cadets in the capital, serving the President. The Domain was the President's creation; and in the Domain they were in the presence of foreigners who had a high idea of the new Africa. Even I, in the Domain, began to feel a little of the romance of that idea.

So foreigners and Africans acted and reacted on one another, and everyone became locked in an idea of glory and newness. Everywhere the President's photograph looked down at us. In the town, in our shops and in government buildings, it was just the photograph of the President, the ruler, something that had to be there. In the Domain the glory of the President brushed off onto all his new Africans.

And they were bright, those young men. I had remembered them as little tricksters, pertinacious but foolish, with only a kind of village cunning; and I had assumed that for them studying meant only cramming. Like other people in the town, I believed that degree courses had been scaled down or altered for Africans. It was possible; they did go in for certain subjects—international relations, political science, anthropology. But those young men had sharp minds and spoke wonderfully—and in French, not the patois. They had developed fast. Just a few years before, Ferdinand had been incapable of grasping the idea of Africa. That wasn't so now. The magazines about African affairs —even the semi-bogus, subsidized ones from Europe—and the newspapers, though censored, had spread new ideas, knowledge, new attitudes.

Indar took me one evening to one of his seminars, in a lecture room in the big polytechnic building. The seminar was not part of any course. It was an extra, and was described on the door as an exercise in English-speaking. But more must have been expected from Indar. Most of the desks were taken. Ferdinand was there, in a little group of his own.

The biscuit-coloured walls of the lecture room were bare except for a photograph of the President—not in army uniform, but in a chief's leopard-skin cap, a short-sleeved jacket and a polka-dotted cravat. Indar, sitting below this photograph, began to speak, easily, about the other parts of Africa he had visited, and the young men were fascinated. Their innocence and eagerness were astonishing. In spite of the wars and coups they were hearing about, Africa was still to them the new continent, and they behaved as though Indar felt like them, was almost one of them. The language exercise turned into a discussion about Africa, and I could feel polytechnic topics, lecture topics, coming to the surface. Some of the questions were dynamite; but Indar was very good, always calm, never surprised. He was like a philosopher; he tried to get the young men to examine the words they were using.

They talked for a while about the coup in Uganda, and about the tribal and religious differences there. Then they began to talk more generally about religion in Africa.

There was some movement in the group around Ferdinand. And Ferdinand—not unaware of me—stood up and asked, "Would the honourable visitor state whether he feels that Africans have been depersonalized by Christianity?"

Indar did what he had done before. He restated the question. He said, "I suppose you are really asking whether Africa can be served by a religion which is not African. Is Islam an African religion? Do you feel that Africans have been depersonalized by that?"

Ferdinand didn't reply. It was as in the old days—he hadn't thought beyond a certain point.

Indar said, "Well, I suppose you can say that Islam has become an African religion. It has been on the continent for a very long time. And you can say the same for the Coptic Christians. I don't know—perhaps you might feel that those people have been so depersonalized by those religions that they are out of touch with Africa. Would you say that? Or would you say they are Africans of a special sort?"

Ferdinand said, "The honourable visitor knows very well the kind of Christianity I mean. He is trying to confuse the issue. He knows about the low status of African religion, and he knows very well that this is a direct question to him about the relevance or otherwise of African religion. The visitor is a gentleman sympathetic to Africa who has travelled. He can advise us. That is why we ask."

A number of desk lids were banged in approval.

Indar said, "To answer that question you must allow me to ask you one. You are students. You are not villagers. You cannot pretend you are. You will soon be serving your President and his government in different capacities. You are men of the modern world. Do you need African religion? Or are you being sentimental about it? Are you nervous of losing it? Or do you feel you have to hold on to it just because it's yours?"

Ferdinand's eyes went hard. He banged the lid of his desk and stood up. "You are asking a complicated question."

And "complicated," among these students, was clearly a word of disapproval.

Indar said, "You are forgetting. I didn't raise the question. You raised it, and I merely asked for information."

That restored order, put an end to the banging of the desk lids. It made Ferdinand friendly again, and he remained friendly for the rest of the seminar. He went to Indar at the end, when the boys in the *jackets de boy* pushed in chromium-plated trolleys and began serving coffee and sweet biscuits (part of the style the President had decreed for the Domain).

I said to Ferdinand, "You've been heckling my friend."

He said, "I wouldn't have done it if I had known he was your friend."

Indar said, "What are your own feelings about African religion?"

Ferdinand said, "I don't know. That's why I asked. It is not an easy question for me."

Later, when Indar and I left the polytechnic building to walk back to his house, Indar said, "He's pretty impressive. He's your *marchande*'s son? That explains it. He's got that little extra background."

In the asphalted space outside the polytechnic building the flag was floodlit. Slender lamp standards lifted fluorescent arms down both sides of the main avenue; and the avenue was also lit with

lights at grass level, like an airport runway. Some of the bulbs
had been broken and grass had grown tall around the fittings.
I said, "His mother's also a magician."
Indar said, "You can't be too careful. They were tough tonight, but they didn't ask the really difficult question. Do you
know what that is? Whether Africans are peasants. It's a nonsense question, but big battles are fought about that one. Whatever you say you get into trouble. You see why my outfit is
needed. Unless we can get them thinking, and give them real
ideas instead of just politics and principles, these young men will
keep our world in turmoil for the next half century."

I thought how far we had both come, to talk about Africa like
this. We had even learned to take African magic seriously. It
hadn't been like that on the coast. But as we talked that evening
about the seminar, I began to wonder whether Indar and I
weren't fooling ourselves and whether we weren't allowing the
Africa we talked about to become too different from the Africa
we knew. Ferdinand didn't want to lose touch with the spirits; he
was nervous of being on his own. That had been at the back of
his question. We all understood his anxiety; but it was as though,
at the seminar, everyone had been ashamed, or fearful, of referring to it directly. The discussion had been full of words of another kind, about religion and history. It was like that on the
Domain; Africa there was a special place.

I wondered, too, about Indar. How had he arrived at his new
attitudes? I had thought of him, since the coast, as a hater of
Africa. He had lost a lot; I didn't think he had forgiven. Yet he
flourished on the Domain; it was his setting.

I was less "complicated"; I belonged to the town. And to leave
the Domain and drive back to the town, to see the shacks, acres
and acres of them, the rubbish mounds, to feel the presence of
the river and the forest all around (more than landscaping now),
to see the ragged groups outside the drinking booths, the squatters' cooking fires on the pavements in the centre of the town—
to do that drive back was to return to the Africa I knew. It was
to climb down from the exaltation of the Domain, to grasp reality again. Did Indar believe in the Africa of words? Did anyone

on the Domain believe? Wasn't the truth what we in the town lived with—the salesmen's chat in the van der Weyden and the bars, the photographs of the President in government offices and in our shops, the army barracks in the converted palace of the man of our community?

Indar said, "Does one believe in anything? Does it matter?"

There was a ritual I went through whenever I had to clear a difficult consignment through the customs. I filled in the declaration form, folded it over five hundred francs, and handed it to the official in charge. He would—as soon as he had got his subordinates out of the room (and they of course knew why they had been asked to leave the room)—check the notes with his eyes alone. The notes would then be taken; the entries on the form would be studied with exaggerated care; and soon he would say, "*C'est bien, Mis' Salim. Vous êtes en ordre.*" Neither he nor I would refer to the bank notes. We would talk only about the details on the declaration form, which, correctly filled, correctly approved, would remain as proof of both our correctness. Yet what had lain at the heart of the transaction would be passed over in silence, and would leave no trace in the records.

So, in my talks with Indar about Africa—the purpose of his outfit, the Domain, his anxieties about imported doctrines, the danger to Africa of its very newness, first ideas being caught most securely by new minds as sticky as adhesive tape—I felt that between us lay some dishonesty, or just an omission, some blank, around which we both had to walk carefully. That omission was our own past, the smashed life of our community. Indar had referred to that at our first meeting that morning in the shop. He said that he had learned to trample on the past. In the beginning it had been like trampling on a garden; later it had become like walking on ground.

I became confused myself. The Domain was a hoax. But at the same time it was real, because it was full of serious men (and a few women). Was there a truth outside men? Didn't men make the truth for themselves? Everything men did or made became real. So I moved between the Domain and the town. It was always reassuring to return to the town I knew, to get away from that Africa of words and ideas as it existed on the Domain (and from which, often, Africans were physically absent). But the Domain, and the glory and the social excitements of the life there, always called me back.

# 8

≈≈≈ Indar said, "We are going to a party after dinner. It's being ≈≈≈ given by Yvette. Do you know her? Her husband, Raymond, keeps a low profile, but he runs the whole show here. The President, or the Big Man, as you call him, sent him down here to keep an eye on things. He's the Big Man's white man. In all these places there's someone like that. Raymond's a historian. They say the President reads everything he writes. That's the story anyway. Raymond knows more about the country than anyone on earth."

I had never heard of Raymond. The President I had seen only in photographs—first in army uniform, then in the stylish short-sleeved jacket and cravat, and then with his leopard-skin chief's cap and his carved stick, emblem of his chieftaincy—and it had never occurred to me that he might be a reader. What Indar told me brought the President closer. At the same time it showed me how far away I, and people like me, were from the seat of power. Considering myself from that distance, I saw how small and vulnerable we were; and it didn't seem quite real that, dressed as I was, I should be strolling across the Domain after dinner to meet people in direct touch with the great. It was strange, but I no longer felt oppressed by the country, the forest and the waters and the remote peoples: I felt myself above it all, considering it from this new angle of the powerful.

From what Indar had said I had expected that Raymond and Yvette would be middle-aged. But the lady—in black slacks in some shiny material—who came to meet us after the white-jacketed boy had let us in was young, in her late twenties, near my own age. That was the first surprise. The second was that she was barefooted, feet white and beautiful and finely made. I looked at her feet before I considered her face and her blouse, black silk, embroidered round the low-cut collar—expensive stuff, not the sort of goods you could get in our town.

Indar said, "This lovely lady is our hostess. Her name is Yvette."

He bent over her and appeared to hold her in an embrace. It was a piece of pantomime. She playfully arched her back to receive his embrace, but his cheek barely brushed hers, he never touched her breast, and only the tips of his fingers rested on her back, on the silk blouse.

It was a house of the Domain, like Indar's. But all the upholstered furniture had been cleared out of the sitting room and had been replaced by cushions and bolsters and African mats. Two or three reading lamps had been put on the floor, so that parts of the room were in darkness.

Yvette said, referring to the furniture, "The President has an exaggerated idea of the needs of Europeans. I've dumped all that velvety stuff in one of the bedrooms."

Remembering what Indar had told me, I ignored the irony in her voice, and felt that she was speaking with privilege, the privilege of someone close to the President.

A number of people were already there. Indar followed Yvette deeper into the room, and I followed Indar.

Indar said, "How's Raymond?"

Yvette said, "He's working. He'll look in later."

We sat down all three next to a bookcase. Indar lounged against a bolster, a man at ease. I concentrated on the music. As so often when I was with Indar on the Domain, I was prepared only to watch and listen. And this was all new to me. I hadn't been to a Domain party like this. And the atmosphere itself in that room was something I had never experienced before.

Two or three couples were dancing; I had visions of women's legs. I had a vision especially of a girl in a green dress who sat on a straight-backed dining chair (one of the house set of twelve). I studied her knees, her legs, her ankles, her shoes. They were not particularly well made legs, but they had an effect on me. All my adult life I had looked for release in the bars of the town. I knew only women who had to be paid for. The other side of the life of passion, of embraces freely given and received, I knew nothing of, and had begun to consider alien, something not for me. And so my satisfactions had only been brothel satisfactions, which hadn't been satisfactions at all. I felt they had taken me further and further away from the true life of the senses and I feared they had made me incapable of that life.

I had never been in a room where men and women danced for mutual pleasure, and out of pleasure in one another's company. Trembling expectation was in that girl's heavy legs, the girl in the green dress. It was a new dress, loosely hemmed, not ironed into a crease, still suggesting the material as it had been measured out and bought. Later I saw her dancing, watched the movements of her legs, her shoes; and such a sweetness was released in me that I felt I had recovered a part of myself I had lost. I never looked at the girl's face, and it was easy in the semi-gloom to let that remain unknown. I wanted to sink into the sweetness; I didn't want anything to spoil the mood.

And the mood became sweeter. The music that was being played came to an end, and in the wonderfully lit room, blurred circles of light thrown onto the ceiling from the lamps on the floor, people stopped dancing. What next came on went straight to my heart—sad guitars, words, a song, an American girl singing "Barbara Allen."

That voice! It needed no music; it hardly needed words. By itself it created the line of the melody; by itself it created a whole world of feeling. It is what people of our background look for in music and singing: feeling. It is what makes us shout "Wa-wa! Bravo!" and throw bank notes and gold at the feet of a singer. Listening to that voice, I felt the deepest part of myself awakening, the part that knew loss, homesickness, grief, and longed for love. And in that voice was the promise of a flowering for everyone who listened.

I said to Indar, "Who is the singer?"

He said, "Joan Baez. She's very famous in the States."

"And a millionaire," Yvette said.

I was beginning to recognize her irony. It made her appear to be saying something when she had said very little—and she was, after all, playing the record in her house. She was smiling at me, perhaps smiling at what she had said, or perhaps smiling at me as Indar's friend, or smiling because she believed it became her.

Her left leg was drawn up; her right leg, bent at the knee, lay flat on the cushion on which she sat, so that her right heel lay almost against her left ankle. Beautiful feet, and their whiteness was wonderful against the black of her slacks. Her provocative posture, her smile—they became part of the mood of the song, too much to contemplate.

Indar said, "Salim comes from one of our old coast families. Their history is interesting."

Yvette's hand lay white on her right thigh.

Indar said, "Let me show you something."

He leaned across my legs and reached up to the bookcase. He took out a book, opened it and showed me where I was to read. I held the book down to the floor, to catch the light from the reading lamp, and saw, among a list of names, the names of Yvette and Raymond, acknowledged by the writer of the book as "most generous of hosts" at some recent time in the capital.

Yvette continued to smile. No embarrassment or playing it down, though; no irony now. Her name in the book mattered to her.

I gave the book back to Indar, looked away from Yvette and him, and returned to the voice. Not all the songs were like "Barbara Allen." Some were modern, about war and injustice and oppression and nuclear destruction. But always in between there were the older, sweeter melodies. These were the ones I waited for, but in the end the voice linked the two kinds of song, linked the maidens and lovers and sad deaths of bygone times with the people of today who were oppressed and about to die.

It was make-believe—I never doubted that. You couldn't listen to sweet songs about injustice unless you expected justice and received it much of the time. You couldn't sing songs about the end of the world unless—like the other people in that room, so beautiful with such simple things: African mats on the floor and

African hangings on the wall and spears and masks—you felt
that the world was going on and you were safe in it. How easy it
was, in that room, to make those assumptions!

It was different outside, and Mahesh would have scoffed. He
had said, "It isn't that there's no right and wrong here. There's
no right." But Mahesh felt far away. The aridity of that life,
which had also been mine! It was better to pretend, as I could
pretend now. It was better to share the companionship of that
pretence, to feel that in that room we all lived beautifully and
bravely with injustice and imminent death and consoled ourselves with love. Even before the songs ended I felt I had found
the kind of life I wanted; I never wanted to be ordinary again. I
felt that by some piece of luck I had stumbled on the equivalent
of what years before Nazruddin had found right here.

It was late when Raymond came in. I had, at Indar's insistence, even danced with Yvette and felt her skin below the silk of
her blouse; and when I saw Raymond my thoughts—leaping at
this stage of the evening from possibility to possibility—were at
first only about the difference in their ages. There must have
been thirty years between Yvette and her husband; Raymond
was a man in his late fifties.

But I felt possibilities fade, felt them as dreams, when I saw
the immediate look of concern on Yvette's face—or rather in her
eyes, for her smile was still on, a trick of her face; when I saw the
security of Raymond's manner, remembered his job and position, and took in the distinction of his appearance. It was the
distinction of intelligence and intellectual labours. He looked as
though he had just taken off his glasses, and his gentle eyes were
attractively tired. He was wearing a long-sleeved safari jacket;
and it came to me that the style—long sleeves rather than short
—had been suggested to him by Yvette.

After that look of concern at her husband, Yvette relaxed
again, with her fixed smile. Indar got up and began fetching a
dining chair from against the opposite wall. Raymond motioned
to us to stay where we were; he rejected the chance of sitting next
to Yvette, and when Indar returned with the dining chair, sat on
that.

Yvette said, without moving, "Would you like a drink, Raymond?"

He said, "It will spoil it for me, Evie. I'll be going back to my room in a minute."

Raymond's presence in the room had been noted. A young man and a girl had begun to hover around our group. One or two other people came up. There were greetings.

Indar said, "I hope we haven't disturbed you."

Raymond said, "It made a pleasant background. If I look a little troubled, it is because just now, in that room, I became very dejected. I began to wonder, as I've often wondered, whether the truth ever gets known. The idea isn't new, but there are times when it becomes especially painful. I feel that everything one does is just going to waste."

Indar said, "You are talking nonsense, Raymond. Of course it takes time for someone like yourself to be recognized, but it happens in the end. You are not working in a popular field."

Yvette said, "You tell him that for me, please."

One of the men standing around said, "New discoveries are constantly making us revise our ideas about the past. The truth is always there. It can be got at. The work has to be done, that's all."

Raymond said, "Time, the discoverer of truth. I know. It's the classical idea, the religious idea. But there are times when you begin to wonder. Do we really know the history of the Roman Empire? Do we really know what went on during the conquest of Gaul? I was sitting in my room and thinking with sadness about all the things that have gone unrecorded. Do you think we will ever get to know the truth about what has happened in Africa in the last hundred or even fifty years? All the wars, all the rebellions, all the leaders, all the defeats?"

There was a silence. We looked at Raymond, who had introduced this element of discussion into our evening. Yet the mood was only like an extension of the mood of the Joan Baez songs. And for a little while, but without the help of music, we contemplated the sadness of the continent.

Indar said, "Have you read Muller's article?"

Raymond said, "About the Bapende rebellion? He sent me a proof. It's had a great success, I hear."

The young man with the girl said, "I hear they're inviting him to Texas to teach for a term."

Indar said, "I thought it was a lot of rubbish. Every kind of cliché parading as new wisdom. The Azande, that's a tribal uprising. The Bapende, that's just economic oppression, rubber business. They're to be lumped with the Budja and the Babwa. And you do that by playing down the religious side. Which is what makes the Bapende dust-up so wonderful. It's just the kind of thing that happens when people turn to Africa to make the fast academic buck."

Raymond said, "He came to see me. I answered all his questions and showed him all my papers."

The young man said, "Muller's a bit of whiz kid, I think."

Raymond said, "I liked him."

Yvette said, "He came to lunch. As soon as Raymond left the table, he forgot all about the Bapende and said to me, 'Do you want to come out with me?' Just like that. The minute Raymond's back was turned."

Raymond smiled.

Indar said, "I was telling Salim, Raymond, that you are the only man the President reads."

Raymond said, "I don't think he has much time for reading these days."

The young man, his girl now close to him, said, "How did you meet him?"

"It is a story at once simple and extraordinary," Raymond said. "But I don't think we have time for that now." He looked at Yvette.

She said, "I don't think anybody is rushing off anywhere right at this minute."

"It was long ago," Raymond said. "In colonial times. I was teaching at a college in the capital. I was doing my historical work. But of course in those days there was no question of publishing. There was the censorship that people pretended didn't exist, in spite of the celebrated decree of 1922. And of course in those days Africa wasn't a subject. But I never made any secret of what I felt or where I stood, and I suppose the word must have got around. One day at the college I was told that an old African woman had come to see me. It was one of the African servants who brought me the message, and he wasn't too impressed by my visitor.

"I asked him to bring her to me. She was middle-aged rather than old. She worked as a maid in the big hotel in the capital, and she had come to see me about her son. She belonged to one of the smaller tribes, people with no say in anything, and I suppose she had no one of her own kind to turn to. The boy had left school. He had joined some political club and had done various odd jobs. But he had given up all that. He was doing nothing at all. He was just staying in the house. He didn't go out to see anybody. He suffered from headaches, but he wasn't ill. I thought she was going to ask me to get the boy a job. But no. All she wanted me to do was to see the boy and talk to him.

"She impressed me a great deal. Yes, the dignity of that hotel maid was quite remarkable. Another woman would have thought that her son was bewitched, and taken appropriate measures. She, in her simple way, saw that her son's disease had been brought on by his education. That was why she had come to me, the teacher at the college.

"I asked her to send the boy to me. He didn't like the idea of his mother talking to me about him, but he came. He was as nervous as a kitten. What made him unusual—I would even say extraordinary—was the quality of his despair. It wasn't just a matter of poverty and the lack of opportunity. It went much deeper. And, indeed, to try to look at the world from his point of view was to begin to get a headache yourself. He couldn't face the world in which his mother, a poor woman of Africa, had endured such humiliation. Nothing could undo that. Nothing could give him a better world.

"I said to him, 'I've listened to you, and I know that one day the mood of despair will go and you will want to act. What you mustn't do then is to become involved in politics as they exist. Those clubs and associations are talking shops, debating societies, where Africans posture for Europeans and hope to pass as evolved. They will eat up your passion and destroy your gifts. What I am going to tell you now will sound strange, coming from me. You must join the Defence Force. You won't rise high, but you will learn a real skill. You will learn about weapons and transport, and you will also learn about men. Once you understand what holds the Defence Force together, you will understand what holds the country together. You might say to me, "But isn't it better for me to be a lawyer and be called *maître?*" I will say, "No. It is better for you to be a private and call the sergeant sir." This isn't advice I will want to give to anybody else. But I give it to you.' "

Raymond had held us all. When he stopped speaking we allowed the silence to last, while we continued to look at him as he sat on the dining chair in his safari jacket, distinguished, his hair combed back, his eyes tired, a bit of a dandy in his way.

In a more conversational voice, as though he was commenting on his own story, Raymond said at last, breaking the silence, "He's a truly remarkable man. I don't think we give him enough credit for what he's done. We take it for granted. He's disciplined the army and brought peace to this land of many peoples. It is possible once again to traverse the country from one end to the other—something the colonial power thought it alone had brought about. And what is most remarkable is that it's been done without coercion, and entirely with the consent of the people. You don't see policemen in the streets. You don't see guns. You don't see the army."

Indar, sitting next to Yvette, who was still smiling, seemed about to change the position of his legs prior to saying something. But Raymond raised his hand, and Indar didn't move.

"And there's the freedom," Raymond said. "There's the remarkable welcome given to every kind of idea from every kind of system. I don't think," he said, addressing Indar directly, as though making up to him for keeping him quiet, "that anyone has even hinted to you that there are certain things you have to say and certain things you mustn't say."

Indar said, "We've had an easy ride here."

"I don't think it would have occurred to him to try to censor you. He feels that all ideas can be made to serve the cause. You might say that with him there's an absolute hunger for ideas. He uses them all in his own way."

Yvette said, "I wish he would change the boys' uniforms. The good old colonial style of short trousers and a long white apron. Or long trousers and a jacket. But not that carnival costume of short trousers and jacket."

We all laughed, even Raymond, as though we were glad to stop being solemn. And Yvette's boldness was also like proof of the freedom Raymond had been talking about.

Raymond said, "Yvette goes on about the boys' uniforms. But that's the army background, and the mother's hotel background. The mother wore a colonial maid's uniform all her working life. The boys in the Domain have to wear theirs. And it isn't a colonial uniform—that's the point. In fact, everybody nowadays who wears a uniform has to understand that. Everyone in uniform has to feel that he has a personal contract with the President. And try to get the boys out of that uniform. You won't succeed. Yvette has tried. They want to wear that uniform, however absurd it is to our eyes. That's the amazing thing about this man of Africa—this flair, this knowledge of what the people need, and when.

"We have all these photographs of him in African costume nowadays. I must confess I was disturbed when they began to appear in such number. I raised the issue with him one day in the capital. I was shattered by the penetration of his answer. He said, 'Five years ago, Raymond, I would have agreed with you. Five years ago our African people, with that cruel humour which is theirs, would have laughed, and that ridicule would have destroyed our country, with its still frail bonds. But times have changed. The people now have peace. They want something else. So they no longer see a photograph of a soldier. They see a photograph of an African. And that isn't a picture of me, Raymond. It is a picture of all Africans.'"

This was so like what I felt, that I said, "Yes! None of us in the town liked putting up the old photograph. But it is different seeing the new photographs, especially in the Domain."

Raymond permitted this interruption. His right hand was being raised, though, to allow him to go on. And he went on.

"I thought I would check this. Just last week, as a matter of fact. I ran into one of our students outside the main building. And just to be provocative, I dropped some remark about the number of the President's photographs. The young man pulled me up quite sharply. So I asked him what he felt when he saw the President's photograph. You will be surprised by what he said to me, that young man, holding himself as erect as any military cadet. 'It is a photograph of the President. But here on the Domain, as a student at the polytechnic, I also consider it a photograph of myself.' The very words! But that's a quality of great leaders—they intuit the needs of their people long before those needs are formulated. It takes an African to rule Africa— the colonial powers never truly understood that. However much the rest of us study Africa, however deep our sympathy, we will remain outsiders."

The young man, sitting now on a mat with his girl, asked, "Do you know the symbolism of the serpent on the President's stick? Is it true that there's a fetish in the belly of the human figure on the stick?"

Raymond said, "I don't know about that. It is a stick. It is a chief's stick. It is like a mace or a mitre. I don't think we have to fall into the error of looking for African mysteries everywhere."

The critical note jarred a little. But Raymond seemed not to notice.

"I have recently had occasion to look through all the President's speeches. Now, what an interesting publication that would make! Not the speeches in their entirety, which inevitably deal with many passing issues. But selections. The essential thoughts."

Indar said, "Are you working on that? Has he asked you?"

Raymond lifted a palm and hunched a shoulder, to say that it was possible, but that he couldn't talk about a matter that was still confidential.

"What is interesting about those speeches when read in sequence is their development. There you can see very clearly what I have described as the hunger for ideas. In the beginning the ideas are simple. Unity, the colonial past, the need for peace. Then they become extraordinarily complex and wonderful about Africa, government, the modern world. Such a work, if adequately prepared, might well become the handbook for a true revolution throughout the continent. Always you can catch that quality of the young man's despair which made such an impression on me so long ago. Always you have that feeling that the damage can never perhaps be undone. Always there is that note, for those with the ears to hear it, of the young man grieving for the humiliations of his mother, the hotel maid. He's always remained true to that. I don't think many people know that earlier this year he and his entire government made a pilgrimage to the village of that woman of Africa. Has that been done before? Has any ruler attempted to give sanctity to the bush of Africa? This act of piety is something that brings tears to the eyes. Can you imagine the humiliations of an African hotel maid in colonial times? No amount of piety can make up for that. But piety is all we have to offer."

"Or we can forget," Indar said. "We can trample on the past."

Raymond said, "That is what most of the leaders of Africa do. They want to build skyscrapers in the bush. This man wants to build a shrine."

Music without words had been coming out of the speakers. Now "Barbara Allen" began again, and the words were distracting. Raymond stood up. The man who had been sitting on the mat went to lower the volume. Raymond indicated that he wasn't to bother, but the song went faint.

Raymond said, "I would like to be with you. But unfortunately I have to get back to my work. Otherwise I might lose something. I find that the most difficult thing in prose narrative is linking one thing with the other. The link might just be a sentence, or even a word. It sums up what has gone before and prepares one for what is to come. As I was sitting with you I had an idea of a possible solution to a problem that was beginning to appear quite intractable. I must go and make a note. Otherwise I might forget."

He began to move away from us. But then he stopped and

said, "I don't think it is sufficiently understood how hard it is to write about what has never been written about before. The occasional academic paper on a particular subject, the Bapende rebellion or whatever—that has its own form. The larger narrative is another matter. And that's why I have begun to consider Theodor Mommsen the giant of modern historical writing. Everything that we now discuss about the Roman Republic is only a continuation of Mommsen. The problems, the issues, the very narrative, especially of those extraordinarily troubled years of the later Republic—you might say the German genius discovered it all. Of course, Theodor Mommsen had the comfort of knowing that his subject was a great one. Those of us who work in our particular field have no such assurance. We have no idea of the value posterity will place on the events we attempt to chronicle. We have no idea where the continent is going. We can only carry on."

He ended abruptly, turned, and went out of the room, leaving us in silence, looking after where he had disappeared, and only slowly directing our attention to Yvette, now his representative in that room, smiling, acknowledging our regard.

After a little Indar said to me, "Do you know Raymond's work?"

Of course he knew the answer to that one. But, to give him his opening, I said, "No, I don't know his work."

Indar said, "That's the tragedy of the place. The great men of Africa are not known."

It was like a formal speech of thanks. And Indar had chosen his words well. He had made us all men and women of Africa; and since we were not Africans the claim gave us a special feeling for ourselves which, so far as I was concerned, was soon heightened by the voice of Joan Baez, turned up again, reminding us sweetly, after the tensions Raymond had thrown among us, of our common bravery and sorrows.

Indar was embraced by Yvette when we left. And I was embraced, as the friend. It was delicious to me, as the climax to that evening, to press that body close, soft at this late hour, and to feel the silk of the blouse and the flesh below the silk.

There was a moon now—there had been none earlier. It was small and high. The sky was full of heavy clouds, and the moonlight came and went. It was very quiet. We could hear the rapids; they were about a mile away. The rapids in moonlight! I said to Indar, "Let's go to the river." And he was willing.

In the wide levelled land of the Domain the new buildings seemed small, and the earth felt immense. The Domain seemed the merest clearing in the forest, the merest clearing in an immensity of bush and river—the world might have been nothing else. Moonlight distorted distances; and the darkness, when it came, seemed to drop down to our heads.

I said to Indar, "What do you think of what Raymond said?"

"Raymond tells a story well. But a lot of what he says is true. What he says about the President and ideas is certainly true. The President uses them all and somehow makes them work together. He is the great African chief, and he is also the man of the people. He is the modernizer and he is also the African who has rediscovered his African soul. He's conservative, revolutionary, everything. He's going back to the old ways, and he's also the man who's going ahead, the man who's going to make the country a world power by the year 2000. I don't know whether he's done it accidentally or because someone's been telling him what to do. But the mish-mash works because he keeps on changing, unlike the other guys. He is the soldier who decided to become an old-fashioned chief, and he's the chief whose mother was a hotel maid. That makes him everything, and he plays up everything. There isn't anyone in the country who hasn't heard of that hotel maid mother."

I said, "They caught me with that pilgrimage to the mother's village. When I read in the paper that it was an unpublicized pilgrimage, I thought of it as just that."

"He makes these shrines in the bush, honouring the mother. And at the same time he builds modern Africa. Raymond says he doesn't build skyscrapers. Well, he doesn't do that. He builds these very expensive Domains."

"Nazruddin used to own some land here in the old days."

"And he sold it for nothing. Are you going to tell me that? That's an African story."

"No, Nazruddin sold well. He sold at the height of the boom before independence. He came out one Sunday morning and said, 'But this is only bush.' And he sold."

"It could go that way again."

The sound of the rapids had grown louder. We had left the new buildings of the Domain behind and were approaching the fishermen's huts, dead in the moonlight. The thin village dogs, pale in the moonlight, their shadows black below them, walked lazily away from us. The fishermen's poles and nets were dark against the broken glitter of the river. And then we were on the old viewing point, repaired now, newly walled; and around us, drowning everything else, was the sound of water over rocks. Clumps of water hyacinths bucked past. The hyacinths were white in the moonlight, the vines dark tangles outlined in black shadow. When the moonlight went, there was nothing to be seen; the world was then only that old sound of tumbling water.

I said, "I've never told you why I came here. It wasn't just to get away from the coast or to run that shop. Nazruddin used to tell us wonderful stories of the times he used to have here. That was why I came. I thought I would be able to live my own life, and I thought that in time I would find what Nazruddin found. Then I got stuck. I don't know what I would have done if you hadn't come. If you hadn't come I would never have known about what was going on here, just under my nose."

"It's different from what we used to know. To people like us it's very seductive. Europe in Africa, post-colonial Africa. But it isn't Europe or Africa. And it looks different from the inside, I can tell you."

"You mean people don't believe in it? They don't believe in what they say and do?"

"No one is as crude as that. We believe and don't believe. We believe because that way everything becomes simpler and makes more sense. We don't believe—well, because of this." And Indar waved at the fishermen's village, the bush, the moonlit river.

He said after a time, "Raymond's in a bit of a mess. He has to keep on pretending that he is the guide and adviser, to keep himself from knowing that the time is almost here when he will

just be receiving orders. In fact, so as not to get orders, he is
beginning to anticipate orders. He will go crazy if he has to
acknowledge that that's his situation. Oh, he's got a big job now.
But he's on the slippery slope. He's been sent away from the
capital. The Big Man is going his own way, and he no longer
needs Raymond. Everybody knows that, but Raymond thinks
they don't. It's a dreadful thing for a man of his age to have to
live with."

But what Indar was saying didn't make me think of Raymond.
I thought of Yvette, all at once brought nearer by this tale of her
husband's distress. I went over the pictures I had of her that
evening, ran the film over again, so to speak, reconstructing and
reinterpreting what I had seen, re-creating that woman, fixing her
in the posture that had bewitched me, her white feet together,
one leg drawn up, one leg flat and bent, remaking her face, her
smile, touching the whole picture with the mood of the Joan
Baez songs and all that they had released in me, and adding to it
this extra mood of moonlight, the rapids, and the white hyacinths
of this great river of Africa.

# 9

It was on that evening, by the river, after he had spoken
about Raymond, that Indar began to tell me about himself. The evening that had excited me had enervated and depressed him; he had become irritable as soon as we had left
Yvette's house.

Earlier in the evening, as we had walked across to the house
for the party, he had spoken of Raymond as a star, someone
close to power, the Big Man's white man; but then, by the rapids,
he had spoken of Raymond in quite another way. As my guide
Indar had been anxious for me truly to understand the nature of
life on the Domain, and his own position there. Now that I had
seized the glamour of his world he was like a guide who had lost
faith in what he showed. Or like a man who, because he had got

someone else to believe, had felt he could let go of some of his own faith.

The moonlight that made me light-headed deepened his depression, and it was out of this depression that he began to speak. The mood of the evening didn't stay with him, though; the next day he had bounced back, and was like the man he had always been. But he was more ready to acknowledge his depression when it came; and what he outlined that evening he returned to and filled in at other times, when the occasion suited, or when he drifted back to that earlier mood.

"We have to learn to trample on the past, Salim. I told you that when we met. It shouldn't be a cause for tears, because it isn't just true for you and me. There may be some parts of the world—dead countries, or secure and by-passed ones—where men can cherish the past and think of passing on furniture and china to their heirs. Men can do that perhaps in Sweden or Canada. Some peasant department of France full of half-wits in châteaux; some crumbling Indian palace-city, or some dead colonial town in a hopeless South American country. Everywhere else men are in movement, the world is in movement, and the past can only cause pain.

"It isn't easy to turn your back on the past. It isn't something you can decide to do just like that. It is something you have to arm yourself for, or grief will ambush and destroy you. That is why I hold on to the image of the garden trampled until it becomes ground—it is a small thing, but it helps. That perception about the past came to me at the end of my third year in England. And oddly enough, it came to me beside another river. You've told me that I've led you here to the kind of life you've always felt you needed. It was something like that, too, that I began to feel beside that river in London. I made a decision about myself then. And it was as an indirect result of that decision that I came back to Africa. Though when I left it was my intention never to return.

"I was very unhappy when I left. You remember that. I tried to depress you—in fact, I tried to wound you—but that was only because I was myself so depressed. The thought of the work of two generations going to waste—it was very painful. The thought of losing that house built by my grandfather, the thought of the risks he and my father had taken to build up a business from nothing, the bravery, the sleepless nights—it was all very painful. In another country such effort and such talent would have made us millionaires, aristocrats, or at any rate secure for some generations. There it was all going up in smoke. My rage wasn't only with the Africans. It was also with our community and our civilization, which gave us energy but in every other way left us at the mercy of others. How do you rage against a thing like that?

"I thought when I went to England I would put all that behind me. I had no plans beyond that. The word 'university' dazzled me, and I was innocent enough to believe that after my time in the university some wonderful life would be waiting for me. At that age three years seems a long time—you feel that anything can happen. But I hadn't understood to what extent our civilization had also been our prison. I hadn't understood either to what extent we had been made by the place where we had grown up, made by Africa and the simple life of the coast, and how incapable we had become of understanding the outside world. We have no means of understanding a fraction of the thought and science and philosophy and law that have gone to make that outside world. We simply accept it. We have grown up paying tribute to it, and that is all that most of us can do. We feel of the great world that it is simply there, something for the lucky ones among us to explore, and then only at the edges. It never occurs to us that we might make some contribution to it ourselves. And that is why we miss everything.

"When we land at a place like London Airport we are concerned only not to appear foolish. It is more beautiful and more complex than anything we could have dreamed of, but we are concerned only to let people see that we can manage and are not overawed. We might even pretend that we had expected better. That is the nature of our stupidity and incompetence. And that was how I spent my time at the university in England, not being overawed, always being slightly disappointed, understanding nothing, accepting everything, getting nothing. I saw and understood so little that even at the end of my time at the university I could distinguish buildings only by their size, and I was hardly aware of the passing of the seasons. And yet I was an intelligent man, and could cram for examinations.

"In the old days, after three years like that, and with some scraped-through degree, I would have returned home and hung up my board and devoted myself to the making of money, using the little half-skill I had picked up, the half-knowledge of other men's books. But of course I couldn't do that. I had to stay where I was and I had to get a job. I hadn't acquired a profession, you understand; nothing at home had pushed me in that direction.

"For some time the boys of my year at the university had been talking of jobs and interviews. The more precocious ones had even been talking about the interview expenses various companies paid. In the porter's lodge the pigeonholes of these boys were full of long brown envelopes from the University Appointments Committee. The dimmest boys were naturally the ones with the most varied prospects; they could be anything; and in their pigeonholes the brown envelopes fell as thick as autumn leaves. That was my attitude to those adventurous boys—slightly mocking. I had to get a job, but I never thought of myself as someone who would have to go through the brown-envelope adventure. I don't know why; I just didn't; and then, almost at the end of my time, with bewilderment and shame I realised that I had. I made an appointment with the Appointments Committee and on the morning put on a dark suit and went.

"As soon as I got there I knew my errand was fruitless. The Committee was meant to put English boys in English jobs; it wasn't meant for me. I realised that as soon as I saw the look on the face of the girl in the outer office. But she was nice, and the dark-suited man inside was also nice. He was intrigued by my African background, and after a little talk about Africa he said, 'And what can this great organization do for you?' I wanted to say, 'Couldn't you send me some brown envelopes too?' But what I said was: 'I was hoping you would tell me.' He seemed to find this funny. He took down my details, for the form of the thing; and then he tried to get a conversation going, senior dark suit to junior dark suit, man to man.

"He had little to tell me, though. And I had less to tell him. I had hardly looked at the world. I didn't know how it worked or what I might do in it. After my three unamazed student years, I was overwhelmed by my ignorance; and in that quiet little office full of peaceful files I began to think of the world outside as a place of horror. My dark-suited interviewer became impatient. He said, 'Good heavens, man! You must give me some guidance. You must have some idea of the kind of job you see yourself doing.'

"He was right, of course. But that 'Good heavens, man!' seemed to me affected, something he might have picked up in the past from someone his senior and was now throwing at me as someone lesser. I became angry. The idea came to me that I should fix him with a look of the utmost hostility and say, 'The job I want is your job. And I want your job because you enjoy it so much.' But I didn't speak the words; I didn't speak any words at all; I just gave him the hostile look. So our interview ended inconclusively.

"I became calmer outside. I went to the café where I used to go for coffee in the mornings. As a consolation, I bought myself a piece of chocolate cake as well. But then, to my surprise, I found I wasn't consoling myself; I was celebrating. I found I was positively happy to be in the café in the middle of the morning, drinking coffee and eating cake, while my tormentor fussed about with his brown envelopes in his office. It was only escape, and it couldn't last long. But I remember that half hour as one of pure happiness.

"After this I didn't expect anything from the Appointments Committee. But the man was, after all, a fair man; a bureaucracy is a bureaucracy; and a couple of brown envelopes did arrive for me, unseasonably, not as part of the autumn rush, choking the pigeonholes in the porter's lodge, but like the last dead leaves of the year, torn away by the gales of January. An oil company, and two or three other large companies with connections in Asia or Africa. With each job description I read, I felt a tightening of what I must call my soul. I found myself growing false to myself, acting to myself, convincing myself of my rightness for whatever was being described. And this is where I suppose life ends for most people, who stiffen in the attitudes they adopt to make themselves suitable for the jobs and lives that other people have laid out for them.

"None of those jobs came my way. There again I found myself amusing my interviewers unintentionally. Once I said, 'I don't know anything about your business, but I can put my mind to it.' For some reason this brought the house down—in this case it was a three-man board. They laughed, the oldest man leading the laughter and in the end even wiping away tears; and they dismissed me. With each rejection came a feeling of relief; but with each rejection I became more anxious about the future.

"Once a month or so I had lunch with a woman lecturer. She was about thirty, not bad-looking, and very kind to me. She was unusual because she was so much at peace with herself. That was why I liked her. It was she who made me do the absurd thing I am now going to describe.

"This lady had the idea that people like myself were at sea because we were men of two worlds. She was right, of course. But at the time it didn't seem so to me—I thought I saw everything very clearly—and I thought she had got the idea from some young man from Bombay or thereabouts who was trying to make himself interesting. But this lady also thought that my education and background made me extraordinary, and I couldn't fight the idea of my extraordinariness.

"An extraordinary man, a man of two worlds, needed an extraordinary job. And she suggested I should become a diplomat. That was what I decided to do, and the country I decided to serve—since a diplomat has to have a country—was India. It was absurd; I knew it was absurd, even while I was doing it; but I wrote a letter to the Indian High Commission. I got a reply, and was given an appointment.

"I went up to London by train. I didn't know London very well, and didn't like what I knew; and I liked it less that morning. There was Praed Street with its pornographic bookshops that didn't deal in real pornography; there was the Edgware Road, where the shops and restaurants seemed continually to be changing hands; there were the shops and crowds of Oxford Street and Regent Street. The openness of Trafalgar Square gave me a lift, but it reminded me that I was almost at the end of my journey. And I had begun to be very embarrassed by my mission.

"The bus took me down the Strand and dropped me at the curve of the Aldwych, and I crossed the road to the building that had been pointed out to me as India House. How could I have missed it, with all the Indian motifs on the outside wall? At this stage my embarrassment was acute. I was in my dark suit and my university tie, and I was entering a London building, an English building, which pretended to be of India—an India quite different from the country my grandfather had spoken about.

"For the first time in my life I was filled with a colonial rage. And this wasn't only a rage with London or England; it was also a rage with the people who had allowed themselves to be corralled into a foreign fantasy. My rage didn't die down when I went inside. There again were the Oriental motifs. The uniformed messengers were English and middle-aged; they clearly had been taken on by the old management, if you can call it that, and were working out their time under the new. I had never felt so involved with the land of my ancestors, and yours, and so far from it. I felt in that building I had lost an important part of my idea of who I was. I felt I had been granted the most cruel knowledge of where I stood in the world. And I hated it.

"It was a minor official who had written me. The receptionist spoke to one of the elderly English messengers, and he led me, with no great ceremony and a lot of asthmatic breathing, to a room that contained many desks. At one of these my man was sitting. His desk was bare, and the man himself seemed quite vacant and easy in his mind. He had small, smiling eyes, a superior manner, and he didn't know what I had come about.

"In spite of his jacket and tie he wasn't what I was expecting. He wasn't the kind of man I would have worn a dark suit for. I thought he belonged to another kind of office, another kind of building, another kind of city. His name was the name of his merchant caste, and it was easy for me to imagine him in a dhoti reclining against a bolster in a cloth shop in a bazaar lane, with his feet bare, and his fingers massaging his toes, rubbing off the dead skin. He was the kind of man who would say, 'Shirtings? You want shirtings?' and, barely moving his back from the bolster, would throw a bolt of cloth across the sheet spread on the floor of his stall.

"It wasn't shirtings that he flung across the desk at me, but my letter, the letter he had written himself, which he had asked to see. He understood that I was looking for a job and his small eyes twinkled with amusement. I felt very shabby in my suit. He said, 'You had better go and see Mr. Verma.' The English messenger, breathing heavily, and seeming to choke with every breath, led me to another office. And there he abandoned me.

"Mr. Verma wore horn-rimmed glasses. He sat in a less crowded office and he had many papers and folders on his desk. On the walls there were photographs, from the British days, of Indian buildings and Indian landscapes. Mr. Verma looked more worried than the first man. He was higher in the service; and he had probably taken the name Verma to conceal his caste origins. He was puzzled by my letter; but he was also made uneasy by my dark suit and university tie and he attempted in a half-hearted way to interview me. The telephone rang a lot and our interview never got going. At one stage, after talking on the telephone, Mr. Verma left me and went out of the room. He was away for a while and when he came back, with some papers, he seemed surprised to see me. He told me then that I should go to an office on another floor; and, giving me real attention for the first time, told me how to get there.

"The room I knocked at turned out to be a dark little ante-chamber, with a small man sitting before an old-fashioned standard typewriter with a wide carriage. He looked at me with something like terror—it was the effect of my dark suit and the tie, my man-of-two-worlds garb—and he calmed down only when he had read my letter. He asked me to wait. There was no chair. I remained standing.

"A buzzer rang, and the typist-secretary jumped. He seemed,

after this jump, to land on the tips of his toes; he very quickly drew his shoulders up and then down into a kind of cringe, making himself smaller than he already was; and with a curious long tiptoeing stride, a lope, he reached the great wooden doors that separated us from the room on the other side. He knocked, opened; and with his hunched gait, his prepared cringe, disappeared.

"My wish for the diplomatic life had by now vanished. I studied the large framed photographs of Gandhi and Nehru and wondered how, out of squalor like this, those men had managed to get themselves considered as men. It was strange, in that building in the heart of London, seeing those great men in this new way, from the inside, as it were. Up till then, from the outside, without knowing more of them than I had read in newspapers and magazines, I had admired them. They belonged to me; they ennobled me and gave me some place in the world. Now I felt the opposite. In that room the photographs of those great men made me feel that I was at the bottom of a well. I felt that in that building complete manhood was permitted only to those men and denied to everybody else. Everyone had surrendered his manhood, or a part of it, to those leaders. Everyone willingly made himself smaller the better to exalt those leaders. These thoughts surprised and pained me. They were more than heretical. They destroyed what remained of my faith in the way the world was ordered. I began to feel cast out and alone.

"When the secretary came back to the room, I noticed that he still walked on tiptoe, still cringed, still leaned forward. I saw then that what had looked like a cringe, that humping of the shoulders as he had jumped off his chair and loped across to the door, wasn't something he had put on, but was natural. He was a hunchback. This was a shock. I began confusedly to think back to my earlier impressions of the man, and I was in a state of confusion when he motioned me through the door into the inner office, where a fat black man in a black suit, one of our black Indians, was sitting at a big black table, opening envelopes with a paper knife.

"His shiny cheeks were swollen with fat and his lips appeared to pout. I sat down on a chair placed some distance away from his desk. He didn't look up at me and he didn't speak. And I didn't speak; I let him open his letters. Not an hour's exercise had he taken in his life, this devout man of the South. He reeked of caste and temple, and I was sure that below that black suit he wore all kinds of amulets.

"At last, but still not looking up, he said, 'So?'

"I said, 'I wrote in about joining the diplomatic service. I had a letter from Aggarwal and I came to see him.'

"Opening his letters, he said, '*Mister* Aggarwal.'

"I was glad he had found something we might fight about.

" 'Aggarwal didn't seem to know too much. He sent me to Verma.'

"He almost looked at me. But he didn't. He said, 'Mister Verma.'

" 'Verma didn't know too much either. He spent a long time with someone called Divedi.'

" 'Mister Divedi.'

"I gave up. He could outplay me. I said, wearily, 'And he sent me to you.'

" 'But you say in your letter you are from Africa. How can you join our diplomatic service? How can we have a man of divided loyalties?'

"I thought: How dare you lecture me about history and loyalty, you slave? We have paid bitterly for people like you. Who have you ever been loyal to, apart from yourself and your family and your caste?

"He said, 'You people have been living the good life in Africa. Now that things have got a little rough you want to run back. But you must throw in your lot with the local people.'

"That was what he said. But I don't have to tell you that what he was really talking about was his own virtue and good fortune. For himself the purity of caste, arranged marriage, the correct diet, the services of the untouchables. For everybody else, pollution. Everybody else was steeped in pollution, and had to pay the price. It was like the message of the photographs of Gandhi and Nehru in the room outside.

"He said, 'If you become a citizen of India, there are the examinations. We have arranged for them to be taken at some of the universities here. Mr. Verma should have told you. He shouldn't have sent you to me.'

"He pressed a buzzer on his desk. The door opened, and the hunchback secretary sent in a tall, thin man with bright, anxious eyes and a genuine cringe. The new man carried an artist's zip-up portfolio, and he had a long green woollen scarf wound about his neck, although the weather was warm. Without reference to me, with eyes only for the black man, he unzipped his portfolio and began taking out drawings. He held them one by one against his chest, giving the black man an anxious open-mouthed smile every time, and then looking down at what he was showing, so that, with his head bowed over his drawings, and with the cringe that was already there, he looked like a man doing penance, displaying one sin after another. The black man didn't look at the artist, only at the drawings. They were of temples and of smiling women picking tea—perhaps for some window display about the new India.

"I had been dismissed. The hunchback secretary, tense over his old, big typewriter, but not typing, his bony hands like crabs on the keys, gave me one last look of terror. This time, though, in his look I thought there was also a question: 'Do you understand now about me?'

"Walking down the steps, surrounded by the motifs of imperial India, I saw Mr. Verma, away from his desk again, and with more papers; but he had forgotten me. The idle merchant-caste man in the office downstairs remembered me, of course. I received his mocking smile, and then I went out through the revolving door into the London air.

"My crash course in diplomacy had lasted a little over an hour. It was past twelve, too late for the comfort of coffee and cake, as a sign in a snack bar reminded me. I set to walking. I was full of rage. I followed the curve of Aldwych to the end, crossed the Strand, and went down to the river.

"As I walked, the thought came to me: It is time to go home. It wasn't our town that I thought of, or our stretch of the African coast. I saw a country road lined with tall shade trees. I saw fields, cattle, a village below trees. I don't know what book or picture I had got that from, or why a place like that should have seemed to me safe. But that was the picture that came to me, and I played with it. The mornings, the dew, the fresh flowers, the shade of the trees in the middle of the day, the fires in the evening. I felt I had known that life, and that it was waiting for me again somewhere. It was fantasy, of course.

"I awakened to where I was. I was walking on the Embankment, beside the river, walking without seeing. On the Embankment wall there are green metal lamp standards. I had been examining the dolphins on the standards, dolphin by dolphin, standard by standard. I was far from where I had started, and I had momentarily left the dolphins to examine the metal supports of the pavement benches. These supports, as I saw with amazement, were in the shape of camels. Camels and their sacks! Strange city: the romance of India in that building, and the romance of the desert here. I stopped, stepped back mentally, as it were, and all at once saw the beauty in which I had been walking—the beauty of the river and the sky, the soft colours of the clouds, the beauty of light on water, the beauty of the buildings, the care with which it had all been arranged.

"In Africa, on the coast, I had paid attention only to one colour in nature—the colour of the sea. Everything else was just bush, green and living, or brown and dead. In England so far I had walked with my eyes at shop level; I had seen nothing. A town, even London, was just a series of streets or street names, and a street was a row of shops. Now I saw differently. And I understood that London wasn't simply a place that was there, as people say of mountains, but that it had been made by men, that men had given attention to details as minute as those camels.

"I began to understand at the same time that my anguish about being a man adrift was false, that for me that dream of home and security was nothing more than a dream of isolation, anachronistic and stupid and very feeble. I belonged to myself alone. I was going to surrender my manhood to nobody. For someone like me there was only one civilization and one place—

London, or a place like it. Every other kind of life was make-believe. Home—what for? To hide? To bow to our great men? For people in our situation, people led into slavery, that is the biggest trap of all. We have nothing. We solace ourselves with that idea of the great men of our tribe, the Gandhi and the Nehru, and we castrate ourselves. 'Here, take my manhood and invest it for me. Take my manhood and be a greater man your-self, for my sake!' No! I want to be a man myself.

"At certain times in some civilizations great leaders can bring out the manhood in the people they lead. It is different with slaves. Don't blame the leaders. It is just part of the dreadfulness of the situation. It is better to withdraw from the whole business, if you can. And I could. You may say—and I know, Salim, that you have thought it—that I have turned my back on my com-munity and sold out. I say: 'Sold out to what and from what? What do you have to offer me? What is your own contribution? And can you give me back my manhood?' Anyway, that was what I decided that morning, beside the river of London, be-tween the dolphins and the camels, the work of some dead artists who had been adding to the beauty of their city.

"That was five years ago. I often wonder what would have happened to me if I hadn't made that decision. I suppose I would have sunk. I suppose I would have found some kind of hole and tried to hide or pass. After all, we make ourselves according to the ideas we have of our possibilities. I would have hidden in my hole and been crippled by my sentimentality, doing what I was doing, and doing it well, but always looking for the wailing wall. And I would never have seen the world as the rich place that it is. You wouldn't have seen me here in Africa, doing what I do. I wouldn't have wanted to do it, and no one would have wanted me to do it. I would have said: 'It's all over for me, so why should I let myself be used by anybody? The Americans want to win the world. It's their fight, not mine.' And that would have been stupid. It is stupid to talk of *the* Americans. They are not a tribe, as you might think from the outside. They're all individuals fighting to make their way, trying as hard as you or me not to sink.

"It wasn't easy after I left the university. I still had to get a job, and the only thing I knew now was what I didn't want to do. I didn't want to exchange one prison for another. People like me have to make their own jobs. It isn't something that's going to come to you in a brown envelope. The job is there, waiting. But it doesn't exist for you or anyone else until you discover it, and you discover it because it's for you and you alone.

"I had done a little acting at the university—that had begun with a walk-on part in a little film somebody had made about a boy and girl walking in a park. I fell in with the remnants of that group in London and began to do a certain amount of acting. Not in any important way. London is full of little theatrical groups. They write their own plays, and they get grants from firms and local councils here and there. A lot of them live on the dole. Sometimes I played English parts, but usually they wrote parts for me, so that as an actor I found myself being the kind of person I didn't want to be in real life. I played an Indian doctor visiting a dying working-class mother; I did another Indian doctor who had been charged with rape; I was a bus conductor no one wanted to work with. And so on. Once I did Romeo. Another time there was an idea of rewriting *The Merchant of Venice* as *The Malindi Banker*, so that I could play Shylock. But it became too complicated.

"It was a bohemian life, and it was attractive at first. Then it became depressing. People dropped out and took jobs and you understood that they had had pretty solid connections all along. That was always a letdown, and there were times during those two years when I felt lost and had to fight hard to hold on to that mood that had come to me beside the river. Among all those nice people I was the only real dropout. And I didn't want to be a dropout at all. I'm not running these people down. They did what they could to make room for me, and that is more than any outsider can say for us. It's a difference in civilization.

"I was taken one Sunday to lunch at the house of a friend of a friend. There was nothing bohemian about the house or the lunch, and I discovered that I had been invited for the sake of one of the other guests. He was an American and he was interested in Africa. He spoke about Africa in an unusual way. He spoke of Africa as though Africa was a sick child and he was the parent. I later became very close to this man, but at that lunch he irritated me and I was rough with him. This was because I had never met that kind of person before. He had all this money to spend on Africa, and he desperately wanted to do the right thing. I suppose the idea of all that money going to waste made me unhappy. But he also had the simplest big-power ideas about the regeneration of Africa.

"I told him that Africa wasn't going to be saved or won by promoting the poems of Yevtushenko or by telling the people about the wickedness of the Berlin Wall. He didn't look too surprised. He wanted to hear more, and I realised I had been invited to the lunch to say the things I had been saying. And it was there that I began to understand that everything which I had thought had made me powerless in the world had also made me of value, and that to the American I was of interest precisely because I was what I was, a man without a side.

"That was how it began. That was how I became aware of all the organizations that were using the surplus wealth of the Western world to protect that world. The ideas I put forward, aggressively at that lunch, and more calmly and practically later, were quite simple ones. But they could only have come from someone like myself, someone of Africa, but with no use at all for the kind of freedom that had come to Africa.

"My idea was this. Everything had conspired to push black Africa into every kind of tyranny. As a result Africa was full of refugees, first-generation intellectuals. Western governments didn't want to know, and the old Africa hands were in no position to understand—they were still fighting ancient wars. If Africa had a future, it lay with those refugees. My idea was to remove them from the countries where they couldn't operate and send them, if only for a little while, to those parts of the continent where they could. A continental interchange, to give the men themselves hope, to give Africa the better news about itself, and to make a start on the true African revolution.

"The idea has worked beautifully. Every week we get requests from one university or the other where they would like to keep some kind of intellectual life going without getting involved in local politics. Of course, we've attracted the usual freeloaders, black and white, and we've run into trouble with the professional anti-Americans. But the idea is good. I don't feel I have to defend it. Whether it's doing any good as of now is another matter. And perhaps we don't have the time. You've seen the boys at the Domain here. You've seen how bright they are. But they only want jobs. They'll do anything for that, and that's where it may all end. There are times when I feel that Africa will simply have its own way—hungry men are hungry men. And that is when I can get very low.

"To work for an outfit like this is to live in a construct—you don't have to tell me that. But all men live in constructs. Civilization is a construct. And this construct is my own. Within it, I am of value, just as I am. I have to put nothing on. I exploit myself. I allow no one to exploit me. And if it folds, if tomorrow the people at the top decide we're getting nowhere, I've now learned that there are other ways in which I might exploit myself.

"I'm a lucky man. I carry the world within me. You see, Salim, in this world beggars are the only people who can be choosers. Everyone else has his side chosen for him. I can choose. The world is a rich place. It all depends on what you choose in it. You can be sentimental and embrace the idea of your own defeat. You can be an Indian diplomat and always be on the losing side. It's like banking. It is stupid setting up as a banker in Kenya or the Sudan. That was more or less what my family did on the coast. What do the banks say in their annual reports about those places? That many of the people are 'outside the monetary sector'? You're not going to be a Rothschild there. The Rothschilds are what they are because they chose Europe at the right time. The other Jews, just as talented, who went to bank for the Ottoman Empire, in Turkey or Egypt or wherever, didn't do so well. Nobody knows their names. And that's what we've been doing for centuries. We've been clinging to the idea of defeat and forgetting that we are men like everybody else. We've been choosing the wrong side. I'm tired of being on the losing side. I don't want to pass. I know exactly who I am and where I stand in the world. But now I want to win and win and win."

# 10

Indar had begun his story at the end of that evening at Raymond and Yvette's. He had added to it at different times later. He had begun his story on the first evening I had seen Yvette, and whenever I saw Yvette afterwards she was in his company. I had trouble with both their personalities: I could pin down neither.

In my mind I had my own picture of Yvette, and this never varied. But the person I saw, at different times of day, in different kinds of light and weather, in circumstances so different from those in which I had first seen her, was always new, always a surprise. I was nervous of looking at her face—I was becoming obsessed with her.

And Indar too began to change for me. His personality too had a dissolving quality. As he filled in his story he became in my eyes quite unlike the man who had presented himself in my shop many weeks before. In his clothes then I had seen London and privilege. I had seen that he was fighting to keep up his style, but I hadn't thought of his style as something he had created for himself. I had seen him more as a man touched by the glamour of the great world; and I had thought that given the chance to be in his world, I, too, would have been touched by the same glamour. In those early days I had often wanted to say to him: "Help me to get away from this place. Show me how to make myself like you."

But that wasn't so now. I could no longer envy his style or his stylishness. I saw it as his only asset. I felt protective towards him. I felt that since that evening at Yvette's—the evening which had lifted me up but cast him down—we had exchanged roles. I no longer looked on him as my guide; he was the man who needed to be led by the hand.

That perhaps was the secret of his social success which I had envied. My wish—which must have been like the wish of the people in London he had told me about, who had made room for him—was to clear away the aggressiveness and the depression that choked the tenderness I knew was there. I was protective towards him and towards his stylishness, his exaggerations, his delusions. I wished to keep all those from hurt. It saddened me that in a little while he would have to leave, to carry on with his lecturer's duties elsewhere. That was what, from his story, I judged him to be—a lecturer, as uncertain of his future in this role as he had been in his previous roles.

The only friends in the town I had introduced him to were Shoba and Mahesh. They were the only people I thought he would have had something in common with. But that hadn't worked. There was suspicion on both sides. These three people were in many ways alike—renegades, concerned with their personal beauty, finding in that beauty the easiest form of dignity. Each saw the other as another version of himself; and they were like people—Shoba and Mahesh on one side, Indar on the other —sniffing out the falseness in one another.

At lunch in their flat one day—a good lunch: they had gone to a lot of trouble: silver and brass polished, the curtains drawn to keep out the glare, the three-stemmed standard lamp lighting up the Persian carpet on the wall—Shoba asked Indar, "Is there any money in what you do?" Indar had said, "I get by." But outside, in the sunlight and red dust, he raged. As we drove back to the Domain, his home, he said, "Your friends don't know who I am or what I've done. They don't even know where I've been." He wasn't referring to his travels; he meant they hadn't appreciated the kind of battles he had fought. "Tell them that my value is the value I place on myself. There is no reason why it couldn't be fifty thousand dollars a year, a hundred thousand dollars a year."

That was his mood as his time at the Domain came to an end. He was more easily irritated and depressed. But for me, even during those racing days, the Domain remained a place of possibility. I was looking for a repeat of the evening I had had—the mood of the Joan Baez songs, reading lamps and African mats on the floor, a disturbing woman in black slacks, a walk to the rapids below a moon and drifting cloud. It began to feel like fantasy; I kept it secret from Indar. And Yvette, whenever I saw her, in harsher electric light or ordinary daylight, confounded me again and again, so different from what I remembered. The days passed; the polytechnic term was over. Indar said goodbye abruptly one afternoon, like a man who didn't want to make too much fuss about a goodbye; he didn't want me to see him off. And I felt that the Domain, and the life there, had been closed to me forever.

Ferdinand too was going away. He was going to the capital to take up his administrative cadetship. And it was Ferdinand whom I went to see off on the steamer at the end of the term. The hyacinths of the river, floating on: during the days of the rebellion they had spoken of blood; on heavy afternoons of heat and glitter they had spoken of experience without savour; white in moonlight, they had matched the mood of a particular evening. Now, lilac on bright green, they spoke of something over, other people moving on.

The steamer had arrived the previous afternoon with its passenger barge in tow. It hadn't brought Zabeth and her dugout. Ferdinand hadn't wanted her to be there. I had told Zabeth this was only because Ferdinand was at the age when he wanted to appear quite independent. And this was true up to a point. The journey to the capital was important to Ferdinand; and because it was important, he wished to play it down.

He had always seen himself as important. But this was part of the new unsurprised attitude to himself that he had developed. From dugout to a first-class cabin on the steamer, from a forest village to the polytechnic to an administrative cadetship—he had leapt centuries. His passage hadn't always been easy; during the rebellion he had wanted to run away and hide. But he had since learned to accept all sides of himself and all sides of the country; he rejected nothing. He knew only his country and what it offered; and all that his country offered him he wished now to take as his due. It was like arrogance; but it was also a form of ease and acceptance. He was at home in every setting, he accepted every situation; and he was himself everywhere.

That was what he demonstrated that morning when I picked him up from the Domain to drive him to the dock. The change from the Domain to the shanty settlements outside—with their scattered plantings of maize, their runnels of filth and mounds of sifted rubbish—jarred more on me than on him. I would have preferred, being with him, and thinking of his pride, to ignore them; he spoke about them, not critically, but seeing them as part of his town. At the Domain, saying goodbye to people he knew, he had behaved like the administrative cadet; with me in the car he had been like an old friend; and then outside the dock gates he had become a reasonably happy, and patient, member of an African crowd, taken with the market bustle.

*Miscerique probat populos et foedera jungi.* I had long since ceased to reflect on the vainglory of the words. The monument had only become part of the market scene on steamer days. Through that crowd we now began to make our way, accompanied by an old man, feebler than either of us, who had taken possession of Ferdinand's suitcases.

Basins of grubs and caterpillars; baskets of trussed-up hens, squawking when they were lifted by one wing by the vendor or a prospective buyer; dull-eyed goats on the bare, scuffed ground, chewing at rubbish and even paper; damp-haired young monkeys, full of misery, tethered tightly around their narrow waists and nibbling at peanuts and banana skin and mango skin, but nibbling without relish, as though they knew that they themselves were soon to be eaten.

Nervous passengers from the bush, barge passengers, travelling from one far-off village to another, and being seen off by families or friends; the established vendors in their established places (two or three at the foot of the monument), with their box seats, cooking stones, pots and pans, bundles, babies; idlers, cripples and scroungers. And officials.

There were many more officials nowadays, and most of them appeared to be active in this area on steamer days. Not all of them were in police or army uniform, and not all of them were men. In the name of his dead mother, the hotel maid, "the woman of Africa," as he called her in his speeches, the President had decided to honour as many women as possible; and he had done so by making them government servants, not always with clear duties.

Ferdinand and myself and the porter made a noticeable group

(Ferdinand much taller than the men of the region), and we were stopped about half a dozen times by people who wanted to see our papers. Once we were stopped by a woman in a long African-style cotton dress. She was as small as her sisters who poled the dugouts in village creeks, and fetched and carried; her head was as hairless and looked as shaved; but her face had plumped out. She spoke to us roughly. She held Ferdinand's steamer tickets (one for the fare, one for the food) upside down when she examined them; and she frowned.

Ferdinand's face registered nothing. When she gave him back the tickets he said, "Thank you, *citoyenne*." He spoke without irony; the woman's frown was replaced by a smile. And that seemed to have been the main point of the exercise—the woman wanted to be shown respect and to be called *citoyenne*. *Monsieur* and *madame* and *boy* had been officially outlawed; the President had decreed us all to be *citoyens* and *citoyennes*. He used the two words together in his speeches, again and again, like musical phrases.

We moved through the waiting crowd—people made room for us simply because we were moving—to the dock gates. And there our porter, as though knowing what was to follow, dropped his load, asked for a lot of francs, quickly settled for less, and bolted. The gates, for no reason, were closed against us. The soldiers looked at us and then looked away, refusing to enter into the palaver Ferdinand and I tried to get going. For half an hour or more we stood there in the crowd, pressed against the gate, in the stinging sun, in the smell of sweat and smoked food; and then, for no apparent reason, one of the soldiers opened the gate and let us in, but just us, not anyone behind, as though, in spite of Ferdinand's tickets and my own dock pass, he was doing us a great favour.

The steamer was still pointing towards the rapids. The white superstructure, with the first-class cabins, just visible above the customs-shed roof, was at the stern end of the steamer. On the steel-plated deck below, just a few feet above the water, a range of iron-clad barrack-like structures ran all the way to the rounded bow. The iron barracks were for the lesser passengers.

And for passengers who were least of all there was the barge—tiers of cages on a shallow iron hull, the cages wire-netted and barred, the wire netting and bars dented and twisted, the internal organization of the cages hidden, lost in gloom, in spite of the sunlight and the glitter of the river.

The first-class cabins still suggested luxury. The iron walls were white; the timbered decks were scrubbed and tarred. The doors were open; there were curtains. There were stewards and even a purser.

I said to Ferdinand, "I thought those people down there were going to ask you for your certificate of civic merit. In the old days you had to have one before they let you up here."

He didn't laugh, as an older man might have done. He didn't know about the colonial past. His memories of the larger world began with the mysterious day when mutinous soldiers, strangers, had come to his mother's village looking for white people to kill, and Zabeth had frightened them off, and they had taken away only a few of the village women.

To Ferdinand the colonial past had vanished. The steamer had always been African, and first class on the steamer was what he could see now. Respectably dressed Africans, the older men in suits, the evolved men of an earlier generation; some women with families, everyone dressed up for the journey; one or two of the old ladies of such families, closer to the ways of the forest, already sitting on the floor of their cabins and preparing lunch, breaking the black hulls of smoked fish and smoked monkeys into enamel plates with coloured patterns, and releasing strong, salty smells.

Rustic manners, forest manners, in a setting not of the forest. But that was how, in our ancestral lands, we all began—the prayer mat on the sand, then the marble floor of a mosque; the rituals and taboos of nomads, which, transferred to the palace of a sultan or a maharaja, become the traditions of an aristocracy.

Still, I would have found the journey hard, especially if, like Ferdinand, I had to share a cabin with someone else, someone in the crowd outside who had not yet been let in. But the steamer was not meant for me or—in spite of the colonial emblems embroidered in red on the frayed, much laundered sheets and pillowcase on Ferdinand's bunk—for the people who had in the old days required certificates of civic merit, with good reason. The steamer was now meant for the people who used it, and to them it was very grand. The people on Ferdinand's deck knew they were not passengers on the barge.

From the rear end of the deck, looking past the lifeboats, we could see people going aboard the barge with their crates and bundles. Above the roof of the customs sheds the town showed mainly as trees or bush—the town which, when you were in it, was full of streets and open spaces and sun and buildings. Few buildings showed through the trees and none rose above them. And from the height of the first-class deck you could see—from the quality of the vegetation, the change from imported ornamental trees to undifferentiated bush—how quickly the town ended, what a narrow strip of the riverbank it occupied. If you looked the other way, across the muddy river to the low line of bush and the emptiness of the other bank, you could pretend that the town didn't exist. And then the barge on this bank was like a miracle, and the cabins of the first-class deck an impossible luxury.

At either end of that deck was something even more impressive—a *cabine de luxe*. That was what the old, paint-spattered metal plates above the doors said. What did these two cabins contain? Ferdinand said, "Shall we have a look?" We went into the one at the back. It was dark and very hot; the windows were sealed and heavily curtained. A baking bathroom; two armchairs, rather beaten up, and one with an arm missing, but still armchairs; a table with two shaky chairs; sconces with bulbs missing; torn curtains screening off the bunks from the rest of the cabin; and an air conditioner. Who, in that crowd outside, had such a ridiculous idea of his needs? Who required such privacy, such cramping comforts?

From the forward end of the deck came the sound of a disturbance. A man was complaining loudly, and he was complaining in English.

Ferdinand said, "I think I hear your friend."

It was Indar. He was carrying an unusual load, and he was

sweating and full of anger. With his forearms held out at the horizontal—like the fork of a fork-lift truck—he was supporting a shallow but very wide cardboard box, open at the top, on which he could visibly get no grip. The box was heavy. It was full of groceries and big bottles, ten or twelve bottles; and after the long walk from the dock gates and up all the steamer steps, Indar seemed to be at the end of all physical resource and on the verge of tears.

With a backward lean he staggered into the *cabine de luxe*, and I saw him drop—almost throw—the cardboard box on the bunk. And then he began to do a little dance of physical agony, stamping about the cabin and flexing his arms violently from the elbows down, as though to shake out the ache from all kinds of yelping muscles.

He was overdoing the display, but he had an audience. Not me, whom he had seen but was yet in no mood to acknowledge. Yvette was behind him. She was carrying his briefcase. He shouted at her, with the security that the English language gave him here, "The suitcase—is the bugger bringing the suitcase?" She looked sweated and strained herself, but she said soothingly, "Yes, yes." And a man in a flowered shirt whom I had taken to be a passenger appeared with the suitcase.

I had seen Indar and Yvette together many times, but never in such a domestic relationship. For a dislocating moment the thought came to me that they were going away together. But then Yvette, straightening up, and remembering to smile, said to me, "Are you seeing someone off too?" And I understood that my anxiety was foolish.

Indar was now squeezing his biceps. Whatever he had planned for this moment with Yvette had been destroyed by the pain of the cardboard box.

He said, "They had no carrier bags. They had no bloody carrier bags."

I said, "I thought you had taken the plane."

"We waited for hours at the airport yesterday. It was always coming and coming. Then at midnight they gave us a beer and told us that the plane had been taken out of service. Just like that. Not delayed. Taken away. The Big Man wanted it. And no

one knows when he is going to send it back. And then buying
this steamer ticket—have you ever done that? There are all kinds
of rules about when they can sell and when they can't sell. The
man is hardly ever there. The damned door is always locked.
And every five yards somebody wants to see your papers. Ferdinand, explain this to me. When the man was totting up the fare,
all the de luxe supplements, he worked the sum out twenty times
on the adding machine. The same sum, twenty times. Why? Did
he think the machine was going to change its mind? That took
half an hour. And then, thank God, Yvette reminded me about
the food. And the water. So we had to go shopping. Six bottles of
Vichy water for the five days. It was all they had—I've come to
Africa to drink Vichy water. One dollar and fifty cents a bottle,
U.S. Six bottles of red wine, the acid Portuguese stuff you get
here. If I had known I would have to carry it all in that box, I
would have done without it."

He had also bought five tins of sardines, one for each day of
the journey, I suppose; two tins of evaporated milk; a tin of
Nescafé, a Dutch cheese, some biscuits and a quantity of Belgian
honey cake.

He said, "The honey cake was Yvette's idea. She says it's full
of nourishment."

She said, "It keeps in the heat."

I said, "There was a man at the lycée who used to live on
honey cake."

Ferdinand said, "That's why we smoke nearly everything.
Once you don't break the crust it lasts a long time."

"But the food situation in this place is appalling," Indar said.
"Everything in the shops is imported and expensive. And in the
market, apart from the grubs and things that people pick up, all
you have are two sticks of this and two ears of that. And people
are coming in all the time. How do they make out? You have all
this bush, all this rain. And yet there could be a famine in this
town."

The cabin was more crowded than it had been. A squat barefooted man had come in to introduce himself as the steward of
the *cabine de luxe*, and after him the purser had come in, with a

towel over one shoulder and a folded tablecloth in his hand. The purser shooed away the steward, spread the tablecloth on the table—lovely old material, but mercilessly laundered. Then he addressed Yvette.

"I see that the gentleman has brought his own food and water. But there is no need, madame. We follow the old rules still. Our water is purified. I myself have worked on ocean liners and been to countries all over the world. Now I am old and work on this African steamer. But I am accustomed to white people and know their ways well. The gentleman has nothing to fear, madame. He will be looked after well. I will see that the gentleman's food is prepared separately, and I will serve him with my own hands in his cabin."

He was a thin, elderly man of mixed race; his mother or father might have been a mulatto. He had conscientiously used the forbidden words—*monsieur, madame*; he had spread a tablecloth. And he stood waiting to be rewarded. Indar gave him two hundred francs.

Ferdinand said, "You've given him too much. He called you *monsieur* and *madame*, and you tipped him. As far as he's concerned, his account has been settled. Now he will do nothing for you."

And Ferdinand seemed to be right. When we went down one deck to the bar, the purser was there, leaning against the counter, drinking beer. He ignored all four of us; and he did nothing for us when we asked for beer and the barman said, "*Terminé*." If the purser hadn't been drinking, and if another man with three well-dressed women hadn't been drinking at one of the tables, it would have looked convincing. The bar—with a framed photograph of the President in chief's clothes, holding up the carved stick with the fetish—was stripped; the brown shelves were bare.

I said to the barman, "*Citoyen*." Ferdinand said, "*Citoyen*." We got a palaver going, and beer was brought from the back room.

Indar said, "You will have to be my guide, Ferdinand. You will palaver for me."

It was past noon, and very hot. The bar was full of reflected river light, with dancing veins of gold. The beer, weak as it was, lulled us. Indar forgot his aches and pains; a discussion he started with Ferdinand about the farm at the Domain that the Chinese or Taiwanese had abandoned trailed away. My own nervousness was soothed; my mood was buoyant: I would leave the steamer with Yvette.

The light was the light of the very early afternoon—everything stoked up, the blaze got truly going, but with a hint of the blaze about to consume itself. The river glittered, muddy water turned to white and gold. It was busy with dugouts with outboard motors, as always on steamer days. The dugouts carried the extravagant names of their "establishments" painted in large letters down their sides. Sometimes, when a dugout crossed a patch of glitter, the occupants were all silhouetted against the glitter; they appeared then to be sitting very low, to be shoulders and round heads alone, so that for a while they were like comic figures in a cartoon strip, engaged on some quite ridiculous journey.

A man teetered into the bar on platform shoes with soles about two inches thick. He must have been from the capital; that style in shoes hadn't reached us as yet. He was also an official, come to check our tickets and passes. Not long after he had teetered out, panic appeared to seize the purser and the barman and some of the men drinking at tables. It was this panic that finally distinguished crew and officials, none of them in uniform, from the other people who had come in and palavered for their beer; and it meant only that the steamer was about to leave.

Indar put his hand on Yvette's thigh. When she turned to him he said gently, "I'll see what I can find out about Raymond's book. But you know those people in the capital. If they don't reply to your letters, it's because they don't want to reply. They're not going to say yes or no. They're going to say nothing. But I'll see."

Their embrace, just before we got off, was no more than formal. Ferdinand was cool. No handshake, no words of farewell. He simply said, "Salim." And to Yvette he gave a nod rather than a bow.

We stood on the dock and watched. After some maneuvering the steamer was clear of the dock wall. Then the barge was attached; and steamer and barge did a slow, wide turn in the river, the barge revealing at its stern tiers, slices, of a caged back-yard life, a mixture of kitchens and animal pens.

A departure can feel like a desertion, a judgment on the place and people left behind. That was what I had been accustoming myself to since the previous day, when I thought I had said goodbye to Indar. For all my concern for him, I had thought of him—as I had thought of Ferdinand—as the lucky man, the man moving on to richer experience, leaving me to my little life in a place once again of no account.

But I didn't think so now, standing with Yvette on the exposed dock, after the accident and luck of that second goodbye, watching the steamer and barge straighten in the brown river, against the emptiness of the far bank, which was pale in the heat and like part of the white sky. The place where it was all going on after all was where we were, in the town on the riverbank. Indar was the man who had been sent away. The hard journey was his.

# 11

It was past two, a time when, on sunny days, it hurt to be in the open. We had neither of us had anything to eat—we had only had that bloating beer—and Yvette didn't reject the idea of a snack in a cool place.

The asphalt surfacing of the dock area was soft underfoot. Hard black shadows had pulled back to the very edges of build-ings, buildings which here on the dock were of the colonial time and substantial—ochre-washed stone walls, green shutters, tall, iron-barred windows, green-painted corrugated-iron roofs. A scratched blackboard outside the closed steamer office still gave the time of the steamer sailing. But the officials had gone; the crowd outside the dock gates had gone. The market around the granite wall of the ruined monument was being dismantled. The feathery leaves of the flamboyant trees made no shade; the

sun struck right through. The ground, hummocked around tufts
of grass, scuffed to dust elsewhere, was littered with rubbish and
animal droppings and patches of wet which, coated and bound
on the underside with fine dust, seemed to be curling back on
themselves, peeling off the ground.

We didn't go to Mahesh's Bigburger bar. I wanted to avoid the
complications—Shoba hadn't approved of Yvette's connection
with Indar. We went instead to the Tivoli. It wasn't far away,
and I hoped that Mahesh's boy Ildephonse wouldn't report. But
that was unlikely; it was the time of day when Ildephonse was
normally vacant.

The Tivoli was a new or newish place, part of our continuing
boom, and was owned by a family who had run a restaurant in
the capital before independence. Now, after some years in Europe, they had come back to try again here. It was a big invest-
ment for them—they had skimped on nothing—and I thought
they were taking a chance. But I didn't know about Europeans
and their restaurant habits. And the Tivoli was meant for our
Europeans. It was a family restaurant, and it served the short-
contract men who were working on various government projects
in our region—the Domain, the airport, the water supply system,
the hydroelectric station. The atmosphere was European; Africans kept away. There were no officials with gold watches and
gold pen-and-pencil sets, as at Mahesh's. While you were at the
Tivoli you could live without that tension.

But you couldn't forget where you were. The photograph of
the President was about three feet high. The official portraits
of the President in African garb were getting bigger and bigger,
the quality of the prints finer (they were said to be done in
Europe). And once you knew about the meaning of the leopard
skin and the symbolsim of what was carved on the stick, you
were affected; you couldn't help it. We had all become his people;
even here at the Tivoli we were reminded that we all in various
ways depended on him.

Normally the boys—or citizen waiters—were friendly and
welcoming and brisk. But the lunch period was more or less
over; the tall, fat son of the family, who stood behind the counter

by the coffee machine, superintending things, was probably having his siesta; no other member of the family was present; and the waiters stood about idly, like aliens in their blue waiters' jackets. They weren't rude; they were simply abstracted, like people who had lost a role.

The air conditioning was welcome, though, and the absence of glare, and the dryness after the humidity outside. Yvette looked less harassed; energy returned to her. We got the attention of a waiter. He brought us a jug of red Portuguese wine, chilled down and then allowed to lose its chill; and two wooden platters with Scottish smoked salmon on toast. Everything was imported; everything was expensive; smoked salmon on toast was in fact the Tivoli's plainest offering.

I said to Yvette, "Indar's a bit of an actor. Were things really as bad as he said?"

"They were much worse. He left out cashing the traveller's cheques."

She was sitting with her back to the wall. She made a small arresting gesture—like Raymond's—with the palm of her hand against the edge of the table, and gave a slight tilt of her head to her right.

Two tables away a family of five were finishing lunch and talking loudly. Ordinary people, the kind of family group I had been used to seeing at the Tivoli. But Yvette seemed to disapprove, and more than disapprove; a little rage visited her.

She said, "You can't tell about them. I can."

And yet that face, of rage, still seemed close to a smile; and those slanting eyes, half closed above the small cup of coffee which she was holding at the level of her mouth, were quite demure. What had irritated her about the family group? The district she had judged them to come from? The job the man did, the language, the loud talk, the manners? What would she have said about the people in our nightclubs?

I said, "Did you know Indar before?"

"I met him here." She put the cup down. Her slanting eyes considered it and then, as though she had decided on something, she looked at me. "You live your life. A stranger appears. He is an encumbrance. You don't need him. But the encumbrance can become a habit."

My experience of women outside my family was special, limited. I had had no experience of dealing with a woman like this, no experience of language like this, no experience of a woman with such irritations and convictions. And in what she had just said I saw an honesty, a daringness which, to a man of my background, was slightly frightening and, for that reason, bewitching.

I was unwilling for us to have Indar in common, as Indar and she seemed to have had Raymond in common. I said, "I can't tell you how much I liked being in your house that evening. I've never forgotten the blouse you wore. I've always been hoping to see you in it again. Black silk, beautifully cut and embroidered."

I couldn't have touched a better subject. She said, "There hasn't been the occasion. But I assure you it's still there."

"I don't think it was Indian. The cut and the work were European."

"It's from Copenhagen. Margit Brandt. Raymond went there for a conference."

And at the door of the Tivoli, before we went out again into the heat and the light, during that moment of pause which in the tropics is like the pause we make before we finally go out into the rain, she said to me, as though it were an afterthought, "Would you like to come to lunch at the house tomorrow? We have to have one of the lecturers, and Raymond finds that kind of occasion very trying these days."

The steamer would have been about fifteen miles downriver. It would have been travelling through bush; it would have passed the first bush settlement. There, though the town was so close, they would have been waiting for the steamer since morning, and there would have been the atmosphere of a fair until the steamer passed. Boys would have dived off dugouts and swum towards the moving steamer and barge, trying to get the attention of passengers. Trading dugouts, poling out from their stations on the bank with their little cargoes of pineapples and roughly made chairs and stools (disposable furniture for the river journey, a specialty of the area), would have been attached in clusters to the sides of the steamer; and these dugouts would be taken—

were being taken—miles downriver, to paddle back for hours, after that brief excitement, through the fading afternoon, dusk and night, in silence.

Yvette had cancelled the lunch. But she hadn't let me know. The white-jacketed servant led me to a room which obviously awaited no visitors and was not at all like the room I remembered. The African mats were on the floor, but some of the upholstered chairs that had been taken away for that evening (and, as I remembered Yvette saying, stored in a bedroom) had been brought out again—fringed imitation velvet, in the "old bronze" colour that was everywhere in the Domain.

The buildings of the Domain had been run up fast, and the flaws that lamplight had hidden were noticeable in the midday brightness. The plaster on the walls had cracked in many places, and in one place the crack followed the stepped pattern of the hollow clay bricks below. The windows and doorways, without architraves or wooden facings, were like holes unevenly cut out of the masonry. The ceiling panels, compressed cardboard of some sort, bellied here and there. One of the two air conditioners in the room had leaked down the wall; they were not on. The windows were open; and with no projecting roof, no trees outside, just the levelled land, the room was full of light and glare and there was no feeling of shelter. What fantasies I had built around this room, around the music that had come out of the record player—there, against the wall next to the bookcase, with its smoked Perspex cover showing dust in the bright light!

To see the room like this, as Yvette lived in it every day, to add my knowledge of Raymond's position in the country, was to catch her unawares and get some idea of her housewifely ordinariness, some idea of the tensions and dissatisfactions of her life at the Domain, which had until then seemed so glamorous to me. It was to fear to be entangled with her and this life of hers; and it was to be surprised and relieved at the disappearance of my fantasies. But relief and fear lasted only until she came in. The surprise then, as always for me, was herself.

She was more amused than apologetic. She had forgotten, but she knew there was something she had had to remember about that lunch. There had been so many changes of plan about the lunch—which was in fact taking place in the staff room of the polytechnic. She went away to make us some scrambled South African eggs. The servant came in to clear some receipts from the oval table, which was dark and highly polished, and to lay the table. "You live your life. A stranger appears. He is an encumbrance."

On the upper shelf of the bookcase I saw the book Indar had shown me that evening in which there was a mention of Raymond and Yvette as generous hosts at one time in the capital—a mention which had mattered to Yvette. The bright light and the altered room seemed to make it a different book. Colour had faded from the backs of books. One book I took out carried Raymond's signature and the date 1937—a note of ownership, but also perhaps at that date a statement of intent, Raymond's expression of faith in his own future. That book felt very tarnished now, with the paper brown at the edges, the red letters on the paper spine almost bleached away—something dead, a relic. Another, newer book carried Yvette's signature with her unmarried name: very stylish, that Continental handwriting, with a fancy y, and speaking in much the same way as Raymond's signature of twenty-three years before.

I said to Yvette while we were eating the scrambled eggs, "I would like to read something by Raymond. Indar says he knows more about the country than any man living. Has he published any books?"

"He's working on this book, and has been for some years now. The government were going to publish it, but now apparently there are difficulties."

"So there are no books."

"There's his thesis. That's been published as a book. But I can't recommend it. I couldn't bear to read it. When I told Raymond that, he said he could scarcely bear to write it. There are a few articles in various journals. He hasn't had time for many of those. He's spent all his time on that big book about the history of the country."

"Is it true that the President has read parts of that book?"

"That used to be said."

But she couldn't tell me what the difficulties now were. All I learned was that Raymond had temporarily put aside his history to work on a selection of the President's speeches. Our lunch began to feel sad. Understanding Yvette's position in the Domain now, knowing that the stories I had heard about Raymond would have been heard by others, I began to feel that the house must have been like a prison to her. And that evening when she gave a party and wore her Margit Brandt blouse began to appear like an aberration.

I said, as I was getting ready to leave, "You must come with me to the Hellenic Club one afternoon. You must come tomorrow. The people there are people who have been here a long time. They've seen it all. The last thing they want to talk about is the situation of the country."

She agreed. But then she said, "You mustn't forget them."

I had no idea what she was talking about. She left the room, going through the door that Raymond had gone through after he had made his exit speech that evening; and she came back with a number of magazines, *Cahiers* of this and that, some of them printed by the government printery in the capital. They were magazines with articles by Raymond. Already, then, we had Raymond in common; it was like a beginning.

The rough-bladed grass of the lawns or open areas of this part of the Domain was high; it almost buried the low-level lights housed in mushroom-like aluminum structures that lined the asphalted avenues. A number of those lights had been smashed, some a long time ago; but there seemed to be no one to mend them. On the other side of the Domain the land for the model farm had become overgrown; all that remained of the project was the Chinese gateway that the now absent Taiwanese or Chinese had built, and the six tractors standing in a line and rotting. But the area where the public walked on Sundays, following a fixed one-way route—watched now by the Youth Guard and not the army—was maintained. New statues were still added from time to time to this public walk. The most recent, at the end of the main avenue, was a bulky sculpture in stone, unfinished-looking, of a mother and child.

Nazruddin's old words came to me. "This is nothing. This is

just bush." But my alarm wasn't like Nazruddin's. It had nothing to do with my business prospects. I saw the empty spaces of the Domain, and the squatters from the villages camping just outside; and my thoughts were of Yvette and her life on the Domain. Not Europe in Africa, as it had seemed to me when Indar was there. Only a life in the bush. And my fear was at once the fear of failing with her, being left with nothing, and the fear of the consequences of success.

But that alarm vanished the next afternoon when she came to the flat. She had been there before with Indar; in that setting, my own, she had for me a good deal of her old glamour. She had seen the Ping-Pong table with my household junk and with one corner left clear for Metty's ironing. She had seen the paintings of European ports that the Belgian lady had bequeathed me with the white studio–sitting room.

It was against this white wall that, after some talk about the paintings and the Hellenic Club, both of us standing, she showed me her profile, turning away when I drew close, not rejecting me or encouraging me, just seeming weary, accepting a new encumbrance. That moment—as I read it—was the key to all that followed. The challenge that I saw then was what I always saw; it was the challenge to which I never failed to respond.

Until then my fantasies were brothel fantasies of conquest and degradation, with the woman as the willing victim, the accomplice in her own degradation. It was all that I knew. It was all that I had learned from the brothels and nightclubs of our town. It had been no hardship to me to give these places up while Indar was around. I had grown to find those occasions of vice enervating. For some time, in fact, though it still excited me to see these women in groups in a bar or a brothel front room, I had shrunk from true sex with bought women, and restricted myself to subsidiary sexual satisfactions. Familiarity of this kind with so many women had bred something like contempt for what they offered; and at the same time, like many men who use brothels alone, I had grown to think of myself as feeble, critically disadvantaged. My obsession with Yvette had taken me by surprise; and the adventure with her (unbought but willing) that began in the white sitting room was for me quite new.

What I have called my brothel fantasies hurried me through the initial awkwardness. But in the bedroom with the very large bed with the foam mattress—at last serving the purpose for which I was certain the Belgian painter had intended it—in the bedroom those fantasies altered. The self-regard of those fantasies dropped away.

Women make up half the world; and I thought I had reached the stage where there was nothing in a woman's nakedness to surprise me. But I felt now as if I was experiencing anew, and seeing a woman for the first time. I was amazed that, obsessed with Yvette as I had been, I had taken so much for granted. The body on the bed was to me like the revelation of woman's form. I wondered that clothes, even the apparently revealing tropical clothes I had seen on Yvette, should have concealed so much, should have broken the body up, as it were, into separate parts and not really hinted at the splendour of the whole.

To write about the occasion in the manner of my pornographic magazines would be more than false. It would be like trying to take photographs of myself, to be the voyeur of my own actions, to reconvert the occasion into the brothel fantasy that, in the bedroom, it ceased to be.

I was overwhelmed, but alert. I did not wish to lose myself in the self-regard and self-absorption of that fantasy, the blindness of that fantasy. The wish that came to me—consuming the anxiety about letting myself down—was the wish to win the possessor of that body, the body which, because I wished to win its possessor, I saw as perfect, and wanted continuously, during the act itself, to see, holding myself in ways that enabled me to do so, avoiding crushing the body with my own, avoiding that obliteration of sight and touch. All my energy and mind were devoted to that new end of winning the person. All my satisfactions lay in that direction; and the sexual act became for me an extraordinary novelty, a new kind of fulfilment, continuously new.

How often before, at such moments, moments allegedly of triumph, boredom had fallen on me! But as a means of winning, rather than the triumph in itself, the present act required constant alertness, a constant looking outward from myself. It wasn't tender, though it expressed a great need for tenderness. It became a brute physical act, an act almost of labour; and as it developed it became full of deliberate brutality. This surprised me. But I was altogether surprised by my new self, which was as far from the brothel man I had taken myself to be, with all his impulses to feebleness, as this act was from the brothel act of surrender, which was all I had so far known.

Yvette said, "This hasn't happened to me for years." That statement, if it was true, would have been a sufficient reward; my own climax was not important to me. If what she said was true! But I had no means of gauging her response. She was the experienced one, I was the beginner.

And there was a further surprise. No fatigue, no drowsiness overcame me at the end. On the contrary. In that room with the window panes painted white, a white that now glowed with the late afternoon light, in that heated room, at the end of one of our heavy, hot days, sweating as I was, with a body slippery with sweat, I was full of energy. I could have gone and played squash at the Hellenic Club. I felt refreshed, revitalized; my skin felt new. I was full of the wonder of what had befallen me. And awakening from minute to minute to the depth of my satisfactions, I began to be aware of my immense previous deprivation. It was like discovering a great, unappeasable hunger in myself.

Yvette, naked, wet, unembarrassed, her hair lank, but already herself again, her flush gone, her eyes calm, sat with crossed legs on the edge of the bed and telephoned. She spoke in patois. It was to her house servant: she was coming home right away: he was to tell Raymond. She dressed and made up the bed. This housewifely attention reminded me—painfully, already—of attentions like this that she gave elsewhere.

Just before she left the bedroom she stopped and kissed me briefly on the front of my trousers. And then it was over—the corridor, Metty's dreadful kitchen, the landing, the yellowing afternoon light, the trees of back yards, the dust in the air, the cooking smoke, the active world, and the sound of Yvette's feet pattering down the external staircase. That gesture, of kissing my trousers, which elsewhere I would have dismissed as a brothel courtesy, the gesture of an overtipped whore, now moved me to sadness and doubt. Was it meant? Was it true?

I thought of going to the Hellenic Club, to use up the energy that had come to me, and to sweat a little more. But I didn't go. I wandered about the flat, letting the time pass. The light began to fade; and a stillness fell over me. I felt blessed and remade; I wanted to be alone for a while with that sensation.

Later, thinking of dinner, I drove out to the nightclub near the dam. It was doing better than ever now, with the boom and the expatriates. But the structure hadn't been added to and still had a temporary look, the look of a place that could be surrendered without too much loss—just four brick walls, more or less, around a cleared space in the bush.

I sat outside at one of the tables under the trees on the cliff and looked at the floodlit dam; and until someone noticed me and turned on the coloured bulbs strung about the trees, I sat in the darkness, feeling the newness of my skin. Cars came and parked. There were the French accents of Europe and Africa. African women, in twos and threes, came up in taxis from the town. Turbanned, lazy, erect, talking loudly, they dragged their slippers over the bare ground. It was the other side of the expatriate family scene that had offended Yvette at the Tivoli. To me it all felt far away—the nightclub, the town, the squatters, the expatriates, "the situation of the country"; everything had just become background.

The town, when I drove back, had settled down to its own night life. At night now, in the increasingly crowded main streets, there was the atmosphere of the village, with unsteady groups around the little drinking stalls in the shanty areas, the cooking fires on the pavements, the barring off of sleeping places, the lunatic or drunken old men in rags, ready to snarl like dogs, taking their food to dark corners, to eat out of the sight of others. The windows of some shops—especially clothing shops, with their expensive imported goods—were brightly lit, as a precaution against theft.

In the square not far from the flat a young woman was bawling—a real African bawl. She was being hustled along the pavement by two men, each one twisting an arm. But no one in the square did anything. The men were of our Youth Guard. The officers got a small stipend from the Big Man, and they had been given a couple of government jeeps. But, like the officials at the docks, they really had to look for things to do. This was their new "Morals Patrol." It was the opposite of what it said. The girl would have been picked up from some bar; she had probably answered back or refused to pay.

In the flat I saw that Metty's light was on. I said, "Metty?" He said through the door, "*Patron.*" He had stopped calling me Salim; we had seen little of one another outside the shop for some time. I thought there was sadness in his voice; and going on to my own room, considering my own luck, I thought: Poor Metty. How will it end for him? So friendly, and yet in the end always without friends. He should have stayed on the coast. He had his place there. He had people like himself. Here he is lost.

Yvette telephoned me at the shop late the next morning. It was our first telephone call, but she didn't speak my name or give her own. She said, "Will you be at the flat for lunch?" I seldom had lunch at the flat during the week, but I said, "Yes." She said, "I'll see you there." And that was all.

She had allowed no pause, no silence, had given me no time for surprise. And indeed, waiting for her in the white sitting room just after twelve, standing at the Ping-Pong table, turning over a magazine, I felt no surprise. I felt the occasion—for all its unusualness, the oddity of the hour, the killing brightness of the light—to be only a continuation of something I had long been living with.

I heard her hurry up the steps she had pattered down the previous afternoon. Out of every kind of nervousness I didn't move. The landing door was open, the sitting room door was open—her steps were brisk and didn't falter. I was utterly delighted to see her; that was an immense relief. There was still briskness in her manner; but though her face seemed set for it, she wore no smile. Her eyes were serious, with a disturbing, challenging hint of greed.

She said, "I've been thinking of you all morning. I haven't

been able to get you out of my head." And as though she had entered the sitting room only to leave it, as though her arrival at the flat was a continuation of the directness of her telephone call, and she wanted to give neither of us time for words, she went into the bedroom and began to undress.

It was as before with me. Confronted with her, I shed old fantasies. My body obeyed its new impulses, discovered in itself resources that answered my new need. New—it was the word. It was always new, familiar though the body and its responses became, and as physical as the act was, requiring such roughness, control and subtlety. At the end (which I willed, as I had willed all that had gone before), energized, revivified, I felt I had been taken far beyond the wonder of the previous afternoon.

I had closed the shop at twelve. I got back just after three. I hadn't had any lunch. That would have delayed me further, and Friday was a big day for trade. I found the shop closed. Metty hadn't opened up at one, as I had expected him to. Barely an hour of trade remained, and many of the retailers from the out-lying villages would have done their shopping and started back on the long journey home by dugout or truck. The last pickup vans in the square, which left when they had a load, were more or less loaded.

I had my first alarm about myself, the beginning of the decay of the man I had known myself to be. I had visions of beggary and decrepitude: the man not of Africa lost in Africa, no longer with the strength or purpose to hold his own, and with less claim to anything than the ragged, half-starved old drunks from the villages who wandered about the square, eyeing the food stalls, cadging mouthfuls of beer, and the young trouble-makers from the shanty towns, a new breed, who wore shirts stamped with the Big Man's picture and talked about foreigners and profit and, wanting only money (like Ferdinand and his friends at the lycée in the old days), came into shops and bargained aggressively for goods they didn't want, insisting on the cost price.

From this alarm about myself—exaggerated, because it was the first—I moved to a feeling of rage against Metty, for whom the previous night I had felt such compassion. Then I remembered. It wasn't Metty's fault. He was at the customs, clearing the goods that had arrived by the steamer that had taken Indar and Ferdinand away, the steamer that was still one day's sailing from the capital.

For two days, since my scrambled-eggs lunch with Yvette at her house in the Domain, the magazines with Raymond's articles had lain in the drawer of my desk. I hadn't looked at them. I did so now, reminded of them by thoughts of the steamer.

When I had asked Yvette to see something Raymond had written, it was only as a means of approaching her. Now there was no longer that need; and it was just as well. The articles by Raymond in the local magazines looked particularly difficult. One was a review of an American book about African inheritance laws. The other, quite long, with footnotes and tables, seemed to be a ward-by-ward analysis of tribal voting patterns in the local council elections in the big mining town in the south just before independence; some of the names of the smaller tribes I hadn't even heard of.

The earlier articles, in the foreign magazines, seemed easier. "Riot at a Football Match," in an American magazine, was about a race riot in the capital in the 1930s that had led to the formation of the first African political club. "Lost Liberties," in a Belgian magazine, was about the failure of a missionary scheme, in the late nineteenth century, to buy picked slaves from the Arab slave caravans and resettle them in "liberty villages."

These articles were a little more in my line—I was especially interested in the missionaries and the slaves. But the bright opening paragraphs were deceptive; the articles weren't exactly shop-time, afternoon reading. I put them aside for later. And that evening, as I read in the large bed which Yvette a few hours earlier had made up, and where her smell still lingered, I was appalled.

The article about the race riot—after that bright opening paragraph which I had read in the shop—turned out to be a compilation of government decrees and quotations from newspapers. There was a lot from the newspapers; Raymond seemed to have taken them very seriously. I couldn't get over that, because from my experience on the coast I knew that newspapers in small colonial places told a special kind of truth. They didn't lie, but they were formal. They handled big people—businessmen, high officials, members of our legislative and executive councils—with respect. They left out a lot of important things—often essential things—that local people would know and gossip about.

I didn't think that the papers here in the 1930s would have been much different from ours on the coast; and I was always hoping that Raymond was going to go behind the newspaper stories and editorials and try to get at the real events. A race riot in the capital in the 1930s—that ought to have been a strong story: gun talk in the European cafés and clubs, hysteria and terror in the African *cités*. But Raymond wasn't interested in that side. He didn't give the impression that he had talked to any of the people involved, though many would have been alive when he wrote. He stuck with the newspapers; he seemed to want to show that he had read them all and had worked out the precise political shade of each. His subject was an event in Africa, but he might have been writing about Europe or a place he had never been.

The article about the missionaries and the ransomed slaves was also full of quotations, not from newspapers, but from the mission's archives in Europe. The subject wasn't new to me. At school on the coast we were taught about European expansion in our area as though it had been no more than a defeat of the Arabs and their slave-trading ways. We thought of that as English-school stuff; we didn't mind. History was something dead and gone, part of the world of our grandfathers, and we didn't pay too much attention to it; even though, among trading families like ours, there were still vague stories—so vague that they didn't feel real—of European priests buying slaves cheap from the caravans before they got to the depots on the coast. The Africans (and this was the point of the stories) had been scared out of their skins: they thought the missionaries were buying them in order to eat them.

I had no idea, until I read Raymond's article, that the venture had been so big and serious. Raymond gave the names of all the liberty villages that had been established. Then, quoting and quoting from letters and reports in the archives, he tried to fix the date of the disappearance of each. He gave no reasons and looked for none; he just quoted from the missionary reports. He didn't seem to have gone to any of the places he wrote about; he hadn't tried to talk to anybody. Yet five minutes' talk with some- one like Metty—who, in spite of his coast experience, had trav- elled in terror across the strangeness of the continent—would have told Raymond that the whole pious scheme was cruel and very ignorant, that to set a few unprotected people down in strange territory was to expose them to attack and kidnap and worse. But Raymond didn't seem to know.

He knew so much, had researched so much. He must have spent weeks on each article. But he had less true knowledge of Africa, less feel for it, than Indar or Nazruddin or even Mahesh; he had nothing like Father Huismans's instinct for the strange- ness and wonder of the place. Yet he had made Africa his sub- ject. He had devoted years to those boxes of documents in his study that I had heard about from Indar. Perhaps he had made Africa his subject because he had come to Africa and because he was a scholar, used to working with papers, and had found this place full of new papers.

He had been a teacher in the capital. Chance—in early middle age—had brought him in touch with the mother of the future President. Chance—and something of the teacher's sympathy for the despairing African boy, a sympathy probably mixed with a little bitterness about the more successful of his own kind, the man perhaps seeing himself in the boy: that advice he had given the boy about joining the Defence Force appeared to have in it something of a personal bitterness—chance had given him that extraordinary relationship with the man who became President and had raised him, after independence, to a glory he had never dreamed of.

To Yvette, inexperienced, from Europe, and with her own ambitions, he must have glittered. She would have been misled by her ambitions, much as I had been by her setting, in which I had seen such glamour. Really, then, we did have Raymond in common, from the start.

# T H R E E

## *The Big Man*

### 12

I often thought about the chance that had shown me Yvette for the first time that evening in her house, in that atmosphere of Europe in Africa, when she had worn her black Margit Brandt blouse and had been lighted by the reading lamps placed on the floor, and every kind of yearning had been stirred in me by the voice of Joan Baez.

Perhaps in another setting and at another time she would not have made such an impression on me. And perhaps if I had read Raymond's articles on the day Yvette had given them to me, nothing would have happened the following afternoon when she came to the flat. I wouldn't have given her cause to show me her profile against the white wall of the studio–sitting room; we might instead have simply gone to the Hellenic Club. Seeing her house in the light of midday had already given me a little alarm. To have understood more about Raymond immediately after might have made me see her more clearly—her ambition, her bad judgment, her failure.

And failure like that wasn't what I would have chosen to be entangled with. My wish for an adventure with Yvette was a wish to be taken up to the skies, to be removed from the life I had— the dullness, the pointless tension, "the situation of the country." It wasn't a wish to be involved with people as trapped as myself.

But that was what I had now. And it wasn't open to me to withdraw. After that first afternoon, my first discovery of her, I was possessed by Yvette, possessed by that person I never stopped wanting to win. Satisfaction solved nothing; it only opened up a new void, a fresh need.

The town changed for me. It had new associations. Different memories and moods attached to places, to times of day, weather. In the drawer of my desk in the shop, where Raymond's magazines had once lain forgotten for two days, there were now photographs of Yvette. Some of them were quite old and must have been precious to her. These photographs were her gifts to me, made at various times, as favours, rewards, gestures of tenderness; since, just as we never embraced when we met, never wasted the sense of touch (and in fact seldom kissed), so, as if by unspoken agreement, we continued as we had begun and never exchanged words of tenderness. In spite of the corrupt physical ways our passion had begun to take, the photographs of Yvette that I preferred were the chastest. I was especially interested in those of her as a girl in Belgium, to whom the future was still a mystery.

With these photographs in my drawer, the view from my shop had a different feel: the square with the bedraggled trees, the market stalls, the wandering villagers, the unpaved roads dusty in the sun or running red in the rain. The broken-down town, in which I had felt neutered, became the place where it had all come to me.

With that I developed a new kind of political concern, almost a political anxiety. I could have done without that, but it couldn't be helped. Through Yvette I was bound to Raymond, and through Raymond I was bound more closely than ever to the fact or the knowledge of the President's power. Seeing the President's photograph everywhere had already made me feel that, whether African or not, we had all become his people. To that was now added, because of Raymond, the feeling that we were all dependent on the President and that—whatever job we did and however much we thought we were working for ourselves—we all were serving him.

For that brief moment when I had believed Raymond to be as Indar had described him—the Big Man's white man—I had been thrilled to feel so close to the highest power in the land. I felt I had been taken far above the country I knew and its everyday worries—the mountainous rubbish dumps, bad roads, tricky officials, shanty towns, the people coming in every day from the bush and finding nothing to do and little to eat, the drunkenness, the quick murders, my own shop. Power, and the life around the

President in the capital, had seemed to be what was real and essential about the country.

When I understood what Raymond's position was, the President had once again appeared to zoom away and to be high above us. But now there remained a link with him: the sense of his power as a personal thing, to which we were all attached as with strings, which he might pull or let dangle. That was something I had never felt before. Like other expatriates in the town, I had done what was expected of me. We hung up the official photographs in our shops and offices; we subscribed to the various Presidential funds. But we tried to keep all that as background, separate from our private lives. At the Hellenic Club, for instance, though there was no rule about it, we never talked of local politics.

But now, taken deep into the politics through Raymond and Yvette, and understanding the intent behind each new official photograph, each new statue of the African madonna with child, I could no longer consider statues and photographs as background. I might be told that thousands were owed in Europe to the printers of those photographs; but to understand the President's purpose was to be affected by it. The visitor might snigger about the African madonna; I couldn't.

The news about Raymond's book, the history, was bad: there was no news. Indar, in spite of his promise to find out about the book (and that farewell hand on Yvette's thigh on the steamer), hadn't written. It didn't console Yvette to hear that he hadn't written me either, that he was a man with big problems of his own. It wasn't Indar she was worried about; she wanted news, and long after Indar had left the country she continued to wait for some word from the capital.

Raymond in the meantime had finished his work on the President's speeches and had gone back to his history. He was good at hiding his disappointments and strains. But they were reflected in Yvette. Sometimes when she came to the flat she looked years older than she was, with her young skin looking bleached, the flesh below her chin sagging into the beginning of a double chin, the little wrinkles about her eyes more noticeable.

Poor girl! It wasn't at all what she had expected from a life with Raymond. She was a student in Europe when they had met. He had gone there with an official delegation. His role as the adviser of the man who had recently made himself President was supposed to be secret, but his eminence was generally known and he had been invited to lecture at the university where Yvette was. She had asked a question—she was writing a thesis about the theme of slavery in French African writing. They had met afterwards; she had been overwhelmed by his attentions. Raymond had been married before; but there had been a divorce some years before independence, while he was still a teacher, and his wife and daughter had gone back to Europe.

"They say that men should look at the mother of the girl they intend to marry," Yvette said. "Girls who do what I did should consider the wife a man has discarded or worn out, and know they are not going to do much better. But can you imagine? This handsome and distinguished man—when Raymond took me out to dinner for the first time he took me to one of the most expensive places. He did it all in a very absent-minded way. But he knew the kind of family I came from and he knew exactly what he was doing. He spent more on that dinner than my father earned in a week. I knew it was delegation money, but it didn't matter. Women are stupid. But if women weren't stupid the world wouldn't go round.

"It was wonderful when we came out, I must say that. The President invited us to dinner regularly and for the first two or three times I sat on his right. He said he could do no less for the wife of his old *professeur*—but that wasn't true: Raymond never taught him: that was just for the European press. He was extraordinarily charming, the President, and there was never any hint of nonsense, I should add. The first time we talked about the table, literally. It was made of local wood and carved with African motifs at the edge. Rather horribly, if you want to know. He said the Africans had prodigious skills as wood-carvers and that the country could supply the whole world with high-quality furniture. It was like the recent talk about an industrial park along the river—it was just an idea to talk about. But I was new then and I wanted to believe everything I was told.

"Always there were the cameras. Always the cameras, even in those early days. He was always posing for them; you knew that, and it made conversation difficult. He never relaxed. He always led the conversation. He never let you start a new topic; he simply turned away. The etiquette of royalty—he had learned it from somebody, and I learned it from him, the hard way. He had this very abrupt way of turning away from you; it was like a piece of personal style. And he seemed to enjoy the stylishness of turning and walking straight out of a room at the appointed time.

"We used to go out on tours with him. We appeared in the background in a few of the old official pictures—white people in the background. I noticed that his clothes were changing, but I thought it was only his way of wearing more comfortable clothes, African-style country clothes. Everywhere we went there used to be these welcoming *séances d'animation*, tribal dancing. He was very keen on that. He said he wanted to give dignity to those dances that Hollywood and the West had maligned. He intended to build modern theatres for them. And it was during one of those animations that I got into trouble. He had put his stick on the ground. I didn't know that had a meaning. I didn't know I had to shut up, that in the old days of the chiefs, to talk when that stick was down was something you could be beaten to death for. I was close to him and I said something perfectly banal about the skill of the dancers. He just curled his lips in anger and looked away, lifting up his head. There wasn't any stylishness in that. All the Africans were horrified at what I had done. And I felt that the make-believe had turned horrible and that I had come to a horrible place.

"After that I couldn't appear with him in public. But of course that wasn't why he broke with Raymond. In fact, he was friendlier than ever with Raymond afterwards. He broke with Raymond when he decided that he didn't need him, that in the new direction he was taking the white man was an embarrassment to him in the capital. As for me, he never spoke to me. But he always made a point of sending me his regards, of having some official come to ask how I was getting on. He needs a model in everything, and I believe he heard that de Gaulle used to send personal regards to the wives of his political enemies.

"That was why I thought that if Indar made some inquiries about Raymond's book in the capital, it would get back to him. Everything gets back to the President here. The place is a one-man show, as you know. And I was expecting to get some indirect word. But in all these months he hasn't even sent me his regards."

She suffered more than Raymond appeared to. She was in a country that was still strange to her and she was dangling, doubly dependent. Raymond was in a place that had become his home. He was in a situation that he had perhaps lived through before, when he was a neglected teacher in the colonial capital. Perhaps he had returned to his older personality, the self-containedness he had arrived at as a teacher, the man with the quiet but defiant knowledge of his own worth. But I felt there was something else. I felt that Raymond was consciously following a code he had prescribed for himself, and the fact that he was following this code gave him his serenity.

This code forbade him expressing disappointment or envy. In this he was different from the young men who continued to come to the Domain and called on him and listened to him. Raymond still had his big job; he still had those boxes of papers that many people wanted to look through; and after all his years as the Big Man's white man, all those years as the man who knew more about the country than any man living, Raymond still had a reputation.

When one of these visitors spoke critically about somebody's book or a conference that somebody had organized somewhere (Raymond wasn't invited to conferences these days), Raymond would say nothing, unless he had something good to say about the book or the conference. He would look steadily at the eyes of the visitor, as though only waiting for him to finish. I saw him do this many times; he gave the impression then of hearing out an interruption. Yvette's face would register the surprise or the hurt.

As it did on the evening when I understood, from something one of our visitors said, that Raymond had applied for a job in the United States and had been rejected. The visitor, a bearded man with mean and unreliable eyes, was speaking like a man on Raymond's side. He was even trying to be a little bitter on Raymond's behalf, and this made me feel that he might be one of those visiting scholars Yvette told me about, who, while they were going through Raymond's papers, also took the opportunity of making a pass at her.

Times had changed since the early 1960s, the bearded man said. Africanists were not so rare now, and people who had given their life to the continent were being passed over. The great powers had agreed for the time being not to wrangle over Africa, and as a result attitudes to Africa had changed. The very people who had said that the decade was the decade of Africa, and had scrambled after its great men, were now giving up on Africa.

Yvette lifted her wrist and looked carefully at her watch. It was like a deliberate interruption. She said, "The decade of Africa finished ten seconds ago."

She had done that once before, when someone had spoken of the decade of Africa. And the trick worked again. She smiled; Raymond and I laughed. The bearded man took the hint, and the subject of Raymond's rejected application was left alone.

But I was dismayed by what I had heard, and when Yvette next came to the flat I said, "But you didn't tell me you were thinking of leaving."

"Aren't you thinking of leaving?"

"Eventually, yes."

"Eventually we all have to leave. Your life is settled. You're practically engaged to that man's daughter, you've told me. Everything is just waiting for you. My life is still fluid. I must do something. I just can't stay here."

"But why didn't you tell me?"

"Why talk of something you know isn't going to come off? And it wouldn't do us any good if it got around. You know that. Raymond doesn't stand a chance abroad now anyway."

"Why did he apply, then?"

"I made him. I thought there was a possibility. Raymond wouldn't do a thing like that by himself. He's loyal."

The closeness to the President that had given Raymond his reputation, and had made people call him out to conferences in different parts of the world, now disqualified him from serious consideration abroad. Unless something extraordinary happened, he would have to stay where he was, dependent on the power of the President.

His position in the Domain required him to display authority. But at any moment he might be stripped of this authority, reduced to nothing, with nothing to fall back on. In his place I don't think I would have been able to pretend to have any authority—that would have been the hardest thing for me. I would have just given up, understanding the truth of what Mahesh had told me years before: "Remember, Salim, the people here are *malins*."

But Raymond showed no uncertainty. And he was loyal—to the President, to himself, his ideas and his work, his past. My admiration for him grew. I studied the President's speeches—the daily newspapers were flown up from the capital—for signs that Raymond might be called back to favour. And if I became Raymond's encourager, after Yvette, if I became his champion and promoted him even at the Hellenic Club as the man who hadn't published much but really *knew*, the man every intelligent visitor ought to see, it wasn't only because I didn't want to see him go away, and Yvette with him. I didn't want to see him humiliated. I admired his code and wished that when my own time came I might be able to stick to something like it.

Life in our town was arbitrary enough. Yvette, seeing my life as settled, with everything waiting for me somewhere, had seen her own life as fluid. She felt she wasn't as prepared as the rest of us; she had to look out for herself. That was how we all felt, though: we saw our own lives as fluid, we saw the other man or person as solider. But in the town, where all was arbitrary and the law was what it was, all our lives were fluid. We none of us had certainties of any kind. Without always knowing what we were doing, we were constantly adjusting to the arbitrariness by which we were surrounded. In the end we couldn't say where we stood.

We stood for ourselves. We all had to survive. But because we felt our lives to be fluid we all felt isolated, and we no longer felt accountable to anyone or anything. That was what had happened to Mahesh. "It isn't that there's no right and wrong here. There's no right." That was what had happened to me.

It was the opposite of the life of our family and community on the coast. That life was full of rules. Too many rules; it was a prepacked kind of life. Here I had stripped myself of all the rules. During the rebellion—such a long time ago—I had also discovered that I had stripped myself of the support the rules gave. To think of it like that was to feel myself floating and lost. And I preferred not to think about it: it was too much like the panic you could at any time make yourself feel if you thought hard enough about the physical position of the town in the continent, and your own place in that town.

To see Raymond answering arbitrariness with a code like the one he had worked out for himself seemed to me extraordinary.

When I said so to Yvette she said, "Do you think I would have married someone who was not extraordinary?"

Strange, after all the criticism, or what I had seen as criticism! But everything that was strange in my relationship with Yvette quickly stopped being strange. Everything about the relationship was new to me; I took everything as it came.

With Yvette—and with Yvette and Raymond together—I had acquired a kind of domestic life: the passion in the flat, the quiet family evening in the house in the Domain. The idea that it was my domestic life came to me when the life itself was disturbed. While it went on I simply lived it. And it was only when the life was disturbed that amazement came to me at the coolness with which I had accepted a way of living which, if it had been reported to me about someone else when I was younger, would have seemed awful. Adultery was horrible to me. I continued to think of it in the setting of family and community on the coast, and saw it as sly and dishonourable and weak-willed.

It was Yvette who had suggested, after an afternoon in the flat, that I should have dinner with them that evening in the house. She had done so out of affection, and a concern for my lonely evening; and she seemed not to see any problems. I was nervous; I didn't think I would be able to face Raymond in his house so soon afterwards. But Raymond was in his study when I arrived, and remained there until it was time to eat; and my nervousness disappeared in the novel excitement I felt at seeing Yvette, so recently naked, corrupt with pleasure, in the role of wife.

I sat in the sitting room. She came and went. Those moments were utterly delicious to me. I was stirred by every housewifely gesture; I loved the ordinariness of her clothes. Her movements in her house were brisker, more assertive, her French speech (with Raymond now at the table) more precise. Even while (all anxiety gone) I was listening to Raymond, it was a thrill to me to distance myself from Yvette, to try to see her as a stranger, and then to look through that stranger to the other woman I knew.

On the second or third occasion like this I made her drive back with me to the flat. No subterfuge was necessary: immediately after eating, Raymond had gone back to his study.

Yvette had thought I had only wanted to go for a drive. When she understood what I had in mind she made an exclamation, and her face—so mask-like and housewifely at the dinner table —was transformed with pleasure. All the way to the flat she was close to laughter. I was surprised by her reaction; I had never seen her so easy, so delighted, so relaxed.

She knew she was attractive to men—those visiting scholars drove home that message. But to be desired and needed again after all that had happened during our long afternoon seemed to touch her in a way she hadn't been touched before. She was pleased with me, absurdly pleased with herself, and so companionable that I might have been an old school friend rather than a lover. I tried to put myself in her place, and just for a while I had the illusion of entering her woman's body and mind and understanding her delight. And I thought then, knowing what I did of her life, that I had been given an idea of her own needs and deprivations.

Metty was in. In the old days, following old manners, I had

taken care to keep this side of my life secret from him, or at any rate to appear to be trying to do so. But now secrecy wasn't possible and didn't seem to matter. And we never worried about Metty in the flat again.

What was extraordinary that evening became part of the pattern of many of the days we were together. The dinner with Raymond in the house, or the after-dinner gathering with Raymond, occurred in a kind of parenthesis, between the afternoon in the flat and the late evening in the flat. So that in the house, when Raymond appeared, I was able to listen with a clear mind and real concern to whatever he had to say.

His routine didn't change. He tended to be working in his study when I—and visitors, if there were visitors—arrived. He took his time to appear, and in spite of his absent-minded air his hair was always freshly damped, nicely combed backwards, and he was neatly dressed. His exits, when they were preceded by a little speech, could be dramatic; but his entrances were usually modest.

He liked, especially at after-dinner gatherings, to begin by pretending to be a shy guest in his own house. But it didn't take much to draw him out. Many people wanted to hear about his position in the country and his relations with the President; but Raymond no longer talked about that. He talked instead about his work, and from that he moved on to general intellectual topics. The genius of Theodor Mommsen, the man Raymond said had rewritten the history of Rome, was a favourite theme. I grew to recognize the way Raymond built up to it.

He never avoided making a political comment, but he never raised the subject of politics himself and never became involved in political argument. However critical our guests were of the country, Raymond allowed them to have their say, in that way he had of hearing out an interruption.

Our visitors were becoming increasingly critical. They had a lot to say about the cult of the African madonna. Shrines had been set up—and were being set up—in various places connected with the President's mother, and pilgrimages to these places had been decreed for certain days. We knew about the cult, but in our region we hadn't seen too much of it. The President's mother came from one of the small downriver tribes, far away, and in our town we had only had a few statues in semi-African style, and photographs of shrines and processions. But visitors who had been to the capital had a lot to report, and it was easy enough for them as outsiders to be satirical.

More and more they included us—Raymond and Yvette and people like myself—in their satire. It began to appear that in their eyes we were people not of Africa who had allowed ourselves to be turned into Africans, accepting whatever was decreed for us. Satire like this from people who were just passing through, people we weren't going to see again but did our best for, people who were safe in their own countries, satire like this was sometimes wounding. But Raymond never allowed himself to be provoked.

To one crass man he said, "What you are failing to understand is that this parody of Christianity you talk so warmly about can only make sense to people who are Christians. In fact, that is why, from the President's point of view, it may not be such a good idea. The point of the message may be lost in the parody. Because at the heart of this extraordinary cult is an immense idea about the redemption of the woman of Africa. But this cult, presented as it has been, may antagonize people for different reasons. Its message may be misinterpreted, and the great idea it enshrines may be set back for two or three generations."

That was Raymond—still loyal, trying hard to make sense of events which must have bewildered him. It did him no good; all the labour that went into those thoughts was wasted. No word came from the capital. He and Yvette continued to dangle.

But then, for a month or so, their spirits appeared to lift. Yvette told me that Raymond had reason to believe that his selections from the President's speeches had found favour. I was delighted. It was quite ridiculous; I found myself looking in a different way at the President's pictures. And though no direct word came, Raymond, after being on the defensive for so long, and after all the talking he had had to do about the madonna cult, began to be more argumentative with visitors and to hint, with something of his old verve, that the President had something up his sleeve that would give a new direction to the country. Once or twice he even spoke about the possible publication of a book of the President's speeches, and its effect on the people.

The book was published. But it wasn't the book Raymond had worked on, not the book of longish extracts with a linking commentary. It was a very small, thin book of thoughts, *Maximes*, two or three thoughts to a page, each thought about four or five lines long.

Stacks of the book came to our town. They appeared in every bar and shop and office. My shop got a hundred; Mahesh got a hundred and fifty at Bigburger; the Tivoli got a hundred and fifty. Every pavement huckster got a little stock—five or ten: it depended on the commissioner. The books weren't free; we had to buy them at twenty francs a copy in multiples of five. The commissioner had to send the money for his entire consignment back to the capital, and for a fortnight or so, big man as he was, he ran around everywhere with his Land-Rover full of *Maximes*, trying to place them.

The Youth Guard used up a lot of its stock on one of its Saturday-afternoon children's marches. These marches were hurried, ragged affairs—blue shirts, hundreds of busy little legs, white canvas shoes, some of the smaller children frantic, close to tears, regularly breaking into a run to keep up with their district group, everybody anxious to get to the end and then to get back home, which could be many miles away.

The march with the President's booklet was raggeder than usual. The afternoon was overcast and heavy, after early morning rain; and the mud in the streets, drying out, had reached the nasty stage where bicycles and even footsteps caused it to fly about in sticky lumps and pellets. Mud stained the children's canvas shoes red and looked like wounds on their black legs.

The children were meant to hold up the President's book as they marched and to shout the long African name the President had given himself. But the children hadn't been properly drilled;

the shouts were irregular; and since the clouds had rolled over black, and it looked as though it was going to rain again soon, the marchers were in a greater hurry than usual. They just held the little book and scampered in the gloom, spattering one another with mud, shouting only when the Youth Guard shouted at them.

The marches were already something of a joke to our people, and this didn't help. Most people, even people from the deep bush, understood what the madonna cult was about. But I don't think anyone in the squares or the market had any idea what the *Maximes* march was about. I don't think, to tell the truth, that even Mahesh knew what it referred to or was modelled on, until he was told.

So *Maximes* failed with us. And it must have been so in other parts of the country as well, because shortly after reporting the great demand for the book, the newspapers dropped the subject.

Raymond, speaking of the President, said: "He knows when to pull back. That has always been one of his great virtues. No one understands better than he the cruel humour of his people. And he may finally decide that he is being badly advised."

Raymond was still waiting, then. In what I had seen as his code I began to recognize a stubbornness and something like vanity. But Yvette now didn't even bother to conceal her impatience. She was bored with the subject of the President. Raymond might have nowhere else to go. But Yvette was restless. And that was a bad sign for me.

# 13

Mahesh was my friend. But I thought of him as a man who had been stunted by his relationship with Shoba. That had been achievement enough for him. Shoba admired him and needed him, and he was therefore content with himself, content with the person she admired. His only wish seemed to be to take care of this person. He dressed for her, preserved his looks for her. I used to think that when Mahesh considered himself physically he didn't compare himself with other men, or judge himself according to some masculine ideal, but saw only the body that pleased Shoba. He saw himself as his woman saw him; and that was why, though he was my friend, I thought that his devotion to Shoba had made him half a man, and ignoble.

I had longed myself for an adventure, for passion and physical fulfilment, but I never thought that it would take me in that way, that all my idea of my own worth would be bound up with the way a woman responded to me. But that was how it was. All my self-esteem came from being Yvette's lover, from serving her and pleasing her in the physical way I did.

That was my pride. It was also my shame, to have reduced my manhood just to that. There were times, especially during slack periods in the shop, when I sat at my desk (Yvette's photographs in the drawer) and found myself mourning. Mourning, in the midst of a physical fulfilment which could not have been more complete! There was a time when I wouldn't have thought it possible.

And so much had come to me through Yvette. I had got to know so much more. I had lost the expatriate businessman's way of not appearing to take too much notice of things, which could end up in genuine backwardness. I had been given so many ideas about history, political power, other continents. But with all my new knowledge, my world was narrower than it had ever been. In events around me—like the publication of the President's book, and the book march—I looked only to see whether the life I had with Yvette was threatened or was going to go on. And the narrower my world became, the more obsessively I lived in it.

Even so, it was a shock when I heard that Noimon had sold up and left, to go to Australia. Noimon was our biggest businessman, the Greek with a finger in every pie. He had come out to the country as a very young man at the end of the war to work on one of the Greek coffee plantations in the deep bush. Though speaking only Greek when he came, he had done very well very quickly, acquiring plantations of his own and then a furniture business in the town. Independence had appeared to wipe him out; but he had stayed put. At the Hellenic Club—which he treated like his private charity, and ruled, having kept it going through very bad times—he used to say that the country was his home.

All during the boom Noimon had been reinvesting and expanding; at one time he had offered Mahesh a lot of money for the Bigburger property. He had a way with officials and was good at getting government contracts (he had furnished the houses in the Domain). And now he had sold up secretly to some of the newfangled state trading agencies in the capital. We could only guess at the foreign-exchange ins and outs, and the hidden beneficiaries, of that deal; the newspaper in the capital announced it as a kind of nationalization, with fair compensation.

His departure left us all feeling a little betrayed. We also felt foolish, caught out. Anybody can be decisive during a panic; it takes a strong man to act during a boom. And Nazruddin had warned me. I remembered his little lecture about the difference between the businessman and the man who was really only a mathematician. The businessman bought at ten and was happy to get out at twelve; the mathematician saw his ten rise to eighteen, but didn't sell because he wanted to double his ten to twenty.

I had done better than that. What (using Nazruddin's scale) I had bought at two I had taken over the years to twenty. But now, with Noimon's departure, it had dropped to fifteen.

Noimon's departure marked the end of our boom, the end of confidence. We all knew that. But at the Hellenic Club—where only a fortnight before, throwing dust in our eyes, Noimon had been talking in his usual practical way about improving the swimming pool—we put a brave face on things.

I heard it said that Noimon had sold up only for the sake of his children's education; it was also said that he had been pressured by his wife (Noimon was rumoured to have a second, half-African family). And then it began to be said that Noimon would regret his decision. Copper was copper, the boom was going to go on, and while the Big Man was in charge, everything would keep on running smoothly. Besides, though Australia and Europe and North America were nice places to visit, life there wasn't as rosy as some people thought—and Noimon, after a lifetime in Africa, was going to find that out pretty soon. We lived better where we were, with servants and swimming pools, luxuries that only millionaires had in those other places.

It was a lot of nonsense. But they had to say what they said, though that point about the swimming pools was especially stupid, because in spite of the foreign technicians our water supply system had broken down. The town had grown too fast, and too many people were still coming in; in the shanty towns the emergency standpipes used to run all day long; and water was now rationed everywhere. Some of the swimming pools—and we didn't have so many—had been drained. In some the filtering machinery had simply been turned off—economy or inexperience—and those pools had become choked with brilliant green algae and wilder growths, and looked like poisonous forest ponds. But the swimming pools existed, whatever their condition, and people could talk about them as they did because here we liked the idea of the swimming pool better than the thing itself. Even when the pools worked they hadn't been used much; it was as if we hadn't yet learned to fit this bothersome luxury into our day-to-day life.

I reported the Hellenic Club chatter back to Mahesh, expecting him to share my attitude or at least to see the joke, bad as the joke was for us.

But Mahesh didn't see the joke. He, too, made the point about the superior quality of our life in the town.

He said, "I'm glad Noimon has gone. Let him get a taste of the good life out there. I hope he relishes it. Shoba has some Ismaili friends in London. They're having a *very* nice taste of the life over there. It isn't all Harrods. They've written to Shoba. Ask her. She will tell you about her London friends. What they call a big house over there would be like a joke to us here. You've seen the salesmen at the van der Weyden. That's expenses. Ask them how they live back home. None of them live as well as I live here."

I thought later that it was the "I" in Mahesh's last sentence that offended me. Mahesh could have put it better. That "I" gave me a glimpse of what had enraged Indar about his lunch with Mahesh and Shoba. Indar had said: "They don't know who I am or what I've done. They don't even know where I've been." He had seen what I hadn't seen: it was news to me that Mahesh thought he was living "well," in the way he meant.

I hadn't noticed any great change in his style. He and Shoba still lived in their concrete flat with the sitting room full of shiny things. But Mahesh wasn't joking. Standing in his nice clothes by his imported coffee machine in his franchise-given shop, he really thought he was something, successful and complete, really thought he had made it and had nowhere higher to go. Bigburger and the boom—and Shoba, always there—had destroyed his sense of humour. And I used to think of him as a fellow survivor!

But it wasn't for me to condemn him or the others. I was like them. I, too, wanted to stay with what I had; I, too, hated the idea that I might have been caught. I couldn't say, as they did, that all was still for the best. But that, in effect, was my attitude. The very fact that the boom had passed its peak, that confidence had been shaken, became for me a good enough reason for doing nothing. That was how I explained the position to Nazruddin when he wrote from Uganda.

Nazruddin hardly wrote. But he was still gathering experience, his mind was still ticking over; and though his letters made me nervous before I opened them, I always read them with pleasure, because over and above his personal news there was always some new general point that Nazruddin wanted to make. We were still so close to our shock about Noimon that I thought, when Metty brought the letter from the post office, that the letter was going to be about Noimon or about the prospects for copper. But it was about Uganda. They were having their problems there too.

Things were bad in Uganda, Nazruddin wrote. The army people who had taken over had appeared to be all right at first, but now there were clear signs of tribal and racial troubles. And these troubles weren't just going to blow over. Uganda was beautiful, fertile, easy, without poverty, and with high African traditions. It ought to have had a future, but the problem with Uganda was that it wasn't big enough. The country was now too small for its tribal hatreds. The motorcar and modern roads had made the country too small; there would always be trouble. Every tribe felt more threatened in its territory now than in the days when everybody, including traders from the coast like our grandfathers, went about on foot, and a single trading venture could take up to a year. Africa, going back to its old ways with modern tools, was going to be a difficult place for some time. It was better to read the signs right than to hope that things would work out.

So for the third time in his life Nazruddin was thinking of moving and making a fresh start, this time out of Africa, in Canada. "But my luck is running out. I can see it in my hand."

The letter, in spite of its disturbing news, was in Nazruddin's old, calm style. It offered no direct advice and made no direct requests. But it was a reminder—as it was intended to be, especially at this time of upheaval for him—of my bargain with Nazruddin, my duty to his family and mine. It deepened my panic. At the same time it strengthened my resolve to stay and do nothing.

I replied in the way I have said, outlining our new difficulties in the town. I took some time to reply, and when I did I found myself writing passionately, offering Nazruddin the picture of myself as someone incompetent and helpless, one of his "mathematicians." And nothing that I wrote wasn't true. I was as helpless as I presented myself. I didn't know where I could go on to. I didn't think—after what I had seen of Indar and other people in the Domain—that I had the talent or the skills to survive in another country.

And it was as if I had been caught out by my own letter. My panic grew, and my guilt, and my feeling that I was provoking my own destruction. And out of this, out of a life which I felt to be shrinking and which became more obsessed as it shrank, I began to question myself. Was I possessed by Yvette? Or was I—like Mahesh with his new idea of what he was—possessed by

myself, the man I thought I was with Yvette? To serve her in the
way I did, it was necessary to look outward from myself. Yet it
was in this selflessness that my own fulfilment lay; I doubted,
after my brothel life, whether I could be a man in that way with
any other woman. She gave me the idea of my manliness I had
grown to need. Wasn't my attachment to her an attachment to
that idea?

And oddly involved with this idea of myself, and myself and
Yvette, was the town itself—the flat, the house in the Domain,
the way both our lives were arranged, the absence of a community, the isolation in which we both lived. In no other place
would it be just like this; and perhaps in no other place would
our relationship be possible. The question of continuing it in
another place never arose. That whole question of another place
was something I preferred not to think about.

The first time she had come back to the flat after dinner at the
house I felt I had been given some idea of her own needs, the
needs of an ambitious woman who had married young and come
out to the wrong country, cutting herself off. I had never felt I
could meet those needs. I had grown to accept, and be excited
by, the idea that I was an encumbrance that had become a habit.
Perhaps she was for me too. But I had no means of finding out
and didn't particularly want to. The isolation that kept me obsessed had become something I saw as necessary.

In time it would all go; we would both return to our interrupted lives. That was no tragedy. That certainty of the end—
even while the boom slackened and my fifteen dropped to fourteen, and Nazruddin and his uprooted family tried to establish
themselves in Canada—was my security.

Quite suddenly, Shoba left us to go and visit her family in the
east. Her father had died. She had gone for the cremation.

I was surprised when Mahesh told me. Not by the death, but
by the fact that Shoba could go back to her family. That wasn't
at all what I had been led to believe. Shoba had presented herself
as a runaway, someone who had gone against the rules of her

community by marrying Mahesh, and was living in this remote place to hide from her family's vengeance.

When she had first told me her story—it had been at lunch on a still, silent day during the rebellion—she had said that she had to be cautious with strangers. It had occurred to her that her family might hire someone, of any race, to do what they had threatened: to disfigure her or to kill Mahesh. Acid on the face of the woman, the killing of the man—they were the standard family threats on these occasions, and Shoba, conventional in so many ways, wasn't too displeased to let me know that the threats had been made in her case. Usually these threats were meaningless, and made only to satisfy convention; but sometimes they could be carried out to the letter. However, as time passed, and Shoba appeared to be forgetting some of the details of her first story, I stopped believing in that drama of the hired stranger. But I took it as settled that Shoba had been disowned by her family.

In my own predicament I had always been conscious of Shoba's example, and it was a letdown to discover that she had kept her lines of communication open. As for Mahesh, he began to behave like the mourning son-in-law. It might have been his way of making a public drama out of the business, taking expensive orders for coffee and beer and Bigburgers (the prices these days!) with an air of tenderness and sorrow. It might have been his way of showing sympathy for Shoba and respect for the dead. But it was also a little bit like the behaviour of a man who felt he had at last earned his place. Well!

But then the joke turned sour. Shoba was to have been away for two months. She returned after three weeks, and then she seemed to go into hiding. There were no invitations to me to lunch; that arrangement—almost that tradition now—at last came to an end. She had hated the political situation in the east, Mahesh said. She had never liked Africans and had come back raging about thieving and boastful politicians, the incessant lies and hate on the radio and in the newspapers, the bag-snatchings in daylight, the nightly violence. She was appalled by the position of her family, whom she had grown up thinking of as solid and secure. All this, combined with her grief for her father, had made her strange. It was better for the time being, Mahesh said, for me to stay away.

But that hardly seemed explanation enough. Was there something more than political and racial rage, and grief for the father whom at one time she had shamed? Was there perhaps a new vision of the man she had chosen and the life she had been living? Some regret for the family life she now saw she had missed, some greater grief for the things she had betrayed?

The air of mourning that Mahesh, in Shoba's absence, had been so glad to put on became a deep and real gloom after Shoba's return; and then this gloom became shot through with irritations. He began to show his age. The confidence, which had irritated me, left him. I grieved for it, grieved that he should have enjoyed it for so short a time. And he, who had spoken so sharply about Noimon, and spoken with such pride about the way he lived here, now said, "It's junk, Salim. It's all turning to junk again."

No longer able to lunch with them or visit their flat, I took to dropping in at Bigburger on some evenings to exchange a few words with Mahesh. One evening I saw Shoba there.

She was sitting at the counter, against the wall, and Mahesh was sitting on the stool next to hers. They were like customers in their own place.

I greeted Shoba, but there was no warmth in her acknowledgment. I might have been a stranger or someone she barely knew. And even when I sat down next to Mahesh she continued to be distant. She seemed not to be seeing me. And Mahesh appeared not to notice. Was she rebuking me for those things she had grown to condemn in herself?

I had known them both for so long. They were part of my life, however much my feelings about them shifted about. I could see the tightness and pain and something like illness in Shoba's eyes. I could also see she was acting a little. Still, I was hurt. And when I left them—no cry of "Stay!" from either of them—I felt cast out and slightly dazed. And every familiar detail of street life at night—the cooking fires gilding the thin, exhausted-looking faces of the people who sat around them, the groups in the shadows below the shop awnings, the sleepers and their boundary markers, the ragged lost lunatics, the lights of a bar fanning out over a wooden walkway—everything had a different quality.

A radio was on in the flat. It was unusually loud, and as I went up the external staircase I had the impression that Metty was listening to a football match commentary from the capital. An echoing voice was varying its pace and pitch, and there was the roar of a crowd. Metty's door was open and he was sitting in pants and undershirt on the edge of his cot. The light from the central hanging bulb in his room was yellow and dim; the radio was deafening.

Looking up at me, then looking down again, concentrating, Metty said, "The President."

That was clear, now that I had begun to follow the words. It explained why Metty felt he didn't have to turn the radio down. The speech had been announced; I had forgotten.

The President was talking in the African language that most people who lived along the river understood. At one time the President's speeches were in French. But in this speech the only French words were *citoyens* and *citoyennes*, and they were used again and again, for musical effect, now run together into a rippling phrase, now called out separately, every syllable spaced, to create the effect of a solemn drumbeat.

The African language the President had chosen for his speeches was a mixed and simple language, and he simplified it further, making it the language of the drinking booth and the street brawl, converting himself, while he spoke, this man who kept everybody dangling and imitated the etiquette of royalty and the graces of de Gaulle, into the lowest of the low. And that was the attraction of the African language in the President's mouth. That regal and musical use of the lowest language and the coarsest expressions was what was holding Metty.

Metty was absorbed. His eyes, below the yellow highlights on his forehead, were steady, small, intent. His lips were compressed and in his concentration he kept working them. When the coarse expressions or the obscenities occurred, and the crowd roared, Metty laughed without opening his mouth.

The speech, so far, was like many others the President had made. The themes were not new: sacrifice and the bright future; the dignity of the woman of Africa; the need to strengthen the revolution, unpopular though it was with those black men in the towns who dreamed of waking up one day as white men; the need for Africans to be African, to go back without shame to their democratic and socialist ways, to rediscover the virtues of the diet and medicines of their grandfathers and not to go running like children after things in imported tins and bottles; the need for vigilance, work and, above all, discipline.

This was how, while appearing just to restate old principles, the President also acknowledged and ridiculed new criticism, whether it was of the madonna cult or of the shortage of food and medicines. He always acknowledged criticism, and he often anticipated it. He made everything fit; he could suggest he knew everything. He could make it appear that everything that was happening in the country, good or bad or ordinary, was part of a bigger plan.

People liked to listen to the President's speeches because so much was familiar; like Metty now, they waited for the old jokes. But every speech was also a new performance, with its own dramatic devices; and every speech had a purpose. This speech was of particular concern to our town and region. That was what the President said, and it became one of the dramatic devices of the later part of the speech: he broke off again and again to say that he had something to say to the people of our town and region, but we had to wait for it. The crowd in the capital, recognizing the device as a device, a new piece of style, began to roar when they saw it coming.

We in the region liked our beer, the President said. He liked it better; he could outdrink anyone of us any day. But we mustn't get pissed too soon; he had something to say to us. And it was known that the statement the President was going to make was about our Youth Guard. For a fortnight or more we had been waiting for this statement; for a fortnight he had kept the whole town dangling.

The Youth Guard had never recovered their prestige after the failure of the book march. Their children's marches on Saturday afternoons had grown raggeder and thinner, and the officers had found that they had no means of compelling children to take part. They had kept on with the Morals Patrol. But the nighttime crowds were now more hostile; and one evening an officer of the Guard had been killed.

It had begun as a squabble with some pavement sleepers who had barred off a stretch of pavement in a semi-permanent way with concrete blocks looted from a building site. And it could easily have ended as a shouting match, no more. But the officer had stumbled and fallen. By that fall, that momentary appearance of helplessness, he had invited the first blow with one of the concrete blocks; and the sight of blood then had encouraged a sudden, frenzied act of murder by dozens of small hands.

No one had been arrested. The police were nervous; the Youth Guard were nervous; the people of the streets were nervous. There was talk a few days later that the army was going to be sent in to beat up some of the shanty towns. That had caused a little scuttle back to the villages; the dugouts had been busy. But nothing had happened. Everyone had been waiting to see what the President would do. But for more than a fortnight the President had said and done nothing.

And what the President said now was staggering. The Youth Guard in our region was to be disbanded. They had forgotten their duty to the people; they had broken faith with him, the President; they had talked too much. The officers would lose their stipend; there would be no government jobs for any of them; they would be banished from the town and sent back to the bush, to do constructive work there. In the bush they would learn the wisdom of the monkey.

"*Citoyens-citoyennes*, monkey smart. Monkey smart like shit. Monkey can talk. You didn't know that? Well, I tell you now. Monkey can talk, but he keep it quiet. Monkey know that if he talk in front of man, man going to catch him and beat him and make him work. Make him carry load in hot sun. Make him paddle boat. *Citoyens! Citoyennes!* We will teach these people to be like monkey. We will send them to the bush and let them work their arse off."

# 14

〰〰 It was the Big Man's way. He chose his time, and what 〰〰 looked like a challenge to his authority served in the end to underline his authority. He showed himself again as the friend of the people, the *petit peuple*, as he liked to call them, and he punished their oppressors.

But the Big Man hadn't visited our town. Perhaps, as Raymond said, the reports he had been receiving were inaccurate or incomplete. And this time something went wrong. We had all thought of the Youth Guard as a menace, and everybody was happy to see them go. But it was after the disbanding of the Youth Guard that things began to get bad in our town.

The police and other officials became difficult. They took to tormenting Metty whenever he took the car out, even on the short run to the customs. He was stopped again and again, sometimes by people he knew, sometimes by people who had stopped him before, and the car's documents were checked, and his own papers. Sometimes he had to leave the car where it was and walk back to the shop to get some certificate or paper he didn't have. And it didn't help if he had all the papers.

Once, for no reason at all, he was taken to police headquarters, fingerprinted and—in the company of other dispirited people who had been picked up—made to spend a whole afternoon with blackened hands in a room with backless wooden benches, a broken concrete floor and blue distempered walls grimy and shining from the heads and shoulders that had rubbed against them.

The room, from which I rescued him late in the afternoon, having spent a lot of time tracking him down, was in a rough concrete and corrugated-iron shed at the back of the main colonial building. The floor was just a few inches above the ground; the door was open, and chickens were scratching about in the bare yard. But rough and homely and full of afternoon light as it was, the room hinted at the jail. The one table and chair belonged to the officer in charge, and these scrappy pieces of furniture emphasized the deprivation of everybody else.

The officer was sweating under the arms in his over-starched uniform, and he was writing very slowly in a ledger, shaping one letter at a time, apparently entering details from the blotched fingerprint sheets. He had a revolver. There was a photograph of the President showing his chief's stick; and above it on the blue wall, high up, where the uneven surface was dusty rather than grimy, was painted *Discipline Avant Tout*—"Discipline Above All."

I didn't like that room, and I thought it would be better after that for Metty not to use the car and for me to be my own customs clerk and broker. But then the officials turned their attention to me.

They dug up old customs declaration forms, things that had been sealed and settled in the standard way long ago, and brought them to the shop and waved them in my face like unredeemed IOUs. They said they were under pressure from their superiors and wanted to go through certain details with me again. At first they were shy, like wicked schoolboys; then they were conspiratorial, like friends wanting to do me a secret good turn; then they were aggressive, like wicked officials. Others wanted to check my stock against my customs declarations and my sales receipts; others said they wanted to investigate my prices.

It was harassment, and the purpose was money, and money fast, before everything changed. These men had sniffed some change coming; in the disbanding of the Youth Guard they had seen signs of the President's weakness rather than strength. And in this situation there was no one I could appeal to. Every official was willing, for a consideration, to give assurances about his own conduct. But no official was high enough or secure enough to guarantee the conduct of any other official.

Everything in the town was as it had been—the army was in

its barracks, the photographs of the President were everywhere, the steamer came up regularly from the capital. But men had lost or rejected the idea of an overseeing authority, and everything was again as fluid as it had been at the beginning. Only this time, after all the years of peace and goods in all the shops, everyone was greedier.

What was happening to me was happening to every other foreign businessman. Even Noimon, if he had still been around, would have suffered. Mahesh was gloomier than ever. He said, "I always say: You can hire them, but you can't buy them." It was one of his sayings; it meant that stable relationships were not possible here, that there could only be day-to-day contracts between men, that in a crisis peace was something you had to buy afresh every day. His advice was to stick it out. And there was nothing else we could do.

My own feeling—my secret comfort during this time—was that the officials had misread the situation and that their frenzy was self-induced. Like Raymond, I had grown to believe in the power wisdom of the President, and was confident he would do something to reassert his authority. So I prevaricated and didn't pay, seeing no end to paying if I should start.

But the patience of the officials was greater than mine. It is no exaggeration to say that not a day passed now without some official calling. I began to wait for their calls. It was bad for my nerves. In the middle of the afternoon, if no one had yet called, I could find myself sweating. I grew to hate, and fear, those smiling *malin* faces pushed up close to mine in mock familiarity and helpfulness.

And then the pressure eased. Not because the President acted, as I had been hoping. But because violence had come to our town. Not the evening drama of street brawls and murders, but a steady, nightly assault in different areas on policemen and police stations and officials and official buildings.

It was this, no doubt, that the officials had seen coming, and I hadn't. This was what had made them greedy to grab as much as they could while they could. One night the statue of the African madonna and child in the Domain was knocked off its pedestal and smashed, as the colonial statues had once been smashed, and the monument outside the dock gates. After this the officials began to make themselves scarce. They stayed away from the shop; they had too many other things to do. And though I couldn't say things were better, yet the violence came as a relief and for a while, to me as well as to the people I saw in the streets and squares, was even exhilarating, the way a big fire or a storm can be exhilarating.

In our overgrown, overpopulated, unregulated town we had had any number of violent outbursts. There had been riots about water, and on many occasions in the shanty towns there had been riots when someone had been killed by a car. In what was happening now there was still that element of popular frenzy; but it was also clear that it was more organized, or that at least it had some deeper principle. Some prophecy, perhaps, had been making the rounds of the *cités* and shanty towns and had found confirmation in the dreams of various people. It was the kind of thing the officials would have got wind of.

One morning, when he brought me coffee, Metty, looking serious, gave me a piece of newsprint, folded small and carefully, and dirty along the outer creases. It was a printed leaflet and had obviously been folded and unfolded many times. It was headlined "The Ancestors Shriek," and was issued by something called the Liberation Army.

The ANCESTORS shriek. Many false gods have come to this land, but none have been as false as the gods of today. The cult of the woman of Africa kills all our mothers, and since war is an extension of politics we have decided to face the ENEMY with armed confrontation. Otherwise we all die forever. The ancestors are shrieking. If we are not deaf we can hear them. By ENEMY we mean the powers of imperialism, the multi-nationals and the puppet powers that be, the false gods, the capitalists, the priests and teachers who give false interpretations. The law encourages crime. The schools teach ignorance and people practise ignorance in preference to their true culture. Our soldiers and guardians have been given false desires and false greeds and the foreigners now qualify us everywhere as thieves. We are ignorant of ourselves and mislead ourselves. We are marching to death. We have forgotten the TRUTHFUL LAWS. We of the LIBERATION ARMY have received no education. We do not print books and make speeches. We only know the TRUTH, and we acknowledge this land as the land of the people whose ancestors now shriek over it. OUR PEOPLE must understand the struggle. They must learn to die with us.

Metty said he didn't know where the leaflet came from. Somebody had just given it to him the night before. I thought he knew more than he said, but I didn't press him.

We didn't have many printeries in the town, and it was clear to me that the leaflet—very badly printed, the type broken and mixed—came from the printing shop that used to do the weekly newspaper of the Youth Guard. That, while it lasted, had been our only local paper, and it was a nonsense sheet—like the wall newspaper of a school, with meaningless advertisements from traders and businessmen and even stall holders in the market, and a few items of so-called news (more like open blackmail) about people breaking traffic rules or using government vehicles as night taxis or building shacks where they shouldn't.

Still, it was very strange. The officers of the Youth Guard, while they had been serving the President, had been hateful to the people they tried to police. Now, humiliated by the President in that "monkey" speech, stripped of power and jobs, they offered themselves to the people as humiliated and anguished men of the region, as defenders of the people of the region. And the people were responding.

It was like the time before the rebellion. But there had been no leaflets then, no leaders as young and educated as these. And there was something else. At the time of the rebellion the town was just beginning to be re-established, and the first disturbances took place far away, in the villages. Now everything was happening in the town itself. There was a lot more blood as a result; and the violence, which at first seemed directed against the authorities alone, became more general. African stalls and shops in the outer areas were attacked and looted. People began to be killed in horrible ways, by rioters and police and shanty town criminals.

Africans and the outer areas first, foreigners and the centre later—that was the way I saw things happening here. So that, having just been freed from a kind of official blackmail against which there was no appeal, I once again had to think of myself as exposed, with nothing to hold on to. I took this fear with me into the familiar streets, this feeling that I was now physically vulnerable. The streets had always been dangerous. But not for me. As an outsider I had so far been allowed to be separate from the violence I observed.

The strain was great. It corrupted everything, and for the first time I considered the idea of flight. If there had been a safe house waiting for me in some far city which would have allowed me in, I believe I might have left during this time. Once there was such a house; once there were several such houses. But there was no such house now. The news from Nazruddin was disheartening. His year in Canada had been bad, and he was uprooting his family yet again, and going to England. The outside world no longer offered refuge; it had remained for me the great unknown and was, increasingly, perilous. What I had once falsely written to Nazruddin had come true. I was in no position to act. I had to stay where I was.

And, forgetting goals, I kept on, living my life: I had learned that years ago from Mahesh. And more and more it happened, in my dealings with people I knew well, that I forgot to study their faces, forgot my fear. In this way fear, the feeling that everything could at any moment go, became background, a condition of life, something you had to accept. And I was made almost calm by something a German from the capital, a man in his late fifties, said to me at the Hellenic Club one afternoon.

He said, "In a situation like this you can't spend all your time being frightened. Something may happen, but you must make yourself think of it as a bad road accident. Something outside your control, that can happen anywhere."

Time passed. No explosion came, no cataclysm such as I had been expecting at the beginning. Fires didn't burn in the centre; the rebels' means were limited. The assaults and killings continued; the police made their retaliatory raids; and something like a balance was achieved. Two or three people were killed every night. But, strangely, it all began to seem far away. The very size and unregulated sprawl of the town muffled all but the most extraordinary events; people in the streets and squares no longer waited for news. News, in fact, was scarce. The President made no statement, and nothing was reported on the radio or in the newspapers from the capital.

In the centre of the town life went on as before. The businessman who came in from the capital by air or by the steamer and put up at the van der Weyden, and went to the better-known restaurants and nightclubs and asked no questions, would not have guessed that the town was in a state of insurrection, that the insurrection had its leaders and—though their names were known only in their own districts—its martyrs.

For some time Raymond had been like a stunned man. At some moment he seemed to have decided that he wasn't going to be called back to the President's favour, and he had stopped waiting, stopped reading the signs. At dinner in the house he no longer analyzed or explained events; he no longer tried to make the pieces fit together.

He didn't talk about history or about Theodor Mommsen. I didn't know what he was doing in his study, and Yvette couldn't tell me; she wasn't too interested. At one time I got the impression that he was reading old things he had written. He mentioned a diary he had kept when he had first come out to the country. He had forgotten so many things, he said; so many things were doomed to be forgotten. That used to be one of his dinner-table themes; he seemed to recognize that, and broke off. Later he said, "Strange, reading those diaries. In those days you used to scratch yourself to see whether you bled."

The insurrection added to his confusion; and after the madonna statue in the Domain had been smashed he became very nervous. It wasn't the President's habit to appear to support those of his men who had been attacked; he tended to dismiss them. And Raymond now lived in fear of dismissal. This was what it had come down to for him—a job, a house, his livelihood, simple security. He was a defeated man, and the house in the Domain was like a house of death.

The loss was mine as well. That house was important to me; and much, as I now saw, depended on the health and optimism of both the people who lived in it. A defeated Raymond made nonsense of my evenings there. Those evenings in the house were part of my relationship with Yvette; they couldn't simply be transferred to another site. That would have meant a new geography, another kind of town, another kind of relationship, not the one I had.

My life with Yvette depended on the health and optimism of all three of us. I was astonished by this discovery. I had discovered it first about myself, when I was under pressure from the officials. I wanted to hide from her then. I felt I could go to her, and be with her in the way I wanted, only in strength, as I had always gone to her. I couldn't present myself to her as a man tormented and weakened by other men. She had her own cause for restlessness; I knew that, and I couldn't bear the idea of the lost coming together for comfort.

It was at this time—as though we understood one another—that we began to space out our meetings. The first days without Yvette, the first days of solitude, subsiding excitement and clear vision, were always a relief. I could even pretend that I was a free man and that it was possible to do without her.

Then she would telephone. The knowledge that I was still needed would be like satisfaction enough, and would be converted, while I waited for her in the flat, into irritation and self-disgust, which would continue right up to the moment when, after pattering up the external staircase, she came into the sitting room, all the strain of Raymond and the intervening days showing on her face. Then very soon, in my own mind, the intervening days would drop away; time would telescope. Physically now I knew her so well; one occasion would very soon seem linked to the last.

But that idea of continuity, however overpowering at those intimate, narrow moments, was an illusion, as I knew. There were the hours and days in her house, with Raymond; there was her own privacy, and her own search. She had less and less news. There were events now we didn't share, and there were fewer things that could be told me without some gloss or explanation.

She telephoned me now every ten days. Ten days seemed to be the limit beyond which she couldn't go. It occurred to me on one of these days—when, the big foam bed already straightened, she was making up her face and considering parts of herself in the dressing table mirror, before going back to the Domain—it occurred to me then that there was something bloodless about our relationship just at that moment. I might have been a complaisant father or husband, or even a woman friend, watching her prepare herself for a lover.

An idea like that is like a vivid dream, fixing a fear we don't want to acknowledge, and having the effect of a revelation. I suppose that, thinking of my own harassment and Raymond's defeat, I had begun to consider Yvette a defeated person as well, trapped in the town, as sick of herself and the wasting asset of her body as I was sick of myself and my anxieties. Now, looking at Yvette in front of the dressing table mirror, seeing her bright with more than I had just given her, I saw how wrong I had been. Those blank days when she was away from me, those days about which I didn't inquire, would have been full of possibilities for her. I began to wait for confirmation. And then, two meetings later, I thought I found it.

I knew her so well. With her, even now, I had never ceased to look outward from myself. No other way would have had meaning, no other way would have been possible. What she drew out of me remained extraordinary to me. Her responses were part of the gift, and I had grown used to them as they had developed; I had learned to gauge them finely. On each occasion I was aware of her sensual memory of me beginning to work, linking the present to the past. But now, on the occasion I speak of, her responses were confused. Something had intervened; some new habit had begun to form, breaking up the delicate membrane of older memory. It was what I had been expecting. It had to be, one day. But the moment was like poison.

Afterwards came that bloodless interlude. The big foam bed had been made up—that housewifely service still, after what used to be passion. I was standing. She was standing too, considering her lips in the mirror.

She said, "You make me look so good. What will I do without you?" That was a standard courtesy. But then she said, "Raymond will want to make love to me when he sees me looking like this." And that was unusual, not like her at all.

I said, "Does it excite you?"

"Older men are not as repulsive as you seem to think. And I am a woman, after all. If a man does certain things to me, I react."

She didn't mean to wound me, but she did. And then I thought: But she's probably right. Raymond's like a whipped boy. It's all he can turn to now.

I said, "I suppose we've made him suffer."

"Raymond? I don't know. I don't think so. He's never given any sign. Of course, he may tell himself something different now."

I walked with her to the landing: the shadow of the house over the yard, the trees above the houses and the wooden outbuildings, the golden afternoon light, the dust in the air, the flamboyant blooms, the cooking smoke. She hurried down the wooden steps to where the sunlight, slanting between the houses, struck full on her. Then, above the noises of the surrounding yards, I heard her drive off.

And it was only some days later that I thought how strange it was for us to have talked of Raymond at that moment. I had talked of Raymond's pain when I was thinking of my own, and Yvette had talked of Raymond's needs when she was thinking of her own. We had begun to talk, if not in opposites, at least indirectly, lying and not lying, making those signals at the truth which people in certain situations find it necessary to make.

I was in bed one evening, about a week later, reading in one of my encyclopaedia magazines about the "big bang" origin of the universe. It was a familiar topic; I liked reading in my encyclopaedias about things I had read in other encyclopaedias. This kind of reading wasn't for knowledge; I read to remind myself in an easy and enjoyable way of all the things I didn't know. It was a form of drug; it set me dreaming of some impossible future time when, in the middle of every kind of peace, I would start at the beginning of all subjects and devote my days and nights to study.

I heard a car door slam. And I knew, before I heard the footsteps on the staircase, that it was Yvette, wonderfully arrived at this late hour, without warning. She hurried up the steps; her shoes and clothes made an extraordinary amount of noise in the passage; and she pushed the bedroom door open.

She was carefully dressed, and her face was flushed. There must have been some function she had been at. Dressed as she was, she threw herself on the bed and embraced me.

She said, "I took a chance. All through dinner I was thinking about you, and as soon as I could I slipped away. I had to. I wasn't sure you would be here, but I took the chance."

I could smell the dinner and the drink on her breath. It had all been so quick—from the sound of the car door to this: Yvette on the bed, the empty room transformed, Yvette in that exclamatory, delighted mood which was like the mood that had overtaken her the first time we had come back to the flat after dinner at the Domain. I found myself in tears.

She said, "I can't stay. I'll just give the god a kiss and go."

Afterwards she remembered the clothes of which so far she had been quite careless. Standing before the mirror, she raised her skirt to pull down her blouse. I, at her insistence, stayed in the bed.

Holding her head to one side, looking at the mirror, she said, "I thought you might have been in your old haunts."

She seemed to be talking more mechanically now. The mood she had brought to the room had left her. At last she was ready. When she looked from the mirror to me she seemed once again, though, to be genuinely pleased with herself and with me, pleased at her little adventure.

She said, "I'm sorry. But I have to go." When she was almost at the door she turned and smiled and said, "You don't have a woman hidden in the cupboard, do you?"

It was so out of character. It was so much the kind of thing I had heard from whores who thought they should pretend to be jealous in order to please. It blasted the moment. Opposites: again this communication by opposites. That woman in the cupboard: that other person outside. That journey out from the Domain: that other journey back. Affection, just before betrayal. And I had been in tears.

It exploded then, all that had been building up in me since she had begun to straighten her clothes. And I was out of the bed, and between her and the door.

"Do you think I'm Raymond?"

She was startled.

"Do you think I'm Raymond?"

This time she was given no chance to reply. She was hit so hard and so often about the face, even through raised, protecting arms, that she staggered back and allowed herself to fall on the floor. I used my foot on her then, doing that for the sake of the beauty of her shoes, her ankles, the skirt I had watched her raise, the hump of her hip. She turned her face to the floor and remained still for a while; then with a deep breath such as a child draws before it screams, she began to cry, and that wail after a time broke into real, shocking sobs. And it was like that in the room for many minutes.

I was sitting, among the clothes I had taken off before going to bed, in the round-backed Windsor chair against the wall. The palm of my hand was stiff, swollen. The back of my hand, from little finger to wrist, was aching; bone had struck bone. Yvette raised herself up. Her eyes were slits between eyelids red and swollen with real tears. She sat on the edge of the foam mattress, at the corner of the bed, and looked at the floor, her hands resting palm outwards on her knees. I was wretched.

She said after a time, "I came to see you. It seemed such a good thing to do. I was wrong."

Then we said nothing.

I said, "Your dinner?"

She shook her head slowly. Her evening was ruined; she had given it up—but how easily! And that head-shaking gesture made me enter into her earlier joy, now gone. My error: I was too ready to see her as someone lost.

She prised her shoes off, using one foot against the other. She stood up, undid her skirt and took it off. Then, just as she was, with her hair done up, her blouse on, she got into the bed, pulled the top cotton sheet over herself and moved to the far side of the bed, always hers. She settled her fluffed-out head on the pillow, turned her back to me; and the encyclopaedia magazine, which had remained on that side of the bed, fell to the floor with its own little noise. And that was how, at this time of farewell, in this parody of domestic life, we stayed for a while, oddly reposed.

She said after some time, "Aren't you coming?"

I was too nervous to move or talk.

A while later, turning to me, she said, "You can't keep sitting on that chair."

I went and sat on the bed beside her. Her body had a softness, a pliability, and a great warmth. Only once or twice before had I known her like that. At this moment! I held her legs apart. She raised them slightly—smooth concavities of flesh on either side of the inner ridge—and then I spat on her between the legs until I had no more spit. All her softness vanished in outrage. She shouted, "You can't do that!" Bone struck against bone again; my hand ached at every blow; until she rolled across the bed to the other side and, sitting up, began to dial the telephone. Who was she telephoning at this hour? Who could she turn to, who was she so sure of?

She said, "Raymond. Oh, Raymond. No, no. I'm all right. I'm sorry. I'm coming right away."

She put on her skirt and shoes, and through the door that she left open she swung out into the passage. No pause, no hesitation: I heard her pattering down the staircase—what a sound now! The bed, where nothing had occurred, was in a mess—for the first time, after she had been: I had had the last of that housewifely service. There were the marks of her head on the pillow, the gathers in the sheet from her movements: things now rare, indescribably precious to me, those relics in cloth that would go so soon. I lay down where she had lain, to get her smell.

Outside the door Metty said, "Salim?" He called again, "Salim." And he came in, in his underpants.

I said, "Oh, Ali, Ali. Terrible things happened tonight. I spat on her. She made me spit on her."

"People quarrel. After three years a thing doesn't just end like this."

"Ali, it isn't that. I couldn't do anything with her. I didn't want her, I didn't want her. That is what I can't bear. It's all gone."

"You mustn't stay inside. Come outside. I will put on my pants and shirt and I will walk with you. We will walk together. We will walk to the river. Come, I will walk with you."

The river, the river at night. No, no.

"I know more things about your family than you, Salim. It is better for you to walk it off. It is the best way."

"I'll stay here."

He stood about for a little, then he went to his room. But I knew that he was waiting and watching. All the back of my swollen hand was aching; my little finger felt dead. The skin was blue-black in parts—that too now a relic.

I was ready when the telephone rang.

"Salim, I didn't want to leave. How are you?"

"Dreadful. And you?"

"When I left I drove slowly. Then after the bridge I drove very fast, to get back here to telephone you."

"I knew that you would. I was waiting for it."

"Do you want me to come back? The road is quite empty. I can be back in twenty minutes. Oh, Salim. I look dreadful. My face is in an awful state. I will have to hide for days."

"You will always look wonderful to me. You know that."

"I should have given you some Valium when I saw how you were. But I thought about that only when I was in the car. You must try to sleep. Make some hot milk and try to sleep. It helps to have a hot drink. Let Metty make some hot milk for you."

Never closer, never more like a wife, than at this moment. It was easier to talk on the telephone. And when that was over, I began to watch through the night, waiting for daylight and another telephone call. Metty was sleeping. He had left the door of his room open, and I heard his breathing.

There came a moment, with the coming of the light, when

suddenly the night became part of the past. The brush strokes on the white-painted window panes began to show, and at that time, out of my great pain, I had an illumination. It didn't come in words; the words I attempted to fit to it were confused and caused the illumination itself to vanish. It seemed to me that men were born only to grow old, to live out their span, to acquire experience. Men lived to acquire experience; the quality of the experience was immaterial; pleasure and pain—and above all, pain—had no meaning; to possess pain was as meaningless as to chase pleasure. And even when the illumination vanished, became as thin and half nonsensical as a dream, I remembered that I had had it, that knowledge about the illusion of pain.

The light brightened through the white-painted windows. The disturbed room changed its character. It seemed to have become stale. The only true relic was now my aching hand, though if I had looked I would have found a hair or two from her head. I dressed, went downstairs and, giving up the idea of a morning walk, began to drive about the awakening town. I felt refreshed by the colours; I thought this early morning drive was something I should have done more often.

Just before seven I went to the centre, to Bigburger. Sacks and boxes of uncollected rubbish were on the pavement. Ildephonse was there, the jacket of his uniform now as worn as the décor. Even at this early hour Ildephonse had been drinking; as with most Africans, he needed just a little of the weak local beer to top up and get high. He had known me for years; I was the first customer of the day; yet he hardly acknowledged me. His beer-glazed eyes stared past me at the street. In one of the lines or furrows of his lower lip he had fitted a toothpick, very precisely, very snugly, so he could talk or let his lower lip fall without the toothpick being disturbed; it was like a trick.

I called him back from wherever he was, and he gave me a cup of coffee and a slice of processed cheese in a roll. That was two hundred francs, nearly six dollars; prices were ridiculous these days.

A few minutes before eight, Mahesh came. He had been letting himself go. He had always been proud of his smallness and spareness. But he wasn't as spare as he had been; I could just begin to see him as a simpler kind of small fat man.

The effect of his arrival on Ildephonse was electric. The glazed look left Ildephonse's eyes, the toothpick disappeared, and he began to jump about, smiling and welcoming the early morning customers, mainly guests from the van der Weyden.

I was hoping that Mahesh would notice my condition. But he made no reference to it; he didn't even seem surprised to see me.

He said, "Shoba wants to see you, Salim."

"How is she?"

"She is better. I think she is better. She wants to see you. You must come to the flat. Come for a meal. Come for lunch. Come for lunch tomorrow."

Zabeth helped me to get through the morning. It was her shopping day. Her business had gone down since the insurrection, and her news these days was of trouble in the villages. Young men were being kidnapped here and there by the police and the army: it was the new government tactic. Though nothing appeared in the newspapers, the bush was now again at war. Zabeth seemed to be on the side of the rebels, but I couldn't be sure; and I tried to be as neutral as I could.

I asked about Ferdinand. His time in the capital as an administrative cadet was over. He was due for some big post soon, and the last I had heard from Zabeth was that he was being considered as a successor to our local commissioner, who had been sacked shortly after the insurrection had broken out. Ferdinand's mixed tribal ancestry made him a good choice for the difficult post.

Zabeth, speaking the big title quite calmly (I thought of the old subscription book for the lycée gymnasium, and of the days when the governor of the province signed by himself on a whole page, like royalty), Zabeth said, "I suppose Fer'nand will be commissioner, Salim. If they let him live."

"If he lives, Beth?"

"If they don't kill him. I don't know whether I would like him to take that job, Salim. Both sides would want to kill him. And the President will want to kill him first, as a sacrifice. He is a jealous man, Salim. He will allow nobody to get big in this place. It is only his photo everywhere. And look at the papers. His photo is bigger than everybody else's, every day. Look."

The previous day's paper from the capital was on my desk, and the photograph Zabeth pointed to was of the President addressing government officials in the southern province.

"Look, Salim. He is very big. The others are so small you can scarcely see them. You can't tell who is who."

The officials were in the regulation dress devised by the President—short-sleeved jackets, cravats, in place of shirts and ties. They sat in neat packed rows and in the photograph they did look alike. But Zabeth was pointing out something else to me. She didn't see the photograph as a photograph; she didn't interpret distance and perspective. She was concerned with the actual space occupied in the printed picture by different figures. She was, in fact, pointing out something I had never noticed: in pictures in the newspapers only visiting foreigners were given equal space with the President. With local people the President was always presented as a towering figure. Even if pictures were of the same size, the President's picture would be of his face alone, while the other man would be shown full length. So now, in the photograph of the President addressing the southern officials, a photograph taken from over the President's shoulder, the President's shoulders, head and cap occupied most of the space, and the officials were dots close together, similarly dressed.

"He is killing those men, Salim. They are screaming inside, and he knows they're screaming. And you know, Salim, that isn't a fetish he's got there. It's nothing."

She was looking at the big photograph in the shop, which showed the President holding up his chief's stick, carved with various emblems. In the distended belly of the squat human figure halfway down the stick the special fetish was thought to be lodged.

She said, "That's *nothing*. I'll tell you about the President. He's got a man, and this man goes ahead of him wherever he goes. This man jumps out of the car before the car stops, and everything that is bad for the President follows this man and leaves the President free. I saw it, Salim. And I will tell you something. The man who jumps out and gets lost in the crowd is white."

"But the President hasn't been here, Beth."

"I saw it, Salim. I saw the man. And you mustn't tell me that you don't know."

Metty was good all that day. Without referring to what had happened, he handled me with awe (awe for me as a violent, wounded man) and tenderness. I recalled moments like this from our own compound life on the coast, after some bad family quarrel. I suppose he recalled such moments too, and fell into old ways. I began in the end to act for him, and that was a help.

I allowed him to send me home to the flat in the middle of the afternoon; he said he would close up. He didn't go to his family afterwards, as was his custom. He came to the flat and discreetly let me know that he was there, and staying. I heard him tiptoeing about. There was no need for that, but the attention comforted me; and on that bed, where from time to time I caught some faint scent from the day before (no, that day itself), I began to sleep.

Time moved in jerks. Whenever I awakened I was confused. Neither the afternoon light nor the noisy darkness seemed right. So the second night passed. And the telephone didn't ring and I didn't telephone. In the morning Metty brought me coffee.

I went to Mahesh and Shoba's for lunch: it seemed to me that I had been to Bigburger and received that invitation a long time ago.

The flat, with its curtains drawn to keep out the glare, with its nice Persian carpets and brass, and all its other fussy little pieces, was as I remembered it. It was a silent lunch, not especially a lunch of reunion or reconciliation. We didn't talk about recent events. The topic of property values—at one time Mahesh's favourite topic, but now depressing to everybody—didn't come up. When we did talk, it was about what we were eating.

Towards the end Shoba asked about Yvette. It was the first

time she had done so. I gave her some idea of how things were. She said, "I'm sorry. Something like that may not happen to you again for twenty years." And after all that I had thought about Shoba, her conventional ways and her malice, I was amazed by her sympathy and wisdom.

Mahesh cleared the table and prepared the Nescafé—so far I had seen no servant. Shoba pulled one set of curtains apart a little, to let in more light. She sat, in the extra light, on the modern settee—shiny tubular metal frame, chunky padded armrests—and asked me to sit beside her. "Here, Salim."

She looked carefully at me while I sat down. Then, lifting her head a little, she showed me her profile and said, "Do you see anything on my face?"

I didn't understand the question.

She said, "Salim!" and turned her face full to me, keeping it lifted, fixing her eyes on mine. "Am I still badly disfigured? Look around my eyes and my left cheek. Especially the left cheek. What do you see?"

Mahesh had set down the cups of coffee on the low table and was standing beside me, looking with me. He said, "Salim can't see anything."

Shoba said, "Let him speak for himself. Look at my left eye. Look at the skin below the eye, and on the cheekbone." And she held her face up, as though posing for a head on a coin.

Looking hard, looking for what she wanted me to find, I saw that what I had thought of as the colour of fatigue or illness below her eye was also in parts a very slight staining of the skin, a faint lividness on her pale skin, just noticeable on the left cheekbone. And having seen it, after having not seen it, I couldn't help seeing it; and I saw it as the disfigurement she took it to be. She saw that I saw. She went sad, resigned.

Mahesh said, "It isn't so bad now. You *made* him see it."

Shoba said, "When I told my family that I was going to live with Mahesh, my brothers threatened to throw acid on my face. You could say that has come to pass. When my father died they sent me a cable. I took that as a sign that they wanted me to go back home for the ceremonies. It was a terrible way to go back

—my father dead, the country in such a state, the Africans being so awful. I saw everybody on the edge of a precipice. But I couldn't tell them that. When you asked them what they were going to do, they would pretend that it was all all right, there was nothing to worry about. And you would have to pretend with them. Why are we like that?

"One morning I don't know what possessed me. There was this Sindhi girl who had studied in England—as she said—and had set up a hairdresser's shop. The sun is very bright in the highlands there, and I had done a lot of driving about, visiting old friends and just driving about, getting out of the house. Every place I used to like, and went to see, I began to hate, and I had to stop. I suppose it was that driving about that had darkened and blotched my skin. I asked the Sindhi girl whether there wasn't some cream or something I could use. She said she had something. She used this something. I cried out to her to stop. She had used peroxide. I ran home with my face scorched. And that house of death became for me truly a house of grief.

"I couldn't stay after that. I had to hide my face from everybody. And then I ran back here, to hide as before. Now I can go nowhere. I only go out at night sometimes. It has got better. But I still have to be careful. Don't tell me anything, Salim. I saw the truth in your eyes. I can't go abroad now. I so much wanted to go, to get away. And we had the money. New York, London, Paris. Do you know Paris? There is a skin specialist there. They say he peels your skin better than anybody else. That would be nice, if I could get there. And then I could go anywhere. Suisse, now—how do you say it in English?"

"Switzerland."

"You see. Living in this flat, I'm even forgetting my English. That would be a nice place, I always think, if you could get a permit."

All the while Mahesh looked at her face, half encouraging her, half irritated with her. His elegant red cotton shirt with the stiff, nicely shaped collar was open at the neck—it was part of the stylishness he had learned from her.

I was glad to get away from them, from the obsession they had forced on me in their sitting room. Peeling, skin—the words made me uneasy long after I had left them.

Their obsession was with more than a skin blemish. They had cut themselves off. Once they were supported by their idea of their high traditions (kept going somewhere else, by other people); now they were empty in Africa, and unprotected, with nothing to fall back on. They had begun to rot. I was like them. Unless I acted now, my fate would be like theirs. That constant questioning of mirrors and eyes; compelling others to look for the blemish that kept you in hiding; lunacy in a small room.

I decided to rejoin the world, to break out of the narrow geography of the town, to do my duty by those who depended on me. I wrote to Nazruddin that I was coming to London for a visit, leaving him to interpret that simple message. What a decision, though! When no other choice was left to me, when family and community hardly existed, when duty hardly had a meaning, and there were no safe houses.

I left eventually on a plane which travelled on to the east of the continent before it turned north. This plane stopped at our airport. I didn't have to go to the capital to take it. So even now the capital remained unknown to me.

I fell asleep on the night flight to Europe. A woman in the window seat, going out to the aisle, rubbed against my legs and awakened me. I thought: But that's Yvette. She's with me, then. I'll wait for her to come back. And wide awake, for ten or fifteen seconds I waited. Then I understood that it had been a waking dream. That was pain, to understand that I was alone, and flying to quite a different destiny.

## 15

I had never travelled on an airplane before. I half remembered what Indar had said about airplane travel; he had said, more or less, that the airplane had helped him to adjust to his homelessness. I began to understand what he meant.

I was in Africa one day; I was in Europe the next morning. It was more than travelling fast. It was like being in two places at once. I woke up in London with little bits of Africa on me— like the airport tax ticket, given me by an official I knew, in the middle of another kind of crowd, in another kind of building, in another climate. Both places were real; both places were unreal. You could play off one against the other; and you had no feeling of having made a final decision, a great last journey. Which, in a way, was what this was for me, though I only had an excursion ticket, a visitor's visa, and I had to go back within six weeks.

The Europe the airplane brought me to was not the Europe I had known all my life. When I was a child Europe ruled my world. It had defeated the Arabs in Africa and controlled the interior of the continent. It ruled the coast and all the countries of the Indian Ocean with which we traded; it supplied our goods. We knew who we were and where we had come from. But it was Europe that gave us the descriptive postage stamps that gave us our ideas of what was picturesque about ourselves. It also gave us a new language.

Europe no longer ruled. But it still fed us in a hundred ways with its language and sent us its increasingly wonderful goods, things which, in the bush of Africa, added year by year to our idea of who we were, gave us that idea of our modernity and development, and made us aware of another Europe—the Europe of great cities, great stores, great buildings, great universities. To that Europe only the privileged or the gifted among us journeyed. That was the Europe Indar had gone to when he had left for his famous university. That was the Europe that someone like Shoba had in mind when she spoke of travelling.

But the Europe I had come to—and knew from the outset I was coming to—was neither the old Europe nor the new. It was something shrunken and mean and forbidding. It was the Europe where Indar, after his time at the famous university, had suffered and tried to come to some resolution about his place in the world; where Nazruddin and his family had taken refuge; where hundreds of thousands of people like myself, from parts of the world like mine, had forced themselves in, to work and live.

Of this Europe I could form no mental picture. But it was there in London; it couldn't be missed; and there was no mystery. The effect of those little stalls, booths, kiosks and choked grocery shops—run by people like myself—was indeed of people who had squashed themselves in. They traded in the middle of London as they had traded in the middle of Africa. The goods travelled a shorter distance, but the relationship of the trader to his goods remained the same. In the streets of London I saw these people, who were like myself, as from a distance. I saw the young girls selling packets of cigarettes at midnight, seemingly imprisoned in their kiosks, like puppets in a puppet theatre. They were cut off from the life of the great city where they had come to live, and I wondered about the pointlessness of their own hard life, the pointlessness of their difficult journey.

What illusions Africa gave to people who came from outside! In Africa I had thought of our instinct and capacity for work, even in extreme conditions, as heroic and creative. I had contrasted it with the indifference and withdrawal of village Africa. But now in London, against a background of busyness, I saw this instinct purely as instinct, pointless, serving only itself. And a feeling of rebellion possessed me, stronger than any I had known in my childhood. To this was added a new sympathy for the rebellion Indar had spoken of to me, the rebellion he had discovered when he had walked beside the river of London and had decided to reject the ideas of home and ancestral piety, the unthinking worship of his great men, the self-suppression that went with that worship and those ideas, and to throw himself consciously into the bigger, harder world. It was the only way I could live here, if I had to live here.

Yet I had had my life of rebellion, in Africa. I had taken it as far as I could take it. And I had come to London for relief and rescue, clinging to what remained of our organized life.

Nazruddin wasn't surprised by my engagement to his daughter Kareisha. He had always, as I realised with dismay, held fast to that idea of my faithfulness which years before he had seen in my hand. Kareisha herself wasn't surprised. In fact, the only person who seemed to examine the event with some astonishment was myself, who marvelled that such a turn in my life could occur so easily.

The engagement came almost at the end of my time in London. But it had been taken as settled from the start. And, really, it was comforting, in the strange big city, after that fast journey, to be taken over by Kareisha, to have her call me by my name all the time, to have her lead me about London, she the knowing one (Uganda and Canada behind her), I the primitive (acting up a little).

She was a pharmacist. That was partly Nazruddin's doing. With his experience of change and sudden upheaval, he had long ago lost faith in the power of property and business to protect people; and he had pushed his children into acquiring skills that could be turned to account anywhere. It might have been her job that gave Kareisha her serenity, extraordinary for an unmarried woman of thirty from our community; or it might have been her full family life, and the example of Nazruddin, still relishing his experiences and looking for new sights. But I felt more and more that at some stage in Kareisha's wanderings there must have been a romance. At one time the idea would have outraged me. I didn't mind now. And the man must have been nice. Because he had left Kareisha with an affection for men. This was new to me; my experience of women was so limited. I luxuriated in this affection of Kareisha's, and acted out my man's role a little. It was wonderfully soothing.

Acted—there was a lot of that about me at this time. Because always I had to go back to my hotel (not far from their flat) and there I had to face my solitude, the other man that I also was. I hated that hotel room. It made me feel I was nowhere. It forced old anxieties on me and added new ones, about London, about this bigger world where I would have to make my way. Where would I start? When I turned the television on, it wasn't to marvel. It was to become aware of the great strangeness outside, and to wonder how those men on the screen had had themselves picked out from the crowd. And always in my mind then was the comfort of "going back," of taking another airplane, of perhaps not having, after all, to be here. The decisions and the pleasures of the day and early evening were regularly cancelled out by me at night.

Indar had said about people like me that when we came to a great city we closed our eyes; we were concerned only to show that we were not amazed. I was a little like that, even with Kareisha to guide me around. I could say that I was in London, but I didn't really know where I was. I had no means of grasping the city. I knew only that I was in the Gloucester Road. My hotel was there; Nazruddin's flat was there. I travelled everywhere by underground train, popping down into the earth at one place, popping up at another, not able to relate one place to the other, and sometimes making complicated interchanges to travel short distances.

The only street I knew well was the Gloucester Road. If I walked in one direction I came to more buildings and avenues and got lost. If I walked in the other direction I went past a lot of tourist eating places, a couple of Arab restaurants, and came to the park. There was a wide, sloping avenue in the park with boys skate-boarding. At the top of the slope there was a big pond with a paved rim. It looked artificial, but it was full of real birds, swans and different kinds of ducks; and that always struck me as strange, that the birds didn't mind being there. Artificial birds, like the lovely celluloid things of my childhood, wouldn't have been out of place. Far away, all around, beyond the trees, were the buildings. There you really did have an idea of the city as something made by man, and not as something that had just grown by itself and was simply there. Indar had spoken of that too; and he was right. It was so easy for people like us to think of great cities as natural growths. It reconciled us to our own shanty cities. We slipped into thinking that one place was one thing, and another place another thing.

In the park on fine afternoons people flew kites, and sometimes Arabs from the embassies played football below the trees. There were always a lot of Arabs about, fair-skinned people, real Arabs, not the half-African Arabs of our coast; one of the newsstands outside the Gloucester Road station was full of Arabic papers and magazines. Not all of the Arabs were rich or clean.

Sometimes I saw little groups of poor Arabs in dingy clothes squatting on the grass in the park or on the pavements of the streets nearby. I thought they were servants, and that seemed to me shameful enough. But then one day I saw an Arab lady with her slave.

I spotted the fellow at once. He had his little white cap on and his plain white gown, proclaiming his status to everybody, and he was carrying two shopping bags of groceries from the Waitrose supermarket on the Gloucester Road. He was walking the regulation ten paces ahead of his mistress, who was fat in the way Arab women like to be, with blue markings on her pale face below her gauzy black veil. She was pleased with herself; you could see that being in London and doing this modern shopping with other housewives at the Waitrose supermarket had excited her. For a moment she thought I was an Arab and she gave me a look, through her gauzy veil, which was meant to get back a look of approval and admiration from me.

As for the fellow carrying the groceries, he was a thin, fair-skinned young man, and I would have said that he had been born in the house. He had the vacant, dog-like expressions that house-born slaves, as I remembered, liked to put on when they were in public with their masters and performing some simple task. This fellow was pretending that the Waitrose groceries were a great burden, but this was just an act, to draw attention to himself and the lady he served. He, too, had mistaken me for an Arab, and when we crossed he had dropped the burdened-down expression and given me a look of wistful inquisitiveness, like a puppy that wanted to play but had just been made to understand that it wasn't playtime.

I was going to the Waitrose place to get a gift of wine for Nazruddin. He hadn't lost his taste for wine and good food. He was happy to be my guide in these matters; and indeed, after years of that Portuguese stuff in Africa, white and meaningless or red and acrid, the range of wines in London was a small daily excitement for me. At dinner in the flat (and before television: he watched for a couple of hours every night) I told Nazruddin about the slave in white. He said he wasn't surprised; it was a

new feature of life in the Gloucester Road; for a couple of weeks
he had been noticing a grubby fellow in brown.

Nazruddin said: "In the old days they made a lot of fuss if
they caught you sending a couple of fellows to Arabia in a dhow.
Today they have their passports and visas like everybody else,
and walk past immigration like everybody else, and nobody gives
a damn.

"I'm superstitious about the Arabs. They gave us and half the
world our religion, but I can't help feeling that when they leave
Arabia terrible things are about to happen in the world. You just
have to think of where we come from. Persia, India, Africa.
Think of what happened there. Now Europe. They're pumping
the oil in and sucking the money out. Pumping the oil in to keep
the system going, sucking the money out to send it crashing down.
They need Europe. They want the goods and the properties and
at the same time they need a safe place for their money. Their
own countries are so dreadful. But they're destroying money.
They're killing the goose that lays the golden egg.

"And they aren't the only ones. All over the world money is in
flight. People have scraped the world clean, as clean as an African scrapes his yard, and now they want to run from the dreadful
places where they've made their money and find some nice safe
country. I was one of the crowd. Koreans, Filipinos, people from
Hong Kong and Taiwan, South Africans, Italians, Greeks, South
Americans, Argentines, Colombians, Venezuelans, Bolivians, a
lot of black people who've cleaned out places you've never heard
of, Chinese from everywhere. All of them are on the run. They
are frightened of the fire. You mustn't think it's only Africa
people are running from.

"Mostly nowadays, since Switzerland closed down, they are
going to the United States and Canada. And they are waiting for
them there, to take them to the cleaners. There they meet the
experts. The South Americans are waiting for the South Americans, the Asians for the Asians, the Greeks for the Greeks. And
they take them to the cleaners. In Toronto, Vancouver, California. As for Miami, that is one big cleaning establishment.

"I knew about this before I went to Canada. I didn't let anybody sell me a million-dollar villa in California or an orange

grove in Central America or a piece of swamp in Florida. You know what I bought instead? You wouldn't believe it. I bought an oil well, part of one. The man was a geologist. Advani introduced him to me. They said they wanted ten of us to form a little private oil company. They wanted to raise a hundred thousand dollars, everybody putting up ten. The authorized capital, though, was to be more than that, and the arrangement was that if we struck oil the geologist was to buy the rest of the shares at nominal rates. That was fair. It was his stake, his work.

"The stake was in order, the land was there. In Canada you can just go and do your own drilling. You can hire the equipment, and it doesn't cost all that much. Thirty thousand for a trial well, depending on where you want to drill. And they don't have the fruits-of-the-earth legislation you have where you are. I checked it all out. It was a risk, but I thought it was only a geological risk. I put up my ten. And guess what. We struck oil. Overnight, then, my ten was worth two hundred—well, say a hundred. But since we were a private company the profit was only a paper profit. We could only sell to one another, and none of us had that kind of money.

"The geologist exercised his options and bought up the remaining shares of the company for virtually nothing. So he acquired control of our company—but all that was in the agreement. Then he bought a semi-bankrupt mining company. We wondered about this, but we didn't question the wisdom of our man now. Then he disappeared to one of the black islands. He had linked the two companies in some way, borrowed a million dollars for our company on the strength of our oil, and transferred the money on some pretext to his own company. He left us with the debt. The oldest trick in the book, and the nine of us stood and watched while it was happening as though we were watching a man dig a hole in the road. To add insult to injury, we found out that he hadn't put up his ten. He had done it all with our money. Now I suppose he is moving heaven and earth to transfer his million to some safe place. Anyway, that was how I achieved the impossible, converting ten into a debt of a hundred.

"In time the debt will settle itself. The oil is there. I might even get my ten back. The trouble with people like us, running about the world with money to hide, is that we are good about business only in our own places. Still. The oil was only a sideline. What I was trying to do was to run a movie theatre, an ethnic theatre. You know the word? It means all the foreign groups in a place. It was very ethnic where I was, but I suppose I got the idea only because there was a theatre for sale, and it seemed a nice downtown property to get.

"Everything was working when I looked at the place, but when I took over I found we couldn't get a clear picture on the screen. At first I thought it just had to do with the lenses. Then I realised that the man who had sold me the place had changed the equipment. I went to him and said, 'You can't do this.' He said, 'Who are you? I don't know you.' So. Well, we straightened out the projectors in the end, we improved the seating and so on. Business wasn't too good. An ethnic theatre downtown wasn't such a good idea. The thing about some of those ethnic groups over there is that they don't like moving around too much. They just want to go home as fast as they can and stay there. The pictures that did well were the Indian pictures. We got a lot of Greeks then. The Greeks love Indian pictures. Did you know that? Anyway. We struggled through the summer. The cold weather came. I threw some switches for the heating. Nothing came on. There was no heating system. Or what was there had been taken away.

"I went to the man again. I said, 'You sold me the theatre as a going concern.' He said, 'Who are you?' I said, 'My family have been traders and merchants in the Indian Ocean for centuries, under every kind of government. There is a reason why we have lasted so long. We bargain hard, but we stick to our bargain. All our contracts are oral, but we deliver what we promise. It isn't because we are saints. It is because the whole thing breaks down otherwise.' He said, 'You should go back to the Indian Ocean.'

"When I left him I walked very fast. I stumbled on an unevenness in the pavement and turned my ankle. I took that as a sign. My luck had run out; I knew that it had to. I didn't feel I could stay in that country. I felt the place was a hoax. They thought they were part of the West, but really they had become like the rest of us who had run to them for safety. They were like people far away, living on other people's land and off other people's brains, and that was all they thought they should do. That was why they were so bored and dull. I thought I would die if I stayed among them.

"When I came to England all my instincts were to go into light engineering. A small country, good roads and railways, power, every kind of industrial facility. I thought that if you identified some area, 'got in good equipment, and employed Asians, you couldn't lose. Europeans are bored with machines and factories. Asian people love them; they secretly prefer factories to their family life. But after Canada I had lost my nerve. I thought I would play safe. I thought I would go into property. That was how I came to the Gloucester Road.

"It is one of the centres of the tourist trade in London, as you see. London is destroying itself for its tourist trade—you can see that here. Hundreds of houses, thousands of flats, have been emptied to provide hotels, hostels and restaurants for the tourists. Private accommodation is getting scarcer. I thought I couldn't lose. I bought six flats in a block. I bought at the height of the boom. Prices have now dropped twenty-five percent, and interest rates have risen from twelve percent to twenty and even twenty-four percent. Do you remember the scandal on the coast when it came out that Indar's people were lending money at ten and twelve percent? I feel I no longer understand money. And the Arabs are in the streets outside.

"I have to charge ridiculous rents to break even. And when you charge ridiculous rents you attract strange people. This is one of my souvenirs. It is a betting slip from one of the betting shops in the Gloucester Road. I keep it to remind myself of a simple girl who came down from the north. She got her Arabs mixed up. The Arab she became involved with was one of the poor ones, from Algeria. She used to dump her rubbish outside her flat door. The Algerian used to gamble on the horses. That was how they were going to make the big time.

"They won, and then they lost. They couldn't pay the rent. I reduced it. They still couldn't pay. There were complaints about the rubbish and the quarrels, and the Algerian was in the habit of pissing in the lift when he was locked out. I asked them to leave. They refused, and the law was on their side. I had a new lock put in one day when they were out. When they came back they simply called the police, and the police opened up for them. To prevent me getting in again, they put in another lock. By this time, on that door, keyholes and their metal surrounds were like buttons down a shirt front. I gave up.

"Every kind of bill was unpaid. I went up one morning and knocked. The flat was full of whispers, but no one opened. The lift was close to the flat door. I opened the door of the lift and closed it. They thought I had gone down, and sure enough they opened up to check. I put my foot in the door and went in. The little flat was full of poor Arabs in undershirts and horribly coloured pants. There was bedding all over the floor. The girl wasn't with them. They had sent her away, or she had left. So for two months, while I had been paying twenty percent interest and other charges, I had been giving free shelter to a whole tentful of poor Arabs. They are a strange people racially. One of them had bright red hair. What were they doing in London? What were they expecting to do? How are they going to survive? What place is there in the world for people like that? There are so many of them.

"Here is another girl who ran out on me. Seven hundred pounds went with her. She came from Eastern Europe. Refugee? But she was a woman. She must have spent quite a bit of money to get these photographic cards printed. Here she is, up to her neck in water; I don't know why she thought she should put that on her card. And here she is, pretending to thumb a lift, in a kind of button-up overall open at the top, and showing a little breast. Here she is wearing a big black bowler hat and black leather trousers and sticking out her little bottom. 'Erika. Model-Actress-Singer-Dancer. Hair: Red. Eyes: Grey-Green. Specialties: Fashion-Cosmetic-Footwear-Hands-Legs-Teeth-Hair. 5'9". 32-25-33.' All that, and nobody wants to buy. All that happened to her was that she became pregnant, ran up a telephone bill of

£1200—twelve hundred pounds!—and ran away one night,
leaving these picture cards of herself. A big pile. I couldn't bear
to throw them all away. I felt I should keep one, for her sake.
"What happens to these people? Where do they go? How do
they live? Do they go back home? Do they have homes to go
back to? You've talked a lot, Salim, about those girls from East
Africa in the tobacco kiosks, selling cigarettes at all hours of the
night. They've depressed you. You say they don't have a future
and that they don't even know where they are. I wonder whether
that isn't their luck. They expect to be bored, to do what they do.
The people I've been talking about have expectations and they
know they're lost in London. I suppose it must be dreadful for
them when they have to go back. This area is full of them, coming to the centre because it is all they know about and because
they think it's smart, and trying to make something out of nothing. You can't blame them. They're doing what they see the big
people doing.
"This place is so big and busy you take some time to see that
very little is happening. It's just keeping itself going. A lot of
people have been quietly wiped out. There's no new money, no
real money, and this makes everybody more desperate. We've
come here at the wrong time. But never mind. It's the wrong
time everywhere else too. When we were in Africa in the old
days, consulting our catalogues and ordering our goods and
watching the ships unload in the harbour, I don't suppose we
thought it would be like this in Europe, or that the British passports we took out as protection against the Africans would actually bring us here, and that the Arabs would be in the streets
outside."

That was Nazruddin. Kareisha said, "I hope you know you've
been listening to the story of a happy man." She didn't have to
tell me.
Nazruddin was all right. He had made himself at home in the
Gloucester Road. The London setting was strange, but Nazruddin appeared to be as he had always been. He had moved on
from fifty to sixty, but he didn't look particularly older. He still

wore his old-style suits; and the broad lapels (with the curling tips) which I associated with him were back in fashion. I didn't think he doubted that his property venture would eventually right itself. What oppressed him (and made him talk about his luck running out) was his inactivity. But he had found in the half mile or so of the Gloucester Road, between the underground railway station and the park, the perfect retirement resort.

He bought his newspaper in one shop, read it with morning coffee in a tiny café that also offered old watercolour paintings for sale; took a turn in the park; shopped for delicacies in the various food shops. Sometimes he gave himself the luxury of tea or a drink in the big, old-fashioned lounge of the red-brick hotel near the station. Sometimes he went to the Arab or Persian "Dancing Room." And there was the nightly excitement of television in the flat. The population of the Gloucester Road was cosmopolitan, always shifting, with people of all ages. It was a friendly, holiday place, and Nazruddin's days were full of encounters and new observations. He said it was the best street in the world; he intended to stay there as long as he was allowed to.

He had chosen well once again. That had always been his gift, to suggest that he had chosen well. At one time it had made me anxious to find the world he had found. Nazruddin's example, or the way in which I had secretly interpreted his experience, had after all helped to determine my life. Now in London, glad though I was to find him in good spirits, that gift of his depressed me. It made me feel that after all these years I had never caught up with him, and never would; that my life would always be unsatisfactory. It could send me back to my hotel room in an agony of solitude and dread.

Sometimes as I was falling asleep I was kicked awake by some picture that came to me of my African town—absolutely real (and the airplane could take me there tomorrow), but its associations made it dream-like. Then I remembered my illumination, about the need of men only to live, about the illusion of pain. I played off London against Africa until both became unreal, and I could fall asleep. After a time I didn't have to call up the illumination, the mood of that African morning. It was there, beside me, that remote vision of the planet, of men lost in space and time, but dreadfully, pointlessly busy.

It was in this state of indifference and irresponsibility—like the lost Gloucester Road people Nazruddin had spoken about— that I became engaged to Kareisha.

One day, near the end of my time in London, Kareisha said, "Have you been to see Indar? Are you going to see him?"

Indar! His name had come up often in our talk, but I didn't know that he was in London.

Kareisha said, "That's just as well. I wouldn't recommend a visit or trying to get in touch or anything like that. He can be difficult and aggressive when he's in the mood, and it isn't funny. He's been like that ever since his outfit folded."

"His outfit folded?"

"About two years ago."

"But he knew it was going to fold. He talked as though he expected it to fold. Lecturers, universities, African interchange —he knew the excitement couldn't last, that no local government really cared one way or the other. But I thought he had his plans. He said he could exploit himself in lots of other ways."

Kareisha said: "It was different when the time came. He cared more about his outfit than he pretended. Of course, there are many things he can do. But he's determined not to do them. He can get a job in a university, certainly in America. He has the contacts. He can write for the papers. We don't talk about it now when we see him. Naz' says Indar's become help-resistant. The trouble is he invested too much in that outfit of his. And after it folded he had that bad experience in America. A bad experience for him anyway.

"You know Indar. You know that when he was young the most important thing to him was that his family was rich. You remember the house they lived in. When you live in a house like that, I suppose you think ten or twelve or twenty times a day that you are very rich or that you are richer than nearly everybody else. And you remember how he used to get on. Not talking about money, but it was always there. You would say that he felt that money had made him holy. All rich people are like that, I suppose. And that was one idea about himself that Indar never lost. His outfit didn't give him back his money, but it made him holy again. It raised him again above everybody else and made him equal with the big boys of Africa, being a guest of the government in this place and that place, meeting foreign ministers and presidents. So it was a blow when the outfit folded, when the Americans decided there was nothing in it for them.

"Indar went to America, to New York. Being Indar, he stayed in an expensive hotel. He saw his American people. They were all very nice. But he didn't like the direction in which they were pushing him. He felt they were pushing him towards smaller things and he pretended not to notice. I don't know what Indar was expecting from these people. No, I know. He was hoping to be made one of them, to keep on at the old level. He thought that was his due. He was spending a lot of money, and the money was running out. One day, much against his will, he even looked at cheaper hotels. He didn't want to do that because he thought that even to start looking for cheaper hotels was to admit that it soon might be over for him. He was appalled by the cheaper hotels. In New York you drop fast, he said.

"There was one man in particular he used to deal with. He had met this man in London right at the beginning, and they had become friends. It wasn't always like that. In the beginning he had thought the man foolish and had been aggressive with him. That used to embarrass Indar, because it was this man who had brought him out of the mess he was in the first time in London. This man had given Indar back his confidence then, had made him think positively about Africa and himself. It was this man who had drawn the good ideas out of Indar. Indar had grown to depend on this man. He thought of him as his equal, and you will know what I mean by that.

"They used to meet in New York. Lunch, drinks, meetings in the office. But nothing seemed to be happening. It was always just back to the hotel, and waiting. Indar was getting lower. The man invited Indar to dinner one evening at his apartment. It was an expensive-looking building. Indar gave his name downstairs and took the elevator up. The elevator man waited and watched until the apartment door was opened and Indar was let in. When Indar went inside he was stunned.

"He had thought of the man as his equal, his friend. He had opened himself to the man. He found now that the man was immensely rich. He had never been in a richer room. You or I would have found it interesting, the money. Indar was shattered. It was only there, in the rich apartment with the costly objects and pictures, that Indar understood that while he had opened himself to the man, and talked of all the little things that made him anxious, he had received very little of that in return. This man was much, much holier. It was more than Indar could bear. He felt he had been cheated and fooled. He had grown to depend on this man. He tested his ideas on him; he looked to him for moral support. He thought of this man as someone like himself. He felt he had been led on all these years, and exploited in the worst way. All that optimism dragged out of him, after he had lost so much. All those constructive ideas! Africa! There was nothing of Africa in that apartment, or in the dinner party. No danger, no loss. The private life, the life with friends, was quite different from the life outside. I don't know what Indar expected.

"During the dinner he focussed all his resentment on a young woman. She was the wife of a very old journalist who had written books that had made a lot of money at one time. Indar hated her. Why had she married the old man? What was the joke? Because apparently the dinner had been arranged around her and the man she was having an affair with. They didn't keep it too secret, and the old man pretended not to notice. He just kept babbling on about French politics in the 1930s, still keeping himself in the centre of things, though, telling about the important people he had met and what they had told him personally. No one paid him the slightest attention, but he didn't mind.

"Still, he had been a famous man. Indar thought a lot about that. He was trying to put himself on the old man's side, to hate the others better. Then the old man noticed who Indar was, and he began to talk about India in the old days and his meeting with

Gandhi in some famous mud hut. As you know, Gandhi and Nehru aren't Indar's favourite subjects. He decided he wasn't doing any social work that night, and he was very rough with the old man, much rougher than anybody else had been.

"So at the end of the dinner Indar was in a state. He thought about the cheap hotels he had looked at, and as he was going down in the elevator he had a wild panic. He thought he was going to pass out. But he got outside all right, and there he calmed down. He had got a simple idea. The idea was that it was time for him to go home, to get away.

"And that's how it has been with him. From time to time that is all he knows, that it is time for him to go home. There is some dream village in his head. In between he does the lowest kind of job. He knows he is equipped for better things, but he doesn't want to do them. I believe he enjoys being told he can do better. We've given up now. He doesn't want to risk anything again. The idea of sacrifice is safer, and he likes the act. But you will see for yourself, when you come back."

Kareisha, talking about Indar, touched me more than she knew. That idea of going home, of leaving, the idea of the other place—I had lived with it in various forms for many years. In Africa it had always been with me. In London, in my hotel room, I had allowed it on some nights to take me over. It was a deception. I saw now that it comforted only to weaken and destroy.

That illumination I held on to, about the unity of experience and the illusion of pain, was part of the same way of feeling. We fell into it—people like Indar and myself—because it was the basis of our old way of life. But I had rejected that way of life—and just in time. In spite of the girls in the cigarette kiosks, that way of life no longer existed, in London or Africa. There could be no going back; there was nothing to go back to. We had become what the world outside had made us; we had to live in the world as it existed. The younger Indar was wiser. Use the airplane; trample on the past, as Indar had said he had trampled on the past. Get rid of that idea of the past; make the dream-like scenes of loss ordinary.

That was the mood in which I left London and Kareisha, to go back to Africa, to wind up there, realise as much as I could of what I had. And make a fresh start somewhere else.

I got to Brussels in the late afternoon. The plane for Africa was leaving from there at midnight. I felt afresh the drama of airplane travel: London vanished, Africa to come, Brussels now. I gave myself dinner and went to a bar afterwards, a place with women. All the excitement lay in the idea of the place rather than the place itself. What followed, some time later, was brief and meaningless and reassuring. It didn't lessen the value of what I had had in Africa: that was no delusion; that remained true. And it removed the special doubt I felt about my engagement to Kareisha, whom I had not yet even kissed.

The woman, naked, unruffled, stood in front of a long mirror and looked at herself. Fat legs, roundish belly, chunky breasts. She said, "I've begun to do yoga with a group of friends. We have a teacher. Do you do yoga?"

"I play a lot of squash."

She paid no attention. "Our teacher says that a man's psychic fluids can overpower a woman. Our teacher says that after a dangerous encounter a woman can become herself again by clapping her hands hard or by taking a deep breath. Which method do you recommend?"

"Clap your hands."

She faced me as she might have faced her yoga teacher, drew herself up, half closed her eyes, pulled her outstretched arms back, and brought her hands violently together. At the sound, startling in the over-furnished little room, she opened her eyes, looked surprised, smiled as though she had been joking all along, and said, "Go!" When I was out in the street I took a deep breath, and went straight to the airport to catch the midnight plane.

# F O U R

## *Battle*

### 16

≋ The dawn came suddenly, in the west pale blue, in the east red with thick horizontal bars of black cloud. And for many minutes it was like that. The scale, the splendour—six miles above the earth! We came down slowly, leaving the upper light. Below the heavy cloud Africa showed as a dark-green, wet-looking land. You could see that it was barely dawn down there; in the forests and creeks it would still be quite dark. The forested land went on and on. The sun struck the bottom of the clouds; it was light when we touched down.

So at last I had come to the capital. It was a strange way to come to it, after such a roundabout journey. If I had come to it fresh from my upriver town it would have seemed immense, rich, a capital. But after Europe, and with London still close to me, it seemed flimsy in spite of its size, an echo of Europe, and like make-believe, at the end of all that forest.

The more experienced among the European passengers, paying no attention to the big photograph of the President with his chief's stick, made a rush at the immigration and customs officials and appeared to force their way through. I wondered at their confidence, but they were mainly people with protection—embassy people, people working on government projects, people working for big companies. My own passage was slower. When I was through, the terminal building was almost empty. The airline posters and the photograph of the President had no one to look at them. Most of the officials had disappeared. And it was fully morning.

It was a long drive into the town. It was like the drive, in my own town, from the Domain to the town centre. But the land was hillier here and everything was on a larger scale. The shanty towns and *cités* (with the maize plantings between houses) were bigger; there were buses, even a railway train with old-fashioned open coaches; there were factories. All along the road were big boards about ten feet high, uniformly painted, each with a separate saying or maxim of the President. Some of the painted portraits of the President were literally as big as a house. We had had nothing like that in our town. Everything in our town, as I realized, was on a smaller scale.

Portraits, maxims, occasional statues of the African madonna —they continued all the way to the hotel. If I had come to the capital fresh from our town I would have felt choked. But after Europe, and after what I had seen of the country from the air, and still with my sense of the flimsiness of the capital, my attitude was different, and I was surprised by it. There was to me an element of pathos in those maxims, portraits and statues, in this wish of a man of the bush to make himself big, and setting about it in such a crude way. I even felt a little sympathy for the man who was making such a display of himself.

I understood now why so many of our later visitors at the Domain found our country, and our awe of the President, comic. What I saw on the road from the airport didn't seem comic, though. I felt it more as a shriek. I had just come from Europe; I had seen the real competition.

Overnight I had changed one continent for another, and this odd sympathy for the President, this vision of the impossibility of what I thought he was trying to do, came just at the moment of arrival. The sympathy wore off as the town became more familiar and I began to see it as a larger version of my own town. The sympathy, in fact, began to wear off when I got to the new big hotel (air-conditioned, shops in the lobby, a swimming pool no one was using) and found it full of secret police. I can't imagine that they had much to do there. They were there to show themselves to visitors. And also because they liked being in the smart new hotel; they wanted to show themselves to visitors in that modern setting. It was pathetic; or you could make a joke of it. But those men weren't always funny. Already, then, the tensions of Africa were returning to me.

This was the President's city. This was where he had grown up and where his mother had worked as a hotel maid. This was where, in colonial days, he had got his idea of Europe. The colonial city, more extensive than ours, with many residential areas rich with decorative, sheltering trees now fully grown, was still to be seen. It was with this Europe that, in his own buildings, the President wished to compete. The city, while decaying in the centre, with dirt roads and rubbish mounds just at the back of the great colonial boulevards, was yet full of new public works. Large areas near the river had been turned into Presidential reserves—palaces with great walls, gardens, state houses of various sorts.

In the Presidential gardens near the rapids (the rapids here matching ours, a thousand miles upriver), the statue of the European explorer who had charted the river and used the first steamer had been replaced by a gigantic statue of an African tribesman with spear and shield, done in the modern African style; Father Huismans would have had no time for it. Beside this statue was a smaller one of an African madonna with a bowed, veiled head. Nearby were the graves of the earliest Europeans: a little dead settlement, out of which it had all grown, out of which our town had been seeded. Simple people, with simple trades and simple goods, but agents of Europe. Like the people who came now, like the people on the airplane.

The rapids made a constant, unchanging noise. The water hyacinths, "the new thing in the river," beginning so far away, in the centre of the continent, bucked past in clumps and tangles and single vines, here almost at the end of their journey.

The next morning I went back to the airport, to take the upcountry plane. By now I was more in tune with the place, and the spread of the capital made a greater impression on me. Always, beside the airport road, there was some new settlement. How did all these people live? The hilly land had been scraped clean, cut up, eroded, exposed. Had there been forest here? The posts that supported the President's maxim boards were often set in bare clay. And the boards themselves, spattered with mud from the road and dust-blown at the bottom, not as fresh as they had seemed to me the previous morning, were like part of the desolation.

At the airport, in the section for internal flights, the departures board announced my flight and one other. The board was electrically operated and, according to a sign it carried, made in Italy. It was a modern piece of equipment; it was like the boards I had seen in the airports of London and Brussels. But below it, around the checking-in desks and weighing machines, was the usual scramble; and what was being checked in, with a lot of shouting, was like the cargo of a market jitney: metal trunks, cardboard boxes, cloth bundles, sacks of this and that, big enamel basins tied up in cloth.

I had my ticket and it was in order, but my name wasn't on the passenger list. Some francs had to pass first. And then, just as I was going out to the plane, a security man in plain clothes who was eating something asked for my papers and decided that they had to be examined more closely. He looked very offended and sent me to wait in an empty little inner room. This was standard procedure. The offended, sideways look, the little private room —this was how middle-rank officials let you know they were going to take some money off you.

But this fellow didn't get anything, because he played the fool and kept me waiting in that little room so long, without coming to collect, that he delayed the flight and was bawled out by an airline man, who, clearly knowing where I was to be found, burst into the little room, shouted to me to get out at once, and sent me running across the asphalt to the plane, last man in, but lucky.

In the front row was one of the airline's European pilots, a small, middle-aged family man; beside him was a little African boy, but it was hard to tell whether there was any connection. Some rows behind there was a group of six or eight Africans, men in their thirties, with old jackets and shirts buttoned right up, who were talking loudly. They were drinking whisky, straight from the bottle—and it was nine in the morning. Whisky was expensive here, and these men wanted everybody to know that they were drinking whisky. The bottle was passed to strangers; it was even passed to me. These men were not like the men of my region. They were bigger, with different complexions and features. I couldn't understand their faces; I saw only their arrogance and drunkenness. Their talk was boastful; they wanted the rest of us to know that they were men who owned plantations. They were like people who had just come into money, and the whole thing struck me as odd.

It was a simple flight, two hours, with a halfway stop. And it seemed to me, with my experience of intercontinental travel, that we had just begun to cruise above the white clouds when we began coming down for that stop. We saw then that we had been following the river—brown, rippled and wrinkled and streaked from this height, with many channels between long, thin islands of green. The airplane shadow moved over the forest top. That top became less even and tight as the airplane shadow grew bigger; the forest we came down to was quite ragged.

After we landed we were told to leave the airplane. We went to the small building at the edge of the airfield, and while we were there we saw the airplane turn, taxi, and fly away. It was needed for some Presidential service; it would come back when it had done that service. We had to wait. It was only about ten. Until about noon, while the heat built up, we were restless. Then we settled down—all of us, even the whisky drinkers—to wait.

We were in the middle of bush. Bush surrounded the cleared area of the airfield. Far away, a special density about the trees marked the course of the river. The airplane had shown how complex it was, how easy it would be to get lost, to waste hours paddling up channels that took you away from the main river. Not many miles from the river, people would be living in villages more or less as they had lived for centuries. Less than forty-eight hours before, I had been in the overtrampled Gloucester Road, where the world met. Now, for hours, I had been staring at bush. How many miles separated me from the capital, from my own town? How long would it take to do the distance by land or by water? How many weeks, how many months, and against what dangers?

It clouded over. The clouds grew dark and the bush grew

dark. The sky began to jump with lightning and thunder; and then the rain and the wind came, driving us in from the verandah of the little building. It rained and stormed. The bush vanished in the rain. It was rain like this that fed these forests, that caused the grass and bright green weeds around the airfield building to grow so high. The rain slackened, the clouds lifted a little. The bush revealed itself again, one line of trees behind another, the nearer trees darker, the further trees fading line by line into the grey colour of the sky.

Empty beer bottles covered the metal tables. Not many people were moving about; nearly everyone had found the place where he was going to stay. No one was talking much. The middle-aged Belgian woman whom we had found in the building waiting to join our flight was still absorbed in the French paperback of *Peyton Place*. You could see that she had shut the bush and weather out and was living somewhere else.

The sun came out and glittered on the tall, wet grass. The asphalt steamed, and for a while I watched that. Later in the afternoon one half of the sky went black, while the other half stayed light. The storm that began with vivid lightning in the black half then spread to us and it became dark and chill and very damp. The forest had become a place of gloom. There was no excitement in this second storm.

One of the African passengers, an elderly man, appeared with a grey felt hat and a blue bathrobe of towelling material over his suit. No one paid him too much attention. I just noted his oddity, and thought: He's using a foreign thing in his own way. And something like that went through my head when a barefooted man turned up wearing a fireman's helmet with the transparent plastic visor pulled down. He was an old man with a shrunken face; his brown shorts and grey check shirt were ragged and soaked through. I thought: He's found a ready-made dancing mask. He went from table to table, checking the beer bottles. When he decided that a bottle was worth emptying he raised the visor of his mask and drank.

It stopped raining, but it remained dark, the darkness of late afternoon. The airplane, at first only a brown smoke trail in the sky, appeared. When we went out to the wet field to board it I saw the man with the fireman's helmet—and a companion, also helmeted—standing unsteadily beside the gangway. He was, after all, a fireman.

As we rose we saw the river, catching the last of the light. It was gold-red, then red. We followed it for many miles and minutes, until it became a mere sheen, a smoothness, something extra-black between the black forests. Then it was all black. Through this blackness we flew to our destination. The journey, which had seemed so simple in the morning, had acquired another quality. Distance and time had been restored to it. I felt I had been travelling for days, and when we began to go down again, I knew that I had travelled far, and I wondered how I had had the courage to live for so long in a place so far away.

And then, suddenly, it was easy. A familiar building; officials I knew and could palaver with; people whose faces I understood; one of our old disinfected taxis; the well-known lumpy road to the town, at first through bush which had distinguishing features, then past the squatters' settlements. After the strangeness of the day, it was like organized life again.

We passed a burnt-out building, a new ruin. It had been a primary school, never much of a place, more like a low shed, and I might have missed it in the dark if the driver hadn't pointed it out to me; it excited him. The insurrection, the Liberation Army —that was still going on. It didn't lessen my relief at being in the town, seeing the nighttime pavement groups, and finding myself, so quickly after arrival, something of the forest gloom still on me, in my own street—all there, and as real and as ordinary as ever.

It was a shock, a puncturing, to find Metty cold. I had made such a journey. I wanted him to know; from him I had been expecting the warmest welcome. He must have heard the slam of the taxi door and my palaver with the driver. But Metty didn't come down. And all that he said when I went up the external staircase, and found him standing in the doorway of his room, was: "I didn't expect to see you back, *patron*." The whole journey seemed to turn sour then.

Everything was in order in the flat. But about the sitting room and especially the bedroom there was something—perhaps an extra order, an absence of staleness—that made me feel that Metty had been spreading himself in the flat in my absence. The telegram that I had sent him from London must have caused him to retreat. Did he resent that? Metty? But he had grown up in our family; he knew no other life. He had always been with the family or with me. He had never been on his own, except on his journey up from the coast, and now.

He brought me coffee in the morning.

He said, "I suppose you know why you come back, *patron.*"

"You said this last night."

"Because you have nothing to come back to. You don't know? Nobody told you in London? You don't read the papers? You don't have anything. They take away your shop. They give it to Citizen Théotime. The President made a speech a fortnight back. He said he was radicalizing and taking away everything from everybody. All foreigners. The next day they put a padlock on the door. And a few other doors as well. You didn't read that in London? You don't have anything, I don't have anything. I don't know why you come back. I don't think it was for my sake."

Metty was in a bad way. He had been alone. He must have been beside himself waiting for me to come back. He was trying to provoke some angry response from me. He was trying to get me to make some protective gesture. But I was as lost as he was.

Radicalization: two days before, in the capital, I had seen the word in a newspaper headline, but I hadn't paid attention. I had thought of it as just another word; we had so many. Now I understood that radicalization was the big new event.

And it was as Metty had said. The President had sprung another of his surprises, and this surprise concerned us. I—and others like me—had been nationalized. Our businesses had ceased to be ours, by decree, and were being given out by the President to new owners. These new owners were called "state trustees." Citizen Théotime had been made the state trustee of my business; and Metty said that for the last week the man had actually been spending his days in the shop.

"What does he do?"

"Do? He's waiting for you. He'll make you the manager. That is what you have come back for, *patron*. But you will see. Don't hurry yourself. Théo doesn't come to work too early."

When I went to the shop I saw that the stock, which had gone down in six weeks, was displayed in the old way. Théo hadn't touched that. But my desk had been moved from its place next to the pillar in the front of the shop to the storeroom at the back. Metty said that had happened on the first day. Citizen Théo had decided that the storeroom was to be his office; he liked the privacy.

In the top drawer of the desk (where I used to keep Yvette's photographs, which had once transformed the view of the market square for me) there were many tattered French-African photo-novels and comic books: Africans shown living very modern lives, and in the comic books they were drawn almost like Europeans—in the last two or three years there had been a lot of this French-produced rubbish around. My own things—magazines, and shop documents I had thought Metty would need—were in the two bottom drawers. They had been handled with care; Théo had had that grace. Nationalization: it had been a word. It was shocking to face it in this concrete way.

I waited for Théo.

And when the man came I could see that he was embarrassed and his first impulse, when he saw me through the glass, was to walk past the door. I had known him years before as a mechanic; he used to look after the vehicles in the health department. Then, because he had certain tribal connections, he had risen politically, but not very high. He would have had trouble signing his name. He was about forty, undistinguished in appearance, with a broad, dark-brown face beaten up and spongy with drink. He was drunk now. But only on beer; he hadn't yet moved on to whisky. Nor had he moved on to the regulation official dress of short-sleeved jacket and cravat. He stuck to trousers and shirt. He was, really, a modest man.

I was standing where my desk used to be. And it occurred to me, noticing how sweated and grimy Théo's white shirt was, that it was like the time when the schoolboys, treating me like prey, used to come to the shop to try to get money out of me in simple ways. Théo was sweating through the pores on his nose. I don't believe he had washed his face that morning. He looked like a man who had added fresh drink, and nothing else, to a bad hangover.

He said, "Mis' Salim. Salim. Citizen. You mustn't take this personally. It has not come about through any wish of mine. You know that I have the highest regard for you. But you know what the situation was like. The revolution had become"—he fumbled for the word— "un pé pourrie. A little rotten. Our young people were becoming impatient. It was necessary"—trying to find the right word, he looked confused, clenched his fist and made a clumsy cuffing gesture—"it was necessary to radicalize. We had absolutely to radicalize. We were expecting too much of the President. No one was willing to take responsibility. Now responsibility has been forced on the people. But you will suffer in no way. Adequate compensation will be paid. You will prepare your own inventory. And you will continue as manager. The business will run as before. The President insists on that. No one is to suffer. Your salary will be fair. As soon as the commissioner arrives, the papers will come through."

After his hesitant start, he had spoken formally, as though he had prepared his words. At the end he became embarrassed again. He was waiting for me to say something. But then he changed his mind and went to the storeroom, his office. And I left, to go and look for Mahesh at Bigburger.

There it was business as usual. Mahesh, a little plumper, was pulling coffees, and Ildephonse was jumping about and serving late breakfasts. I was surprised.

Mahesh said, "But this has been an African company for years. It can't be radicalized any more. I just manage Bigburger for 'Phonse and a few others. They formed this African company and they gave me a little part in it, as manager, and then they bought a lease from me. That was during the boom. They owe the bank a lot. You wouldn't believe it when you look at 'Phonse. But it's true. That happened in a lot of places after Noimon sold out to the government. That gave us an idea which way the wind was blowing, and some of us decided to compensate ourselves in advance. It was easy enough then. The banks were flush with money."

"Nobody told me."

"It wasn't the kind of thing people would talk a lot about. And your thoughts were elsewhere."

That was true. There had been a coolness between us at that time; we had both been scratchy after Noimon's departure.

I said, "What about the Tivoli? All that new kitchen equipment. They invested so much."

"That's crippled with debt. No African in his right mind would want to be the trustee of that. They queued up for yours, though. That was when I knew you hadn't done anything. Théotime and another man actually came to blows, right here in Bigburger. There were a lot of fights like that. It was like a carnival after the President announced the measures. So many people just going into places, not saying anything to the people inside, just making marks on doors or dropping pieces of cloth on the floor, as though they were claiming a piece of meat in the market. It was very bad for a few days. One Greek burnt down his coffee plantation. They've calmed down now. The President issued a statement, just to let everybody know that what the Big Man gives the Big Man can take away. That's how the Big Man gets them. He gives and he takes back."

I spent the rest of the morning at Bigburger. It was strange for me, wasting the working day in chat, giving news, asking for news, watching the coming and going in Bigburger and the van der Weyden across the road, and all the time feeling myself separated from the life of the town.

Mahesh had little to tell me about Shoba. There was no change there. She still hid with her disfigurement in the flat. But Mahesh no longer fought against that situation or seemed irritated by it. It didn't make him unhappy—as I had feared it might—to hear about London and my travels. Other people travelled; other people got away; he didn't. For Mahesh it had become as simple as that.

I became Théotime's manager. He seemed relieved and happy, and agreed to the salary I suggested for myself. I bought a table and chair and set them next to the pillar, so that it was almost like old times. I spent many days assembling old invoices, checking stock and preparing the inventory. It was a complicated document, and of course it was padded. But Théotime approved it so readily (sending me out of the storeroom while he struggled to sign *Cit:Theot:*) that I felt that Mahesh was right, that no compensation was going to be paid, that the most I could expect, if anybody remembered, were government bonds.

The inventory only reminded me of what I had lost. What remained? In a bank in Europe I had about eight thousand dollars, proceeds from my gold dealings in the old days; that money had just stayed and rotted, losing value. There was the flat in the town, for which there would be no buyer; but the car would fetch a few thousand dollars. And I had about half a million local francs in various banks—about fourteen thousand dollars at the official rate of exchange, and half that on the free market. That was all; it wasn't a great deal. I had to make more, as fast as I could; and the little I had, I had to get out of the country.

As manager in the shop I had opportunities; but they were not extraordinary. And so I began to live dangerously. I began to deal in gold and ivory. I bought, stored and sold; or, acting for bigger operators (who paid directly to my bank in Europe), I stored and shipped on, for a percentage. My suppliers, and sometimes the poachers, were officials or army people, and these people were always dangerous to deal with. The rewards were not great. Gold only sounds expensive; you have to handle kilos before your percentage amounts to anything. Ivory was better, but ivory was more difficult to store (I continued to use the hole at the bottom of the staircase in my yard) and trickier to ship. For shipping I used one of the ordinary market vans or jitneys, sending the stuff (larger tusks in mattress consignments, smaller pieces in sacks of cassava) with other goods, always doing so now in the name of Citizen Théotime, and sometimes getting Théotime himself to pull a little political rank and give the driver a good talking to in public.

Money could be made. But to get it out of the country was another matter. Money can be got out of countries like these only if you deal in very large sums and can get high officials or ministers to take an interest; or if there is a certain amount of business activity. There was little activity now, and I had to depend on visitors who for various reasons needed local currency. There was no other way. And I had to trust these people to pay up when they got back to Europe or the United States.

It was a slow, tout-like, humiliating business. I wish I could say that I discovered certain rules about human behaviour. I wish I could say that people of a certain class or country were to be trusted and people of another class and country not trusted. That would have made it much simpler. It was a gamble each time. I lost two-thirds of my money in this way; I gave it away to strangers.

I was in and out of the Domain on this money business; it was there that I made many of my contacts. At first it made me uneasy to be there. But then I proved Indar's point about trampling on the past: the Domain quickly ceased to be what it had been for me. It became a place where honourable people—many of them first-time lawbreakers, who were later to use their respect for the law to cheat me with a clear mind—tried to get better rates than the ones we had agreed on. What was common to these people was their nervousness and contempt—contempt for me, contempt for the country. I was half on their side; I envied them the contempt that it was so easy for them to feel.

One afternoon I saw that Raymond and Yvette's house had a new tenant, an African. The house had been closed since I had come back. Raymond and Yvette had gone away; no one, not even Mahesh, could tell me where or in what circumstances. The doors and windows of the house were wide open now, and that emphasized the shoddiness of the construction.

The new man, barebacked, was forking up the ground just in front of the house, and I stopped to have a chat. He was from somewhere downriver, and friendly. He told me he was going to grow maize and cassava. Africans didn't understand large-scale agriculture; but they were passionate planters in this smaller way, growing food for the house and liking to grow it very close to the house. He noted my car; he remembered his bare back. He told me he worked for the government corporation that ran the steamer service. And to give me some idea of his standing, he said that whenever he travelled on the steamer he travelled first class and free. That big government job, this big government house in the famous Domain—he was a happy man, pleased with what he had been granted, and asking for nothing else.

There were more households like his in the Domain now. The polytechnic was still there, but the Domain had lost its modern, "showplace" character. It was scruffier; every week it was becoming more of an African housing settlement. Maize, which in that climate and soil sprouted in three days, grew in many places; and the purple-green leaves of the cassava, which grew from a simple cutting even if you planted it upside down, created the effect of garden shrubs. This piece of earth—how many changes had come to it! Forest at a bend in the river, a meeting place, an Arab settlement, a European outpost, a European suburb, a ruin like the ruin of a dead civilization, the glittering Domain of new Africa, and now this.

While we were speaking, children began to appear from the back of the house—country children still, bending a knee at the sight of the adult, before coming up shyly to listen and watch. And then a large Doberman came bounding out at me.

The man with the fork said, "Don't worry. He'll miss you. He can't see very well. A foreigner's dog. He gave it to me when he went away."

It was as he said. The Doberman missed me by about a foot, ran on a little way, stopped, raced back, and then was all over me, wagging his docked tail, beside himself with joy at my foreigner's smell, momentarily mistaking me for somebody else.

I was glad for Raymond's sake that he had gone away. He wouldn't have been safe in the Domain or the town now. The curious reputation that had come to him in the end—of being the white man who went ahead of the President, and drew on himself the bad things that should have fallen on the President—that reputation might have encouraged the Liberation Army to kill him, especially now, when the President was said to be planning to visit the town, and the town was being made ready for that visit.

The rubbish hills in the centre were being carted away. The corrugated streets were being levelled and graded. And paint! It was everywhere in the centre, slapped onto concrete and plaster and timber, dripping on the pavements. Someone had unloaded his stock—pink and lime and red and mauve and blue. The bush was at war; the town was in a state of insurrection, with nightly incidents. But suddenly in the centre it seemed like carnival time.

# 17

Citizen Théotime would come in in the mornings, red-eyed and tormented-looking, high on his breakfast beer, with a couple of comic books or photo-novels to see him through office hours. There was an informal system of magazine exchange in the town; Théo always had something new to look at. And oddly, his comic books or photo-novels, tightly rolled up, gave him a busy, businesslike air when he came into the shop. He went straight to the storeroom, and could stay there without coming out for the whole morning. At first I thought it was because he wanted to be out of the way and not to be any trouble. But then I understood that it was no hardship for him. He liked being in the dark storeroom with nothing in particular to do, just looking at his magazines when the mood took him, and drinking his beer.

Later, when he became easier and less shy with me, his storeroom life became fuller. He began to be visited by women. He liked them to see him as a real *directeur*, with a staff and an office; and it pleased the women too. A visit could take up a whole afternoon, with Théotime and the woman chatting in the way people chat when they are sheltering from the rain—with long pauses and long hypnotized stares in different directions.

It was an easy enough life for Théotime, easier than anything he could have imagined when he was a mechanic in the health department. But as he gained confidence, and lost his fear that the shop might be taken away from him by the President, he became difficult.

It began to worry him that as a *directeur* he didn't have a car.

Some woman had perhaps given him the idea, or it might have been the example of other state trustees, or it might have been something he had got from his comic books. I had a car; he began to ask for lifts, and then he required me to drive him to and from his house. I could have said no. But I told myself it was a small thing to do to keep him quiet. The first few times he sat in the front; then he sat in the back. This was a four-times-a-day duty.

He didn't stay quiet for long. It might have been my easiness, my wish to appear unhumiliated: Théotime was soon looking for new ways of asserting himself. The trouble now was that he didn't know what to do. He would have liked to live out his role in fact—to take over the running of the shop, or to feel (while enjoying his storeroom life) that he was running the shop. He knew, though, that he knew nothing; he knew that I knew he knew nothing; and he was like a man enraged by his own helplessness. He made constant scenes. He was drunken, aggrieved and threatening, and as deliberately irrational as an official who had decided to be *malin*.

It was strange. He wanted me to acknowledge him as the boss. At the same time he wanted me to make allowances for him as an uneducated man and an African. He wanted both my respect and my tolerance, even my compassion. He wanted me, almost, to act out my subordinate role as a favour to him. Yet if, responding to his plea, I did so, if I took some simple shop document to him, the authority he put on then was very real. He added it to his idea of his role; and he would use that authority later to extort some new concession. As he had done with the car.

It was worse than dealing with a *malin* official. The official who pretended to be offended—and bawled you out, for instance, for resting your hand on his desk—was only asking for money. Théotime, moving quickly from a simple confidence in his role to an understanding of his helplessness, wanted you to pretend that he was another kind of man. It wasn't funny. I had resolved to be calm about my dispossession, to keep my mind on the goal I had given myself. But it wasn't easy to be calm. The shop became a hateful place to me.

It was worse for Metty. The little services that he had done for Théotime in the beginning became things that he was required to do, and they multiplied. Théotime began sending Metty out on quite pointless errands.

Late one evening, when he returned to the flat after being with his family, Metty came into my room and said, "I can't take it, *patron*. I will do something terrible one of these days. If Théo doesn't stop it, I'll kill him. I'd rather hoe in the fields than be his servant."

I said, "It won't last long."

Metty's face twisted with exasperation, and he did a silent stamp with one foot. He was close to tears. He said, "What do you mean? What do you mean?" and went out of the room.

In the morning I went to collect Théotime to drive him to the shop. As a well-to-do and influential local man, Théotime had three or four families in different parts of the town. But since becoming a state trustee he had (like other trustees) picked up a number of new women, and he lived with one of them in one of the little back houses in a *cité* yard—bare red ground intersected with shallow black drains all down one side, scraped-up earth and rubbish pushed to the edge, mango and other trees scattered about, cassava and maize and clumps of banana between the houses.

When I blew the horn, children and women from the various houses came out and watched while Théotime walked to the car, with his comic book rolled up. He pretended to ignore the watchers and spat casually on the ground once or twice. His eyes were reddened with beer and he tried to look offended.

We drove out of the bumpy *cité* lane to the levelled red main road, where the buildings were freshly painted for the President's visit—each building done in one colour (walls, window frames, doors), and each building a different colour from its neighbour.

I said, "I want to talk to you about Citizen Metty's duties in our establishment, citizen. Citizen Metty is the manager's assistant. He is not a general servant."

Théotime had been waiting for this. He had a speech prepared. He said, "You astonish me, citizen. I am the state trustee, appointed by the President. Citizen Metty is an employee of a state establishment. It is for me to decide how the half-caste is to be used." He used the word *métis*, to play on the adopted name of which Metty had once been so proud.

The vivid colours of the buildings became even more unreal to me. They became the colours of my rage and anguish.

I had been growing smaller and smaller in Metty's eyes, and now I failed him altogether. I could no longer offer him the simple protection he had asked for—Théotime made that plain during the course of the day. So the old contract between Metty and myself, which was the contract between his family and mine, came to an end. Even if I had been able to place him in another establishment in the town—which I might have been able to do in the old days—it would have meant that our special contract was over. He seemed to understand this, and it made him unbalanced.

He began to say, "I am going to do something terrible, Salim. You must give me money. Give me money and let me go away. I feel I'm going to do something terrible."

I felt his pain as an extra pressure. I mentally added his pain to mine, made it part of my own. I should have thought more of him. I should have made him stay away from the shop, and given him an allowance from my own salary, while that lasted. It was, really, what he wanted. But he didn't put it like that. He involved it in that wild idea of going away, which only frightened me and made me think: Where is he going to go?

So he continued to go to the shop and Théotime, and became more and more tormented. When he said to me one evening, "Give me some money and I will go away," I said, thinking of the situation in the shop, and trying to find comforting words, "It isn't going to last forever, Metty." This made him scream, "*Salim!*" And the next morning, for the first time, he didn't bring me coffee.

That happened at the beginning of the week. On Friday afternoon, after closing up the shop and driving Théotime to his yard, I came back to the flat. It was a place of desolation for me now. I no longer thought of it as my own. Since that morning in the

car with Théotime I had felt nausea for the bright new colours of
the town. They were the colours of a place that had become
strange and felt far away from everywhere else. That feeling of
strangeness extended to everything in the flat. I was thinking of
going to the Hellenic Club—or what remained of it—when I
heard car doors slam.

I went out to the landing and saw police in the yard. There
was an officer—his name was Prosper: I knew him. One of the
men with him had a fork, another a shovel. They knew what they
had come for, and they knew exactly where they had to dig—
below the external staircase. I had four tusks there.

My mind raced, made links. Metty! I thought: Oh, Ali! What
have you done to me? I knew it was important to let someone
know. Mahesh—there was no one else. He would be at his flat
now. I went to the bedroom and telephoned. Mahesh answered,
and I only had time to say, "Things are bad here," before I heard
footsteps coming up. I put the phone down, went to the bathroom, pulled the lavatory chain, and went out to see the round-
faced Prosper coming up alone, smiling.

The face came up, smiling, and I retreated before it, and this
was how, not saying anything, we moved down the passage before I turned and led Prosper into the white sitting room. He
couldn't hide his pleasure. His eyes glittered. He hadn't yet decided how to behave. He hadn't yet decided how much to ask
for.

He said, "The President is coming next week. Did you know
that? The President is interested in conservation. This is why this
is very serious for you. Anything might happen to you if I send in
my report. This is certainly going to cost you a couple of thousand."

This seemed to me very modest.

He noticed my relief. He said, "I don't mean francs. I mean
dollars. Yes, this is going to cost you three or four thousand
dollars."

This was outrageous. Prosper knew it was outrageous. In the
old days five dollars was considered pretty good; and even during
the boom you could get many things done for twenty-five dollars.

Things had changed since the insurrection, of course, and had become very bad with the radicalization. Everyone had become more greedy and desperate. There was this feeling of everything running down very fast, of a great chaos coming; and some people could behave as though money had already lost its value. But even so, officials like Prosper had only recently begun to talk in hundreds.

I said, "I don't have that kind of money."

"I thought you would say that. The President is coming next week. We are taking a number of people into preventive detention. That is how you will go in. We will forget the tusks for the time being. You will stay in until the President leaves. You might decide then that you have the money."

I packed a few things into a canvas holdall and Prosper drove me in the back of his Land-Rover through the brightly coloured town to police headquarters. There I learned to wait. There I decided that I had to shut out thoughts of the town and stop thinking about time, that I had as far as possible to empty my mind.

There were many stages in my progress through the building, and I began to look upon Prosper as my guide to this particular hell. He left me for long periods sitting or standing in rooms and corridors, which gleamed with new oil paint. It was almost a relief to see him coming back to me with his chunky cheeks and his stylish briefcase.

It was near sunset when he led me to the annex in the yard at the back, where I had once gone to rescue Metty, and where I now had to be fingerprinted myself, before being taken to the town jail. The walls had been a dusty blue, I remembered. Now they were a brilliant yellow, and *Discipline Avant Tout*—"Discipline Above All"—had been freshly painted in big black letters. I lost myself contemplating the bad, uneven lettering, the graining of the photograph of the President, the uneven surface of the yellow wall, the dried yellow spattering on the broken floor.

The room was full of young men who had been picked up. It was a long time before I was fingerprinted. The man at the table behaved like an overworked man. He didn't seem to look at the faces of the people he fingerprinted.

I asked whether I couldn't get the ink off my hands. It wasn't a wish to be clean, I decided after I had asked. It was more a wish to appear calm, unhumiliated, to feel that the events were normal. The man at the table said yes, and from a drawer brought out a pink plastic soap dish with a slender-waisted wafer of soap streaked with black lines. The soap was quite dry. He told me I could go outside and use the standpipe.

I went out into the yard. It was now dark. Around me were trees, lights, cooking smoke, evening sounds. The standpipe was near the open garage shed. The ink, surprisingly, washed out easily. A rage began to possess me when I went back and gave the man his soap and saw the others who were waiting with me in that yellow room.

If there was a plan, these events had meaning. If there was law, these events had meaning. But there was no plan; there was no law; this was only make-believe, play, a waste of men's time in the world. And how often here, even in the days of bush, it must have happened before, this game of warders and prisoners in which men could be destroyed for nothing. I remembered what Raymond used to say—about events being forgotten, lost, swallowed up.

The jail was on the road to the Domain. It was set a good way back, and in the space in front there had grown up a market and a settlement. This was what registered—the market and the settlement—when you drove by. The concrete jail wall, no more than seven or eight feet high, was a white background. It had never seemed like a real jail. There was something artificial and even quaint about it: this new jail in this new settlement, all so rough and temporary-looking, in a clearing in the bush. You felt that the people who had built it—village people, establishing themselves in a town for the first time—were playing at having a community and rules. They had put up a wall just taller than a man and put some people behind it; and because they were village people, that was jail enough for them. In another place a jail would have been a more elaborate thing. This was so simple: you felt that what went on behind the low wall matched the petty market life in front.

Now, at the end of the lane, after the lights and radios of the little huts and shacks and stalls and drinking booths, that jail opened to let me in. A wall taller than a man is a high wall. Below electric lights the outside wall gleamed with new white paint; and again, but in large black letters about two feet high, was *Discipline Avant Tout*. I felt damned and mocked by the words. But that was how I was expected to feel. What a complicated lie those words had become! How long would it take to work back from that, through all the accumulated lies, to what was simple and true?

Inside, behind the jail gates, there was silence and space: a large, bare, dusty yard with rough low buildings of concrete and corrugated iron arranged in squares.

The barred window of my cell looked out on a bare courtyard, lit by electric lamps high up on poles. There was no ceiling to my cell; there was only the corrugated-iron roof. Everything was rough, but everything held. It was Friday night. And of course Friday was the day to pick people up: nothing would happen over the weekend. I had to learn to wait, in a jail that was suddenly real, and frightening now because of its very simpleness.

In a cell like mine you very quickly become aware of your body. You can grow to hate your body. And your body is all you have: this was the curious thought that kept floating up through my rage.

The jail was full. I found that out in the morning. Quite a time before, I had heard from Zabeth and others about the kidnapping operations in the villages. But I had never suspected that so many young men and boys had been picked up. Worse, it had never occurred to me that they were being kept in the jail past which I drove so often. In the newspapers there was nothing about the insurrection and the Liberation Army. But this was all that the jail—or the part of it I was in—was about. And it was awful.

It had sounded, bright and early in the morning, like a class of some sort: people being taught poems by many instructors. The instructors were warders with big boots and sticks; the poems were hymns of praise to the President and the African madonna; the people being compelled to repeat the lines were those young men and boys from the villages, many of whom had been trussed up and dumped in the courtyard and were being maltreated in ways I don't want to describe.

These were the dreadful sounds of the early morning. Those poor people had also been trapped and damned by the words on the white jail wall. But you could tell, from their faces, that in their minds and hearts and souls they had retreated far. The frenzied warders, Africans themselves, seemed to understand this, seemed to know that their victims were unreachable.

Those faces of Africa! Those masks of child-like calm that had brought down the blows of the world, and of Africans as well, as now in the jail. I felt I had never seen them so clearly before. Indifferent to notice, indifferent to compassion or contempt, those faces were yet not vacant or passive or resigned. There was, with the prisoners as well as with their active tormentors, a frenzy. But the frenzy of the prisoners was internal; it had taken them far beyond their cause or even knowledge of their cause, far beyond thought. They had prepared themselves for death not because they were martyrs; but because what they were and what they knew they were was all they had. They were people crazed with the idea of who they were. I never felt closer to them, or more far away.

All day, through the mounting and then lessening heat of the sun, those sounds continued. Beyond the white wall was the market, the outside world. Every image that I had of that world outside was poisoned for me by what was going on around me. And the jail had seemed quaint. I had thought that the life of the jail would match the market life outside. Yvette and I had stopped at a stall one afternoon to buy sweet potatoes. At the next stall a man was selling hairy orange-coloured caterpillars— he had a big white basinful. Yvette had made a face of horror. He, the vendor, laughing, had lifted his basin and pushed it into the window of the car, offering it all as a gift; later, he had held a squirming caterpillar over his mouth and pretended to chew.

All that life was going on outside. While here the young men and boys were learning discipline and hymns to the President. There was a reason for the frenzy of the warders, the instructors. I heard that an important execution was to take place; that the President himself was going to attend it when he came to the town; and that he would listen then to the hymns sung by his enemies. For that visit the town had burst into bright colour.

I felt that almost nothing separated me from those men in the courtyard, that there was no reason why I shouldn't be treated like them. I resolved to maintain and assert my position as a man apart, a man waiting to be ransomed. The idea came to me that it was important for me not to be touched physically by a warder. To be touched in one way might lead to more terrible things. I determined to do nothing to provoke any physical contact, however slight. I became cooperative. I obeyed orders almost before they were given. So at the end of my weekend, with my rage and obedience, my exposure to the sights and sounds of the courtyard, I was a hardened jailbird.

Prosper came for me on Monday morning. I was expecting someone to come. But I wasn't expecting Prosper, and he didn't look too happy. The loot-glitter had gone from his eyes. I sat beside him in his Land-Rover and he said, almost companionably, as we drove through the jail gates, "This business could have been settled on Friday. But you've made it much worse for yourself. The commissioner has decided to take a particular interest in your case. All I can say is that I hope it goes well for you."

I didn't know whether this was good news or bad news. The commissioner might have been Ferdinand. His appointment had been announced some time before, but so far he had not appeared in the town; and it was possible that the appointment had been rescinded. If it was Ferdinand, however, this wasn't the best way for me to meet him.

Ferdinand, progressing through the world, had, as I remembered, accepted all his roles, and lived them out: lycée boy, polytechnic student, new man of Africa, first-class passenger on the steamer. After four years, after his time as an administrative cadet in that capital so dominated by the President, where would he be? What would he have learned? What idea would he have about himself as one of the President's officials? In his own eyes he would have risen; I would have got smaller. It had always unsettled me a little—the knowledge that the gap between us would get bigger as he grew older. I had often thought how ready-made and easy the world was for him, the village boy, starting from nothing.

Prosper delivered me to the people in the front office of the secretariat. There was a wide verandah all around the inner courtyard, and on three sides the verandah was screened from the sun by big reed blinds. It gave an odd feeling, walking through the thin stripes of light and shadow, watching them appear to move over you as you moved. The orderly let me into a room where, after the shifting verandah dazzle, spots of light momentarily danced before my eyes; and then I was let into the inner office.

It was Ferdinand, strange in his polka-dotted cravat and short-sleeved jacket, and unexpectedly ordinary. I would have expected style, a certain heartiness, a little arrogance, a little showing off. But Ferdinand looked withdrawn and ill, like a man recovering from fever. He wasn't interested in impressing me.

On the newly painted white wall was a larger-than-life photograph of the President, just the face—that was a face full of life. Below that face, Ferdinand seemed shrunken, and characterless in the regulation uniform that made him look like all those officials who appeared in group photographs in the  newspapers. He was, after all, like other high officials. I wondered why I thought he would be different. These men, who depended on the President's favour for everything, were bundles of nerves. The great power they exercised went with a constant fear of being destroyed. And they were unstable, half dead.

Ferdinand said, "My mother told me you had gone away. I was surprised to hear that you were still here."

"I went to London for six weeks. I haven't seen your mother since I've come back."

"She's given up the business. And you must do that too. You

must go. You must go right away. There's nothing here for you.
They've taken you into jail now. They haven't done that before.
Do you know what it means? It means they'll take you in again.
And I won't always be here to get you out. I don't know how
much Prosper and the others wanted from you. But next time it
will be more. That's all that it is about now. You know that.
They haven't done anything to you in jail. That's only because it
hasn't occurred to them. They still think you are not that kind of
man. You are a foreigner; they are not interested in you in that
way; they just beat up bush people. But one day they will rough
you up and then they will discover that you are like everybody
else, and then very bad things will happen to you. You must go.
Forget everything and go. There are no airplanes. All the seats
have been reserved for officials coming up for the President's
visit. That's standard security for these visits. But there's a
steamer on Tuesday. That's tomorrow. Take it. It may be the
last. The place will be full of officials. Don't draw attention to
yourself. Don't take too much luggage. Don't tell anyone. I will
keep Prosper busy at the airport."

"I will do what you say. And how are you, Ferdinand?"

"You don't have to ask. You mustn't think it's bad just for
you. It's bad for everybody. That's the terrible thing. It's bad for
Prosper, bad for the man they gave your shop to, bad for everybody. Nobody's going anywhere. We're all going to hell, and
every man knows this in his bones. We're being killed. Nothing
has any meaning. That is why everyone is so frantic. Everyone
wants to make his money and run away. But where? That is what
is driving people mad. They feel they're losing the place they can
run back to. I began to feel the same thing when I was a cadet in
the capital. I felt I had been used. I felt I had given myself an
education for nothing. I felt I had been fooled. Everything that
was given to me was given to me to destroy me. I began to think
I wanted to be a child again, to forget books and everything
connected with books. The bush runs itself. But there is no place
to go to. I've been on tour in the villages. It's a nightmare. All
these airfields the man has built, the foreign companies have
built—nowhere is safe now."

His face had been like a mask at the beginning. Now he was showing his frenzy.

I said, "What are you going to do?"

"I don't know. I will do what I have to do."

That had always been his way.

On his desk there was a glass paperweight—small flowers set in a half-sphere of crystal. He put the paperweight on the flat palm of his left hand and looked at it.

He said, "And you must go and get your steamer ticket. That was where we last met. I've often thought about that day. There were four of us on the steamer. It was midday. We drank beer in the bar. There was the director's wife—you left with her. There was the lecturer who was your friend. He travelled down with me. That was the best time. The last day, the day of leaving. It was a good journey. It became different at the other end. I've had a dream, Salim. I've had a terrible dream."

He took the paperweight off his palm and rested it on the desk again.

He said, "An execution is to take place at seven in the morning. That is what we are meeting for. We are going to witness the execution. It is one of us who is going to be executed, but the man doesn't know. He thinks he is going to watch. We are meeting in a place I can't describe. It may be a family place—I feel the presence of my mother. I am in a panic. I have soiled something in a shameful way and I am trying hard to clean it or to hide it, because I have to be at the execution at seven. We wait for the man. We greet him in the usual way. Now, here is the problem in the dream. Are we going to leave the man alone, to be driven alone to the place of his execution? Will we have the courage to be with him, to talk in a friendly way to the last? Should we take one car, or should we go in two cars?"

"You must go in one car. If you go in two, it means you are halfway to changing your mind."

"Go and get your steamer ticket."

The steamer office was famous for its erratic hours. I sat on the wooden bench outside the door until the man came and opened up. The *cabine de luxe* was free; I booked it. This took most of the morning. The market outside the dock gates had built up: the steamer was due that afternoon. I thought of going to see Mahesh at Bigburger, but decided against it. The place was too open and central, and there were too many officials there at lunchtime. It was strange, having to think of the city in this way.

I had a snack at the Tivoli. It looked a little demoralized these days, as though awaiting radicalization. But it had kept its European atmosphere, and there were European artisans and their families at the tables and men drinking beer at the bar. I thought: What is going to happen to these people? But they were protected. I bought some bread and cheese and a few expensive tins—my last shopping in the town—and decided to spend the rest of the time at the flat. I wanted to do nothing else. I had no wish to go anywhere or look at anything or talk to anyone. Even the thought of having to telephone Mahesh was like a burden.

Late in the afternoon there were footsteps on the external staircase. Metty. I was surprised. Normally at this time he was with his family.

He came into the sitting room and said, "I heard they let you out, Salim."

He looked wretched and confused. He must have spent some bad days after reporting me to Prosper. That was what he wanted me to talk about. But I didn't want to talk about it. The shock of that moment of three days before had vanished. My head was full of other things.

We didn't talk. And soon it was as though we had nothing to talk about. There had never been a silence like this between us before. He stood around for a little, went to his room, then came back.

He said, "You must take me with you, Salim."

"I'm not going anywhere."

"You can't leave me here."

"What about your family? And how can I take you with me, Metty? The world isn't like that nowadays. There are visas and passports. I can hardly arrange these things for myself. I don't know where I'm going or what I'll do. I hardly have any money. I'm scarcely able to look after myself."

"It's going to be bad here, Salim. You don't know what they're talking about outside. It's going to be very bad when the President comes. At first they were only going to kill government people. Now the Liberation Army say that isn't enough. They say they have to do what they did the last time, but they have to do it better this time. At first they were going to have people's courts and shoot people in the squares. Now they say they have to do a lot more killing, and everybody will have to dip their hands in the blood. They're going to kill everybody who can read and write, everybody who ever put on a jacket and tie, everybody who put on a *jacket de boy*. They're going to kill all the masters and all the servants. When they're finished nobody will know there was a place like this here. They're going to kill and kill. They say it is the only way, to go back to the beginning before it's too late. The killing will last for days. They say it is better to kill for days than to die forever. It is going to be terrible when the President comes."

I tried to calm him down. "They always talk like this. Ever since the insurrection they've been talking of the morning when the whole thing is going to go up in flames. They talk like that because that is what they would like to happen. But nobody knows what is going to happen. And the President is smart. You know that. He must know they're preparing something for him here. So he'll get them excited, and then he may not come. You know the President. You know how he plays on the people."

"The Liberation Army isn't just those boys in the bush, Salim. Everybody's in it. Everybody you see. How am I going to make out alone?"

"You have to take your chance. That's what we've always done. Everybody has done that here. And I don't think they'll trouble you—you don't frighten them. Hide the car, though. Don't tempt them with it. Whatever they say about going back to the beginning, they'll be interested in the car. If they remember and ask you about it, tell them to ask Prosper. And always remember that the place is going to start up again."

"How am I going to live then? When there is no shop, and I have no money? You gave me no money. You gave it away to other people, even when I was asking you."

I said, "Ali! I gave it away. You're right. I don't know why I did that. I could have given some of it to you. I don't know why I didn't. I never thought of it. I never thought of you in that way. You've just made me think of it. It must have driven you crazy. Why didn't you tell me?"

"I thought you knew what you were doing, Salim."

"I didn't. I don't know now. But after this is over you'll have the car and you'll have the flat. The car will be worth quite a lot, if you keep it. And I'll send you money through Mahesh. That will be very easy to arrange."

He wasn't comforted. But it was all I could do now. He recognized that and didn't press me any further. Then he left to go to his family.

In the end I didn't telephone Mahesh; I thought I would write him later. Security at the docks the next morning wasn't extraordinary. But the officials were tense. They were like people with a job to do; and that was to my advantage. They were less interested in a foreigner who was leaving than in the African strangers in the market encampment around the monument and the dock gates. Still, I was constantly stopped.

A woman official said, when she gave me back my papers, "Why are you leaving today? The President is coming this afternoon. Wouldn't you like to see him?" She was a local woman. Was there irony in her voice? I was careful to take all irony out of mine. I said, "I would like to, citizen. But I have to go." She smiled and waved me on.

At last I went aboard the steamer. It was hot in my *cabine de luxe*. The door faced the river, which dazzled; and the sun fell on the deck. I went around to the shaded side, which overlooked the quay. That wasn't a good idea.

A soldier on the quay began to gesture at me. Our eyes met, and he began to scramble up the gangway. I thought: I mustn't be alone with him. I must have witnesses.

I went down to the bar. The barman was standing in front of his empty shelves. A fat man with big, smooth arms, a steamer official of some sort, was drinking at a table.

I sat at a table in the centre, and the soldier soon appeared in the doorway. He remained there for a while, nervous of the fat man. But then, overcoming his nervousness, he came to my table, leaned over and whispered, "*C'est moi qui a réglé votre affaire.* I fixed it for you."

It was a smiling request for money, from a man who might soon have to fight a battle. I did nothing; the fat man stared. The soldier felt the fat man's stare and began to back away, smiling, saying with his gestures that I was to forget his request. But I took care after that not to show myself.

We left at about midday. The passenger barge was not towed behind these days—that was now considered a colonial practice. Instead, the barge was lashed to the forward part of the steamer. The town was soon past. But for some miles that bank, though overgrown, still showed where in colonial days people had laid out estates and built great houses.

After the morning heat it had turned stormy, and in the silver storm light the overgrown, bushy bank was brilliant green against the black sky. Below this brilliant green the earth was bright red. The wind blew, and ruffled away reflections from the river surface near the bank. But the rain that followed didn't last long; we sailed out of it. Soon we were moving through real forest. Every now and then we passed a village, and market dugouts poled out to meet us. It was like that all through the heavy afternoon.

The sky hazed over, and the sinking sun showed orange and was reflected in a broken golden line in the muddy water. Then we sailed into a golden glow. There was a village ahead—you could tell from the dugouts in the distance. In this light the silhouettes of the dugouts and the people in them were blurred, not sharp. But these dugouts, when we came to them, had no produce to sell. They were desperate only to be tied up to the steamer. They were in flight from the riverbanks. They jammed and jostled against the sides of the steamer and the barge, and many were swamped. Water hyacinths pushed up in the narrow space between the steamer and the barge. We went on. Darkness fell.

It was in this darkness that abruptly, with many loud noises, we stopped. There were shouts from the barge, the dugouts with us, and from many parts of the steamer. Young men with guns had boarded the steamer and tried to take her over. But they had failed; one young man was bleeding on the bridge above us. The fat man, the captain, remained in charge of his vessel. We learned that later.

At the time what we saw was the steamer searchlight, playing on the riverbank, playing on the passenger barge, which had snapped loose and was drifting at an angle through the water hyacinths at the edge of the river. The searchlight lit up the barge passengers, who, behind bars and wire guards, as yet scarcely seemed to understand that they were adrift. Then there were gunshots. The searchlight was turned off; the barge was no longer to be seen. The steamer started up again and moved without lights down the river, away from the area of battle. The air would have been full of moths and flying insects. The searchlight, while it was on, had shown thousands, white in the white light.

*July 1977–August 1978*